Traitor

THE CHANGE SERIES

Stranger

Hostage

Rebel

Traitor

TRAITOR

·THE CHANGE, BOOK 4·

Rachel Manija Brown
and Sherwood Smith

BOOK VIEW CAFE

BOOK VIEW CAFÉ

TRAITOR

ISBN 978-1-63632-266-7

Published by Book View Café
304 S. Jones Blvd., Suite #2906
Las Vegas, NV 89107
www.bookviewcafe.com

First edition published 2017 by Book View Café

To everyone who waited for it

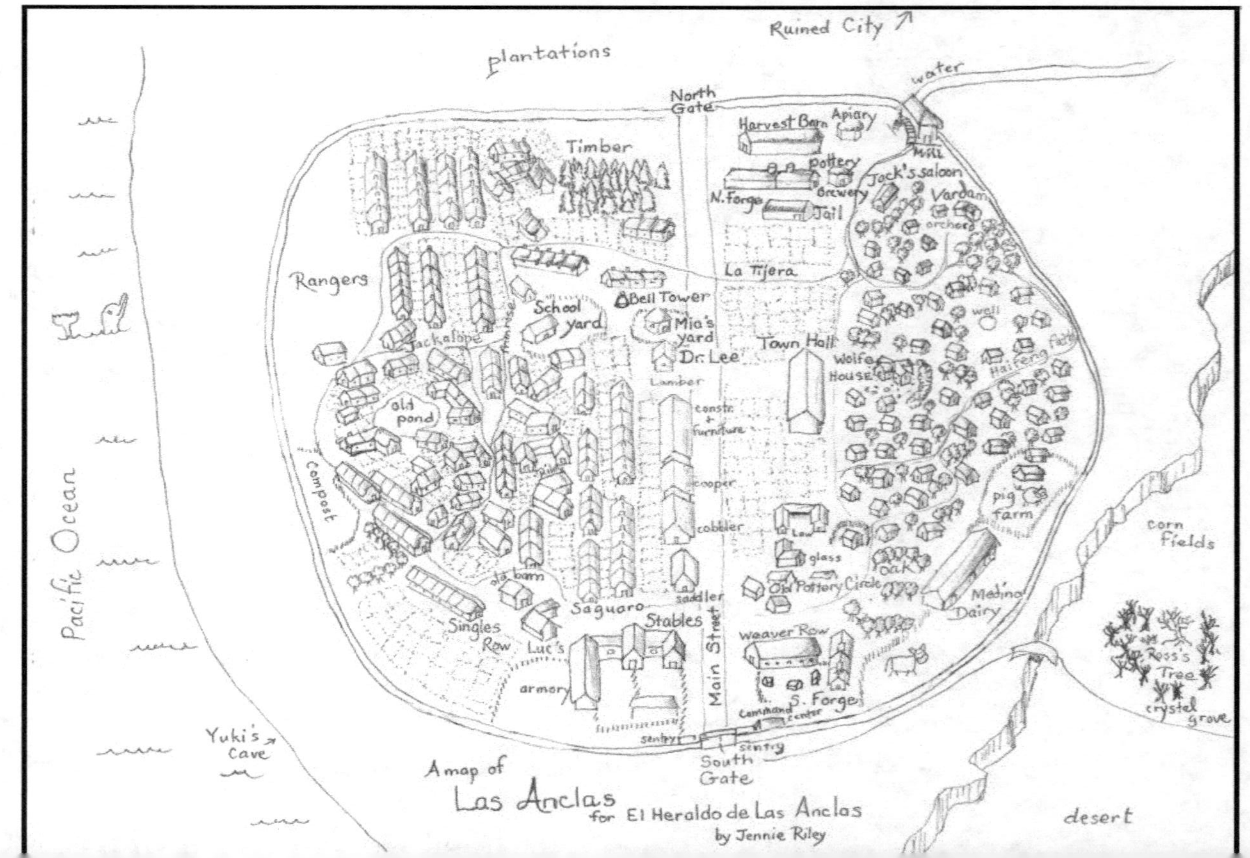
Ruined City
plantations
water
North Gate
Harvest Barn
Apiary
Mill
pottery
Jack's saloon
Timber
N. Forge
Brewery
Vardam
Jail
orchard
La Tijera
Rangers
Bell Tower
well
School yard
Mia's yard
Town Hall
Jackalope
Dr. Lee
Wolfe House
Halfern
Lumber
old pond
constr. + furniture
Compost
cooper
pig farm
cobbler
Lau
corn fields
old barn
glass
Oak
saddler
Old Pottery Circle
Saguaro
Stables
Medina Dairy
Singles Row
Luc's
Main Street
Weaver Row
Pacific Ocean
armory
S. Forge
Command Center
sentry
sentry
Yuki's Cave
South Gate
Ross's Tree
crystal grove
desert
A map of
Las Anclas
for El Heraldo de Las Anclas
by Jennie Riley

·WHAT CAME BEFORE·

STRANGER

Lone prospector Ross Juarez is chased through the desert by a bounty hunter sent by the tyrant king Voske, who is after an ancient book Ross found. While escaping the bounty hunter, Ross is hit by a shard from a deadly crystal tree and rescued by the sheriff of the walled town of Las Anclas. Dr. Lee and his mechanic daughter Mia take Ross in. Ross learns to read from teenage schoolteacher Jennie Riley, who is also a Ranger — the elite defense force led by Captain Sera Diaz. Ross strikes up a romance with both Mia and Jennie, with the agreement of all three of them.

Ross learns that he now has the power to communicate with and control the crystal trees. While exploring his power, he discovers a secret tunnel leading from within the town to outside its walls, meant to let the children escape if the town is invaded. Meanwhile, aspiring prospector Yuki Nakamura wonders if Ross could train him, and Yuki's drummer boyfriend Paco Diaz, Sera's son, urges him to ask. Felicité, the daughter of the mayor and the anti-Changed defense chief Tom Preston, despises Ross as a Changed mutant, but she herself is secretly Changed – she grows scales and gills when her skin gets wet, and has constructed an entire persona to conceal this.

Voske attacks Las Anclas, but is driven away when Ross uses the crystal trees to kill many of Voske's soldiers, though the effort almost kills him, too. Sera Diaz is killed in battle. Jennie sees Voske's face and realizes that Voske must be the biological father of Sera's son Paco. Ross agrees to train Yuki to prospect, sells the book to Mr. Preston, and becomes a citizen of Las Anclas.

Hostage

Ross is kidnapped by King Voske and taken to Gold Point, Voske's town. There he meets Voske's daughter, Princess Kerry. While Voske forces Ross to prospect for him, Las Anclas mounts a rescue mission led by Jennie. Jennie's team is unable to rescue Ross, but they kidnap Kerry and take her to Las Anclas in the hope of doing a hostage exchange. When Kerry arrives, everyone realizes by their resemblance that Voske is Paco's father. Paco, distraught, quits drumming and devotes himself to becoming a Ranger. Kerry learns what life is like in a free town and is befriended by Mia.

When Las Anclas votes to execute Kerry if Voske refuses to do the exchange, Mia, Jennie, and Yuki free Kerry in exchange for her promise of freeing Ross. Paco and Yuki break up, and Jennie is banned from the Rangers for life. Kerry returns to Gold Point, where Ross has attempted to kill Voske and is being held for execution. She breaks Ross free and decides to move to Las Anclas. She leaves behind her boyfriend Santiago, as Voske would kill Santiago's family if he fled. Ross and Kerry blow up the Gold Point dam to cover their escape. Yuki leaves Las Anclas to go prospecting, and Kerry becomes a citizen of Las Anclas.

Rebel

Ross's younger sister Summer, whom he hadn't known existed, tracks him down. While they deal with their new and difficult relationship, Las Anclas is plagued by a series of mysterious fires. Becky Callahan, Dr. Lee's timid apprentice from an emotionally abusive home, Changes and gains the ability to touch an object and hear the thoughts of people who handled it. Sheriff Crow enlists Becky to help her track down the arsonist. Paco Diaz becomes a Ranger, and Becky's brother Henry Callahan is rejected. An election is held. Felicité's father Tom Preston is voted out. Ironmonger Noah Horst becomes the new defense chief, and Mr. Preston becomes captain of the Rangers.

While Ross, Summer, Mia, Jennie, and Kerry take a trip down the coast, they learn that Yuki is prospecting successfully. Kerry's long-lost brother Sean warns her that Voske intends to attack Las Anclas by sea. When they return, a huge fire threatens Las Anclas. Becky discovers that her brother Henry, Felicité's boyfriend, is secretly Changed and setting fires with his power in the hope of being a hero. During the fire, while she's with Henry, Felicité begins to sweat and Change from the heat. She can only preserve her secret by going to a cooler area, so she takes Henry into the secret tunnel. When Henry is revealed as the arsonist, Felicité warns him not to tell anyone about the tunnel, as she knows her father will execute him to preserve the secret. Henry is exiled from Las Anclas, and Becky becomes the sheriff's apprentice.

·CAST OF CHARACTERS·

Authors' Note

Some characters have been omitted to avoid spoilers. Occupations, relationships, and Change powers are current as of the beginning of *Traitor*.

CITIZENS AND FORMER CITIZENS OF LAS ANCLAS

The Callahan Family

Mr. Callahan. A trader. Left the town and his family years ago.
Martha Callahan. His wife, a clothing designer and tailor.
Henry Callahan. Their son, exiled for arson in *Rebel*. Felicité Wolfe's ex-boyfriend. Changed: creates fireballs. 19.
Becky Callahan. Their daughter, the sheriff's apprentice. Brisa Preciado's girlfriend. Changed: can sense impressions of the past from objects. 18.
Rosa Callahan. Mr. Callahan's sister. A weaver.
Grandma Ida. Mrs. Callahan's mother.
Grandma Alice Callahan. Mr. Callahan's mother. Killed in battle in *Stranger*.

Kerry Ji Sun Cho.

Formerly Kerry Voske, crown princess of Gold Point. Daughter of King Ian Voske and Min Soo Cho; Voske's oldest surviving daughter. Works as a pat-roller and in the town stables. Changed: creates invisible objects made of force fields. 19.
Whisper. Her brown rat.

Nugget (Nebraska Gold). Her gold stallion.
Sally (Seattle Silver). Her silver mare.
Penny (Pennsylvania Copper). Her copper mare.
Katana (Kansas Steel). Her steel colt.

The Crow/Koslova Family

Tatyana Koslova. A rat breeder and trainer.
Noemi Crow. Her wife, a rat breeder and trainer.
Elizabeth Crow. Their daughter, the sheriff. On the town council. Changed: strength, speed, and a skull-like face.

The Diaz Family

Serafina "Sera" Diaz. Captain of the Rangers. Killed in battle in *Stranger*.
Francisco "Paco" Diaz. Her son, a Ranger. Used to drum in the town band. Voske's biological son. Yuki Nakamura's ex-boyfriend. 19.

The Juarez Family

Ross Juarez. A prospector; also assists Mia Lee with mechanical jobs. Mia Lee and Jennie Riley's boyfriend. His power to control the singing trees is not a true Change. 19.
Summer Juarez. His sister. A student. Changed: agility and the ability to leap weightlessly. 15.
Spring Juarez. Her twin. Changed: telekinetic. Killed while forced to work for bandits.
Rusty. Ross's burro.

The Lee Family

Dante Lee. A doctor. Changed: can push time forward for people's bodies; he uses this to help them heal faster, but it also ages them. On the town council.
Mia Lee. His daughter, the town mechanic. Ross Juarez's girlfriend. 18.
Grandma Lee, Aunt Olivia Lee, Aunt Renata Lee, and **other relatives.**
Spanner, a tabby cat. **Phillips,** a calico cat. **Fluffy**, a black

cat.

The Lowenstein/Nakamura Family

Rivkah Lowenstein. The chief archer. Changed: cat's eyes.
Yuki Nakamura. Her adopted son. Left town to become a prospector in *Hostage*. Paco Diaz's ex-boyfriend. 18.
Meredith Lowenstein. Her biological daughter, her mother's apprentice. 17.
Kogatana. Yuki's gray rat.
Tigereye (Tennessee Bronze). Yuki's bronze mare, given to him by Kerry Cho.

The Preciado Family

Mrs. Preciado. A fieldworker.
Mr. Preciado. Her husband, a fieldworker.
Cisco Preciado. Their son, a fieldworker. 21.
Dominica Preciado. Their son, a fieldworker. 19.
Brisa Preciado. Their daughter; has not yet settled on an apprenticeship. Becky Callahan's girlfriend. Changed: makes rocks explode. 18.
Juanita "Nita" Preciado. Their daughter. 7.

The Riley Family

Sam Riley. A patrol rider. Changed: far-seer.
Judith Riley. His wife, a horse trainer. Her skill with horses may or may not be an actual Change. Deaf.
Jennie Riley. Their biological daughter. Changed: telekinetic. Formerly a Ranger, she was fired and banned in *Hostage*. Now teaches at the one-room schoolhouse. Ross Juarez's girlfriend. 19.
Jose Aldana. Their foster son. An apprentice printer/librarian. Changed: creates small earthquakes. 16.
Yolanda Riley. Their foster daughter. An apprentice farmer. Changed: controls the wind. 15.
Dee Riley. Their biological daughter. One of the "Terrible Trio." Changed: creates small vortexes. 13.
Tonio Bailis. Their foster son. Changed: bioluminescence. 10.

Grandma Riley. Mr. Riley's mother. Changed: freezes liquids.
April Riley. Mrs. Riley's niece. Changed: has wings. 3.
Aunt Flora Riley. Mr. Riley's sister. A patroller.

The Vardam Family

Ravi Vardam. Owner of a large orchard. Changed: chameleon skin. Killed in battle in *Stranger*.
Anjali Vardam. His wife. Co-owner of the orchard.
Indra Vardam. Their son, a Ranger. 19.
Sujata Vardam. Their daughter, a Ranger. 18.
Priya Vardam. Ravi's mother, a judge.

The Wolfe/Preston Family

Valeria Wolfe. The mayor of Las Anclas. On the town council.
Tom Preston. Her husband. Captain of the Rangers.
Felicité Wolfe. Their daughter. The council scribe and her mother's assistant. Henry Callahan's ex-girlfriend. Changed: grows scales and gills when water touches her skin. 18.
Will Preston. Their son. 12.
Julio Wolfe. Mayor Wolfe's nephew. A Ranger.
Grandma Lili Wolfe. Mayor Wolfe's mother, a retired teacher and current council member. Changed: fire-starter.
Wu Zetian. Felicité's golden rat.

The Town Council

Dr. Dante Lee
Sheriff Elizabeth Crow
Guild chief Jamison Appel
Teacher Lili Wolfe
Judge Marina Lopez
Defense chief and ironmonger Noah Horst
Mayor Valeria Wolfe

The Rangers

Captain Tom Preston
Frances Carillo
Paco Diaz
Grandpa Rajamouli
Indra Vardam
Sujata Vardam
Julio Wolfe
Other Rangers

The Terrible Trio

Dee Riley, 13
Nhi Tran, 13
Zaida "Z" Kabbani, 12

OTHER CITIZENS OF LAS ANCLAS

"Uncle" Omar Anders. A Ranger. Left Gold Point for Las Anclas with Sera Diaz and Tom Preston 19 years ago. Deceased.
Jamison Appel. Guild chief, on the town council.
Anna-Lucia Benisti. The saloon manager and baker. Dr. Lee's girlfriend.
Peter Chang. Student. 13.
Amy Chen. A butcher.
Carlos Garcia. An apprentice farmer. 19.
Amir Hassan. Beekeeper.
Nasreen Hassan. Mr. Hassan's daughter, an apprentice beekeeper. 18.
Noah Horst. Defense chief and ironmonger.
Paula Horst. Mr. Horst's sister.
Tommy Horst. Mr. Horst's son, an apprentice ironmonger. 18.
Luc Hsing. Owner of Luc's, a restaurant.
Rabbi Litvak. Changed: empath. Lives outside of town due to his Change.
Jack Lowell. The owner of the saloon. Sheriff Crow's ex-fiancé.
Tania Medina. A falconer. 23.
Alfonso Medina. Tania's brother. Dr. Lee's apprentice.

Changed: gecko-like fingers and toes. 18.

Josiah Rodriguez. The former town mechanic, now retired.

Hans Ruiz. A student. 14.

Constanzia Salazar. A weaver. Changed: a sparkling aura.

Hattie Salazar. Mrs. Salazar's daughter. 8.

Rico Salazar. Mrs. Salazar's son. Changed: fire-starter. 15.

Faviola Valdez. An apprentice fisher. 18.

Grandma Radha Thakrar. A brewer.

Ed and Rick Willet. Brothers, troublemakers, town drunks.

CITIZENS OF GOLD POINT

The Royal Family

Ian Voske. The king. Changed: silver hair.

Min Soo Cho. Voske's wife and Kerry's mother. Changed: activates the Change in others.

Deirdre Voske. Former crown princess. Changed: created storms. Died of over-using her power in *Stranger*.

Sean Voske. Former crown prince. Changed: evades notice (unless he consciously turns it off.) Disappeared at age 19.

Bridget Voske. Princess. Changed: makes non-living things decay. 13.

Owen Voske. Prince. Changed: telekinetic. 11.

Fiona Busisiwe Voske. Princess. Changed: teleports objects. 9.

Connor Voske. Prince. Changed: makes flowers bloom. 7.

Thandi Nkosi. Voske's wife. Sean and Fiona's biological mother, and Owen's adoptive mother. A soldier. Changed: alters gravity.

Coronet (California Silver). Voske's silver stallion.

The Flores Family

Santiago Flores. Kerry's boyfriend. Changed: heats up rocks. 19.

Mr. and Mrs. Flores. His parents.

Maria-Luisa Flores. His aunt, a horse trainer.

Maria-Pilar Flores. His cousin, a soldier. Changed: casts illusions. 19.
Diego Flores. His brother. 18.
Maria-Luz Flores. His cousin. 15.
Maria-Delia Flores. His sister. 12.
Maria-Elena Flores. His cousin, Maria-Pilar's sister. 6.
San Ramon-Nonato Flores. His brother. 1.

OTHER CITIZENS OF GOLD POINT

Luis Zavaleta. A soldier, Sophie's fiancé. Changed: a healer, but his power causes burns and can also be used to harm. 19.
Sophie Rosenfeld. A soldier, Luis's fiancée. 19.

·1·

FELICITÉ

LAS ANCLAS – WOLFE HOUSE

FELICITÉ HEFTED A HAMMER, then yanked down the towel covering her mirror. One good blow, and she'd never again have to see her hideous mutant face.

"Wu Zetian, go to your house," Felicité ordered.

Her golden rat gazed at her with shining black eyes. Felicité stroked the only creature in the world who had seen her repulsive monster face and loved her anyway.

"Darling, I'll be fine. I'll feel much better once this is done. But you need to stay safe." Felicité gently tapped the rat under her chin. "Go."

Wu Zetian scurried into her house, and Felicité covered it with the towel. Then she turned back to the disgusting, ugly mirror framing her disgusting, ugly face.

She hit the mirror with all her strength.

Cracks spiderwebbed across the mirror. She struck it again. A few shards fell to the floor, but most stayed in place.

"Felicité!" It was Grandmère's voice! She sounded like she was right outside the bedroom door.

Felicité had thought it would only take one blow, and that no one would hear her if she shut her door and waited till everyone was asleep. She couldn't even do *this* right. And there was still the long mirror in her bathroom. She swung the hammer again and again, until there was nothing left but shards. Felicité stood in a sea of shattered glass, each fragment reflecting her hideousness.

"Felicité! Open this door immediately!" The door

rattled, but the lock held.

She bolted for the bathroom. She had to destroy the last mirror before her grandmother fetched the key. She swung the hammer feverishly, glass tinkling down, until someone grabbed her arm. Felicité jumped. She hadn't heard anyone come in.

"Felicité, what are you doing?" Grandmère was in her nightgown, her usually neat hair rumpled. Mother was at her shoulder with a robe over her gown. Her hair was tied back, and she looked very tired.

Felicité's angry triumph faded, leaving her numb and empty. The mirrors were gone, but she was still a monster. She was thousands of monsters scattered across the floor.

"Felicité," Grandmère said gently. "Why don't you put down the hammer, and come talk to us?"

"I'm *done* talking!" Felicité screamed. Oh, it felt good to scream! For years, she'd been so careful to modulate her voice properly, like a future mayor, and for what? She'd never be a mayor. Everyone hated her — but no one more than she hated herself.

She looked around for something else to destroy. The bathtub! The place where the monster came out. Felicité hadn't dared to get into it for months. She threw the hammer as hard as she could. A huge crack appeared in the porcelain. Felicité smiled. Now they'd have to get rid of the tub.

Mother went out, and Grandmère spread out the bath towels to cover the broken glass. Felicité turned her hot, angry gaze to her, then saw a vein flicker in the delicate hollow in her grandmother's temple. A wave of guilt washed away the anger. She'd never seen her grandmother so upset. Not even when Grandmère's own Change had emerged at menopause and she'd nearly burned down the schoolhouse, or the night she'd left Las Anclas to live in a fireproof house outside its walls, not knowing if she'd ever be able to control her Change and come back.

"I just…" Felicité's voice trailed off. There was no way she could explain what she'd done. Her mother and Grandmère must think she'd lost her mind.

Maybe she had.

"Darling, let us tend to your feet." Grandmère took a

bottle of disinfectant alcohol from the cupboard as Mother reappeared with bandages. They returned to the bedroom, where Mother pulled off the bedding and dropped it over the broken glass. Felicité's feet made red prints on the coverlet. They sat on the bed with Felicité in the middle, and Mother pulled Felicité's feet into her lap. They left red smears on her grass-green silk nightdress embroidered with spring wildflowers.

Felicité ruined everything.

"Would you like your rat with you, dear?" Grandmère asked.

Of course she wanted her rat. Wu Zetian was the only friend she had left. Felicité whistled. Wu Zetian poked her pink nose out, then leaped into her lap. Felicité held her close as Grandmère disinfected the cuts and Mother wrapped them.

"Darling," Grandmère said as she eased on a pair of clean stockings. "Everyone understands that you couldn't possibly have known that Henry Callahan was using a secret Change power to set fires. Even I thought he had grown out of his mischievous stage. When he came over for dinner, he seemed quite a charming young man."

Felicité snapped, "That's not what *Daddy* said. *Daddy* said I should have known better. *Daddy* said he'd never liked Henry in the first place."

A flicker of irritation tightened Grandmère's mouth. "Tom doesn't know what it's like to be a young woman. But I know, and your mother knows, and neither of us blame you."

Mother said with her usual composure, "You don't have to punish yourself for something you had nothing to do with. Love is a wonderful thing, but it can blind y—"

"*Daddy* said I didn't even love him!" Felicité shouted. "*Daddy* said he was one of my 'little flirts.'" Mother's brows drew together and Grandmère opened her mouth, but Felicité didn't stop. "*Daddy* said if Henry really loved me, he wouldn't have put me in that position. *Daddy* —"

Grandmère interrupted her. "Your father isn't here. When he returns, he can speak for himself. I understand how much it hurts. But Felicité, you are no longer a child."

Gently but firmly, Mother said, "You've graduated from school. You are the mayor's assistant, an adult."

Grandmère added, in a similar tone, "One of the things — one of the hardest things — that adulthood means is this: you need to carry on with your responsibilities even if your heart is breaking inside."

"What do you know about that?" Felicité demanded. "Either of you?"

Felicité's parents hated Changed people. Grandmère didn't, but when she'd Changed, she hadn't had a choice over whether to hide it or not. And Grandmère had never cared a whit for Daddy's opinion, so she wouldn't have hidden it anyway. Most importantly, *her* Change wasn't monstrous. It was a power, not a hideous deformity. *She* had never had to keep a secret or lose the love of the person who'd admired her for her brains, her inner strength, and her *normality*.

Unable to say any of that, Felicité muttered, "You were never publicly humiliated when the entire town found out that you'd been duped by a Changed criminal. People stare at me like I'm the biggest fool they've ever seen. And I'm stuck here for my entire life. I made one mistake, and it'll follow me forever."

"It seems like forever," said Grandmère. "But that's because you haven't been alive for very long. I am old enough to assure you that these moments are universal, and that they pass. Every adult in town once believed they'd be humiliated for the rest of their lives." When Felicité shook her head in disbelief, Grandmère said, "Name any adult, and I'll tell you a low point in their lives."

"Oh, really? How about those Rileys, who everyone thinks so perfect?"

Grandmère smiled. "Certainly. Let's begin with Jennie's father, Sam. He was so popular that the entire town celebrated his wedding — his first wedding — which was the most elaborate many of us had ever seen. Do you know how long that marriage lasted?"

Felicité shrugged. She knew Mr. Riley was divorced from one of the Lee women, but she couldn't remember which. Jennie and Mia used to bore everyone to death at school about how they could have been sisters.

"Two months," Mother said, holding up two fingers. "Sam Riley and Olivia Lee were about your age. Both their families thought they were too young, but they insisted. By the week before the wedding, they knew it was a mistake."

Grandmère added crisply, "They went through with it because they were too embarrassed to admit it. And when they broke up two months later, some people laughed when they went around giving back their gifts."

"Really?" Felicité asked, interested despite herself.

"Really," said Grandmère. "You see, you didn't even know about that. That's because time passed, and people forgot. They both made happy second marriages."

Mother stroked Felicité's bandaged foot. "I promise, darling, in a few months, the only looks anyone will give you will be of respect and admiration."

Because they don't know I'm a monster, Felicité thought. *And you'd drop my foot in a hurry if you found out.*

Grandmère went on, "By this time next year, most people won't think about it. In time, they won't even remember."

"But I will," Felicité said.

Grandmère patted her back. "Of course you will. But adults have to go on with hurt inside. When your grandfather — my husband — died of a heart attack, I had a schoolhouse of children waiting for me. School was dismissed for a few days, but the children couldn't go untaught forever. That entire year, I felt as shocked and hurt as if he'd died an hour ago. But I still had to teach science and math and reading. And I had to care for the children. Can you imagine how trivial the problems of a seven-year-old felt to me that year? But they were serious to that child, and we both felt our hurts would last forever."

Felicité vaguely remembered her grandfather as an old man who let her hunt for the candy hidden in his coat pockets. She'd been sad when he died, but she'd also wondered if she was supposed to feel something different, something more. Now she understood what it must have been like for Grandmère. For Mother, who had lost *her* daddy.

People said no one can walk in someone else's shoes. Yet she'd briefly felt like she was walking in Grandmère's. If she told her grandmother her secret, might she understand? After all, she was Changed herself. Felicité imagined saying, "Grandmère, there's something I haven't told you…"

Yes, Grandmère would sympathize—with the Change. She'd tell Felicité to stand up with pride and announce it to the entire world. But Grandmère didn't care what Daddy thought. Daddy didn't love her, nor did she love him. Grandmère had seen his disgust and horror when she lit candles with her power, and it didn't bother her at all.

And Mother? She'd probably give Felicité the look of controlled distaste she turned on flying roaches, too dignified to recoil in the horror she felt in her heart—

The familiar creak of the front door opening broke into her thoughts.

"Oh! Tom must be back!" Mother hurried out of the room, smiling. Grandmère followed her, not looking half so pleased.

Felicité froze. She'd looked forward to Daddy's return from his trip, but she didn't want him to know about her breaking the mirror and bath. At best, he'd be disappointed in her loss of control. At worst, he might start to wonder…

Wu Zetian clawed at Felicité's ankle, tail lashing, teeth bared. Felicité looked down at her golden rat, alarmed. Wu Zetian *never* scratched her. And she knew Daddy's scent. Felicité got up, then winced as she put weight on her bandaged feet.

She stepped onto the landing and peered down the staircase. All the lights were out. As her eyes adjusted to the moonlight coming in through the windows, she made out black-clad, masked figures hurrying quietly toward the doorways—and up the stairs!

Felicité dashed toward her room. Just as her fingers touched the doorknob, she was yanked backward. As she started to scream for help, a gloved hand clamped around her mouth. She smelled the sharp sweat of a man. Struggling, Felicité was dragged back to the landing.

Mother stood before her room, the moonlight pale on her blood-smudged nightrobe, her long black hair streaming down. She brandished a heavy vase. A black-clad figure knocked the vase out of her hand with a shattering crash, then shoved past her into her bedroom. Cold light glinted on drawn steel. Mother stared up at Felicité, her eyes round with shock.

"Let go of my daughter!" Mother snatched up another vase. An invader knocked it out of her hand with a sword, and it, too, smashed on the floor. Two more invaders grabbed her.

Felicité had never seen her mother fight, not even in training. But with wild fury in her eyes, Mother clawed at a masked face, screaming, "Let my daughter go!"

The invader caught her wrist before she could hurt him. Mother kicked out, but the enemy swept her feet out from under her. Horrified, Felicité saw Mother fall to the floor. Two enemies pinned her down, one clamping a hand over her mouth. More enemies emerged from the bedroom and thundered up the stairs, drawn steel gripped in gloved hands. Felicité struggled uselessly as they streamed past her.

Golden light flared with shocking brightness from Grandmère's door downstairs. Two figures were silhouetted in the doorway — on fire! One let out a strangled scream.

A man yelled, "Drop and roll!"

Grandmère bounded into the living room, a small figure with hands upraised. As a fireball blossomed in her hand, an enemy punched her in the jaw. The fireball went out as Grandmère crumpled to the floor. The enemy drew back a boot to kick her.

Felicité had been frozen in shock, but now hot anger surged in her. She struggled hard, trying to bite the hand over her mouth like she'd once bitten Jennie. But her captor had her lips pressed hard against her teeth, preventing her from biting.

"Remember our orders," a woman said in a low voice. "The prisoners aren't to be harmed."

Prisoners. Terror pooled in Felicité's stomach.

She'd seen those black-clad figures before. In the battle of Las Anclas, when she'd thought she and Daddy would die together in a last stand, they'd instead witnessed Ross's singing tree kill a team of elite soldiers. Their black uniforms became the obsidian of a new grove of crystal trees outside the town walls.

These were Voske's soldiers.

She heard shouts from outside, but no alarm bells. Felicité couldn't understand how so many soldiers could have gotten into Las Anclas with no alarm being raised. The Rangers patrolled outside every night, and sentries manned the walls.

Voske's soldiers came downstairs. One carried her little brother Will tucked under his arm, limp. Fresh terror chilled her at the thought that they'd killed him. But she didn't see any blood. He was probably still asleep. It took Mother ten minutes of shaking to get him up in the morning. As Mother struggled uselessly on the living room floor, Will was set down on his feet with a pair of enemies holding him up by the arms.

"Wake up, William," the enemy woman spoke again. "William! Wake up."

As Voske's soldiers shook her little brother, Felicité tried to think of something she could do. She couldn't fight. Could she send Wu Zetian with a message? She didn't see her rat anywhere. With a lurch in her belly, Felicité hoped her pet was safe.

Where was Sheriff Crow? Where were the Rangers? What had happened to the sentries who were supposed to watch for invaders? Felicité looked around frantically for the help that ought to be coming. But all she saw were enemy soldiers calmly putting out the fire Grandmère had set and carrying the badly burned soldier to the couch. One lit a candle in the stairway lamp.

"Wha—?" Will mumbled.

"William." The enemy woman spoke in a sweet, low tone that reminded Felicité of her own voice when she needed people to do what she said. "Where is your father?"

Clearly not really awake, Will mumbled, "Daddy took the Rangers on a scouting trip. Wouldn't let me come. I'm old enough."

"What a shame," the woman said, oh so very sweetly. "I'm sure you'd have been such a help. Where did they go?"

"Gold Point." Will yawned, blinking. "Dunno if they got there yet. Daddy said there might be mudslides."

The woman nodded at a man, who went out. Felicité

tried to stamp on the feet of the soldier holding her. But all she did was hurt her cut soles on his boots.

Daddy will kill you all when he finds out about this, Felicité thought fiercely.

What would Daddy do if he were here? She made herself calmly evaluate the situation, putting together everything she knew. The alarm bell had never rung, so it couldn't be a big attack. There were only a few enemies, like the team that Voske sent to try to break Kerry out of jail. Once Sheriff Crow found out where they were, she'd come and kill them all, like she'd killed Kerry's would-be rescuers. Everything would be all right. They simply had to wait for the sheriff to arrive.

"Where is Kerry Voske?" the woman went on.

"Kerry Cho," Will muttered sleepily. "She's gone. Went to see the Catalina Players with Jennie and Ross and Mia. And that stupid Summer. She broke my arm. I hope she falls in a pit mouth. Hey," Will yelped, now thoroughly awake. He tried to pull away from the people holding him. "Who *are* you? Let me go!"

A soldier put a hand over his mouth, stifling his cries. Others carried Grandmère from the hall and laid her on the living room carpet. Though she was still unconscious, her hands had been tied with her palms together, preventing her from using her powers. Kerry had been bound like that when she had been a prisoner in Las Anclas.

This is Kerry's fault, Felicité thought furiously. Voske must have sent a team after her again, only this time to kill her rather than rescue her. But why would they look *here?*

The woman's head turned from Mother to Felicité to the servants, who had been herded out from the back rooms, and spoke to them all. "We can do this two ways. You can agree not to yell or fight—which as you see, won't do any good—or we can do whatever we need to do to keep you quiet."

She nodded at the soldiers holding Mother. The tall one lifted his hand from her mouth. Mother said, "Leave my children alone, and we'll cooperate." She turned to Felicité, then to Will. "Don't fight."

Will exclaimed indignantly, "But these are bad guys! Daddy said—"

"William, we shall wait." The steel in Mother's voice silenced him immediately.

An enemy laughed, then stopped abruptly when the woman in charge turned her masked face to him. "Very good." The enemy commander pulled off her mask. She looked about Daddy's age, with her tight black curls clipped short. "Everybody, sit down."

Felicité was freed at last. Her knees wobbled as she walked downstairs and joined Mother and Will on a couch. The burned soldier lay on another. The servants silently sat on the third, which they had never been permitted to use before. Mother's fingers slid over Felicité's and gripped tightly. The only human sounds were the hissing breaths of the badly burned soldier. The one with the lesser burn sat on a chair getting his wound tended. As time passed, ticked off by the clock on the mantelpiece, and no rescue came, dread curdled inside Felicité. What was going on? Could the sheriff still be asleep? The bell had never rung...

The front door opened, bringing a surge of cool air. The candle in the stairwell lamp guttered, throwing wild shadows. The soldiers all saluted. In the flickering light, a tall black-clad man walked in, his boots treading on the ancient carpet that no shoes had ever walked on. Candlelight glinted on metallic silver hair.

Felicité's heart thundered in shock and recognition. She'd glimpsed him at a distance, near the end of the battle for Las Anclas. He'd tried to kill Daddy with a rifle, but Mia Lee had distracted him. He'd been too far away for her to see his face, but she would never forget the glitter of silver hair in the moonlight.

Voske himself was inside her house.

Felicité stared, numb, at his face. He looked like Paco. He looked like Kerry. There were those sharp cheekbones, the pointed chin and nose, the upward slanting eyebrows. And Kerry's eerie smile.

He stepped aside, beckoning.

Felicité had thought she couldn't be more shocked and horrified, but when she saw the person who walked in behind King Voske, dressed in the same black as his soldiers, she knew that until now, she hadn't even known what shock and horror were.

Looking right at her, his familiar grin wide, was Henry Callahan.

Shock jolted through her. Her stomach churned with sickening realization. Now she knew why the alarm bells hadn't rung. She knew why rescue hadn't come — why rescue would never come.

Las Anclas had been conquered from within.

The enemy had come in through the secret tunnel that ran from the mill outside the town walls to the town hall. It had been created as a last resort, so the children could escape if Las Anclas was taken. That tunnel had been the town's biggest secret, and Felicité had revealed it to Henry…and let him walk into exile without telling anyone what she'd done.

Las Anclas had fallen to Voske. And Kerry had nothing to do with it.

It was all Felicité's fault.

·2·
BECKY

LAS ANCLAS – TOWN CENTER

"ELIZABETH!"

The low voice shattered Becky's dream. She leaped out of bed, still blinking sleep from her eyes, and snatched up her dart gun. She slept in her clothes when it was her turn to be deputy at the jail, so all she needed to do was jam her feet into her shoes.

She'd been sleeping in the deputy alcove with the door open, as it was the size of a closet and got stuffy. When she stepped out, dart gun ready, she saw a man with blond hair. For a heart-stopping instant, she thought it was her brother Henry, returned from exile. Then she recognized Jack, Sheriff Crow's ex-fiancé.

The sheriff appeared at her bedroom door, in pajamas and with her rifle cocked. "Jack?"

"Enemies in town," Jack whispered. "They came out of the town hall and spread out in all directions."

"Voske!" Sheriff Crow said in a muffled gasp, buckling a belt over her pajamas. "How could he have found out about the tunnel?"

Jack shrugged. Becky was already putting on her dart belt. "What tunnel?"

"Later," said the sheriff. "Becky, go to the bell tower. Ring the alarm. Don't stop for *anything*." She shoved two pistols into her belt and offered a third to Jack.

He shook his head. "You know I can't shoot worth a damn. I'll ring the bell."

"I'll go to the town hall." Sheriff Crow handed the

third pistol to Becky. "Cover Jack."

It felt like a dream, but her body knew better — Becky was trembling so hard, her dart case rattled in her belt.

"You can do this," said Sheriff Crow.

Becky wasn't so sure. She'd faced down drunks and belligerent election campaigners, but this was war. She hadn't fought in the battle of Las Anclas — she'd been Dr. Lee's apprentice then and spent the entire battle in the field hospital. And what was that stuff about a tunnel?

"Becky, *run*," the sheriff commanded her.

Becky obeyed automatically, grabbing Jack's elbow and bolting outside. The sheriff was already tearing past Jack's saloon, her Changed speed making her a blur. But before she reached the town hall, a swarm of black-clad soldiers charged her. Sheriff Crow punched and kicked through the middle of them. Becky longed to watch, but the sheriff had ordered her not to stop for anything. That included Sheriff Crow herself.

They bolted across pocket gardens, trampling spring plantings underfoot. Despite the urgency, Becky felt guilty over every plant she crushed underfoot. She fixed her gaze on the bell tower. It wasn't far. They only had to get through the gardens and across Main Street. Becky could run it in three minutes...if no one stopped her.

But more soldiers appeared, spreading out wide to block them. Becky tried to scream out an alarm. Nothing came out but a croak. Jack panted beside her as he leaped the low fences dividing the gardens. Her entire body tensed when a soldier raised his crossbow. But he didn't shoot. Instead, the soldiers charged her and Jack.

Becky raised her dart gun and shot the crossbowman. She missed. Though she'd practiced daily since she became the sheriff's apprentice, Sheriff Crow had warned her it was almost impossible to hit a target while you were running yourself. In Becky's mind, the sheriff's dry voice spoke: *"Don't waste your ammo."*

Jack faltered, looking around wildly. The soldiers closed in, blocking him from darting between the surgery and Mia's cottage toward the bell tower. Jack glanced desperately back at the sheriff. Becky followed his gaze.

Sheriff Crow hadn't made it to the town hall. She was fighting off a horde of soldiers, far too many for even her

Changed strength to handle. She didn't seem wounded. They were trying to capture her, too.

Becky forced her gaze back to the enemies closing in on her and Jack. She halted, planting her feet firmly on either side of a row of cabbages, slapped a new dart into her gun, pulled the lever back, took aim with both hands, and shot at the enemy at Jack's left.

He froze, paralyzed by the cloud viper venom in the dart, then toppled into a tangle of tomato vines.

She ran three steps, her fingers working automatically to reload, stopped, and dropped the one at Jack's right. Jack leaped between the two fallen soldiers and pelted for the bell tower.

Becky followed. One attacker shot low—aiming for her legs—but she'd already leaped over a pumpkin vine. The crossbow bolt was a wink of light as it passed a finger's breadth from her knee. She shot at him, then jagged aside as she slapped in a dart and yanked back the slide.

Becky heard the voices of the enemies: "Shoot to kill?"

"No. Our orders to capture stand."

That didn't make Becky feel any better. She bent low, pumping her legs hard as she ran after Jack. A warning shot zipped in front of her. Black-clad soldiers ran everywhere. She couldn't get past them. Caught at the edge of the gardens, with one foot on Main Street and the other in someone's carrots, Becky kept reloading and shooting. But she knew she and Jack would never reach the bell tower.

She looked back. Even more enemies surrounded Sheriff Crow—and they were now shooting to kill. The sheriff wove among them so fast that some shot each other. She kept fighting, trying to get back to Jack and Becky, but more enemies leaped over their fallen allies, maneuvering to encircle her.

Becky continued to shoot as she tried to widen the field of her vision. Dr. Lee ran out of the surgery, his hair undone and hanging around his shoulders. An enemy grabbed him. Dr. Lee's bare hand reached up to touch the soldier's cheek. Sick and stunned, Becky knew he was about to break his own moral code and use his Change power to kill. In another instant, that man would be dead of old age.

But Dr. Lee chose otherwise. The second passed, and he dropped his hand in surrender.

Jack said hoarsely, "Bell tower's blocked. I'm going to help Elizabeth." He started running back through the gardens. A soldier intercepted him in a flying tackle, throwing him to the ground.

A fresh mob of soldiers poured in through the rear gate, which now stood open to the enemy. Only Sheriff Crow was still fighting, whirling and leaping past a line of enemies. But a larger line was closing in on her, and even she couldn't keep up her amazing speed forever.

Becky saw that Sheriff Crow wasn't planning to survive the battle. *She's making her last stand right here.*

It was so pointless. Dr. Lee had surrendered, and he hadn't been harmed. The soldier was holding Jack down but hadn't hurt him. Becky herself could have been shot, but she hadn't been. But the soldiers fighting with the sheriff were using crossbows and swords. They meant to kill her if she didn't surrender.

It was too late for Jack and Becky. But there was one thing she could still do. She remembered how Sheriff Crow had taught her to yell. Putting all the force of the sheriff into her own voice, she screamed, "SHERIFF CROW, RUN!"

The sheriff stilled for an instant. Becky's heart banged against her ribs. Then Sheriff Crow leaped, smashed aside a crossbow, and shot away at her blurring Change speed—not toward Becky and Jack, but away, toward the back wall.

Elated, dizzy, Becky stumbled toward her, stopping every other step to load and shoot the enemies firing at Sheriff Crow, covering her escape. Becky kept shooting until her darts ran out. She dropped the dart gun and snatched for her pistol.

Before she could touch it, someone tackled her from behind, throwing her face-down into the mud. Her pistol was yanked from her belt, and her hands were wrenched behind her and tied. Her eyes stung with tears. She forced her head to turn.

She didn't see the sheriff's body. Maybe, maybe, maybe, she'd escaped. Becky clung to that hope.

·3·
PACO

LAS ANCLAS - BEACH

HORSE HOOVES THUDDED INTO the packed beach sand. Paco absently drummed a counterpoint on his saddle. He and Grandpa Rajamouli had the midnight perimeter patrol. They hadn't seen anything but a glittering streak of blue phosphorescence on a gentle wave, three washed-up jellyfish, and a spiky little creature that had scuttled back into the ocean before Paco had gotten a good look at it. Grandpa Rajamouli hadn't been able to identify it, either.

Yuki would have tried for a closer glimpse. And he'd have kept an eye out each patrol afterward, until he either figured out what it was or named it himself.

Paco noticed his fingers tapping and clenched his fist tight. Yuki had loved his drumming, but Yuki was gone. Mom had loved his music, but she was dead. If he'd only trained for the Rangers when she'd encouraged him! He'd have been a Ranger by the time Voske attacked, and then he'd have been with Mom when she needed him. Instead, he'd spent his precious time—*her* precious time—on useless music. And here he was, still drumming!

"Hey," said Grandpa Rajamouli. "Don't stop. We don't need to be *that* stealthy. That was a nice rhythm you had going there."

"It was distracting me," Paco said, trying to hide his self-loathing.

"Distraction isn't too bad on a quiet night like this," Grandpa Rajamouli responded with cheer. "That's why we ride in pairs, so we can talk and not drift off in the saddle."

Paco took a deep breath of the cool sea air. He glanced back at the floodlit walls of Las Anclas, then at the ocean, black and empty except for a dim moon trail. The shoreline lay colorless in the moonlight. Where under this dark sky was Yuki? Did he look up and think of home, of Paco?

Grandpa Rajamouli patted his horse's side. "Don't tell my family, but it's good to be a Ranger again."

"I remember when you retired," Paco said, glad to be distracted. "You said you wanted to spend the rest of your life playing with your grandkids."

"I did when they were five." Grandpa Rajamouli chuckled ruefully. "Now they're teens. They don't want piggybacks from Grandpa, they want to go dancing at Luc's." He sent Paco a sharp look. "Why aren't you at Luc's when you're off duty? My grandkids say you never drum anymore. They miss it."

"I need to train. I don't have time for music."

Grandpa Rajamouli laughed. "You new Rangers are all like that, on fire for training day and night. We were, too, back in my day. In fact, after Voske's attack, when Tom Preston asked me to come out of retirement, *I* was like that for a couple months."

Paco smiled a little. It had been oddly comforting when Grandpa Rajamouli had rejoined the Rangers. When Paco was small, he'd been Uncle Rajamouli, one of the older Rangers. He'd often had dinner at their house, a cheerful presence.

"It paid off," said Paco. "Hope when I'm your age, I'm in such good shape."

Grandpa Rajamouli laughed again, clearly pleased by the compliment. Paco meant it. Grandpa Rajamouli might have gray hair and a lot more wrinkles than when he'd last been a Ranger, but he was strong. Paco had sparred with him enough to know what a formidable opponent he still was.

A glimmer of light across the dark ocean caught Paco's attention. He whipped around in the saddle, his hand dropping to his sword. "Those lights!"

Grandpa Rajamouli reacted a heartbeat slower. He shaded his eyes from the moon. "Those aren't Voske's ships. Or any ship. Look closer. They're in the sky."

He was right. The lights weren't the rocking yellow specks of Catalina's lantern-lit fishing boats. Ever since Kerry's report that Voske might be planning an attack by sea, whenever Paco saw those bobbing lights, he wondered if it was a Catalina fishing boat or a Gold Point warship in disguise. But these lights floated in the sky, pearly bubbles catching the moonlight.

"Oh. They're the jellyfish." Paco had always enjoyed watching the giant flying jellyfish floating over the ocean, drifting to and from Catalina. He craned his neck, trying to see the riding basket he knew dangled beneath them, but it was too dark.

Julio and Frances rode up from the other end of the beach. Pointing at the opalescent jellyfish, Julio said, "We should catch one! We could use it to sneak up on your giant lobsters, Paco." He punched Paco lightly in the ribs.

Irritated, Paco jerked away. Fuego sidled underneath him, his ears flicking back. Paco tried to breathe out his irritation; he was upsetting his horse. "You didn't see those lobsters, Julio. The queen was big as a house. And she took over—" Paco broke off. He didn't want to mention Kerry, especially around the tactless Julio. Paco was not going to lose his temper while he was on patrol. "People's minds."

Julio laughed. He was a good fighter, but he didn't take anything seriously. Paco had been relieved when Mr. Preston had taken charge of the Rangers away from him.

Grandpa Rajamouli fixed him with a frown. "Julio, we're probably seeing those jellyfish more than usual because Catalina is worried about Voske attacking them, after our trouble last year. My guess is, the entire coast is on watch, right down to the Fire Lands in the south. And queen lobsters are equally serious business. So is this patrol."

Julio chuckled, then said, mock-solemn, "Got it. Lobsters and jellyfish are serious." He saluted sharply and rode back toward his proper patrol route.

Frances gave Grandpa Rajamouli a long-suffering smile and followed Julio.

Paco took a last look at the jellyfish as he and Grandpa Rajamouli continued their round. Julio had been kidding about using the jellyfish as weapons, but if Yuki had been there, he'd probably be thinking along the same lines. Only Yuki would have an actual plan to capture a wild one—

Paco had to stop thinking about Yuki. And about anything in the past. He was on patrol, protecting his town, and that was all he was going to focus on.

They had just reached the turn-around point when Fuego sidled more sharply and both horses' ears flattened.

"What?" Grandpa Rajamouli only got out the one word.

Black-clad figures appeared out of the darkness, like an army of shadows. There seemed to be a hundred of them, rapidly closing in, steel gleaming in the moonlight.

This was no surprise exercise.

Paco ripped out his sword and slashed at the nearest one. He heard Grandpa Rajamouli grunt with effort, followed by the clash of steel.

Paco forced Fuego around in a circle. The attackers were on foot, so he had the advantage of fighting downward. But there were so many of them. He kneed Fuego as he struck at another figure. The red-gold gelding plunged and kicked, and Paco let him. He did not want the attackers killing Fuego, his favorite horse. He had to get to higher ground, get out of this trap—

"That's him," someone barked sharply.

Paco didn't know who 'him' was, but he sensed a subtle hesitation in the fighter attacking him. Paco didn't hesitate. His sword bit into flesh. He yanked his weapon free and whirled it overhead and down at an enemy on the other side. The enemies wore black masks, but that one's bare neck gleamed pale in the moonlight. Paco's sword struck something, and the blade bounced back hard enough to reverberate up his arm. A Change power! They'd left their throat open as a tempting target—

Paco kneed Fuego away as attackers closed in from the other side. He regripped his sword and swung it down in a killing arc, again and again and again, Fuego dancing this way and that, sometimes rearing and striking with his hooves.

He lost count of the strikes of steel against steel. Though he landed some blows and saw enemies fall, more crowded in. Where was Grandpa Rajamouli? Paco had to back him up, but he didn't dare look farther than the attackers pressing up on all sides.

A gigantic force slammed into him, nearly knocking him from the saddle. As he struggled to regain his seat, he was yanked from the saddle and flung down to the sand.

Heavy boots stomped on his sword arm. Ignoring the agony in his shoulder, he hitched one hip up and swung his foot in a roundhouse kick, shattering an attacker's kneecap. The man doubled over. But before Paco could do anything else, he was flung over, his face shoved into the sand. Grit filled his mouth, eyes, and nose. For a panicked instant, he couldn't breathe. Someone grabbed his hair and jerked his face up. Many hands ripped his sword away, nearly breaking his fingers. More hands yanked his arms behind his back and bound his wrists tightly.

The enemies hauled him to his feet. His vision swam dizzily, and his right arm ached where all those boots had landed. He spat sand and tried to blink it out of his eyes. He had to see what was going on. Where was Grandpa Rajamouli? Where was Julio? The bells should be ringing the alarm. But all he heard was the heavy breathing of his attackers.

One soldier pulled off his mask. He was Paco's age, with short black hair and blunt features. This seemed to be the commander. He waved his hand in a circle, and the nearest soldiers promptly closed in around Paco. One held Fuego by the reins. Paco was relieved that the horse wasn't hurt.

To Paco's surprise, the commander took out a watch. The only watch he'd seen before belonged to Mr. Preston, who used it to time drills; Mr. Preston had said once, "We need to get Mia to learn how to make watches. It's the only sure way to run simultaneous attacks." Then he'd laughed, and said, "Once I can bring myself to let her take mine apart."

Simultaneous attacks. This was a full-scale invasion. Why didn't the bells ring? Why didn't he hear fighting?

The young commander used his mask to wipe sweat off his forehead. "Diwanji, take charge of the dead and wounded. Hettick, fall back to West Company. I'll take my team to report."

The enemies forced Paco to walk. He saw Grandpa

Rajamouli lying in the sand, his open eyes staring sightlessly up at the moon. Blood pooled blackly beneath him. Paco started toward him, but the soldiers yanked him back.

"Halt." The commander left the formation and dropped to his knees, reaching out to the enemy soldier who lay beside Grandpa Rajamouli. It was a young woman, her mask ripped off in the battle, her eyes closed. The commander touched the side of her neck, then drew back his hand.

"Oh, Sophie," he murmured.

The only other noise was the soft splash and hiss of waves. The dead soldier's face was clear in the strong moonlight. Scars dappled one cheek in an oddly familiar pattern. With a lurch in his belly, Paco remembered the handprint scar on Ross's neck.

"She's dead." The commander looked up. "Diwanji?"

"We've got her." Two soldiers knelt beside her with a stretcher.

Paco desperately looked for Julio and Frances and the other Ranger pair on beach patrol, but only saw their horses being led away from the beach.

They couldn't *all* be dead.

They didn't kill me, Paco thought grimly. He twisted the ropes binding his wrists, ignoring the hot pain. At first he welcomed the slickness of blood, but the ropes only pulled tighter: the enemy knew how to tie knots.

As they started moving again, he searched for more prisoners. But another twenty paces brought him to more figures lying in the sand. His gaze swept past the black clad enemies, then hitched to a stop. Julio lay as still as the enemies — as still as Grandpa Rajamouli — his sword half-buried in the sand near his limp fingers. Beyond him, moonlight glinted on Frances's red hair. She was dead, too. Paco knew from Voske's invasion what that looked like, how the dead lay.

It was the sight of Julio lying there lifeless that made Paco feel as if he'd been asleep, and now he was waking up. Grandpa Rajamouli dying was terrible, but old people died. *Parents die.* Cold pooled inside Paco.

Julio was only five years older. He was always lucky. He never got hurt. His ready laughter rang in Paco's memory. It was so impossible for Julio to be dead that it made the possible seem unreal.

Paco had to pull himself together if he wanted to fight back effectively. He had to think. Plan. But no thoughts came, only the sound of his heart drumming in time to the throb in his wrists, and the chuff of feet in sand. What sort of person was he, to notice rhythms when all the Rangers but him were dead?

Longing stabbed through him. He wanted Yuki by his side more than he had wanted anything in his life. Yuki would know what to do. They would fight together…

No. He couldn't think about that. Yuki was gone. Thinking about him would only make the pain worse. Paco was alone. He had to accept that. Think. Plan. Yuki was good at thinking and planning—

As he renewed his struggle to loosen his bonds, he was vaguely aware of the commander giving orders, and soldiers taking off in different directions.

Every thought fled when he saw the gates of Las Anclas, standing wide open and guarded by the enemy. The town had been taken.

That was why the bells had never rung.

The pocket watch.

Simultaneous attacks—

Voske was back. And this time he'd won.

The commander grabbed Paco by his shoulders, jerking him close. Paco jumped, startled. Everyone else seemed to have been sent away. There was no one within earshot as the commander demanded in a harsh whisper, "Where's Kerry?"

Only then did Paco remember that she was far away, off traveling with Ross and Jennie and Mia and Summer. Relief washed through him, followed by a burst of rage. Of course, Voske's first thought after taking the town would be to murder his renegade daughter—exactly as Kerry had predicted.

Paco said fiercely, "Go to hell."

The commander's face twisted with…frustration? Anger? "No, it isn't—" His gaze lifted to the watching sentries on the wall. "Come on."

The commander didn't speak again as he pushed

Paco through the gates that were never opened at night. Someone on the wall yelled, "Santiago! You got him!"

The enemies on the wall cheered. The commander — Santiago — jerked his hand, cutting them off.

Paco knew why his capture was worth a cheer. He was Voske's —

He was *not* Voske's son. Mr. Preston's voice echoed in his ears: *"Ian Voske is nothing to you. You are your mother's son."*

But Voske obviously wanted something from him. Maybe to kill him in place of Kerry. He'd heard Kerry say to Ross that when Voske took the town — she'd always said *when*, not *if* — she'd fight to the death rather than face a public execution. And Ross had said, *"So will I."*

Bitterness flooded Paco. Fine. He could face a firing squad. He was not afraid to die.

As they walked up Main Street, he saw enemy soldiers everywhere, moving in ordered ranks throughout the town. A fire burned at the armory, with a bucket brigade of enemies working to put it out. But there was no fighting in the streets. Voske had taken the town almost without a fight. How had he done it? It could never have happened if Mr. Preston had been here.

Enemy soldiers swarmed around the town hall. Their eyes widened when they saw Paco. Santiago said, "I have to report to the king. Is he here?"

"He's setting up headquarters at Preston's house — it's the biggest one, on the hill over that way. You're to report there with...him." The soldier's stare flicked away as he turned to a pair of enemies. "Escort them."

It was surreal to walk the familiar paths with enemy soldiers. Paco'd had dinner at Wolfe House on New Year's, the night before Mr. Preston had left with half the Rangers.

At least Mr. Preston was alive. At least Indra was alive, and Sujata, and the other Rangers who had gone with Mr. Preston. Jennie was alive. And Ross. And Mia, Kerry, and Summer. And Yuki. That would be a good thought to die with: Yuki was alive. *I hope he never comes back. I hope he spends the rest of his life exploring, like he always wanted, and never finds out what happened to me.*

Wolfe House was lit up, with soldiers walking in and

out. As Paco and Santiago approached, they all side-eyed Paco. His rage burned hotter. He jerked his head, flinging the hair out of his eyes. Let them stare.

The front door opened, silhouetting a tall figure, the light a golden nimbus around his hair. His head turned, and the light fell on his face. Shock jolted through Paco when he recognized Henry Callahan. Paco had never expected to see Henry again after he'd been exiled for arson.

Henry grinned. "Hi, Paco. Having fun?"

He wore black fatigues like the Gold Point soldiers. Henry had to have something to do with this invasion, or why would he be walking around free in an enemy uniform? Once again, Paco saw Grandpa Rajamouli lying dead. Julio. Aunt Frances, who had been one of mother's best friends. The gates open wide to the enemy.

All his anger focused into his voice. "I'm going to kill you."

Paco watched the smile wipe itself from Henry's face.

Everyone in earshot stilled. Paco swayed on his feet, blood dripping down his fingers from where the ropes had lacerated his wrists, his emotions tangled up with the fury he fought to control. Though he was surrounded by armed guards, with his hands tied, he could see they believed his threat.

It felt like when he was onstage at Luc's. He'd lift his hand, and everybody would fall silent in expectation as he took his place behind his drum. Focus, Yuki had called it, something he'd been taught as a prince. He'd said Paco had it instinctively. He wished that focus would help him now. He wrenched his hands in futility, ignoring the agony in his wrists.

Henry recovered first, his old grin twisting into an ugly jeer. Before he could say anything, Santiago said, "Let's go."

Santiago entered Wolfe House without taking off his boots, grinding sand and dirt into the ancient carpet the Wolfe family so prized. Paco hesitated, unable to pull off his boots with his hands tied. Santiago glanced back impatiently. Feeling all wrong —but *everything* was wrong —Paco walked shod into the brightly lit living room. None of the Wolfe family were in sight. Gold Point soldiers stood in a semi-circle around a tall man with short silver hair.

"Reporting in, sir," Santiago said.

The man turned. Shock hit Paco once again. He'd known that he and Voske must look alike. He'd seen his own features in Kerry's face, but she was a girl, and she also shared features with her mother. This man looked like Paco would if he was eighteen years older, with lighter skin and silver hair.

Paco's wildfire fury cooled to ice.

Voske gave him a little smile, as if he could see inside Paco's brain. He kept his gaze unswervingly on Paco as he said, "Santiago. Your report?"

"Mission successful," Santiago said. "All dead."

"And your company?"

"Seven dead, eighteen wounded. I don't know how bad," Santiago stated flatly.

Still watching Paco, Voske asked, "How many was he responsible for?"

"Six wounded." Santiago's voice roughened. "Two dead."

"Well." Voske smiled. It was the same cool, knife-edged smile that Kerry had given Las Anclas when she'd been a hostage. "You will remember, Santiago, that battle plans never survive contact with the enemy."

Another jolt wrung through Paco: Mr. Preston often said the same thing to the Rangers.

Voske addressed Paco for the first time. "Anything to say?"

Paco gritted his teeth and said nothing.

Voske had still not shifted his gaze away. "Santiago, what did he have to say on your way here?"

Santiago cleared his throat. "He didn't talk until we saw Henry just now. Henry asked him if he was having fun, and he said, 'I'm going to kill you.'"

Paco waited for him to report that he'd refused to give away Kerry's whereabouts, but Santiago said no more. Had he forgotten? Surely Voske had ordered him to ask.

Santiago spoke again. "Sir, Sophie was one of the dead. Shall I tell Luis?"

Voske's eye contact broke for the first time, and his

expression altered subtly. Regret? Annoyance? "No. Leave that to me. Good job, Santiago. You've earned some rest. Take a room upstairs. But before you go, please untie our guest."

Guest? Paco had expected him to summon a firing squad. It had to be some mind game first. As Santiago worked at the tight, blood-sticky knots, Paco tried to think. What would Yuki do? No, he shouldn't be thinking of Yuki, except to be glad that he was safe somewhere else.

A soldier entered and saluted. He was pale, his freckles standing out. "Sir. My teams have reported in, confirming that Tom Preston is not in Las Anclas. Neither are Ross Juarez and Prin—uh, your dau—uh, Kerry Voske."

As Paco's hands fell to his sides, tingling unmercifully, Voske's posture stilled. No one breathed for a painful moment, then Voske said, "Where are they?"

"We interrogated several citizens to get their whereabouts," the soldier replied. Paco remembered what Ross had looked like on his return from Gold Point, and his blood chilled. "Two weeks ago, Tom Preston and half the Rangers left to spy on Gold Point. He didn't tell anyone when they expected to return. One month ago, Ross and, uh, Kerry left to travel north up the coast, with three others. They said they'd return any time between another month and, uh, now."

"Tell Axel and Loretta to report to me," said Voske. The soldier saluted again, looking relieved, and rushed out.

Then began the longest wait of Paco's life. Voske sat down on a couch. He didn't even look at Paco, who stood where he was, blood dripping off his wrists to land on the Wolfes' carpet, splat, splat, splat. A small eternity later, two soldiers hurried in and saluted. The man was big and husky, an obvious fighter. The other was a woman, slight and middle-aged. Probably she was either a crack shot or had a Change power.

"Axel," Voske said, "Loretta. I know you two are used to operating as the leaders of independent teams. But I want you to work together for this mission. Find Ross Juarez and my daughter Kerry, and the others traveling with them. Bring them back alive. Preferably, unharmed."

"Yes, sir," the man said.

The woman gave an unnerving smile. "We'll find them."

Voske gave a short nod. "You can get the details from Jasper."

They saluted and left as quickly as they had come in.

Where would Ross and the rest even be by now? Still in the desert? Paco tried to reassure himself that Jennie would notice the team before they got close, and she and Ross and Kerry—even Summer and Mia—would fight them off. Then he pictured Frances and Julio and Grandpa Rajamouli, all lying dead on the sand.

Voske indicated the couch he was sitting on. "Please. Sit down, son."

Son. Paco's stomach lurched. He wanted to share that couch with Voske about as much as he wanted to jump into a pit mouth's maw, but he was already light-headed. He needed all his strength for whatever came next. Paco sank down at the far end.

Voske smiled that eerie smile, as if he watched the antics of a puppy. "Would you like something to drink? You must be thirsty."

He did not look away as he snapped his fingers. A man ran toward the kitchen. Voske was king of Gold Point, and this was how kings behaved. When Voske last attacked Las Anclas, and Yuki had wanted Ross on his team, Mr. Preston had tried to dismiss Ross, saying he couldn't even shoot a crossbow. Yuki had used a similar voice and manner to order Ross to throw a knife. Ross had obeyed instantly, and Mr. Preston had listened.

The aide-de-camp reappeared with Grandma Wolfe's prized silver tray, a crystal pitcher of water, a bowl of fruit, sliced bread, and two crystal glasses. He set it on a table and backed away. Voske indicated the tray, a gesture that was more command than invitation. Paco's tongue moved in his dry mouth, sand gritting in his teeth. His arm throbbed in counterpoint to the slam of his heart against his ribs. But he didn't move.

Voske poured water into a glass and held it out, gazing straight at Paco.

What would Yuki do? This time Paco did not dismiss the thought. Faster than the thump of his heart streamed memories of Yuki talking about the kinds of lessons a prince learned, like how to deal with an enemy. You never escalated aggression. But you also never pretended friendship. If the enemy was fooled, they'd think you weak; if they weren't, they'd know you to be a fool yourself. A prince learned to control his body, so that it would reveal no more than his words.

And there, clear in Paco's mind, was an image of thirteen-year-old Yuki when he'd first arrived, his manner that of a prince who did not know if the people of Los Anclas were friends or enemies.

He felt his body assuming Yuki's posture as he reached to take the glass. Paco drank the water in three gulps, then set the glass down, still mirroring Yuki's movements. It had always been that way. When a Ranger demonstrated a fighting technique, Paco had found himself mirroring that Ranger's style as well as the movement. When he learned a new beat, he'd always mirrored his teacher's style. *Focus.*

Voske's slanted brows hitched up, and Paco wondered what the enemy king saw besides Paco's bloody fingerprints on the glass. This was some sort of duel, one without swords. And he wasn't going to let Voske win.

Yuki, show me what to do.

Voske set his booted feet on the delicate table, crossed them at the ankles, and leaned back. "Talk to me, son. What have they told you about me?"

Paco breathed in and out, flexing his fingers. He had enough feeling back to use his hands. He could launch himself and be on Voske in a heartbeat, both hands closing around his throat. Except...

One of Voske's arms lay along the back of the couch with his fingers a foot away from Paco's shoulder. His other hand rested lightly on his knee. A posture of relaxation—a *pose* of relaxation. But he wasn't relaxed. Paco saw the curve of hard muscle shaping his sleeve, his controlled breathing. Mr. Preston waited like that before a sparring match began. Voske was clearly a trained fighter, and he was ready.

His gaze went past Voske, to the soldiers standing ready at the doors. They were watching him. If he tried to attack Voske, he'd be jumped in an instant.

Paco let his breath trickle out. He tried to ease his own posture to neutrality. "You put people's heads on pikes."

The corners of Voske's mouth deepened. "That's all? Of course I do. It's effective."

Paco tried to keep his voice calm. "It wasn't effective against Ross. Or didn't he blow up your dam?"

Voske's smile didn't change, but the skin tightened under his eyes. Then they crinkled with appreciation. Voske was enjoying himself. "Ross and I will have a conversation about that stunt of his. Later than I'd planned, it seems. But soon."

"His *stunt* kept him from being tortured to death."

"No," Voske said. Paco's heart jolted. "Only postponed it. More water?"

"I'm fine," Paco said hastily. But Voske had shaken him, and he knew that Voske had seen.

"Suit yourself. It's been a long night, but quite successful. The last time I was here, I seriously underestimated Las Anclas—or rather, I underestimated my old friend Tom Preston. Do you know why I retreated?"

"Ross killed your covert team with his crystal tree."

"That was a setback, but not why I retreated. I was low on ammunition and supplies. We could have held Las Anclas in a siege situation while I summoned reinforcements. But when we attacked again, we'd have had to bludgeon this town into wreckage and bury half the inhabitants. Then I'd have to build it all up again. My towns thrive, or what's the point? Yes? You were going to say something?"

Paco gritted his teeth. He'd wanted to scorn that *My towns thrive*, but he remembered Yuki's description of how wealthy Gold Point was in comparison to Las Anclas, with electric lights everywhere.

Voske's smile deepened again. "They thrive because effort is rewarded. This is what Las Anclas is going to learn, as soon as it settles down and understands that I mean what I say. Cooperation, effort, and loyalty are rewarded. Stupidity and trouble have consequences, which are visible to everyone entering the gates. A skull sitting on a pike is more effective than a hundred speeches. But we were talking about my last visit."

Paco kept himself still, his gaze on his hands, his wrists sluggishly bleeding.

Voske continued, "I decided that what was required was a surgical strike. And your friend Henry Callahan provided the means."

"He's not my friend." The words were out before Paco could stop them. He heard petulance in his voice, and he shut his teeth hard.

"Really? He claimed to be popular before Tom Preston found out about his Change power—a very useful one—and threw him out. Typically short-sighted. And an advantage for us. Would you like to know how we met?"

That question had been burning in Paco's mind ever since he'd seen Henry, but he forced himself not to blurt anything out. Yuki wouldn't. Yuki would think first. So, Paco considered Henry, who was careless and short-sighted. He'd been exiled for starting a dangerous fire, apparently in the hope of being a hero and impressing Mr. Preston. It would be just like Henry to plunge into the desert without more than a cursory glance at the maps he'd been given.

"I assume he wandered into your territory, and a patrol found him," Paco said.

Again, that eerie smile curved Voske's lips, doubly unnerving for being so familiar. Surely that wasn't what Paco's own smile looked like. "Very good. Half-right. You're overestimating Henry's skills at desert travel and underestimating my reach. Henry never got anywhere near Gold Point. He stumbled into a scout camp of mine above your reservoir. I'd been considering plans revolving around that, but once I spoke with Henry, I got a much better idea."

In a disturbingly friendly tone, as if he was an older Ranger advising Paco, Voske said, "Flexibility is important. Sticking to outdated ideas makes you weak, not strong. We welcome Changed people in Gold Point. Henry appreciated that. In return for nothing more than good treatment and acceptance, he told us about your secret tunnel."

"Tunnel?" Paco repeated blankly.

"You didn't know about it? Yes, there's a tunnel that leads from the mill to the basement of your town hall. It was intended as an escape. Of course, all ways out are also ways in. I'm impressed by how long it managed to stay secret. But Henry's girlfriend — Tom's teenage daughter — told him, and he told us. I'll enjoy discussing that with Tom when we catch up with him."

For a wild moment, Paco wondered if Voske was lying about everything — Henry, the tunnel, Felicité — but Paco had seen Henry, so that part had to be true. And a tunnel made so much sense. No wonder the alarm had never been rung. No wonder the town had been taken so easily.

"Would you like to know exactly how I took Las Anclas?" Voske inquired.

Paco didn't want to give Voske anything, not even a nod. But Voske waited, his expression bland, and Paco knew that unless he gave Voske that little concession, he would never tell.

Yuki's cool voice spoke in Paco's mind. *"A meeting with an enemy is still a meeting. Gather information. If they want some small concession that costs you nothing but pride and might gain you a lot, give it to them."*

Paco nodded.

There was the smile again. Paco gritted his teeth. "I gave out watches to my company commanders, so we could synchronize our attacks to the minute. One company split into teams, to take out your perimeter patrol at the same time. They were the ones you fought with, son. Another company split to simultaneously take down the wall sentries."

Cold fear and grief churned in Paco's belly. He knew that night's sentry roster. Were they all dead? Brisa Preciado. Ms. Lowenstein — had Yuki lost his mother?

Voske shook his head, denying Paco's thought as if he'd read his mind. "Bound and gagged, Paco. Not killed. Some were wounded, if they fought hard. But there was no need to kill mere citizen sentries."

Paco veered between wanting to believe Voske, and wanting to deny every word that came out of the tyrant's mouth. He stayed silent, waiting.

Voske went on, "The third company subdued the sentries at the mill. Then we used the tunnel to muster inside the town hall. From there, we split into three teams.

One went to open the front gate and secure the armory, one to capture the bell tower and open the back gate, and the third here to Tom Preston's house, which is large and central, and makes an excellent headquarters. It was all over in fifteen minutes. The shortest battle I've ever fought. If you can term it a battle. More of an exercise." Voske explained things exactly as Mr. Preston did, clearly and simply and to the point.

Paco's thoughts roiled. If Mr. Preston had been there, the "exercise" would have been a battle. Maybe they'd still be fighting now. Maybe they'd have won. Or would Mr. Preston and Sujata and the other Rangers be dead, too?

And Felicité. How could that girl have betrayed a secret that even Paco, a Ranger, hadn't known, to the last person who should have been entrusted with it? He'd never taken Henry or Felicité seriously, but those two had caused the fall of Las Anclas. Grandpa Rajamouli—Frances—Julio—all those deaths were the fault of that stupid girl with her huge hats and spying rat, and Henry's big mouth!

Paco couldn't help the stiffening of his hands, so he pressed them against his sides.

Voske noted the movement. Nothing seemed to escape those watchful eyes. "Your wrists will need attention. Anyway, it's all over now. Tomorrow we shall encourage Las Anclas to return to normal. I want a thriving town. Then everyone wins."

Paco couldn't resist. "Not Grandpa Rajamouli. Or Julio. Or Aunt Frances."

"I take it these are your fellow Rangers? Well, they were military, and that's what happens in an engagement. The same could be said for young Sophie, among others in my army. I'll have to break it to Luis gently. He and Sophie were planning to marry this year. You weren't the one who killed her, were you?"

Paco remembered the girl lying dead by Grandpa Rajamouli, with fingerprint scars on her face. "No."

"Just as well."

A shadow flickered in the window, and Voske was there, peering out.

Paco jumped. The man had moved from lounging on the couch with his feet on the table to across the room with jaw-dropping speed.

"Hawk." Voske sauntered back to the couch and put up his feet again, smiling as if daring Paco to try to attack him.

He *was* daring Paco to try to attack him. Paco saw with sickening conviction Voske had just demonstrated exactly how futile it would be to try to jump him. He was faster than Paco. He was faster than Jennie. He might even be faster than Ross, who was the single quickest person Paco had ever seen short of Sheriff Crow, whose Change power lent her superhuman speed.

Voske snapped his fingers at a pair of soldiers. "Escort my son to the infirmary."

Paco couldn't bear facing anyone else. "I'm fine."

"Suit yourself. Take him to his residence. When I have more leisure, we will continue our discussion."

The soldiers flanked Paco and escorted him out. The entire town was lit up, the streets as busy as if it were the middle of the day, but only enemies were in sight. At Singles Row, he looked away from Julio's room.

Paco wasn't going to be killed like the other Rangers. Voske obviously wanted something from him. But the realization brought him no comfort whatsoever. He'd been ready to face death. He'd always been ready, ever since Voske's previous attack, when Dr. Lee told him his mother was dead.

One soldier guarded him while the other searched his room and confiscated his weapons. When they were done, they shut him inside. Paco didn't bother trying to open the door. He knew the guards would be there. But he did go to the window, though he knew what he'd see outside. Sure enough, Voske's soldiers were on guard.

Paco closed the curtains and uncovered the bright-moth cage. The golden light illuminated the little silver statuette of a dancer that Yuki had given him.

"Keep it for me," Yuki had said.

Paco's wrists stung as he picked it up. He gripped the cool metal tight against his aching chest. He'd probably never see Yuki again. But he held onto the statuette, and Yuki's promise to come back.

·4·
BECKY

LAS ANCLAS - JAIL

BECKY SAT ON THE narrow jail cot, with Brisa curled into her lap. Becky held her tight. Brisa's sleeping face was streaked and puffy with tears, her black hair sticky with blood. Becky had often cried in Brisa's arms. For the first time, Becky had held Brisa as she wept.

At the first battle of Las Anclas, Brisa had succeeded in her part of Jennie's mission, and had been sent back before Sera Diaz had been killed and Indra wounded. On the mission to rescue Ross, no one had been seriously hurt, and Brisa's kindness to Kerry had probably been one of the factors leading to Kerry switching sides.

But this battle was different. Soon after Becky had been locked into the jail cell, Brisa was shoved in and fell sobbing into Becky's arms. Her sentry outfit was soaked with blood.

Becky's heart lurched. "Sit down. I've got to stop the bleeding."

"I'm not hurt. I exploded one rock, and then they all jumped me." Brisa gulped back tears. "It's Ms. Lowenstein's blood. She fought so hard, but there were so *many*. She might be dying. Or dead. If she was still alive when she got to the infirmary, Dr. Lee could save her, right?"

The image of Mr. Gutierrez and a bottle of poppy elixir flashed into Becky's mind. Dr. Lee couldn't save everyone. "Where was she hit?"

"I don't know," Brisa wailed. "It all happened so fast. There was blood everywhere. Oh, Becky, it's like a nightmare. I'm so glad you're here with me."

Brisa had cried herself to sleep. Becky was exhausted, but her mind wouldn't stop spinning in circles. Had Sheriff Crow escaped? Or was she dead? Had Becky killed her or saved her by telling her to run? Sheriff Crow had put Jack in Becky's charge, and she'd failed to protect him. Where was he? Was *he* dead?

And what about Ms. Lowenstein? "Blood everywhere" could mean anything from a superficial scalp wound to a severed artery to... Becky swallowed, thinking of the bloody ruin of Mr. Gutierrez's stomach.

Nausea surged in her own gut as she imagined the infirmary now. She knew exactly what it must be like. She'd lived it. The wounded crying like children. The dead, forever silent. Dr. Lee running from person to person, deciding in desperate moments who he could help, who was beyond help, and who might beg him for a merciful death. He probably needed her aid. He'd only been training Alfonso for a few months. Guiltily, she couldn't help being glad she was in the cell with Brisa instead of at the field hospital.

She looked around wearily. Judge Lopez, Mr. Horst, and Mr. Appel were in the cell across from hers, sitting silently on a cot in their nightclothes. She'd glimpsed a few wall sentries in the other cells before she was locked into this cell, alone at first.

Where were the rest of the council? Becky hastily added them up. Mr. Preston was out of town. Dr. Lee must be in the infirmary. Mayor Wolfe and Grandma Wolfe would have been sleeping at home. She hoped they'd been captured and held there rather than killed. And what about Felicité? She could only fight with a crossbow, and she didn't keep one in her home. Surely Voske wouldn't hurt a harmless girl with no important position... who was the daughter of the mayor and his old enemy, Mr. Preston. Kerry had told Becky how Voske held people's families hostage to keep them obedient, and how he didn't hesitate to execute them if they disobeyed. Would he kill her for Mr. Preston's disobedience to him years before Felicité's birth?

To Brisa, it all felt like a nightmare, but to Becky, it was inescapably real.

The outer door opened, and a tired-looking soldier walked in. The guards outside the cells saluted. The soldier met Becky's eyes and pointed. "Wake her up."

Her heart pounding, Becky gently squeezed her girlfriend's shoulders. "Wake up, Brisa. Someone wants to talk to you."

Brisa raised her tear-stained face.

"You," the man said. "Exploding rocks girl. What's your name?"

Brisa glanced nervously over her shoulder, looking to Becky for a cue.

"Just tell him," Becky whispered.

"Brisa Preciado," Brisa said in a small voice. It made Becky's heart hurt to hear how frightened Brisa sounded. Brisa wasn't afraid of anything.

"What's your job in town?"

"Um… Well…I'm a student…I mean, I'm an apprentice, too…. I'm a lot of apprentices…" Brisa's confusion and fear was making her babble.

Becky jumped in. "She's had a lot of apprenticeships. Right now, she's assisting the town veterinarian, but she only started that last month. Before, she was with the weavers."

The man turned to Becky. "She's not a soldier? What about her Change power?"

In a wobbly voice, Brisa said, "I was just doing my sentry duty. I tried out for the Rangers, but I didn't make the cut. Mr. Preston said I was enthusiastic but he was being *sarcastic!*" She burst into tears.

Becky stroked Brisa's back, but her eyes were on the soldier. She could see that he did not perceive Brisa as a threat.

"You," snapped the soldier. "Sheriff's apprentice. Make her pay attention."

Brisa gulped and looked up. "I *am* paying attention!"

"Good. We're letting you free. Go home and stay there until further orders. These are the rules. If you and your family obey orders and don't give us trouble, life will go back to normal. Who's the youngest member of your family?"

"My little sister Nita. I mean Juanita. She's five."

"Excellent. If you or anyone in your family attempts

to fight back, in any way, Nita will be executed. Do you understand?"

Brisa exclaimed shrilly, "She's *five* – " She cut herself off. Visibly terrified, she nodded.

"Tell me you understand. Repeat to me who dies if any of you fight back."

"Nita," Brisa whispered. "I understand."

"Then go home. Inform your family of the rules."

The guard unlocked the door. Brisa looked uncertainly at Becky.

"Go," Becky said. "It's okay, Brisa. He'll just say the same thing to me."

Brisa stroked her hair with a trembling hand, then fled.

Becky knew the soldier wasn't going to say the same thing to her. He'd asked Brisa what her job was, but he already knew Becky's. What would Voske do to the sheriff's apprentice?

He slammed the cell door shut behind Brisa, then went to another cell and began the same questions. Becky's head ached with a sickening throb. She lay down and dozed fitfully until the squeak of the cell hinges brought her leaping to her feet. This time the soldier was a woman. "Becky Callahan, come with me."

Becky's legs shook as they left the jail. She had no idea how much time had passed, adding to her disorientation. It was dark—surely past midnight—but the streetlamps had been lit. Soldiers were everywhere, but she saw no one she recognized. Many pocket gardens had been trampled, but there was no other visible damage. There had been more after Voske's first attack on Las Anclas—the one that had failed.

Becky didn't dare ask where they were going and was puzzled when she was led to a very familiar road. She'd walked that path to parties and get-togethers, back when she'd been one of Felicité's best friends. She hadn't been to Wolfe House since the party Felicité had thrown a month before Voske had first tried to invade Las Anclas.

The soldier led her up the neat brick path and past the roses. Golden light spilled from the windows and open door of Wolfe House, but it was no longer inviting. The house was surrounded by guards in black Voske uniforms.

They halted on the porch. A guard said, "I'll tell the king you're here."

Becky was appalled when the guard stepped inside without taking off his dirty boots. Then his words sank in. The king! Voske himself was inside that house.

It was impossible. Everything was impossible, unreal. She stared blankly at the shoe rack, unable to think. Then a voice she knew shocked her back into awareness.

"My sister?"

What was *Henry* doing here? He'd been exiled months ago! Why would he come back now?

An unfamiliar man's voice replied, "Yes. You've been so important to me, Henry, of course I want to get to know your sister. But she may not be like you. She may be loyal to Las Anclas. Do you know what she's been doing since you left?"

"Since I left?" Henry's words came in a quick pattern that Becky recognized from before their father had left. He used to echo Dad's words to give himself time to come up with a plausible lie to protect himself, and sometimes to protect her.

Henry continued in that hasty voice, "Of course I don't know what she's been doing since I left, but I promise you, Becky's completely harmless. She couldn't stick it out as the doctor's apprentice because the sight of blood made her sick. But she's like me in one way — she has a Change power. You'd like it, sir. It's very useful. She can touch objects and see who handled them last. Yes! You could use Becky!"

Sir? That had to be Voske himself. Who else could make Henry sound that terrified?

"Harmless, is she?" Voske asked. "Henry, what did she do after she failed to stick it out as the doctor's apprentice?"

The nausea roiling inside Becky burned up toward her throat. She knew that silence. It was Henry frantically thinking of another lie. Or considering which would be worse, to lie or to tell the truth.

"Well, Mom had already thrown her out of the house. Becky told her she'd Changed, and like I told you, our mother hates Changed people. Mom knocked her down, and Becky didn't fight back. She went crying to Aunt Rosa, who told the sheriff—Becky was too scared to tell on Mom herself—and the sheriff felt so sorry for her that she made her into a, a sort of a, a *pet!* The sheriff called her an apprentice, but she wasn't really. She's a tiny little thing. You'll see. Can't fight at all—cries if a bird gets a hurt wing."

Becky's shoulders hunched up to her ears. It was crushing to hear, but Henry was obviously trying to protect her. Trying to save her life.

If only she could turn time backwards, to before Henry had set his first fire. Back to when she'd been friends with Felicité, before she'd fallen in love with Brisa, and both Becky and Henry had echoed their parents' bigoted opinions. Becky had done it out of fear, but she'd thought Henry had been sincere. How could she have been so stupid? If they'd trusted one another—if they'd had one honest conversation—he could have told her about his Change, and she'd have warned him not to start fires, and then—

"Henry." Voske didn't shout like their dad had before he struck out, usually at Henry. Even so, the back of Becky's neck tightened. "Let me tell you what your sister did last night. She used a very interesting weapon, which I feel quite certain that you knew about. What do you know about your sister's dart gun, Henry?"

Henry's voice came even quicker, near panic. "The dart gun! Yes! She got that right before I left. But that's what I mean about her being harmless. It just paralyzes people. Like I said, she can't stand to hurt anyone."

Voske's voice softened, and Becky's heart crowded her throat at the threat that she felt more than heard. "What kind of fool do you take me for? That's a sheriff's weapon, to keep civilians in line when you don't want to kill them. Your sister took down more of my soldiers than any other single person in Las Anclas but the sheriff herself."

Becky thought, *I did?* In the midst of her fear, a small warmth bloomed in her chest.

Voske went on, "Do you know why the sheriff survived the teams sent to kill her? Your sister singlehandedly covered her escape."

The warmth glowed brighter. Sheriff Crow was alive. Becky had saved her. No matter what happened to Becky now, at least she had that.

Voske's voice hardened. "I expect that some people probably did think she was the sheriff's pet, but I know what she's capable of. If you ever lie to me again, your sister will have a tragic accident, and only you will know who killed her. Not me, Henry. You. Run along."

Henry appeared at the door. He wore the black Gold Point uniform, the freckles standing out in his pale face. He froze when he spotted Becky. His mouth formed the shape of the word, "Sorry," and then he bolted across the garden in panicked flight.

Voske said, "Becky?"

She jumped. The woman nudged her. "Go in. The king is waiting."

Becky slid off her shoes and walked inside. Her building horror worsened as she saw her dirty socks adding to the boot prints on the ancient carpet. Felicité had said it had been passed down from her ancestor, a French queen.

Becky forced herself to look up and was shocked again when she saw Voske's face. He looked so much like Paco, though older and with silver hair, but his expression was all wrong.

"I gather you were surprised to see your brother here, Becky?" Voske held no weapons and sat in a relaxed posture, but she felt as if he was pointing a gun at her face.

She looked down at her grubby socks, unable to speak.

"We encountered one another in the desert," Voske said. "Unlike many in Las Anclas, I appreciate Change powers. He showed me the way into this town. It seems the tunnel was only known to a few. I guess you weren't among them."

Becky must have reached the limit of horror and shock that a person could experience. Now she just felt numb. But her mind raced. The sheriff had mentioned a tunnel, and Jack had clearly known about it. Becky couldn't imagine why her brother would know about something that was obviously a town secret.

She wished she couldn't believe that Henry had told Voske about it.

"Henry appreciates being valued for his abilities," Voske went on. "He discovered, as your fellow townspeople will, that I appreciate enterprise."

It sure hadn't sounded like it. Becky gritted her teeth against letting that thought out. She dared a glance at Voske, to discover him watching her. A tide of heat crept up her neck and face. She had never been able to hide her expression, ever.

Sure enough, Voske said, "My recent words might not have sounded like appreciation, but your brother has developed some bad habits. He needs boundaries and consequences."

So Voske had wanted her to hear that conversation. Why?

He spoke again, his tone friendly. "You must be longing for a hot bath and a good bed. You shall have them presently."

Once he mentioned beds and baths—especially baths—she did long for them. But she didn't believe for an instant that he'd let her have them.

"You appreciate a hot bath, don't you?" Voske went on.

Warily, Becky said, "Everybody appreciates hot baths."

"Ah, but you're a connoisseur, aren't you? You like them scented, with…roses."

She felt like she'd been plunged into freezing water. How could Voske know that roses were her favorite scent—especially in the bath? He'd read her mind!

His smile widened. "You remind me of one of my wives. Min Soo doesn't fight, but she has inner strength. As you also possess. I value such people. Min Soo will tell you the same, when she arrives. She is very beautiful and appreciates beautiful things. I think you'll like her."

Anyone who'd marry Voske had to be terrifying. Becky's shoulders hunched up to her ears. Voske seemed to read her mind once more. "You've heard terrible things about me. Everyone seems to bring up heads on pikes, which I assure you is a rare necessity. I would much rather reward people. A town needs its ordinary, productive citizens—such as your council members. Mr. Appel, Mr. Horst, and Judge Lopez are all on their way home. You're the sort of person who needs to make up her own mind. I respect that. So, as I told your brother, I don't underestimate you. I'd like to make use of your skills. For now, in the infirmary."

"The infirmary?" If she had to help Dr. Lee give someone a merciful death...

"Some of your townspeople are badly hurt. So are many of mine. They need care by trained hands. But first, we need to understand one another, Becky. You might be tempted to, shall we say, help my more badly wounded soldiers to succumb—"

I would never, Becky thought in horror. But she was too unnerved to speak.

For the third time, he seemed to read her mind. "Yes, you are revolted by the idea. Excellent. But what about Dr. Lee?" Watching her closely, he said, "Might Dr. Lee put a wounded soldier out of their misery, for the good of the town?"

"Dr. Lee?" Becky exclaimed. "He wouldn't kill *anybody*. Everybody knows the reason he won't even go on patrols is in case they might run into human enemies." She halted, remembering Mr. Gonzalez. But that was different.

"But he has an exception, doesn't he?" Voske asked. He *did* read minds! "To save Las Anclas..."

"No, no. That's not why. If someone's dying anyway and can't be saved. And even then, only if they ask."

"Ah. I see. But back to you, Becky. I respect you enough to remind you of consequences. I'm told you're close to Brisa Preciado. Brisa has a very useful Change talent. However, I have plenty of skilled Changed people. She's not essential. If you give me any trouble, Brisa will suffer the consequences. Do you understand?"

Becky nodded, sick terror pooling in her stomach.

Voske was still watching her, smiling. "I want to hear you say it."

Becky remembered the soldier using the same words on Brisa. Now she knew where they came from. She forced the words out. "I understand."

"Good! Then we're done. Get some rest, then report

to the infirmary. They will be expecting you."

Becky stumbled back to the porch, where she had left her shoes so many times. Two pairs of Felicité's shoes were on the rack, and she wondered again where Felicité was. If she was alive. But she didn't dare ask.

The soldier who'd brought her was waiting. "I'll escort you to your home."

And find out where I live. But it wasn't as if she could hide. And Henry had mentioned Aunt Rosa, so Voske already knew he had more than one person he could threaten to keep Becky in line.

Becky found her aunt sitting at the kitchen table, her eyes frightened. But she looked relieved when she saw Becky. "Do you know what's happening? Soldiers banged on my door and said if I stayed inside, I wouldn't be hurt. Is Sheriff Crow...?"

"She escaped." Becky told her aunt everything. The worst part was about Henry. She felt the old impulse to hide it, as she'd always hidden the bad things at home, but Henry had run off in a Gold Point uniform. The entire town would know soon enough. Miserably, Becky concluded, "I don't know what to do."

"You don't have to do anything right now," Aunt Rosa said, recovering some of her old briskness. "Sheriff Crow is free, thanks to you. So is Tom Preston, with the Rangers he took with them. And your friend Kerry, thank goodness, along with Mia and Ross and Summer and Jennie. They won't abandon us."

"Sheriff Crow is the only one who knows what's happened."

"Then she'll probably find the others and tell them. As for you, here's what you'll do." Aunt Rosa got up and began slicing bread. Having a purpose seemed to cheer her. "You're going to eat this bread and cheese, and while you do, I'll draw you a good hot bath."

"Not a bath!" Becky blurted out. Then, at her aunt's bewildered stare, she forced herself to sound more reasonable. "I mean, not with rose petals."

"Rose petals?" Shaking her head, Aunt Rosa said, "Becky, you need to eat and rest. Everything else can wait."

Becky thanked her, though she thought she'd never

sleep again. Her appetite woke as her aunt cut a thick slice of the Medinas' delicious, crumbling cheese. She devoured the food, drank two glasses of water, and headed to the bathroom. Unsettled, Becky breathed in the steam of the unscented water. How had Voske known that she loved the scent of rose petals in hot water? Only Brisa knew that, and Voske hadn't had a chance to talk to her. *Could* he be telepathic? They could never defeat him if he could look into their minds and see their plans.

Becky drew in a deep breath. She had to stop frightening herself. At the very least, she wasn't going to be afraid of baths. She threw off her grimy clothes and stepped in. The hot water stung at first, then felt incredibly good. Purple bruises she didn't remember getting had blossomed everywhere, vivid against her pale skin. The water soothed her, and she had to force herself to get out before she fell asleep in the tub.

She pulled on clean clothes, the sort she'd wear if she were going to sleep in the deputy's closet, before she poured herself into bed. She had a feeling she should be ready for anything.

Becky woke abruptly to banging at the front door. Her hand dropped automatically to her hip, but she found no weapon. Memories flooded her mind as she stumbled out of bed. She was unsurprised to open the door to one of Voske's soldiers.

"Come with me," the soldier said.

Becky followed her into the quiet street, heart racing. It was barely dawn. She hoped she wouldn't be led straight back to Voske—surely, he had better things to do than to bother with her—but he'd said she'd taken down more of his soldiers than anyone but Sheriff Crow. Maybe he'd only let her sleep so he could enjoy her shock when she was led to her execution.

But the soldier took her to the infirmary. The realization left her both relieved and nauseated. The familiar smell of antiseptic and cleaning fluid threw her back to the days when she'd felt so helpless, caught between her mother and a job that didn't suit her. But she remembered what Sheriff Crow had taught her—and what she'd done for Sheriff Crow—and squared her shoulders. She was *not* helpless.

Dr. Lee came out of the surgery, his shoulders slumped and dark smudges under his eyes. "I'm sorry you have to be here. But Alfonso was so exhausted, I ordered him to take a nap."

Becky was sure Dr. Lee hadn't taken any naps himself. "I want to help. Honestly. Dr. Lee, who's..." She was such a coward, afraid to ask who was dead. She forced herself to go on. "Is Ms. Lowenstein...?"

"Alive." His encouraging smile was more tired than convincing. "She's in critical condition. If I was allowed to heal her... but Voske forbade me to use my powers except with his express permission. He said she was lucky he was giving her any chance at all."

Becky was filled with a horribly familiar mixture of relief and horror. "If you're not allowed to heal anyone, what have you been doing here?"

"Most of what I do doesn't involve my powers. Voske did order me to use them on his most critically wounded soldiers. Which I would have done anyway," he added, raising his voice as if he thought someone was listening at the door. Her skin crawling, Becky realized that probably someone was. "Voske also sent a healer to assist me with the Gold Point patients, but he overextended his Change power and passed out."

Silence fell. Becky realized that he hadn't answered the question she'd initially meant to ask. "Dr. Lee..."

"Becky, please sit down."

Her knees wobbly, Becky sank down in the nearest chair. She knew what was coming: he'd taught her how to break the news of a death. You had to make them sit down first, in case they collapsed. "Who's dead?"

"I'm sorry to tell you..." Dr. Lee began, then paused.

Becky recognized that, too. Pause, to give them time to brace themselves for what was coming. "Dr. Lee, please just tell me."

"All the Rangers but Paco."

All the Rangers? Becky couldn't take it in. Julio was dead? *Sujata* was dead? No, Sujata and Indra had been among the Rangers who had left with Mr. Preston a month ago. And there it was again, that nauseating feeling of relief mixed with horror.

Watching her carefully, Dr. Lee said, "Grandpa Choi and Ken Thomas were killed trying to protect the mill. That's it. Voske clearly wanted most people taken alive. The majority of the wounded are Gold Point soldiers."

But Julio was dead. And Frances, who just two nights ago sat in the jailhouse with Sheriff Crow, chatting as they cleaned weapons and ate apple crumble. Even old Grandpa Rajamouli. It was hard to take in. At least Paco was alive.

"Paco," Becky said urgently. "Is he badly wounded?"

"He wasn't hurt at all. Just captured."

Becky should have been glad, but her heart sank. Voske obviously could have killed him if he'd wanted to. She wondered if Voske expected Paco to switch sides.

Dr. Lee took her into the infirmary. The worst injured lay in the secluded annex, Las Anclas and Gold Point patients side by side, separated only by cloth hangings. Soft moans and the hissing breathing of people in pain sounded behind the hangings.

Dr. Lee gave her crisp, quiet instructions, recounting the injuries and what each patient needed, keeping the more difficult tasks for himself. Becky knew where everything was. She loaded a tray with bandages and antiseptic and went to the first little alcove to check on Ms. Lowenstein. She was pale and deeply asleep, her neck, side, and one leg bandaged.

Soldiers tromped into the infirmary, making her jump. They walked around with their hands on their swords, as if they expected the wounded patients might leap up and attack them. Some even stomped upstairs to nose into the bedrooms.

"Get out." Becky tried to keep her voice low. "Shoes off! It's unsanitary!"

They ignored her. The ones upstairs clattered back down, and they assembled near the door. "All clear," said one. The snub-nosed young soldier at the door leaned out and called, "All clear, sir!"

Voske walked in. The soldiers saluted. Becky froze. Dr. Lee stepped out of the surgery. His operating coat and gloved hands were stained with blood.

"I need to talk to Luis," Voske said. "Where is he?"

"Resting in my office." Dr. Lee pointed. "He collapsed this morning."

Voske's smile was frightening, but seeing it vanish was even worse. His voice was soft and distinct. "What did you do to him?"

"Nothing," Dr. Lee said steadily. "I believe he overtaxed himself. I set up a makeshift bed and left him to recover in complete quiet."

"Show me," Voske said curtly.

Becky followed them into the office, feeling as if she was pulled by an invisible string. She didn't know what she could do, but she couldn't leave Dr. Lee to face the enemy alone. A tall, well-built boy about Becky's age sat on a folding camp bed, breathing as if just sitting up required an enormous effort. His brown skin had a grayish cast, his shoulders were hunched in pain as he pressed his knuckles to his forehead. He looked so exactly like Ross had when he'd overused his powers and landed in the infirmary that Becky had to stop herself from going to fetch the willow bark tea.

"Luis," Voske said in that scarily soft voice.

Luis dropped his hands and squinted up at the king of Gold Point. "Sir. I—I'm sorry. I think I passed out. I know you told me to be careful. But there were six wounded from Sophie's company, and three of them were really bad. I thought I could heal them all, but…" He turned a questioning glance to Dr. Lee.

"They're alive," Dr. Lee said to Luis, and to Voske, "Two are severe. I just finished removing bone fragments from the third one's shattered knee. You can see her in the infirmary."

"In a moment," Voske said, no longer in that terrifying whisper. "Luis, I gave you strict instructions not to overextend yourself."

"But I couldn't let them die. They're Sophie's comrades. I knew she'd be in here first thing asking about them…What?" That last word came out in a small voice as Luis stared up at Voske.

Voske spoke with what sounded like genuine regret. "Sophie died a hero's death. It was fast. Santiago will tell you—"

"No," Luis said, almost voicelessly, and then on a rising scale, "No, no, no, *no!* She *can't* be dead! We didn't even—she was still mad at me because I wouldn't kiss her, after—and I burned her! I *burned* her!"

Voske snapped at Dr. Lee and Becky, "Get out."

As they backed out, she heard Luis whispering, "No, no, no."

Dr. Lee led her into the surgery. She could hear Luis sobbing through the closed door. As they cleaned up the surgery, Dr. Lee said, "You remember those burn scars on Ross's neck? That wasn't from torture. It's a side effect of Luis's power."

"That must be awful for him." Becky hadn't been able to handle the controlled violence of surgery. She couldn't imagine what it would be like to have a healing power that *burned* people.

"His power takes a toll on him, as mine does on me. I don't think he fully understands it, or his limits."

Voske came back in. "I've ordered Luis to use his powers only in life-or-death situations, and only once in a day. Did any of the Las Anclas wounded see him healing my people?"

"No," Dr. Lee said. "We had the privacy curtains up."

Voske gave a short nod. "Good. No one is to know about his power. That will be revealed when I choose to reveal it. None of my people would ever say a word I don't want them to say, so if anyone from Las Anclas finds out about Luis, I'll know it came from one of you."

Dr. Lee said evenly, "I never talk about my patients, and I taught Becky not to either."

"Excellent," said Voske. "Luis needs to continue his training in the basics, but I've given him liberty for a day. I'll rotate the company medics through in his place."

"I'm putting him in your charge, Becky," said Dr. Lee. "You can teach him the basics, and..."

Teach him the basics, and keep an eye on him, Becky finished silently.

·5·

FÉLICITÉ

LAS ANCLAS – WOLFE HOUSE

FÉLICITÉ HUNCHED MISERABLY IN the corner of the fruit shed.

No! It was *not* a fruit shed. It was her own basement pantry. It only reminded her of a fruit shed because that was the only other place she'd ever been locked into. At least when Jennie had tied Félicité up and locked her into the Vardams' fruit shed, she'd had Wu Zetian for company. Not to mention the knowledge that sooner or later, the traitors would have to release her and confess their misdeeds.

Félicité had been locked up ever since Voske's invasion, with no company but phosphorescent spiders and some scuttling creatures she could hear but not see. If the trays of food they dumped at the top of the stairs came twice a day, she'd been there for four days, with no idea of what was going on or if her family was still alive.

The bell rang out a deep toll. It was the pattern that called the townspeople to assemble at the town square. Félicité instinctively jumped to her feet, then froze. A soldier opened the door and called, "Come out."

Her feet had fallen asleep, but she hurried up the stairs. If she'd learned one thing in the last few days, it was to obey orders quickly. She followed the soldier out of the fruit—the pantry!—and into the kitchen. Its familiar warmth and breakfast smells were a brief comfort, but she was hustled through without even seeing what was being served, let alone be given any of it.

"Go to your room and get dressed," said the soldier.

"You have five minutes."

Felicité bolted upstairs, passing several soldiers as she went. She listened for any familiar voices. Her mother. Will. Grandmère. Even the servants. But the voices she heard were unfamiliar, and therefore enemies. There was no one in Las Anclas whose voice she didn't know.

She slammed her bedroom door, then rushed to Wu Zetian's house. Felicité was immensely relieved to see that her rat was alive and unhurt. Wu Zetian nuzzled her but didn't emerge from her house.

"Smart rat," Felicité said. "Stay inside."

Wu Zetian was alive. Daddy was surely alive. He would come rescue her. Felicité just needed to wait.

She flung open her wardrobe and stared blankly. She couldn't wear anything she'd worn while dating Henry, but last year's clothes were in the attic.

The soldier banged on the door and shouted, "One minute!"

Felicité nervously snatched up the closest dress to her hand. It was the worst possible choice, the starflower dress that she'd worn on her first date with Henry. His horrible mother had made him a suit to match. Felicité began to hurl it away, but a fist thudded against the door. "Get on with it!"

"I'm coming," Felicité called, panicked. She yanked off the nightgown she'd worn for days, scrambled into the starflower dress, then grabbed a random scarf within reach and wound it around her neck. A hat snatched off the top shelf completed her outfit.

The soldier marched her downstairs without a word, though not without a scornful glance. She thrust Felicité into Daddy's office.

Voske himself was seated behind Daddy's desk. Alone. Felicité froze in terror.

The last time she'd seen him, he'd been in black fatigues. He now wore a long black tunic over black pants stuffed into high-topped boots. Both pants and tunic were embroidered in red. The outfit was similar to the formal pants and blouse Kerry had popularized, except that Kerry wore a blouse and a short jacket instead of a tunic.

Voske gave her mismatched clothing and unwashed skin a contemptuous look. "I would have sent you to bathe, but your bathtub was broken in what I can only assume was some childish tantrum."

Felicité couldn't deny it. In any case, her throat was too dry to speak.

"Don't imagine I'll let you get away with behavior like that. Or more serious offenses. Keep quiet and do exactly as you're told, and no harm will come to your little brother."

"Will?" Felicité gasped. "No, please don't hurt him."

"That will be up to you. Outside." He snapped his fingers.

To her immense relief, she found Becky, Mother, and Will outside, guarded by a group of soldiers. Mother looked exhausted and her dress was wrinkled, as if she too had been wearing it for days. Will looked around curiously, his eyes wide under his uncombed hair.

Felicité scurried to her mother's side and whispered, "How's Grandmère?"

"Her jaw was broken," Mother whispered back.

Felicité winced. Dr. Lee could heal her, but he'd probably been forbidden. After all, Grandmère had burned two of Voske's soldiers.

"She'll heal," said Becky. "I've been coming to check on her."

Mother caressed Felicité's shoulder. "How are *you?*" she murmured softly.

"Fine." Felicité glanced nervously from Mother to Becky to Voske, uncertain how much she was allowed to say. But Voske was busy speaking to his soldiers.

Becky said, "I'm so glad you're okay. I was so worried about you. No one would tell me where you were."

"I've been locked in the basement." Felicité decided that the enemy king didn't care if they spoke to each other, or he'd have stopped it by now. This could be her only chance to make up with Becky. No matter what else happened, at least she could try her best to do that. "I'm glad *you're* okay. Is Brisa all right?"

"She's fine." Becky's voice was as sympathetic as her expression.

Voske snapped his fingers. "Come along."

He went first, surrounded by his guards. Mother led

the way after him, dignified despite her rumpled dress. The girls and Will followed, with more soldiers behind them. When they passed the Callahan house, Becky edged away, almost going off the path. A soldier held up a warning hand. Felicité hastily stepped between Becky and the house that must hold so many bad memories. Now she could get out that long-overdue apology —

But when they turned onto Town Hall Path, they found Paco waiting with a group of guards. He wore clothing like Voske's, except that it was red trimmed with black instead of black trimmed with red. Voske must have forced him to wear it, just like Voske had rushed her getting dressed and ensured that she looked awful. She tried to convey her sympathy with a glance.

Paco shot her a look of cold contempt, as if she was a bug he planned to step on. Horrified, she wondered if he'd changed sides. Henry had. Kerry had rejected Voske and the life of a princess to come to Las Anclas. Maybe Paco wanted to take Kerry's place and become a prince. The earth felt unsteady beneath her feet. Except for Mother, Grandmère, and Becky, she had no idea whom she could trust anymore. Paco looked so much like Voske…

Felicité took a deep breath. Maybe he'd been glaring at the guards beside her, not her. She couldn't leap to the conclusion that he was a traitor just because of his facial structure and his clothes. She whispered, "Did Voske make you wear those clothes?"

In a voice as cold as Voske's own, Paco said, "Don't talk to me about my *clothes*. You told Henry about the tunnel."

The shock of his words reverberated through Felicité. She froze. Mother stumbled right into her. Felicité stared into Mother's eyes, willing her to have not heard. But the blank shock in her mother's face made it clear that Mother had.

"I —I didn't mean—" Felicité stammered, unable to find any excuse or explanation. She looked desperately at Becky, hoping that at least her friend would believe or somehow understand. But Becky, too, looked shocked and horrified.

"*You* told Henry?" Becky asked. "Felicité, why?"

The reasons that had felt so logical at the time

streamed into her head. *To save the town. To save Henry. To stop Henry from finding out that I was a monster.*

But she couldn't say any of it. None of it had been worthwhile. She hadn't saved the town, she'd destroyed it. She hadn't even saved Henry. All she'd saved was her repulsive secret.

Paco spoke as if he was quoting someone. "'Every way out is also a way in.' *You* gave Voske the key to Las Anclas. Every Ranger who died, *you* let in the soldiers who killed them."

He walked ahead, not giving her a chance to respond. Becky followed him, her face pale and shocked. Betrayed. Felicité stumbled along alone, desperate to find something to say. There had to be some way to explain, some way to make everyone not hate her…

Voske glanced at Mother, smiling. "You and Tom raised a fine daughter there." His mocking tone cut like a knife.

Felicité suspected that Voske had known that would happen. That was why Paco had been kept waiting. But had Voske guessed what Paco would say, or had he and Paco set it up together?

Mother's breath drew in sharply. Felicité braced herself to hear something terrible, like *"She's not my daughter."* But Mother said nothing.

Mother wasn't looking at her at all.

Following her gaze, Felicité saw that the entire town had gathered in the square, facing a platform in front of the town hall. The last time that had been set up, it had been a stage for the Catalina Players. A row of chairs lined the back of the platform. Henry sat there alone, wearing a Gold Point uniform and backed by soldiers. In the middle of the platform waited a block of wood, an empty basket, and an enormously muscled Gold Point soldier. Felicité looked from the wood to the basket to the man, baffled.

Then she saw the axe.

Soldiers shooed Becky into the crowd, and herded Felicité, Mother, Will, and Paco to the chairs on the platform. Felicité dropped into one, her knees watery, her insides roiling. After all the stories she'd heard, both as rumors and from Kerry Voske's own lips, she was finally going to see an execution.

Soldiers forced five people onto the platform. Felicité recognized Mr. Horst, the Willet brothers, Tommy Horst's hot-tempered Aunt Paula, and one of the brewery women. All had their hands tied behind their backs.

Voske was actually going to kill them in front of everyone.

This was what Felicité had been trying to prevent when she'd warned Henry to say nothing of the tunnel. She'd known Daddy would have him shot to protect the town.

The town had voted for Kerry to be executed if Voske refused the hostage exchange. Felicité remembered every detail of that vote. She'd recorded it herself. Now, in place of Mr. Horst's heavy, battered features, she imagined Kerry's sharp ones. If Felicité had been old enough to vote then, she too would have voted for Kerry's death.

She'd had no idea what that would actually mean.

Voske stepped onto the platform. *Why doesn't everyone attack him?* Felicité thought wildly. But armed guards surrounded the crowd, weapons at ready.

People whispered, then fell silent.

Voske spoke loudly. "Citizens of Las Anclas. A rebellion was attempted last night. As you can see, it was not successful. Because it occurred so early in the new regime, before I'd had a chance to assemble you to explain my rules, I'm sparing the families of the rebels. I will not be so merciful if this occurs again. You all now know the penalty for rebellion: not just the perpetrator, but their entire family."

The huge soldier — the headsman — stepped forward. Mr. Horst was shoved down on his knees before the block.

"No, you can't!" Felicité barely recognized Tommy Horst's voice. Tommy stumbled forward, waving his arms frantically. Behind him, Mrs. Horst bent double, her hands covering her face.

Soldiers instantly grabbed him. Big and strong as he was, he couldn't wrest free. "Let him go, let him go," Tommy sobbed.

The soldiers looked up at Voske, waiting for orders. Voske murmured to an aide-de-camp, then said, "Thomas, is it?"

Tommy gulped. "You'll let him go?"

"No," Voske said. "You are all here to see thatalways keep my promises."

"But he's the defense chief," Tommy wailed. "He's supposed to fight back!"

Voske's voice remained calm and even. "Every action has consequences. Even that pathetic attempt at rebellion, which had no more of a chance than a rat nipping at my boot. Thomas, you now have a choice: you can join your father up here, or you can join my army. Do well, and you will prosper. The choice is yours. Make it now. There will be no second chance."

Felicité's empty stomach churned with horror. She held her breath, watching Tommy's tearstained, ravaged face. The soldiers let him go. He drew a breath, turned toward his father, and lifted his foot.

Paco used the voice Felicité had only heard when he led the band at Luc's. It carried, and it had force. "*No, Tommy.*"

And, as if in distant echo, Mr. Horst wheezed, "No, Tommy. No."

Tommy lurched as if he'd been smacked, and his foot slammed back down. He sobbed again.

Felicité flicked a glance Voske's way. She caught a brief tightening of his expression. Then he smiled as Tommy turned uncertainly toward his mom. She grabbed him and held on.

Voske sat down and spoke to Paco. "Excellent leadership potential, son. I like that."

Then he gave a nod to the waiting headsman.

It was really going to happen. At the battle of Las Anclas, Felicité had been faced with the choice of seeing things that would be burned into her mind's eye forever, or not looking. She'd chosen to look. She wouldn't make that mistake again.

Instead, she turned her gaze to her family. Mother's eyes were like black mirrors. Will leaned forward, looking more excited than anything else. Felicité wanted to tell him to look away, but she couldn't speak without catching Voske's attention.

Voske reached out and with what would have been a fond gesture from anyone else, tousled Will's hair. Will jerked up and stared at him. "You see, William? Thomas obeyed me, and I spared him. When you're in a position of power, always remember to keep your promises."

The thud from the stage made Felicité jump. She forced herself not to look up. It was bad enough to hear the gasps and stifled screams. A minute later, Ed Willet argued and pleaded until she heard another thud.

Grandma Ida Callahan's voice rose in a shriek of fury. "You blood-thirsty *monster* — "

Startled, Felicité glanced up. At a casual sign from Voske, a guard raised his pistol and shot Becky's grandmother in the head. She crumpled without a sound, as Mrs. Callahan screamed and people backed away from them both.

Felicité pressed her hand against her mouth, biting down on her knuckles.

Don't look.

She didn't even hear the next three thuds. The crowd broke up under the eyes of Voske's soldiers. But while no one fought back, Felicité saw plenty of angry glances. Some of them weren't directed at the soldiers or Voske, but at her.

Becky must have told. Or Henry. Or Paco. All it would take was a word. By the end of the day, everyone would know that she was the one who betrayed the town.

·6·
PACO

LAS ANCLAS – TOWN CENTER

FELICITÉ'S GIANT HAT DIPPED down as she fixed her gaze on the floorboards of the execution platform. She may have chosen not to watch, but she was to blame for this nightmare. Paco took in the rest of her family: Mayor Wolfe, clearly in shock. Will Preston, letting Voske treat him like a son out on a picnic. Uneasy, Paco wondered if Will was too young to understand.

Henry stared straight ahead, his face blank.

Thud.

The voices of the Willet brothers rose in panicky anger.

"You can't do this!"

"I take it back! I'll do whatever you say!"

For the first time, the headsman spoke. "Shut up."

It was too late for Ed and Rick Willet. Paco's only choice was whether to watch and have the sight of their wretched deaths fixed in his head for the rest of his life, or be like Felicité, and turn his gaze away in cowardice.

Setting his jaw, Paco looked straight at the headsman, the upraised axe, and Ed Willet flung down to his knees before the block. This obscenity *should* stick in his memory. He'd see, and he'd remember, and some day, he'd get justice for them all. Even this pair of drunken idiots would not have died in vain.

As he watched the axe rise and fall, Paco forced himself to think one step beyond, not merely about revenge, but about the so-called 'rebellion.' It was easy to figure out what must have happened. He'd known Mr. Horst and the Willets and the others his entire life. Mr. Horst was brave, but he wasn't an experienced military leader like Mr. Preston. Still, he was the defense chief, and the Willets and those other two would have done whatever he said. Mr. Horst must have just shoved weapons into their hands and yelled, "Fight back!"

Paco wouldn't make that same mistake. Voske wasn't only smarter than Mr. Horst. Voske seemed to be smarter than practically everybody, and way more experienced in warfare. With an anguished wrench of longing in his chest, Paco wished Mr. Preston was there. *He* might be smarter than Voske. And Mom—

Paco couldn't think about his mother. Mr. Preston wasn't there. Mom was dead. Yuki was exploring somewhere, hundreds of miles away. Jennie and Indra and Sujata were gone. He tried to halt the grind of his mind in familiar circles. He'd slept for two days after the attack. The guards had brought him meals, but he'd barely touched them. Last night the orderly had not only brought food, but clothes in Voske's colors. He'd been informed by an enormous guard that if he didn't put them on, they'd be put on him.

During those two days' wakeful moments, he'd fantasized about Mr. Preston galloping in to retake the town at the head of an army he'd found…somewhere. But fantasy wouldn't get rid of Voske. Las Anclas would have to rescue itself, and that meant working with the people who were actually there.

They had to do a better job than Mr. Horst.

The headsman wiped off his axe, and two soldiers picked up the basket containing the heads of the executed people. Paco suppressed a surge of nausea: he knew where they were taking those heads.

Voske walked to the front of the platform. This time, instant silence fell. "You may return to your jobs."

The crowd scattered like phosphorescent roaches when you lit a lantern. Voske walked off the platform. The guards closed in, forcing Paco and the Wolfe family to follow. Paco caught a glimpse of Henry's blond head, then Henry took off.

That's right, Henry. You come near me, and you'll see I keep MY promises.

Since Paco was being herded along in Voske's wake, the king was probably planning another conversation. Paco wrenched his mind back to retaking the town. He had to get help, of course. But he wasn't going to make the same mistake as Mr. Horst, and approach people simply because they were convenient, or big and strong. He needed people who were trustworthy, intelligent, and could keep their mouths shut.

Diego Martinez, his first boyfriend? Diego was great on horseback, but he was more interested in painting than in fighting. Paco needed fighters.

He thought back to the Ranger candidates he'd trained with, the ones who hadn't been chosen. Tommy Horst. Mr. Preston had liked him and had encouraged him to try again. But while Tommy might make a good Ranger, he was all wrong for a secret resistance plot. He was like Julio. He was brave and he could fight, but he was impulsive and had never kept a secret in his life.

Meredith Lowenstein. The only reason that Meredith hadn't been chosen was that Mr. Preston wanted her as an archer instead. Yuki had trusted her with his life. She was a little reckless, but she was a lot smarter than Tommy. Paco could trust her — if he could get her alone.

Jose Riley was a good scrapper, though he was only sixteen. He could keep his mouth shut, and his Change power to create small earthquakes could be very useful.

Yolanda Riley was even younger than Jose, too young to even try out for Rangers, but she was the best fighter of the younger students. She'd gone on a mission with Jennie the first time Voske had attacked the town, and she'd done well.

Brisa Preciado, who'd also gone on the mission with Jennie? Paco hesitated. Mr. Preston had turned her down when she'd tried for the Rangers. She had courage, a good heart, and a very strong Change power, but discreet she was not. Maybe he could recruit her at the last moment, when she wouldn't have time to blab by accident.

Was that it? Three people he could trust, and two he'd have to recruit five minutes before everything went down? As he passed the law guild, he glanced back at the front gate, where soldiers were rebuilding the burned armory. A company rode out to patrol, and the walls had twice as many armed sentries as Las Anclas could normally muster.

A sense of futility hit him like a punch in the gut. Who did he think he was, plotting to take the town back with a handful of teenagers, no weapons, at a hundred to one odds? He remembered Voske's scornful dismissal of Mr. Horst's desperate attempt to defend the town as a rat nipping at his heels.

But what other choice did he have? *Surrender is not a choice.*

At the threshold of Wolfe House, Paco stooped to remove his boots.

"Don't bother." Voske gave a careless wave at the new doormat on which he was wiping off his own boots.

Startled, Paco peered inside the house. The carpets were gone, leaving polished hardwood floors. A desk had replaced the satin chairs. The sofa was gone. Except for the crystal chandelier still hanging from the ceiling, the parlor now looked like an office—far larger than the small room Mr. Preston had used as his office.

"Valeria, go stay with your mother," Voske said to the mayor.

Mayor Wolfe walked stiff-backed and silent toward the far wing.

"Félicité, run along," Voske said.

The girl looked around in panic, seeming not to know where to go, then bolted upstairs. Paco heard a door slam.

"William, go to school," Voske said.

"But Grandmère's hurt," Will protested.

"You have a new teacher. On your way, William." Voske indicated the door, and Will took off.

Voske took a seat behind the desk, waving back his ever-present guard. "You're in need of a job, son." He sat back, clearly waiting for a response.

Paco said nothing. He'd give Voske as little as possible. It was obvious that the man listened to everything and forgot nothing.

"How would you like to be king's aide?"

"What?" Paco blurted out.

"King's. Aide." Voske articulated the words. "You're quite suited. Intelligent. Well-mannered. Dressed for the role." Voske's eerie smile, which Paco had seen so often on his half-sister's face, parted his lips. "And, of course, you're my son."

All of Paco's resolve deserted him in a blinding rush of fury. "I am not your son! I'm my mother's son. And you *killed* her." He punched the wall, his shirt cuffs pulling against the scabbed rope cuts on his wrists. They tore open and bled.

Voske held up his hand. The soldiers who had started to rush him stopped short. Paco drew in a shuddering breath, his empty stomach roiling as he braced for the order to be taken out and shot. Like Henry's grandmother. Gritting his teeth, Paco lifted his chin and straightened his spine. If that was his fate, he'd meet it on his feet.

"What do you expect me to do?" Voske asked. "Do you really think I'd throw away your life in a fit of temper like you just displayed? I have plans for you. I've had plans since before you were born. Do you know what your real name is?"

The floor seemed to shift under Paco's feet. Bewildered, he said, "Paco Diaz." Then he saw what Voske must have meant, and added, "Francisco. Francisco *Diaz*."

Voske's eerie smile widened. "You have more than one name. I see your mother didn't tell you the one we chose together. It's Liam. Unusual, isn't it? It was her choice, in fact."

"You're lying," Paco blurted out. "That's the sort of name you give *your* kids. It's…um Irish!"

"Yes, it's Irish. Part of my heritage. Your heritage, too. And out of all those possible Irish names, that's the one Sera liked for you."

Paco stared at Voske, trying to read his face. Could that possibly be true?

"I attacked Las Anclas to get *you* back."

Paco took a step away, as if he could put distance between himself and Voske's words. "I don't believe you. You attacked Las Anclas because that's what you do. You take over towns to add to your empire."

"Ah, but why do I want an empire?" Smiling, Voske said, "One town is a kingdom. An empire is a legacy. Immortality. I was going to give Las Anclas to you, my firstborn son. Did you really think I'd forgotten about you?"

Again, Paco felt that unsteady sensation. Then he remembered Kerry saying that Las Anclas was to be *her* town. Voske was manipulating him. Recognizing it steadied him, and he returned to the subject that Voske had so skillfully deflected. "Who cares! My mother left you, and you killed her."

Voske didn't reply immediately. But neither did he smile again. The longer he and Paco watched each other, the more certain Paco felt that Voske was actually going to tell him the truth. About something.

"Your mother was my first love," said Voske. "You never get over your first love."

That was it. That had the ring of truth. And it was the last thing Paco wanted to hear. He willed Yuki's image away.

Voske went on, "I never ordered her death. Sera died in the chaos of battle. If I'd known who fired those shots, I'd have killed them with my own hands. But I don't know. And nobody will ever know. I'm sure you've tried to find out. Haven't you?"

That, too, had the ring of truth. Paco had asked Jennie's team, but no one had seen who'd pulled the trigger. "You gave the orders. You attacked our town."

"I did, but this, right here, is how I wanted the annexation to go. With as little bloodshed as possible. I can't tell you how much I regret Sera's death. And that is what you and I have in common."

Paco grasped at the shreds of his self-control. He'd walked into this room with a plan, but he couldn't even remember what it was. He looked into that half-familiar face, a distortion of his own, and saw the reflection of his own grief. He was certain that on some level, at least, Voske had once loved Mom. Maybe he even regretted her death. But what had he planned to do to her once he conquered this town if she had still been alive? His instinct screamed that Voske did not tell the whole truth.

And then Paco had it. Voske had sidestepped when Paco had accused him of taking over towns to add to his empire, shifting the subject to Paco himself, then to his mother. With a mental wrench that almost felt physical, Paco brought his mind back to what mattered: that Voske was a conqueror. What's more, he enjoyed conquering.

Paco had seen that at their first meeting.

He remembered reading one of Jennie's old books. Most of it was confusing, but one image had stayed with him, of a hall of mirrors with every mirror different and every one distorted. A character got lost among the many images of himself, until he didn't know which way to turn or which was real.

Voske uses truth like the distorted mirrors. Remember that!

Paco backed up, almost colliding with an armchair.

Voske snapped his fingers. "Santiago!"

The snub-nosed soldier who had captured Paco hurried in. "Yes, sir?"

"I'm assigning you to Prince Liam, as his honor guard. Protect him with your life."

The young soldier saluted. "Yes, sir."

"Santiago here will protect you, Liam. You have freedom of the town, within ordinary limits." Voske gave Paco a long, considering glance, then in a tone that would have sounded kind coming from someone else, he said, "Go get those wrists tended. As for my offer, think about it."

Paco walked out, struggling to hide his fury. He half-expected to be halted, maybe with a bullet in the back of his head. But nothing happened, except Santiago falling in beside him.

Ignoring him, Paco headed straight for the infirmary. He hoped Ms. Lowenstein would be awake by now. If she was, she'd be worried about him.

Santiago walked close beside him. Too close. It made Paco uncomfortable. As he started to edge away, Santiago murmured, "You knew Kerry, didn't you?"

"Not really." Paco stared straight ahead.

Sounding frustrated, Santiago said, "But she was okay the last time you saw her, right?"

Paco stopped so suddenly that Santiago was forced to back up or collide with him. "She's gone. You can't hurt her now."

"I don't want to—" The soldier broke off, glancing around. "Never mind."

Paco hurried ahead, not giving Santiago a chance to talk again.

Dr. Lee met them at the infirmary, his round face calm, his gaze steady. "Paco! Becky and I were having breakfast." His gaze fell to Paco's wrists. "Why don't you join us? Becky can patch you up once you're done."

Paco followed Dr. Lee into the kitchen, where he looked around curiously. He'd been there maybe once or twice in his entire life. Usually, his time in the infirmary had begun and ended in the surgery. The kitchen had a big table laden with food. A tabby cat and a black cat wound around Dr. Lee's feet, meowing. A calico cat leaped from the top of a cupboard, her flaps of furry skin spreading out, and sailed through the air to land on Dr. Lee's shoulder. She meowed loudly, right in his ear.

Becky twitched at the sight of Santiago, her gaze darting to Dr. Lee. She settled down when Dr. Lee waved her to sit.

Paco didn't recognize the soldier who also sat at the table, but Santiago apparently did. He started toward him, his hand reaching out, as the other soldier got up. Then it was like an invisible barrier sprang up between them. Santiago froze in place, and the other guy actually jumped back.

"Sorry," Santiago exclaimed, just as the other muttered, "Sorry."

Paco was bewildered. What was going on with those two? Ex-boyfriends?

"Luis, this is Paco," said Dr. Lee.

Luis! That was the soldier whose girlfriend had died. No wonder those two were acting so strange. Paco didn't want to feel sorry for anyone from Gold Point, and he was so unsettled himself that he didn't have a lot of sympathy to give. But an unexpected pang of sympathy went through him as he recalled how people had tiptoed around him after his mother had died.

Dr. Lee removed the calico cat from his shoulder and set down a plate of scrambled eggs with salsa. "Eat up, Paco. Santiago, you, too."

For the first time since the invasion, Paco felt hungry. He was mildly surprised that he was still capable of hunger, or of enjoying the burn of hot salsa. It was just as well. He couldn't imagine talking with not one but two Gold Point spies at the table.

Santiago pushed his eggs around. In a discouraged tone, he said, "I know Kerry's gone, but..."

"Kerry was doing fine when I saw her last, Santiago," said Dr. Lee.

Paco almost choked on his eggs. Why was Dr. Lee talking to the enemy?

"She rode out on Nugget," Dr. Lee went on. "He looked like he was in a bad mood, but he gets like that."

"She's the only one who can handle him," Santiago said with a sudden smile. Paco crushed the thought that he too liked Nugget, Kerry's temperamental stallion. He didn't want to have anything in common with that spy.

"I packed her lunch myself," Dr. Lee said. "Well, I packed everyone's lunches. But I slipped some extra bean-paste dumplings into hers. The savory type. She doesn't like sweets."

Santiago's smile twitched wider. "I know."

Now Paco was fascinated. Was Dr. Lee doing some spying himself? Why not? After all, Paco was plotting to retake the town. Just because the military adults were gone or wounded or out of action, didn't mean all the adults were useless. Maybe Dr. Lee had a plan of his own. But how could Paco find out with these Voske spies squatting right there, ears wide open?

Dr. Lee was still talking to Santiago. "...and Kerry named the new foal Katana. It means—"

"Sword," Paco said automatically.

Everyone stared at him. Hot blood rose to his face. "My boyfr—my ex-b—an old friend of mine taught me some Japanese."

Santiago laughed. "Old friend, huh?" To Dr. Lee, he said, "Of course she'd name a steel foal 'Sword.' Katana. Katana Steel. Kansas Steel?"

As Dr. Lee nodded, everything fell into place in Paco's mind, like the puzzles Ross had set Yuki to teach him prospecting. Santiago wasn't asking about Kerry because he was her enemy. He was in love with her. Dr. Lee wasn't fishing for information, he was comforting Santiago. Kerry had practically lived with the Lees. She'd been under Mia's guard, just as Paco was under Santiago's.

Nothing was as it seemed. Nothing.

Paco turned to Dr. Lee. "Is Ms. Lowenstein conscious? Could I speak to her?"

Dr. Lee set down his teacup. "She was still unconscious when I last saw her, but she might be coming around now. Meredith's with her. Becky, why don't you disinfect Paco's wrists while I go check."

While Becky daubed Paco's scrapes with stinging witch hazel, he considered Santiago. He tried to think of what he could say to confirm his guess without giving himself away if he was wrong. It was too bad he didn't know Kerry better. But maybe he didn't need to know that much.

"I was there when Katana was born," Paco said. "Kerry loves horses."

This time a brilliant smile lit up Santiago's entire face. Then Paco was sure. No one reacted like that to a minor comment about a person unless they loved them. But it didn't mean Santiago was an ally. He might happily stab Paco in the back if he thought it would save Kerry. Paco understood that. He'd kill Santiago without hesitation if it would save Yuki.

"There," Becky said, tying off the last bandage. "You'll need to come back tomorrow so I can change the bandages."

Paco blinked. There was no need to change the bandages—then he caught her steady gaze. There was more to Becky than people assumed. "Right. Of course."

It was strange how easily you got used to speaking without words. He'd always done it before because he didn't need words. So many of his conversations with Yuki had been at least half conducted with their bodies alone. Now it was a necessity rather than a pleasure, but the same understanding and communication was there.

Dr. Lee appeared in the doorway. "She's awake."

Paco followed him, with Becky and Santiago trailing. Behind him, he heard Santiago say in a low voice, "Luis, please don't do anything…anything reckless."

Paco glanced back. The expression on Santiago's face was pure desperation. Was Santiago worried that Luis would try to kill whoever had killed his girlfriend? Or that he might try to kill *himself*? Luis didn't return Santiago's gaze but stared fixedly ahead.

Paco's neck chilled. That was a guy who might do

absolutely anything.

After the first battle of Las Anclas, there had been so many wounded that Dr. Lee had made up pallets on the floor. But the infirmary was half empty. Dr. Lee pulled aside a curtain, revealing Ms. Lowenstein looking pale and small, lying on her back with one leg pulled up in traction. Meredith sat beside her, holding her hand.

"Paco! Oh, I'm so glad to see you," Meredith said. Then she gave him a second look. "What're you wearing? It looks sort of like those outfits Kerry designed—"

"Oh," Santiago said unexpectedly. "Of course she did." He laughed, a sound unsettlingly out of place in the hushed room. Then the amusement wiped itself right off his face. "It's the royal colors. The king chose the style himself."

"What?" Meredith exclaimed. Then, scowling fiercely, she muttered, "Don't worry, Paco. I know he held you at gunpoint."

Paco had to warn Meredith before she blurted out something she'd be made to regret. Unable to think of any way to summarize everything he'd learned or guessed, he finally said, "Meredith, it's so much harder than that."

Ms. Lowenstein startled Paco by whispering, "I know." As if those two words have exhausted her, she closed her eyes.

She had been his mother's best friend, along with Mr. Preston, Uncle Omar, and Sheriff Crow. She must know so much! If only he could talk to her in private.

Paco realized that he'd found the first recruits of his army right here, in the infirmary. Dr. Lee, Ms. Lowenstein, and Meredith, he'd trust with his life. He didn't know Becky well, but Sheriff Crow had trusted her, and that told Paco a lot.

He wondered about Santiago. He was clearly on Kerry's side, but whose side was Kerry on? He hadn't forgotten how she'd tried to recruit *him* before she'd switched sides. And he hadn't missed how she'd covered it up, either. She wasn't with Voske, but she might just be out for herself. Paco put a mental question mark by Santiago.

With spies everywhere, he would watch, wait, listen, and learn. He'd build his secret army one person at a time.

And when the time was right, they'd strike back.

·7·

FELICITÉ

LAS ANCLAS - WOLFE HOUSE

FELICITÉ COULDN'T BEAR ONE more moment cooped up in her room. It was starting to feel like a fruit shed.

Early on, Voske had made her and her family sit down for dinner with him, but Grandmère couldn't speak or eat solid food, Mother refused to say a word in Voske's presence, and Felicité was too frightened to speak or eat. Will ate normally and answered Voske's questions, but even he seemed uneasy. After three nightmarish dinners, Voske clearly got bored with them and let them eat in their rooms. And there Felicité gladly stayed, hiding from the town that hated her.

But after more than a week of lurking in her room, she couldn't stand it any longer. She clicked her tongue at Wu Zetian, who rocketed out of her rat house. "I'm glad *someone* is happy to go outside."

But even her rat knew something was wrong. Her golden fur was dull. She wasn't washing herself as much as normal. Just like Felicité.

She was glad the smashed mirrors had never been replaced. She had to look awful, with her dirty skin, greasy hair, and the worn dress she'd fished out of the attic. She slunk to the landing, hoping Voske was away. She didn't hear his voice. It seemed safe enough. Maybe she could finally talk to Mother or Grandmère alone! But when she got downstairs, she found guards outside their room.

Felicité hurried by, and almost collided with Clara coming out of the kitchen with a lunch pail. She was startled to see something so normal. Will was still going to school, and still forgetting to take his lunch pail. But how normal was it, really? Maybe this was her chance to learn more.

"I'll take Will's lunch to the school." Felicité was relieved when Clara gave it to her. There were so many new rules, she felt like she might get in trouble for breathing.

Felicité walked outside with Wu Zetian at her heels, blinking in the noon light. She hadn't seen sunlight in days. Even outside, everything looked strange. Normal, and yet not. The neighboring homes were the same, except they had their curtains drawn. People worked their garden patches, but in silence — or was that only when she passed by? Voske's soldiers walked along the paths in pairs.

As she passed the town hall, she spotted Abner Ghenouie, her father's favorite bootmaker. He used to slip her fresh salt-water taffy when she went along with Daddy to be fitted for shoes and boots. Felicité smiled, about to greet him. He curled his lip at her like she was a slug he'd stepped on with his bare foot in the middle of the night. She flinched, her stomach lurching.

That was why she'd stayed inside so long. She'd feared meeting a look like that. Now that she'd experienced it, she wanted to run back to her house. Only it was Voske's house now. She kept her gaze on her sandals and tried to walk as if she didn't care. She couldn't see anyone's face, but she felt their gazes stabbing into her. They hated her, and she deserved it.

As Felicité entered the schoolyard, she heard the teacher's voice. "Line up properly for lunch. Dismissed!"

The kids didn't run out like they used to. They marched out like soldiers, two by two. Someone had trained them hard. The older teenagers looked sour, but the six-year-olds grinned as if they were having fun.

Felicité waited at the edge of the yard, Wu Zetian quiet at her side, as the kids marched to the old picnic tables. They used to be scattered under the big black oak, but now they were arranged in neat rows. The kids didn't sit down but stood rigidly behind the benches.

A tall woman left the schoolhouse. She was about

Mother's age, wearing a Kerry-style short jacket and riding trousers. The teacher surveyed the students, taking her time about it, before saying, "You may be seated."

Thump! The kids sat down at the same time. A pair of eight-year-olds attacked their lunch pails, pulling things out. An older kid hissed, "Stop!"

But it was too late. The two children froze as the teacher approached. "Amy and Esteban, what are the lunch rules?"

"We have to wait?" Esteban Rios said. Amy Lee's lip quivered.

"Nobody eats until we thank the king," the teacher said.

"Oh yeah. Thank-you-King-Voske!" Esteban said it as if spitting out the words. His mother Magali had been a wall sentry the night of the invasion. She'd fought back and had died of her wounds the next day.

"Those aren't the words. Children, what are the words?"

Felicité's skin crawled as the entire school chorused, "King Voske, thank you for the food we eat and the safe school we learn in."

"Very good, children." The teacher turned to Amy and Esteban. "What are the words?"

The two kids stumbled through the sentence, Amy getting the first part right and trailing off toward the end, and Esteban mumbling at random parts. The teacher shook her head. "You will have to do better than that. 'King Voske, thank you for the food we eat and the safe school we learn in.'"

Everyone waited with their hands in their laps, except for the bratty thirteen-year-old girls who proudly called themselves the Terrible Trio. Felicité could see that they had their hands at their sides and all their fingers crossed.

The teacher made Amy and Esteban repeat it three times, until they not only said it right, but with the right sing-song rhythm. Then she said, "No lunch for either of you today. You can sit and watch the other children eat. But if you remember whom to thank tomorrow, you'll get lunch then. Tell me you understand."

In tearful, trembling voices, Amy and Esteban said,

"I understand."

"Good. The rest of you may begin eating."

Tell me you understand. Voske had used those words to threaten her family. Felicité glanced at her brother, half-hoping and half-fearing to see him looking rebellious, but he was patiently waiting while the other kids ate. He'd never been so disciplined in his life. It gave her the creeps.

She remembered Jennie overseeing the schoolyard. Felicité had always thought Jennie was too lenient with the annoying younger kids, and much too strict with her. But right now, she'd have given anything to see Jennie overlooking the little kids having a food fight while scolding Felicité for not trying hard enough in training.

Felicité assumed her best fake smile as she approached the teacher, wondering where Jennie was now. Voske had made sure everyone knew he'd sent crack teams of "scouts" (presumably assassins) after Jennie and her party. Felicité hoped Jennie would kill them all. She pictured Jennie standing tall and heroic, sword in hand. For the first time in her life, the image filled her with pleasure rather than jealousy or anger. She hoped Jennie and Ross and Mia—even Kerry and Summer—had escaped the assassins, and met up with Daddy, and—

"Yes, Felicité?" The voice broke into her thoughts. The teacher knew who she was. Everyone knew who she was. The older kids were glaring at her and Wu Zetian.

Felicité looked away. "I have Will's lunch."

"William," the teacher said. "You may get your lunch pail."

The entire school watched as Will scampered up. He avoided Felicité's eyes as he grabbed his lunch, muttering, "You didn't have to. I coulda shared with Xavier."

She realized that Will was ashamed of her. Felicité dared a glance at the rest of the students. Every single one looked at her with anger, hatred, or disgust. Even the smallest kids, who probably didn't even know what she'd done, were copying the expressions of the older ones.

The entire town hated her. Her own brother hated her. Felicité scooped up Wu Zetian and fled.

She didn't stop running until she felt a runnel of sweat drip down her back, followed by the prickle of scales forming along her spine. She froze, horrified, and frantically scrubbed at her face, telling herself, *The scales are under my dress. No one can see.*

Breathing slowly, she forced herself to set her rat down and walk at a sedate pace. A whisper floated on the air from the direction of Jack's saloon, "Traitor."

Felicité was so shocked by the word that she didn't take in the sound. She had no idea if the speaker had been a man or a woman, let alone their identity. It could have been anyone.

It could have been *everyone*.

Her steps slowed even more when she saw Wolfe House, the home her family had always taken great pride in. The biggest house in town, on the crest of The Hill.

It was no longer her home.

Tears stung her eyes as she passed her mother's roses. She scrubbed her sleeve fiercely over her face. At the door, she automatically stooped to take off her shoes, then remembered that Voske didn't want them to do that. It felt so wrong to walk over the floors with her shoes on.

With her gaze fixed on the polished wood floor, she was startled by a voice. "Felicité."

Voske himself stood in the office doorway. "Where are you going?"

She heard her own nervous stammer as she said, "My-my room."

"You no longer have a room in this house," Voske said.

"What do you mean?"

With exaggerated patience, as if he was explaining something to a slow child, he said, "My wife Min Soo is arriving tomorrow. She will of course have the best bedroom. That's currently occupied by your mother and grandmother. Today they are moving into your room, and you are moving out."

"Out?" she repeated. "Where?"

"That's up to you," Voske said with a little smile. "I really don't care. Stay with friends."

"Friends!" Felicité screamed. All the fury she'd pushed down, lest it harm her family, exploded out of her. "I don't *have* any friends, because of *you!* It's all *your* fault! When Daddy gets here, he'll take back this house! And then he'll *kill* you!"

Felicité shook with anger. Voske would probably kill her, but she didn't care. At least she'd told him what she thought. "I can't wait to see *your* head on a pole! At least I never turned on my Daddy, like Kerry turned on you!"

Voske's eyes narrowed. Felicité wished she hadn't mentioned Kerry. But then he laughed derisively. "Daddy?" The word sounded absurd, coming from his lips. "How old *are* you?"

The hot rage began to seep out of Felicité as she faced the man who had taken over her town and home. He didn't look angry, as if she was an enemy. He looked at her as if she were a fly not even worth swatting.

"Have you wondered why I no longer trouble to lock you up? It's because unlike your mother, you don't have any value to me as a hostage. The town cares about your mother. They care about your grandmother. They even care about your little brother. But nobody cares about you. There's no point in me holding you hostage, because nobody would care if you died."

Felicité sucked in a breath to deny it, but nothing came out.

"Go on," Voske said. "Name one person in town who cares about you. You can't, can you?"

All that came to her was that whisper of *traitor*, and the hateful looks she'd been given. Voske was right. Nobody did care about her.

"It's your father's fault, really," Voske went on in a conversational tone. "If he'd raised you differently, you might have come out...well, not as clever as any of my children, of course, but at least not so pathetic that you couldn't even make yourself popular in a tiny town that your own parents ruled. You might have known something of politics. You might have known, for instance, not to betray the town's most important secret, much less to someone like Henry Callahan. You'd have been better off telling your little brother."

While Felicité stood frozen, he walked past her. "Run along." He headed down the path without even bothering to see if she obeyed him.

Felicité stumbled outside in the opposite direction, tears blurring her vision. She swiped at them desperately. She couldn't have scales growing over her face. But why bother? She'd betrayed Las Anclas to keep her secret, but she'd lost everything that made it matter. If the entire town found out that she was a monster, it wouldn't actually make her life any worse.

She wandered blindly through the garden until she bumped into the low stone wall around the well. Felicité sat on the edge and stared into the circle of dark waters, so very far down. Wu Zetian jumped into her lap, but not even her rat could comfort her.

She tried to think of someone, anyone, who might take her in. Becky and Nasreen must hate her now. Sujata was gone. Maybe one of the servants, but she didn't think any of them had particularly liked her, even before she'd ruined everything.

The only servant she'd been close to was her old nanny, now long-gone. Nanny Shelley had been very fond of Felicité, and Felicité had adored her. But then she'd gotten pregnant and grown claws, and Daddy had fired her. Felicité had been secretly relieved when Nanny Shelley had left town, so she didn't have to fear seeing her and her claws on the streets. Later, she'd wished she'd at least said good-bye.

Everyone who'd ever loved Felicité had been driven away, or was gone forever, or hated her, or was a prisoner, or was a traitor, or was dead. Because of her. She might as well walk out the town gates and die in the desert. Voske certainly wouldn't stop her.

Tears trickled down her cheeks, but she wiped them away as fast as they welled up. She would not give Voske the satisfaction of seeing her Change. He could take everything else from her, but her secret was her own.

"Felicité?" The whisper was so quiet, she thought she'd imagined it.

"Felicité? I need to talk to you."

She glanced up. It was Henry, still wearing that black uniform. His Gold Point uniform.

"Go away," she said, stroking Wu Zetian's golden fur.

Henry didn't move. "I heard what the king said."

"Listening at the door?" Of course he had. He was a spy. A traitor. People hated her, but she had never meant for the secret to get out. Henry had led the enemy into the town. He wore the uniform of the army that had murdered his own grandmother.

"Go away," Felicité repeated. "I don't want to talk to you."

"But I want to talk to you," Henry said. "I *need* to. Felicité, I never thought it would go like this. Can I please at least apologize?"

"You can't possibly say anything that will make this better," she said dully. "Just go away, Henry. Play with your Gold Point *friends*."

Sunlight caught in his golden hair. She remembered how handsome she'd once thought he looked wearing black, such a contrast with his pale hair. She remembered how she'd enjoyed running her hands through that hair, and down over his shoulders. All those feelings were utterly gone. She was empty inside, as if she'd never feel anything for anyone ever again. She couldn't even find the energy to demand again that he go away.

Desperately, Henry said, "They're not my friends. Felicité, I'm so sorry. I should have told you about my Change. I couldn't tell my family, but I should have told *you*. That fire was an accident!"

"It could have killed people, Henry."

"But it didn't! And I wouldn't have done it again. I was alone and mad, and I got captured by Voske, and he tricked me into telling him about the tunnel. He said he had a place for Changed people. For *me*. Me and anyone I wanted to have with me. I thought there could be a place for *us*."

"There is no us, Henry." But she could tell he wasn't listening.

As he rushed on, making himself the hero of the story, it occurred to her that he'd always done that. And she'd gone right along with it because she'd been telling herself her own story about the future, with herself as the mayor and Henry by her side.

Felicité put out her hand, palm out. "Just stop. No matter what you say, Mr. Horst is still dead. Julio is still dead. Your own grandmother, Henry!"

"I know." He licked his lips, his gaze sliding away. Even he couldn't reinvent *that*. "After the fire, you said we had to go on with our lives. Start over. Let's do it.

Together. Come stay with me. They gave me Julio's room in Singles' Row —"

A surge of revulsion wrung through Felicité, making her recoil.

Henry reddened. "Or my mother. She's always saying she needs help around the house. You could stay with her, if you don't mind doing Becky's old chores..."

Like Cinderella, Felicité thought bleakly. But her charming prince was a traitor.

Henry opened his mouth to say something, but she couldn't bear to hear it. She couldn't bear to look at his face, or anyone's face, especially her own.

Nothing mattered any more.

"Go to Will, Wu Zetian," Felicité whispered, and kissed her rat on the nose, her salt tears running. If she was really going to do this, she couldn't leave Wu Zetian to hopelessly search for her forever. She held her rat up to her face. Wu Zetian didn't blink, her bright black eyes curious. Felicité leaned in close, choking down tears, and whispered, "Go to Will. Obey Will. Obey Will. Obey Will."

Wu Zetian seemed to stare at her in shock and betrayal, as if waiting for Felicité to take it back. With a stab of pain, Felicité pushed Wu Zetian off her lap. The rat leaped down and ran off.

Felicité tried to make her hands release their hold on the low stone wall, but they clung of their own accord. She wished Henry would push her in, so she wouldn't have to do it herself. But he never would. She needed to push herself. Deliberately she looked into his face, that face that she'd once loved enough to betray everyone. She never wanted to see it again. She never wanted to see *herself* again.

Felicité lifted her hands and let herself fall backwards. She immediately had the sick sense that she'd made a horrible mistake. But it was too late.

She fell through the cool air, her skirts flapping wildly. The shock of cold water made her gasp. The last thing she saw through the water closing over her was Henry's horrified expression. Then she drifted down, down, down. The surface blurred into shifting colors that faded with every thundering drumbeat of her heart.

Though she'd meant to drown when she let go, her

body panicked and she held her breath, her lungs burning as her entire body began the familiar prickling.

Go ahead, she thought. *Finish the Change. Die a monster.*

A cool sense of release flooded through her, startling her into opening her mouth. A few bubbles escaped, jewel-like as they wobbled upward, glinting with light from the surface far above. Her lungs no longer hurt, nor did she feel as if she were suffocating. She wasn't breathing, but somehow, she didn't need to. A rush of sweetness ran through her veins, originating in…her gills.

Felicité touched her neck and felt the gills gaping along the sides of her throat. She blinked at her fingers, seeing the webbing stretching with silver scales between them. The water, so dark when she was holding her breath, had lightened: her eyes, like the rest of her, were changing.

The well had no bottom, but opened out into an underground lake that she'd never known was there. It glimmered in a hundred shades of blue and green and silver. Currents curled slowly through the water as tiny fish darted about.

Fascinated, she swam into the lake, leaving behind the column of weak light below the well opening. As she swam, her body continued to change. It was painless, and though her mind protested that it was bizarre and monstrous, physically it felt as natural as the movement of her legs while walking.

Her hip bones shifted within her, pushing against the sodden weight of her dress. With a lunge and a wrench, she tore the buttons apart and shimmied out of her clothes. They floated down and out of sight in a sodden mass.

The muscles in her legs contracted, pulling them together. As soon as they touched, they fused all the way down to her ankles. Fear flashed through her: would she sink if she couldn't use her legs?

Then she remembered her swimming lessons before she'd Changed. Daddy had taught her a powerful swimming stroke meant to break yourself out of an undertow.

She heard his voice in her mind: *"Kick with your legs straight together and scoop your arms overhead and down."*

When she tried that, she stopped sinking and skimmed through the water. The webs between her fingers propelled her, and as she kicked her legs, it got easier and easier to use them to swim. But they didn't feel quite like legs.

She bent in the middle, looking upside down at herself. Her brown skin had become bronze scales, her breasts streamlined into barely discernable mounds. The bones in her feet tickled as they spread into fins. No, a fluke! Her knees were gone entirely, her lower body a slim, powerful shape that narrowed in toward that webbed fan.

She snapped her lower body with a surge, making a thousand bubbles whirl around her in a glittering cascade, crystalline and clear. Then she shot to the surface, splashing up as she tossed her hair back.

A slick membrane slid away from her eyes, and her vision sharpened. She looked up into a cavern with rock formations like sea sculptures reaching down from above. Minerals glittered in striations, and here and there, phosphorescent patches glowed.

It was strange, and quiet, and beautiful.

She dipped her head into the water. That membrane slid back over her eyes, protecting them and sharpening her focus below the surface. Everything tightened into extraordinary clarity. The underwater cavern was bright, strange, beckoning. A break in the rocky dome on the other side widened into a vast tunnel, angling upward.

She swam toward it to see where it went, her gills fluttering with each stroke of her heart. She put her hands before her and snapped her lower half in a sinuous, powerful stroke that sluiced her through the water like an arrow to a target, bubbles streaming along her smoothly scaled flank with a whisper-soft tickle.

The tunnel angled again, water surging through a massive crack in the earth. Here and there mysterious barnacle-covered objects jutted out: remnants of the old days. She was tempted to explore them, but what would she do with them? She thought of Yuki, who had never known about these mysterious artifacts right below Las Anclas. Could he and Ross find them if she told them?

She wasn't telling anyone anything. *That* had

changed forever.

Her gills sensed the presence of salt in the water as she swam upward. It made no difference except to the light, which became greenish. Dazzling sunlight lanced down in golden shafts, now diffuse, now bright as the currents shifted. She had come out from under the shelf of the shore, directly into the little harbor.

She surfaced and looked eastward toward Las Anclas. She could make out the bell tower a mile or two away, the western wall barely visible below it. Tiny gleams of light winked on the metal of rifles as Voske's soldiers patrolled the sentry walk.

Felicité turned her face outward, sank below the surface, and swam out to sea.

·8·

BECKY

LAS ANCLAS - AUNT ROSA'S HOUSE

BECKY AWOKE FROM A familiar dream of being in her old house, hiding from her mother. Dr. Lee had told her the nightmares would eventually lessen, then disappear as she got used to her new life. He'd been right…for a while. But ever since Voske had taken Las Anclas, the nightmares had returned.

It was still dark, so she couldn't use Dr. Lee's technique of counting everything in the room that was different from her old one. Becky began to reassure herself by touching the bed Aunt Rosa had given her—so much more comfortable than her old one—when a noise startled her. As she began to gasp, a hand came down over her mouth. She reacted fast, as Meredith had trained her, yanking at the vulnerable thumb as she jerked her head away.

"Ow," a muffled voice complained as the hand let go. "Did you have to break my thumb? I just didn't want you yelling."

"Henry," Becky whispered, though she didn't know why she shouldn't yell. "What are you doing here?"

"I have to talk to you."

"Why?" The roiling emotions from the nightmare twisted inside her as she reached for her bedside lamp and the tinderbox.

"No lights," Henry murmured hoarsely. She would have ignored him, except for the quaver in his voice. Henry was upset. Very upset. "Becky, Felicité is dead."

Becky was speechless with shock and horror. Then

rage burned through her. She welcomed it. Anger hurt less than grief. "Voske murdered —"

"No! She threw herself down the well."

She didn't believe it. Henry was lying or repeating a lie, and that fed her fury. "Felicité would never! Not to her family — her grandmother — Voske must have had someone push her in and said she did it herself!"

"She *did* do it herself," Henry said. Becky's eyes had begun to adjust to the darkness. He sank down on the floor with his knees up and leaned against her bed. "I saw it. I was *there*. No one knows. Except you, now."

Becky didn't want to believe it. She fell back on her sheriff training. Say as little as possible and let the person you're interviewing talk freely. "What happened?"

"Voske kicked her out of Wolfe House. I found her sitting on the edge of the well. I told her she could live with me, and she just…did it. I saw her sink, Becky. I lowered the bucket as far as it would go, so she could see it and grab on. But she was *gone*. I snuck into our house and hid out. Why did Felicité do it? I don't get it." He sounded more upset than he'd been on the day he'd been exiled. Then he'd been mostly angry. Now, he sounded *hurt*.

Becky's sheriff training told her things she didn't want to believe: the ring of truth in his voice. The little details, like lowering the bucket, that liars didn't tend to invent. Henry behaving in a characteristic manner, with his lack of responsibility. She seized on the last. It was easier to focus on how to talk to Henry than on the idea of Felicité being dead. "Henry, I'm not saying that committing suicide was justified. I can't even imagine how her mother's going to feel when she finds out. But everybody blamed Felicité for what *you* did."

"I didn't want it to be like this," he burst out, his voice raw. "I didn't mean for any of this to happen."

"You told Voske about the tunnel."

"Yeah, but he tricked me. I was all ready to resist torture, but he didn't even interrogate me. He was nice to me. Interested in me. We talked, that's all."

"That *was* the interrogation," Becky said, disgusted. Yes. Disgust was good. Better than picturing Felicité drowning. "He was getting information out of you. Like a vampire tree sucking blood."

"I'd never have said anything if I'd known anything would happen to *Felicité*."

Becky almost snapped that Felicité could easily have died in the fire he'd set, but she stopped herself. She couldn't stand to hear more of his excuses. Her emotions were so jangled, she didn't know what to think. Was Felicité really dead? It seemed impossible. It *should* seem impossible. But Becky remembered glaring at Felicité when she'd learned what her old friend had done. Then she'd seen Felicité, so shocked and miserable, so...*small* beneath her giant hat, forced to watch those hideous executions.

It wasn't as if Becky had never made mistakes. Even terrible mistakes. If only she'd stayed closer to Henry. If only she'd told Dr. Lee what was happening in her house. Maybe then everything would have been different. But that was how it went. You think you're right and you act—or in her case, you don't act—without knowing what the result will be. And when you learn the consequences, they've already happened, and you can't go back and change your decision.

Henry was still talking. "...and Voske said he re-warded people who—"

Light flared under Becky's door, and it opened. Aunt Rosa stood in her nightgown, holding a lamp. "I heard voices. Henry, you know you're not welcome here."

Becky burst out, "Felicité is dead."

Aunt Rosa's eyes widened. "What?"

"She killed herself. Nobody knows," Henry said. "I snuck in to tell Becky. She and Felicité were best friends."

Becky had started to feel sorry for Henry, but he was lying again. She and Felicité hadn't been *best* friends since they were thirteen, when Felicité had replaced her with Sujata and Nasreen.

"If this is true, her mother deserves to hear it from one of us. Not one of *them*," said Aunt Rosa. Becky's insides squeezed at the thought of breaking that news. "Exactly what happened?"

Henry said, "Voske kicked her out of Wolfe House to make room for his wife and daughter. I tried to stop her, but she threw herself down the well."

That wasn't quite what he'd told Becky, but she kept quiet. Then she wondered if that was one of those decisions she'd been thinking about, the kind she'd regret later. Why should she keep protecting Henry, even in such a small way?

Aunt Rosa gave a short nod. "I'll walk up to Wolfe House at first light. Go away, Henry. Life right now is hard enough without staying up all night."

Henry walked out. All dark clothes look black in the night, but she could see from the cut that he still wore the Voske uniform. The sight of her brother in it made her sick.

"I'm so sorry, Becky," said Aunt Rosa. "Do you want to talk?"

Becky shook her head and got back into bed. She shut her eyes, but all she could think about was Felicité. Why hadn't she come to Becky? Angry as Becky was, she would still have asked Aunt Rosa if they could set up the truckle bed for her.

But Felicité couldn't have known that. Becky again regretted the accusing look she'd shot at Felicité the day of the execution. *That* was the terrible mistake Becky had made, the one she could never take back. And now she was living with the consequences.

Becky awoke to a knock at the front door. She leaped out of bed and rushed to open it. Before she even got there, she remembered that Felicité was dead. Becky wished she could go back to sleep and forget again, but she had to open the door.

A soldier with a stack of papers thrust one into her hands. She was surprised to see that it was the newspaper. The headline read *El Heraldo de Las Anclas* — in the same font, too.

But Jennie isn't here. Becky stared, bewildered. Jennie was the one who wrote the newspaper.

The soldier spoke in a quick monotone. "You have

one day to read the paper. If you're not here to receive it, it will be slipped under your door. Today's edition will be picked up for recycling tomorrow. If you're not here to hand it over, leave it weighted down outside your door. Don't damage it in any way." He marched to the next house.

Becky ducked inside to look at it. Instead of Jennie's alliterative headlines—the one that came instantly to mind, with a stab of bitterness, was "Voske Vanquished"—the chief story was titled "Las Anclas Welcomes a New Era."

It began, *With the coming of a new era, Las Anclas will welcome the advent of electricity in all homes. And that is only the beginning of the greatness that lies in store. With its entry into the Voske Empire, Las Anclas will enjoy the prosperity and...*

Becky skipped to the next article: "Daily Quote from the King." *Great effort brings great rewards.*

"Ugh!" she said aloud.

The final article was headlined "Crime and Punishment." *Five criminals were executed for rebellion. One criminal was executed for offending the dignity of the crown.*

It took her a moment to realize that the "one criminal" must be her Grandma Ida, shot dead just for yelling. Dignity! Voske didn't even give them the dignity of names.

She wanted to rip up the page and stuff it into the stove, but that would undoubtedly offend the dignity of the crown. Gritting her teeth, she left it weighted down with a rock and headed to Dr. Lee's.

She was so tired and upset that she didn't even look forward to breakfast with Dr. Lee, which had been her sole comfort since the invasion. She was further alarmed when she arrived at the infirmary kitchen and saw not only Dr. Lee and Meredith, who often joined them, but Paco, in that black and red outfit Voske forced him to wear, looking even more tense than usual.

Becky's heart banged against her ribs. What new awful thing had happened?

"I was with Santiago, of course," Paco was saying.

Becky was surprised Santiago wasn't there now—once he'd been assigned as Paco's personal guard, she'd always seen them together. She had wondered if Paco knew that Santiago was Kerry's boyfriend, but she didn't dare ask. And even if he did know, did it change anything? Paco had avoided Kerry as much as possible.

Becky gritted her teeth. She had no idea what was safe to say to whom. Especially if Voske could read minds!

"Voske and his wife were talking in his office. She said..." Paco imitated a sweet, breathy woman's voice. With a stifled gulp of nervous laughter, Becky thought that he'd never make the Catalina Players. "'It desolates me to have to tell you, Ian dear, but you did ask me to be vigilant. I do not wish to make any accusations, and of course you might have given Custer Bern permission to sit in your throne, but—' and Voske said, 'What? Custer Bern did what?' He sounded furious. Santiago hustled me out of there."

Paco might not be a good actor, but Becky was sure he'd repeated the exact words he'd heard. He could hear a complicated rhythm once and perform it perfectly.

"Hmm," said Dr. Lee. "It seems this Custer Bern was left in charge of Gold Point while Voske is here. And that you all had better be very careful around Voske's wife."

"She's a spy and a tattletale," Meredith said. "Ugh."

"How's your mom today?" Becky asked, nerving herself to share her own horrible news.

Meredith brightened. "Better. She was awake this morning."

Dr. Lee glanced out the window, then closed it, though the day was already hot. Paco got a broom out of the cleaning closet and leaned it against the hall door so it would noisily fall over if anyone walked in. Then he picked up a canister of flour and tossed a handful on the floor. Spanner, the tabby cat, leaped down from a high cupboard, his skin flaps outstretched. He glided down to the flour and rolled in it.

"What's going on?" Becky's voice squeaked as her heart crowded her throat. She felt like one more piece of shocking news would make her explode into a million pieces.

Dr. Lee patted her shoulder and put a platter of kimchi quesadillas on the table. In the midst of this nightmare, he was reassuringly himself, his mostly-gray ponytail neat behind his rounded shoulders. He was a short man and not a fighter, but calm and strength seemed to flow from him to her, like it did from Sheriff Crow. Dr. Lee would never fall into pieces. Neither would Meredith or Paco. If they could stay calm, she could at least try to do the same.

The four of them crowded around the table, leaning in. Becky remembered crowding around the table in Felicité's room when they were all ten. She and Sujata and Felicité used to have 'secret meetings' to decide whom to invite to Felicité's tea parties. *Felicité.* Becky's throat hurt even more. Despite the tempting smell of melted cheese and caramelized kimchi, she couldn't force herself to eat. She *had* to tell them about Felicité. But she could not get the words out.

Dr. Lee said gently, "We all know about Felicité, Becky. Your aunt stopped by earlier this morning. I want to assure you —"

Meredith broke in. "I'm sorry, Becky. I know you two used to be friends. But you deserved better. She was selfish, she was vain, she let Voske into this town —"

Dr. Lee raised a hand. "Meredith, Felicité didn't —"

Meredith charged on. "She did! And now look what she's done. She took the coward's way out and left us with the mess she made. How dare she!"

"Meredith, please keep your voice down." Dr. Lee indicated the door.

Becky turned to Meredith, angry, miserable, sorry, and saw a gleam of moisture in Meredith's eyes. Meredith scowled at the table, her arms crossed tightly, and Becky wondered if she was seeing how Meredith showed loss.

Dr. Lee said gently, "We'll take time later to talk about how Felicité's action makes us feel. That's important. But we don't have many opportunities to speak freely together. Let's move on to the purpose of this meeting."

"What purpose?" Becky asked, wiping her eyes on her sleeve.

Meredith hissed in a long breath. Then she announced in a determined voice, "We're having a secret meeting to plan our rebellion."

"It is not a rebellion." Dr. Lee's voice was

uncharacteristically sharp.

Meredith's red brows shot up. "That's what the paper called it." She jerked her thumb at the new version of *El Heraldo*, which was on the floor weighted down by the mulch bucket.

"We don't accept Voske's words," Dr. Lee said. "A rebellion is a conflict against an established government. Voske's using every tool he has to make us accept him as our king, all the way down to his language. But he's not our rightful leader—this town is run by a council we choose by election. He's a tyrant who took this town by force. What we're organizing is a *resistance*, a fight against an invader."

"Okay." Meredith jerked her chin down. "But if we're not rebels, what are we? We need a name. A secret name, since this is a secret group."

There was a pause. Becky supposed the others were thinking about a name. But all she could think of was water closing over Felicité's head.

"We should be the Rats," Paco said. "Voske called Mr. Horst and his fighters rats nipping at his boots. Their resistance failed, but they fought back, and they died for our town. If they're rats, we're rats, too."

"I like that." Becky tried to make her voice sound firm. She was still the sheriff's apprentice. "Our trained rats helped us win against Voske's last attack."

"And if any Gold Point poke-nose overhears us talk about rats, they'll think we mean the ones with four legs." Meredith grinned. It was the first time Becky had seen anyone but Voske look genuinely happy since the invasion.

Paco turned to Becky. "Our goal is to take Las Anclas back. Becky, do you want to be a part of this?"

"Oh, yes," Becky breathed, then stopped, waiting for...what? For them to have second thoughts about her? But they had chosen her. They had trusted her with their secret. And they simply waited, giving her time to think.

So, she thought. Yes, she was afraid, but she had been afraid when she tried to protect Jack and covered the sheriff's escape. The first lesson she had learned from Sheriff Crow was that being afraid didn't mean you couldn't act. You didn't just give up. Down deep, she was aware of a whisper, *The way Felicité did.*

As she looked from Dr. Lee's solemnity to Meredith's glee to Paco's determination, she felt a sense of rightness. Las Anclas wasn't going to give in to Voske's tyranny. She would be a part of taking the town back. She could see Sheriff Crow's nod of approval.

"Yes," Becky said again. "I do."

Dr. Lee held up his hand. "This isn't something to rush into. Noah Horst had no real plan and chose his fighters because they were there when he decided to do it. He was brave, but courage is not enough. We have to be smart, and we have to be cautious."

Meredith elbowed Becky. "Paco talked to me this morning, when I came to see Mom, and we decided to invite you and Dr. Lee. But we need to figure out who else to talk to."

Becky's inside swooped between fright and a weird flash of amusement. It really was like the secret meetings of her childhood, only their invitations weren't to a "select" tea party. Making the wrong decision meant people would die. "I wish we knew where Sheriff Crow was. She'd help us."

Dr. Lee refilled her glass of barley tea. "I'm sure she's trying to help us now."

"How do you know?" Becky asked. "Have you—"

He shook his head. "I don't know any more than you do. But I feel certain that Sheriff Crow is going to look for aid."

"Mr. Preston. And the Rangers." Meredith said in a softer voice, "The Rangers still alive."

"How can she even find them?" Paco asked. "They must have gone to ground."

"If anyone can find them, it's Sheriff Crow." Becky knew that in her heart.

Meredith crossed her arms. "I hope so. But we need people inside the town."

"We need people who can keep a secret for a long time," said Paco. "People who can think strategically, as Mr. Preston says. People who can fight."

"Everyone doesn't have to be a warrior." With a smile, Dr. Lee indicated himself. "I've already been talking to Jack Lowell and Anna-Lucia. We should bring them in."

Meredith snapped her fingers. "Great idea! Jack hears everything. And how about Jennie's parents?"

"I agree," Dr. Lee said. "I have a long list of adults in mind. But you may know the teenagers better."

Becky had already thought of someone quiet, smart, and capable. And as soon as Dr. Lee pointed out that they didn't have to be fighters, she was sure. "Alfonso —"

Simultaneously, Dr. Lee said, "Such as my apprentice, Alfonso Medina." They smiled at each other. Then he went on, "If Paco and Meredith agree, I'll speak to him when he arrives to work today."

"I don't really know Alfonso," Paco said. "He's so quiet."

"He's smart. And quiet means he can *definitely* keep things to himself." Meredith had never looked so serious.

"If you all think he'd a good choice, then I'm for him," Paco said. "Who else?"

Dr. Lee held up one hand. "We need to be careful how many people we talk to at a time. Especially with teenagers. I suggest that the four of us agree on whom to talk to before we do it. And that we approach people one by one."

"How about Jose and Yolanda Riley?" Paco suggested. "They're young, but..."

"Yes!" exclaimed Meredith. "They fought on Jennie's team."

"They did," said Dr. Lee. But his tone held reservation. "But Yolanda especially can be impulsive, and Jose will fall in with her. Also, as you say, they're fighters. They're not planners. My suggestion is that we wait to bring them in *after* we have a solid plan. What do you think?"

Paco gave a thoughtful nod. "You're right. What we need now are people who can think ahead and keep a secret."

Meredith gave Becky a quick look. Becky knew what she was thinking. Brisa had also been on Jennie's team. "I know, Meredith. Brisa is fearless, but she'd be the first to admit that you can read her mind by looking at her face." Then panic flashed through Becky. "I've been wanting to tell you. Voske really can read minds."

"No, that was just a rumor he spread," Dr. Lee reassured her. "He actually spied with the help of a Changed woman who could see through the eyes of hawks."

"It's not a rumor," Becky insisted. "He's telepathic. When he talked to me, he knew everything I was thinking before I said it. He'll know what we're planning as soon as he sees any of us!"

"Really?" Meredith said doubtfully. "Then why does he need spies?"

"Because he's not telepathic," Dr. Lee said. "He likes to make it seem like he is to frighten people and keep them in line."

"He is," Becky insisted. "I was going to warn you all, but I didn't have the chance. When he talked to me, he knew things that nobody could have told him. Things I was thinking that I hadn't said yet."

"Henry blabbed all the town secrets." Meredith shrugged.

"This is stuff Henry doesn't know about." Becky pushed around a shred of kimchi. "There's no way he could have known...this stuff...except by reading my mind."

Dr. Lee seemed undisturbed. "Becky, can you repeat the conversation you had with Voske, as best as you remember it?"

Becky drew on her sheriff training, to remember not only what people had said, but how they said it. She repeated the interview she'd had with Voske, all the way down to his knowledge that her favorite bath scent was rose petals.

"Brisa is the only person who knows that, and he never talked to her. I know what we said about her being bad at keeping secrets, but *this*, she wouldn't have mentioned. It's..." Becky couldn't help blushing. "It's *private*."

"Oh. It's a sex thing." Meredith rolled her eyes.

Though Becky knew it was only because Meredith had never had any interest in sex, she blushed harder, hoping that nobody was picturing *anything*.

There was the tiniest tremble of laughter in Dr. Lee's voice as he said, "I hate to do this to you, Becky, but the roses are a perfect example of how Voske makes people think he's reading their minds. It's similar to something you've all seen me do. You must have noticed that I can tell when someone's worried. I'm sure you can all think of a time when I asked you about something you were dying to talk about, but afraid to bring up."

He looked at each of them in turn, as he said, "Haven't I?"

They all nodded. Becky remembered trying to hide from Dr. Lee for fear that if she gave him the chance to talk to her privately, he'd somehow find out what was going on in her home. Everyone knew that about Dr. Lee. He knew things about people.

Dr. Lee went on, "I'm not telepathic. And neither is Voske. Both of us are good at reading expressions, then asking questions to confirm what we've guessed. It has a name, even. It's called cold reading. The first requirement is knowing a lot about human nature. We can guess what people are probably thinking, because we've seen so many people in similar situations before. As for the roses, *you* told him about them, Becky."

"What?" Becky exclaimed. "No, I didn't!"

"You did. He asked if you liked scented baths, he saw from your expression that you did, and then he mentioned a scent that most people like. Your face told him he was correct, so he didn't keep guessing. If he'd been wrong, he'd have kept on guessing."

Becky's spine crawled as Dr. Lee imitated Voske's voice: "You like jasmine...violets...roses...Yes, you love roses. Well, if you ever want to bathe in rose petals with your girlfriend again, you'll do as you're told."

"Eww." Meredith crossed her arms. "That is *completely* creepy."

In his normal voice, Dr. Lee said, "And if he'd done that, Becky, you'd have been so shocked once he said roses that you'd have forgotten his earlier guesses, the ones that were wrong. You'd only remember that he'd read your mind and known your favorite scent. It's a very easy way to find things out about people. You use the knowledge you already have, take your best guess, and see if it's right. If their face doesn't show that it is, you take your next guess. If you're good at cold reading, and Voske and I both are, it rarely takes more than three guesses."

Becky wondered if Voske had done something similar to Henry. Now that Dr. Lee had explained it, she realized it wouldn't have been hard at all.

"Three guesses, huh?" Paco asked. "But if someone knows how to do that themselves, they'd notice if you did it to them, right?"

His calculating expression was so like Voske's that it unnerved Becky. *It's just his face,* she told herself. *His bones.*

Dr. Lee looked alarmed. "Paco, do not practice this on Voske. He *will* notice."

"Teach me to do it," Paco said. "I'll practice on someone else."

"Ugh!" Meredith exclaimed. "Why do you want to learn that? It's creepy!"

"You can use it to help people. Find out what's on their minds that they're afraid to talk about." Dr. Lee looked sad, and Becky wondered if he was wishing he'd tried it on Felicité. "It's a double-edged sword. Like my power. If I wanted to, instead of healing people, I could age them until they died."

He looked at Paco again. This time, Becky knew that Dr. Lee was trying to read his expression. "I'm serious, Paco. Don't try it on Voske."

"I'll be careful," Paco said. And that was the most Dr. Lee could get out of him.

Becky urgently said, "There's something else you all need to know. Santiago is Kerry's boyfriend. He loves her, and Kerry trusted him with her life. He lied to Voske for her! Maybe we can trust him, too. I'm sure he'd do anything to save her."

Only Meredith seemed surprised. "Oh, he's *that* Santiago!"

Paco nodded. "I figured that out. But it doesn't mean we can trust him. If he lied to Voske to save Kerry, he might turn in anyone he thinks is a danger to her. Like us. We tell him nothing."

"Agreed," Dr. Lee said with a soft sigh. "We must always err on the side of caution when it comes to telling anyone what we're planning."

Footsteps sounded outside the kitchen. Meredith grabbed the broom and began sweeping up the flour.

Becky began collecting the plates, her hands shaking. Santiago walked in and almost collided with Meredith. He stepped in the flour, then backed away hastily, his socks leaving white prints in the hall.

"Oh, oops. Sorry," Santiago exclaimed. "Can I help?"

Meredith snorted. "I think you've 'helped' enough already."

"Becky, I've made more medicine for Grandma Wolfe." Dr. Lee handed her a bottle of poppy infusion. Becky's hands trembled as she took it, though she knew it was a mild dose that would do nothing but ease pain. "Can you deliver it to Wolfe House, and see if there is anything else she needs?"

Becky flinched inwardly at the thought of facing Grandma Wolfe and the mayor. Would they blame her for glaring at Felicité the last time they saw each other?

Dr. Lee gave her a sharp look. "Becky. It was *not* your fault. No one in this town has committed suicide in your lifetime, but people have in mine. Everyone who cared about Felicité, and even some people who didn't, are blaming themselves. But you didn't make her kill herself. That's something *she* did."

Becky gulped back the tears that threatened to fall at the thought of Felicité's blaming herself.

"We'll walk with you," Santiago offered.

"It's all right," Becky said, then regretted it. He'd clearly meant it as a kindness.

"We have to go that way anyway. We have orders," Santiago said. Paco's expression hardened.

The three of them put their shoes on and left the infirmary. Hammering echoed from the town hall on the other side of the town square. Paco asked, "What's going on?"

"They're building a bigger stage," said Santiago. Becky gritted her teeth, wondering if it was to accommodate more executions.

"Oh?" said Paco in an overly innocent voice. "For a dance?"

Becky shot him a suspicious look, just as Santiago gave him a baffled one.

"No," Santiago said. "It's for Opportunity Day."

Becky almost tripped over level ground. Kerry had

told her about Opportunity Day, when her mother forced often deadly Changes on random citizens. It had never occurred to Becky that Las Anclas would also be subjected to that atrocity.

"Voske is going to make us do that?" Paco sounded as horrified as Becky felt.

Santiago gave him a warning look. Loudly, he said, "It's a great honor."

Paco's fists clenched. Becky quickly said, "Paco, you were talking about dances. Santiago, you have dances at Gold Point, right?"

"Yeah, of course. At celebrations or the military club. Or restaurants that have a dance floor." With a glance at Paco, Santiago added, "Being a soldier is just my job, you know. I have a life."

"Of course you do," Paco said. "So. you dance. With boys...girls?"

"Girls," Santiago said absently.

"You like the ones with long black hair, don't you?" Paco asked.

Becky almost dropped the medicine bottle. He was doing that *thing* that Dr. Lee told him not to do! And he sounded so unnatural, too. Santiago would notice for sure, and report it to Voske! She glared at him.

"Yeah, in braids—" Santiago began, then looked horrified. "I like all kinds of girls. Blondes! Redheads! Not just with long hair! Short is good, too!"

Paco held up his hands. "Sure. Okay, got it. Just girls. I liked girls sometimes, too, when I was younger. Especially to dance with. But once I got older, dancing was all I wanted to do with them."

Becky edged closer to Paco and jammed her elbow into his ribs, hoping that he would get the signal that his attempt to cover up sounded incredibly fake. To her immense relief, Santiago wasn't paying attention. He pointed at the town hall. Sounds of hammering came from inside as well as outside.

"Oh, look. Here we are," Santiago said in a cheery voice that sounded equally fake. Rehearsed. "Prince Liam, you and I are supposed to help the carpenters."

"My name is *Paco*." Paco stopped walking. "And I don't know anything about carpentry. I worked with glass."

"Oh, it doesn't matter," Santiago said, in that same falsely cheery tone. "They just need a few extra guys to hammer in some nails. Someone else is doing the skilled labor."

That made no sense. Unskilled people would just get in the way of the carpenters, who could hammer in their own nails. Voske had some reason to want Paco to work on that stage. Paco's expression froze over.

Becky hurried on alone, wondering what Voske was doing with Paco. Maybe Voske was trying to intimidate him by forcing him to work on one of the Gold Point things that Voske had imposed on Las Anclas. And have everyone see it.

When she reached Wolfe House, she nearly dropped the bottle again. Voske himself stood in the doorway. "Good morning, Becky."

Becky said nervously, "I brought the medicine. For Grandma Wolfe."

Voske snapped his fingers, summoning an aide. "Take that to Mrs. Wolfe." The soldier took the bottle upstairs. Apparently, Grandma Wolfe and Mayor Wolfe had been moved out of the master bedroom.

Becky started backing away, but Voske held up his hand. She froze in place. "Becky, I'd like you to meet Min Soo. Why don't you go introduce yourself? She's expecting you." With a lazy wave of his hand, he indicated the master bedroom.

Expecting *her?* Becky felt sick. He watched with that eerie smile as she walked slowly across the parlor — now Voske's office. And that wasn't all that had changed. Mayor Wolfe had decorated the master bedroom with simple elegance. The bed was now completely hidden by a pink silk canopy and curtains. The chairs beside it were lavishly carved and upholstered in pastel silk. Servants were busy moving in new furniture.

Where was Voske's wife?

Someone softly snapped fingers from within the curtained bed. Two servants instantly set down the trunk they were carrying, ran to the bed, and ceremoniously pulled the curtains. At first, all Becky could see was pink. Then her gaze was drawn to a woman in a pink and white hanbok, lounging against a pile of silk pillows. Her blue-black hair was swept up to the top of her head and captured with a golden ornament. A cascade of peach-colored silk ribbons hung down on one side of her face.

Brisa would love this. Then Becky came to her senses. This had to be Voske's wife.

"You must be Becky," the woman said sweetly. "Do come in. Sit down."

Becky dropped nervelessly into a mauve chair as Min Soo gestured gracefully with her perfectly manicured hands. "Would you care for some candied rose petals?"

"Sure," Becky said, hating the way her voice squeaked. "Thank you."

They were in a lacquered box on a small table. Like the chairs, its legs were carved into dragon claws. Becky took one rose petal, then a few more, and stuffed them into her mouth. The candies were sweet and crunchy, and while she was chewing, she didn't have to talk.

"I see that you like them," Min Soo said, smiling. Becky nodded. "I remember another guest who also liked them. Ross Juarez."

Becky choked, then tried not to cough up chewed rose petals.

"Are you all right, my dear?" Min Soo asked. "Water, please."

A servant set down a stack of fluffy towels — pink — and brought a crystal glass of water. Becky drank gratefully. As she looked for a place to set the glass down, Min Soo said, "Is Ross a friend of yours?"

"No, I barely know him," Becky said. The servant took the glass from her hand, making her jump.

"Oh, what a disappointment," Min Soo said with a rueful little smile. "Such an interesting young man. I had hoped to meet his friends. With whom would you suggest I begin?"

Becky was appalled. She couldn't refuse to answer, but she couldn't sic Min Soo on anyone, either. Luckily, his actual friends were safely out of town. "He's… er…close to Jennie Riley and Mia Lee." She decided not to mention Kerry.

She looked at Min Soo with new interest. She wasn't only Voske's wife, she was Kerry's mother. Kerry had said she'd spent most of her life not getting along with her. But she'd changed her mind and even changed her name, taking on her mother's.

"Yes, the girls he's traveling with now," said Min Soo. "But he also took his little sister. And my daughter. Surely, she's a friend of his, too. A *close* friend."

Becky tried to figure out who knew what. Henry must have told Voske that Ross was dating both Mia and Jennie. To protect Santiago, when Kerry had fled Gold Point, she'd left a note saying she'd fallen in love with Ross and was running away with him. Min Soo must think Ross was dating Mia, Jennie, *and* Kerry. Becky bit her lip against the giggle that threatened to spill out. Apparently Voske didn't know *everything*.

Min Soo's eyes narrowed. "Yes, he's very handsome. I hope you weren't too sad to be left behind. Was it because you were needed in town...?"

Becky blinked, baffled.

"Or was he just a little flirt before you found Brisa?"

Becky's jaw dropped. "Flirt?" Then she understood what Min Soo was doing, and the flutter of laughter froze into fear. Min Soo was doing that cold reading thing, and Becky had fallen for it! She'd just told Voske's wife...what *had* she told her? Becky began a frantic mental review of the conversation.

"Oh, my mistake." Min Soo laughed a little. "You're not interested in boys at all, are you?"

Becky shook her head, then wondered if she shouldn't have revealed that. But everyone in town knew she only liked girls. And what did it matter who Ross dated?

"Have more rose petals, Becky," Min Soo said in her soft, soothing voice. "Tell me about Las Anclas. What is your recommendation for the best place to eat?"

At least *that* was a safe enough a question. "Everybody likes Jack's."

"Oh, thank you. And what are some of his best dishes?"

Becky said cautiously, "It depends on what you like."

"Does he make good desserts? I love sweets."

Becky began to relax. This was the Min Soo Kerry had told her about, who loved fancy desserts, pretty clothes, and roses. "Jack's desserts are simple. But you'd like the ones his pastry chef Anna-Lucia makes. Um, if you like fancy things."

"I do indeed," Min Soo said. "You're a good observer. You must feel so lost with Sheriff Crow gone."

Becky's stomach twisted into a knot of grief and fear. "I…"

Min Soo smiled gently. "It's hard, I know. But people do adjust. There are other people who care about you. Brisa, your aunt, and I'm sure many more."

Becky nodded, and wondered what Voske's wife was reading in her face.

"It's been lovely talking to you, but I don't want to keep you from your work," said Min Soo. "We'll have more chats, once I settle in."

Becky leaped up, ready to escape. "Uh, thank you. For the candies."

"Take them. Share them with your girlfriend. The box, too. Keep it." Min Soo smiled. "Or give it to her."

"Thank you." Becky picked up the box as carefully as if it contained a scorpion and fled with it, her heart hammering. She couldn't possibly share such a tainted gift with Brisa, nor did she want it in her room. But she couldn't throw it away, either. Maybe she'd stash it in Aunt Rosa's attic.

As she walked, she reviewed the conversation, trying to commit it to memory as Sheriff Crow had taught her. There might be something in it that would help the Rats.

·9·
PACO

LAS ANCLAS - INFIRMARY

PACO VOLUNTEERED TO COLLECT Ms. Lowenstein's breakfast tray, hoping to catch her awake—and alone. But Luis fell into step with him as soon as he saw where Paco was headed. Luis didn't even make an excuse about needing to see her too, but just trailed behind him. As always, he had his hands jammed in his pockets.

Ms. Lowenstein was asleep, her cat eyes closed. She'd only eaten a few bites of her breakfast. Paco took the tray, and Luis followed him right back out. Paco had thought he'd get used to Luis's presence, as he had Santiago's, but he hadn't. It was like a black cloud hung over the guy, even when all he was doing was sorting pills or feeding table scraps to the potted surgical plants. When Becky's aunt had told them that Felicité had committed suicide, Paco would have sworn that Luis looked *jealous*.

Becky came in. Several days after Felicité's death, her eyes were still red and swollen, her face still puffy. "Hi, Paco." Her voice wavered. She ducked her head and hurried into the surgery.

Paco said to Luis, "She and Felicité were old friends. Mind if I talk to her alone?"

Luis never let Paco speak to Ms. Lowenstein alone, though Dr. Lee sometimes got a chance to do so. Because Voske suspected Paco of plotting, but not Dr. Lee? Because Voske wanted to intimidate Paco with visible surveillance? Voske was like the Go master Yuki had on his ship, who'd instructed him on a board game that was meant to teach him strategy. Voske didn't think two or three moves ahead, like a good player. He thought twenty moves ahead, like a *great* player.

Paco had never cared for chess, but he'd enjoyed Go. Maybe because only he and Yuki played it, so it was something special the two of them shared. Well, he'd practice his Go skills right now, and see what orders Voske had given to Luis about Becky.

Luis nodded as if he understood. "Go ahead."

So Voske thought Becky, or maybe all teenagers, were either harmless, in which case it didn't matter if they spoke privately, or potential trouble-makers, in which case he wanted to lull them into a false sense of security so he could close a trap around them later. It was like Yuki had said about Go: the possible moves were infinite.

Paco found Becky rearranging bottles in the medicine cabinet. He recognized the blind look in her eyes. She'd keep on rearranging those bottles until something brought her attention back.

"I'm sorry, Becky." He'd already said that once, and he knew it wouldn't fix anything. But he couldn't think of anything else he could say.

"It hits me at night. I can't get past how I left Felicité thinking I hated her." Her voice had gone tiny, like it had been before Sheriff Crow had taken her on as apprentice. Even if Luis was listening at the door, Paco was certain he couldn't hear her.

"I should've told her I knew she didn't want Voske to attack." Becky sniffed, but it didn't keep back the tears. "I don't know why she told Henry about that tunnel. Maybe he tricked her. Maybe she just wanted them to share a secret. Who knows. But I let her believe that I thought she wanted to help Voske. And she didn't. I know she didn't. She must have thought everyone believed she was a traitor."

Paco had never liked Felicité, but he knew Becky was right. Everybody knew Felicité wanted — had wanted — to be mayor of Las Anclas someday. She'd never have deliberately betrayed the town. She'd been stupid, but Henry was the traitor, not her. He didn't want to feel guilty over Felicité. But Becky's grief-stricken face made him wish he hadn't been so harsh with her. He'd been like everyone else in town, blaming her for something that really was Henry's fault.

Paco searched for words of comfort, though nice words would not bring Felicité back. "If you'd known she was thinking of killing herself, you'd have talked her down, right? She didn't tell anyone, so you couldn't."

"Yeah. Dr. Lee said the same thing." And Becky returned to endlessly rearranging bottles, obviously not comforted at all.

Paco left her to it. He had another job to do. Dr. Lee's apprentice Alfonso had agreed to join the Rats. He and Meredith had come up with two possible teenage recruits. Dr. Lee had suggested that Paco go to the school to check them out, so he needed an excuse to go there.

Paco's mind felt stuffed to bursting with secrets and plots and excuses. It was like he needed to study for a final exam before he did *anything*.

To get to the school to see the potential Rats, he had to collect Meredith's "forgotten" lunch, and make sure some spy saw him do it. He opened the door, but Luis was nowhere in sight. So. he really hadn't been spying on Paco, the one time that Paco wanted a spy! Frustrated, he glanced into the kitchen. Dr. Lee was chopping turnips. Luis was sitting at the table, staring at a wall the same way Becky had stared into the cabinet.

Paco was about to join him when he spotted Santiago through the window. He must have finished his morning drill. Perfect timing. When Santiago came in, Paco said, "Morning. Dr. Lee made some new kimchi."

Santiago grinned as he followed Paco into the kitchen. Paco set Ms. Lowenstein's plate on the side table, and Dr. Lee frowned at the uneaten meal. "So. she's still not—" He broke off when he caught sight of Santiago. "Paco! Will you do me a favor? Meredith forgot her lunch."

Before he could continue his lines, Santiago cut in with a hopeful expression. "I hear you have new kimchi?"

Dr. Lee smiled at him. "I do. Watermelon-cucumber! Nice and refreshing. I packed some in Meredith's lunch. But I'll give you a dish to eat on the way."

He tried to pass Paco the lunch, but Santiago intercepted it. "Prince Li—he doesn't have to go to the school. Send someone else."

Paco bit down on his annoyance, his thoughts spinning frantically. He, Meredith, and Dr. Lee had assumed a forgotten lunch was a simple, foolproof excuse to send Paco to the school. "What's the matter with the school? Am I banned from it permanently, or just today?"

"You're not banned at all," Santiago said with a laugh. "I was just trying to save you from getting trapped with a bunch of little kids. Unless you like having your ears yakked off by squeakers."

Dr. Lee said calmly, "Oh, Paco shouldn't get trapped. My Mia used to forget her lunch all the time. It only takes a few minutes to drop it off."

"It might take longer today," said Santiago. "It's Princess Bridget's first day at school. And because he's a prince—I mean, because he's the king's—well, anyway, if he shows up, the teacher will invite him to stay. And Bridget's been telling everyone she's dying to meet her new brother."

Paco winced inwardly. He was no brother to any child of Voske's.

Santiago went on, "If she asks you to stay, and she will, you can't say no. She's Crown Princess now."

Santiago seemed genuinely friendly, and that made it hard not to like him. But he was still the enemy. Paco couldn't let his guard down. He forced a smile. "I've got nothing else to do. And I don't want to stick someone else with the kids, but if you want to stick someone else with me..."

Santiago laughed. "No, it's fine. I'm used to little kids. I'll come back for the kimchi. Or maybe Meredith will let me have some of hers."

They went out. The permanent stage he and Santiago had worked on was being painted. Voske's royal colors, black and crimson, crept across the raised viewing boxes at the back of the stage. No matter how Voske tried to pretty it up, it would never make Paco think of anything but the headsman and his axe and basket.

Santiago grabbed his arm. "About Opportunity Day—I have to tell you—"

"I know what it is," Paco said. Kerry had bragged about it when she'd been a hostage in Las Anclas. And after Ross had come back from Gold Point, he'd gone pale every time it had been mentioned in his earshot.

Voske had made it clear that if there were no volunteers, someone would be "chosen." Paco doubted there'd be any volunteers. If they selected candidates by lottery, as Kerry had described, it would undoubtedly be fixed anyway.

"No, you don't," Santiago began. But they'd reached the schoolyard by then. He glanced around, then stopped talking.

An almost visible cloud of gloom hung over the school Paco had attended. The voices he heard through the windows sounded angry and upset and anxious.

Faviola Valdez's voice rose above the rest, tight with anger and grief. "I *know* Felicité. Yeah, she was upset. Of course she was! But she loved her family. Her mother. Her father, especially. She'd never do anything to hurt him, and this will *destroy* him when he finds out. Voske had her killed, just like he killed Mr. Horst and —"

A woman's cold voice interrupted her. "Felicité Wolfe killed *herself.*"

Paco glanced in the window. A tall woman with graying hair stood over Faviola, her posture straight as a ruler. She clapped her hands with a sound like a gunshot. "Everyone! Assemble."

The students scrambled into an orderly line-up. Faviola didn't move but was hauled into place by her friends. Paco mentally marked her down as yet another person who could fight, but not disguise her feelings.

"Some false rumors are being spread about the death of your former classmate, Felicité Wolfe," said the teacher. "Let me correct them for you now, so you will all know the truth and be able to correct others. She didn't die in an accident, and she wasn't executed. She took her own life."

Paco was certain that Voske had told her to say that. Her words were very precise, as if they'd been rehearsed.

Voske must have been as surprised as anyone when Felicité killed herself. He'd have known people would assume he had her murdered. Paco would have thought that himself if he hadn't heard the story directly from Becky's Aunt Rosa. What point was Voske trying to make by insisting on the truth when no one would believe it?

The teacher went on, "I've been told that Felicité was

popular, in a small way, in the old Las Anclas. But she didn't fit into the new, *better* Las Anclas. So, like a coward, she drowned herself. Have you ever seen a drowned corpse? A rat, perhaps, that fell into a well and couldn't get out? They swell up like balloons. Disgusting. And that's what happens to those who don't fit in."

And there it was. That last remark had to be planned to hammer it in to even the smallest kids: people who don't fit in under Voske's rule will die gruesomely. It was a lesson that worked to his advantage whether people believed that Felicité had committed suicide or had been murdered.

The teacher said, "Before I dismiss you for lunch, what was today's daily quote from the king?"

A ragged chorus arose, chanting, "Rebellion destroys public order." Yolanda and Jose exchanged sour looks, and one of the Preciado boys rolled his eyes.

"Excellent. That will be the topic of today's essay. You may discuss your ideas during lunch. Dismissed."

The students filed out and sat down at the picnic tables in orderly rows. Paco walked up to the teacher, Santiago following at his heels.

"Excuse me." Paco held up the lunch box. "Meredith forgot her lunch."

"You may give it to her," the teacher said.

As she took the lunch box, Meredith said loudly, "Paco, want to—"

At the same time, the teacher said, "Please join—"

But a young girl's voice rose above the other two, and continued when they broke off. "Prince Liam!"

"Just call me Paco." He couldn't decide which he hated more, Liam or Prince.

Bridget sat at the head of the table, a skinny thirteen-year-old with long black braids. She wore the Voske family colors in a heavily embroidered dress. Her blouse was bright red around the collar, then gradually darkened until became a swirling black skirt. It must have taken some weaver six months to make that one dress.

Bridget pointed regally. The teacher hastened to bring a chair and set it next to Voske's daughter. Paco sat down. This close to Bridget, he could see the details of the embroidery. Scorpions chased each other around her collar, stinging each other and writhing in their death throes. Snakes around her waist rose up to attack deer and rabbits. The detail was incredible. The embroiderer had actually silk-stitched drops of venom, and conveyed pain and fear on the tiny faces of the victims.

Bridget grinned. "Like my skirt? You have to get right up close."

She spread it out so Paco could see that the black embroidery on black fabric was crystal trees rising up from fallen humans—just like the obsidian grove that had grown from Voske's own soldiers outside the walls of Las Anclas.

He jerked his gaze upward, but that brought his gaze level with the blouse again. It wasn't merely bright red and dark red; it was the color of blood from an artery and blood from a vein. Given the rest of the dress, she must have requested exactly that.

The teacher set a plate before him, and the students spoke in unison, thanking Voske for the food and for the "safe" school. Paco's stomach churned. There was no way he could force anything down his throat with those words ringing in his ears, and that horrific dress sitting beside him. And on Voske's daughter, too.

"I was telling everybody about Opportunity Day," Bridget said. "You'll have a seat in the royal box. Next to me! We go in order of age. And now it's you, then me."

Paco glanced at the next table, where Santiago had been seated next to Meredith. He hadn't been given his own plate of food and was eating her watermelon-cucumber kimchi. Paco wished Bridget would stop talking so he could observe Tammy and Rogelio, the teenagers Meredith and Alfonso had picked as potential Rats. Paco knew them by name and sight, but he'd never spoken to either of them.

Bridget poked his arm. "Do you have any questions about Opportunity Day?"

"I know what it is," he replied. But that didn't work any better on Bridget than it had on Santiago.

"Ah, but you don't know what happens to the candidates who *don't* get good powers." Bridget looked around as if she expected a reply.

Nobody spoke until the teacher said, "You may

converse with Princess Bridget."

That 'may' sounded like a 'must' to Paco. Sure enough, an older teenager nervously blurted out, "No. What happens?"

Will Preston said eagerly, "Something gross?"

Bridget replied to Will. "Oh, yeah. I've seen lots of gross stuff."

Another ten-year-old said in a tone just like Will's, "Sometimes people die, right? They just drop dead!"

"Yeah, but there's no blood or anything," Bridget said carelessly. Then her voice lowered to a thrilling note. "The gross stuff isn't the failed candidates, it's some of the powers. See, we have a test table with things they can use to show their power. One of them is a live mouse in a cage. The gross things happen to the test mice. There was one woman who touched a mouse, and at first, we thought nothing had happened, but then it started *squealing*."

Paco tried to shut out Bridget's words as he watched the students' reactions. The younger kids mostly seemed excited, though some looked horrified. Dee Riley, who was such an animal lover that she'd once adopted a larval pit mouth, drew in an angry breath. To Paco's relief, Z Kabbani and Nhi Tran did something below the table that made her jaw snap shut.

The older teenagers did not seem to appreciate Bridget's graphic description of the melting mouse. Of the two possible Rats, Tammy was visibly holding herself back from lunging across the table to punch Bridget. Paco sympathized, but the last thing the Rats needed was a recruit who let all her emotions show on her face. The other one, Rogelio, was staring at his plate, stone-faced. Now that was the emotional control the Rats needed.

"...and then the mouse *exploded!*" Bridget exclaimed. Paco had lost track of whether it was the same mouse or a different one. For the sake of the mice, he hoped it was the same one.

Rogelio leaped to his feet.

"Sit down," snapped the teacher.

"I'm gonna barf!" Rogelio looked both panicked and green, and Paco realized that his stone face had been a desperate attempt to hold back nausea.

"Go, go!" said the teacher.

Rogelio bolted, his hand clamped over his mouth.

So much for new recruits. As Yuki had often grumbled, discretion and subtlety were virtues sorely lacking in Las Anclas.

A wave of longing for Yuki slammed into Paco like a tidal wave. If Yuki was there, they'd have an ally who'd never let a secret slip. If Yuki was there, Paco would apologize for pushing him away. If Yuki was there, Paco would hold him tight, comforted by the heat of his body, and lose himself for a few precious moments.

If Yuki was there, Voske would hold him hostage to ensure Paco's loyalty.

"Princess Bridget!" It was a little girl, waving frantically from another table. "Did you get your powers on Opportunity Day?"

"No, I was born with mine," Bridget replied. "And I'm too young, anyway. Opportunity Day is for eighteen and up. There's no point doing it for someone who might get their powers in the regular way. We don't know why some people die, or why a lot of the Opportunity Day powers have nasty side effects. It might be that Min Soo's power is dangerous all by itself, and those people would have been fine if they'd gotten their powers naturally. But *I* think there's something that usually stops people from Changing if their powers would kill them or do something really bad to them, and what Min Soo does is turn that part off."

Bridget spoke with a scientific relish that reminded Paco of Mia, if Mia had been a horrible person with no conscience and a taste for gore.

"But if I'd gotten mine on Opportunity Day, it *might* have been gross," Bridget went on. "See, people usually can't control their powers very well when they first get them, even if they do get them naturally. So, if I'd tried to do this..."

Bridget made a hand gesture so dramatic that Paco guessed she didn't need to make it at all, concluding in a point at the boots of Horacio, a boy at the next table.

A foul odor rose up as the boots faded from glossy black to a dull green, then gray, then began to liquefy.

"Hey!" Horacio yelled.

"Eeeewwww!" rose up in chorus all around him.

Horacio leaped up, madly shaking first one foot then the other as slime splattered off his bare toes. "Are my feet okay?"

"Oh, yes," Bridget assured him. "Your feet are fine. I have perfect control. But if I'd gotten my power on Opportunity Day—well, and if my power worked on living things—I probably would have rotted off both your feet. Right down to the bone!"

The teacher handed a wet cloth to Horacio. He scrubbed frantically, but his alarm faded to annoyance as he saw that his feet were unhurt. In fact, they looked extra clean compared to his legs. Fascinated despite himself, Paco wondered if Bridget had actually dissolved the dirt off his skin.

"I just got those broken in!" Horacio exclaimed. "And they fitted perfect!"

Bridget sounded sincerely apologetic as she said, "Oh, I'm sorry. I forgot, not everybody is as wealthy as we are in Gold Point. Don't worry. I'll have the best shoemaker in Las Anclas make you new boots. As a gift. No, two new pairs!"

That seemed to reassure Horacio, who sat back down. It didn't reassure Paco at all. Voske's daughter seemed just like him.

"What do you say to the princess, Horacio?" the teacher put in.

"Thanks," Horacio said enthusiastically. "Wow. *Two* new pairs!"

"Thank you, *Princess Bridget*," said the teacher.

As Horacio echoed her words, Paco was relieved to see that everyone was done eating. The teacher said, "Princess Bridget, would you like to lead the students inside?"

Paco and Santiago headed back toward the infirmary. As soon as they rounded the bell tower, Santiago looked around, then grabbed Paco by the arm. No one was within earshot, but he whispered, "I have to talk to you. Privately."

Wondering if this was some ruse of Voske's, Paco cautiously replied, "Okay."

Looking frustrated, Santiago said, "Where's private?"

If that was the ruse, it wasn't a very smart one. Paco shrugged. "Got me."

Santiago shot him an irritated glance, then pointed to Mia's scrap yard. "Let's go in there."

Santiago ducked down behind a lean-to made of sheet metal. To Paco's astonishment, it concealed a futon, a blanket, and a pillow, now covered with dust and soggy leaves. Paco opened his mouth to say that he wasn't interested, then saw the bewilderment on Santiago's face.

"Oh. I wasn't expecting..." Santiago began, then blushed dark red. "Okay, this isn't what it looks like. This is Mia Lee's cottage, right? Does she *sleep* out here?"

"Maybe?" Paco eyed the pillow. "The last time I was inside Mia's place, there was an engine on her bed. I assumed she took it off at night, but maybe not."

"There were two, actually—" Santiago made a cutting-off motion with his hand. "Forget the engines. That's not what I wanted to talk to you about." He met Paco's gaze, his expression earnest. "Listen. Don't volunteer for Opportunity Day."

"Are you kidding? I don't want to melt mice." Paco was fairly sure this wasn't a Voske ruse. If it wasn't, his reply should relieve Santiago.

But he looked just as worried as he had before. "Okay, good. But you have to tell your friends not to volunteer either. I know this seems weird coming from me, but you have to believe me."

Unless Voske was trying to figure out who Paco's friends were, which made no sense since Henry would have already told him, this seemed to be Santiago's own suggestion. All the same, Paco wasn't going to give his guard any information. "Why would it seem weird coming from you?"

"Oh, I thought you knew. I volunteered for Opportunity Day. I wanted to get a power." Santiago gave a brief chuckle. "And to impress Kerry. But I was the last volunteer. Even when I did it, it was starting to scare people. You need to tell everyone you care about not to do it."

"Don't worry about it, Santiago," Paco said. "Rumors travel fast in Las Anclas. The entire town will have heard about the exploding mouse within an hour of school getting out. No one will volunteer."

"That'll put off some of them." Santiago shot him a surprisingly sharp glance. "But you're in the Rangers. You have to know people who'd love to blow up a mouse. Even if none of the Rangers were like that, some people who tried out for them are, right? There's some in every army."

Paco found himself running through everyone he knew who liked violence. Like Henry. Or who were daring, and craved action. Like Meredith.

"And powers," Santiago went on. "Powers are cool. I wanted one enough to risk my life for it. You can't tell me you don't know anyone who really wants one."

Paco shrugged, unwilling to give Santiago anything that could get passed on to Voske. But he knew people like that, too. Most of them were too young to volunteer. But not all. Once again, Meredith's name topped the list. He needed to warn her. And at that, he knew that regardless of whether Santiago was trustworthy in general, he was sincere about this. He'd done Paco a favor, and he might have saved Meredith's life. Paco couldn't just walk away from him without a word.

"Thanks." He made sure Santiago could hear his sincerity as he said, "I appreciate it. I'll pass the word on."

Santiago looked relieved. He sat down on the futon. Leaves crunched, and several brilliant blue millipedes scuttled out. "Thank *you*. It was driving me crazy, listening to Bridget and wondering how many people she'd convinced to volunteer."

The lean-to was low. It was making Paco's neck ache to stand bent over so he wouldn't hit his head. He used the pillow to brush away the leaves, disturbing more millipedes and a six-legged lizard, and sat down next to Santiago. He wouldn't try Dr. Lee's cold reading again, but there couldn't be any harm in asking a real question. "Why is it so important to you?"

"Because I saw Luis get his power." As soon as the words were out of Santiago's mouth, he nervously looked around. "Don't tell the king I said that. We're not supposed to say anything in Las Anclas about Luis's power. Not even that he has one."

Paco thought back to every time he'd been spied on

by Luis, or even seen him around. That blank, black-cloud stare. The grim face. Hands shoved in his pockets.

Had Paco ever seen his hands out of his pockets? He remembered a few times when he had…but Luis had worn gloves. He always wore long-sleeved shirts, no matter how hot it was. And there was that time he and Santiago had recoiled from each other, when Santiago had offered his condolences about Sophie.

"What can he do with his hands?" Paco asked.

"It's not just his hands," Santiago whispered. "It's his whole body. He burns people. He can control it now, most of the time, but not when he first got his power. He and I and Sophie, his fiancée who died, used to train together. At the start of his Opportunity Day, he was a regular guy who used to ride and dance and have fun. He and Sophie were like me and —" He broke off. "They were in love. She ran onstage when he Changed. She touched his face, and it burned her fingers nearly down to the bone."

Paco remembered the beach where the Rangers had died. Santiago had bent over a girl with finger-shaped scars on her cheek. "But he touched her, too, right? There were scars on her face."

Santiago nodded. "Yeah. Sophie was fearless. She was trying to help him learn control. And he *can* control it now. Mostly. That was from one time he slipped up."

Paco remembered where he'd seen similar scars. "Ross has scars like that. A whole handprint. On his throat. You can't tell me that was a slip."

Santiago's voice dropped to the barest whisper. "You're not going to tell the king I told you any of this, right?"

"I don't tell your king anything."

"It wasn't a slip. Luis was ordered to torture Ross. The worst part is, right after that, Luis found out that he could use his power to heal, too. But the king keeps making him use it to torture people, too."

Paco shuddered involuntarily. "And Luis does it?"

Santiago sighed. "Luis is a soldier. Like me. Like you. We're loyal to our towns. If we're ordered to fight, we fight. If we're ordered to do…other things, we have to do them. I was on duty in the king's honor guard once when the king made Luis, uh—he calls it experiments. With prisoners."

"Like Ross?" Paco heard his voice rise in anger and hoped it hadn't carried out of the scrap yard. For the first time, he joined Santiago in nervously glancing around.

When no one appeared to drag them away, Santiago went on in a low voice. "Yeah. Afterward, the king told me I'd never have to guard him again when he did anything with Luis. He said it distracted me."

Before Paco could let his anger slip out, Santiago said, "But that's not the point. The point is, Luis was like me and you. We're fighters. We're not torturers. The way he is now, that's not because of Sophie dying. He was like that before we came here; it's just worse now. Opportunity Day destroyed him."

An unsettled silence fell as Paco thought about that handprint scar on Ross's throat. He'd known it must be the brand of some Change power, but he'd assumed Ross had gotten it in a fight. Now he understood why Ross wouldn't talk about Gold Point. He imagined being chained up while that hand reached out for him. And then, worse, he imagined having that power and being forced to use it on helpless prisoners.

Paco wanted to kill Voske more than he'd wanted anything in his life.

But the tyrant was always ready to fight, he was faster than Paco, and he always had guards close enough to jump him before he could get to the king. But maybe at Opportunity Day, Voske would let his guard slip… No, he couldn't think like that. He'd be like Mr. Horst, acting too soon and throwing away his life.

For the rest of the afternoon, as Paco and Santiago "helped" the carpenters finish the royal seats and set up torches on poles around the stage, he kept thinking about Luis. And Ross. Voske had sent assassins after Ross, but Paco was confident that Ross, Jennie, and Kerry wouldn't let themselves be caught by surprise. Especially now that he knew what had happened to Ross, and what Kerry had escaped. Those two had to have grown eyes in the backs of their heads.

When the bells rang the watch change at sunset, Paco thankfully took his leave of Santiago and stopped by the infirmary, where he found Dr. Lee and Alfonso. Alone.

Paco hastily gave his negative report on the potential Rat recruits, then filled them on his conversation with Santiago.

Dr. Lee listened with his usual calm, but Alfonso shuddered in horror. "Good thing I'm already Changed," he said, holding up the gecko pads of his fingers. "But I'll make sure no one in my family volunteers."

"Is there anything we can do to protect people?" Paco asked. "Maybe if we figure out who Voske's decided to have 'volunteer…'"

"Paco, I don't see anything we can do," Dr. Lee said. "We don't even know if the powers really are random. For all we know, Voske's wife controls who lives, who dies, who gets a power, and what it is. The best we can do is make sure this is the only Opportunity Day Las Anclas ever holds."

·10·
JENNIE

THE DESERT – OUTSIDE THE RUINED CITY

JENNIE RODE ON POINT, a little ahead of the group. In the distance, the crystal trees surrounding the ruined city sparkled in the afternoon light.

They'd had a great time visiting Corymbia City, the extraordinary town built high above the ground into the towering redwoods and sequoias, but Jennie was ready to come home. All that was left was for Jennie and Kerry to camp for a couple days with the horses while Ross took Mia and Summer into the ruined city.

Jennie smiled to herself at the memory of how earnestly and unselfishly Mia had offered to let Jennie take her place. Mia had learned a lot since their first disastrous trip into the ruined city, when she'd accidentally caused the collapse of a building, resulting in Ross losing a set of tools that had belonged to his grandmother. She'd worked hard since then to master the basics—along with designing a collapsible grabbing tool that she'd used to recover his precious crowbar and pry bar.

The joy that had brightened Ross's—and Mia's—faces when he'd gotten his tools back had made that expedition a memorable one. And Jennie enjoyed getting a glimpse of ancient history and watching Ross at his most skilled. But Ross could only take two people through the ring of singing trees around the ruined city, each holding his hand, and Jennie was just as happy to skip the final prospecting trip. Her scalp itched from days of camping—more days than she'd expected, after Summer talked Ross into making a detour to prospect in ruins southeast of

Corymbia City.

Jennie ran her hand over her braids, now beginning to fray into fuzz. Clean hair, clean clothes, how she missed them! She couldn't wait to sleep in a bed again, eat Ma's cooking, and hear the voices of her family as they sat around the table. Maybe the best part of a journey was coming home, and enjoying how everything she took for granted felt new again.

It was interesting how voices echoed in forests, she thought as she idly listened to Kerry and Summer. Ross's burro Rusty flicked his long ears. What did burros hear?

"...but my favorite play was *The Princess and the Pit Mouth*," Kerry said.

Jennie glanced back to her, mildly envious of how Kerry had remained somewhat fresh-looking in the blue riding clothes she'd designed herself, her shining black hair braided into a coronet. Her trained rat Whisper sat on his saddle perch, whiskers trembling as he sniffed the air.

"The best play was the one with the nine travelers and the evil gold ring," Summer stated with her usual confidence in her own opinion. Then, in the wistful voice she always used when talking about her dead twin sister, she added, "Spring would have loved the dances." Her hand reached out, curling around air. "Spring *did* love them."

It was touching how Summer kept the memory of her lost twin alive. And who knew? Maybe Spring did watch over Summer, and they really had enjoyed the plays together. Jennie couldn't quite believe to the extent that Summer did, but she was sure that death was not the end. She liked to think that her old mentor Sera Diaz was with her in more than memory, and sometimes saw her and was proud.

Summer went on, more brightly, "But *everything* the Catalina Players do is wonderful. This whole trip was awesome! A perfect birthday!" She sidled a glance at her brother, and commented in a wheedling tone, "*Almost* perfect."

Ross was such a contrast to his sister. He was quiet and rarely smiled, whereas Summer lived at the pitch of enthusiasm or irritation. People frequently overlooked him. It didn't help that he often let his long hair shadow his face, so no one could see how handsome he was. Like

Summer, he was wiry. But beneath his shabby clothes, he was solid muscle, and one of the most formidable fighters she'd ever known. He'd had to be.

"Almost?" Mia asked.

Summer scratched absently behind one ear. The skinny girl was cheerfully grubby, except for her blue-black hair. She and Ross shared those long, sooty-black eyelashes and rippling falls of fine hair. "Spring says, if we find anything *really good* in the ruined city, *then* it will be perfect. It was her birthday, too. It'll be her present."

"We already got some really good finds," Ross pointed out. "You can pick out one for Spring, if you like."

Summer flung back her hair, every line of her leaf-light body expressive of disdain. Jennie wondered if she'd been as dramatic when she was fifteen. That had only been four years ago, but it felt like forty.

"Huh!" Summer snorted. "You call those dinky tool thingies we found in that cave good? 'Good' would be a *car!* Or crown jewels! I bet scavengers got all the good stuff ages ago. If you'd let me dynamite deeper into that cave, I bet we'd have found better stuff."

Ross flashed a quick, laughing look Jennie's way. It amazed her that he was still unaware of how handsome he was, especially when that rare, sweet smile appeared. Though it had been less rare of late. Ross, usually as twitchy as a horse scenting danger on the wind, had relaxed more than she'd thought possible on this trip. Though he had come to love Las Anclas, he was in his element on the road.

The smile turned wry as he spoke to his sister. "Summer, if I'd let you blast that cave, we'd still be trying to dig our way out from under it."

Summer slumped, muttering, "Because you don't let me practice with dynamite."

Mia said consolingly, "When we get to the ruined city, you can go in first. I mean, me and Ross will be going in first, too, but you can take the first step in." She turned to Kerry, the tools on her overalls rattling. "Are you sure you don't mind staying with the horses and Rusty the whole time? You've never gotten to see the ruined city. I wouldn't mind staying with the animals so you can see it."

"It's no sacrifice for me." Kerry gave the little smile

that meant she was secretly amused. But there was nothing unkind in it. It was the way Jennie and Kerry had exchanged smiles as the ridiculous fake heads had gone bouncing across the stage when they'd watched their first play. It wasn't a Voske smile.

Voske. Silver hair glinting in moonlight. Sera falling lifeless.

Jennie shivered. She welcomed the distraction when Summer said, "At least you can let me light the dynamite while you're *right there.*"

"No!" The rest of them all spoke at once. Jennie could practically hear Summer's eyes rolling.

Ross flicked a serious look at his sister, his shoulders tightening under his battered leather jacket that had survived countless knife fights, attacks by animals, and carnivorous plants. "We're not using dynamite in there. It's much too dangerous."

Summer thumped her arms across her chest but didn't argue. Though brother and sister had survived on their own for most of their lives, they'd finally found a balance with one another. "Can we dynamite something in Las Anclas when we get back?"

"I'll start *teaching* you to use dynamite when we get back," Ross said firmly. "But it takes a long time to learn to use it safely. I didn't have time to finish teaching Yuki before he left, so he doesn't carry any."

Jennie smiled, remembered the amazing stories they'd heard about Yuki's journeys when they'd traveled into the Saigon Alliance months ago. Summer looked mollified, but made a token protest, "You think everything fun is too dangerous."

Kerry's golden stallion shied, and her rat Whisper let out a high-pitched squeal. Ross snatched up a throwing knife, and Jennie drew her sword. Kerry dropped the reins and flung up both her hands. Shards of glittering white shattered against an invisible shield.

"Ambush!" Kerry yelled. "The ice—that's Axel—"

Everything went black. Jennie blinked desperately, swiping at her eyes with her free hand, but there was nothing on her face. She swung her sword in an arc in front of her, in case whoever had caused the blackout was trying to sneak up.

Her vision snapped back. At least six people had charged them from behind, swinging swords and shooting arrows. Their weapons bounced off Kerry's shield, but every muscle in her body trembled as she fought to maintain it.

Jennie tried to scan for the bigger picture. She had to get a sense of the enemy numbers so they could figure out how to fight back once Kerry's shield failed—as it would at any moment.

Once again, everything went black. In the moment before her vision returned, she realized that if Kerry knew the person with the ice power, he had to be someone from Gold Point. And even worse, he hadn't tried to kill them. The ice had been aimed at their horses' legs. Voske had sent a team to capture them alive.

Jennie's vision returned, but the air had clouded as if they'd ridden into a thick fog. She could see vague shapes moving outside of Kerry's shield, but no details.

Kerry gasped, "I can't hold it much longer!"

Ross glanced at Jennie, his eyes wide and desperate. "I can't let them take me. Or you." His gaze flicked to Mia. Then to Summer, and to Kerry. "I can't let them take any of you."

Kerry nodded hard. Blood trickled down her chin from where she'd bitten her lip. She shoved Whisper into her shirt as she said flatly, "I won't be taken alive."

Ross said hoarsely, "I think…"

From within the mist a voice boomed, "Surrender!"

Ross stilled, his profile distraught as he muttered, "I think I can get us all through the crystal trees. If we take hands."

"With the horses?" Jennie asked softly.

He had that inward-turning look she'd seen before, as if what he was watching was miles away from any of them. "No. Too much. Let 'em go."

Jennie beckoned to the others, whispering, "At the next blackout. Dismount. Take hands and run. Ross will lead us."

The world darkened. She vaulted free and smacked her mount on the rump to send her running. Then she reached out, fumbling until she caught two hands. She knew them by feel: one strong, the same size as hers, callused in the same places as hers from weapons practice. That was Ross. The other was small, with calluses from tool use. That was Mia.

"Kerry?" Jennie whispered. "Summer? Are we all holding hands?"

Nervous murmurs of assent reached her ears. Jennie whispered, "Run!"

Jennie kept up with Ross easily, but Mia lagged. Jennie held onto her little hand and hauled her along. If Mia tripped, Jennie could half-carry her. She knew the dangers of the desert and could only hope they weren't running straight into a pit mouth.

The sun abruptly jabbed her eyes. They were tearing across the sand, straight for the crystal trees. Ross had Summer on his other side. Jennie dared a quick glance behind her. Mia, clutching Kerry's wrist, had an enormous pack bouncing against her spine. Jennie had to bite back the impulse to tell her to drop it—Mia couldn't without letting go.

Kerry had her free hand up. An arrow glanced off an invisible shield.

Jennie muttered under her breath, "Guess they'd rather kill us than lose us."

"No," Kerry cried—and stumbled, falling flat, her hand tearing out of Mia's.

Jennie recognized that kind of fall as sheer exhaustion. Whisper squeaked, leaping clear from within Kerry's embroidered shirt. The rest of them stumbled to a halt.

"I lost my shield," Kerry gasped, dragging herself to her knees. Whisper scrambled up her arm and nosed his way back into her shirt.

Still holding onto Jennie with her one hand, Mia plunged her free hand behind her and unhooked her skunk gun. As Ross hauled Kerry to her feet, Mia let loose an oily, reeking spray at their attackers. One swore as his sword squirted out of his grasp. Another dropped her crossbow, screaming, "My eyes!" Another began gagging and retching; he must have had his mouth open. Jennie exulted.

The gun sputtered to a stop, the nasty oil spent. Mia clipped it back on to her overalls and grabbed Jennie's hand again. Ross hauled them toward the crystal trees.

They were still so far away. Jennie had thought they were closer—until she saw sunlight glimmer off crystal, so close that she could have reached out and touched it.

They were already within the tree line.

Shock ran cold through her body. The crystal trees closest to them had lost their color, turning to crystal so clear that it was impossible to see except when the sun struck a facet. A delicate tinkle, like a wineglass breaking, was followed by another. And another.

And then the screams began.

Jennie kept her eyes forward. If she had learned one thing in the last year, it was that some sights were impossible to forget. She said quietly, "Don't look."

"Forty-one, forty-two..." Mia was quietly counting steps, as if numbers would help. Maybe they did. It was better to listen to her than to their attackers' dying curses and moans.

They moved on through the singing trees. Rays of sunlight blazed off trees of brilliant vermillion, deep violet, cool emerald. The forest seemed impossibly large, and the unnervingly sweet chime never quite died away. Fear squeezed Jennie's heart when she saw Ross's head thrown back, his sightless eyes turned skyward. Abruptly, his knees buckled. Summer and Jennie had to hold him up, Jennie taking most of his weight. His head lolled.

"Come on," Jennie said hoarsely. "I don't think he can hold out much longer."

Exhausted as they were, they forced themselves into a quicker march. The trees fell silent. That silence pressed down on Jennie, and she cast worried looks at Ross every other step. She told herself that she'd seen him pass out from over-using his power before, and he'd be all right. She told herself that the crystal trees that had killed their attackers hadn't been his tree, the scarlet tree grown from his own blood, and so the deaths shouldn't affect him too much. She told herself that he obviously could get more than two people at a time through the crystal forest, because he was doing it.

But other worries squirmed into their place. Voske had sent another kidnap team after Ross, and presumably Kerry as well. What was he planning now? He no longer had his spy hawks, so how had that team found them?

Jennie's right foot came down on nothing. She pitched forward, her hands pulling out from Ross's and Mia's grip, and fell hard. Her ankle twisting painfully beneath her. The others collapsed around her.

She instinctively flung her arms over her face, but there was no deadly tinkling of crystal shards. Her heart thumped frantically as she lowered her arms. Ross lay sprawled on the ground, unmoving. The others sat up slowly.

A single tree branch bent down, its delicate ruby twigs prodding at Ross as if it was trying to wake him up. Jennie froze in terror, not even daring to touch him herself. The ruby branch slowly straightened up again.

With a breath that sounded like a sob, Mia flung herself beside Ross, one hand patting desperately at his throat.

"He's breathing," Jennie whispered. "See, his chest is moving."

"But he's not holding our hands." Summer had never sounded so frightened.

Mia turned to Jennie. "You fell. Are you all right?"

As soon as Mia spoke, the pain crashed over Jennie in waves. She withdrew her foot gingerly from a hole in the ground. How had she missed such an obvious danger?

"I saw a lizard scuttle away from there." Kerry pointed to a lizard with a red diamond pattern twisting around its green body, eyeing them from beside a sapphire tree. It gave a slow blink and vanished, replaced by a green plant with red flowers.

"Those lizards cast way better illusions than rabbits," Mia breathed.

"Rabbits couldn't live here. The trees will kill anything warm-blooded." Jennie didn't need to add that they had to get out of there before Ross's control over the trees wore off.

She tested her foot and swore under her breath. She couldn't bear any weight on it. Mia shrugged out of her pack as she stared in worry at Ross. Jennie dropped to her knees on his other side. Kerry stayed at a distance, her hands clutching Whisper's warm little body close as she eyed Ross's chalky face.

"You and me. We'll carry him," Kerry said to

Summer, who nodded violently. They pulled him upright, his head drooping.

"Lean on me, Jennie," Mia said.

This time it was Jennie counting steps as they trudged past the silent, glittering trees. After a while, they were replaced by trees that looked more metallic than crystalline. She recognized them from an earlier journey into the ruined city. Beyond the bronze and silver and copper trees, she saw honeycomb-shaped pillars with dragonfly things flitting about them, their wings like thin glass.

With infinite relief, Jennie staggered with the others into the ruined city, out of the range of the deadly trees, and breathed in the strangely acrid air. Straight rows of chin-high mounds extended in a line, too regular for nature. Enormous butterflies sailed through the air, sometimes in flocks, sometimes alone. The ground was covered with blue-purple moss and many-colored mushrooms. Creatures like fat hairless bears the size of a thumbnail rolled and crawled among the moss, along with weird insects.

Mia thoroughly poked at the ground, scaring off the many-legged insects, and they all sank down with relief. Kerry and Summer laid Ross down, and Jennie checked him again. He was very pale, but breathing as if he was deeply asleep.

Kerry straightened in dismay. "It just hit me—we ditched our supplies along with the horses."

"My drawings of Corymbia City," Summer wailed.

"We'll just have to go back again," Jennie comforted her. "And you can make new sketches."

Summer brightened. "When the Catalina Players are there again!"

"I've got my pack." Mia dragged it off her back and pounced on it with a grin. "I saw that look you gave me, Jennie. But aren't you glad now I brought it?"

"Now I'm glad," Jennie admitted.

Mia opened it, and her expression changed from delight to dismay. Jennie realized what had happened even before Mia pulled out a chunk of petrified redwood she'd bought in Corymbia City as a gift for her father, followed by a beautifully carved wooden jack-in-the-box, also purchased in Corymbia City, as a gift for April Riley, the winged toddler.

"Um," Mia said.

"The supplies are in the bottom, right?" Kerry spoke with a distinct lack of hope.

"Um," Mia said again. "It's more efficient to keep the supplies in one pack and the gifts and prospecting finds in another, so I don't have to dig through the gifts when I need things we can actually use."

"And you had to grab your pack in the blackout," Kerry said glumly. "I don't suppose you bought anyone anything useful as a gift?"

"Me and Jennie and Ross are the only people who like useful gifts. And we're all here already, so…"

Jennie slid her coat off and laid it over Ross. Summer, following her lead, folded hers and put it under his head.

"Is anyone wearing a canteen?" Jennie asked.

Summer shot her hand into the air. "I am! I'm never without a canteen."

Kerry smiled at her. "Let's go find some water. There's no way Ross is waking up until tomorrow morning."

Jennie called after them, "He might not be up for taking us back out tomorrow. See if you can find some food too."

As they cautiously made their way into the ruined city, Summer's voice floated back to Jennie, "I can snare a rabbit! Actually, I don't need to snare a rabbit. I can catch them with my bare hands! When I was alone in the desert…"

Mia turned to Jennie. "Let's see your ankle."

Jennie stretched out her leg, wincing. As she'd feared, her ankle was already swollen and stiff. She carefully worked her toes as Mia felt along her ankle. Jennie forced herself to breathe through the pain.

Mia sat back on her heels. "I'm not as good as Alfonso or Becky, but I did learn some things from Dad. It's not broken. Just a nasty sprain. Rest it and keep it elevated."

"Oh, good." Jennie prodded a nearby rock to make sure it wasn't alive, then rested her injured ankle on it.

Mia hopped to her feet, then yanked a long knife from her overalls. "I'll find a sturdy branch and make you a crutch. At least I have my best tools. See? If I wear them,

I never lose them." She patted her clattering set of implements as she trotted off.

It wasn't long before all three were back. Kerry held two plump rabbits, while Summer's leather canteen was full. Mia returned with a set of branches and set to work fashioning one into a splint and another into a crutch. Summer dressed the rabbits, and soon they were sizzling over the fire.

Jennie said to Kerry, "You recognized the man with the ice power."

Kerry looked grim. "Yeah. And I'm not sorry the trees killed him. He was one of Voske's best scouts. And interrogators. His team all have useful Change powers. That fog — that was Tina Musashi. And the blackout was Lalo Estrada."

"Well, they're all dead now," Summer said with a fierce grin.

Jennie caught Kerry's mouth twisting in sadness before it smoothed into a practiced calm. Kerry had known everyone in that team, and Jennie realized that she grieved for at least one of them.

"We don't know that the trees got all of them," Jennie said to Kerry.

Summer waved her hand dismissively. "Nah, they definitely got the whole bunch. And if Voske sends another team, Ross will have his trees kill them all, too."

Jennie didn't think another team would be likely to make the same mistake, but she held her tongue. The last thing they needed was to get Summer wound up, while they weren't even out of danger yet. Anything might be lurking in the ruined city.

Uneasily, Jennie said, "They wanted you — us — alive."

Kerry gave a sharp nod. "Voske wants to hold a public execution for me and Ross in Gold Point. A long execution."

"Well, he won't get one," Summer frowned. "Will the horses be all right in the desert? And Rusty? Ross loves him."

"Sure," Kerry said. "They'll kick up their heels for a while, then they'll wander back to Las Anclas. They're much too smart to walk into a pit mouth, and they'll stick together in a herd to fight off anything that attacks them."

"But their tack," Summer said worriedly. "You have to take it off every day, or it'll give them sores."

Kerry smiled. "It'll be gone by the time they get back to Las Anclas. The royal horses can undo their tack with their tails if they have enough time to work at it. Nugget used to drive the stable hands crazy taking off the other horses' tack."

Summer sat back with a sigh of relief.

Jennie checked the rabbits. "Done. Let's eat, divide up the watches, and get some sleep. First thing in the morning, we'll forage more thoroughly."

"I'll take the first watch," Mia said. "I want to get this crutch finished."

The last thing Jennie was aware of was the steady slice, slice, slice of Mia's carving knife on the wood.

Jennie awoke to a scream. She jolted up, snatching for her sword. Her sprained ankle hit the ground painfully. Summer knelt by Ross's side, her hands scrabbling at the air several feet over his head. Jennie's heart seemed to stop. Had he died in the night?

Mia was also running her hands over the air, but her expression was puzzled rather than grief-stricken. As Jennie watched, caught between terror and bafflement, Kerry also poked at the air. Her fingernail made a ticking sound, like tapping glass. "It's like one of my shields."

A breath of wind blew aside a stand of glimmering reeds, and a ray of sunlight struck Ross…and glinted off something surrounding him.

He lay unmoving within a cocoon of crystal.

"I'll *smash* it," Summer shrieked. "Where's a rock—"

"No." Jennie caught her wrist. "Look at that stuff."

Summer yelled tearily, "I am! It's exactly like the trees. He'll suffocate!"

"Summer, think," Jennie said urgently. "If it's the same crystal as the trees, what happens when it shatters?"

She dropped the rock, horrified.

Jennie knelt down carefully by Ross. "Look. He's breathing just fine."

"I can't believe I didn't see it forming," Mia said. "I was right next to him."

"I couldn't even see it until a ray of sun glittered off

it," said Jennie. "At night, it would have been completely invisible. Maybe the trees made it to protect him."

Mia said hopefully, "Maybe it's to help him recover."

Summer chimed in, "It's probably to protect him from all the dangerous beasts here. When me and Kerry were fetching water, I saw bees the size of sand tigers! BEES!"

"More like the size of dogs," Kerry said. "But yeah. Bees should not be that big."

"I'm sure Ross will be fine," Jennie said, speaking with more certainty than she actually felt. "His power can be hard on him and scary to watch, but he's always recovered. Right now, we need to get more water and food. I'm sure we'll be here for at least another day. I can watch over him while the rest of you forage."

"You can't do it alone," Mia said. "What if something fast attacks you? Or more than one thing?"

"I'll stay," Kerry said. "Mia, you know the most about the area."

"And *I'm* the best hunter," Summer put in.

Jennie was glad to see that Mia didn't flinch at the idea of being alone with Summer. The trip really had helped them all get along better.

Mia and Summer took off. Kerry said glumly, "Bees again! When I was a prisoner in Las Anclas, Mia and I got attacked by bees. I've never liked them since. And I didn't like them much before."

Jennie could just barely see the tip of the white tower they'd explored the first time she'd been in the ruined city. She pointed. "See that? It's their hive. We got attacked by them, too, when we accidentally disturbed their larvae."

"Ugh!" Kerry shuddered.

Leaves rustled from beyond the clearing. Jennie's hand tightened on her sword, and Kerry gripped an invisible weapon. Just as Jennie was beginning to think it was a false alarm caused by their bee conversation, she heard a strange, low groan. Then footsteps, at once heavy and skittering. Jennie stood up, bracing her back against a tree. She gripped Mia's crutch in one hand and her sword in the other.

A creature burst into the clearing, moving astonishingly fast. It was long and low, and seemed entirely composed of plates of green armor and rows of sharp teeth.

At both ends.

The creature lunged at them, snapping at them both from either end. Kerry charged it. Jennie recognized from the angle of her attack that she'd created a pair of spears. They hit the creature hard, flipping it over. But it quickly regained its footing and seemed uninjured.

"My spears bounced off its armor," Kerry gasped.

"Try staves," Jennie suggested.

She had barely enough time to switch the crutch to her right hand before a pair of the creatures darted into the clearing. She caught the nearest one with the tip of the crutch, flipping it as Kerry had done. It hit the ground, one end whipping around, and snapped its teeth. Crunch! The end of her crutch vanished into its gaping maw.

Jennie switched weapons again and stabbed at that maw with her sword. The creature jerked backward. "Go for the inside of the mouth!"

The creatures slithered backward as Jennie jabbed at their fangs. They might not be able to kill the beasts, but if they put up enough of a fight, maybe they could chase them off. They slowly herded the creatures out of the clearing. Kerry flipped one into a bush full of chittering insects. The bugs rose in an angry pink swarm and attacked the beast. The creature snapped at the bugs, then let out a long, groaning howl. It seemed to be a signal. All three beasts turned tail—or rather, turned mouth—and rushed away.

Jennie leaned on the mangled crutch, gasping. Her ankle was on fire.

Kerry offered her a shoulder. "I really don't like it here."

"At least it wasn't bees," Jennie said.

"At least bees are only dangerous on one end," Kerry retorted.

They limped back into the clearing. Jennie's gaze went to Ross, though she knew his glass cocoon would have protected him.

There was nothing left but a pile of glittering sand. The cocoon was gone.

And so was Ross.

·11·
ROSS

THE RUINED CITY

ROSS AWOKE LYING ON some spongy surface. He couldn't move his hands or feet. With the caution of experience, he kept his eyes closed and thought back to the last thing he remembered. They'd been attacked by Voske's team, and he'd had to take everyone into the crystal forest. He'd opened the door in his mind as wide as it went, but it hadn't been enough to protect all five of them. Frantic, desperate, he'd blown up the mental wall and the door with it. That was the last thing he remembered.

He reached out to the crystal trees, so he could sense any people around him through their body heat. But he felt nothing. How could he have gotten so far from the forest that he couldn't sense any trees at all? Could Voske's team have dragged him to Gold Point?

That panicked him enough that he opened his eyes. He was somewhere up high, looking across a flat surface overgrown with fungi into a tangle of jungle. The white tower of the bees speared up in the distance.

He was still in the ruined city, so why couldn't he feel the crystal trees? He reached out again. Nothing. Not even an emptiness. It was as if he was trying to lift something telekinetically like Jennie, or to jump like Summer.

It was as if he'd never had a power at all.

"Wakey-wakey!" It was a woman's voice.

Ross turned his head. A middle-aged woman sat nearby, smirking at him. His muscles contracted, and ropes tightened around his ankles and wrists. So, he was a prisoner. Had the team that had attacked them somehow followed him safely through the forest? And where were the girls?

A big man stepped in front of him, grabbed the front of his shirt, and yanked him into a sitting position. Ross braced for a splitting headache caused by the sudden movement, but it didn't come. Nor did he feel weak or dizzy. But rather than being relieved, that made him even more unsettled. If the cost of his power was gone, did that mean his power was gone too?

"You're awake. You're taking us back through the crystal forest. Now." The man spoke as if it didn't even occur to him that Ross might disobey.

So, they had tagged along with him. "Where are the people I was with?"

"Dead," said the woman. "Unless you cooperate."

Ross tried to hide his relief. They must not have even been captured, or these two would be brandishing them. Stalling for time, he said, "I want to see them. So, I know they're alive."

"You're in no position to be dictating terms, boy," the man said.

"If you're good, you'll get your reward," said the woman.

The big man scowled at her. "Shut up, Loretta."

"You don't get to order me around, Axel," snapped Loretta. "You shouldn't even be here."

"*You* shouldn't be here," retorted Axel. "I ordered you to guard the road out."

"You're not part of my chain of command," said Loretta haughtily. "I take orders only from the king."

While they argued, Ross quietly felt around behind him with his fingertips. Amidst the spongy stuff he was sitting on, he felt something hard and almost sharp. A bit of shell or rock? He caught it between finger and thumb, flipped it up, and began to gently saw it against the ropes that bound his wrists.

A new voice spoke. "The prisoner is trying to cut through his ropes."

The bit of hard stuff was snatched away from him. Ross craned his head around and was astonished to recognize the teenage girl holding a broken bit of crab shell. She was one of Santiago's...sisters? Cousins? He'd met her at the Flores family quinceñera at Gold Point.

"Good work, Maria-Pilar," Axel said.

Maria-Pilar. She was Santiago's cousin. She'd created illusions at the quinceñera, delighting the children with unicorns and dragons. Santiago had told Ross all about her. She'd lost her two front teeth on her seventh birthday and hadn't been able to eat the walnut birthday cake she'd asked for. She'd won medals for archery.

Ross tried to read in that familiar face whether she might be talked into helping him, or if she saw him as merely an object to earn a reward from Voske. The Flores family was close, much like the Rileys. She had to remember that Ross had saved her cousin's life. But it was her little sister whom Voske held hostage for their continued loyalty. Ross wouldn't risk Summer's life for anyone.

Her face was completely expressionless. If he hadn't known better, he wouldn't have even thought she'd recognized him.

Axel slapped Ross across the face, knocking him back onto his elbows.

The big man raised his hand to slap him again, but Loretta caught his wrist. "He's supposed to be unharmed. The first cut goes to the king." She turned a malicious smirk on Ross. "That doesn't go for your friends."

Axel glowered at him. "Take us through."

Ross had no idea if he could get through the crystal trees now, even if he'd wanted to. He still couldn't feel them. He had to stall. "So, you can drag me back to Gold Point for a day-long execution? I'd rather have you beat me to death right here."

"Oh, we won't touch *you*," Loretta said with false sweetness. "You can watch while we beat your little friends to death. One at a time. Your choice."

"You don't have them." Ross thought of how he'd bargained for supplies in exchange for his prospecting finds. Better yet, he thought of how other, more successful prospectors bargained. "What can *you* offer *me*?"

"Nothing," said Axel. "And we can get them any time we want."

The look Loretta shot him made it clear that it was a lie. Ross suppressed a fierce smile. They must not have enjoyed fighting Jennie and the others before they'd run for the trees. And he bet that either only these three had tried to follow him, or only these three had survived. So, they were outnumbered, too.

"You can't get out of here without me, and I'm not going back to Gold Point." He flicked a glance at Maria-Pilar, then stared hard at Axel and Loretta. "I'll lead you through if you give me half an hour's head start. Then you can chase me all you like."

Axel grinned. "You got it. An hour, even. Makes no difference to us."

"Okay," Loretta said, holding up her hand in the universal gesture. "Deal."

Ross cursed inwardly. He knew they had no intention of honoring the bargain, but he hadn't expected them to agree that fast. Where was Summer? Where were Jennie, Mia, and Kerry? What would happen if these Voske soldiers found them?

He tried to calm himself the way Dr. Lee had been teaching him. *Think logically,* Dr. Lee always said. Jennie was powerful, fast, and skilled; he'd seen her defeat men of Axel's size. Kerry wasn't as strong as Jennie, but she was a trained fighter, and she knew what lay ahead if they captured her. Summer had her Changed agility and knew some vicious tricks for getting free of far larger opponents. It was Mia he worried about most. He'd lose his mind if Axel or Loretta, with their taste for torture, laid a hand on her.

"Tomorrow." As Axel's fist rose threateningly, Ross added in haste, "Not today. Your king knows I can't use my power more than once a day."

"Tomorrow morning, then." Loretta shot Axel a meaningful look. "We need the time anyway."

Time for what? Ross wondered.

$$\cdot 12 \cdot$$

Mia

The Ruined City

Mia had been fighting tears for the last two hours and fifty-three minutes. Now fifty-four minutes. She couldn't stop thinking about that awful thing Summer had blurted out about maybe the trees having *eaten* Ross. Mia had seen how the trees could grab control of Ross. Or maybe he was wandering around lost — or getting attacked by giant bees, or by the two-mouthed creatures that had attacked Jennie and Kerry and —

Kerry nudged her. "I'm sure he's fine. He's tough."

Mia scrubbed her eyes. "I know. I *know*. I'm just afraid we'll never find him if he can't hear us. This place is huge!"

"We will find him, but we can't yell," Jennie said, leaning on the bitten-off crutch. Mia wished she could borrow some of that confidence. Jennie, so big and beautiful and brilliant, would find him if anyone could. "You saw that monkey-creature drag a deer up a tree. If Ross got grabbed by…something…the last thing we want to do is startle it."

"Summer's searching from the treetops," Kerry put in. "If he's in sight, she'll find him."

Mia sucked in a deep breath, trying to squash the thoughts of terrible things that could have happened to him. She lifted her gaze — and saw the biggest ruined building yet. Ross would love to prospect it, and if he was hurt, he could have taken shelter inside. "Let's look there."

She forced herself not to rush in, but to stop and assess it exactly as Ross had taught her. The floor looked intact. The entire front had collapsed, so there were no doorways that could fall on her head. Enough sun shone through that she could see a maze of toppled shelves. The floor was littered with broken glass and bits of metal. She poked around with a stick before she stepped in. Nothing stirred.

"Ross?" Mia glanced behind her, making sure everyone had noticed that she didn't yell.

She wiped her eyes on her shirt, then went in, skirting a mass of tumbled shelves. A few glass jars were unbroken. Mia picked one up, peering at the murky contents. "Pickles! This must be a city pantry!"

Kerry looked up from some fallen brooms. "I think it's a store. A food store."

"I don't think the pickles would still be good," Jennie said. "But grain might be edible, if the container stayed dry and airtight."

Mia pushed her way through overgrown greenery and an incredible amount of empty metal cans. At the back, she found an entire barrel. She pried it open, hoping for grain, but it was full of glittering white fragments. She sniffed it. Salt! Enough salt to keep Jack in business for a year.

Kerry called out, "Hey! I found honey."

Mia said, "Dad says honey stays good for thousands of—"

"I found Ross!" Summer landed lightly in the doorway.

Mia whipped around. "Is he all right?"

Jennie was already hobbling toward Summer. "Where?"

"He's okay, but he's been captured." Summer scowled. "They've got him on a rooftop."

"The monkeys?" Mia gasped.

"No! Axel, the ice-throwing guy who attacked us. And a woman, Loretta."

Kerry's breath hissed in. "She's the leader of a different scout team. She turns into a shadow."

Summer shrugged. "Whatever she does, there's only three of them. I could have taken them all, but you said I should come back and report."

Mia doubted that even Summer believed she could

have taken them all, or she would have. Sure enough, she added. "That Axel guy is huge. And Ross is tied up, so he couldn't help."

"Good thing you didn't try," said Kerry. "Loretta can walk through walls. She'll just disappear, and the next thing you know, she's carving out your heart with a knife."

"Is that how they followed us?" Jennie asked. "She made them all into shadows?"

Kerry shook her head. "She can only affect herself. Summer, you said there were three of them. Who's the third?"

"She's your age. Axel and Loretta went away — only to the other edge of the roof, or I'd have rescued him right then! Ross said to her, really quietly, 'I know about Maria-Elena. I know you're protecting her.'" Summer's imitation of Ross's inflections was eerily accurate.

"That's Maria-Pilar!" Bizarrely, Kerry sounded…*happy?* "She's Santiago's cousin."

Then Mia understood. Kerry and Maria-Pilar were probably friends. Or had been friends? Would they be enemies now? Either way, Kerry was glad that Santiago hadn't lost a member of his family.

More somberly, Kerry went on, "My father promoted her to Axel's team just before I left Gold Point. Like Santiago being promoted to Voske's honor guard, it's a promotion you can't say no to. Maria-Elena is her little sister. If Maria-Pilar didn't show gratitude and enthuse-asm, Maria-Elena would pay the price."

"Ugh!" Summer exclaimed. "Well, Axel and Loretta came back right after that. They told Ross he had to take them through the crystal forest as soon as they found *her.* They didn't say who 'her' was."

Kerry's lips were a white line. "Me."

Mia broke in. "Okay. Axel shoots ice arrows. Loretta becomes a shadow. What can Maria-Pilar do?"

"She casts illusions over herself," said Kerry. "Very realistic ones."

Jennie's hand fell to the hilt of her sword. "We'll need weapons. All we have is my sword, which is too heavy for you two." She indicated Mia and Summer, then raised her voice over Summer's protest, "And Kerry's weapons, which no one else can use. Summer, could you tell how they got onto the roof? Did they climb a staircase or a tree?"

"A rope ladder," Summer said. "On a grappling hook. The only other way I saw up there is the way that only *I* can use. Drop down from the trees above."

Mia thought furiously. If Summer could drop down from a tree, she could drop things *from* a tree. Boiling oil? They didn't have that, and it could splash on Ross. Rocks?

Mia grabbed Jennie's sleeve. "Salt bombs! There's a barrel in the pantry. I mean the store." She dashed back in, broken glass crunching underfoot.

Mia was so engrossed in making the salt bombs that she only stopped when Jennie patted her shoulder. "Summer says that's as many as she can carry."

Mia blinked up. Apparently, some time had passed. She had a vague recollection of someone handing her water. And leftover rabbit.

"I could carry more," Summer said. "But not if I'm carrying a person, too."

"Let's see if you'll be carrying a person," said Jennie. "Mia, can you stand up?"

Mia got up. Summer grabbed her around the waist and hefted her into the air.

"Hey!" Mia squawked.

Summer thumped her back down. "Not with all those tools, I can't. I could if she takes them off."

Mia clutched protectively at her tools. "Could what?"

With a slight smile, Jennie said, "It's your plan, Mia. Summer can't lift Kerry."

Mia had suggested the plan but had never expected to be a part of it. No one ever wanted her for hand-to-hand combat—she was a terrible fighter, too young, too short, too everything. But here, now, was her chance! And to rescue Ross, too!

But without her tools. Her hands closed protectively

over her front.

"I didn't say you have to go naked," Summer said.

Jennie grinned. "Mia *is* naked without her tools."

Fighting a blush at the word *naked*, Mia gritted her teeth. "I'll do it. I know exactly what to do. And it's for Ross."

"*I'll* do all the fighting," said Summer with a confidence Mia wished she shared.

There was no time to waste. It was sundown. Summer led them through the ruined city to a huge tree. Mia looked up and up and up. She'd never been afraid of heights before, but…

Her hands ran down her body, over all the empty pockets and loops. She really did feel naked. She glanced at the mesh bag full of bombs that Summer had strapped to her front. Summer crouched down. "Hop on."

Mia got on her back, piggyback style. She hadn't done that since she was a little kid, and her father had given her rides. She clutched at Summer, her heart pounding. With a tremendous jerk, they hurtled into the air. Summer grabbed a branch, stopping them with another tremendous jolt. Mia clenched her teeth to stop herself from screaming. It looked so graceful and easy when Summer leaped. It looked *fun!*

Summer dropped down like a rock, again stopping herself by grabbing a branch. She hung, swinging like a pendulum, then dragged herself upward, panting with effort. Mia clung desperately to her.

Summer whispered, "Get off me."

Mia grabbed onto the branch and edged away from her. The rooftop was thirty-two feet, seven inches below. Mia gulped, then took note of where everyone was. There was Ross, with his hands tied behind his back. His head was lowered, his hair hiding his face. There was Axel—he was huge—a middle-aged woman who had to be Loretta, and a teenage girl, Maria-Pilar.

Mia murmured into Summer's ear, "Drop two on Loretta."

Summer whispered back, "I know the plan."

She grabbed a salt bomb in each hand. Mia took the other two. They locked eyes, then Mia gave a brief nod. She threw one bomb at Axel and one at Maria-Pilar, hoping her aim was good and Ross's fast reflexes would ensure that he'd have his eyes closed by the time they hit. But she had no time to check. Mia lunged at Summer and grabbed tight.

With a terrifying drop in the pit of her stomach, she plunged down to the roof. They landed so hard that Mia's teeth knocked together. She leaped off Summer's back and bolted for Ross, drawing her knife. The air was full of salt, making her eyes sting. She tasted it with every breath.

Someone was screeching. Mia hoped it was Loretta. She skidded to her knees beside Ross and sawed frantically at the ropes around his wrists. One strand, two. Three. She was almost through when a huge hand knocked her sprawling.

She scrabbled desperately, aware of the roof's edge close by. Mia looked up just as Ross yanked the last of the rope free. Axel roared and charged. Ross swept his hand along the roof, slinging dirty salt straight into the man's face.

Mia looked around to see what she could do. Summer and Maria-Pilar were grappling. Loretta rolled around on the rooftop, clutching her face and screaming orders and threats. Ross dodged a shower of ice knives from Axel — trying to get to *her*. She could see the desperation in his eyes.

Mia spotted Ross's belt with his knives. As she snatched it up, Ross side-stepped to avoid a punch, darted in close and turned. Quick as a blink, his elbow struck Axel behind the ear. The big man crumpled to the ground.

From below, Kerry shouted, "Get down!"

Ross grabbed Mia's arm and bolted with her toward the rope ladder. He hooked it in and dropped it down. She scrambled down first, her legs shaking badly, and dropped the last few feet. Ross landed neatly beside her, glanced up, and lunged to scramble back up the ladder. Summer and Maria-Pilar were still grappling, dangerously close to the edge. Maria-Pilar flung Summer away from her and rolled. As Maria-Pilar tried to get up, her foot struck the grappling hook. It flew off, taking the ladder with it.

Ross tumbled a few feet, the rope ladder landing on top of him. "Summer!"

Summer leaped off the roof and landed beside Mia, as light as a feather. "Ahh, much better."

"Let's go," Kerry said sharply, one hand curled protectively around Whisper's head poking out from her shirt collar.

Ice arrows hissed and whistled down as they ran. They rounded the corner of the building and charged into the shadows of gigantic mushrooms. Their brightly colored caps reminded Mia of Felicité's giant hats.

As they paused to look back, Mia was relieved to see all three of their enemies stomping angrily around on the rooftop. Kerry had thought Loretta's shadow power wouldn't help her jump up or down, and Mia rejoiced to see that she was right.

"Where's Jennie?" Ross asked.

Mia touched his arm. "She's waiting for us. She sprained her ankle."

She glanced back at the roof. Alarm burned through her when she saw the enemy team tearing up clothing—no doubt to tie into a rope. "Come on!"

Summer bounded ahead, floating from branch to branch. Kerry couldn't keep up with her, but she easily outdistanced Mia. Kerry stopped, glancing back, but Mia waved at her to keep going. Ross had fallen in at Mia's side.

"I'm so—" Mia began, then had to side-step a hairy caterpillar that reared up to the height of her knees, its toothy jaws snapping. "I'm so glad—" She ran out of breath, gave up, and just ran, panting.

Ross put his arm around her. His presence, even more than his physical support, made her feel like she could run forever, though her lungs said otherwise.

"Salt bombs were a great idea." *He* could talk easily while running flat-out.

"Thanks," Mia gasped, then managed to get out, "So glad you're all right. I was so worried."

"Me too," he said. "About all of you."

She was relieved and happy that he was fine, apart from some bruises—she angrily hoped that Loretta and Axel's eyes still burned—but he sounded strange. Tense. More tense than just being captured and having to fight could account for.

"Did they torture you?" Mia demanded, then coughed.

"No," he said shortly.

She peered at his face, but he avoided her eyes. That told her more than eye contact would have. He *wasn't* all right.

They skirted the big white tower and its bees, and arrived at the clearing where they'd left Jennie, right at the edge of the crystal forest. She was sitting on a boulder with her foot propped on Mia's useless backpack full of gifts, which didn't sound like a heroic pose but looked like one when it was Jennie. Her face brightened when she saw them.

"Ross!" Jennie exclaimed. "I'm so glad to see you. Let's get out of this place. I can't wait to go home."

Ross still had his arm around Mia, so she felt it when his muscles stiffened. "We can't get out. I've lost my power."

·13·
ROSS

THE RUINED CITY

EVERYONE STARED AT HIM. For an unsettling heartbeat or two, it was as if he'd gone back in time, to when he was a stranger to Las Anclas. Everyone had stared then, too.

"What?" Mia asked, her brow puckered worriedly.

Jennie reached out a protective hand. "What happened, Ross? Are you okay?"

He was not a stranger. There was genuine concern in all their faces, though they showed it differently: Mia mirroring his own anxiety; Jennie's steady, empathetic gaze; Kerry's wariness in high alert; Summer scowling, her way of showing concern that she would never admit to.

He wondered if she'd hidden her feelings as much before her twin Spring was killed by bandits. And he wondered how much the sister he would never meet had been like Summer. He hoped that someday Summer would tell him. If they ever got out of the ruined city, that was.

"I'm fine." He tried to sound convincing. At least he could reassure them, even if he couldn't reassure himself.

"You didn't look fine when we woke up. You were in a crystal cocoon!" Mia exclaimed. "I thought you were *dead*."

"A crystal cocoon?" The image chilled him. "I don't remember that. I remember trying to protect you all from the singing trees, then I woke up on that rooftop. I can't feel the trees. It's not that they're hard to reach. It's that they aren't there at all."

Jennie's worried expression smoothed into reassureance. "I think you just used too much of your power bringing us all in. Those enemies must have tagged on, or they wouldn't be here. You were supporting far more people than you thought. In the battle of Las Anclas, I used my powers so much that I couldn't pull anything for a while. It was more than an hour before I could even move a pebble."

"That's right," Kerry said. "You saw me lose my shields fighting those guys yesterday. Your power will come back."

Summer gave an enthusiastic nod. Mia looked at him with the absolute trust that he'd always found so touching—and unnerving. He never wanted to betray that trust. They all believed in him. Only Ross wasn't reassured. He didn't know how to explain it to them, but it didn't feel as if he'd burned out his power. It felt *gone.*

Jennie said briskly, "We just have to avoid Voske's team until your power comes back. I bet you'll be fine tomorrow."

Kerry glanced around. "We'll need a good place to hide out. Loretta can walk through walls."

"Bet she can't climb trees," Summer caroled.

"Unfortunately, at the moment, *I* can't climb trees," Jennie said.

Ross held out his hand to her. Her warm, strong hand met his in a brief clasp, then he slung her arm around his shoulder. Mia threw them a quick, approving nod.

Whisper scampered at Kerry's heels as they headed farther into the city. Ross kept a lookout for a hideout, noting and dismissing ruined structures as too unstable, too overgrown with possibly toxic fungus, too noticeable to prying eyes, too likely to trap them all if Loretta walked through the wall. He kept feeling for the crystal trees, like a child feeling for a lost tooth with his tongue. But there was never anything there. He felt certain that if he got within range of one now, it would kill him.

A ruin rose before them, a tangle of walls and bridges and massive steel girders. There were parts he wouldn't want to stand on, but others looked remarkably stable.

"What about that?" Kerry asked. "Loretta can't walk through steel. We—Voske tested her."

Jennie glanced at Ross. He could see that she was

tired and in pain, though she said nothing.

"Is it safe?" Mia asked.

"Parts of it." Ross wouldn't have chosen it on his own, but at least partially safe from Loretta sounded good. "Follow me. Kerry, better pick up your rat. Don't step anywhere I don't step."

Kerry stuffed Whisper into her shirt. Ross spotted Summer starting to rise up on her toes. "No jumping. I'll tell you where it's safe."

"Okay, okay," Summer muttered.

There was movement in the corner of his eye. A shadow with nothing to cast it, slipping up toward Summer.

"Summer!" Ross shouted.

The shadow flickered. Loretta was already behind Summer, reaching around to slit her throat.

The dagger ripped from Loretta's grip and smacked into Jennie's palm. Loretta snatched another knife from her belt, but Summer was already flying away. Ross leaped for Loretta and hit the ground hard. She was gone. He looked around wildly, but all the shadows were still.

Kerry flung out her hands, and ice daggers shattered against her shield. Ross threw Loretta's knife at Axel, who was lurking behind a tree. The big man ducked, and the knife only grazed his shoulder.

"Follow me!" Ross shouted as he sprang back to Jennie's side.

He wished he had more time to evaluate the building, but he could only take his best guess on the most stable parts. He led them up a partially collapsed staircase and onto a landing with broken footbridges projecting out from it. Summer crouched on a steel girder. Ross beckoned, and she leaped from the girder and landed lightly by his side. Sunlight shone bright on the staircase, so he'd see any shadow that tried to flit up it.

"Surrender now!" Axel's voice echoed hollowly. "Our deal is still good! It goes for your friends, too! But not if you make us fight for it!"

Mia whispered, "I'll look for a way out."

Ross divided his attention between the staircase and Mia, gesturing her away from unsafe areas.

Loretta called out, "Did you know we've taken over

your town?"

Ross froze. Her tone had the ring of truth. More than that, he *felt* it was true. He'd always believed Voske would come back. He felt Jennie stiffen beside him.

Summer shrieked, "Go kiss a pit mouth, you liar!"

"It's true," Loretta called. "I can tell you who died."

Ross heard Jennie gritting her teeth. Mia's voice rose up shrilly. "You're lying!"

"All your Rangers are dead," Loretta shouted. "I killed one myself. A middle-aged woman with short red hair? She put up a good fight till I cut her throat."

"Frances?" Jennie's voice was barely audible.

Ross forced himself to stop thinking about Las Anclas. He couldn't fight if he was distracted. They'd already gotten to Jennie.

Kerry said loudly, "She's trying to destroy our morale. I knew the names and descriptions of the Rangers from when we had Prudence spying with her hawks. Frances is probably at the stable right now, picking out a horse to ride."

"Wrong!" Axel shouted. "I killed Julio Wolfe. I had some fun with him first. Somebody should tell him he's weak on his left side defense. Oops! Too late, he's dead! I have proof right here. I always take souvenirs of my kills. Shall I show you?"

Ross had been scanning the area while Axel spoke. The staircase had acquired some extra bits of rubble. Maria-Pilar! Loretta was probably sneaking up the staircase right now.

Ross whispered to Kerry, "Can Loretta get through your shield?"

Kerry shook her head.

Jennie, who had followed his gaze, whispered, "Shield us. Now."

Axel bellowed, "I can tell you whose heads are on your gates! There's five of them. So far. Not the Rangers, though. They got buried. After I took my souvenirs."

"I found a way out," Mia held aside vines from a hole in the wall. "There's a steel ladder inside."

Ross beckoned to Summer. "Fly around. Yell at them. Act like you're going to attack. That girder there is safe. I don't trust that one over there. When I yell your name, jump on it and rebound fast back up here."

Summer grinned. She flitted to a footbridge, crouched low with her long hair brushing the steel support, and screamed, "You killed the Rangers? I'll kill you! I'll take my own souvenirs!"

As she continued yelling, the extra bits of rubble flickered, then vanished. A small gray lizard scuttled away down the steps. A shadow crept toward a partially collapsed wall below where Summer was crouched — a partially collapsed wall that hadn't been there before. As Axel and Summer continued exchanging threats and insults, Ross waited while the shadow crept closer. Then he shouted, "Summer!"

She leaped off the footbridge to the off-balance girder, both feet slamming into it, and rebounded onto the landing. The girder creaked, swayed, and fell with a crash. A huge cloud of dust rose up, and Loretta and Maria-Pilar began coughing.

"Now," whispered Ross.

They all scrambled for the hole and went down the ladder. Ross helped Jennie as much as he could. Her breath hissed every time she put weight on her bad ankle. At the bottom, he led them through a tunnel of fallen walls precariously balanced on each other. Hanging vines shifted, their tendrils reaching for them.

Mia's voice was tremulous. "That couldn't have been true, what they said about Las Anclas? Right?"

"No way," Summer said. "They were only trying to trick us. *I* didn't fall for it."

Kerry lifted her hand, and a tendril reaching for Mia fell to the floor, cleanly sliced through. "I know I said they were only trying to destroy our morale, but I also know that Voske was planning to invade even before Ross and I blew up the dam. He never forgives a strike against him. That was the biggest one anyone has ever pulled off."

Ross couldn't help imagining Las Anclas turned into a smaller Gold Point. All those people he knew, with those terrible fake smiles. He hadn't liked the noise and chaos of the election, but that was how freedom worked. Everybody got a chance to try to make their ideas a reality. In Gold Point, only Voske's ideas mattered, and any others couldn't even be spoken.

Jennie's voice echoed in the small space. "They were bluffing. Kerry was right the first time. They were using old knowledge to try to scare us. Axel easily could have fought with Julio the first time they attacked Las Anclas."

"Axel wasn't there," Kerry said, then quickly added, "But someone else could have told him."

"You're right," said Jennie. "It was a lie. We shouldn't even think about it."

Kerry jerked away from something with a soft exclamation of disgust. "Ugh! Something…slimy. How's your power, Ross? Has it come back yet?"

Unease surged in him again. "No."

Mia laid a comforting hand on his shoulder. "It'll be back tomorrow. Or the next day. It took a couple days after the battle at Las Anclas. So, we just need to stay alive till then."

Just, Ross thought grimly.

·14·
FELICITÉ

THE SEA

A BEAM OF SUNLIGHT pierced the water, illuminating the multi-colored veins in slowly waving kelp strands. Phosphorescent jellyfish undulated upwards, the delicate tracery of their tentacles glimmering blue. Felicité swam toward the light.

Everything was so beautiful underwater. A broader shaft of light struck a long and sinuous fish into glittering gold. As it swam into shadow, the gold dimmed to ochre. A clear note faded away as the fish vanished. The undersea world was not silent. Fish sang to one another, high and low. She'd never known the world beneath the water was so wonderful.

The seawater was soft against her skin. Currents caressed her like silk ribbons. Felicité snapped her fluke, sending herself spinning in a tight circle. It was so easy to move through the water, like a dream of flying. She'd never felt so strong or agile. Underwater, even the simplest movement was a delight.

The light shaft blurred as the jellyfish surrounded her. They undulated closer. Curious, or threatening? She decided not to wait to find out. Giving a hard snap of her lower body, she gloried in the rush of speed as she arrowed upward past the softly drifting jellyfish, toward the blue surface.

The current was warmer and more forceful, gathering her up. She swam with it, enjoying how the water tumbled her around. Felicité had no fear of being overpowered by it. She was fast and powerful in the water, able to break free of any current and outswim any creature. She loved the beauty beneath the waves, but she loved her own fearlessness the most. She'd been afraid for so long. Afraid of Voske. Afraid of her secret being discovered. Afraid of being rejected by the ones she loved. Afraid of her own body, and what it meant…

Felicité frowned, swishing her tail to resist the playful current. It had been a long time since she'd had thoughts like that. How long, she didn't know. Time had been only measurable by moonlight shimmering silver on the surface of the sea, followed later by golden shafts of light slanting down. There were no calendars, no schedules. No expectations. She'd explored and experienced underwater life, detached from the horrors at home.

Why bother being human? The human world was no longer home. That had been taken away forever — not only by the murdering tyrant, but by her own body. But she no longer cared that she was a monster. Daddy would never see her again. She'd learned to relish how fast she could swim away from the restless prowl of gigantic sharks and the marching ranks of queen lobsters as large as a house. She could swim in the midst of a school of a thousand fish, their small bodies slipping over hers, softer than silk. Then — in a single flip — they'd turn and dart away.

The same way that she had always intuitively known that if she ever let herself stay submerged, her entire body would change, she knew that if she pushed those thoughts out of her mind and swam deeper, swam farther, and never surfaced, eventually she'd forget everything, all the way down to her name. She'd never again feel regret or shame. There would be nothing but peace and beauty and the song of the sea.

But when she slept, memories drifted into her dreams like ink poured in water, and she awoke to the emotions of memory-suffused dreams. What had Mother thought when she learned that Felicité had thrown herself down the well? What had Becky thought? Or Grandmère?

Felicité swam upward. She wasn't ready to stop being human. She'd surface, get some sun and air on her face, and decide what to do about those lingering regrets. She could always swim out to sea again…

The current strengthened as she rose up, the water

curling into a wave that caught her. The world filled with bubbles, and she was flung onto a hard surface.

The water slid away behind her, leaving her gasping on a beach. The sunlight dazzled her. She recognized nothing. Where was she?

Another surge of water broke over her, carrying her a little farther up the beach.

Felicité tried to scramble to her feet. Her fish tail, so marvelous to swim with, gave a revolting flap, sending up a spray of sand and water. She clawed her soggy hair out of her eyes.

"A mermaid!"

A boy on fire was running toward her. The membranes slid away from her eyes as she blinked, focusing. The boy glowed with a flickering aura, sometimes red, sometimes golden, like leaping flames. A Change. A hideous—

Well, it wasn't quite hideous. But still, a Change.

He was tall and broad-shouldered, wearing an elegant, embroidered overcoat. Beneath the fiery Change aura, his face was surprisingly handsome. His hair was long, a glossy blue-black that contrasted strikingly with the aura.

Felicité wanted to hide her hideous self in the water, but the tide had receded.

"You're beautiful," said the boy.

She looked around to see if he was addressing someone else, but they were alone on the beach. The boy blushed—the flames glowing rosy—as he said, "Welcome to Catalina. Uh, can you speak?"

Felicité drew in a deep breath. Her gills were already closing, now that she was in the air. "Did you call me a mermaid?"

That seemed to embarrass him even more. "Well— you look like one. I'm sorry. I shouldn't have said that." He looked away as he shrugged off his coat, then held it out toward her. "Are you cold? Would you like my coat?"

Felicité remembered her clothes sinking to the bottom of the artesian well. She was naked! She looked down at herself as she snatched the coat. For an instant, she was relieved to see that he hadn't seen her breasts. They were still only little mounds covered in bronze scales. Then horror seized her. She was still Changed. Still covered in scales. Out of the secret deeps of the ocean, in the glaring light of day, she was still a tailed and finned fish-monster.

She desperately rubbed the boy's coat over her body, hoping against hope that the Change wasn't permanent. Her skin prickled, and her internal organs began their shift. The skin over her tail split painlessly as her flesh and bones pulled apart into legs. A moment later, she was a Norm again.

The boy stood with his face averted. She scrambled to her feet and pulled the coat around her. It covered her entire body, falling to her ankles. Felicité forced her mind away from her overwhelming relief that she wasn't trapped in that monster body and thought fast. He'd welcomed her to Catalina. The Changed island.

She glanced across the ocean, to the horizon where Las Anclas lay. The glorious undersea detachment had disappeared. Guilt clawed at her as she remembered how she'd destroyed her town and abandoned her family. If she was someone else, she wouldn't want anything to do with Felicité Wolfe.

She didn't want to be Felicité Wolfe anymore. She wished that girl *had* drowned in the well.

The boy cleared his throat. "Are you okay?"

"Almost," she said quickly.

He'd called her a mermaid. Norms told tales of mutant fish-women who dragged sailors from their boats to drown and ate them with their sharp teeth. In the stories Changed people told, sailors fell in love with beautiful mermaids, though she'd never understood how anyone could be attracted to a monster with a slimy, scaly fish tail. But on Catalina, the island of the Changed, those must be the stories they told. Felicité recalled an especially stupid story about a lovely mermaid who became human at the price of forgetting everything about herself, even her name.

Felicité wished she could forget everything about herself.

"I'm Isais Aldana," said the boy, still with his back turned. "What's your name?"

In a flash, the idea came to her: she couldn't forget, but she could say she had. She could leave everything behind.

"Noelle." It was her middle name. It wasn't difficult to make her voice shake as she said, "I don't remember anything else. I don't even know how I got here."

Isais's aura shaded eggshell blue. Gold rippled through it as he turned to see her standing up, her monster tail gone. A Norm. "Why don't you come with me? I'll take you to my family's place. We're used to refugees in Catalina."

"Thank you."

Smiling, Isais led her off the beach and on to a pathway of pebbles that shimmered in the bright sunlight. Felicité's skin had become very sensitive after her long immersion, especially her feet. The pebbles stabbed and bruised and burned her soles. She winced, trying to step lightly.

His aura rippled blue again. Based on his expression, that indicated concern. "Do your feet hurt? Can I carry you?"

Felicité suppressed another flinch. Henry had also been considerate and look what he'd done. But this boy wasn't Henry. And she was no longer Felicité. "Yes, please."

Isais slid an arm around her shoulders and the other under her knees and picked her up. She enjoyed how strong he was as he walked steadily up the path. His aura glittered at the edges of her vision as pebbles gave way to scrubby bushes.

A herd of rainbow-furred mutant goats came leaping down the path, blatting mockingly. A scrawny boy pursued them. The boy gestured, and a brilliant light flared in front of the goats. They turned and charged back into their corral.

The boy slammed the gate behind them, then called cheerfully over his shoulder, "Most salubrious morning, Prince Isais! Eh—who've you got there?"

Prince? Catalina wasn't a monarchy. Her parents had told her they had an elected council of Changed people, plus the occasional token Norm.

Isais snorted. "Don't call me that unless you want to bow three times!" To Felicité, he said, "Werner's just giving me a hard time. I'm not a prince. My parents are ambassadors, and we use whatever titles give us equal negotiating positions with the leaders of the towns we deal with. I've gone to a few banquets as a prince. Here we are!"

Felicité gazed upon the most beautiful building she had ever seen. It was like a castle from the book of fairy tales in the Las Anclas library, but prettier. It seemed made of mother of pearl, and the sun struck rainbow glimmers off its towers, arches, and spires. Isais might not really be a prince, but he lived in the most royal house imaginable. The way Daddy had talked about Catalina, she'd pictured slimy monsters in grubby mud huts.

Isais stepped through the arched entryway "My parents are at a council meeting up at Avalon, but I'd be glad to show you around. Would you like a bath first? And, um, some clothes? Whoever gets elected ambassador gets to live in this house with their family, so all the impressive clothes live here, too."

"Thank you." The drying salt and sand on her skin made her itch all over. "I'd like that very much. Though this is a beautiful coat."

"Thank you. I did the embroidery myself. Would you like to keep it?"

Felicité admired the intertwined leaves around the cuffs, and the gold and red dragon rippling down the front. It must have taken him six months to embroider this coat. And he was giving it to her? She glanced up to see him smiling at her in a very familiar way. He was flirting with her. He liked her.

How could he? He'd seen her monster form.

But he was Changed himself, though it wasn't in a monstrous way. And she'd returned to her Norm body. He'd probably pushed aside the memory of her hideous fish tail. Felicité knew all about how you could choose not to think about things.

She smiled back. If he liked her, even crusted in salt and with stringy hair, and was willing to pretend he'd never seen that ghastly thing on the beach, she was certainly willing to go along with that.

"Do you think you can walk here?" he asked.

"Let's find out," she said.

He set her down. The tile floor was cool and soothing

underfoot. A woman with feathery, moth-like antennae came through a door painted with sea anemones and rainbow shrimp. She stopped in surprise at the sight of Felicité.

"This is Dorothy," Isais said to Felicité. "She works here. Dorothy, Noelle just arrived. Can you give her some nice clothes? And the princess room."

Dorothy, a kindly-looking woman whose smile reminded Felicité of her old Nanny Shelley, said, "Come this way, Noelle."

"When you're ready, come downstairs," said Isais. "I'll give you the royal tour!"

Dorothy led her up a spiral staircase and into a room even bigger than the master bedroom at Wolfe House. As Felicité's toes wriggled in the softest rug she had ever felt, Dorothy opened a door to an entire room of clothing in every size and style.

"Take anything you want. I'll lay out a couple dresses while you bathe."
Dorothy took down one of deep blue silk with a bodice sewn with pearls, and another of floating gauze in crimson and gold. Felicité had never seen such elegant gowns.

"The bathroom is through that door." Dorothy's antennae swiveled toward it.

It was another huge room, with a sunken pool lined in blue tile. A waterfall outside the windows had been siphoned off to pour from a decorative fountain and fill the pool. The water steamed gently, heated from below.

Felicité's skin crawled at the sight of that inviting pool. As soon as she sank into it, she'd be a monster again. Fine. She'd just scrub herself with a dampened towel. She shut herself into the bathroom and headed for the rack of fluffy towels.

She caught sight of herself in a full-length mirror. Felicité froze. The only familiar sight was her tangled, salt-stiffened hair. The face in the mirror was the face of a monster. Her features had returned to normal, but a glittering mask of bronze scales framed her eyes and curved along her cheekbones. No one could ever mistake that face for the face of a Norm.

Her hands flew up, rubbing at those hideous scales.

How could she have missed that her face had been wet this entire time? She'd thought Isais had been talking to—flirting with—giving his beautiful coat to a pretty Norm girl!

The scales on her face were smooth and soft and completely dry.

Horrified, she yanked off the coat and stood naked before the mirror. Bronze scales twined down her arms like vines, fanning out over the backs of her hands and twisting around every finger. Lines of scales traced across her chest and wound around her legs. There were even circles of tiny scales around her toes, like little rings. And nothing was wet but her hair.

This was what she'd dreaded ever since she'd first Changed. No one would ever see her as a Norm again. She was a monster forever.

Felicité bit her lip to hold back her tears.

She'd never see Daddy again. She hoped he'd never find out what had happened to her.

·15·
FELICITÉ

CATALINA

AS SHE HAD EVERY morning since she'd come to Catalina, Felicité woke up hoping that the monster scales had vanished in the night. She hadn't let a drop of water touch her skin. She'd scarcely even let herself drink any water, and she was so thirsty.

Surely this time… She forced herself to walk to the mirror.

A scaly monster stared back at her.

She wanted to smash that mirror, like she'd smashed her mirror in her old room. But even if she destroyed its reflection, the monster would remain.

There was a tap at the door. "It's Dorothy, with your breakfast."

As always, Felicité called, "Please leave it outside the door."

"We're a little concerned about you. May I bring it in, Noelle?"

Felicité wanted to scream out her refusal. But the requests to enter had gotten more forceful by the day. Eventually they'd come in no matter what she said.

They've already seen the monster, she told herself. *They'll be repulsed, but they won't be shocked.*

"Yes, it's all right," she said, as politely as she could manage.

Dorothy's antennae canted alertly as she set the tray on a side table. She didn't really resemble Nanny Shelley except in that tender smile, and the soft expression of her eyes. As if she really cared about Felicité.

Felicité's throat ached, but she forced a smile. "As you can see. I'm perfectly fine. I just..." *I'm just too much of a monster to let anyone see me?* How was that going to sound here on Catalina, which Daddy called Monster Island?

Dorothy's antennae trembled gently. "Noelle, this island has been a refuge for many generations. People come here to escape all kinds of dreadful situations, often ones they don't want to discuss. No one will ask you any questions. But if you want to talk, we'll listen." She smiled, her eyes crinkling. "All of us who work at the palace are good listeners. It's part of the job!"

"Thank you," Felicité managed, her throat aching even more.

"You're welcome. By the way, Isais would very much like to see you when you're ready. If you are, you'll find him on the terrace." Dorothy went out.

Felicité stared blankly at the steaming teapot. Isais had seen her. All of her. And he hadn't run away screaming. Well, he was Changed, too. But *his* Change enhanced his handsome looks. Whereas *hers*...

She turned back to the mirror, eyeing the bitter smile on that monster face. Why not take a bath? A good, long bath, and while she was at it, she'd drink half the jug of water. Then she'd put the ugliest dress in that closet, take her monster face down to that handsome boy, and watch him throw up his breakfast at the sight of her.

Felicité began with the water, drinking until she sloshed. It soothed her dry throat, eased her headache, and made her feel steadier. She resented her body's need for water, and its happiness when that need was fulfilled. The huevos rancheros with chorizo and the chilaquiles verdes were delicious, and she resented that too. The monsters shouldn't make a better breakfast than the Wolfe's cook Clara.

She marched to the ever-brimming, ever-hot sunken tub, tore off her nightgown, and plunged in. This time, the Change happened immediately. Her gills opened. Her organs shifted. Membranes grew over her eyes and nostrils. Her legs fused, and the fluke fanned out. Mermaid? Ha! She was an ungainly, hideous *fish monster*.

She could never face Daddy again. Just as well she'd never see him. Or Mother. Or Will, or Grandmère. Even if

Voske dropped dead tomorrow, she could never go back to Las Anclas.

Mayor Felicité Wolfe. What a joke.

She wept, and couldn't tell underwater if her fish eyes could shed actual tears.

She cried below the surface until she was exhausted, then brought her head and shoulders up. The gills sealed instantly despite her hair hanging over them in wet clumps. The auburn dye had mostly washed off in the ocean, leaving it dark brown — the only normal feature she had left. She sat up farther, raising her webbed hands. As soon as the air contacted her skin, the webs receded smoothly, softly, as if her Change had always been meant to work that way.

Felicité slathered on the herbal-scented soap and scrubbed her scalp until it tingled. Then she scrubbed all over, longing for the scales to scrub away, but all they did was gleam brighter. She toweled herself vigorously, but not desperately. There was no point. The scales were there to stay.

"Time to meet the monster you hauled off the shore, Isais," she said aloud.

To her annoyance, she couldn't find a single ugly dress. This was not Wolfe House, with an attic full of castoffs to be repurposed. Everything was exquisitely made and fashioned to fit most body types, with ties and sashes to perfect the fit. Well, a pretty dress would make the contrast with the monster face that much worse. She selected a short dress of wine-red silk with black lace straps and a tight bodice decorated with flecks of sparkling quartz, and sturdy but pretty sandals of bronze leather.

She twitched her hips and watched the skirt flare out above her knees. Was this how Elizabeth Crow had felt when she first dressed up after her Change, and saw her normal body and monster face? Or had she still been too sad about losing her baby to care what she looked like?

Thinking about Sheriff Crow made Felicité uncomfortable. That was part of the world she'd left behind. And no one who'd loved Elizabeth Crow before she'd Changed had stopped loving her afterward, so the comparison was pointless.

She picked up a scarf to conceal any gills that might appear and a hat to keep off any possible rain, then gave a bitter laugh. What was there to hide?

Felicité marched down to the terrace. Would Isais take one look at her and run screaming? Or had he been trained well enough make pleasant conversation with the fish monster, only occasionally letting his disgust show?

Isias sat at a little table with a vase of blue roses — a color she'd always believed was impossible for roses — and lilies that glimmered with their own light. Even the flowers here were Changed. He wore a white shirt and black pants, both perfectly tailored. Embroidered kelp twined up the sides of his pants, and sea horses swam among coral on his shirt. She recognized the embroidery as his own.

His phosphorescent fire seethed with hues of gold and peach and lavender and deep blue. "Noelle! I'm so glad you're feeling better. Would you like anything? The kitchen is standing by, ready to make tea — coffee — hot chocolate?"

"I just ate breakfast, thank you." Felicité searched his eyes for the disgust. But it simply wasn't there. He was looking at her the way every boy and girl who had ever had a crush on her looked at her. As if she was perfect. She had the absurd thought that he might be blind. But that was ridiculous. He'd called her a mermaid. He'd seen her naked and given her his coat.

He was seeing her now.

Isais spoke with the hopeful tone of a boy asking out a girl he likes. "The stable has a pair of horses ready if you'd like to ride. There's also a game of pitch pot this afternoon, if you don't mind a crowd. And I have my sailboat ready, if you'd like to see the island from the sea."

Ever since she'd Changed, she'd stopped swimming and sailing and anything else to do with the sea. If she got splashed now, then she'd see the disgust. "Let's go on your boat."

"Good choice. It's a beautiful day for sailing." Isais led the way through the castle. As he passed one door, he called, "Gretchen! It's the boat!" He was answered by a giggle. Felicité gave him a questioning glance, and he blushed. "She's the cook's apprentice," he said, which explained nothing.

He took her into a sheltered garden. It was a sea of blue roses, from shell pale to sky blue to deep cobalt. Isais asked, "Which is your favorite?"

Felicité touched the velvety petals of a translucent blue-green rose.

"Of course. Like the ocean." He plucked it and gave it to her. It was such a romantic gesture that she felt a bit giddy, as if she was a normal girl being courted by her crush. Then she saw the fish scales on her hand that held the rose.

"I've always loved the sea," said Isais. "I thought I'd be a fisher, until Mom and Dad started including me in diplomatic functions, if visitors had a kid to be entertained. I loved meeting kids from up and down the coast, and even the meetings turned out to be more interesting than I expected. Here we are!"

The ground dropped off abruptly into a cove. A boat was moored there, a beautiful little craft with a figurehead carved into a sea horse.

"Isais, wait!" A high voice floated on the breeze. A girl came running up with a huge picnic basket. "Here's your pastries!"

"Thanks, Gretchen." Isais set the basket in the boat and helped Felicité in.

He pushed off, then adjusted the ropes. With a rattling thud, a sail opened up. The boat seemed to come alive, surging into the water. Automatically, Felicité put up her hand to adjust her hat. But there was no hat. There would never be a hat again. For the first time since she'd turned thirteen, the sun warmed the top of her head.

As the boat picked up speed, leaping and splashing, she fought the instinct to clench her fists and brace for the first cold drops of water that would bring out the monster. The monster was already there, facing this handsome boy.

"I hope you like the palace," Isais said. "Do you know what makes the iridescence?"

"Abalone shells." She'd seen that same shimmer underwater, the living shells slowly opening and closing. Some had been as large as a house.

"Oh, did you see those when you were—" He broke off, his aura darkening. "Sorry, Noelle. I shouldn't have asked. People come to Catalina to make a new start, and lots of them don't like to talk about the life they had before. That includes their Change. Sometimes people don't want to use it or even think about it. We're used to that. No one will ask you questions. Or say anything about your Change, unless you say it's okay." He paused, giving her a long look.

He actually looked hopeful! As if he wanted permission to talk about the fish monster. Well, she wasn't going to give it. She couldn't imagine why he'd want to talk about it. The image flashed into her mind of her hideous tail flopping on the beach. Isais had seen that...and on an indrawn breath, as if beholding something wonderful, he'd said, "You're a mermaid."

Was it possible that he *liked* it? She shuddered.

Sounding somewhat discouraged, he said, "If there's anything you want people to know, you're welcome to bring it up yourself."

He seemed to assume she'd been persecuted by Norms. Like Nanny Shelley...

Felicité supposed she could say she'd fled Las Anclas because of Voske's attack. But if she revealed where she was from, they might figure out who she was. So, she wouldn't. He and Dorothy had promised that no one would ask. If she never said a word about her past, everyone would assume she was still recovering from whatever cruel things Norms had done to her.

Norms like Daddy.

So long as she kept her secret, she could be Noelle forever.

Isais tied the sail's rope to a handy knob and sat down on the deck. "Time for pastries." He opened the picnic basket. "Topfenschnitten!" The word sounded alarming. Something must have shown in her expression, because he laughed. "It's kind of like cheesecake."

It tasted like cream with a hint of lemon, rich and refined. Isais smiled to see her enjoyment. "Have you ever had rice dumplings? We're a bit past the Lantern Festival, but they're so good I talked the cook into making them anyway."

Rice was a rare delicacy in Las Anclas. "I haven't. But I do love rice."

He piled them on her plate. "Oh, hey, I just remembered. Some of my friends are having a party tonight. Not a huge one! Just ten of us. There'll be music and dancing. Do you think you might like to come?"

Felicité recognized that overly casual tone. He was trying to conceal just how much he wanted her to say yes. But to show her monster face to ten teenagers, to see ten looks of horror and disgust?

Shyly, looking down, Isais mumbled, "I'd really like to show you off to them."

She searched his face for the slyness that would prove that this was all a cruel joke. But all she could see was the shy hopefulness of a boy with a crush.

He was sincere. She could no longer deny it. And there was more than that. The conviction that everyone would see her as a hideous monster was her expectation, not an objective fact. She'd been brought up to believe that visible Changes were monstrous. But even in Las Anclas, not everyone had seen it that way. At the party on the night Voske had attacked the first time, all those men had competed to dance with the sheriff. No one had made them do that. They had seen Elizabeth Crow as beautiful.

Isais saw *her* as beautiful. It was unsettling. It was kind of frightening. And it was kind of wonderful.

This is me, she thought, looking down at the sea spray shining on the brown skin and bronze scales of her forearms.

"I'd like that," she said.

·16·
PACO

AS THE SUN SET on Opportunity Day, Paco discovered that his closet had been invaded while he was forced to ride on patrol with Voske's soldiers. A new set of clothes, red with black trim, hung with a note attached: *Wear these to Voske House for dinner.*

He wished he could rip up both the clothes and the note.

Choose your battles, his mother had always told him. Fighting back had to benefit the resistance. Destroying the Voske clothes was pointless.

He put them on. The previous outfit had been in his general size, but this one had been tailored exactly to his body, as if he'd been measured in his sleep. The idea made his skin crawl. Undoubtedly someone had just borrowed another outfit of his to use as a pattern, but even that was a reminder that Voske controlled every aspect of his life.

My outer life, he reminded himself. *My mind is my own.*

As Paco walked toward *Wolfe* House, he caught some side glances from Las Anclas citizens. He wanted to shout that he'd been forced into the outfit. But he kept his lips shut tight and his gaze forward.

Wolfe House had been redecorated *again*. A tapestry hung in the dining room, with embroidered butterflies with long trailing wings glowing under the light of the chandelier. The hallway entrance was hidden by a folding screen with a blue-green dragon dancing across the panels.

A small, graceful woman came in. "Good evening! I

am Min Soo Cho. I'm so pleased to meet you at last."

That makes one of us, thought Paco. He gave Kerry's mother a brief nod.

Bridget bounced in, wearing a black and red dress. "Me too! Well, we met yesterday, at the schoolhouse. It's *tiny*. And it has chalk slates instead of paper."

"I first learned on a chalk slate," Min Soo murmured, her voice too sweet to be reproachful. "I have fond memories of my school, which was even smaller than the one here." She smiled at Paco. "Do have a seat, dear boy. Let's get to know one another."

He had intended to sit as far from Voske as possible, but Min Soo towed him to a seat. "You'll sit in the place of honor, at the king's right hand." She seated herself gracefully at the foot of the table.

Servants in black and red livery came in, bearing dinner on gold trays. Bridget ran to sit across from Paco. Henry walked in and began to head for Paco's seat, stopped short, and sat beside Bridget.

"Hi, Paco," Henry said. *Grinning.* A surge of hatred almost choked Paco.

"He's *Prince* Liam," Bridget said.

Paco unclenched his jaw to say, "Please just call me Paco."

"But you *are* a prince. And you can have a middle name, of course—mine's Suzanne—but Father gives us our first names." Bridget studied Paco earnestly under slanted brows. She reminded him of a little fox. "Father told us all about you. He said that one day we'd all be reunited as a family."

Paco's stomach churned as he clamped down on making a reply to *that.*

"I'm sorry about your mom," Bridget went on. She actually did look sorry. "It'd be worse than being poisoned, worse than being boiled in oil, if *my* mom died."

"Worse than being beheaded?" Paco hated himself as soon as it was out.

Bridget looked puzzled. Min Soo said smoothly, "My dears, let's talk about more pleasant subjects. Bridget, have you made any friends at school?"

"Not really. I like Yolanda Riley. She spars so well! But she doesn't talk to me."

"Some people take time to get to know you," Min Soo said. "But those often turn out to be the ones most worth knowing."

Voske walked in from behind the folding screen, and the servants filed out. Paco wondered if the screen had been placed to enable eavesdropping. As Voske helped himself to steamed fish, he said, "It's good that you're taking note of the most promising students at drill, Bridget. We can invite them to train for your future honor guard."

He'd been listening, all right. Paco regretted his remark about beheadings. He'd revealed his true feelings and gotten nothing in return.

"Meredith is promising too," Bridget said. "She's the best of the big girls. Jose is the best of the big boys."

Voske gave her a smile, then turned to Paco. "Liam, has Santiago told you about Opportunity Day?" Paco nodded, but Voske didn't let it go. "What did he tell you?"

Paco stuffed asparagus into his mouth as he thought rapidly. "Just that people are picked to try for powers."

"Unless they drop dead," Bridget said, her fork suspended in mid-air. "You were there at school when I told everybody about that. And the mouse," she added with an air of triumph, and took a huge bite of fish.

"You visited the school?" Voske asked.

He had to already know that. But if Voske wanted to know every detail of Paco's days, he could have them. "Yesterday I went by to take Meredith's lunch to her. Dr. Lee makes her lunch, since she's a terrible cook. She forgot to take it. Dr. Lee said his daughter Mia used to forget her lunch all the time, too."

It was almost fun to be deliberately boring. Maybe that could be a weapon in this duel with Voske?

But Voske cut in smoothly, "You aren't eating much, son. Don't like sea fish? Perhaps you're used to it, living here next to the sea? Or do you dislike the preparation?"

Paco couldn't say that Voske calling him *son* had ruined his appetite. Nor could he criticize that food and get the cook into trouble. The way Voske watched everything he did, no matter how inconsequential, made him feel like he was trapped in a tiny cell with glass walls. "The fish is fine."

"Then eat up." Voske watched Paco choke down a bite, then returned to eating.

Paco had been so distracted by first Min Soo, then Voske himself that he only noticed then that the forks had been blunted, and nothing had been served that required a sharp knife to cut. The tyrant planned *everything*.

A blinding wave of rage hit Paco. Voske thought he was safe, but if Paco moved fast enough, he could put the butter knife through his eye…

Voske looked deliberately from Paco to the cutlery and *smiled*. Paco remembered how Voske had taunted him by sitting beside him on the couch when they'd first met, and how fast Voske had gone to the window. If Paco tried to attack him now, he really would be a rat who nipped at Voske's boot and was easily kicked away. He stared down at his plate of soft food, overcome by a sense of futility.

"Min Soo, please tell Liam more about Opportunity Day, so he doesn't think it's all about exploding mice." Voske chuckled, and Bridget instantly followed up with a loud giggle. Paco was revolted.

Min Soo smiled at Paco. "Opportunity Day is just that, an opportunity. Many wish to take it, knowing that even in the rare occasions when something unfortunate does occur, their families are rewarded. We're giving Las Anclas the same opportunity that we give the citizens of Gold Point."

"Opportunity Day is great," Bridget put in. "We have a banquet. You'll love it! Not like that mopey Ross Juarez. He didn't appreciate *anything*."

Paco flicked a look Voske's way, but the king's amused expression hadn't changed.

Bridget went on, "He slumped around like, oh, like a slumping thing. I'd been so excited to meet him—he has such a cool power—but he was the most boring person I ever met. I think *you'll* love it, because you're a *real* prince. And you look like one. Don't you think so, Henry?"

With a jolt, Paco realized that he'd actually forgotten that Henry was there.

Henry flashed his *just kidding* smile. "We always knew he was a prince. Just like his boyfriend. Oh, I mean his *ex*-boyfriend."

"Ah, the mysterious prince from the floating island,"

Voske said. Paco gritted his teeth. Of course, Henry had blabbed about Yuki.

Voske said, in a deceptively mild voice, "One's first serious romance, though few of them last, is very telling about one's character. The prospector prince sounds like he's got courage and ambition. Two qualities notably lacking in Felicité Wolfe. For example."

Henry flushed. Paco was not grateful to the king for needling Henry on his behalf. Every reminder of Felicité made him feel guilty for taking out his anger on her. She'd made a terrible mistake in trusting Henry. But *she* hadn't revealed the tunnel to Voske.

Henry muttered to his plate, "What was she supposed to do, when she got kicked out of her own house?"

"What was she supposed to do?" Voske opened his hands. "Anything. It was a test of her mettle. If she'd tried to attack me, I'd have respected the attempt. But she took the coward's way out."

A brief silence fell, broken by Min Soo's pleasant voice. "Who would like apricots and cream, anyone?"

"Me!" Bridget exclaimed.

"No, thanks." Paco and Henry spoke simultaneously. Paco suppressed a scowl.

Min Soo passed the dessert dishes, praising the quality of the apricots. She was obviously trying to establish a pretense of a normal family dinner. Paco pushed around the food left on his plate, remembering his mother and real love and laughter around their little dinner table. But his mother was gone, and he couldn't imagine ever experiencing that kind of happiness again.

·17·
PACO

ALL OF LAS ANCLAS had been summoned to stand before the stage, flanked by guards. Electrical lights shone on the Voske family in the raised seats at the back of the stage, so the entire town could see them—and Paco, who'd been seated between Min Soo and Bridget. Voske's honor guard stood behind them, with Santiago at Paco's chair; Paco remembered their conversation and did not dare look his way.

Henry Callahan wasn't grinning as he took the empty seat beside Bridget. Maybe he, like Becky, was grieving over Felicité. Paco didn't feel sorry for him. It was too bad he was already Changed. Paco wouldn't care in the slightest if he dropped dead.

A brilliant spotlight illuminated the testing table. It was as Bridget had described, containing a number of objects, a potted plant, and—Paco winced—a caged mouse.

Voske stepped forward. The crowd quieted instantly. "Min Soo?"

Her robes of white and red swirled as she walked up and ceremoniously held out her hands. Bridget leaned forward, expectant glee on her face. Paco shifted his gaze to the captive audience. Some townspeople stared at Voske with hatred, a few at Bridget and Min Soo, and many at Henry. Some stared at Paco.

He wanted to jump up and shout, "*I don't want to be here either! How can you not know that Voske forced me here, just like he's forced you to stand and watch while he does something terrible to one of you?"*

Voske lifted his voice. "Welcome to Las Anclas's first Opportunity Day. What a historic occasion! Do we have any volunteers?"

Nobody spoke. The crowd seemed to shrink into itself, as if everyone was trying to make themselves invisible. Voske let the silence stretch until it felt like forever. Then he said, "Since we have no volunteers, one of you will be chosen."

Henry stirred. It would be just like Voske for Henry to get the "honor" of pulling a name out of a basket.

Voske held out his hand. "Liam, step up."

Startled, Paco stumbled to his feet. Horror churned inside him as he stood beside Voske, with the entire crowd staring at him.

Voske smiled. "I give you the honor of selecting today's candidate. You may choose anyone eighteen or older who isn't already Changed."

Paco's heart thundered as he gazed at the horrified, angry faces before him. He had no idea what to do. He could refuse—

"And should you decline the honor," Voske said, "three randomly selected candidates will be given the opportunity to Change, instead of the customary one."

A red haze of fury blurred Paco's vision. He couldn't let three people risk death. Voske had forced him into a corner with nothing to do but comply. His thoughts felt locked in place, like a jammed rifle. He scanned the crowd, hoping some idea would come to him.

He could choose someone he hated. Henry Callahan—no, he was already Changed. Paco didn't hate anyone else. Mrs. Callahan...

No, he couldn't condemn someone to possible death just because he *disliked* them.

Maybe someone old who would die soon anyway? But who was he to make that decision? And you never knew how long old people might live. Great-Grandma Riley was over ninety and still going strong. He'd rather cut off his own hand than pick her.

He'd rather choose *himself.*

Certainty flooded through him, along with the knowledge that he had to move quickly, before Voske stopped him. Paco spoke as if he was on stage at Luc's, making sure his voice carried. "I choose myself."

Before anyone could speak, Paco strode up to Min Soo. For the first time, he noticed her palms. They were terribly scarred, as if she'd grabbed a handful of red-hot coals. That must have been from when she'd Changed Luis.

In the instant before he touched her, a flood of horrific images flashed through his mind: that soldier girl dead on the sand, with fingerprint scars on her face. Ross riding back from Gold Point with that bandage wrapped around his throat. Bridget's glee as she'd said, "And then the mouse exploded!" And, lingering in his mind, the deadness in Luis's eyes.

He grabbed Min Soo's hands and gripped them hard.

Her eyes flickered from him to over his shoulder. She was probably waiting for some instruction from Voske. Paco gritted his teeth, unsure whether he hoped that Voske would call it off or not. The waiting made him feel sick. Voske must have nodded, because she turned back to Paco with a look of cool certainty. She squeezed his hands.

Paco's breath caught in his throat. Between one heartbeat and the next, something altered inside him. He couldn't describe it, even to himself, yet he was certain that something was different. He was Changed.

Min Soo released his hands and looked at him curiously. "Do you feel anything?"

She didn't know. He could feel it, but she couldn't.

He had to keep his Change hidden. Whatever it was. He tried to look puzzled as he said, "Should I?"

He could see that he'd fooled her. Her eyebrows puckered in doubt, then her face smoothed into relief. She was probably glad that she hadn't killed Voske's "son."

She said softly, "Yes, you'd feel it. You definitely don't feel different?"

For the first time since the invasion, Paco felt strong and in control. It was like playing at Luc's. He knew how to make the crowd cheer, and he knew how to convince Min Soo. "Well, um, I was kind of nervous. And now I'm not?"

Min Soo gave him a small smile. "That's not what I

meant." Then, pitching her voice to be heard across the crowd, she announced, "No Change."

Paco returned to his seat, glancing at Voske as he went. The king stared at him narrowly, and Paco sensed cold anger. Whatever Voske had intended, it hadn't been this.

Then Voske smiled broadly at the crowd and lifted his voice. "That's my son! Willing to risk his life for the chance of power. Too bad you didn't get one, Liam. But I salute your courage. Perhaps next month, someone will volunteer. Or perhaps not."

Voske looked straight at Paco as he spoke, and Paco knew that on the next Opportunity Day, he would have to choose again.

Voske called out to the crowd, "Dismissed."

People practically tripped over their own feet getting out of the square. Paco caught a glimpse of Meredith's bright red hair. He saw her look of relief, before she, too, vanished into the night. Then he was alone on the stage with the Voske family, their guards, and Henry.

Voske's fake smile tightened, and Paco wondered if he was about to get executed before he even found out what his power was.

Min Soo's voice rose sweetly. "Ian, dear, let's go have tea. I don't think we need Liam. He must be so disappointed. Let's not force him to keep up that strong, brave front."

The tic in Voske's jaw eased. "I agree. Son, you're dismissed. I'll talk to you tomorrow."

Paco made himself walk off the stage rather than run, though he couldn't wait to get away from Voske. He headed into the first empty space he saw, the lumber yard, to gather his thoughts. Probably he ought to go talk to Dr. Lee. But he wasn't *sure* he had a power. Maybe he'd imagined that strange feeling. And the last thing he wanted was to be questioned about Opportunity Day. The only person he wanted to see right now was Yuki. If only he could go home and find Yuki waiting for him.

A wave of exhaustion hit him, nearly making him stagger. The short walk to Singles Row seemed like a ten-mile hike through the desert. He could see his room so vividly in his mind's eye: the bed he'd forgotten to make that morning, the window with the curtains that he now always kept closed, the table with the covered cage of brightmoths and Yuki's silver dancer.

With all his heart, Paco longed to be home *now*.

A flash of heat startled him, as if he was suddenly in front of a fire. His vision blurred. Something punched him sharply in the arm. Then he was falling.

He slammed hard onto cool tiles.

Paco rolled over, staring in confusion at his own room. He was lying on the floor. No, he'd *fallen* to the floor. He raised the arm that had felt the punch. A piece of his red Voske shirt was missing, as if it had been sheared off.

From the lumberyard to his room in one heartbeat. He'd wanted to be in his room, and he was there.

Paco had found his power.

·18·
PACO

LAS ANCLAS – PACO'S ROOM

PACO WOKE WITH A start. He'd apparently fallen asleep on top of the covers, fully dressed. After *teleporting*. Unless that was a dream.

He patted his shirt. A piece of cloth was missing from his sleeve.

It had all really happened.

Pre-dawn light shone dimly through the curtains as he leaped up, full of energy and anticipation. If he acted at once, he ought to have enough time to test his new power. The night before, he'd longed to be back in his room, he'd pictured it, and he'd been there. He could try that again right here in his room.

He backed up to the door. The room was small, so he wanted to give himself as much space as possible. He looked at his window, fixed it firmly in his mind —

— then stopped, his heart abruptly pounding, and inspected his shirt again. It looked like a piece of cloth had been cut out with scissors. And the floor was bare. That bit of cloth was just...gone.

Uneasily, Paco fingered the hole in his sleeve. He'd have to make up some accident, probably tear it more himself, if he had to wear it again. But more importantly, what did it *mean?* He'd never heard of any person having this power. He knew the word 'teleport,' but only in the context of teleporting small items, like squirrels could teleport an apple from his hands to their paws. This, as Yuki would say, was new territory.

He had to try it anyway. When he was a kid, he'd

hoped he'd get a power. He'd thought about it all the time for the year or so before he hit puberty. Then he turned thirteen, then fourteen, and finally resigned himself to it never happening. Women were lucky. They had an entire lifetime of chances.

No, *he* was lucky. He had the perfect power for his circumstances—one that would allow him to escape. He could find Mr. Preston and the surviving Rangers and help them take back Las Anclas!

Paco started to visualize Mr. Preston, then hesitated. The only time he'd teleported before, he'd pictured a place, not a person. And he had no idea where Mr. Preston was. What would happen if he tried to teleport to a person rather than a place? Would he arrive wherever they were? Would his attempt simply fail? Or would he be lost forever in some…otherness?

And what about that missing piece of cloth? Would that happen every time he teleported? Had he done something wrong? Did it depend on some unknown factor? He wished Mia Lee was with him. She could do an experiment to determine exactly what was going on. But since he didn't have Mia, he'd have to do his own experiments.

Paco stared across the room, focusing intently on the curtains, the floor, the whitewashed adobe walls. He tried to think himself there.

Nothing happened.

He tried harder. Still nothing.

The night before, he hadn't been looking at the place where he arrived. Maybe that was the problem. He closed his eyes and visualized himself standing at the window.

Still nothing.

Frustrated, Paco opened his eyes. Why couldn't he do it again? Was the distance too short? Or could his power be to teleport between the lumberyard and his room? That would be terrible! Or maybe he just wasn't doing it right. Once again, he thought back to the night before. He'd pictured his room because he'd wanted to be there so much. He'd *longed* to be there.

His gaze fell on the silver statuette Yuki had given him. It wasn't Yuki, but...

He longed to be beside that statue, which he so often

looked at, imagining that Yuki had come back.

Thud!

Paco staggered, his arms swinging wildly. He stopped himself just before he knocked the statuette off the table.

He'd done it!

He picked up the statuette, wondering exactly how far his power could take him. *Could* he go all the way to Yuki? What if all it took was picturing Yuki and imagining himself there beside him?

For a wild moment, Paco was tempted to try it immediately. But that hole in his shirt stopped him. He checked himself all over. Nothing new seemed to be missing.

Maybe it was the distance that mattered. From one end of the room to the other was about fifteen feet. From the lumberyard to his room was about a thousand yards. Once again, he wished Mia was there. She'd not only already know exactly how far it was from the lumberyard to his room, she could eyeball any distance and tell him exactly how far it was, down to the inch.

At least he knew — well, he guessed — that he could teleport some distance between fifteen feet and nine hundred yards without losing anything. And teleporting a thousand yards, he'd only lost a small piece of cloth.

Paco considered distances, and safe places. Not that there were many of those left in Las Anclas. Then he thought of the perfect place for his second experiment: the new barn, rebuilt after Henry had burned it down. It was only about a hundred yards from his room, and it was empty, waiting for spring hay. If he arrived inside it, he'd be safe.

He set the statuette down. The barn itself was new, but he used to practice the drums in the old barn, while Yuki stood and listened. It was where they'd shared their first kiss. That would be easy to long for.

With confidence, Paco pictured the barn and longed to stand in the spot where he and Yuki had first kissed.

The ground slammed into his face. Something hard crashed on top of him, hitting his arm and back. Bewildered, he tried to roll away, but the thing hit him again. For a disoriented moment, he had no idea what was hitting him or why. There was a wooden slab close overhead. It was the underside of a table. He was lying on the floor of the barn, with a table on top of him. He couldn't move his leg.

He looked around. The barn was full of furniture and boxes. Cautiously, he tried to wriggle out from under the table, but every time he moved, it moved with him. He twisted the other way, trying to figure out what he was caught on. It felt like his pants had snagged on a nail.

He groped down his leg, trying to find the place where it had caught. He sure couldn't see it. His fingers touched soft cloth, then hard wood.

Paco froze.

His pant leg was joined to the leg of the table. He could actually see where the black cloth merged with the wood. He must have teleported so close to the table that his pant leg had materialized *inside* it.

A bead of cold sweat slid down his spine. One inch farther to the side, and his leg would have been inside that wood.

He had to get free. He put his hand in his pocket, then remembered that he didn't have his knife—Voske's soldiers had confiscated anything he could use as a weapon. He looked around desperately. What was all this furniture anyway? The table he was stuck to was intricately carved and inlaid with threads of real gold. It had to be Voske's.

He looked for anything he could use to cut himself free—a saw, a sickle, even a pry bar—but there was nothing but boxes and more fancy furniture.

Paco braced one hand on the underside of the table, grabbed his pant leg in the other, and shoved in opposite directions. His pants tore free, and the table fell again with a crash that made him flinch. He must be making so much noise. He had to get out of there fast, in case someone had heard.

He was about to teleport back to his room—he'd definitely longed to be there—when his gaze fell on that table leg. A swatch of cloth was embedded in the wood. Paco crouched down and ripped at it. Some of it came free, leaving threads dangling from the wood and a clear line of black cloth running through the pale wood and gold thread of the table. There was no way anyone could miss that.

He thought fast, his heart pounding. *He'd* never known another teleporter, but Voske might. For all Paco knew, Voske had seen the remains of other teleporting experiments. If he did, he'd figure out that it had to be Paco.

He picked up the table in both hands and smashed it against the nearest wooden box, frantic to break the leg off. He had to get rid of it somehow.

The box smashed open. But the table only bounced. A thread of gold fell off. Paco clenched his teeth and smashed the table again, this time against the floor. The top cracked with a sound like a gunshot.

From outside came a distant, "Hey! Did you hear that?"

Frantically, Paco glanced around. Inside the broken box, white stone gleamed. He yanked at the stone. It came free, though he staggered at the weight. It was a marble statue. Perfect.

As running footsteps approached the barn, Paco swung the statue into the table. The leg finally came free in a shower of splinters. As the door rattled, he gripped the table leg and longed with all his heart to be back in his room.

Paco staggered and fell beside his bed, the table leg clattering with a noise that sounded like thunder. He rolled onto his back, gasping for breath. Safe.

No. He still had the table leg in his hand. Soldiers could come in this room at any moment. He couldn't just hide it either. People came in his room when he wasn't there, bringing new clothes. They probably searched for weapons while they were at it.

He looked down at the ripped pants, then at the hole in his sleeve. The two holes in his sleeve. There was another hole in the other leg of his pants. The Voske outfit was completely destroyed. How could he possibly explain that? Moths? Giant mutant moths?

Feverishly he scrambled out of the clothes and flung them and the table leg into his closet. He was yanking on new clothes when he heard footsteps.

The closet would be the first place anyone would

look. As someone knocked at his door, he yelled, "Just a minute! I'm not dressed!"

He scooped up the clothes and the table leg, looked around wildly, then shoved them under his mattress. They made a bulge, so he pulled up the bed cover and sheets, and dumped them in a pile on top so it looked like hadn't made his bed.

"Hurry up," someone unfamiliar shouted. "You'll be late to breakfast with the king."

Paco clawed his fingers through his hair, smoothing it down as best he could, while he tried to make sure his face didn't give away his panic.

He opened the door. The soldier outside flung out a hand, shouting, "Stop!"

Paco froze. What had he forgotten? How had the guard known—

The guard exclaimed, "Don't step on it!"

Paco looked down. There by his feet lay the repulsive parody of *El Heraldo*. Since the guard was watching, he picked it up. Paco, a fast reader, couldn't help registering the first few sentences at a glance:

PRINCE LIAM SHOWS HIS METTLE!

In a stunning display of courage and ambition, Prince Liam Voske volunteered for Las Anclas's first Opportunity Day…

Stifling his fury, Paco put the paper on a table and left with the soldier. He could think of nothing but the tell-tale table leg under the mattress. What if some servant was sent to tidy up and make his bed?

Outside, it looked like an ordinary day in Las Anclas, when the worst thing anyone had to worry about was tomato worms. People were busy working in their pocket gardens, giving him a pang of nostalgia. But no one greeted him, or even looked at him. Nor did they chat with each other. The silence was so oppressive that he was almost relieved when they reached Wolfe House. The relief vanished when he actually had to walk inside. Paco gritted his teeth, preparing himself for another tense meal.

Voske was in the parlor, listening to a messenger's low, urgent report. Paco's tension intensified as Voske's expression hardened. Then he turned to Paco with that eerie smile. Paco's heart thudded against his ribs.

"A learning opportunity has come up," Voske said. "Come along, son."

Paco followed him out. He wasn't sure whether to be relieved to miss breakfast, or to be worried about the "learning opportunity."

Courage and ambition, he thought, furious and disgusted. He was certain that Voske had written the article himself.

Four armed guards flanked them as Voske led him to the new harvest barn. Paco's hands went clammy. Voske gestured at the soldiers guarding the barn to stay outside, and led Paco inside.

He knows, Paco thought, cold with terror. Could he teleport away? But where could he go? He clenched his fists, forcing himself to stay in control. If there was any chance that Voske didn't know what he'd done, he couldn't give it away.

He stole a glance at Voske, expecting to see accusation, but Voske wasn't looking at him. He was studying the heap of tumbled furniture and the ruined table. By the time Voske turned back, Paco had conjured up a look of puzzled curiosity.

"Who here would be stupid enough to vandalize my property?" Voske asked.

Paco's heart sped like a runaway horse. "I would have said the Willet brothers. But they're dead."

Voske bent to examine a curled wire ripped out of the inlay. "There's a leg missing. That's odd. It suggests that this wasn't just about destruction. What do you think, son? Why would someone take one table leg with them?"

Paco drew in a breath, trying to read Voske's face, like Dr. Lee had said Voske could read his. Was Voske playing with him? Did he already know everything? Or did he actually want Paco's opinion? Either way, his only chance was to play along. "Got me."

"Think about it," Voske said. "Why would someone smash a table, run away, and take one leg with them?"

Run away. Voske really didn't know. Paco could see it in his face. Voske was testing him, but not because he knew about his power.

"Maybe they were so panicked they ran without even realizing they were holding it," Paco suggested.

"Maybe," Voske said. "Any other reason you can think of?"

Paco tried to figure out what he was getting at. "They needed a weapon?"

Whatever Voske was fishing for, that wasn't it. The searching gaze eased. "Do you understand symbolism? I own this table. Anything that's done to it could be seen as a strike against me. A piece stolen from it could be used as some kind of cowardly threat. Perhaps a scarecrow left in the town square, with silver paint on its head and the table leg through its heart."

That was awfully detailed for an example. Voske seemed to be speaking from experience. Paco wondered who had done that, and what had happened to them. Since Voske seemed to expect a reply, Paco said, "Okay..."

"This will be your first task as king's aide," Voske said. "Find out who vandalized my property and locate the table leg. Before it's used. Understand?"

Paco wanted to retort that he wasn't the king's aide. But when he'd thought of refusing to choose someone on Opportunity Day, Voske had threatened to choose three victims. And he held families hostage. Paco had no family left, but Voske could threaten his friends. Clamping down on his fury, Paco said, "I understand."

Voske led him back to Wolfe House, the four guards flanking him. Santiago was waiting outside, puffing as if he'd run straight from the training ground.

"Santiago, you'll assist the prince," said Voske. "He has some investigating to do."

It was only then that Paco took in that he'd been assigned to investigate himself. And the table leg was in his room, hidden by nothing but a mattress covered by a heap of blankets. For all he knew, someone was heading there right now to tidy it up for him. He had to get back there and destroy it.

But Voske made him have breakfast with his family first, leading an interminable chat about everyone's plans for the day, as if it was a normal day among normal people. Paco couldn't think of anything but getting rid of that table leg.

When the meal finally ended, Paco left with Santiago. He had to get rid of him before he could do anything about the table leg. Maybe he could send Santiago on an 'investigative' errand. But as soon as they were out of earshot of Wolfe House, Santiago lowered his voice. "We need to talk in private. Let's go to your place."

"No!"

Santiago looked at him in surprise. "Why not?"

"My room's a mess," Paco said. "Let's go to Mia's yard instead."

Santiago cast him a wry glance. "You think I've never seen a messy room?"

Paco bit back the urge to argue. It would seem suspicious if he made an issue of avoiding his room. "Okay."

He was immensely relieved to find that his room was untouched. Paco sat on the pile of blankets. The table leg jabbed into his thigh. Santiago sank onto Paco's one chair. "You call not making your bed a mess? A mess is dirty clothes all over the floor, and half-eaten food everywhere."

Paco shrugged. "What did you want to tell me?"

"It's not what I want to tell you. It's what you have to tell me. What are we investigating? Tell me exactly what happened."

Paco recounted his visit to the barn. Santiago listened, serious and intent, then said, "That table leg had better not have been destroyed. We *have* to find it."

"What if we don't?" Paco asked. "It's just a table leg. It's not important."

"Weren't you listening to the king? All that stuff about symbolism: he was teaching you, like he teaches the other princes and princesses. He won't accept failure."

"I'm not a sheriff. I have no idea how to investigate anything. What am I supposed to do, go door to door looking for it?"

Santiago didn't smile. "That's not a bad idea. Let's start with the houses near the barn. See if anyone saw anyone running away."

Paco hated to leave the room — at least while he was sitting there, no one could look under the mattress — but he had no alternative.

He spent an agonizingly endless day facing frightened, angry, and suspicious citizens of Las Anclas, asking them questions he knew they couldn't answer. He'd known all of them his entire life, but not one seemed to realize that he was being forced into this position. They looked at him like they looked at Henry. Like he was a traitor.

The sun was setting when they ran out of houses with people who could possibly have seen anyone going to or from the barn. Paco said with relief, "That's it. No one saw anything. I guess that's it for the day. See you tomorrow!"

"Wait," said Santiago. "Let's get dinner and make a plan. Why don't we try that restaurant Dr. Lee always goes to?"

Paco suppressed a sigh of impatience. "Jack's? Sure."

Only soldiers were present at Jack's. It was strange to sit in the familiar saloon without hearing the normal chatter or hear any music playing. Santiago said cheerfully, "Two for dinner. Bring on your best. We're starved."

"Coming right up." Jack gave Paco an odd, almost apologetic glance before he returned with a platter of tacos.

Paco almost spat out his first bite. The meat had no seasoning, the salsa was inedibly salty, and the tortillas had been made with stale flour.

Santiago muttered, "That's your famous cook?"

Paco suspected that this was Jack Lowell's quiet resistance—letting Gold Point know they were not welcome. He forced a shrug. "We like his meals."

"Maybe it tastes better with whiskey," Santiago muttered. "A lot of whiskey."

When they were done, Anna-Lucia came up to take their plates. She gave them a big, fake smile and said, "Tonight's dessert is prune whip. Delicious *and* healthy!"

Paco shuddered. Santiago said, "No, thank you," and drank an entire glass of water. "About tomorrow. Since no one saw anything, we'd better start house-by-house searches. I can call up two search teams. Any idea where they should start? You know those people. Anyone sound like they were holding out?"

Paco was so exhausted that his anxiety had dulled, but at the words "house by house" his heart thudded against his ribs again. He had to get rid of that table leg that night. "Nope," he said, striving to keep his voice even. "They all sounded honest to me."

"That thing could be anywhere," Santiago said with a sigh. "And once we start searching, if we don't pick the right area first, whoever has it will know to hide or destroy it. Well, maybe we'll get lucky."

"Yeah," Paco said. "Maybe we will."

It had been so impossible to ditch Santiago that Paco was surprised when he waved good night outside of Singles Row and Santiago actually walked away. But of course, the guards were still there. Paco shut the door on them.

Alone at last. And the bed was still unmade. He had no time to lose. If he got caught, it'd be his head in the basket. He pulled out the leg and studied the area where the cloth had joined the wood. It was much too big to burn inside his room without smoke getting out. He had to teleport it away.

He ran through all the places that would normally be private. The beach was patrolled, if his power could even reach that far. The town hall had been turned into a barracks, and the officers had been temporarily quartered in citizens' homes. He couldn't be sure any room in town would be empty.

The only house he was sure didn't have extra soldiers bunking in was Wolfe House, which was the last place he could ever go.

Or was it?

Voske's voice spoke in memory, *"Do you understand symbolism?"*

Paco hefted the broken table leg. Voske thought it could be used as a threat. Paco could make it a lot more threatening than just leaving it in the town square. The more he thought about it, the more the idea appealed to him. Let Voske find out what it felt like to have people come into *his* space and threaten *him*.

But first, he had to get rid of the cloth that that had

melded to the wood. Only a Change power could do that.

He got out his glass-making toolkit and chipped away at the wood around the cloth until that chunk came loose. Working slowly to minimize noise, Paco sawed the leg in half, hiding where he'd extracted the cloth. The narrow slice containing the cloth was small enough to burn, so he shut himself into his closet and burned it with a candle flame. He rubbed the ash into the tile grouting throughout the entire room.

Paco was left with two pieces, but at least the incriminating cloth was gone. He sat on his bed to wait. He almost dozed off but jerked awake when the town bell tolled for the midnight watch change. Now everyone but the sentries would be asleep.

The impulse to defy Voske suddenly seemed less compelling. He'd be going straight into the tiger's den—Yuki's term for deadly danger. If Voske was working late, Paco would be dragged straight to the execution platform.

Paco grinned suddenly. He could *teleport*. No one could drag him anywhere!

If he made it to Wolfe House, then he'd know he could travel at least two thousand yards. If he could go that far, then he didn't need to worry about whether he could teleport by visualizing a person. He could just teleport outside the walls and into the desert. Once he was out of sight of the sentries, he could look ahead and jump as far as the eye could see.

For the first time since the invasion, he felt free. He'd plant the table leg at the heart of Voske's power, then disappear beyond the walls.

He needed supplies for a journey. Paco headed to his closet, then stopped. He didn't want to ruin any more clothes by teleporting in them or be burdened with a pack. He'd go naked, then come back, pack clothes and supplies, and rejoin the Rangers.

Paco stripped off his clothes, then picked up the two pieces of wood. He knew exactly where to go. He pictured the room that had once been the Wolfes' parlor and was now Voske's office, called up all the rage he'd felt since the invasion, and longed to be where he could strike back at his enemy.

His body jolted, white heat burning along his arm.

He swayed, his bare feet cold on the hardwood floor. He was in Voske's office. It was dark. He was alone.

His arm burned like he'd been slashed. Blood welled up on his forearm from a deep gouge. He clamped his arm against his side to keep the blood from dripping. What had happened?

Another shock hit him when he looked at the two pieces of the table leg. The one he held in his wounded arm was noticeably shorter, as if a saw had sheared off the end.

Parts of...things...got lost when he teleported. Just like the missing piece of his shirt. This time it had been a piece of the table leg. And a piece of *him.*

Had he gone too far? If he tried to teleport out, would he lose a bigger piece? A finger? An eye? Cold with terror, he laid the pieces of table leg on the floor, then pressed his palm over the gouge in his arm. Was there any way he could walk out of there?

The steady tramp of feet sounded outside. Wolfe House was patrolled by guards. Of course.

He thought quickly. He must have jumped too far. In that case, he'd have to go back in shorter steps. He forced himself to calm down and think carefully. He could teleport from his room to the barn—a hundred yards— without anything disappearing. When he'd teleported from his room to the lumber yard—a thousand yards— he'd lost a piece of clothing. So, he could safely teleport a thousand yards from Wolfe House.

No, he couldn't. He wasn't wearing any clothes. That must have been the problem this time. No clothes, but he'd carried the table leg. Counting his heavy boots, his clothes and the table leg probably weighed about the same amount. But he'd teleported twice as far as he ever had before.

If he teleported far enough, he lost mass. He could practically hear Grandma Wolfe's voice in his head: *"Weight depends on gravity; a Change power that alters gravity can make an object weigh less or more. But mass is the amount of matter in an object, and that doesn't change unless it's physically removed."*

He was going to leave the table leg behind anyway. He thought briefly about grabbing some random thing to teleport with, in the hope that he'd lose it rather than more of himself. But what vanished seemed random. He imagined arriving in his room missing a finger and still holding some possession of Voske's that he'd have to get rid of all over again, and shuddered.

He had to teleport in shorter jumps. He could try five hundred yards. With any luck, he'd lose nothing. He'd have to go inside a building to avoid being spotted by the guards. Who lived near the Wolfes?

Footsteps overhead startled him. He froze. They started down the stairs. He had to leave now.

The Callahans lived nearby. Only Mrs. Callahan remained in the house, and she'd be asleep. He'd only been inside the house once, fetching Henry when he'd been late for Ranger practice. Paco frantically tried to remember where the furniture had been. There'd been a giant sofa on the left side of the parlor off the front hall. Or was it the right?

The footsteps reached the landing. Hot blood oozed down his side. He had no time left. The entryway just inside the Callahans' front door was surely safe. As the footsteps reached the office door, Paco longed to be out of there.

He arrived in a dark, stuffy space. He staggered and crashed into…something. Full of other…somethings. He grabbed frantically with his free hand, trying to catch whatever it was, seized a shape he recognized — he must have tripped over an umbrella stand — and righted it. As he straightened up, his elbow smacked into a delicate glass thing. It shattered on the floor before he could catch it.

Mrs. Callahan's voice rose in a shriek. "Who's there? Get out!"

Near panic, Paco cast about mentally for somewhere else to go. The glaziers' shop was nearby. He'd worked there as an apprentice. It felt like a lifetime ago. But he remembered the quiet happiness of piecing glass together to make a stained glass window and longed to be back there.

Another hard jolt. He staggered. He was alone in the workshop. Moonlight shone through the stained glass windows and skylight, casting a kaleidoscope of muted color over the vases and bottles and windowpanes.

A chill seized him. Taking off his clothes had been a stupid idea. This had to be the coldest night in months. He clutched his arms around his body and caught his breath.

A mostly-finished stained glass window was on the worktable. It featured a rising sun, much like the sun he'd made for the Rileys' window, and a man in a heroic pose astride a rearing horse, sword in hand. The man had silver hair, and wore black and red. It was Voske. The walls of Las Anclas rose up beneath the sun.

Paco raised his fist to smash the repulsive thing, but he caught himself. The doors were locked. And he'd broken something at Mrs. Callahan's, which was undoubtedly also locked. The last thing he needed was Voske realizing that somebody could get into locked buildings.

Raising his fist made his arm hurt more. Blood oozed between his fingers. He hoped he hadn't gotten any blood inside the Callahan house. And he had to get out of the glazier's workshop before any dripped on its floor.

He thought of what was near the glazier's. His memory caught on warm greenery, and Dr. Lee's calm voice in the days after Paco's mother had died. Dr. Lee had asked Paco to help him carry clippings into the greenhouse in his garden patch and had stood in front of a kitten-vine and talked for a while as green tendrils slowly and stealthily undid his ponytail. Even in the midst of his grief, Paco couldn't help smiling. Only now did Paco realize that Dr. Lee had undoubtedly stood there on purpose.

Paco thought of the greenhouse and longed to once again experience kindness.

Another jolt. He shivered, deeply chilled. Even the greenhouse was cold. He breathed in the green scents of herbs and medicinal plants. The kitten-vine tickled his back with playfully reaching tendrils. Just as he had on that day long ago, Paco couldn't help a brief smile.

He was close enough to his room now. One more jump. He longed for his bed.

Nothing happened.

Paco fiercely pressed down his terror and thought. He didn't really long for his bed. By now his room felt like a trap. But it did have something he longed for. Or rather, as Voske had taught him, it had something that symbolized someone he longed for.

Paco thought of Yuki, his long black hair, silky between Paco's fingers, and Yuki's fingers, so long and elegant as they curled around that beautiful silver statuette that he'd bravely risked his life to find.

Another jolt. Paco fell against the table holding the statuette. He caught it before it could topple, staggered to his bathroom, and pumped water over the cut on his arm. He wrapped the washcloth around the cut and rinsed off the rest of the blood.

Slowly the truth seeped into his mind, worse than the pain of the gouge: he couldn't teleport his way out. If he carried anything with him, he might arrive without an arm. Or his head. And a man with no food or water or weapons would die very quickly in the desert.

He could travel in the blink of an eye, but he was still trapped.

·19·
BECKY

LAS ANCLAS

BECKY AWOKE TO BANGING on the door. It felt as if she'd just climbed into bed, but her window showed the faint blue of impending dawn.

"Get up and get dressed," a man shouted. "You have two minutes."

Becky leaped out of bed, almost tripping over the blankets that came with her. She dragged on last night's jeans over her pajama bottoms, feverishly yanking down the hems, and buttoned a jacket over her pajama top. Aunt Rosa stood by, looking worried and angry, as two soldiers hurried Becky outside.

"What's wrong?" Becky asked, her heartbeat frantic in her ears. Had one of the Gold Point patients died? Was Henry in trouble?

Had the Rats been caught?

Nobody spoke until they reached Wolfe House. The entire bottom floor was lit up, light shining from the windows onto the well where Felicité had drowned. *Felicité is dead.* Every time she remembered it, it felt like she'd been told for the very first time.

A soldier gave her a yank. "Stop dawdling. The king wants you."

A sweet scent drifted up from the rose bushes. They'd been overgrown and neglected the last time she'd been at Wolfe House. Now someone was clearly taking as good care of them as Mayor Wolfe had.

Voske was waiting for her in his office, his icy expression reminding her of how he'd looked when he'd had Grandma Ida shot. "Dismissed." The soldiers saluted and wheeled about, leaving her alone with the angry king. "Becky, come here."

Becky stopped short when she saw two pieces of wood, maybe bits of a chair leg, lying on the floor. Puzzled, she glanced up.

The angry lines in Voske's face had smoothed out, leaving only a calm, slightly smiling mask. "Good morning, Becky. Tell me who touched these."

Becky tried to swallow in her dry throat as she obediently knelt down and touched the nearest piece of wood. A rush of emotion overwhelmed her, reminding her of the time she'd waded in the surf and an undercurrent knocked her down and swept her out to sea. But that had been cold. This was hot.

Voske's fury filled her mind. As quickly as it had come, it vanished, as if she had been washed up on shore. Then she heard his cold voice in her mind: Voske's thoughts.

This is defiance. Threat. A war gauntlet thrown at my feet. Covert, leaving no trace. A lone rebel? Conspiracy? And why is a piece of the table leg missing? It must have been so they can use it later. The symbol of their rebellion? Will they carve it and put it on a pole like a banner? Who? Is Sean back? He can walk unseen. How do I find them? I'll start with the sheriff's apprentice...

The shock of seeing herself as Voske saw her—capable, intelligent, wearing fear as nothing more than an exceptionally convincing disguise—pulled Becky out of the stream of Voske's thoughts. She blinked at the wood. It had seemed a long time while enduring it, but it had been barely a couple beats of her heart.

She took in a breath, and again touched the table leg, reaching beneath the fury. She saw a strong brown hand. A boy's hand. She reached deeper.

Parts of...things... get lost when I teleport.

Have I gone too far?

Becky recognized Paco's voice. She felt his anger swamped by terror as he clapped his bleeding arm against his side.

Shock hit her again, this time cold as that sudden wave rising from the ocean. Paco could *teleport*?

Her hand tightened on the wood. She couldn't tell Voske. He'd kill Paco.

He'd kill *her* if he found out that her power enabled her to hear his thoughts.

Desperately, she reached for the layers below. These were mere flickers, some more vivid than others: Voske himself, touching it and appreciating the carving. Min Soo brushing her fingers over it to check for dust. A woman's callused hands rubbing sandpaper over the unvarnished wood, then her satisfaction with its satiny feel.

Becky kept her eyes closed as she ordered her thoughts. *Calm.* She took a breath the way Dr. Lee had taught her and relaxed her muscles the way Sheriff Crow had taught her. Only Sheriff Crow, Dr. Lee, and Brisa knew that she could hear thoughts and feel emotions with her power. Everyone else thought she could just see pictures. Becky had blurted it out to her mother at their last confrontation, but Mom had been too busy uttering threats and laying blame to listen. All Becky had to do was give Voske a plausible story that didn't involve Paco. Or reveal the king's own thoughts.

Her stomach clenched as she imagined opening her eyes and lying to a man who thought like *that*. He'd see through her before she even opened her mouth.

Calm.

Becky had spent her entire life keeping secrets. She could keep this one.

"Becky? What do you see?"

"A man's hand. He's wearing a gold ring on his little finger." She opened her eyes. "Oh…that's your hand. I recognize the ring. You touched it, didn't you?"

"No," Voske said. "Wait. Yes, I did. When I first bought it. I remember testing the finish. Nothing else?"

She shook her head. "I can only see people who touched it with bare skin. It's no use if they wear gloves."

"Try the other piece," Voske said.

Becky reached for the second piece of wood. She took her time handling it, thinking out what to say. "Sorry. All I can see is a woman's hands sanding it, before it was joined to the rest of…whatever it was. A table? A chair?"

She almost wished she could read his mind again. Did he believe her? His face showed nothing. Then he smiled. "Thank you, Becky. You've been very helpful."

Paco burst in, with Santiago right behind him. Paco's gaze lit on her, and he flinched. A heartbeat later, his face smoothed into a blank mask. Just like Voske.

Voske also noticed the flinch. "Liam? You seem alarmed."

Becky's heart almost stopped.

"Is Becky in trouble? Why is she kneeling on the floor?" Paco looked at the wooden pieces, and his brows pulled together is puzzlement. "What are those—wait, are they…?"

"The missing leg from my table," Voske said in that soft voice that made Becky's neck tighten. "How do you think it got here, boys? And why?" He addressed them both, but Becky noticed that his gaze didn't waver from Paco.

Santiago looked from the wooden bits to the king. "Maybe whoever took it got scared. Could be our investigation got too close. So, they tried to return it to you, sir. Could it have been tossed in through a window?"

"The windows were shut."

"No one could get past the guards," Santiago said with confidence. "Someone might have a Change power that transports things from a distance. Like a squirrel. But why it's broken…" He shook his head slowly. Becky wondered if he knew he was drawing the king's attention away from Paco. Could it be deliberate? "A Change power might break up things if they pass through walls. But I'm just guessing, sir," he finished apologetically.

"Liam?" Voske inquired. "Have you anything to offer?"

"I think Santiago's right. Whoever took it saw us searching, and decided to give it back before we could find it. As for how it got in…" Paco shrugged. "Yeah, it'd have to be a Change power. Maybe someone who can turn invisible?"

Becky immediately thought of Kerry's brother Sean, who could go unnoticed until someone consciously looked for him. Apparently Voske did too, because quickly glanced around before turning back to Paco. He said in that calm, pleasant voice that terrified Becky, "Why are you wearing a coat?"

"It's chilly outside."

It *was* cool, but not enough to need a coat.

"Take it off," Voske ordered.

Becky bit her lip, remembering the gouge on Paco's arm. But he looked embarrassed rather than afraid as he took off his coat, revealing a bandage. He must have prepared an excuse. "I searched a tool shed for the table leg, and I tripped and fell on a saw. It was careless."

"Liam, why are you lying to me?" Voske sounded disappointed rather than angry. "Let me see that wound."

The room was so silent that Becky could hear birds scolding outside as Paco unwrapped his makeshift bandage. She forced herself not to look startled when she got a good look at the wound. The only time she'd ever seen anything like it, it was in the surgery, when Dr. Lee had cut out dead flesh with a scalpel. But the cut was too narrow for that to make sense.

Voske examined the wound, which bled sluggishly. "This is too clean for a saw. It was made by a blade."

Close, but not quite. Becky had to stop believing that Voske knew everything. He knew battle and torture, but he wasn't a doctor. Or even a former doctor's apprentice.

"Who did it? Who dared to attack my son?"

He's looking for someone to punish. She didn't know whether to be terrified or relieved.

"No one attacked me. This was my own fault." Paco went on, as if he was reluctant to admit it, "I'm not going to tell you if it'll get someone else's head on a pike."

Voske smiled suddenly. "You were sparring with someone. It's tempting to use regular blades instead of blunted ones, isn't it? Gives the fight an edge of real danger."

Paco rewrapped the bandage and said nothing.

Voske turned on Santiago. "Where were you, Santiago? I assigned you to prevent such accidents."

Paco blurted out, "It's not his fault. I made him do it."

"I'm so sorry, sir." Santiago glanced at Paco. "I thought you'd block me."

"I should have. I was overconfident." Admiringly, Paco added, "You're fast."

Becky was positive that they'd improvised that story on the spot. But Santiago had fallen in as if they were the kind of friends who could finish each other's sentences.

Voske was smiling again, but this time it reached his eyes. He looked genuinely amused. Then the smile faded. "Santiago, you're an excellent soldier. But actions have consequences. You did injure the prince."

Santiago's expression shuttered. "Yes sir."

"Ten lashes," said Voske. "Tomorrow at dawn."

"It was *my* fault," Paco protested. "I'll take the lashes."

Voske gave them the eerie smile that had no humor in it. "You get to watch. Santiago, report to detention. Liam can spend the day on patrol. Dismissed, all of you."

Becky rose on wobbly legs and fled. She couldn't go talk to Paco; Santiago was with him. But if she hurried, she could catch Brisa before school started. She desperately needed Brisa's warm arms around her, to smell Brisa's sweet scent of wildflowers, and to pour every detail of her terrifying morning into her girlfriend's sympathetic ears.

At the schoolyard, she found Brisa with a group of girls. She wore a pink silk dress, the sleeves edged with delicate lace. More of that lovely lace made up the top of the bodice, so fine that she could see Brisa's creamy brown skin through it. The dress was short and low-cut, showing off the gorgeous curves of Brisa's breasts and hips. Pink silk ribbons fluttered from Brisa's pigtails, along with ribbons of pink lace.

For a delicious moment, Becky forgot everything and simply stood there, adoring her pretty girlfriend. Then Brisa spotted her.

"Becky!" Brisa cried happily. "Do you like my new dress?"

"I love it," Becky said. "You look beautiful."

Brisa drew her away from the other girls, and they kissed. Becky ran her fingers along the soft silk of the dress and the even softer smoothness of Brisa's warm skin. "Where did you get it?"

"It's not just the dress. Look!" Brisa held up a beautiful enamel box. Just like the one Min Soo had given Becky. As Becky stared in horrified realization, Brisa popped it open. The scent of roses and sugar drifted up. "I saved the best ones just for you."

The smell made Becky feel sick. She whispered, "Min

Soo."

"She called me in last night. I was scared. You were at Dr. Lee's, and I was all alone. But I shouldn't have worried. She just wanted to meet me, because I'm your girlfriend."

Becky was so horrified, she couldn't speak.

Brisa twirled, sending the dress flaring out around her thighs. "Wasn't it sweet of her to give me this dress? It's a princess dress! Like I've wanted my entire life. It's even pink—my favorite! Min Soo said it had been made for her, but it didn't fit. She thought it might fit me, and it did!"

Even if Becky hadn't had a dressmaker for a mother, she'd have known no tailor would deliver a dress to Min Soo that was far too big. That dress had been made for Brisa. It fit *her* perfectly.

"What did you talk about?" Becky asked carefully.

Brisa beamed at her. "Clothes, mostly. She showed me her hanbok, and said they wouldn't suit me, but you'd look lovely in them. She said we have the same taste for beautiful things. And we talked about *you*—how smart and brave and pretty you are. She said I had excellent taste in girlfriends, too!"

"Brisa," Becky said. "She's Voske's *wife*."

"Kerry was Voske's daughter," Brisa pointed out. "Don't hold it against her, Becky. She didn't have to be so kind to me. I'm nobody!"

Becky's eyes stung with tears, but she gritted her teeth and fought them back. Brisa was the sweetest girl in Las Anclas, and she came from a family where everyone was kind. She didn't understand the evil in people, and Becky didn't want to force her to.

But Becky understood exactly what Min Soo was doing, and why. And she also understood that the Rats had been right. Brisa could never play a role the way Paco could. The way Becky could.

She loved Brisa as much as she ever had. But the comfort of sharing all her thoughts had to end. At best, it would put Brisa in danger. At worst, Brisa could bring down the entire resistance.

But there was one thing Becky had to warn her about. "Brisa, what exactly did you tell Min Soo about me?"

Brisa gave her a hurt look. "Nothing. Min Soo did all the talking. I just agreed."

"Thanks, Brisa. As nice as she seems, I still want to keep some things secret, just between me and you. Like my family. And my power."

"Of course I won't tell her anything about that." Brisa looked even more hurt. "I never told anyone you heard Henry's thoughts. They all think you recognized his hands."

"I don't want anyone to know I can hear thoughts at all!" Becky trembled, remembering Voske standing over her as she knelt on the cold floor.

"Becky, I *know*. I've never told anyone, and I never will." Brisa held her tight, and kissed her with her warm, soft lips. But for the first time in her life, Becky didn't enjoy it.

"Here, have something sweet." Brisa giggled. "Something else sweet."

Becky took the rose petals Brisa held out. She'd eaten other things she didn't like. They couldn't be as bad as Henry's uncooked potato and unwashed rutabaga stews.

They were worse.

·20·
PACO

LAS ANCLAS

AFTER AN ENDLESS DAY riding with Voske's patrollers, Paco was released at sundown. When he got back to his room, he found that someone had raided his closet, adding Gold Point fatigues and another suit in Voske colors. His sliced and torn clothes were gone. At least Voske would assume they'd been ruined knife fighting.

He'd gotten rid of the table leg just in time.

His arm throbbed, his head ached, and he went to bed without eating. Then he lay there picturing Santiago getting flogged at dawn because of Paco's lie. The delay had to be a deliberate cruelty. If the punishment had been immediate, at least it would have been over by now. The wait was agonizing—and it had to be far worse for Santiago.

After a sleepless night, it was almost a relief to finally get up. But there was no getting out of what was to happen next. Paco reluctantly pulled on the fatigues, glad he had no mirror. He didn't want to see himself dressed like a Gold Point soldier, with Voske's own face looking back at him.

As he walked out, he kept coming back to that lie he'd told. He couldn't have known what Voske would do, but Paco should have known he wouldn't placidly accept evidence of covert defiance.

Leaving the table leg at Wolfe House had been stupid. *Paco* was stupid. He should have thought up a better lie. He'd panicked at the thought of Voske executing anyone Paco claimed he'd fought with and assumed that

Voske wouldn't hurt one of his own soldiers who'd done nothing wrong. Now he knew better. *No one* was safe around Voske. He had to remember that. He had to think ahead every single time he was forced to be around the tyrant.

He reached the Ranger training ground, which he'd known his entire life. He'd played on its edges as a child while his mother had practiced. He'd trained there himself, just months ago.

Some of it was the same: the sparring area, the mud pit, the monkey bars, and the climbing wall. But the net Paco had crawled under so many times was now a tangle of barbed wire. Sharpened stakes had been hammered into the ground. A troop of soldiers dodged around them at top speed as Paco passed by. On the other side of the ground, pairs of soldiers sparred with staves. Except for the instructors shouting instructions and corrections, everyone was silent. It was an atmosphere utterly unlike the camaraderie of the Rangers when his mother had been alive.

But the worst change was a wooden pole with manacles attached. Paco started to look away, then reminded himself that he refused to close his eyes to Voske's deeds. He would watch and remember.

A soldier saluted him and said, "This way, sir." She led him to a bench near the flogging post.

His heart sank further when he saw Henry Callahan sitting there, his hair pale against his black fatigues. Henry's face looked hollow under the cheekbones, as if he hadn't been eating. Paco had no sympathy for the traitor. At least the king wasn't in sight. He'd dreaded having to hide his emotions from Voske. But this wasn't a public spectacle. Those were exhibitions of power to civilians. Voske wanted his soldiers looking unbeatable, so their punishments were kept private.

Paco sat as far away from Henry as he could and stared out over the city wall.

Someone barked an order, and all training ceased. The area filled up with neat rows of Voske's elite guards. A burly man carrying a whip walked up to the post. Another soldier brought a pair of water buckets. Santiago came behind them, accompanied by two other soldiers, one man and one woman. His snub-nosed face was grim and set. Paco's stomach churned.

The three soldiers halted in precise step. An officer pointed at the woman. "Patroller Lindsay! Three lashes for drunkenness."

The woman took off her shirt, revealing a sleeveless singlet. She marched up to the post, where the man tending the buckets put her hands into the manacles.

"Having fun, Your Highness?" Henry taunted—quietly, so no one would overhear.

Paco was briefly relieved at the distraction. But that 'Your Highness' jibe threw him back to the nightmarish day he found out who his father was, and Henry's taunt, *Of course a prince would only want to date another prince.* Henry's nose was still crooked from where Yuki had broken it.

"Are *you* having fun?" he retorted, so corrosively that he was surprised at the sharpness of his own voice.

Henry flinched back. But though he was a traitor, he'd never been a coward. "It *was* fun," he muttered, with a hint of the old Henry. "The first few days. Watching them make each other bleed. Now it's just…what they do. Make everyone bleed."

Snap! Paco clenched his fists at the crack of the whip on human flesh. The woman yelped a curse.

Henry muttered, "She's a tough one."

Paco ignored him.

"The howlers are the worst," Henry commented as the whip cracked again.

He wanted to talk? Paco gave in to the fury boiling in his guts and whispered, "And you still brought Voske here."

"I didn't *bring* him. He was coming anyway. This way saved lives."

"I hope that helps you sleep at night," Paco retorted.

The whip cracked for the last time, and the woman was unshackled and led away. Blood seeped through her ruined singlet.

Paco meant to ignore Henry, but he couldn't help himself. "What are the buckets for?"

"When they pass out. That guy tosses water in their face to wake them up before they finish." Henry didn't seem to be joking.

The second soldier to be whipped had a bony, scowling face. He tossed down his shirt, and Paco saw that his back was criss-crossed with white scars.

This would happen to Santiago. He'd wear scars like that for the rest of his life. And all because of Paco's stupid, futile gesture with the table leg. What did he *think* Voske would do in retaliation? That was the problem, he *didn't* think. He'd just acted, like a little kid.

As the officer barked out the name and punishment of the scarred man, Henry whispered, "What really happened on Opportunity Day?"

Paco's entire body chilled. Henry knew! Paco whispered, "Nothing."

As the whip cracked, Henry whispered back, "Liar."

Paco clenched his fists. "You're the liar. You lied about setting those fires. You even lied about your Change!"

Henry muttered, "You wanted to Change all along. You set the whole thing up so you could make a big splash volunteering and impress Voske."

Paco fought not to reveal his relief. Of course, Henry hadn't realized he'd been Changed. No one could possibly know. Henry had set fires to impress Mr. Preston. No wonder he assumed Paco had tried to impress Voske. "Think whatever you like."

Henry let out a sigh. "Being the prince won't protect you forever."

"Protect me from what?"

"Paco, look where you are. Sitting right next to me. Wearing the same uniform. What do you think everyone believes about you?"

"They know I'm not a traitor like you."

Henry snorted softly. "Do they? Just wait till people start throwing rocks at *you* from behind walls. Wait till *you* get into bed and find scorpions or broken glass. Have fun checking your food and water to make sure nobody spat in it. Or put poison in it."

It couldn't happen to a more deserving person. But Paco didn't say it. As the man in the shackles yelled and cursed, Paco realized uneasily that he *was* a liar. Like Henry, he'd even hidden a Change.

"Ten!"

The shackles clattered open, and two soldiers helped the big man away. Paco caught himself looking away from his torn and bloody flesh and dragged his gaze back. He'd look, no matter how much it sickened him.

Santiago took off his shirt, his lips compressed into a tight line.

"Got it in for that guy?" Henry asked. "Was it worth taking the cut on your arm?"

Paco turned on him. "Shut up."

He forced himself to watch Santiago get shackled to the post. He drew his breath in and held it as the sergeant raised the whip and struck. Santiago jerked but made no sound other than a hiss of breath. Each crack of the whip made Paco flinch as if he'd been lashed himself. He wished he was the one standing there. No, he wished it was Voske chained there — it was by his will that so much blood had been shed. Without Voske, Las Anclas would be safe.

Without Voske, his mother would be alive.

On the fifth stroke, Santiago let out a choked yell. On the eighth, his knees buckled, and he sank down, head drooping, hanging by his wrists. The man with the bucket tossed its entire contents into Santiago's face.

Santiago stiffened and tried to stand. But he couldn't. The last two blows were delivered as he knelt with his arms forced upward in a way that made Paco's own wrists and shoulders hurt just watching.

Paco sprang to his feet. "I can help. I'll take him to Dr. Lee."

Santiago raised his dripping face. Paco pulled Santiago's arm over his own shoulders and tried to take Santiago's weight against his side, but it was awkward when he couldn't put his own arm around Santiago's back.

"I'm sorry," he whispered. "I'm sorry, I'm sorry."

Santiago was silent for a few slow, painful steps, then breathed, "S'okay. Would've happened anyway…"

The words jolted Paco as he realized what they meant. Santiago was supposed to protect him. If anything happened to him, Santiago would be punished.

How could Paco explain this to Kerry if he ever saw

her again? But there was nothing to explain. This was the world Kerry had grown up in. Paco had only recently learned about the need to think ahead, and the unavoidable, terrible choices. Kerry had dealt with that since childhood. He'd judged her when he'd never had any idea why she was the way she was.

Halfway to the infirmary, Santiago began shivering violently. Paco slid his hip under Santiago, bent, and took most of the other boy's weight onto his own back. Santiago's breath shuddered at every jolting step.

At the infirmary, Dr. Lee was silent and grim. He measured out a poppy infusion, which sent Santiago to sleep. Alfonso went to work on the brutal lashes, his motions quick, gentle, sure. How many wounds like this had the two of them seen since the invasion? Paco stayed and watched, helpless but unwilling to leave. As he waited by Santiago's side afterward, he reviewed everything he'd done that had brought this about. Every thought. Every action. Every mistake. It seemed as if everything he'd done had been a mistake.

It was afternoon when Santiago stirred and let out a soft groan. "Paco?"

"Here. Drink some water." It was awkward, trying to hold his head while disturbing his back as little as possible, but at last Santiago lay back down with a trembling sigh.

"Shall I ask Dr. Lee for more medicine?" Paco asked.

"Wait." Santiago groped for his wrist. Paco braced for questions. He owed Santiago that much. "Who...were you trying to protect? Who attacked you?"

"Nobody."

Santiago didn't accept that. "Was it one of us, or one of you?"

Paco owed him the truth, but how much truth? Santiago had courageously gone along with Paco's story, though he had to have known what was coming. But if Paco made up some tale — threw in some random name — would Santiago feel obliged to report it to the king? Paco looked down at Santiago's feverish face and resolved to protect him from his own honesty. In Voske's world, honesty could get you killed.

"I can't tell you," Paco said at last. And let Santiago

come to whatever conclusions made sense to him.

Santiago let out a long sigh and closed his eyes.

Dr. Lee returned and examined him, then turned to Paco. "Let him sleep. You come eat. Meredith brought over some tamales from Luc's. And I want to look at that knife wound on your arm." His voice flattened on the words 'knife wound.'

Everything Paco had fiercely suppressed hit him at once: gnawing hunger, thirst, the throb in his head timed with the throb in his arm. It hurt as badly as it had after he'd teleported. The hastily applied bandage might as well have been glued on. Dr. Lee had to soak it off.

Paco's breath hissed between his teeth as Dr. Lee cleaned the wound and applied a fresh bandage. The whole time, he thought of Santiago lying on his stomach with his back laid open. Paco only had one cut. Santiago had ten.

"Drink this." Dr. Lee put a cup in his hand.

Paco recognized the sharp smell of willow bark tea, and gratefully gulped it down. It was bitter and made his mouth feel dry, but it would dampen the pain. The doctor led him into the kitchen. Becky was sitting at the table, her eyes wide. It was a stiflingly hot night, but Dr. Lee closed all the windows.

Then he sat down across from Paco. "Now talk."

·21·
FELICITÉ

CATALINA

FELICITÉ MET THREE OF Isais's friends outside the palace.

"Noelle! Like my wing rings?" Paloma twirled, her wings snapping out. The iridescent membranes gleamed in the sun, and four little silver bells rang. When they'd first met, Paloma had said with a smile that her wings were useless for anything but being pretty, but they were a great way to wear extra earrings.

"I love them. Your dress, too," Felicité said. Paloma's dress of floating blue gauze made her look like she really was light enough to fly. She was beautiful, with her shimmering wings and long black hair like Sujata's. Her personality was a little like Sujata's, too, before Voske had first attacked Las Anclas.

Felicité steered her thoughts away from that and turned to Shobha, who wouldn't call attention to herself. "And you look gorgeous, too."

Shobha smiled but didn't reply. She reminded Felicité a little bit of Becky. But Shobha was quiet because she was self-contained, not because she was scared.

"Crimson is your color," Felicité said. "Come on. Twirl!"

Shobha twirled, sending her flame-colored skirt flaring around her slim hips.

Paloma clapped. "Now, that is a dancing dress. Too bad we aren't the ones dancing tonight—oops!"

"Oops?" Felicité asked. "Are we watching a dance?"

Nicolas grinned, reminding her of—

She halted that train of thought. Nicolas wasn't like

Julio Wolfe or Carlos Garcia or anyone in Las Anclas. He was only himself, a Catalina boy with a sly sense of humor and a set of extra joints in his fingers.

"Not telling," said Nicolas. "But we're positive you'll like it."

Felicité smiled at them all, certain that she would. They weren't just Isais's friends, they'd become her friends, too. As Isais had promised, no one had asked awkward questions. They didn't care about her past. It was so *freeing*. The past was the past. She was Noelle. Every day got easier.

Paloma tapped Shobha on the shoulder. "Time to make me even prettier."

"If I do it now, it'll wear off by the time we arrive," Shobha pointed out.

Paloma shrugged. "Then you'll do it again!"

"Okay." Shobha lifted her hand. "What color do you want?"

Paloma turned to Felicité. "I love your color sense, Noelle. What do you think?"

Felicité glanced at Shobha. "Can you do iridescent, to match her wings?"

Shobha traced her fingers over Paloma's hair, leaving streaks of iridescent color that glowed like jellyfish. "What about you, Noelle?"

Felicité wrinkled her nose. Putting colored streaks in her hair would only call attention to the last traces of old dye. "It would be a waste. Is there anyone in Catalina who can dye hair? I could pay in work, since I don't have anything for trade."

"It's free while you're a guest of the palace," Paloma said. "So, you'd better get it done before you find a permanent place to stay."

"We'll take you to Camille," Shobha said softly. "She's the best."

Nicolas took Shobha's arm. "Let's go. You can do my hair when we get there."

Felicité linked arms with Paloma as they walked. She hadn't had this kind of lighthearted outing with friends since she was twelve. After she'd Changed, she'd had to watch every word she spoke and be wary of every activity. She'd always had to have an excuse ready when Sujata wanted to go swimming, or Nasreen invited her to enjoy the hot spring behind the Hassans' house.

She'd never have to worry about that again.

She only wished Wu Zetian was with her, frisking at her heels. Felicité was sure Will was taking good care of her, but she missed her beautiful golden rat.

They came to a bowl-shaped meadow bright with wildflowers, with a view of the ocean. It was full of people sitting on the slopes on blankets and folding chairs, facing down into the center. As she surveyed the crowd, her gaze snagged on a familiar profile. Did she know that middle-aged woman with a pair of little girls? Felicité's gaze traveled down the woman's arms, outstretched to rest on each little girl's shoulder, and her nerves chilled when she saw those lizard-like claws.

The woman's head turned, and Felicité saw her face. *Nanny Shelley?* Felicité ducked back a step, so Paloma hid the woman from view. She had to get away, to hide. What if Nanny Shelley recognized *her?*

"Noelle? Are you okay?" Paloma slowed down to give Felicité a look of concern.

Wild excuses streamed through Felicité's mind — the excuses she used to make if it unexpectedly began to rain — and then she caught herself. She was Noelle. And she was eighteen years old. She was no longer the chubby-cheeked eight-year-old who'd hugged her nanny around the waist. There was no way that Nanny — that *Shelley* — would recognize her. Especially with her mask of bronze scales.

Felicité was not going to cower in fear any longer. She stepped out from behind Paloma's wings and looked straight at Shelley. With a smile, Felicité said, "I'm fine."

Paloma followed her gaze. "You see that woman with the two girls? That's Shelley Stolz. She's kind of a hero to us."

Nicolas spoke up. "Ten years ago, we had a drought. It was so bad, we sent a delegation to that pack of bigots across the ocean to ask for help."

Felicité knew the alarm she felt was showing on her face — but that was fine. It was appropriate for a refugee from Norm prejudice.

Paloma took up the story. "Las Anclas is disgusting!

It makes me so mad that the town closest to us is the worst town on the coast!"

"Except for Gold Point," remarked Nicolas.

"Gold Point is inland," Paloma retorted. "It doesn't count."

Felicité could barely hear them, she was trying so hard to not reveal anything that might give her away. She made what she hoped was a noncommittal sound.

Paloma went on, "Las Anclas kicked out our delegation! They didn't even give them a glass of water! Shelley lived in Las Anclas then. She'd Changed a few months before, when she was pregnant, and she got fired from her job for it. Can you imagine? When she saw what her own town did to us, she realized she'd rather die of thirst with us than stay with those bigots in Las Anclas. She took her entire family and moved here."

"That girl on the left is the baby she was carrying," said Shobha. "She gave up everything so she and her baby could have a better life."

Everyone was looking at Felicité as if she was supposed to say something. The only thing she could think of was, "And the other girl? Did she have twins?"

"Oh, no, the other one is her charge," Nicolas said. "She's a nanny."

Felicité had never been so relieved in her life when Isais hurried up, carrying two giant picnic baskets. "Sorry I'm late. I promised I'd help with the costumes. You look beautiful, Noelle. And you, too, Paloma. Shobha."

"And what about me?" Nicolas fluttered his eyelashes.

Cheerfully, Isais said, "You too."

Felicité only partly heard the banter. Her mind had caught on the word *costumes*. For a dance. Right? For a dance?

Paloma spread out a blanket and plopped down on it. "Sit by me! It's the best view of the ocean *and* the stage."

"The stage?" Felicité echoed. "For the dance? Or is it a concert?"

"Surprise!" Isais said. "We're seeing a play!"

A sickening wave of horror washed over her. A play. That meant the Catalina Players. They'd recognize her for sure, even with her Change. She could see Grandma Wu now, pointing dramatically from the stage, while her trained voice called out, "That's Felicité Wolfe, Tom Preston's daughter, the traitor from the bigoted town of Las Anclas! Cast her out before she brings ruin on us all, like she did to her own town!"

That would be the end of her romance with Isais—the end of her friendship with Paloma and Shobha and Nicolas—the end of Noelle—the end of her chance to have a new life as a new person. She'd been such a fool to imagine she could start anew, after what she'd done.

"Noelle?" Isais was saying. "Noelle, are you feeling ill? Is it the heat?"

Ill! Yes, that was her chance! She could have him carry her back to the palace with her face buried in his shoulder. Then she saw a group of people in costumes walking to the stage. They weren't the Catalina Players. She'd never seen any of them before.

She shook her head. "I was just wondering what we're seeing. A…play, did you say? What's that?"

They eagerly began to explain it to her. She listened, smiling and nodding, until Nicolas said, "We have a theatre troupe called the Catalina Players, who travel from town to town. They *only* do theatre—it's their job. But other people put on plays for fun, for each other. The group that's doing the play practices in secret, then puts it on for us. I have no idea what this one is even about."

"If you enjoy it, we can see the Catalina Players later," Isais said. "They're gone now, up north somewhere. Won't be back for months."

"Oh, let me know when they come back," Felicité said, immensely relieved. She'd find a way to be gone.

She smiled at them all. "I'm so excited to see the play!"

·22·

PACO

LAS ANCLAS

PACO SQUARED OFF WITH an elite guard. While Santiago recovered, Paco had been forced to spend his time with Voske's honor guard. That included training—and today, sparring. It was so strange to be on the old Ranger grounds, sparring like he used to spar with the Rangers, but with enemies.

He glared at the big guy. *Let's see how good your training is.*

"Go," shouted the commander.

Paco feinted to the left, then leaped. He easily brushed aside the block his enemy flung up, whirling in with a hard punch to the man's unprotected face. But instead of side-stepping or blocking, his enemy skidded backward, his expression tight and worried. What a coward!

Then Paco remembered that Santiago had been *flogged* for accidentally hurting Paco—in a supposed sparring match. No wonder this soldier didn't dare fight him! Paco skidded to a halt, pulling his punch. While everyone else continued to fight hard, trusting in each other not to do any real harm, Paco and his opponent stood still.

"Go on," said the commander. "I haven't called a halt yet."

Gritting his teeth, Paco threw a slow punch at his opponent, which was blocked with equal care. They resumed the match at half speed, as if they were both giving a lesson to a young, inexperienced fighter. Paco felt like a fool, and he was sure his opponent did, too. Paco had never hated a training session that much in his entire life. When the commander finally called a halt, he turned away in relief.

Santiago approached, back in uniform, but moving stiffly. Guilt surged in Paco. But Santiago showed no trace of anger, or even bitterness or resentment. It was as if he didn't feel that anything of importance had happened. That was life under Voske's rule. It was normal to be punished for someone else's deed.

Santiago said, "We're to report to the king."

"You're dismissed," said the commander. It was hard to tell from such a flat tone, but Paco was sure the man was as glad to see him going as he was to be gone.

When they were out of earshot, Paco said, "I'm sorry. I had no idea that would happen."

Santiago gave him a searching glance. "You still won't tell me who attacked you?"

Paco hated to lie to Santiago, especially after Santiago had taken such a big fall for him. Finally, he said, "I'm sorry I used you as my excuse."

"It doesn't matter," Santiago said with a slight shrug. "I was supposed to keep you safe. As soon as I saw the bandage, I knew what was coming."

Paco was unsurprised when Santiago followed him into his room on Singles Row. He'd probably sleep curled up on Paco's floor from now on, and Paco had no one to blame but himself.

Santiago stood looking at the statuette as Paco changed from fatigues to the royal clothes. "Where did you get this? It looks like an artifact."

"It's not mine. I'm just keeping it for someone."

Santiago had reached out to touch it but pulled his hand back when Paco said that. "Who?"

Before the flogging, Paco would have said it was none of his business. But he owed Santiago. He looked down at the graceful statue of the dancer and could almost see Yuki's strong and graceful hands holding it. Paco had never felt so lonely in his life. "My boyfriend—my ex-boyfriend—Yuki Nakamura."

"Is he still here?" Santiago asked.

If Yuki had been in town Paco would never have

mentioned him at all. But Yuki was safe from Voske, far away. "No. He's a prospector."

Santiago's face, so easy to read, revealed regret. Or was it loneliness? "I guess you haven't heard from him since he left, huh?"

Paco didn't reply. How could he hear from Yuki?

Santiago went on, "But he's safe wherever he is, right?"

Another absurd question. How could Paco possibly know that? Then it occurred to him that Santiago might not really be talking about Yuki. He remembered Dr. Lee explaining about cold reading and was unable to resist another try.

"It's hard to worry about someone who's far away." Watching Santiago closely, Paco added, "Someone you love, who might be in danger. It makes you feel so helpless."

Santiago whirled around and slammed his fists against the doorframe. "Every night," he said to the door two inches from his nose. "Every night I dread hearing a report that she's been found. Ever since she left, I lie awake at night thinking I should have gone with her. But Maria-Elena is our hostage. She's only six—seven now. I couldn't risk it. And now Kerry's out there somewhere, all alone."

"She's not alone," Paco said slowly, thinking. Santiago didn't know Jennie or Mia. "Ross is with her."

Santiago turned around, laughing bitterly. "Oh, right. Ross."

"With both his girlfriends," Paco added. "And his sister."

"Ross has *two* girlfriends? And a sister? He said his family was dead..." Santiago's eyes widened with alarm. "Please don't tell the king I—"

Paco said deliberately, "I would die before I told Voske anything."

Santiago dropped onto Paco's bed as if all the strength had gone out of him. "How is she? Is she happy here? Does she talk about me?"

"I don't know." Those were such intimate questions, about a person he'd avoided as much as possible.

Impatiently, Santiago said, "You must know. You're

her brother."

If anyone else had said that, Paco would have instantly denied it. But Santiago loved Kerry. It was strange, now that he thought about it: conniving Kerry and straightforward Santiago. What did they see in each other?

Or maybe there was a lot to Kerry that Paco had never seen. "I think she was happy. She loves her horses. Her best friend is Mia Lee, but she has others. There's this whole group of girls she hangs out with. I'd tell you more if I knew more, but the truth is, we're not close."

Santiago gave a gloomy sigh. "Let's go, then. We can't be late."

Paco stood up, trying harder for what he knew about Kerry. "Did you see the rat she had with her when she came back to Gold Point?"

"Yeah! Does she still have it?"

"No, that was Yuki's rat. Kerry just borrowed her. But she has her own rat now, a little brown thing named Whisper. I think—" Paco corrected himself; he was on sure ground now. "I know she really loves him. And he's with her."

"Oh. Good." With his hand on the doorknob, Santiago whispered, "Please. Tell me more about her later."

At Wolfe House, he found Voske at the dining table. "Liam, we'll discuss your orders for the day over breakfast. Santiago, report back in an hour."

Santiago saluted sharply and left. Paco wondered why Santiago couldn't stay and eat, then realized it was another lesson on power. Just like the golden plates were a lesson on how power leads to wealth.

"Help yourself," Voske said.

Paco normally would have loved a breakfast of crispy bacon, eggs scrambled with chorizo, tortillas, toast, and three kinds of jam. But not with Voske.

Will Preston burst into the dining room, then skidded to an alarmed halt. Voske flicked him an irritated glance. "William, you should be at school."

"I had to clean Wu Zetian's house. It smelled. Felicité…" Will gulped down tears. "She ditched Wu Zetian! Trainer Crow says when animals depend on you,

you can never let them down. *I* won't let Wu Zetian down."

Voske said, his voice softening, "I like to see you taking responsibility, William. That's what a prince does. Go to the kitchen. They'll make you a burrito to eat on the way. Tell your teacher I gave you permission to be late."

Will flashed a big smile before he left, obviously as thrilled at Voske's approval as he was relieved not to be in trouble.

"That's what a prince does." Paco was so filled with loathing that it turned his stomach.

Voske picked up his fork as if nothing had happened. "How did training go?"

"Fine."

Voske looked askance. "I'd have thought you'd prefer a real challenge."

Paco gritted his teeth. Someone had obviously reported that joke of a sparring match.

"It won't happen again. The commander will talk to them." Voske smiled. "I imagine you'll enjoy getting a chance to really fight again."

"I won't enjoy it when they get flogged for landing a hit on me!"

Voske smiled slightly. "They won't. I didn't order your match with Santiago. That's the difference."

Paco was filled with such blinding rage that he was strongly tempted to try stabbing Voske in the throat with his blunted fork. His mother had always said that if you put enough force into it, any hard object could be a weapon...

A clamor of voices arose outside. Voske was at the window in an instant. It was always shocking how fast he could move. He was quicker than anyone Paco had ever known, other than Sheriff Crow and *maybe* Ross. He was certainly far faster than Paco. It was a depressing reminder of how pointless it would be to try to jump him, even if Paco was willing to throw his life away in the effort.

Voske turned to Paco with the cold smile that always promised violence. "Come along. This will be interesting."

Paco was certain that wouldn't be the right word for whatever fresh horror awaited. But he followed Voske to

Main Street, where soldiers were bringing in several horses and a burro. Paco's throat closed when he saw the sweat-streaked golden stallion and the silver mare. Those were Nugget and Sally, Kerry's horses. And Ross's burro, Rusty. The buckskin gelding Sidewinder. Paco's own favorite horse, the red gelding Fuego. And gentle Buttermilk, a mare Mia liked to ride. The patrol had brought in all the horses that Jennie's party had taken.

Had Jennie and her party been captured? Killed?

None of the horses wore any tack, other than makeshift leads on all but the royal horses. Kerry's horses had been herded rather than led in. Both plunged and kicked when anyone got near them. When a soldier tried to grab Nugget's mane, the golden stallion reared, striking out with his front hooves. The man threw himself aside.

A soldier ran up to Voske and saluted. Like the rest of them, he was muddy and looked exhausted. "Sir, we've been tracking these horses for over a week. We finally caught up with them at the eastern edge of the crystal forest." His voice cracked on "crystal," and he shuddered.

Paco inwardly exulted. Jennie and her group were still free.

Voske's voice was cold and sharp as shattered ice. "Those are royal horses. Where is my daughter?"

There was a long silence, then the leader nervously saluted again. "Sir, we ventured as close as we dared to the singing trees. Fermor there nearly got nailed by crystal shards." He pointed to another man, who saluted with a shaking hand. "There was a little grove of black crystal trees with the remains of Gold Point issue packs beneath them. I think one was Axel's—he's the only one who wears a shirt that big. And I saw some sugar skulls. Maria-Pilar likes to snack on those."

Paco exulted even more fiercely. Ross must have led Voske's assassins straight into the crystal forest. Good riddance!

Voske's smile was gone. "Post more sentries around the crystal forest. Have them stay out of sight. We want the targets to think it's safe to leave." To the other guards, he said, "Put the royal horses in my stable." To Paco, he said, "Come with me."

Paco's gnawing tension spiked as they returned to

the house. He could *feel* Voske's cold fury. But there was no sign of it in his face. "This is an exercise in leadership. You must always think ahead. Ross Juarez escaped my scouts. What do you think he'll do next?"

"He's long gone," said Paco, hoping it was true. "Those horses could have been living on winter grasses for weeks. I think he walked straight through the ruined city and out on the other side."

"Convenient," Voske remarked. "If they did do that, where did they go?"

Paco wondered that himself. He wanted to believe it was true, but it seemed more likely that they were still in the ruined city. There was no way for them to know Las Anclas had been invaded. And if they were in the ruined city, they'd undoubtedly leave soon, if they hadn't already.

"Back the way they came, I guess." Paco shrugged. "North."

Voske gave him a sharp look. "And why would they do that?"

"I can't think why they'd want to stay in the ruined city. It's full of giant bees."

They stared at each other, neither willing to give an inch. Then Voske smiled slightly. "Go back to your room. I'll send Santiago to you when he returns."

Paco had to warn Ross and the others before the sentries reached the forest. And he had very little time to do it.

He hurried back to his room and changed into old work clothes and a battered old pair of shoes. He'd have to teleport in jumps of five hundred yards or less, without being seen, until he got to the crystal forest itself. Since he didn't know its exact size, he'd have to take his best guess. Paco shuddered involuntarily, remembering the dying screams of a coyote that had wandered too close to a tree. He'd rather risk getting a limb amputated cleanly by his own teleportation than be eaten alive from within.

He planned out his route, then began. He pictured the greenhouse and longed for Dr. Lee's kindness. And he was there.

He pictured Ross's room, the only part of the surgery that was likely to be empty. He'd helped Mia and Jennie install its glass ceiling, in those terrible days after his mother's death, and had felt some comfort in the concentration required and the knowledge that he was doing some good. Paco longed to be doing good again. And he was there.

The next part was tricky. He couldn't go to the school, which was occupied. There were homes near it, but he wasn't close to anyone who lived in them. There was nothing he could long for there.

But beyond the houses, there was an orchard. As a little boy, he'd been sent with other children to pick apples. In those days the orchard had seemed like a great forest. They'd run through the orchard, chasing each other and climbing the trees and filling their baskets in between games. Mom had picked him up, congratulated him on how many he'd picked, and promised him they'd eat pie made from his own apples. He longed for his mother, so hard that it made his heart hurt. And he was there.

The next jump was outside the gates, into the fields where he and Yuki had ridden patrols. There was a spot on a ridge where they had shared lunch and kisses. He longed for Yuki. And he was there.

Every jump after that was into the desert that symbolized Yuki to him. He looked for landmarks—a twisted cactus that Yuki would love to examine, a towering boulder Yuki would enjoy climbing, a patch of shade that would be perfect to sit in and kiss—and he was there.

He paused atop a low hill dotted with hexagon cactuses. The crystal forest was a sparkling line on the horizon. It was the first time he'd ever been alone in the desert. Standing under the vast blue sky, he shivered. Strange. He should feel better now that he'd finally escaped Voske and his spies. Instead, he felt cold and uneasy, though the sun was shining bright.

About five hundred yards away, he saw a gully with a little stream running through it and a black oak growing on the bank. Paco pictured Yuki sitting beneath it with Kogatana curled up in his lap, and teleported.

He fell hard against the trunk and grabbed it to stop himself from hitting the ground. He was shaking with chill, his fingers almost too numb to feel the bark. It was hard to catch his breath, as if he'd been training for hours.

Paco had never been bothered by teleporting before, but he'd also never teleported more than twice in one day. He'd probably worn himself out.

And he hadn't even gotten into the crystal forest yet.

He decided to take a brief rest first. Paco lay down in the warm sand, trying to soak up as much heat as possible. As the deep chill slowly faded, he wondered why he'd gotten so cold. It was a typical day for early March, warm in the sunshine. Tired, he understood. But too much training normally made you overheat. He felt as if he'd been swimming too long in wintry seawater.

Why *did* parts of his clothing—and parts of his body—vanish if he teleported too far? He didn't feel himself going anywhere but his destination. So where did the missing parts go? Some cold place that he was in for too short a time to see?

He forced himself to his feet and faced the crystal trees. Now he couldn't plan how far he'd go. He had no idea how far to go or what the destination looked like. He'd never before attempted to teleport to a place he'd never seen.

He thought about the people he was trying to find. Summer, he didn't know. He liked and trusted both Ross and Mia, but not enough to *long* for them. Jennie, though, was a close friend and a strong shoulder to lean on. There was nothing he needed more than that. He could easily long for Jennie's friendship.

Kerry was there, too. Once she'd symbolized Voske to him. Every time he'd seen her, he'd thought of his mother's death, and he'd hated her for it. But that hatred was gone now. Since the invasion, he'd begun to understand what she'd had to deal with growing up, and the courage it had taken to break away from Voske. Longing welled up in him to have a conversation with his sister, and this time do it right.

There was a shout. Something struck him, and he fell to his hands and knees. They were too numb to hurt.

A bewildering onslaught of colors, sounds, and smells assailed him. He couldn't make sense of any of it.

"Hey!" a shrill voice rose. "Who's—"

Jennie's familiar voice exclaimed, *"Paco?"*

"Paco!" Mia shrieked. "Behind you!"

He looked over his shoulder and flung himself away from a glutinous column the size of a man, translucent and glistening like a slug trail. Within its body floated countless skeletons of small animals.

Ross yelled, "Paco, duck!"

He flung himself flat. Something shattered over his head. A man's voice he didn't recognize exclaimed, "Prince Liam?"

Paco turned violently. The two team leaders Voske had sent after Ross and Kerry were right there, inside the ruined city, their uniforms in tatters.

The woman asked, "Prince Liam, did you bring reinforcements?"

Paco's fury and confusion surged up. "My name is Paco!"

A knife flew through the air, straight for Loretta's heart. She vanished, and a shadow flickered away from where she had been. Axel raised his hands, and white daggers of ice hurtled toward Jennie and Ross. Paco snatched the knife from the ground and lunged at Axel. He caught an instant of astonishment on the enemy's face before the big man blocked him with a shield of ice. At last Paco could let loose his pent-up fury. Axel staggered back from his onslaught, then snarled and raised his hands.

Loretta screamed, "Axel, no! We can't hurt him! He's the prince!"

Paco pressed his attack, but Axel bolted away. He disappeared into a forest of enormous mushrooms, followed by a flitting shadow. A coyote-sized mushroom near Jennie vanished, replaced by a teenage girl in tattered black fatigues. She dashed after Axel and Loretta.

"Hey, how—" Summer began.

Jennie held up her hand. "Wait. Can you go up in the trees and guard us?"

"You bet! I can listen from there, too." Summer leaped onto a mushroom cap as big as a bed, then floated up into a tree. She called down, "They took off! Can't see them anywhere. I'll keep watch."

The excitement of the fight melted away, leaving Paco cold and exhausted. He sat down on the ground before he could fall over.

"Wait, wait," squeaked Mia. "There might be skittery — well, too late now."

"Are you all right?" Jennie asked.

Paco nodded. "Just tired."

The others sat down, too, Mia carefully inspecting the ground first. They were all dirty and ragged, scratched and bruised. Ross had such dark shadows under his eyes, he looked like he'd been repeatedly punched in the face. Jennie favored one leg. Mia had several painful-looking bug bites. Kerry's hair was tangled and full of leaves. And though Summer was keeping a lookout, none of them let go of their weapons. Every so often, they all scanned the area.

Kerry's little brown rat scampered up, and she scooped him up and cuddled him. Paco thought of Yuki cuddling Kogatana, and his heart twisted.

They all looked at Paco, different faces with the same expression. It was one he'd come to recognize, and wished he hadn't. They had a question they'd already guessed the answer to but were putting off asking because knowing for sure would be unbearable. Probably Voske's soldiers had taunted them about the invasion.

Paco wouldn't prolong the agony. Flatly, he said, "Voske took over Las Anclas."

Then he had to watch their reaction to him taking away their last, forlorn hope.

"Is Santiago...?" Kerry began, then broke off.

Paco had first met her when she was a prisoner who'd known she'd probably be executed, and he'd seen her fight for her life. But he'd never seen anything like the teeth-gritted terror on her face now. Quickly, he said, "He's fine. I mean —" He too broke off, thinking of the flogging.

"I understand," said Kerry, looking immensely relieved.

"Your horses are fine, too," Paco added. "They showed up today without any tack. Sidewinder and Buttermilk and Fuego as well. And your burro, Ross."

Ross actually smiled at that.

"How in the world did you get here, Paco?" Jennie asked.

"I teleported," he said. "I Changed."

Mia began to say, "But aren't you too old?" and Summer called down, "Have you been keeping it a secret? Like—"

"No." Paco knew he had to explain, but the words choked him. He looked at Kerry and saw that she knew.

"Opportunity Day," she said. It wasn't a question.

Paco nodded. A long, terrible silence fell.

Mia stirred uneasily, and Jennie said, "Let's talk when we're out of here. Paco, can you take us all? Maybe one at a time?"

"I can't take anyone out. I can't even carry anything with me. If I go too far, I lose parts of my clothes. Parts of *me*." He looked down and was unsurprised to see half his pant leg gone and a gash in his calf. Wearily, he thought, *Now I'll have to explain that.*

Jennie and Kerry wore twin expressions of horror. Mia's glasses twinkled as she bent in to examine the gash. "Even Dad's best scalpel doesn't cut that clean. Do you know why…?"

Paco shook his head. He should have been glad they were all alive and more-or-less well—he *was* glad—but he also felt cold and sick and exhausted. And he had to recount all the grotesque details of the invasion and watch their faces when the news hit them. It was yet another unbearable thing that he nonetheless had to bear.

Maybe he could at least delay it. "I can't stay long. I have to get back before Voske notices I'm gone. I came to warn you that Voske has sentries watching the crystal forest, with more on the way. You'll have to be careful when you leave. It would be better if you go now, before the rest arrive."

As soon as he said that, he realized that it didn't matter if Voske noticed that he was gone. He could go with them. They had weapons and food and water, and Ross knew the desert. They could go in search of Mr. Preston and the other Rangers, and—

"We can't leave." Ross was staring at the ground. Mia took his hand and Jennie put her arm around him, but that only made him look guilty as well as miserable. "I lost my power."

His words hit Paco like a punch to the gut. "What do you mean? Permanently?"

"No!" Summer declared from above. "He wore himself out saving our lives. He just needs to rest. But we can't, because those Voske creeps keep trying to kill us!"

Mia spoke more to Ross than Paco as she said, "His power *will* come back. He's lost it before when he overused it."

"For a few days." Ross sounded miserable. "It's been a lot longer than that now. I think it might really be gone."

"How long have you been here?" Paco asked.

"About two weeks," said Jennie. "Ross found us a fantastic hiding space."

"It even had preserved, edible food," Mia put in excitedly. "*Ancient* food!"

Kerry glanced at Paco over Mia's head and made a face that suggested that it had tasted ancient, too. Paco tried to convey his silent commiseration. For that instant, they shared their amusement.

"Edible might be stretching it," Jennie said dryly.

"Mia thought it was an underground shop. It was very well-hidden," said Kerry. "Unfortunately, Axel's team found it a couple days ago. We've been chasing each other around the ruined city ever since."

Paco had been distracted by the news about Ross's power and the specter of centuries-old food. He wasn't prepared when Jennie asked abruptly, "When did they take the town?"

"A month ago." It seemed impossible that it had only been a month. It felt like an eternity.

Mia's eyes gleamed with tears behind her greasy glasses. "My father?"

"He's fine," Paco hastened to say. "All your family is fine. Jennie, yours too."

"Thanks. But this is Voske," Jennie spoke in a dull, flat voice. He could tell she was bracing for the worst. "Everyone isn't fine. Who died?"

"Grandpa Choi. Ken Thomas. Magali Rios. They were on sentry duty, and they refused to surrender." Then he uttered the words he knew would hurt the most. "And all the Rangers who were still in town. Except for me."

Just as Paco had dreaded, he had to watch the news hit her. He thought he might have looked like that the night his mother died. Jennie scanned the forest again, but it was like Becky endlessly rearranging medicine bottles. Paco wondered how much she really saw. "And the other team of Rangers, with Mr. Preston?"

"They're still away," Paco said swiftly. "Voske hasn't found them. I'd know."

Jennie's shoulders slumped with relief, but then she said, "Who else?"

Paco cleared his throat. "Mr. Horst and Tommy's Aunt Paula, the Willet brothers, and Grandma Thakrar's brewing assistant. They tried to fight back, and Voske had them all executed. He had Grandma Callahan shot, just for shouting at him."

As he recited the details, he relived the same shock and horror he'd felt as he'd watched the axe come down. He stopped, unable to bring himself to tell them about Felicité, too.

In a hard voice, Jennie said, "That's not all. Is it?"

"No." Paco felt like he was in a never-ending nightmare. "Felicité. She killed herself."

Mia gasped, recoiling. Even Kerry looked upset. Paco suspected that none of them liked Felicité any more than he did, but no one wanted to hear that.

Giving the news in bits was as excruciating for them as it was for him, he could see that now. He hurried on, "Voske moved into Wolfe House and threw her out. And I think she felt guilty, too."

"Guilty about what?" Mia asked.

"Voske's soldiers came in through a tunnel. It was a secret, but Felicité knew about it. She told Henry before he was exiled, and Henry told Voske. Henry came back to town with the conquerors. Wearing their uniform and everything."

Mia and Ross glanced at each other, and Paco wondered if they'd known about the tunnel too. If they had, it had been a secret they'd kept.

Jennie wiped her eyes, drew in a shaky breath, and lifted her chin. "How did Felicité kill herself? Did anyone see her body?"

"No. Henry said he saw her throw herself into the well at Wolfe House."

"So, the only witness was Henry?" Jennie asked.

"Do you think he lied?" Paco asked.

"Of course," Kerry said. "I expect Voske ordered him to say it was suicide."

Jennie wiped her eyes again. "I just don't see Felicité killing herself."

"No. No way." Mia sounded more angry than sad. "Voske murdered her."

"It'd be just like him," said Summer from the tree. She, too, sounded angry.

Paco wouldn't put it past Voske, but Felicité's suicide had been more shocking than surprising to him. He'd seen her sneaking around with her head down, and how everybody glared at her with contempt or pity.

Ross said quietly, "I don't know. It's hard to understand unless you've been there. But I lived in Gold Point. Felicité was living under Voske, too. We don't know what he could have done to her." His fingers drifted up to his throat, tracing the handprint scars.

Paco's stomach clenched. Mia began crying soundlessly.

"I have to go," Paco said. "I've already been here too long."

Mia scrubbed tears from her face. "Paco, will you talk to my dad about Ross? Ask him if he has any ideas."

"I will," Paco promised. "I'll come back when I can."

Kerry touched his arm. "Be careful. I know what it's like."

There was a time when he would have shouted that she didn't know anything about him. But now he understood that she, more than anyone, really did know. "I'll try."

Paco pictured the gully with the stream and the oak, imagined Yuki leaning against the tree, and longed for him.

He collided with something and fell down. He tried to get to his feet but fell back into a shallow stream. His hands and feet were like blocks of ice.

A boy about his own age pulled him out of the water. Paco was astonished to see yet another version of his own face. This boy had darker skin and a broader chest and wore his hair in cornrows. But there was that sharp chin, those prominent cheekbones, those slanted eyebrows.

The boy stared back at him, his mouth open. "You

must be Paco."

"You must be the invisible son. Um..." Paco's brain felt as frozen as his fingers and toes.

"Sean." Sean flashed a friendly grin utterly unlike Voske's, then sobered. "I didn't know you could teleport. I saw the teams chasing Kerry and her friends into the ruined city. I've been waiting to see if they come out. Do you know if she's all right?"

Paco's thoughts began to return to their usual speed, and he recalled Kerry saying, *"Sean ran away. Just like me. He would never spy for our father—uh, for the king."*

"She's fine," Paco said. "But she can't get out."

Sean blew out an exasperated breath. "I'm always too late! I was too far away to help her, but close enough to hear when the trees killed the team chasing them." He shuddered. "Axel deserved it, but I feel terrible about Maria-Pilar."

"Axel made it into the ruined city, unfortunately. Plus, Loretta and some teenage girl who can make herself look like a giant mushroom."

Sean's expression eased. "That's Maria-Pilar! Oh, I'm so glad."

Paco had begun to shiver again. He didn't care about some random Voske soldier that Sean happened to like. "There's a company on the way to watch the crystal forest. I don't want to run into them, and I have to get back before anyone realizes I'm gone. Santiago is probably banging on my door right now."

"You know Santiago!" Sean exclaimed. "Maria-Pilar is his cousin. He's an old friend of mine. And he'd do anything for Kerry. You need to get him on your side."

"I know he loves Kerry. But Voske's holding his family hostage." Paco thought about Santiago's awful dilemma, with the girl he loved on one side and his little cousin on the other. What would Paco have done if Voske had held his mother hostage, while searching for Yuki to have him executed? Paco turned away from that impossible choice and looked for a third option. "Why don't *you* help us? You want to save Kerry, right?"

Sean flexed his hands, his expression troubled. "Yeah. But I'm not actually invisible. I can go unnoticed, but not if people look for me. And my father looks for me all the time."

"If you came inside, I could tell you where Voske will be," Paco promised. "There're places you could hide, where he'd never go. You think Santiago is the person we need. I think you're the person we need."

Sean gazed out at the crystal forest, obviously torn. Then he, too, chose not to choose. "You'd better go back. If they realize you're missing, they won't hurt *you*."

"They'll hurt Santiago. I know." Paco longed to run away, but he owed Santiago, and he had to report to the Rats. At least now he knew he *could* leave. "If you decide to help us, meet me at the cave on the beach, by the breakwater."

Sean looked hopeful. "Will you bring Santiago?"

"I can't teleport another person. It'd probably kill us both."

Sean grimaced. "All right. If he's willing, I'll bring him."

Paco was astonished. "You can make other people invisible?"

"*Unnoticed*. But yes. I don't spread it around."

"Then come tonight, after moonrise."

Paco teleported back, taking the same route in reverse, forcing himself to focus. Every jump was harder and left him colder and more exhausted than the last. Spinning shards of ice seemed to flicker around him, brighter and colder with each succeeding jump. When he reached Ross's room, he fought an almost overwhelming urge to collapse into the bed. But he couldn't implicate Dr. Lee if he was discovered there.

Paco longed desperately, miserably for his own bed—and slammed onto it, shivering convulsively. His eyes burned. With numb, shaking fingers he rubbed his eyes, and discovered ice crystals clinging to his eyelashes. He rolled off his bed to the floor, then noticed new stabs of pain.

He had two more cuts, one over his ribs and another in his leg. There was blood all over his shirt and what remained of his pants.

The cold made his blood sluggish. He had to force himself to rip up his ruined shirt for bandages, then shove the pant remnants into a pair of old boots at the back of his closet. He had so much to hide, it felt impossible to keep up with it all. And now Axel, Loretta, and Maria-Pilar knew that he could teleport. If they got out of the ruined city, they'd tell Voske.

But he couldn't give up yet, much as he longed to. He was clumsily buttoning a fresh shirt with still-cold fingers when someone banged on his door.

"Paco? Are you in there?" Santiago shouted. He sounded alarmed.

"Yeah."

The door burst open. "Where were you?" Santiago demanded, uncharacteristic irritation in his open face. Irritation and worry. And then confusion. "What's wrong?"

Paco had no idea what he looked like, but he had to go with it. "I'm sick. I woke up feeling lousy, but I didn't want to say anything. Voske..."

"Yeah, no one wants to look weak in front of the king. But where were you? I came here earlier, but you weren't here."

"I tried to go to the doc's," Paco said, hating how lies had to multiply and multiply. "But I got dizzy. I sat down for a while in someone's garden. Then I came back here. I was about to go to bed."

"Uh-huh." In a movement too quick for Paco to block, Santiago yanked his shirt up, revealing the makeshift bandages. "How'd you get these?"

Paco's mind went completely blank.

"Don't worry," Santiago said. "I won't tell the king. And I already know, sort of. Before Opportunity Day, you weren't getting cut up. You also weren't having unexplained absences. Then there was that broken table. What power did you get?"

Santiago could so easily have threatened him, or even said, *"I took a flogging for you. You owe me."* But he'd reassured Paco instead.

"Teleporting," Paco admitted. Though he was still tense, it was a relief to stop lying. "The table leg was one of the first times it happened. I got too close to it, and it merged with my pant leg. I had to get rid of it."

Santiago looked horrified. "Do you have to cut out bits of stuff from your body whenever you get too close to something?"

Paco's stomach lurched at the thought. "No. The cuts just happen when I jump too far. I overdid it today. I really do feel sick."

Santiago put the back of his hand to Paco's forehead. "You feel like a dead fish."

"Thanks," Paco said wryly. "But listen, the important part is that I got into the ruined city. Kerry is fine. So's your cousin who went after her. Uh, Maria something."

Santiago sat down heavily on the bed as if his knees had given out. He put his hands over his face, and said in a muffled voice, "I hoped Kerry was alive. I thought she probably was. But I didn't *know*. And I was sure Maria-Pilar was dead." He dropped his hands and rubbed at his wet eyes. "What are they doing in there?"

Paco told him the whole story. Santiago was pleased to hear about Sean, and worried about Kerry being stuck in the ruined city. And then, since there was no point in hiding it anymore, he told Santiago about the Rats.

Santiago groaned. "This is so dangerous. If you get caught teleporting, you're dead. If you get caught planning a resistance, you're dead but even more painfully. And so am I. And so is Maria-Elena. She's *seven*."

"I know. I didn't want to involve you." All the talking had tired him out. Paco lay down, shivering again.

"I involved myself," Santiago said gloomily. "Listen, we're due back at headquarters. I'll tell the king you're sick. He'll send Dr. Lee to you."

"Thanks." Paco lay back with a sigh. At least he didn't have to see Voske again that day. And though Santiago might not join the Rats, Paco was confident that he wouldn't betray them either. Either way, it was a relief to not have to hide from him.

He had to appreciate those small victories, in the midst of so many defeats.

·23·
PACO

LAS ANCLAS

A BANG ON THE door made Paco tense for trouble. The only people he expected were Santiago or Dr. Lee, and neither pounded the door like that.

"Come in," he said from his nest of blankets. He was still shivering.

When Dr. Lee entered, Paco opened his mouth to exclaim in relief. Then he saw the doctor's grim face, and the words froze in his throat. Just as well. Voske was right behind him.

Paco let his breath out in a whoosh.

Voske sidestepped the doctor, frowning down at Paco. "Santiago said Liam looks terrible. I see that he does. What's wrong with him? He was fine two hours ago."

"It's a kind of flu, distinctive for its rapid onset. Here, this will ease the discomfort." Dr. Lee opened a vial of willow tincture and lifted Paco's head. Paco, aware of that makeshift bandage around his ribs, kept the covers pulled up to his shoulders as he swallowed the bitter, astringent potion.

Paco braced himself as the king laid a hand callused from sword work over his forehead. "He's clammy."

Dr. Lee nodded. "That's one of the symptoms, along with chills and joint pains."

"We have illnesses like that in Gold Point, though they don't come on so fast. Son, rest up. Santiago will bring your meals." Voske left.

Dr. Lee closed the door behind him. Softly, he said, "What happened?"

Paco forced himself to sit up in bed, shivering, to reveal his seeping bandages. "I had to warn them about the company coming. I saw Mia. She's fine." He told Dr. Lee everything. Dr. Lee's smile broadened at the ancient food, but he looked grave at the rest, and even more so at Paco's injuries. "I don't think these are cuts at all, in the sense of having been made by a sharp object. The flesh seems to be simply...gone."

Paco's skin crawled. "Where am I going, that's so cold, and...takes things from me?"

"It may not be a place you go." Dr. Lee's tone, thoughtful and interested, eased Paco's visceral terror of the unknown. "The cold may mean you're using so much energy that you're draining your own body heat, and possibly the heat from the air around you. Something similar may be happening with the missing parts. You're only able to transport a certain amount of mass over a certain distance. Anything more simply doesn't arrive. Perhaps it's consumed, like the heat."

That took him straight back to horror. His whole body shook with chills, making the bed frame creak.

"*Please* be more cautious," Dr. Lee urged him.

"I will," Paco said, and meant it. His teeth were chattering.

Dr. Lee frowned over him. "I have to heal these wounds completely, or Voske will notice them. It goes against my grain to take so much time for what are essentially minor injuries, but...one month."

The doctor touched him, and his wounds become pale scars on his brown skin. The constant throb of pain that he'd been enduring for days pulsed weaker and weaker, then vanished. Suddenly, he felt well again.

Dr. Lee stuffed the bloody shirt strips in his doctor's bag, along with Paco's ruined pants. "Take advantage of your 'illness' and get some rest. You could use it. As for Mia's question about Ross, you can't lose a Change power. You can only exhaust it temporarily. But Ross's power doesn't come from a Change."

Paco felt more discouraged than ever. Did that mean they would be trapped in the ruined city until they died?

"But," Dr. Lee went on, "Ross also has a history of forgetting things that were too traumatic to remember. I wonder if something like that might have happened again. Instead of trying to force his power to work, he should relax and try to remember what happened just before he lost it. And ask him to think about whether there could be any reason he might not want to have his power anymore."

"I'll tell him." Paco rubbed his forehead. "I wish I hadn't had to decide on the spot about Sean and Santiago. It was easier when it was just *us*. Now we've got two of *them*." But it was getting harder to make that distinction. Kerry had once been them but was now us. Henry had once been us but was now them. And some people in Las Anclas clearly thought Paco was now one of *them* too.

Dr. Lee said, watching Paco closely, "But that line isn't so clear now, is it?"

Paco smiled slightly. "You're doing that cold reading thing again."

He slept for the rest of the day and awoke at nightfall. Though he was still tired, he didn't dare go back to sleep again. When the position of the moon marked midnight, he remembered training on the beach with Rangers who were dead now and longed to see them again.

It took three jumps to get to the breakwater. He breathed in the briny night air as gooseflesh rose on his chilled skin. But he'd planned his jumps well. He had no cuts and had lost no bits of clothing.

The tide was out, leaving the beach slick in the light of the sinking moon. He clambered over slippery rocks to the cave. At first, he saw only Santiago's stocky form, but then he remembered that he had to look for Sean. Once Paco looked, he saw him.

"Will you help us?" Paco said to Sean.

"I'll help Kerry once she gets out of the ruined city," Sean said guardedly. "But I'm not staying inside Las Anclas, and I'm not killing anyone. I left Gold Point so I wouldn't have to do that sort of thing."

Paco bit back a sigh. Sean had already said he couldn't get anywhere near Voske, even if he had been willing to kill his own father. But Paco had hoped Sean could sneak up on some of Voske's commanders.

"Take Kerry to Catalina," Santiago pleaded. "Or anywhere far away."

"She won't go," said Sean. "You know that. This is her home now."

"Sean's right," Paco said. "Once they get out, none of them will just run. They'll want to take the town back."

"Impossible," muttered Santiago.

Paco plowed on. "We'll need to hide them somewhere. Dr. Lee will help—"

"She can't hide in the infirmary," Santiago protested. "We're in and out of there all the time."

We. Santiago meant Gold Point soldiers. Paco hoped he hadn't made a terrible mistake in arranging this meeting.

"When we come up with a good hiding place, will you help us get Kerry and the others there?" Paco asked. There was that *we* and *us* again.

"I will," said Sean.

"This is such a bad idea," Santiago muttered. "But yeah, of course I'll help her."

Paco hesitated, then said, "Will you join the resistance?"

Sean folded his arms. "I already said what I'd do. And that's it."

Santiago actually clutched his head. Then he dropped his hands, heaved an enormous sigh, and said, "Yes."

When Santiago knocked on his door the next morning, he looked so tired and stressed that Paco's claim that he was still "sick" died unspoken. He got up and they headed for Wolfe House. When they neared Main Street, and the stable that was now reserved entirely to Voske, they passed a group of angrily muttering soldiers.

"I wish the king would shoot him."

"Not a royal horse, not a chance. No matter how many walls—or heads—that crazy beast kicks in."

Paco never addressed soldiers unless he had to, except for Santiago. But he couldn't let that go by. "Are you talking about Nugget, the golden stallion?"

The soldiers jerked to attention. "Yes, sir!"

Santiago eyed Paco gloomily, undoubtedly weighing whether Voske would be angrier if they were both late or if he arrived alone. Since the other soldiers were listening, Paco said to Santiago, "The king won't want a royal horse to injure himself kicking at walls. Tell him I'll be there soon. I think I can get Nugget to calm down."

Santiago's expression eased slightly as he saluted, then ran off toward Wolfe House. The soldiers escorted Paco to what had been the town stable. Voske had reserved it entirely for his and his honor guard's horses, relegating the others to a hastily converted barn. Before they reached the stable, noise reached them: *Bang!* Thump. *Bang!* Thump. It sounded like Nugget was alternately kicking the wall and an overturned water barrel.

"This I gotta see," a soldier muttered as they entered the stable yard.

A tall woman poised warily out of kicking range, trying to soothe Nugget. She looked tired and tense, and Paco guessed she'd been ordered to get control of Nugget, or else. The stallion's ears lay flat, his eyes rolling, and streaks of sweat marred his glossy coat. An overturned water barrel lay in the stall, and the straw near it was soaked.

Paco said, "That's not his stall."

"No?" the woman asked. "Which one is his?"

Paco pointed to where a silver horse, much taller than Sally, stood in a large loose box, his ears wary and twitching. From the next one over, the copper mare Penny peered, ears alert and curious. Paco glimpsed her steel colt Katana between the bars.

"That's *Coronet*'s box." From the way the woman said 'Coronet,' Paco knew he was the king's favorite.

Paco shrugged. "Nugget's had that stall longer."

The woman snapped her fingers at a stable hand. "Turn Coronet into the far paddock." And to Paco, "Nugget won't let anyone near him. We've given him water, but he kicks it over."

"Let me try." Paco slowly approached the angry stallion, talking softly. He dipped a feed bucket into the oat sack and shook it gently. "You know me, Nugget. Let me in, and you can have your own stall back. Come on..."

Nugget kicked the back wall. Moving slowly, speaking softly, Paco came closer and held up the bucket as an offering. Nugget breathed in his face, then lowered his muzzle and munched some oats. Paco slowly reached up to stroke him between the ears the way Kerry did. The golden stallion stood still and tense. Paco kept rubbing until Nugget's eyes looked less fierce.

"Halter," Paco said, holding out the bucket. The woman took it away and placed a halter in his hand.

Paco let himself into the box. Nugget reared, eyes rolling, but Paco didn't flinch. When Nugget stood still, Paco slowly worked the halter over the stallion's head. The stallion twitched his ears at the other humans, making it clear he didn't want them around. They backed away. Nugget regally ignored them and allowed Paco to lead him into his own box. Paco slipped the halter free, and watched with pleasure as Nugget bent his head to the water barrel.

He turned around. Voske was right behind him, with, Santiago at his elbow.

"Good job, Liam," Voske said. "You've inherited a sense of authority with the royal horses." Paco had been warm with pride, but that 'inherited' doused it cold. Voske indicated Nugget. "He's yours, son. A royal stallion. His full name is Nebraska Gold."

The last thing Paco wanted was for an innocent animal to become a hostage. But how could he refuse a gift from the tyrant? He thought of playing Go with Yuki, and said, "I'd be glad to help with Nugget, but I don't want to own a horse."

There was a little pause, and then Voske said, "Why not?"

"It's extra work. I'm fine with riding whichever mounts are in the day's rotation."

Voske gave him a long look, then shrugged. "As you like. Take it easy today. I'm glad you're feeling better, but don't overdo it. Report to me tomorrow for the orders of the day."

Paco gritted his teeth and said nothing. He could feel the others staring at him. Waiting for him to salute? To thank Voske for his offer? Paco would rather be put up against a wall than thank Voske for anything.

The king began to walk out. Just as everybody in earshot breathed easier, he paused at the stable door. "Liam? One more thing. Opportunity Day is the day after tomorrow."

Paco felt as if the earth had dropped right out from under his feet. "What? But it hasn't been a month since the last one."

Voske smiled. "Yes, but you didn't choose anyone. Remember, son, a king isn't bound by rules—not even the rules the king himself sets. Opportunity Day isn't once a month. Opportunity Day is whenever I say it is."

·24·

BECKY

LAS ANCLAS

BY DINNER TIME, THE news had spread all over Las Anclas that another Opportunity Day had suddenly been declared. When Paco arrived at the infirmary, looking grim, Dr. Lee dispatched Luis to take a refill of willow bark to the chief medic at the barracks. Then the Rats gathered in the kitchen, curtains closed. Alfonso guarded the door while Dr. Lee fixed dinner.

Becky listened in amazement and relief as Paco told the Rats about his visit to the ruined city and Santiago's recruitment. She was so glad everyone was all right— Kerry, especially. Becky hadn't realized how close she and Kerry had become until she heard the news and felt like a weight had been lifted from her back.

The kitchen had been cozy, with the good news and the smell of simmering onions and the purring of cats, but it became tense the instant they start discussing Opportunity Day.

"I'm the *perfect* volunteer," Meredith said. "I don't care how dangerous Paco's power is. I do dangerous things anyway. And my mom is Changed, so I know I'll get something. If we can't launch our uprising—"

As Meredith said the word 'uprising,' Alfonso hissed, "Shh!" He leaped from the door to the table, and everyone picked up waiting implements and started cleaning the kitchen or helping Dr. Lee cook.

Santiago walked in. Hesitantly, he said, "I just got off duty."

"Welcome among us, Santiago," said Dr. Lee.

"Thanks. If that's the right word." Santiago heaved a deep sigh. "But I know it's what Kerry would want. And it's the only way to keep her alive."

Dr. Lee looked closely at him, making Becky wonder if he was doing that cold reading. His next words confirmed it. "If it helps, we have no intention of launching a slaughter against people you've known and worked with all your life. We just want to govern ourselves and live in peace. If the king won't let us—if he coerces us into military action—we want to limit that to the leaders. Not those merely following orders because they have to."

Santiago whooshed out his breath. "I can live with that."

Dr. Lee then said musingly, as he added garlic to the onions, "I wish I knew what motivated the king to suddenly declare an Opportunity Day. Do you know?"

Santiago shrugged, looking away. Paco seemed to about to say something, then shook his head.

"Paco?" Dr. Lee prompted.

"I don't know. I can't read his mind. I don't want to read his mind," Paco added with suppressed violence.

"It doesn't really matter. What does is being ready for it. A few of the adult resistance and I met at Jack's for some quick discussion over boiled brussels sprouts and Zucchini pie." Dr. Lee made a face. "Voske took this town by sneaking in and attacking key people at the same time. We can use the same strategy against him. Each volunteer will attack a specific person in Voske's chain of command."

"We need more weapons," Paco said. "They have theirs, but Voske confiscated all of ours."

Dr. Lee nodded. "We also need information. Like, where exactly does Min Soo fit in? What are her motives for giving up the luxury of Gold Point to live far less comfortably here?"

Santiago held up a warning hand. "You have to be careful around her. She got Commander Custer Bern shot."

"Who?" Meredith asked.

"He *was* the man the king left in charge of Gold Point while he's here. Custer Bern was one of the king's earliest supporters. We thought he was untouchable. But Min Soo claimed she'd caught him sitting in the king's throne. We just found out that he was shot by a firing squad. And recently Min Soo got Chandra Kim demoted from the captain of the honor guard. We'd thought she was untouchable, too. Now she's helping Tommy Horst build the new generator."

"Voske has every advantage," Meredith burst out. "We need more people on our side."

"I agree," said Santiago. "You should recruit Luis."

"The torturer?" Paco exclaimed. "No."

"You don't know him," said Santiago. "I do. And if anyone has reason to want to end Voske's tyranny, beginning with ending Opportunity Day, it's him."

Dr. Lee was also shaking his head. "I don't question his motives. But I have concerns about his state of mind. He's under too much of a burden already."

"We're *all* under a burden: Voske!" Meredith rolled her eyes. "When can Ross and the others get out and help us?"

"I'll go find out tonight," Paco said.

Dr. Lee shook his head. "Paco, do not go to the ruined city. You were very lucky that Voske didn't discover your power last time. We can't risk that again, just for you to get an update."

"Fine." Paco hit the wall lightly with his fist. "Meanwhile, I still have to choose someone tomorrow. Who might drop dead."

Santiago said softly, "Or end up like Luis."

Meredith shrugged. "Like I said, I volunteer."

"No!" Paco exclaimed.

Meredith glared at him. "I've always wanted a power, and I'm not planning to get pregnant. I don't want to wait until I'm fifty!"

Dr. Lee inquired, "Would you rather get a good power at menopause, or force it prematurely and risk dying or a getting a power that will ruin your life?" When Meredith scowled, Dr. Lee went on, "By the way, I've already had this conversation with your mother. She agrees with me."

Meredith instantly deflated.

Dr. Lee went on, "I believe that the person who has the best chance of survival is someone who does not have the genetic capacity to Change. My theory is that those are the people who don't Change at Opportunity Day — because they *can't*. Unfortunately, there's no way to test that. The best we can do is have someone who, as far as they know, has never had anyone in their family Change."

Becky tried to think of who she knew with no Changes in their entire family tree. Tommy Horst?

Dr. Lee said, "Such as Jack Lowell."

"No!" That came from everyone, not just Becky. She felt sick. She remembered when Sheriff Crow — Elizabeth Crow then — Changed and lost her baby. Becky had been cleaning the infirmary floor when Jack Lowell stumbled out of the surgery and collapsed sobbing on the porch outside the door.

"I don't want to pick Jack." Paco's face flushed dark with anger.

"It's not up to you," said Dr. Lee. "Jack has volunteered. This is his contribution. Respect it."

The instant Becky awoke the next morning, she remembered two things: Felicité was dead, and Opportunity Day was tomorrow.

She'd started writing letters to Felicité in her head, saying all the things she wished she'd said when Felicité was alive.

I wish I'd told you I didn't blame you. I wish I'd asked you if Voske would let you move in with me. I wish I'd told you it was Henry's fault. Not yours. No, I wish I'd told you it was Voske's fault. I wish I'd just asked you how it all happened.

Becky imagined herself putting pen to paper, watching the black ink flow as she wrote to Felicité, who was in some other town. She'd be curious about what was going on in Las Anclas. Would she think it was funny how Jack was resisting Voske by cooking the worst possible food that wasn't obviously a deliberate insult?

I didn't even know lardy cake existed. One taste, and you wish it didn't…

Now Becky wrote in her mind, *When I heard about Opportunity Day, I was almost glad you weren't here to see it. I thought you'd seen enough terrible things that you weren't strong enough to bear. But now I think that was wrong of me. I think you made an impulsive decision in a moment of despair, and if someone had stopped you, you'd never do it again. I wish someone had.*

She picked up Grandma Wolfe's medicine and headed to what she would always and forever think of as *Wolfe* House. Once everyone would have been chatting outside the stores or while working in the pocket gardens. Now everything was silent. Curtains pulled. It was as if all of Las Anclas had become like the Callahan house, dark and closed into itself. Becky shivered.

And there was the well at Wolfe House, where Felicité had drowned.

After the guards inspected her for weapons, she went inside with her shoes on, feeling like every speck of dust she carried inside was a betrayal of Felicité.

Bridget was waiting for her. "Can I help you with the medicine?" Without waiting for an answer, Bridget followed her up to Felicité's room. Wu Zetian's cage had been moved to Will's room, Felicité's mirror was gone, and an extra bed had been moved in.

Bridget barged into the bedroom after a quick knock. "Here's your medicine, Mrs. Wolfe! How are you feeling?"

Grandma Wolfe had always been smiling ever since Becky's first day of school. There was no smile in the part of her face visible around the bandage.

"Does your broken jaw still hurt?" Bridget asked. "Can you talk even if it does hurt?"

Becky fitted the straw into the cup and held it up for Grandma Wolfe to drink. She and the mayor obviously wanted Bridget gone. But the girl kept right on chattering about the broken arm she'd had once.

"All done," Becky cut in loudly. "See you tomorrow."

She wondered if the mayor and Grandma Wolfe knew that tomorrow was Opportunity Day. She couldn't wait to get out of that house, but as they descended the stairs, Bridget chirped, "Becky, let me show you my invertebrates!"

The last thing Becky wanted to see was Voske's daughter's invertebrates. But she dared not refuse. "Sure."

"You must have seen lots of broken bones." Bridget sounded thrilled.

Becky tried not to flinch. "Not really. What sort of invertebrates do you have?"

"Just you wait!" Bridget bounded to what had previously been Grandma Wolfe's room, which Becky had used in sleepovers. The bed with the coverlet of embroidered roses was the same, but the shelves that used to hold vases of blooming roses were now crammed with terrariums full of horrifying creatures.

Becky tried to keep her gaze out of focus as Bridget pointed them all out. "Tailless whip scorpions! Venomous land crabs! Hairy slime crawlers! And my very favorites, fanged rainbow spiders. They're very rare."

Bridget took out a pair. Each one covered her entire palm. The spiders did have gleaming rainbow carapaces where they weren't hairy, but Becky couldn't help fixating on their huge fangs and eight eyes.

"This is Lilabella." Bridget hefted the spider in her left hand. "And this is Clarabella. Aren't they darling?"

For a horrifying moment, Becky thought Bridget would demand that she hold them. But the girl was too engaged in holding them close to her own face and nuzzling them. Clarabella scuttled up Bridget's arm and onto her shoulder. Bridget set Lilabella on her other shoulder, reached into a jar, and fed each of the spiders a live cockroach.

Becky tried not to show any fear. Then she realized that Bridget wasn't trying to scare her. She wasn't even paying much attention to Becky. Bridget cooed to her spiders the way Brisa cooed to the Preciados' house cats.

It was the first time Becky had seen Bridget caring for another living being. "I thought you didn't like animals."

Surprised, Bridget turned to her. "Oh, I love animals. They're so fascinating."

"But...the exploding mouse?"

"Powers that work on living things are so interesting," Bridget said earnestly. "A lot of the ones that kill can also cure. And! You can think of it the other way around — powers that cure can also kill. Like how an axe can chop off a head or do an amputation."

Becky decided not to mention that you didn't perform amputations with an axe. The casual way Bridget talked about chopping off heads made her queasy. It didn't help when she plucked another live roach from the jar and popped it into her spider's waiting jaws.

"You don't mind killing roaches," Becky said. "Don't you like them?"

Bridget shrugged. "Spiders eat roaches. Chickens eat spiders — not my spiders, of course, but spiders in general. We eat chickens. And after we die, the roaches eat us. It's so elegant how it all fits together, don't you think?"

The last thing Becky wanted was a lesson on the circle of life from Voske's daughter. Unenthusiastically, she said, "Sure."

Bridget eyed her, then returned the still-munching spiders to their terrarium. "I guess you don't want to see the slime molds."

Bridget sniffed hard, and a tear slipped down her face. Then another.

Becky was appalled. Would Bridget report her for being insufficiently enthusiastic over slime molds? "I do want to see them!"

"It's not that." Bridget's face crumpled. "I wish my mom was here." A muffled sob escaped her. "I wish I could make friends. I like Yolanda, but if I try to share my lunch with her, she looks at me as if it's poison. Min Soo said you make friends by being kind, but when I offered to help Yolanda with her biology, she pretended she didn't hear me. I finally asked her why she didn't like me, and she gave me this *stare*, and she s-said...my father is holding April hostage — you know, the flying toddler — and she said I think hurting little animals is funny."

Alarmed, Becky said, "Have you told your father?"

"No!" Bridget raised puffy eyes and looked at Becky like she was an idiot. "I told you, I *like* Yolanda."

Did she dare? Her heart pounding, Becky strove for a neutral tone. "What does that have to do with it?"

Bridget shot her an exasperated look. "Because *obviously*, if *I* tell Father, he'll order Yolanda to be my friend or he'll hurt April. I want Yolanda to actually like me, not to fake it. And I don't want to get April hurt. She's just a *baby*."

"Your father wants you to rule Las Anclas someday, right?" Becky asked cautiously. Bridget nodded, sniffing. "If you ruled it now, would you ever hurt April?"

"No! Of course not."

"Even to make her family obey you?" Becky asked.

Bridget looked away, chewing her lip. Then back. "Isn't that how a smart ruler ensures loyalty?"

"Wouldn't loyalty be stronger if it was given freely?" Becky's heart was crowding her throat. Bridget could repeat this entire conversation to Voske.

"I don't know." Bridget began sniffling again.

Becky found herself feeling sorry for Bridget, who was just a kid. A bright kid. She reminded Becky a little bit of Mia, and also a little bit of Dr. Lee, when he'd talked about how you needed pain to tell you when you were hurt, and that sometimes you needed to amputate a limb to save a life. Abruptly, Bridget's talk about broken bones took on a new meaning.

"Bridget, are you interested in medicine?"

"Of course." Bridget wiped her nose on her sleeve. "That's why I wanted to see you treat the prisoner."

"Would you like to see the town doctor treat a patient?"

Bridget's expression cleared like magic. "Would I!"

"He has a surgery scheduled for noon."

"Ooh, a surgery!" Bridget looked thrilled. "What is it?"

"He has to remove a bone chip from a patient's leg. He thought he got it all, but there seems to be another."

"How does he know there's another?"

A host of gruesome details flashed into Becky's mind, reminding her of why she'd stopped being his apprentice. "He'll tell you."

"Girls?" Min Soo appeared at the open door. "Becky! How lovely to see you!"

Becky tried not to flinch, all the while thinking of how the very next day, Min Soo would grab Jack's hands and do…*something* to him. Kerry had given Becky a much-too-vivid description of the Opportunity Day when Min Soo had Changed Luis.

Min Soo straightened Bridget's braids. Her palms

were terribly scarred, as if she'd thrust them into a fireplace.

"Becky let me watch her give Mrs. Wolfe the medicine," Bridget said. "And she said I could watch the doctor! I'll skip school. It's so boring here, and Father said I could for worthwhile lessons. Shall I wear my predator dress or my parasite dress?"

Becky couldn't help a glance at Min Soo. She caught a flash of disgust followed by a wryly humorous glance her way, then Min Soo said firmly, "The predator dress."

Bridget stepped out, and Min Soo murmured, "You really don't want to see the parasite dress."

"I don't," Becky said honestly.

"Come. Let's find something pretty for you."

"Me?" Becky said.

"Yes. Join us for breakfast. I would love to see you in robin's egg blue, to bring out your lovely eyes..."

With gentle insistence, she brought Becky into her rooms, and pulled out a hanbok, similar in design to the lovely red one that Kerry had on the wall of her room. This one was deep blue with a white cloud pattern, and not a ruffle or ribbon in sight.

Becky couldn't help smiling. "It's gorgeous."

"Try it on." Min Soo walked to the door. "Come out when you're ready."

Becky stared at that shut door. Maybe she could learn something. She hastily put on the hanbok. Then, her heart pounding, she touched the desk carved with oak leaves. She saw Kerry, sitting in a cushioned chair and wearing a gold crown, scowling like a thunderstorm. Kerry had already told her how she and her mother hadn't gotten along, but it was startling to see her wearing a crown.

Becky touched a chair. Min Soo's thoughts came through sharp and clear. *How do I get through to her? She can't just charge through life waving those weapons of hers. If she doesn't learn to use soft power, she'll never survive being Ian's daughter.*

Becky released the chair, glancing nervously at the door. Kerry had said that her mother had good intentions behind her obnoxious lessons, but Becky wondered if Kerry had known that Min Soo had meant to save her from her father.

She touched an end table, and her knees almost buckled as powerful emotions surged through her. Grief. Anger. Guilt. The sense of being trapped. Love.

Becky gazed through Min Soo's eyes at an unfamiliar boy. He had the Voske features but dark skin and cornrows beneath his golden crown. His face was tear-stained, ravaged as if he'd been crying for a long time.

"I'm so sorry, Sean," Min Soo said. "I truly can't control it. I wish I could."

"I know," Sean said, his voice broken. "It's too late for Leila. But this can't ever happen again. Promise me you'll stop doing Opportunity Day."

"I can't," Min Soo whispered. "I wouldn't survive a day. Nobody says no to your father. You know that..." And the memory was gone.

Becky yanked her hand away. She didn't dare touch anything else. Min Soo would take one look at her and *know*. But now she knew that Min Soo wasn't doing Opportunity Day by choice.

That wouldn't save Jack, of course.

Becky walked to the bathroom, splashed some water on her face, and stared into the mirror until she was satisfied that her expression showed nothing. Then she went out. Bridget had returned, swirling her blood-red skirts. This dress had spiders embroidered around the collar, sleeves, and hem. Their glittering obsidian eyes seemed to follow you every time Bridget moved.

"I did the embroidery on these spiders here," Bridget said proudly. "And this pit mouth in the back. It didn't come out that great, which is why it's in the back."

Min Soo said smoothly, "They're both still very good. A pit mouth is an extremely difficult subject. So many tiny fangs."

Though Becky didn't want to look too closely, she did glance at the spiders that Bridget had sewn. Min Soo was right. Bridget's embroidery was excellent. Dr. Lee would say she had the hands of a surgeon.

"The hanbok is exquisite on you, Becky." Min Soo looked pleased with herself.

In the dining room, Becky took the offered seat next to Bridget's. She was unnerved to see Voske at the head of the table, and surprised to see Henry, who looked at her with no expression. His face was sharp-boned, and the black uniform hung loose on his thinner body.

"Father," Bridget said. "Becky offered to introduce me to the town doctor, so I can see a surgery. Can I skip school for that?"

Voske glanced at Becky, whose heart instantly began pounding.

"Certainly," said Voske. "Get to know the people you will be ruling. Becky, why don't you accompany Bridget for as long as she wishes to remain in the infirmary." He gave Becky a terrifying smile. "I like seeing the two of you making friends. Bridget, I think Becky is an excellent influence."

Becky's stomach churned at those words. But Bridget's face lit up. She seized Becky's hand and said, "You'll have to show me all your favorite places."

Voske looked at Becky. "That was an excellent idea, to introduce Bridget to Dr. Lee. You understand the princess's interests and strengths." Bridget beamed, and Becky managed a nervous half-smile. "I can see you working together in the future. Every ruler depends on an intelligent and loyal second in command."

Bridget beamed. "Oh, I'd love to have Becky."

Second in command? Was Voske playing another mind game? Or could he mean it? She wasn't sure which was more horrifying, the thought of working within Voske's empire, or how happy Bridget looked at the idea of her doing it.

The instant Voske left the table, Bridget jumped up, obsidian spider eyes winking. "Let's go!"

Becky didn't breathe easily until they were walking away from Wolfe House. As usual, the street was quiet as people went about their daily work. She stole a glance at Bridget, who was uncharacteristically silent.

Tommy Horst passed them with a wheelbarrow full of bricks, heading toward the construction zone. Becky waved to him. "Hi, Tommy."

"Becky," Tommy said shortly. He ignored Bridget.

Bridget gave a sigh. "He doesn't even know me, and he still doesn't like me."

Becky felt her way carefully. "It's not personal. It's because your father is very powerful."

"Of course he is. He's a king. But he doesn't only hold hostages. He rewards hard work. He *likes* giving rewards. If they were nice to me, he'd reward them. Like he's planning to reward you!" Quickly, she added, "Don't worry. I know that's not why you're doing it."

With a lurch in her stomach, Becky thought that the people of Las Anclas were lucky that Bridget wanted real friends, not fake ones. If she wanted to *make* them be nice to her, she could do it.

"Everyone's so gloomy all the time," Bridget went on. "Even though Father's already rewarded them with electric lights and stuff."

Even more cautiously, Becky said, "People here were used to freedom. No one likes having things taken away from them."

"They still have freedom, as long as they don't raise a rebellion."

Becky was surprised by intensity of her own anger at that word. Bridget was only saying what she'd been taught. It would be madness to correct her. And yet Becky couldn't help wanting to give her a new perspective. She chose each word before speaking, like she had in the bad old days with her family. "They miss our elections. And the freedom to criticize the candidates. They used to be able to argue with the town council if they didn't like a decision."

Bridget tossed her a skeptical look. "Elections are pointless. People vote for the strongest person in town, or else. So why bother?"

"Who do you think the strongest person in Las Anclas was, before your father took over the town?"

"Tom Preston, of course. I've been hearing about *him* all my life. He runs the Rangers, and he's the military commander—"

"Defense chief."

"Right, you call it defense chief," Bridget agreed. "And his wife was the mayor."

"He was voted out of being defense chief in the last election," Becky said.

"Really?" Bridget stopped dead, jewel-eyed spiders staring from her collar. "What did he do to the people who made him lose?"

"Nothing. He just said he'd run again next time. People spoke their minds and made their wishes known, and nobody got hurt. That's freedom."

"It sounds more like disorder. If everyone does what they want, then nothing gets done. Towns need a good strong leader, somebody who rewards effort and loyalty." Bridget's voice rose with conviction.

Miss Chen, the butcher, was walking toward Jack's with a basket of sausages. She caught Becky's eye and mouthed the words, *Be careful.*

When they arrived at the infirmary, Dr. Lee came out of the back room. As Bridget slipped off her shoes, copying Becky, Dr. Lee gave Becky a surprised glance. Before she could explain, Bridget said eagerly, "Becky invited me to see a surgery and Father said I should get a lesson in medicine!"

"Welcome, Bridget," Dr. Lee said. "The surgery will be later, but I'm happy to give you a tour. Shall I start with the medical plants?"

"Yes! I want to see *everything*," Bridget declared.

Becky trailed behind as Dr. Lee introduced Bridget to the surgery, the infirmary, and the supply chests and cupboards. On Becky's own first tour, she hadn't asked a tenth as many questions. But Dr. Lee didn't seem impatient. In fact, he seemed to sincerely enjoy Bridget's enthusiasm.

When Dr. Lee offered them lunch, Bridget said, "Thank you, Dr. Lee. This is so exciting! Can you show me your power? I think it's a little bit like mine. Look! I can do it slowly if I really concentrate!"

She held out her hand over a plump green tomato in a basket. It slowly swelled and ripened to a beautiful red. "See? Ripe is halfway to rot!"

"Thank you for showing me, Bridget." Becky could see that Dr. Lee was really interested. "That is indeed similar to mine. Can you do it to anything living?"

Bridget shook her head regretfully. "I could only do it to the tomato because it was already picked."

"Hmm. I wonder if dissolving stitches..." Dr. Lee tugged at his ponytail. "Hmm."

Bridget bounced on her toes. "Is it time for the surgery? Can I watch?"

"Certainly," Dr. Lee said. "If the patient gives permission. But I think she will."

"Oh, good. Can you tell me what you'll do, so I'll know what to look for?"

When Dr. Lee finished describing the surgery, Bridget pointed to a scalpel. "How did you start learning to do surgeries? Did you practice on animals?"

Becky's stomach roiled. But Dr. Lee said simply, "Yes. Eventually. You start with dead animals before you ever operate on a live one. And before you operate on dead animals, you practice on slabs of meat. And before that, fruit."

"Fruit?" Bridget repeated.

"Some fruits have a very similar texture to flesh. Like plums." He took a plump red plum out of the fruit basket. Becky wondered if she would ever eat a plum again. "Want to try?"

"Oh, yes," Bridget said.

Dr. Lee fetched a scalpel and put the plum on a plate. "Your first patient."

Bridget giggled and held out her hand for the scalpel.

"Watch me first. Don't hesitate with the first incision. One bold stroke."

Becky remembered that phrase well. It had taken her multiple tries to get used to that idea, even with a plum. It just felt so violent.

Dr. Lee demonstrated one bold stroke on the plum. Then he handed Bridget the scalpel. "But not too bold. Don't hit the pit. Go about half an inch in."

Bridget seized the scalpel. With her forehead creased in concentration, she gave one bold stroke to the plum.

"Very good," said Dr. Lee.

Bridget beamed. "I wish you were my teacher. What we do in school isn't half this interesting. And when I ask questions like I asked you, like how much blood you can lose before you die, everyone looks at me like I'm a slug they stepped on with bare feet when they got up to go to the bathroom in the middle of the night."

Dr. Lee looked at her thoughtfully. "I know someone who had a problem like that. It wasn't blood and bones she was interested in. It was...other things."

Becky knew who he meant. She'd seen Mia try to talk

to other kids about machinery. They hadn't looked at her like she was a slug, more like they were bored and she was boring.

"But she found people to talk to, who had similar interests," Dr. Lee went on. "You can always talk about blood and bones to me or Alfonso. And maybe someday..."

Becky realized that Dr. Lee was not only thinking forward to when Mia would return, he was imagining a time when it would be safe for Mia and Bridget to meet. How did he keep his hope when everything seemed so hopeless?

"Well, it's time to prepare for the surgery. Becky, why don't you go tell Alfonso to come in? I know this won't be a treat for you."

Becky fetched Alfonso, then went to work with Luis. They used kelp sutures on a man who'd been flogged. She would have thought that she'd feel Luis's silent horror, but she felt nothing. It wasn't only that he was quiet, it was that his emotions seemed locked up behind a wall thicker than the one surrounding Las Anclas.

She was relieved when Bridget came bouncing out of the surgery, exclaiming, "It was so cool! Dr. Lee let me hold the retractor!"

Dr. Lee, following at a more sedate pace, said, "Bridget was an excellent assistant. Right, Alfonso?"

Alfonso said softly, "She didn't let a drop of arterial blood spill."

Becky was impressed. Dr. Lee might have been being kind, but Alfonso never spoke unless he had something he really wanted to say. And if Becky had heard anyone talk like Bridget about surgery when she was younger, she'd have known that she could never be a surgeon.

·25·
PACO

LAS ANCLAS

THE MORNING OF OPPORTUNITY Day, Paco used the excuse of his recovering from his "illness" to get up and dress slowly, hoping he'd not only miss breakfast, but that Voske would be too busy to bother with him. But when he arrived at Wolfe House, he found Nugget saddled and waiting with Coronet, the temperamental royal horses held by nervous stable hands.

Of course, Voske wouldn't be busy. He was a king. He gave orders, and others toiled. The tyrant did exactly what he wanted to do. Voske had begun taking Paco for occasional rides through Las Anclas and its environs, and he wasn't going to forego it today.

"Come along, son." He glanced back, and Paco wondered what he was waiting for. A salute? Perhaps a *"yes sir!"*

Paco would cut out his own tongue first.

When they got outside, Nugget plunged, ears back, tail whisking. But as Paco approached, his ears twitched forward and he settled down, allowing Paco to mount him. Coronet reared, ears back. But Voske walked up to him and snapped his fingers. Coronet stopped, his flanks trembling, and Voske mounted.

Paco glanced back and saw Bridget and Becky leaving Wolfe House. Good for Becky. He hoped she'd get lots of useful information, even if it did come with a dose of hideous, tail-lashing invertebrates.

The honor guard fell in behind them as Nugget and Coronet trotted off. Though Paco loathed these rides with

Voske, he had come to appreciate Nugget. The sense of controlled power coming from the golden stallion was incredible. He was so much more than just pretty.

Paco caught Voske watching him enjoy riding Nugget. All his pleasure in the horse turned to ash.

Voske led the way up the path past Luc's. So, this would be a ride around the inner circle of the town. Paco braced inwardly. People backed hastily out of their way, even those carrying heavy loads. They were people he'd known all his life, familiar faces with unfamiliar expressions. Fear. Disgust. Anger. Suspicion. Here and there, sympathy. He knew how it looked, riding with the conqueror, both on royal horses, both dressed in royal colors, both with the Voske face. Voske did it deliberately.

All the same, he hoped that people understood that these rides were not by his choice. Exactly what did they expect him to do? Refuse, and end up with his head next to Mr. Horst's on the gate?

At Main Street, Voske said, "The weather is perfect. Let's give them a gallop."

Paco's heart sank as they trotted toward the gate. When they drew near the wall, a tendril from an eater rose snatched at his hair. He jerked his head back —and saw the heads. Paco recoiled so violently that Nugget laid his ears back and side-stepped.

Voske glanced over. Smiling. "If you gave them a good look every time you rode by, you'd be used to them by now."

I'll never get used to that, Paco wanted to shout. *I don't want to get used to that.* "No one does that. So what good are they?"

"They deliberately don't look, so they don't ever get used to them. That keeps them fresh in their minds." Voske gave him that smile with his teeth showing. "And every time, they remember who has the power to display their heads."

Those words echoed in Paco's ears as he sat onstage that evening, listening to Voske address the crowd.

"Today, Las Anclas has the honor of witnessing its second Opportunity Day. Our first one was quite a surprise. We got something better than a citizen getting a Change. You all got the privilege of witnessing the courage of my firstborn son, who wanted to be the first volunteer. And so…" Voske turned to Paco. "Prince Liam now has the honor of choosing the first citizen of Las Anclas to take this Opportunity!"

A lot of people took a step back. Meredith stayed where she was, glaring up at him. Paco took his time, as Dr. Lee had cautioned him to do, as if he was still unsure. Voske couldn't suspect that they'd planned it in advance.

Jack was among those who had stepped back. He was looking down as if he was afraid to meet Paco's eyes. Paco raised his hand and pointed. "Jack Lowell."

Jack looked around as if there might another Jack Lowell nearby, then his shoulders slumped. But he started uncertainly forward, and Paco had to admire how much Jack let what had to be real fear show.

Voske turned to Paco and said loudly, "Interesting choice, son. Please enlighten the citizens. What inspired you to choose *this* man?"

Paco had prepared for that. But he'd assumed the question would come at the private dinner afterwards, not in public. Reluctantly, he began, "He's strong and healthy. And young…ish. He should be able to handle it." He shut his mouth with a snap, hoping Voske wouldn't demand the rest of his reason.

But Voske smiled wider. "Strong and healthy. Young…ish. That's true of many people. Why him?"

Paco mentally sent an apology to Jack. He couldn't look at him as he said, "He's not married. He doesn't have children. His only family is an elderly grandmother. So…"

Disapprovingly, Voske murmured, "Sentimental." More loudly, he said, "Ah, yes. You chose someone expendable. Ruthless, son. But tactically excellent."

Paco locked his jaw against a surge of fury as Jack shuffled onto the stage.

"What do I do?" Jack said. "I couldn't see last time."

"Just take my hands," Min Soo said. "It'll only take a

moment."

He laid his palms on hers. She closed her eyes. Three, four, five heartbeats passed, then she stepped backward. "How do you feel?"

Jack blinked. "Am I supposed to feel something?"

Min Soo announced, "No Change."

Jack drew in an audible shuddering breath, then fled the stage. Voske said to the crowd, "That's the way it goes. Unusual for it to happen twice in a row. We'll almost certainly have better luck next time. Dismissed."

The crowd dispersed, many shooting anxious glances over their shoulder. And the usual glares at Paco, which felt like invisible knives. He could barely even feel relieved that at least he hadn't gotten Jack killed.

Bridget spoke up. "Can I choose someone next time?"

Voske smiled at her, then at Paco. "No, let's wait until he chooses someone who Changes. The next one will be your turn."

Paco made it through his dinner with Voske, then went to his room and threw up.

The next morning at Wolfe House, the atmosphere was like the air before a thunderstorm. Even Min Soo looked nervous. Bridget ate methodically, never raising her eyes from her plate. Henry played with his silverware without eating. Paco took a bite that tasted of ash.

Abruptly Voske said, "Has anyone but me been thinking about the ruined city?"

Paco jumped. That was the last thing he'd expected Voske to bring up.

"Always," Min Soo said softly, leaving Paco to wonder if she meant Kerry.

"I've summoned a team to extract our fugitives from the ruined city, if they're still in it, and track them down, if they're not." Voske paused as if waiting for a reply. No one spoke. "Where they are and why can be determined by considering how they think. Give me a reason why they might have left, and a reason why they might have stayed."

This again. Paco had to squelch his longing to be somewhere else in case he accidentally teleported.

"Bridget," Voske said. "You know Kerry quite well, and you met Ross. We'll skip the others, as you haven't met them. What do you think?"

Bridget perked up. "It turned out that Ross was quietly plotting the whole time he was in Gold Point. So, if he's still in the ruined city, it's because he needs more time to plot. If he left, it's because he finished plotting and he's gone off to set his plan into action. Kerry..." She gave her father a nervous glance. "I thought I knew her, but then she betrayed us. So, I actually don't know her well enough to say."

"Fair enough," said Voske. "Henry, what do you think? You know all of them."

Paco's head throbbed. He didn't care what Henry thought. You couldn't believe anything he said.

Henry jerked his shoulders up. "They're all cowards. Either they were so scared they ran, or they were too scared to run. Ross came here half-dead, with nothing. I don't know why all the girls think he's so cool. He's probably sitting in a corner feeling sorry for himself. Jennie talks real big, but obviously she's too scared to come here. Mia's probably building some useless contraption. That brat Summer's probably jumping up and down, bragging about killing sand tigers."

He sidled a furtive look at Voske. "Kerry, well, let me put it this way. I was the only person who didn't trust her when she came to Las Anclas."

"You didn't trust her when she came to Las Anclas?" Voske inquired. "You mean, you believed she was loyal to me?"

Paco pictured a cat keeping silent to lure a mouse out of a hole, then slapping it across the room. Henry's fork clattered to his plate. He mumbled, "I just thought she was a liar. In general."

Voske turned the full force of the eerie smile on Paco. "And you, Liam?"

Paco couldn't just babble randomly, like Henry had. Coming from him, Voske would take that as defiance. He pictured Yuki's slim fingers moving a Go piece. Click, down on the board. *Redirect.* "I think they haven't come out because they're all dead."

Voske's eyebrows slanted more steeply. "What makes you think that?"

Paco tried to figure out what Voske already knew about Ross's power. But he had no way of knowing. He'd have to stick as close as possible to the truth—or what Paco himself had believed to be the truth, before he'd teleported into the ruined city. "Ross has only ever been able to take two people through the crystal forest at a time. And five of them went in. I think he tried to protect all of them, and they all died."

He could see that Voske was taking him seriously. Voske looked genuinely approving. "Yes. That matches with what I know."

Good. Now Voske was underestimating their numbers.

Bridget suggested, "Maybe he tried to protect all five of them, but it only worked for the usual two. So, two are dead. There could still be three left."

Voske gave a nod. "Very good, Bridget. If we assume that Ross is still alive, which two do you think he protected?"

"Well, um, Kerry betrayed us because she fell in love with him, so he must have picked her. And his sister. Of course he'd protect his sister. Anyone would." Bridget had started out nervous but ended confident. Paco wondered how close she'd been to Kerry.

"Henry?" Voske asked.

"Definitely his brat sister." Henry shrugged. "Maybe he flipped a coin for the other spot."

Voske gave him a look that made Paco's guts clench, then said, "Liam?"

Much as Paco hated responding to that name—much less agreeing with Henry—he said, "Yeah. If Ross could protect anyone, he'd have protected his sister." He wondered if it would help to continue the confusion over Ross's supposed love affair with Kerry, then decided Voske was too good at catching outright lies. "No idea about the others."

An aide came in and saluted. "Erik Dente is here, sir."

Bridget gave a squeal of delight.

"Rather late, but that's the team I mentioned," said Voske. "Bridget, you may go."

She ran out, leaving Paco wondering who Erik Dente was to get Bridget so excited. A favorite uncle?

"Liam, come with me." Voske led the way to Main Street. The streets, though usually bustling with morning activities, were utterly deserted.

The area just inside the gate was swarming with roaches the size of large dogs. They were black, their carapaces gleaming, and they made a soft chittering sound. Bridget was in their midst, surrounded by waving feelers and scrabbling legs. For an instant, Paco thought they were eating her. But her squeals were pure joy.

"Erik, welcome," Voske said to the man leading the roaches. "Here at last."

"I'm so sorry, sir," said Erik. "A flock of cloud vipers attacked us, and the roaches stampeded. It took me two days to round them up. But I didn't lose a one."

Someone in the saddlery lifted a shade, then slammed it back down.

"Let's review your orders," said Voske.

Review, Paco thought. So, Erik already knew what he was supposed to do. Bridget was playing with the roaches. *This is just for me.*

"I'm to take my roaches to the edge of the ruined city," the trainer began.

To Paco, Voske explained, "Erik has already tested the roaches' ability to pass harmlessly through the local crystal trees. He believes it's because they're cold-blooded. Perhaps the trees can sense the heat generated by mammals. Isn't that interesting?"

Paco's mind was already racing ahead to why Voske would want to send a swam of giant roaches through crystal trees. He barely managed a nod.

Voske spoke to Erik. "Before we release them into the forest, I want to see a demonstration. On a live target."

Paco's stomach lurched.

Erik didn't flinch or even look surprised. "Yes, sir. I'm sure you'll be pleased with their performance. Shall I choose a prisoner?"

"No, use Terry Nelson. He's in detention again for

drunk and disorderly—for the last time. This will be a private demonstration, just for the army. Then give the roaches the night to rest. Release them at dawn."

"Yes, sir!"

"Give them the command to capture any humans within the forest. Not to kill. You'll probably lose some roaches, but it's an acceptable margin."

Paco, picturing those hideous bugs swarming Jennie and Mia and the others, had to force himself to keep a stone face. He wished he had a weapon. How he *longed* to jab steel between Voske's ribs.

He felt Voske watching him as the tyrant added, "You must order the roaches to keep their prisoners together. This is very important. If they're separated, the crystal trees will kill all but Ross Juarez."

"Yes, sir," said Erik. "But I don't need to give them a special order. The swarm is already trained to stay together and keep their captives at the center."

"Excellent work. Come along, Bridget!"

Bridget reluctantly left the roaches. They surged after her in a glittering wave.

Erik cracked his whip down on their carapaces. "Back! Back!"

As the roaches skittered into a formation, Bridget said, "Erik, they were just saying hello."

"Princess, they're not pets. They need discipline." The whip came down across their lowered feelers. The roaches chittered in pain.

Paco was surprised to see tears in Bridget's eyes. She gulped and said to her father, "I know they're not pets. But that's no reason to be cruel to them. *I* think the roaches could be trained without the whip. They're *smart*."

"Bridget, Erik gets results. If someone is an expert, you don't interfere with their methods." To the roach master, Voske said, "Now go."

Erik cracked his whip and rode away, his roaches scuttling after.

·26·
PACO

LAS ANCLAS AND THE RUINED CITY

PACO AWOKE AT DAWN. He hated that he'd have so little time to give the warning about the roaches, but he couldn't teleport through the desert without being able to see where he was going. At least Voske hadn't forced him to watch the "demonstration" with the roaches. As he dressed, he reviewed his teleporting stops, picturing each precisely, concentrated, and jumped.

There. First step done. A swift look around. No one. He checked himself. He'd calculated well. Nothing missing, not even a thread of cloth. Second stage.

A chill wrung through him as he looked around, remembering that Voske had the crystal forest surrounded. He'd chosen well, nothing near the gully. And he was intact. This next one would increase the chill, but at least he expected it now. Jump. Pause, brace, jump.

Once the worst of the shivering abated, he shut his eyes and brought up an image of Jennie, tall and strong and confident. It would be so good to have Jennie by his side, sword in hand…

Jump! He staggered, shivered, and there was Jennie, whirling around, sword raised. She lowered her weapon, grinning in weary relief. "Paco!"

They were on top of a hill, with a view of the entire ruined city. He could see the ring of crystal trees, and even some of the desert beyond. Everyone looked exhausted. Even Summer looked wilted, something he had not thought possible. They were filthy to the eyebrows, but Ross managed a half-smile. "Good to see you."

Paco wished he could give them some good news—they looked in desperate need of it—but he said, "Voske is sending a swarm of giant attack roaches to drag you out."

"Oh, Erik Dente is here?" Kerry asked. "You know, those roaches—"

Paco hurried on, "They were released at dawn, so they'll arrive...I don't know, as fast as they can scuttle. They're cold-blooded, so they can get through the forest."

"But we can't," Ross said, sounding bitter.

Paco began to say, "About that—"

A flicker in the corner of his eye resolved into Loretta. She hurled something at Ross, and vanished as soon as it left her hands. A web of green strands hit Ross and clung. The tendrils tightened around his legs, and he fell hard. The more he struggled, the tighter they contracted.

The shadow reappeared as Loretta, a knife in both hands. She darted at Jennie, who brought up her sword.

Axel charged Jennie from the other direction. Paco moved to intercept the big man, but the dirt crumbled away at his feet. A yawning maw gaped below, like a pit mouth but with slick, writhing tentacles instead of fangs. He scrambled backward.

Something fell over his head, draping down to his ankles. A girl's voice exclaimed, "Got him!"

Paco instinctively tried to throw the stuff off, but it tightened around him, knocking him off his feet. He hit the dirt hard. Axel roared, "You idiot! He can teleport! Now you've wasted the net!"

Paco had never tried to teleport out of something covering him. He glanced around: Ross still entangled, Summer frantically cutting at the vines covering him, Jennie and Kerry fighting the disappearing and reappearing Loretta, and Axel going straight for Mia, knife high. He longed to strike back at Axel—and there he was, within arm's reach. He kicked Axel's ankles out from under him.

An unpleasantly familiar skittering, chittering noise rose up from all around them. Paco yelled, "It's the roaches!"

Kerry shouted, "Freeze!"

Paco froze. And then the roaches were upon them.

Paco had to bite his lip to stop himself from flailing at those tickling legs. Axel slashed an ice knife at the nearest roach, kicked at another, and smashed a third. The roaches went into a frenzy as they rushed him, scrabbling right past Paco to bury Axel in shiny black bodies.

Axel emerged from the mass, slashing wildly and flinging out ice daggers. The roaches pursued him.

Kerry stood absolutely still as roaches swarmed past her. Jennie and Mia clung to each other, wild-eyed, while Summer perched atop a tree far too slender to support the weight of a giant roach, even if they could climb. Ross lay still and entangled, his eyes clenched shut. Loretta and Maria-Pilar had vanished.

Paco was startled by a howling groan. A pair of long, low, scaled creatures streaked out of the trees and lunged at Axel, teeth at both ends snapping. Axel hesitated between fighting the roaches and fighting the armored things—and then all four jaws were on him, yanking him off his feet. His cursing swiftly turned to screams which abruptly cut off. Then there was only rapid crunching. In what seemed like an impossibly short time, there was nothing left, and the creatures dragged their swollen bellies back into the underbrush.

It had all happened so fast, Paco was stunned.

After a thunderous pause, Summer said, "If they have mouths at both ends, how do they—"

"In the middle," Mia said, subdued. "I saw when Jennie flipped one over."

"Gross!"

"You asked."

The roaches had scattered at the approach of the double-mouthed creatures, vanishing into the nearby trees. Their chittering changed to occasional squeaks.

Paco stared into the trees. "The guy who had them said they'd drag you all out alive."

Kerry glanced in the direction of the squeaks. "Before we got attacked, I was going to say that my sister Bridget likes those roaches. She said that if you left them alone, they'd leave you alone. They were trained to attack anything that fought them."

Kerry cocked her head. "Can you see them from where you are, Summer?"

"Yeah," Summer said. "They're rolling around in the moss and climbing mushrooms and stuff like that. I think they're having…roach fun."

"Maybe they'd rather have roach fun than go back," Mia suggested.

Thoughtfully, Kerry said, "I think you're right. Bridget always did say their master was cruel to them."

Paco went to help Jennie, who had cut the vines around Ross and was peeling them off, one at a time, leaving a slime trail over his jeans and leather jacket. Kerry kept a lookout in all directions, hands at the ready.

Summer dropped from her perch. There was a thump and a yelp. A boulder blurred and became Maria-Pilar, flat on the ground with Summer on top of her.

"I surrender," gasped Maria-Pilar.

"Where's Loretta?" Jennie demanded.

"Ran off. I don't know where," Maria-Pilar's voice was muffled by dirt.

"It's a plot!" Summer exclaimed.

"Move over, Summer." Mia had picked up the net that had been dropped over Paco. As Summer eased aside, Mia dropped the net over Maria-Pilar. The wiggling vines instantly tightened.

There was another squeak from behind the glittering line of shrubs.

"Are those roaches coming back?" Ross asked.

"I'll see!" Summer leaped to the top of a tree, then called down, "Nope. Still just doing roach stuff."

Kerry glanced in the direction of the squeak. "I think they've found a place where no one will ever bother them again."

"Good." Maria-Pilar shuddered, and the vines tightened even more.

Jennie eyed her as Kerry knelt beside Maria-Pilar. Her rat popped out of her shirt, whiskers trembling as he sniffed at the girl in the net.

"Maria-Pilar, would you be willing to join us?" Kerry asked.

Jennie held up her hand. "Hold on. She's been fighting us the entire time we've been in here."

Maria-Pilar glanced around nervously, staring into every shadow.

Kerry spoke to Maria-Pilar. "I think Loretta's gone for now. I've noticed you've always been a little too late or a little too noisy when Axel and Loretta attacked us. Nothing obvious enough that they'd notice, but enough that we've always had just enough warning of their approach. And I *know* you're a far better fighter than you've showed us the past few days." She looked up at Jennie. "I couldn't say anything about it before because you can never tell for sure if Loretta's around." To Maria-Pilar, Kerry said, "Am I right?"

Maria-Pilar's gaze again flicked around. She whispered, "Of course you are. I couldn't do anything to get you killed. But I've been terrified that Axel or Loretta would notice and kill me. It's been hell, Kerry. Everyone I liked on my team is dead. I don't want to spend the rest of my life chasing around this weird place, attacking you guys. But I *had* to."

"How convenient," Summer said. "Don't trust her. She'll turn into a mushroom and stab us in the night."

Kerry pulled a clinging vine away from Maria-Pilar's face. "If we can get out and leave Loretta here, Voske will never know you're still alive. Your family will be safe."

Maria-Pilar's eyes closed, but tears leaked from beneath her lashes.

"Don't buy those fake tears," said Summer. "They're probably an illusion!"

Kerry wiped the tears from Maria-Pilar's dirty face. "They're real."

Maria-Pilar looked up at Summer. "What a joke. You don't believe I'd rather be with you, but *she* sure will."

Jennie folded her arms. "What can you give us?"

Maria-Pilar tried to straighten, and the vines writhed and tightened. "I could cast illusions for you, even tied up. If you stay close to me, I could cover a couple of you."

Kerry chuckled. "Remember when you covered me and Santiago so we could jump out at Domingo?"

Maria-Pilar gave a small smile. "For a big guy, he squealed like a two-year-old."

Ross said to Maria-Pilar, "I remember you from Gold Point. And I remember how hard you and your family worked to protect your little sister."

Kerry nodded. To the others, she said, "If Maria-Pilar

had wanted to kill us, her team would have been more successful. Did you hear Axel screaming at her just now?"

"I'm not stupid enough to drop a net over a teleporter unless I wanted him to escape. But I had to be convincing." Maria-Pilar glanced at Ross. "Like when we first got you. I had to report you sawing those ropes — Loretta was about to notice anyway."

Ross nodded. "I remember. You're right."

"Convinced?" Kerry looked around at them all.

"Any objections?" Jennie asked.

Summer tilted her head. "It *was* stupid to throw a net over a teleporter."

"If Kerry trusts her, I trust her," said Mia.

Jennie gave Maria-Pilar a long, considering look, then said, "Ross told me about Voske holding Santiago's six-year-old cousin hostage. That's your sister?"

Maria-Pilar nodded. "She's seven now."

Jennie glanced at Paco, surprising him. He hadn't thought he'd be a part of this decision, as it wouldn't affect him. Then he realized that she wanted his opinion because she trusted his judgement. It warmed him inside. Then he thought about Maria-Pilar. It was safer to err on the side of caution, but the choked-up way she'd mentioned her sister's age convinced him. He nodded.

"Cut her loose," Jennie said.

Kerry began sawing at the vines with an invisible knife.

"I'm glad you're with us," said Ross. "Especially if we're stuck here for good."

Mia and Summer's voices collided. "No, we're not!" "You'll figure it out!"

Paco raised his voice. "Ross, I asked Dr. Lee about your power. He thought it wasn't really gone. He asked me to ask you what you've been doing to try to get it back."

Ross tensed. "I've been trying as hard as I can. I concentrate and concentrate, but there's just nothing there."

Paco saw the teeth-gritted intensity in Ross's haggard face and felt more hopeful. "Dr. Lee thought that you might be trying too hard. Like that vine net you were caught in. The harder you struggle, the tighter it holds you. He thought maybe something bad had happened right before you lost your power. Something you wouldn't want to remember. Something you *couldn't* remember unless you relaxed enough to just let it in."

Ross looked doubtful, then said, "Well, it's not like it's been very relaxing in here. I could try again. Or maybe, try less."

Jennie grinned at him. "Here's something relaxing to think about. Now it's six against one."

Ross managed a brief smile.

Kerry said to Maria-Pilar, "Santiago will be so glad you're with us."

The mention of Santiago reminded Paco of passing time. "I have to get back. *When* you get out, go to the grove of black trees outside Las Anclas. I'll throw in a rock with a note. It'll tell you where to go."

As he readied himself to teleport, the last thing he heard was a squeak from a happy roach.

·27·

FELICITÉ

CATALINA

"IT'S SUCH A PERFECT day for the beach," said Paloma.

Felicité didn't even flinch. Paloma loved swimming, but Shobha wouldn't even put a toe in the water. Nobody cared that Felicité claimed to also prefer to bask in the sun. Well, Isais always gave her that hopeful look, but by now it had started to seem less hopeful and more resigned.

"I love your new hair, Noelle," said Isais.

Felicité ran her fingers through her newly dyed hair, letting some locks dangle before her eyes. The hairdresser had perfectly captured the intense blue-green of the ocean in sunlight. Felicité could still hardly believe she'd had the nerve to choose that color. No one in Las Anclas would ever dye their hair such an unnatural shade, even if they were Changed. But in Catalina, it was fashionable. And it was a wonderful contrast with her bronze scales.

Paloma turned a handspring, her wings fluttering in the breeze, then laughed. Felicité couldn't help thinking of Sujata, who had been so good at gymnastics and had also loved to swim in the ocean. Then she shut those thoughts away. She'd never see Sujata again. That life was *over*.

Paloma stretched her hands toward the sky. "After a long day at the sewing machine, I need to move. And I mean more than my feet on the treadle." She spun around on her toes and danced backward. "Noelle, you've got such exquisite taste. Do you like sewing? Maybe you could work with me!"

Felicité couldn't admit that her clothes had been both made and mended by others. Noelle would not have had servants. "Sorry, I'm all thumbs."

She was relieved that the rules about not quizzing people on their pasts meant that they couldn't ask what her apprenticeship had been. She'd only ever worked as a scribe and a mayor's assistant, preparing for a future she'd never have. That was a problem. Guests at the palace usually stayed for a few days to a month, before finding a job and a place in the community. Noelle needed a job that required her to leave periodically, like every time the Catalina Players were in town.

"What about being a diplomat?" Isais suggested. "You have such lovely manners, and you get along with everyone."

Diplomat! Mother was the finest diplomat Felicité had ever seen. A mayor had to be. Mother's training had allowed Felicité to become Noelle, who got along with everyone. Everyone liked Noelle. It was easy to be Noelle, who had no past, only a future. One she could make herself.

They reached the white sand of the beach. The boys tore their shirts off, leaving only their shorts, and dove into the water. Paloma shed her dress, revealing a bathing suit underneath, and jumped in after them.

Nicolas called out, "The water is perfect. Want to just get your feet wet, Noelle?"

Paloma waved. "Come join me! We'll have a water fight. Girls against boys!"

"I don't want to wash out my gorgeous new hair dye," Felicité called back. "We've got the masquerade ball tonight."

"It doesn't wash out that easily." Paloma paused, then said, "If you don't know how to swim, I'd be happy to teach you."

Isais looked uncomfortable—for her sake. The pressure the others were giving her was friendly, but it was still pressure.

From the towel beside her, Shobha took her hand. "You don't have to. You can stay with me."

Once again, Felicité was reminded of Becky. Oh, how she missed Becky. How she regretted that last stupid, *stupid* year when they had barely spoken. It still hurt to realize that Becky had been enduring abuse for all those years, and Felicité hadn't known. She'd even begun to resent Becky for not telling her, especially when Becky got that Change, a useful Change, that didn't show.

All those reasons sounded so babyish now, so *selfish*. Now she had nothing but the memory of a year of silence when they could have talked. If anyone would have understood about Felicité's Change, it would have been Becky. She would never see Becky again. She would never see Wu Zetian again. She would never see her family again. She had to leave all that behind. She was *Noelle*.

She got up and ran toward the water.

"Noelle?" The voice sounded like a seagull's cry as she splashed into a wave, and then dove under.

The Change began. Impatiently she slipped out of her clothes and tossed them up on the sand, moments before her fluke would have torn them apart. Giving her fins a strong flip, she surged upward through the bubbles streaming from her gills and broke the surface.

"Noelle, is that you?" Paloma gasped. "You're gorgeous!"

Noelle slapped the water with her fluke. "It's me."

Paloma turned to Isais. "Did you know?"

Isais was grinning. "It's been killing me not to say anything! Isn't she fantastic?"

Shobha walked down to the water and cautiously stuck a toe in.

"Got over your horror of cold water, Shobha?" Nicolas teased.

"Nope," Shobha said, pushing out into the surging waves. "But it's not every day that I get to swim with a mermaid!"

Noelle swam underwater, glorying in her speed and strength. She surged up again, then turned in the air, and came down, slapping a huge wave of water at the boys.

Paloma shouted with laughter. "Battle on!"

They splashed and ducked in a grand water fight. Then Noelle swam underwater to Isais and tugged at his hand. He ducked down and they looked at each other through the clear water. His black hair waved about his face and his aura coruscated in shimmering rainbows. She cupped his face in webbed hands. When he drifted toward her, laughing a little so that bubbles escaped from his lips, she drew nearer, and nearer, and kissed him.

He kissed her back, then they surfaced, Isais laughing at the sky breathlessly. "Watch out! You almost made me forget that I can't breathe underwater."

"Sorry!"

"So, we'll just have to try until we get it right," he whispered.

It was a perfect moment in a perfect day. Her new life was perfect. She had become a new person. While swimming in the ocean, she had been nameless. What was more natural than to have a new name for a new life?

And what better way to begin life as Noelle than by capping off a perfect day with a masquerade ball?

When they finished swimming, the girls held up a towel for her to Change and dress behind. Paloma offered to sew her a wrapper that was easy to slip on and off. Then everyone parted to dress for the ball.

Isais escorted Noelle to the palace. As they walked by the blue roses, he said, "I'm so proud of you, Noelle." He gave her a soft kiss, which she returned eagerly. "I'll introduce you to some diplomats tonight."

Would he turn out to be The One? Or was that just a stupid dream belonging to the Felicité she no longer was? She shrugged internally. It was the first day of her new life. She had plenty of time ahead to figure that out.

She luxuriated in a bath. It was so wonderful not to be afraid of water. After she dressed, she admired herself in the mirror. Her hair looked gorgeous, complementing the bronze scales around her eyes. Her dress was the lightest gauze in shades of blues and sea-greens, seeming to float around her. She decided not to wear a mask, because she had the perfect mask.

The girl in the mirror had a new place, new friends, and a new life. She was Noelle.

The palace ballroom was enormous, a half-sphere of iridescence. This was a *real* ball, in a splendid palace with an orchestra playing up in a gallery. So superior to poky Las Anclas, whose celebrations either took place in the town hall, which was basically a very large barn, or outside on the ground, bordered by vegetable patches. The little town band played on a bare platform.

Isais was waiting for her, striking in deep midnight

blue, which enhanced his aura of color. He smiled and held out his hand, and they walked in together. They'd just found and greeted their friends, everyone admiring everyone else, when the brass trumpets rang out a fanfare, announcing the first waltz. She turned to Isais to invite him to dance at the same time he turned to her, and they laughed. Isais was a wonderful dancer, of course. She floated in his arms, glorying in her new life.

She rarely sat down but danced every dance. Late in the evening, the orchestra struck up another waltz while Noelle was chatting with Shobha, whose deep brown skin looked spectacular against the golden silk of her gown. Shobha held out her hand, and they twirled to the center of the ballroom, with everyone else dancing around them. As they whirled past a tall, framed mirror, she saw her sea-colored gown fluttering against Shobha's gold. So elegant, so civilized. Truly, the perfect life.

As the orchestra brought the waltz to an end, she caught sight of Isais up to the dais with his parents, the ambassadors. All three were in earnest conversation, as several council members drew near. They all looked very serious.

Noelle made her way to Isais's side. "Isais?"

He turned her way. "There's nothing wrong, just work—news on the way. I'll find you when I'm done. Unless you'd like to join me?"

News meant the intrusion of the outside world. She was torn. Staying in this perfect moment would cap the perfect day, but she had a creeping sense of urgency. She knew that she'd be asking him about the news as soon as he got back, so why not hear it firsthand? "I'd like to come."

He took her hand. "This is part of diplomacy—we're never truly off-duty. But I like it that way. There's always something going on."

Exactly the way she'd felt... No. That life was gone.

"Hang on. I want to show you something cool first." He led the way up a magnificent spiral staircase, tiled in gleaming, iridescent mother-of-pearl. Isais had taken her up to the tower once before, and proudly pointed out the beautiful view of the mainland coastline. She'd consciously avoided looking in the direction of Las

Anclas.

To Noelle's relief, Isais pointed not out but up, into the star-studded black of the night sky. She gasped. A luminescent bubble trailing gleaming streamers was slowly floating down toward them. She couldn't get any sense of its size. It looked like the moon. "What is that?"

Isaias said with pride, "It's a flying jellyfish."

Noelle remembered the slow dance of the jellyfish deep in the ocean. And the tiny pale bubbles of jellyfish in the sky, seen from Las Anclas.

Isais misinterpreted her expression. "They only sting on command. We're perfectly safe."

"I know. I'm more used to them in the sea. And none this big." The jellyfish descended closer, and she saw that it was the size of the Las Anclas schoolhouse. It had a basket suspended beneath its body. "Are those people in that basket?"

"Yes! The jellyfish riders have spent hundreds of years learning to raise, train, and steer them. We have a landing platform in the garden, but this is the best place to see them float in. We use them for transportation sometimes, but mostly they carry messages." He took her arm. "Come on, let's go meet them."

"Will they mind if I'm there?" She was intrigued.

"No. If it were secret, we wouldn't have seen them come in. The riders can command them to change color — to night-black, for instance."

They headed for the jellyfish platform at the back of the garden. The basket was just touching down when Isais and Noelle arrived.

Two people hopped out of the basket. Noelle's step faltered. One of them looked nearly skeletal, like Sheriff Crow, but over their entire body. The second jellyfish rider had grayish skin lightly coated in translucent slime, like some deep-sea creature accidentally caught in a net and dragged up to the surface.

Isais greeted them with enthusiasm, seizing the skeletal person's hand and smiling at the slimy one. "Cathy! Jim! Great to see you!" He turned to Noelle, saying "And this is Noelle, a newcomer to Catalina. Noelle, this is Cathy, and this is Jim. Don't shake Jim's hand."

Noelle gave Jim a graceful curtsey. Cathy stepped forward, her hand outheld. "Hi, Noelle."

Noelle glanced at Isais, who was smiling at her, clearly expecting her to shake that bundle of sticks covered in stretched skin. Noelle forced herself to take it. It felt exactly like she'd imagined. "Pleased to meet you, Cathy," she said in her sweetest voice.

The ambassadors emerged from the palace door and greeted them with real pleasure. Mrs. Aldana, Isais's mother, asked, "What news do you bring us?"

Cathy laughed. Noelle turned away from those grinning teeth. "You'll *never* guess who insisted on sending out a call for allies."

"King Voske, of course," Mr. Aldana said with a chuckle.

"Almost as good — Tom Preston of Las Anclas!" Jim hooted with laughter.

Noelle was frozen, her nerves chilling to the bone. *Daddy?*

Cathy, also laughing, said, "Preston turned up at Dai La and requested an alliance."

"*What?*"

For a horrifying instant, she thought she'd exclaimed aloud. Then she realized that her thought had been spoken by everyone else.

Cathy went on, her tone jeering, "The Saigon Alliance turned him down, of course. So, he demanded that a jellyfish be sent to request an alliance with Catalina. The nerve of him! He couldn't even stand to look me and Jim in the face when we went to Las Anclas to ask for help with the drought. So, the council sent us to deliver his request, and then deliver your reply to him personally."

"Should we even bother unhitching the jellyfish?" Jim patted the tether. "We can take your 'not a chance' and be back in Dai La in time for breakfast."

Felicité — Noelle — Felicité forced her face to remain a pleasant mirror while inwardly, her thoughts raced and her heart pounded. Daddy was alive! And looking for help. And these people were *laughing at him*.

Isais exclaimed, "What a turnaround! I remember the drought when I was ten. We were living on nothing but dried fish and seaweed. I still can't stand seaweed. I remember how excited I was when we sent a boat to Las Anclas. I thought it would come back full of juicy fresh fruit and baked bread."

Jim gave a disgusted snort. "I still can't believe that Tom Preston wouldn't even let the Rileys give us a drink of water before he booted us out."

Cathy's teeth were bared in her skull face. "He even had the Rangers lined up there, fully armed, like he thought we might steal that glass of water."

"The council has already discussed this," said Mrs. Aldana. "We thought Preston might get desperate enough to ask for an alliance with Catalina to save his bigoted town. Tell him we're giving him the same answer he gave us eight years ago when we asked him for help to save our town. No."

Felicité suppressed the wild urge to shout, "You're talking about my father! Yes! The daughter of your worst enemy is living in your own house!"

She imagined their reactions. Shock. Horror. Anger. Betrayal. And then… What would they do? Throw her out of the palace, of course. Exile her from Catalina? Yes. Of course they'd exile her. They'd boot her out, exactly like her father had booted out Jim and Cathy.

She could always return to the underwater world, where everything was beautiful and peaceful. There was no Felicité Wolfe there. There was no Noelle, either. She could stay there forever, until even the memory of what she'd lost was gone.

Or she could say nothing. She could stay Noelle forever. It wasn't a lie, really. She *was* Noelle. She was the beautiful mermaid who couldn't speak of her tragic past. Wasn't that more true than the life she'd led in Las Anclas, lying to everyone, even lying to herself, believing that she was a hideous monster who had to pretend to be a Norm?

The conversation continued, but Felicité didn't hear a word.

Her father was alive. He was still fighting for his town. His family. He thought he was still fighting for her. And Mother and Grandmère and Will. He had to know that Voske had either killed his family or taken them prisoner. He must be longing to know if they were all right, longing to get any news of them, even to know if they were still alive. It had to be eating him up inside to be so far away.

She folded her forearms tightly across her cramping belly. She could tell herself she didn't care, but her body didn't lie. Her father was trying so desperately to find someone who'd help him fight Voske. It wasn't funny at all. But the Saigon Alliance and Catalina only saw him as a villain. To them, he was Evil Tom Preston—just as she'd once seen Catalina as the Land of Monsters.

There was nothing that could ever change their minds.

Change, she thought. Maybe a Changed person could. Like her.

She stood very still, thinking it through. She *was* Changed. She was from Las Anclas. Mother had trained her in diplomacy since she was six years old. She remembered all her lessons in how to request an alliance, temporary or permanent, for war or for trade. She pictured herself standing before the council of Saigon, making that request. The image came easily. Of course she could do that.

But if she did, she'd also have to stand in front of her father.

She imagined his disgust. His horror. His betrayal, once he realized that she had been lying to him for years. This could be the last time she would ever see him.

And it would be the last time she would ever see Catalina. She would never find out if Isais was a brief flirtation, or something more. She'd never see Paloma and Shobha and Nicolas again. It might be the last time anyone would ever look at her in the water and see her as a beautiful mermaid.

Or maybe she could save Las Anclas and keep what she had, by working a little diplomacy right here, as Noelle.

She faced them all. "There might be another way of looking at things." She could hear mother's voice: "*Find common ground. If you offer a way to compromise, both sides give a little, but get something, too.*"

The others turned to her, looking surprised. Isais said, "Noelle is interested in becoming a diplomat."

Mrs. Aldana gave her a nod. "What do you have to

say, Noelle?"

What could she give Catalina? "The drought was ten years ago. That's a long time. Mr. Preston did ask for an alliance, and that suggests that things are different now."

Jim snorted. "Things are different, all right. Voske's got that town. And it couldn't happen to a worse bunch of bigots. If we agreed to that alliance, Preston would take what he wanted from us and turn around and stab us in the back. If Voske gets kicked out of Las Anclas, Preston and his wife will go right back to ruling that town. And they hate Changed people. They were willing to let every soul in Catalina starve to death, just because of who we are."

Sickness churned inside Felicité. Daddy would never go back on an alliance, but Jim was right about how he felt. He wouldn't be able to look at *her* face.

And if they found out who she really was, it wouldn't matter if they liked Noelle. She was the daughter of the hated Tom Preston.

"Good try, Noelle," Mr. Aldana said. "You've the makings of a diplomat if you can find a way to defend Tom Preston!"

The adults all chuckled, but not at her. They returned to their conversation.

Isais hastened to reassure her. "They're not laughing at you. They're laughing at Dad's joke about Preston and his family. They really did like what you said."

Preston and his family. Had Isais ever heard of *her?* The Catalina players had put on a show mocking her, but they couldn't have played it in Catalina, could they?

"Thank you," she said. "Have you ever been to Las Anclas?"

"No, but the Catalina players have. They put on a play making fun of Preston and his family."

"Family? What do you know about Tom Preston's family?" Her fingers tightened on her skirts. She didn't want to lie outright, in case she did decide to reveal herself. Her words sounded stilted, but Isaias replied easily.

"He has a daughter and a son. The son is a kid. He wasn't in the play. The daughter has a funny name. Funella? Anyway, she's supposed to be as bad as her parents." Isais frowned.

Felicité held her breath.

He went on, slowly, "Or maybe not. I know one of the teenage players pretty well. Rosalind told me the whole story. I wish I remembered it better. At the time I was more interested in hearing about the wildfire they'd helped fight than in Tom Preston's daughter. But Rosalind said they all ended up feeling bad about making fun of her. Grandma Wu actually apologized, and that's not something she normally does. So maybe Fussilla's not like her father."

Felicité clutched her arms tightly against her chest. So, *this* was her choice. She didn't have to be Noelle to stay in Catalina. She could be Felicité here. She wouldn't even have to explain why she'd left. Everyone would assume it was to get away from her father. She'd never have to see him again, and he could go on remembering her as the beautiful Norm daughter he loved.

"Noelle?" Isais asked. "Are you cold? We could go back in. They're playing another waltz."

"Just a moment," Felicité said, pretending to look out to sea.

This was the true choice. It was much simpler than the dramatic scenarios she'd thought of before. She could stay in Catalina and wash her hands of her family, and her past, and her town. Like Becky. And Dr. Lee. Sujata. Nasreen. Even the people she didn't particularly like, but who didn't deserve to live under Voske's tyranny.

Or she could leave Catalina, and fight for her town.

"Excuse me," she said loudly.

The general conversation broke off, as Isais gave her a concerned glance. She spoke as soon as she saw that everyone was looking at her.

"My name is Felicité Noelle Wolfe. I'm Tom Preston's daughter."

I'm Tom Preston's daughter. Her words echoed in her own ears.

The adults stared at her with a variety of expressions of shock that in another time, maybe another life, might have once been funny.

Then Isais reached out and clasped her hands. In a voice throbbing with emotion, he said. "Oh, Noelle. You are so brave. I don't even have words."

When Felicité didn't reply, he went on, "Forced to hide your own true, beautiful self from your oppressive town and your own family! It must have been so terrible for you, especially when your town was taken over! But look at you, you escaped all that. You took your destiny into your own hands, and braved incredible dangers under the sea to seek out a place where you could make your own future."

Felicité had guessed that Isais would feel something like that, but she hadn't expected him to be quite so eloquent. A part of her loved him for it. He was a genuinely good person—and so romantic.

Unfortunately, now was not a time when she could revel in that. She had business to attend to. "Thank you." More loudly, looking at the adults, she repeated, "Tom Preston is my *father*. So—"

Isais's aura flickered with the rose and gold colors it went when he told her how beautiful she was. Or took her to a particularly romantic spot. "Yes! And you came here! That's the bravest part of all. It's like the Catalina Players' play about the Montagues and the Capulets!"

"Noelle—or do you prefer Felicité?" Mr. Aldana said. "You don't need to be afraid. Many refugees come here because their families didn't accept them. We would never hold your parentage against you."

Even fifteen minutes ago, she would have been so happy and relieved to have heard that. But now, it was just another step in the dance of diplomacy.

"That's very kind of you," she replied. "I've seen how welcoming Catalina is to refugees. As I'm sure you're aware, one third of Las Anclas is Changed. My father isn't only fighting for the Norms in the town. Everyone in Las Anclas is suffering under Voske's tyranny."

She turned to Jim and Cathy. "You mentioned the Rileys, who offered you hospitality. They're still in Las Anclas. And they need help."

The smiles faded. They looked at one another. Then Mrs. Aldana said gently, "Yes. We are aware. Our laughter was inappropriate. But don't take it as a sign that we didn't regard this decision seriously. We did, and it's final. But also, know that you are as welcome here as you ever were."

She scoured her memory of Mother's lessons, trying to find something that would persuade them as she gazed at the winking lights across the bay. Those lights were Voske's lamps, so his sentries could prevent anyone from escaping Las Anclas. Anyone—like Becky. Like her little brother Will. Her Grandmère. Tommy Horst, whose father had been grotesquely murdered. Townspeople she'd known all her life. How many more executions had Voske forced Las Anclas to watch since Felicité's escape?

"In that case, I request transportation to Dai La," she said.

·28·
FELICITÉ

DAI LA

FELICITÉ STEPPED OUT OF the jellyfish basket onto the landing platform in Dai La. The flight had taken all night, in which time she had passed through the absolute terror of swinging in the sky, to an attempt to practice diplomacy on the unreceptive Cathy and Jim, to a state of mingled boredom, anxiety, and exhaustion.

The weak dawn light illuminated hanging bridges and houses on stilts as Felicité hefted her carryall and stepped onto the platform's tower. She held onto the rail until her body stopped feeling that it was swaying. Below her lay not a town, but a *city*, with round homes connected by a maze of bridges and staircases built over the waters of the bay.

Rainbow-feathered parakeets flew everywhere, chirping and singing. One landed on Cathy's outstretched forearm. She removed a tiny paper scroll from a carrying case attached to its leg, then stroked it gently. The bird chirped at her. Felicité missed Wu Zetian so much. Maybe now she'd get to see her again.

"Thank you for the ride. Do you have any idea where I should start looking for my father?"

Cathy did not look away from the bird. "Nope."

"Good luck," Jim said briefly. Felicité felt the *You'll need it* that went unsaid. At least he hadn't said it aloud. She'd take that as a tiny victory.

She decided to start with the council building, which Jim and Cathy had pointed out to her from the air. She descended the platform and marched straight toward it.

Or she tried to, at least. It became immediately apparent that there were no straight lines in this city. Felicité walked along a bridge, dodging the strange, fat, hairless little black creatures that trotted with purpose like rats did in Las Anclas, clearly with jobs to do. Too bad she couldn't get directions from one.

The bridge ended in a choice of three rope ladders. She marched up a woman watering a small garden patch in pots on a platform. "Excuse me. I'm looking for Tom Preston."

The woman glared at her like she was a tomato worm. "Never heard of him." As Felicité turned away, the woman added, "And I'm glad of it!"

Felicité crossed a randomly chosen rope bridge and approached a teenager who was delivering newspapers by levitating them alongside him. "I'm looking for Tom Preston."

"What do you want *him* for?" The newspapers bounced aggressively.

"I have business with him."

"Too bad. He's probably gone by now. Good riddance." A newspaper hurled itself against a door.

Felicité worked her way down to sea level. She balanced nervously on a floating platform and shouted to a pair of fishers in a boat. "Do you know where I could find Tom Preston?"

"Him?" one of them said. "You're too late. He got kicked out yesterday."

"Not yet," the other said. "He's probably lurking at the Tian An Inn."

"Before they toss him out on his ear," the other one said.

"Thanks," Felicité forced herself to say. She gathered up her skirts and ascended the limpet-studded steps. She'd carefully selected an elegant but business-like dress to wear to Dai La. She should have worn pants. *Canvas* pants, she thought as her silk dress snagged on a barnacle.

At the top of the stairs, something tugged at her dress. A striped creature the size of a dog was using its long rubbery snout to pull at her skirt. Felicité yanked her skirt away, then gasped in dismay when she saw a big mouthful of scarlet silk vanishing into the creature's jaws.

Her skirt now had a noticeable chunk missing, edged in drool.

A girl panted up to her. "Spot! Spot! Oops, sorry about that. Mini-tapirs are so slippery."

Felicité shook out her skirt (the drool clung) and asked, "Can you please direct me to the Tian An Inn?"

"Oh, you're new in town! Spot can take you." The girl knelt down and said earnestly to the tapir, "Tian. An. Inn. Then return."

The tapir whuffled at her with its snout, then trotted off.

"Hurry!" the girl said. "Follow Spot!"

Felicité picked up her skirts and hurried after the creature. The animal stopped before a two-story building and chomped off another bite of her skirt, leaving more drool. Then it trotted away.

At least I don't have to say thank you, she thought wearily.

This was it. Her father had to be here.

Her stomach roiled once again. She forced herself to march inside. At the counter, a person with feathers covering most of their face looked up from an abacus. "May I help you?"

Dread tightened her throat. "I'm looking for Tom Preston."

The feathered clerk blinked. "Room twelve."

Felicité reminded herself of Mother's admonition about deep breaths before tackling difficult situations, but she couldn't catch her breath. Her heart was pounding so loudly in her ears that when she knocked on the door, she could barely hear the sound.

He opened the door and looked out at her. It was Daddy. Finally.

She stared at him, unable to speak.

Daddy continued looking at her, then said, "Yes?"

She had braced herself for horror, disgust, anger — anything but him not even recognizing her.

"Daddy." Her throat was so dry that the word came out in a whisper. Loudly, she said, *"Father."*

He stared at her, his blue eyes shocked behind his glasses. Then his brows drew together. She could imagine herself in his eyes: familiar features, except for the scales.

Familiar eyes, until she blinked.

"It's me," she began.

"Felicité?" It was his turn to whisper. "You're *alive!* What happened to you?" The shock and disbelief in his voice made her take a step back. He reached out as if to hug her, then dropped his hands. "Your mother? William?"

"They're alive, too," she managed, her throat tight. "Last I saw."

Her father hustled her inside and closed the door behind them. He wiped his hands over his face, then blinked at her. He looked every bit as tired as she felt.

"I thought you were dead." He wiped his eyes again before resettling his glasses, then let out his breath in a whoosh. "What happened? What did they do to you?" When she didn't immediately answer, he said, "It was Min Soo, wasn't it."

Of course, he thought it was Min Soo. Of course, her Change was some hideous punishment Voske had forced on her. If her father believed that it wasn't her fault, he would forgive her. But there was no fault here, and she didn't want forgiveness. There was nothing to forgive.

She crossed her arms. "Nobody did it to me. It just happened."

"But you're eighteen! It can't just happen."

"It happened when I was thirteen. I woke up late, and I splashed my face with cold water. I looked in the mirror and saw fish scales all over my face. When I blinked, I saw this." She leaned toward him, widening her eyes, and blinked, feeling the nictitating membrane slide over her eyes.

Her father recoiled a step. "No. Impossible."

"Yes," she said. "It *happened*. I was *there*. And I hid it ever since. Never went swimming again. Never got sweaty. I had to put up with Jennie Riley calling me lazy all the way through school because I couldn't train hard enough to sweat. I hid my face under hats. My neck under scarves, no matter how hot it was. I let everyone laugh at me, just to hide *this*."

Silence fell. Her father stared down at his hands. Felicité couldn't even breathe.

Then he looked up at her. "I don't understand. What

happened to bring you here? Like this? We heard rumors that you were *dead*."

Felicité swallowed, wondering exactly how detailed those rumors had been. She had a vivid flash of herself falling, the gray stone walls of the well blurring around her. "I came from Catalina, where I heard that you were trying to get the alliance to help against Voske. I came here to *help* you."

He looked up, hopeful and surprised. "Catalina agreed to ally with us?"

"No. Catalina said no."

He snatched off his glasses again and pressed his thumbs in his eyes, then rubbed his hands over his face with a shaky hand. "I've had no luck getting the Saigon Council to listen to me. I've told them and told them that they need to take on Voske before he's ready to attack them. And he will attack them. That's what he does. They need to strike him now, while he's lingering in Las Anclas and some of his other towns are starting to pull away. But they won't listen to me, even when I explain in the simplest terms."

He sounded so much like the daddy she'd known, talking over the dinner table about how the Las Anclas council wouldn't listen. He'd explained to her as the future mayor and had listened to her ideas.

"Who else is out there other than Catalina and Saigon?" Felicité asked. "What about Corymbia City?"

"That was my next stop, if Catalina wasn't willing. In fact, I've been hoping that I might have some allies there already. I assume Jennie Riley and her group are still there. They didn't come back, right?"

"No." It was strange how she'd almost forgotten them, after how much thought and emotions she'd given them in the past. Ross, who'd been the cause of so many bad things that had happened to her. Jennie and Kerry, her enemies. It all seemed so unimportant now.

"Excellent," said her father. "What happened to Sheriff Crow?"

"She got over the wall. I don't know where she went."

Her father took a deep breath. "Excellent. She's probably in Corymbia City too. I'll have to—"

Felicité recognized the signs of her father beginning a lengthy plan. She interrupted him. "What happened to *you?*"

He blinked at her, a little surprised. "The Rangers and I came across Voske's tracks on our way back home. We scouted close enough to see that the gates and walls were undamaged, and there was no smoke rising from the town. That's when we knew the town had been taken by surprise from the inside. There was no other way to sneak a large force inside the walls except through the tunnel."

Felicité's stomach churned. She had actually managed to forget about that for a while.

He went on, "The only people who knew about that tunnel were the council and Mia Lee. The council never left town, so they couldn't have fallen into Voske's hands. One month after Mia left town, Voske invaded through the tunnel. She must have been captured and interrogated." But he sounded doubtful.

Felicité stood there paralyzed, unable to speak. She had to tell him, but that would be the thing that would make him hate her. All along, she'd been worried about her Change, when what she should have been worried about was her betrayal.

He looked at her, then away. "The other possibility, which I find less likely, is that Henry Callahan fell into Voske's hands. The timing works for that, too. But Henry didn't know about the tunnel. Unless someone told him." Once again, he looked at her.

He knew. He knew it was her.

"I didn't *tell* him," Felicité said quickly. "I had to *show* him. It was the only way to get from the mill back to you to warn you about the fire spreading that way."

Her father stared at her. With a sinking feeling, she realized that he hadn't known. He spoke in a low voice, like someone had hit him and knocked him down. "Then Sujata was right. I didn't believe her. I thought you would never—"

"It was to save the town!"

Now he looked angry, as well as hurt and bewildered. "But why didn't you tell me you told him? If it was to save the town, you should have known I wouldn't be angry with you! You telling him wasn't the problem. You *not* telling *me* about it was!"

"I *couldn't* tell you!" Felicité shouted. "You would have killed him! You were ready to kill Kerry Voske, and she hadn't done anything but be born to the wrong father!"

Her father stared at her. "It's not the same thing."

Anger choked her voice. "Tell me you wouldn't have had Henry killed."

"I wouldn't have had any choice." He sounded confident, even self-righteous. As if no one could possibly find any fault with him. "The council was unanimous about exile, and he couldn't go out carrying a secret like that—and now you see why! With Henry Callahan, it wouldn't have even taken torture. He probably bragged about it to Voske. You should have told me the night of the fire, and I would have taken care of the problem. This is the kind of decision you have to make as a future mayor—"

The heat that had been building in Felicité's body burst into flames. Her voice rose to a scream. "Future mayor? I'm never going to be mayor. Las Anclas is *gone!* And you're blaming me? This is *your* fault!"

Her father stared incredulously.

"*You're* the one who made me believe I was a monster. You fired Nanny Shelley because she Changed! You drove out the delegation from Catalina because you didn't like how they looked. I was so scared of you finding out that I was Changed, I gave away the secret of the tunnel so Henry wouldn't learn my secret. We *didn't* have to go through the tunnel. Yes, the flames were coming at us, but we could have run through the town. I wouldn't do it because I was sweating, and I was afraid that everyone would see my scales. That *you* would see them and throw me out like Mrs. Callahan threw out Becky."

A grimace tightened his face. "I would never—"

She spoke over him. He'd had his say for her entire life. Now she was going to have hers. "In Catalina, no one cared how I looked. If I'd been born to the Rileys, they wouldn't have cared! It's only because you hate Changed people that I thought it was better to take Henry through the tunnel than to have my pointless secret get found out."

"I don't *hate* Changed people," her father began.

"No. You despise the ones with visible Changes. You taught us to despise them, and I did. I despised them, and I despised myself. For *years*. It would have been for the rest of my life, except..." She halted herself before revealing that she'd thrown herself down the well and gulped in a breath. "You would have killed Henry. He wasn't even a person to you. He was just a 'problem.'"

Once again, her father pressed his thumbs into his eyes, and held them there. He looked haggard, even more than after the battle of Las Anclas.

She was still furious, but his silence left room for her to feel other emotions. He must have spent this entire time believing that she, Mother, and Will were all dead. She remembered the open disgust that everyone in Catalina and Dai La showed when she mentioned her father's name. But here he was, still trying to get help for Las Anclas.

He dropped his hands. "Wait. Felicité, what did you mean by 'except?' What happened?"

She didn't want to tell him. No matter how angry she was, she didn't want to hurt him like that. But she was done with hiding. *No more secrets,* she thought. "I tried to kill myself. I jumped into the well in our rose garden. I intended to drown."

Her words struck him with the force of a sword. His face blanched. "What made you despair like that? Voske?"

When Felicité thought back to that moment, it seemed as if it had happened in another life. Slowly, she said, "Partly. He threw me out of the house to make room for his family moving in. I felt so guilty about telling Henry about the tunnel. I hated myself. But when I threw myself into the water, I didn't die. I turned into a mermaid, and I swam out to sea."

For the first time, she realized that if she hadn't been Changed, she'd have died. As much to herself as to her father, she said, "It was my Change that saved me. It gave me a second life." She lifted her hands, with their scale patterns that she now saw as beautiful. "I can't Change back now. This is what I look like when I'm out of water."

He looked at her hands, and he didn't flinch. "But you came anyway. That took a lot of courage."

"I came for Las Anclas. Catalina said no. But I want

to talk to the council here. I want to help you argue our case. And I can give them—and you—everything I observed about conditions inside Las Anclas."

He studied her with an expression she'd never seen directed at her, so it took her a moment to recognize it. It was how he looked at successful Ranger candidates: with pride and respect. "I was about to go receive the answer from Catalina. I know what it is now, but I'll take your words to them. Wait here, all right? We'll talk when I return."

"All right."

"Felicité. You're my daughter. Nothing will alter that." He started forward, as if he was going to hug her, then turned around and left.

What had that hesitation meant, when he hadn't hugged her? Was it disgust? Or was it acknowledgment that she'd grown up? Was he seeing her anew, the real Felicité?

She sat alone in the room, glad to have a moment to think. Her entire body ached from staying up all night. Though exhaustion pulled at her, she couldn't imagine sleeping. After all this time, she'd finally told her father exactly what she thought—even the thoughts she hadn't known she had.

And she'd survived. They both had. All her secrets were out. She had nothing left to hide. It was a strange feeling, as if she could do anything, or as if anything might happen. It felt *good*.

Sujata burst into the room, then stopped as if she'd run into a wall. "Felicité! You're Changed. Were you always Changed?"

"Yes, I—"

But Sujata didn't wait for the rest. She flushed with fury. "Did you tell Henry about the tunnel to hide your stupid secret?"

"Yes, but—"

White lightning blasted across Felicité's vision, followed by stinging pain. Next thing she knew, she was sitting on the floor, her cheek throbbing. Sujata stood over her, her hand poised to slap again. "Get up."

Felicité croaked, "Not if you're going to attack me again."

"I should. But I won't." Sujata's hand dropped. "Start talking."

Felicité stared up at Sujata in her Ranger fatigues, her hair pulled back into a plain ponytail. Paloma wasn't like this Sujata. She was like the Sujata who had been. That Sujata would never have left her house like this. They used to plan what dresses they'd wear to school, so they'd be coordinated. Sujata's gorgeous black hair was always elegantly arranged.

It was like Sujata had become a different person. But then, so had Felicité.

Felicité got up and brushed herself off. She'd been so relieved once she'd told her secrets to her father that it hadn't occurred to her that she'd have to do it more than once. She'd have to keep telling and telling her secrets until everybody knew. "I Changed when I was thirteen. But it didn't become permanent until I left Las Anclas."

Sujata nodded slowly. There was at least one thing Felicité didn't need to explain: why she'd never told anyone. "When was that? After Voske attacked?"

"Yes. Soon after." She saw Sujata's lips trembling, and quickly added, "Your family is fine. Well, nobody is fine with Voske as king, but they're alive. Unharmed. When I left, Voske was pretending that life is back to normal. Gold Point normal."

"And the Rangers?" Sujata must have read the answer in Felicité's face, because she gave an angry sob. "*All* of them?"

"Not Paco. Voske is treating him like a son."

Disgust tightened Sujata's face, followed by anger, even as tears poured down her face. "This is all because of *you*. How *could* you tell Henry Callahan, of all people, about that tunnel? *My parents* didn't even know."

"Henry and I were—"

"Don't you dare yak on about *in love*," Sujata cut in, sharp as a knife. "Or I'll knock you down again. You and I grew up with Henry. You couldn't trust him with a tomato plant."

"It wasn't about Henry," Felicité said. "It was about me. My Change."

"Me, me, me. It's always *me*, with you," Sujata snapped back.

Felicité realized then that there was no point in defending herself. She would never retrieve their friendship. "I gave my father a report on Las Anclas. He's back at the council now."

Sujata sucked in an unsteady breath. "I hope it works, because I got nowhere talking to people just now. And I'm sure none of us have had any better luck." She hesitated, chewing on her lip as if she was trying to control her temper. "How's Paco holding up?"

Felicité winced, remembering the last time she'd been face to face with Paco. He'd been so angry, but his fury was cold. He'd looked just like Voske. But she, of all people, wasn't going to judge on appearances. "He's fine. He's—

"He isn't *fine!*" Sujata yelled. "He can't be."

The rest of the Rangers walked in, looking dispirited. Indra stopped in surprise when he saw Felicité. The others halted behind him.

Sujata turned to her brother. "Mr. Preston was right. They're all dead. Except for Paco. He's being forced into Kerry's place." She glared at Felicité. "And she *did* tell Henry about the tunnel. They're…all…*dead.*"

Felicité had once dreamed of marrying tall, handsome Indra, and ruling the town with him. That dream, like so many others, seemed to come from another life. He gave Felicité a cold look, then put his arm around Sujata. The other Rangers sank onto the bench along the wall as if someone had punched them in the stomach. Felicité stood there uncertainly. They were shutting her out as clearly as if they'd physically booted her out the door. She didn't belong in their circle of grief, but where could she go?

The silence stretched painfully until her father returned. He took in the situation at a glance. "Felicité, go next door to Sujata's room and change your clothes. The council wants your perspective and report."

Felicité couldn't get out of there fast enough.

·29·

FELICITÉ

DAI LA

THE MEETING ROOM INSIDE Dai La's town hall reminded Felicité painfully of the one in Las Anclas. And like Las Anclas's town council, most of the leaders of the Saigon Alliance were middle aged or old. But that was where the resemblance stopped. Several had visible Changes which they didn't make the slightest effort to hide. And even the ones who looked like Norms might not be — a gray-haired man idly twirled a pencil in midair just above his open palm.

Her father turned to the council. "This is my daughter, Felicité Wolfe, who just arrived from Catalina — "

An old woman cut in abruptly, "She can speak for herself."

The council's eyes trained on Felicité. She was glad she'd ordered her thoughts on the walk over. Emulating Mother's Council Voice, she gave her report, beginning with Voske's attack. She made sure to include everything she could about how the town was organized now, from the location of the sentries to the new electric spotlights.

When she finished, the old woman said in a less abrupt voice, "Thank you for that well-organized presentation, Felicité."

Felicité's father spoke up. "You can see from this detailed report that time is absolutely of the essence. Voske will attack Catalina and the towns of the Saigon Alliance next. It's only a matter of when. The moment to strike is now, while he's still establishing control."

He laid out a military strategy with precision and

clarity, just as he explained such things to Las Anclas's council. But the Saigon Alliance council wasn't giving him the same respectful attention he'd always received in Las Anclas. They looked annoyed, frustrated, and even bored. His authority in Las Anclas meant nothing here.

The old woman was watching Felicité more than her father. Other council members also eyed her, looking puzzled and expectant — almost as if they were waiting for *her* to speak. Finally, the telekinetic man interrupted him in the middle of a sentence. "Mr. Preston, we've heard all this before."

Felicité recognized that her father was about to reply, and said quickly, "Do you have any questions on my report?"

She caught a startled look from her father. The man with the twirling pencil plucked it out of the air and asked, "Do you have an estimate for how many soldiers were in town when you left?"

Felicité gave them her best estimate, adding that she couldn't be exactly sure, as there might be more stationed outside the north gates. As she answered more questions, she felt the mood in the room change. With a shock, she realized that she was getting the respectful attention that her father hadn't. Was it what she was saying, as an eye-witness...or who she was? Or who she *wasn't?*

After the last question, her father spoke again. "With these numbers, the best and safest approach would be a two-pronged attack, from the sea as well as land — "

He was interrupted by one of the younger council members, a woman in her thirties with feathery moth antennae. They swiveled toward her father as she said, "And exactly why should we defend a town where we've never been welcome?"

Felicité recognized her father's expression. He was going to ignore what the woman was really saying and repeat his old argument about how it was in Saigon's own best interest to help Las Anclas.

Felicité jumped in to stop him. "I'm Changed. One third of the population of Las Anclas is Changed. It's not a town made up of bigoted Norms, though we do have them." She was careful not to meet her father's eyes. "It's a town with a lot of different people, just like you have here. Changed. Norms. Old people. Children. In fact, you've met some of them. Just a few months ago, you had visitors from Las Anclas."

The woman with the antennae spoke up. "Yes! I remember Jennie Riley, and that lively little girl Summer. My daughter was on the patrol that met them."

Another person spoke up, "That's right. They were friends of Yuki, the prospector. One of them rode a metallic horse like he had."

A third person exclaimed, "Oh, Yuki! He's the one who saved my grand-nephew!"

Felicité smiled at them. "Yes, Yuki's from Las Anclas. And his mother and sister and boyfriend are still there. I'm certain that if he knew what had happened, he'd be riding back as fast as he could."

The council members exchanged looks, then the old woman spoke up once more. "We need time to consider this new information. Please return at dawn."

Once they were outside, her father turned to her. "I've never been more proud of you, Felicité. You got through to them in a way I never could have." But before she could enjoy the moment, he went on, "I really hope this works. I'm so worried about your mother and Will. The only hope I have to hang onto is that Voske will keep Valeria alive because he'll want me to be there to watch him execute her. As for William, he'll try to turn him against me, so he's likely to treat him reasonably well. But he could get impatient."

Felicité glumly followed him back to the inn. Now she had the rest of the day to stew in anxiety with the grieving, resentful Rangers. She was relieved when her father suggested that she get some rest. Unfortunately, Sujata's room was the only one with an extra bed. Felicité was so exhausted that she fell instantly asleep.

She woke to a dark room and the sound of muffled weeping. For a disoriented moment, she couldn't remember where she was or how she'd gotten there. Then it all came rushing back. She lay awake in a heavy silence only broken by the sounds of Sujata's tears. She knew better than to say anything.

When Sujata finally fell asleep, Felicité tiptoed onto the balcony to watch the stars fade into the brightening sky. *Are you watching these same stars, Mother? Are you wondering if I'm seeing them, too? Or do you believe I'm dead?*

Everything inside Felicité hurt. She'd made peace with Daddy — with Father. The word "daddy" would forever remind her of Voske's whip-sharp sarcasm as he'd drawled, "How old *are* you?" The worst part was that for once, Voske had been right: Felicité had kept herself a child when she was around her father, the Norm child she'd been before she Changed.

That was over now. Father had accepted her, because loving parents never stopped loving their children, no matter what. But she felt no triumph in that, not with Mother still locked up in Las Anclas, believing her daughter was dead by her own hand.

I'm coming, Mother, she promised the fading stars.

At dawn, she and her father walked to face the council. The only sounds beside the wash and hiss of the sea were the cries of sea birds, and the *tic-tic-tic* of little trotting hooves. Gritting her teeth, she walked into the town hall at her father's side.

The old woman announced, "Here is our final decision. If you two can convince Catalina to ally with you, then the Saigon Alliance will as well."

Felicité was taken aback. She'd expected a yes or no, not an entirely new task — and one she'd already failed at! But Father seemed pleased. Maybe he knew something she didn't.

The old woman went on, "The jellyfish is standing by, ready to leave immediately, while the wind holds."

Father nodded. "May I request that my Rangers be informed where we are going, and to wait for our return?"

"It will be done," the council woman promised.

They walked up to the landing tower. The pearlescent jellyfish glowed softly in the morning sunlight, looking just like the jellyfish that had brought her. Felicité laughed at herself. Of course, all jellyfish looked alike to her.

Then she saw the jellyfish riders. It was Cathy and Jim. And the instant they saw Father, they looked like they'd just whiffed a very spoiled fish. Felicité remembered what they'd said about Father. And she remembered what he'd said about them. Did he still see Jim as "that thing fished up from the bottom of the sea," and Cathy as "that thing straight out of a nightmare."

"Thank you so much for waiting for us," Felicité said, drawing on Mother's most gracious manner. Oh, this was going to be incredibly awkward.

"We're not waiting for *you*. The council commandeered us." Jim addressed Father, not Felicité.

Father gave an uncertain glance at the basket. This was clearly his first time in a jellyfish. And it was steered by people who loathed him.

Felicité was determined to be diplomatic, no matter how everyone else behaved. "We're going to Catalina as envoys. May I introduce my father, Tom Preston? Father, this is Cathy, and this is Jim."

Jim offered his slime-gleaming hand for a handshake. Isais had said not to touch Jim—was he planning to get revenge by burning or poisoning or *melting* Father?

Felicité, standing so close, saw the tension in Father's jaw as he slowly lifted his hand. At the last moment, Jim stepped back and Cathy took his place. Her skeletal hand stuck out like a bundle of bare bones. Father sucked in a breath, then closed his fingers around Cathy's. With the slightest tremble in his voice, he said, "Pleased to meet you, Cathy. Jim."

Neither of the jellyfish riders said they were pleased to meet him. Cathy jerked her skeletal thumb at a bench, and Felicité and her father sat down. Jim cast off the ropes, and the jellyfish rose up into the dawn sky. The motion was as smooth as if she was floating underwater. There was nothing but the glow of dawn over the land and sea, the brilliance of the stars in the west, and the glimmering bubble of the jellyfish above.

Felicité glanced at her father, wondering how he was taking being suspended in the air. He sat with a stolid expression, but his fingers clutched his knees so tightly that the tendons in his forearms pressed against his shirtsleeves.

Cathy was the first to speak. "Have you had a chance to get some breakfast?"

Felicité shook her head. "There wasn't time."

"I have rice balls." Cathy opened a basket, revealing rice balls wrapped in seaweed. "These are smoked fish, these are cucumber, and these are pickled plum."

Felicité gratefully helped herself to one of each. "Father, do you want to share mine?"

"No need," Cathy said with a big, toothy smile on her skull face. "We've got plenty. Here you go!" She plunged her bony fingers into the basket, pulled out a rice ball, and held it out to Father.

Felicité felt her father stiffen beside her. Was he going to refuse? Oh, no, he wasn't. Mother would not have let him if she'd been here! She turned to him with Mother's best smile. "That's the plum. It smells delicious!"

Her father's cheeks ridged with color, but he got the hint. He pried his fingers off one knee and accepted the rice ball. Felicité stared him until he actually took a bite. "Thank you. Very tasty."

The jellyfish swayed higher into the air as the sun crested the distant hills and flooded the sky with pale blue. Father got down two rice balls, and Felicité ate all of hers as the gondola swung over the sea. She felt better once she'd eaten, but also more aware of the tense silence.

"Who made the plum sauce?" she asked. "It's the best I've ever had."

"Cathy's wife," said Jim. "She owns a restaurant in Avalon, on Catalina's south coast. Cathy, give her one of Guadalupe's cabbage rolls."

Cathy stiffly offered her one. Felicité suspected that it had been meant for Cathy's own lunch, but that made it even more rude to refuse. She accepted with a smile. "Thank you so much. How long has your wife had the restaurant?"

That was apparently the magic question. Cathy was clearly proud of her wife's successful restaurant, and after recounting its history, the conversation led to her family. She had a husband, a wife, and three children, while Jim declared that he preferred the freedom of a single life.

As Felicité used every trick she knew to make the ride less painful, she was aware of her father's silence. He knew where she'd learned those skills. When she'd spoken to the Saigon council, it was Father's training that enabled her to answer questions about Voske's soldiers. And it was Mother's that let her assess the mood of a room.

But none of it would have mattered if she hadn't been

Changed. Felicité knew perfectly well that it was her bronze scales that had made them pay attention to her in the first place and believe her when she talked about Changed people in Las Anclas. She wondered how her father felt, knowing that it was her Change that had enabled this second chance.

The conversation moved from family to hobbies. When Cathy said she was planning to enter a regional competition when she got her next free rotation, Felicité suppressed a yawn so firmly her eyes watered. She was proud of her sprightly tone as she asked, "Oh, really? What is your sport?"

"I'm a swimmer," Cathy said.

"She's won the silver medal three times," Jim put in. "Only one faster is a woman from way down south."

Father finally spoke up. "Swimming? Long distance, or short? I used to do long."

Cathy and Jim eyed him with less sourness, though they weren't anywhere near what she'd call friendly. But they were being polite, which, as Mother always said, was the first step to negotiation and compromise.

She sat back as Cathy and her father fell into a conversation about speed versus stamina, and lake versus ocean swimming. Her determination to keep things civilized was actually working! Even so, it was a relief when they came close enough to Catalina to see trees and buildings, and then distinguish the glistening spires of the palace.

Her father looked up suddenly, his glasses winking in the sunlight. "I have to say something before we land. I remember you both, and I know you remember me. I wanted to tell you that I was wrong to turn you away. I know it's much too late, but I'm sorry. I apologize to you both."

"Okay. You've apologized. That's more than I expected." Cathy didn't sound very impressed.

"Yup," Jim said.

Cathy's eyes glittered from the caverns of their sockets. "But what happens after the apology? If anything."

"I don't know what will happen with Las Anclas," Father said. "But I can promise you that from now on, I'm going to work on being better."

"Okay," Cathy said again, but this time she smiled. "I

can accept that."

"Grab on," Jim said. "This part can get a little dicey as wind currents whip up these little canyons."

Felicité gripped one of the woven handholds by the bench. Her father also held on. The basket swung like a bell as it dropped toward the palace. To her surprise and delight, she saw Isais's brilliant aura within the small group of upturned faces.

"Noelle—Felicité!" Isais shouted. "You came back!"

As the basket was secured, Felicité performed introductions. The ambassadors did not look happy to see her father or hear the message from the Saigon Alliance.

Mr. Aldana began, "We already sent our message. Nothing has changed."

"Something has," said Felicité. "Your reasons for saying no were based on your opinion of my father, and his actions eight years ago. You said he was the same person now. I say he's not."

Her father cleared his throat and addressed the ambassadors. "I apologized to Jim and Cathy, and I apologize to you as representatives of the people of Catalina. I didn't help you, and I'm sorry. It was wrong."

Felicité looked past the ambassadors to Isais, who was looking from her to her father and then back again. He seemed bewildered. This was clearly not the evil Tom Preston he'd imagined, who'd throw out his Changed daughter. She gave him a little nod, and he smiled suddenly. He understood that things were different now.

Father went on, "I can't speak for Las Anclas. Even if Voske wasn't occupying it right now, I don't have a position on the council anymore. I was voted out. So, I can only speak for myself. But I can tell you that eight years ago, if I hadn't been in charge, you would have gotten a different reception. Whatever you think of me, I am not Las Anclas. And it's the people of the town who need your help."

Jim stepped forward. "I'll never forget that he kicked me out, but I've also never forgotten that other citizens of Las Anclas would have helped me—would have helped Catalina—if he hadn't stopped them. Those are the people trapped there now."

"He shook my hand." Cathy shrugged. "I'll call that a good start."

The ambassadors glanced at Isais, who grinned at them hopefully. Mrs. Aldana nodded, and Mr. Aldana said, "My suggestion is that we all start over. Come inside. We'll talk over lunch."

·30·
Ross

The Ruined City

"How about here?" Summer asked eagerly. She'd found them an open rooftop, accessible by swinging along rope-like vines. With clear sunlight in all directions, a sneaking shadow would be very obvious. She peered even closer into Ross's face. With great intensity, she said, "This is relaxing, right? Right?"

"Summer," Jennie said. "Remember what we said about not pressuring Ross."

"I'm not pressuring him! I found him a perfect spot to be relaxed in! You're relaxed, right, Ross?" Summer threw herself on her back along a tree branch. "Look how relaxed *I* am!"

Ross had never felt less relaxed in his life. Mia had suggested that he not count how many times he'd tried to get his power back, which had ensured that he kept count from that point on. He was now at try number nine. It would have been more, except that trying twice in close succession guaranteed that he'd get nowhere at all, instead of halfway there and then failing.

"What about dinner first?" Kerry suggested.

The thought of having to choke down dinner, knowing that he'd have to try again afterward, while everyone attempted to talk about anything but his power, made him fling himself down almost as fast as Summer had. "It's fine. I'll do it now."

He breathed out the way Dr. Lee had taught him, closed his eyes, and tried to relax his muscles. His foot cramped. His spine twitched. He opened his eyes and saw a row of staring faces: Mia hopeful, Jennie concerned, Kerry interested, Summer expectant, Maria-Pilar puzzled.

"This." He waved a hand at the row of eyes. "Is still not helping."

Jennie cleared her throat. "Let's cook some dinner. Everyone who's not cooking, keep watch for Loretta. Looking *away* from Ross."

He closed his eyes and tried not to think about how even if no one was watching him, they were thinking about him. Ross returned to the exercises Dr. Lee had taught him. First, relax your toes. Then, your ankles. By the time he got to his knees, he knew it wasn't going to work. But if he opened his eyes, he'd just become the focus of everyone's attention again.

He couldn't stop thinking about all his failed attempts, even though he was sure that was the exact wrong thing to do. Every time, if he got relaxed enough, he'd see the door, reach for the handle...and then he'd abruptly lose it all, heart pounding, more on edge than if he was waiting for a battle to begin.

He had no idea what was wrong, other than that if it really depended on him not worrying, it would never happen. Maybe he needed to be more alone? If the others spread out enough that he couldn't see them, but they could still guard him from Loretta...but even that didn't feel like enough distance. It was strange. When they were eating or on the move, he felt calmer when they were together. It was only when he was trying to relax with everyone staring at him that their presence bothered him.

What if he was going about it the wrong way? He felt safe with Jennie and Mia. He felt *relaxed* with Jennie and Mia. Maybe he needed more presence, not less.

Or maybe he needed more than presence alone. He'd gotten advice from them—he'd gotten advice from everyone, eventually including Maria-Pilar—but he'd never managed to explain exactly what it felt like when he tried and failed. It was hard to put into words, and even harder to talk about failure. But maybe their advice was unhelpful because they didn't understand what he was trying to do, as if they were trying to tell him how to prospect a structure they'd never seen.

He opened his eyes. If he hadn't been so tense, he'd

have laughed at the way everyone was very obviously trying not to look at him. Except for Summer, who kept sneaking peeks.

"Look," he said. Sure enough, they all swung around. "Let me tell you how this feels to me."

There was their incredibly intense attention again. Five people all staring hard at him. No. He couldn't think of them as five people staring. It was Mia and Jennie, who he loved. It was Summer, his sister. Kerry, his friend. Maria-Pilar, his ally. They were people he trusted. They were people who wished him well. They were people whose words he wanted to hear.

"To control the trees—" No. That wasn't right. He didn't control them. He communicated with them. "To talk to them, I imagine a door. It has to be a door, because I need to close it again. So, I don't feel them all the time."

Hope shone bright in Mia's eyes, and Jennie was nodding encouragingly. Maria-Pilar looked unnerved. Ross went on, "Normally, I open the door to talk to them. As if they were people in another room. But now I can't open the door."

"Can you picture a lever?" Mia suggested.

Ross shook his head. "It's not that the door's stuck. It's that when I touch it, it goes away. Everything goes away. I'm back in my body again."

"How do you feel when you're back in your body?" Jennie asked.

Ross gazed down into the fire. "Scared."

"Of the trees?" Maria-Pilar asked tentatively.

"No. I know them. They know me. It's that…" When he tried to figure out what he was scared of, it was like hitting a blank wall. Like the wall he'd kept coming up against before he met Summer, when he'd tried to remember his family. "It feels like other things I can't remember. Things I can't remember because they were bad."

Summer blurted out, "Like how you can't remember how our dad was killed."

"Not helping," Jennie murmured.

Ross forced himself to say, "No. It *is* helping. I think there's something that bad. Something that scares me more than being trapped here forever."

Five varieties of uneasy expressions surrounded him

now.

Then Mia looked up, her glasses flashing as she gave him that wonderful Mia smile, full of hope and trust. "How about if we hold your hands?"

Summer rolled her eyes. "He doesn't have five hands."

"But we could all hold hands," Jennie suggested. "In a circle."

"Will that help?" Kerry asked. "If it's worse than being trapped here forever..."

"What it might help with is giving me the courage to see what it actually is." Before Ross could lose his nerve, he held out his hands.

Mia and Jennie scooted over to take one hand each. Kerry took Mia's hand and reached for Maria-Pilar's, but Summer snatched Kerry's. Maria-Pilar settled between Summer and Jennie.

Ross closed his eyes. He relaxed his muscles, one by one, helped by his lingering amusement at Summer's grab for Kerry. By the time he got to his forehead, his mind drifted easily.

He floated in a thousand sparks of light and life, spread out over a vast plain. Most of them formed a circle. Some distance away, a set of black lights clustered around the brightest light of them all, a brilliant ruby scintillation standing alone. He was part of a network of trees, all singing to each other, observing the other fragments of life around them. But he wasn't a tree...was he?

The trees claimed him as one of them. A little different. Not entirely crystal. But close enough. Close enough to perceive him and everyone around him as one of them. Of course they wouldn't hurt him. He was crystal, drinking in sunlight.

As his attention wavered, a tree became aware of the body heat of the figures around him. Surely those were seed-food. Ross extended his tree-awareness. There was no seed-food here. All were trees. If he believed that he was a tree, they would believe it, too. They would trust his senses.

He didn't breathe. He didn't feel as humans felt. Trees felt neither pain nor love. He felt nothing but his roots sinking into the ground, strengthened by the warm sun, and his thorns seeking out the heat of warm blood.

He was at the door now. This time, he would open it. Even if he couldn't step through, he would see what was inside.

Ross opened the door.

When he opened his eyes again, he found that his palms were slick with sweat. His hair was wet with it. But he wasn't hot. He was cold and shivering, his heart pounding with the aftermath of terror. Everyone was eyeing him worriedly.

"I opened the door." His voice came out so hoarse that he stopped and cleared his throat. "I saw what I was afraid of. When I took you all through the forest, it was more people than I'd ever been able to get past the trees before. To protect you all, I had to convince the entire forest that I was a tree. I convinced them so well, they spun crystal around me. I was lucky to be able to come back from that."

"You could have become a tree?" Summer gasped.

"Worse. I would have had a human body with the mind of a tree." With everyone still holding hands, he felt them all shudder.

Encouragingly, Jennie said, "But now that you've faced your fear, do you have your power back?"

Ross extended that inner sense. He had his power back, all right. In the instant that he'd opened his mind to the trees, he'd felt the tree awareness pulling at him. He'd slammed the door—no, but there was no door. He'd cut himself off. Now he felt nothing.

Only then did he recall exactly what he'd done to get them all through the forest. He'd opened the door in his mind, then realized he had to open it wider. It couldn't go wide enough. No door would. He'd had to blast down the entire wall he'd put up so long ago to protect his mind from the trees. That wall was gone for good.

"Yeah, my power's back. But I did something permanent to myself the last time I used it. I could get you out of here, but I don't think I'd stay human if I did it."

Mia said earnestly, "But the hand-holding. That helped! Would it help more if I held *you*? Really tight? Maybe skin to skin?" She turned bright red. "I didn't mean that. I only meant my hand! Holding yours. Hand! And maybe face." She muttered, "Andifyouneedmorenotinfrontof-everybodyelse. Okay?"

Ross was too distracted by the image of "skin to skin" to reply. There hadn't been any of that since they'd come to the ruined city, except for the occasional brief kiss.

"I think Mia's onto something," Jennie said.

Summer burst in, "Not if I have to hear you three snogging. I'd rather live here for the rest of my life!"

Jennie chuckled. "Not like that. Ross, see if it helps to think of what makes you human. Your feelings. Your body. Your relationships."

Ross was thrown back to the night he lay in Voske's hell cell, his ribs shattered, awaiting his execution at dawn. He'd thought he was dying, and what he'd believed to be his last thought was of Mia and Jennie. Maybe if he kept the people he loved in his mind, he could fight back against the pull of the trees.

He again took Jennie's strong hand and Mia's small one. Each girl gripped him back firmly. Trustingly. When Summer groaned, Ross added that to the things that kept him human: his sister, at the age where romance was gross. Kerry, who had saved his life. Maria-Pilar, who turned herself into all kinds of weird creatures to amuse Summer. He opened his mind. When the trees tried to absorb him, he thought of those five people.

But the singing trees were a huge, powerful web of connection. Five relationships, no matter how strong, weren't enough. But he cared about more than five people. Sheriff Crow, who had saved his life when he was a stranger to her. Dr. Lee, who had taken him in. Yuki, who had studied so hard to learn from him. The trees' grip loosened, their inhuman insistence on sun and light and blood fading slightly.

It still wasn't enough.

He ran through everyone he liked in Las Anclas, then *everyone* in Las Anclas. Everyone in Gold Point who wasn't thirsting to kill. All the animals in both towns. All the life in the ruined city. Each connection a lifeline, until he sensed that his web of relationships was strong enough for the trees to accept his own web of connection.

But there was a price. For him to sustain that web, he'd have to stay connected to it. Forever. What would that mean? Would he be pulled into everyone's emotions? If anyone died within that web, would he feel that death, the way he'd experienced the deaths of the six people Voske forced to die? The deaths of the soldiers his crimson tree had killed?

There was no way for him to tell. But whatever the price was, he'd have to pay it. He had to get the people he loved to safety.

Ross opened his eyes. "You were right, Jennie. Mia. Thinking about my relationships worked. I can get us all out of here." He decided not to mention the still-unknown price. He'd deal with that when he got to it.

"All of us at once?" Mia asked.

He nodded. "I don't think that'll be a problem anymore."

Jennie's hand dropped to the hilt of her sword. "We'll still have to dodge the soldiers surrounding the crystal forest."

"They won't be a problem, either," Ross said. "I can see them as lights. You, too. Animals. Other trees. Everything living is a light to the trees. They'll see us as human-shaped trees."

"Wow," Summer exclaimed. "*That* is cool. Everything else about the trees is super creepy."

He smiled at his sister. "I can even sense the roaches. Seems like they've moved in for good."

"But they're cold-blooded," said Kerry. "I thought that was why they could get through the crystal trees."

"They sense much more than just heat. I wasn't deep enough in to feel it before. Cold-blooded creatures don't make good food, and a new tree can't grow from them. But the trees know the roaches are there. They know everything living within their range." He shut up when he saw all five girls look horrified.

Mia looked around wildly. "They're watching me? Right now?"

Jennie patted her shoulder. "I'm sure they're not interested in you personally."

"I don't want them interested in me at all," Mia muttered. "Yeah. Let's get out of here. Soon. Now."

Summer bounced to her feet. "So, we sneak to Las Anclas, climb over the wall, and kill Voske?"

"No," Jennie said. "We stick to our plan and get Paco's message out of the grove of black crystal trees."

Summer subsided, grumbling. They packed up the camp and climbed down from the rooftop, keeping an eye out for Loretta. Mia shoved her glasses up her nose, hoisted her pack, then said nervously, "Do we all take hands again?"

Ross suspected that it was no longer necessary—he could sense their lights without actual physical touch. But he wasn't *sure.* "Yes."

They made a human chain as they walked toward the trees. Wisps of fog drifted, felt more than seen. Ross closed his eyes, settling into the trees' awareness. Before, he could only sense the trees by entering into their world so completely that he lost all track of everything else. But now that other vision enabled him to walk through the forest and see exactly where he was going.

A new light suddenly appeared a little way behind them. Ross recognized Loretta; the trees recognized seed-food. Before he could react, the nearest trees exploded their pods. Everyone with Ross jolted. Summer shrieked. Loretta howled in rage, then pain. Her screams rose, then abruptly cut off.

Ross froze, bracing himself for the agony of her death. But he felt nothing.

"What happened?" Summer gasped.

"Loretta," Maria-Pilar whispered, "She can only stay a shadow for a few minutes. The trees got her when she materialized."

Mia's grip tightened convulsively on Ross's hand. Jennie's low voice was tight with tension as she said, "I can carry you."

"I'm fine," Ross said. "Her death didn't hurt me."

Mia relaxed, and Jennie muttered, "Thank God." But Ross's own relief was mixed with worry. He'd felt Loretta's death as a singing tree would feel it, as a light blinking out. He reached out for his web of connections, assuring himself that he was still human.

Lights were scattered across the desert, some human-shaped and in orderly groups and pairs. Ross made sure they were well away from any of them when they emerged from the crystal forest, and as they made their way across the desert.

They hid from patrols three times as they approached Las Anclas, dropping into ditches and ducking behind boulders. Ross had to force himself to stay on his feet; breaking through to the trees had exhausted him almost as much as it had when he'd first gained his power. But he couldn't rest. He was the only one who could keep them safe from Voske's soldiers.

At last, they came to his crimson tree and its company of obsidian trees. The trees felt curious as Ross led the girls among them, hands clasped. Summer spotted the rock with a piece of paper tied around it. She whispered, "It says 'Medina dairy barn.'"

Mia murmured, "Makes sense. Even Voske wouldn't spy on cows."

Ross sensed that the sentries along the wall were turning back at the same place Las Anclas's sentries had. He whispered, "Everyone follow me over the wall. We'll have to move fast."

It was only when they reached the wall that he realized that they'd have to release hands to climb it. He could feel the knowledge hitting them through the tension with which Mia and Jennie gripped his hands, and the way Summer and Kerry froze. They all turned to him. He nodded in what he hoped was a reassuring manner, then let go of Mia and Jennie's hands. Jennie stifled a gasp.

Ross held up his empty hands so everyone could see. Behind them, the crystal trees remained silent. Still. Drawing a shuddering breath that he was sure everyone could hear, Ross quickly scaled the wall. As he reached the top, Summer floated down beside him. Ross scrambled down, and Summer jumped. Together they ran through the timber forest, toward the dairy barn. The other three pelted in his wake.

He dashed inside the barn, the others following. Moonlight filtered through high windows and cracks in the walls, but he couldn't see much more than silhouettes. The barn smelled like hay and grain and cow manure: familiar, comforting smells. A warm, wet nose prodded at the back of his neck, and a cow mooed softly in his ear. With a grin, he scratched the cow between the ears.

At last, he was back in Las Anclas.

·31·
KERRY

MOONLIGHT TRACED SILVERY LINES across the hayloft floor. Everyone else had fallen asleep, but all Kerry could think of was Santiago. He was so close to her now, and yet they were still apart. And her father...

"Kerry?" Jennie whispered. "Go to sleep. I'm taking the first watch."

She was so startled when Jennie first spoke, she materialized a sword. She let it vanish. "I'll take it. I can't sleep anyway. I keep thinking of how close Voske is."

She could practically feel his angry awareness, like the lidless eye ceaselessly watching in the Catalina Players' play about the evil ring. But this was no lantern high on a stage, covered with translucent red leaves. It was real.

"What was it like, growing up with him as a father?" Jennie asked, then quickly added, "Never mind. That was nosy. And I don't want to stir up terrible memories."

Kerry was surprised, both at the tactless question and the backtracking coming from the indefatigable Jennie. Maybe even Jennie could get soggy from days of broken sleep followed by a very long trek. "It wasn't terrible. Well, it was, and it wasn't. Anyway, I don't mind you asking."

"I've been assuming you had to become an expert at flattery and hiding your true self to survive," Jennie said.

"Yes and no," Kerry said thoughtfully. "What you saw when you took me hostage *was* my true self. At least, it was the self my father wanted me to be. I was a different person with Santiago, though I didn't realize it until I was away from him. Santiago was always…decent. To everybody. A lot like Dr. Lee."

"My parents are like that."

"Yes." Kerry hadn't spent as much time with Mr. and Mrs. Riley, but she'd seen that. "As for flattery, Voske hates bootlickers."

"What *does* he value?"

"Loyalty. Ambition, of a sort. Loyalty is proved by instant, cheerful obedience. He values ambition only from the loyal and obedient. Your goals have to be his goals. He also values martial excellence. He used to call me and Sean his good little soldiers."

"Ouch," remarked Jennie.

"Yeah. I never heard that again after Sean ran off. But he was proud of us when we excelled. He was a good teacher. He took the time to explain things. We all strove to please him because we wanted to. We believed our father was the smartest and the best and the most powerful, and isn't power more important than anything else?" Kerry heard her voice sharpening to bitter sarcasm, and consciously breathed out her rising anger.

"How did he get that way?" Jennie asked. "Or did no one dare to talk about it?"

"I know his first kill was his older brother. And then he rebelled against his mother, my grandmother…" Kerry shrugged. "That's really all I know."

"I know more." Maria-Pilar sat up, a shadow in the shadows.

"You do?" Kerry asked. "Santiago never talked about it."

"He couldn't. Our entire family warned him not to get involved with you." Maria-Pilar's quiet voice rang with conviction. Kerry didn't doubt her, though Santiago had never said a word about that either. "Then, when he did anyway, we all got warned to speak carefully around you. For both your sakes. Talking about old enemies of the king might get mistaken for support of them. But Grandpa always said things were much worse under your grandmother, when she was queen. She was *terrifying*. It wasn't just her skeleton hand—lots of people have Changes like that—it's the way she used it to kill anyone who crossed her. It's why they helped the king rebel against her."

"And then he became just like her." Kerry could practically feel all that history weighing on her. "And now my younger brothers and sisters are going down the same road I was walking before I came to Las Anclas."

"You weren't *that* bad." Maria-Pilar's voice was part joking, part not. "I liked you. Eventually."

"I was awful. I was even mean to Mia. Who could be mean to Mia?" Kerry remembered her astonishment at the Lees' effortless, unthought kindness. As if everybody thought that way.

"Thank you," Jennie said.

"For what?" Kerry asked.

"For being honest," said Jennie. "For seeing Mia's worth."

Kerry huffed a soft laugh. "I could say the same about you."

"Go to sleep," Jennie said. "Both of you."

"What about you?" Kerry asked.

"I'll take first watch. Now that we're not dodging Loretta, I want to think about everything Paco told us." Jennie added, "And what he didn't tell us."

When Kerry woke again, it was still dark. Whisper's little body was warm against hers. Everyone else seemed to be asleep. Kerry was surprised, then supposed that Jennie must have somehow determined that it was safe. She felt as if she could sleep for a week, but her danger sense hummed, and her body was one gigantic itch. She might as well do a perimeter check.

She moved her rat off her chest, murmuring, "Stay, Whisper." She groped for the ladder, silently descended, and tiptoed through the cows. She peeked out the door. Beyond the timber stand was the south forge, and north of that Weavers' Row, now lit up and ringed by guards. But they were far enough away that they wouldn't see anyone leaving the dark barn. She opened the door.

The hinge creaked, making her jump. The cows placidly continued to munch. Kerry slipped out and began moving from tree to tree until she heard footsteps. She backtracked into the timber stand, below a tall tree with no low branches. She created spike-studded gloves around her hands and equally spiky shoes over her real ones, and scrambled straight up until she crouched within thick foliage.

A man marched along, the light from Weaver's Row outlining a stocky body, blunt features —

She drew in a breath. *"Santiago?"*

She hadn't known she'd spoken aloud until his head jerked upward, eyes round, mouth open. His lips formed the name *Kerry*.

She dropped down and hurled herself at him. His arms crushed her against him. His heartbeat hammered frantically against her ribs as he whispered, "I dreamed you were dead."

"Santiago," she murmured against his lips, and then they were wildly kissing.

Oh, yes. This was what she'd thought she'd never have again outside of memory.

"I'm so glad to see you," he said when they had to breathe. "Alfonso told us you were all safe in the barn, but Dr. Lee forbade the rest of us from going in."

Jennie must have spoken to Alfonso while everyone slept. Of course she wouldn't have just dozed off.

"I've been patrolling as close as I dared," he went on. "If anyone asks, I'll say I'm guarding the new armory over there at Weavers' Row."

"Where are the weavers?"

"Sent to work from home, to make cloth for our uniforms."

Voske had taught Kerry all about symbolism. She wondered if he was making a deliberate statement to the people of Las Anclas by evicting the weavers, and putting both them and their old workplace into service for his wars. Belatedly, she said, "Good thinking. I mean, about your saying you're on guard."

His arms tightened around her. "I *so* wanted to sneak into that barn. And kiss you. Just to make sure you were really here. Really alive."

"It's dark in there. You'd probably have kissed a cow."

Santiago gave a short laugh. Then a shuddering sigh. "Kerry, that's the first time I've laughed since the night before you said, 'If we ever see each other again, shoot me first.' I was so afraid that someday I'd have to do it."

His starlit face was uncharacteristically bleak. She'd known she'd broken his heart when she'd left Gold Point alone, and she'd known what a terrible burden she'd laid on him when she'd told him to kill her rather than let her be captured by her father. But now she saw the cost of that burden in his tense, tired face. "I'm sorry, Santiago. I *had* to leave. You understand, don't you?"

"Yeah," he whispered into her hair. "I don't suppose you'd consider leaving again? The king's orders about you stand."

The giddiness of joy leached out of her, and the night air was suddenly cold on her skin. "This is my home now. I came back to fight for it."

Santiago looked resigned, not surprised. "There's something I need to tell you. One of the Rangers killed Sophie during the initial attack."

"Oh, no," Kerry exclaimed softly. Sophie had been one of her few real friends in Gold Point. "I hoped I'd see her again someday, to explain why I had to leave. The four of us had so much fun together. How is Luis?"

"About how you'd expect." He sighed, then ran his fingers along her collarbone, under her shirt. "I can't believe I'm really touching you."

"Same here." Despite everything, joy bloomed in Kerry's chest. She'd spent months trying to get used to the knowledge that she'd never see Santiago again. And here he was, living and breathing in her arms.

One more kiss, and then she made herself let go.

·32·
MIA

LAS ANCLAS – MEDINA DAIRY BARN

MIA AWOKE CURLED UP against Ross. Slivers of moonlight slanted down between warped barn planks, picking out bits of straw, the scuffed toe of Jennie's boot, and a lock of Ross's blue-black hair against the battered arm of his leather jacket.

Everyone else seemed to be asleep. She should go back to sleep, too. She tried calculating square roots, but that didn't help. She tried counting cows. Then she tried counting cars. It was so frustrating to keep seeing cars in the ruined city, and never have enough time to take them completely apart. Someday she'd go back, pry those cars open, and acquire enough intact parts to recreate…

"Mia?" Jennie's calm voice broke into her thoughts.

"I'm awake, too," Kerry said. "I did a perimeter check. I ran into Santiago! He said you spoke to Alfonso?"

"He showed up after you all went to sleep," said Jennie. "He said he took over feeding and milking these cows since the Rats decided we could stay here. They'll bring us food and water as soon as they can."

"It's so weird to have to hide in my own town," said Mia.

"I know." Jennie gave Mia a comforting touch on her shoulder. "I keep thinking of what it must have been like for Paco and the others who've been here the whole time."

A rush of tears surged up in Mia, and she gulped them back. "Like Felicité."

In the silvery moonlight, she saw Jennie and Kerry exchange glances, as if they knew something she didn't.

"What?" Mia demanded.

Kerry propped her chin on her fists. "I know we all thought Voske killed her and ordered Henry to say she committed suicide. But when he kills someone important—like Tom Preston's daughter—he likes people to see the body."

Mia instantly pictured Felicité's head atop a pole. Hat and all. She shuddered.

Kerry went on, "So why would Voske tell Henry to say she killed herself in the only way that wouldn't leave a body? I think it's because he doesn't have a body."

"Then you think it was suicide after all?" Mia couldn't decide which was worse.

"No," said Kerry. "I think she isn't dead."

Jennie was nodding. "Me too. It doesn't make sense that Voske would kill Tom Preston's daughter and not make more hay of it. I don't think Voske had anything to do with it. I think she's hiding somewhere and Henry's covering for her."

Mia hugged her knees to her chest. She wanted to believe it. "I hope you're right. But it's hard to imagine Felicité and Henry being smart enough to fool Voske for weeks."

"Henry was smart enough to hide his Change for years," Kerry pointed out.

"And desperation and danger change people," Jennie said. "I bet she's hiding, trying to figure out how to contact her father and help retake the town."

Mia ground her chin into her knee. "That sounds like what *you'd* do, Jennie. I know she fought in the first invasion, but she went right back to her old self afterward. 'Oh no, rain! My hair!' I hope she's hiding. But if she is, I don't think she's doing anything *but* hiding."

Kerry smiled. "I don't think she's hiding. I think she's hidden. I bet Voske came up with the suicide story, and he's got her locked away somewhere." Her teeth shone white as her smile widened into a grin. "Here's where we differ, Mia. I *do* think she's plotting from wherever Voske has her locked up."

The barn door creaked open. Ross was instantly on his feet, knife in hand, followed by Summer and Maria-Pilar. Mia was briefly torn between alarm and hope, then saw the shadowy figure outlined in moonlight. She'd know that silhouette anywhere. Mia hurled herself at the ladder, only stopped from falling off the edge by Ross grabbing the back of her overalls. She detached herself and slithered down, then lunged at her dad.

"Hi, Mia. I'm so glad you're okay," he breathed against the top of her head.

"I smell like cows," Mia sobbed into his shirt. "No, *worse.*"

"I'll live," Dad said with a quiet laugh.

A slighter figure had entered behind him, moonlight glinting on blonde hair.

"Becky?" Mia asked, then hugged her, too.

Jennie stuck her head over the edge of the loft. "Come on up."

They all climbed up, and Dad opened a satchel and pressed a bun—a hot bun!—into Mia's hand. "It's stuffed with braised pork."

"My favorite!" Mia took an enormous bite. The bun was fluffy, the filling savory and delicious. Pork took hours to braise. Dad must have been cooking all night.

He and Becky passed out buns, dried fruit, jerky—not the boring travel jerky, the good, spiced stuff he made himself—and a canteen of barley tea. Mia was blissfully happy, being with Dad and eating his food. She only came down to earth when she realized that it was all food that didn't have much smell and wouldn't leave a trace—no seeds, pits, shells, or bones. The need to hide crept into everything, even Dad's cooking.

The barn door creaked open, then shut. "It's Paco."

"And Santiago."

"And me," came a voice Mia didn't recognize. "Sean."

"Sean!" Kerry exclaimed in delight. Mia realized that it was Kerry's unnoticeable brother. Between the dim light and his dark clothes and skin, he probably didn't even need a Change to go unseen. "What are you doing here?"

"I thought you might need me," Sean replied.

"And me!" It was Meredith's voice. "Out of the way, cow. Ugh! Don't lick me."

They climbed up and sat with the others in the hay-scented dimness.

"We can't stay here for very long," said Jennie. "Dr. Lee, do you have any idea where we can hide?"

"Yes," Dad replied. Just hearing his voice made Mia felt so much better. "Becky came up with the perfect place."

"My old house is empty," said Becky. "Henry moved into Singles Row, and Mom moved into with my distant cousins. She told Aunt Rosa our house is haunted by a poltergeist."

Mia had never been inside the Callahan house. As far as she knew, nobody ever went in but the Callahans. She'd even seen people veer off to one side as they walked past it. But that made it an excellent hiding place, haunted or not.

"I'm the poltergeist," Paco said wryly. "I teleported inside in the middle of the night and tripped over the furniture."

Mia was relieved to hear it. She wasn't particularly afraid of ghosts, but she didn't think the ghosts of long-dead Callahans would be friendly.

Paco went on, "I checked the house tonight, and it's still empty. Santiago says it's being saved for reinforcements who were supposed to come here but got sent to put down a rebellion in a different town. There'll be plenty of warning time if the reinforcements do show up."

"I hope that town succeeds," said Kerry.

"It sounds like Voske's army is getting spread thin," Jennie said thoughtfully. "Well, let's go. It's night and it's quiet out. We won't get a better chance. We'll have to move from hiding—"

"I'll take you," said a male voice.

Mia flung herself backward and fell into a hay bale. Some guy had appeared out of nowhere—

Oh. It was Sean. She'd forgotten about him.

"Sorry," Sean said. "Okay, when we go out, everyone put a hand on me or each other. Stay as close as you can. I've never tried to cover this many people before."

"Santiago and I will go ahead," said Paco. "If any patrol sees us, they won't think anything of it."

They climbed down, and everyone but Paco and Santiago clustered around Sean. Mia grabbed his sleeve and took Ross's hand. She hated the idea of Voske's soldiers patrolling Las Anclas, and Ross had to hate it even more. His strong fingers closed tight over hers as they crept in an awkward bunch to the Callahan house along silent pathways. The house was dark, musty, and dusty. Mia stifled a sneeze.

"Watch out for the furniture," Becky said, just as Mia's knee banged into something hard and unforgiving. *Like Mrs. Callahan,* Mia thought.

Becky opened a door in the back of the pantry and took them down a flight of stone steps and into the cold cellar. The air felt thick and smelled like old onions. Becky lit a pair of lamps. The walls were lined with shelves of preserves and sacks of flour and beans. A string of desiccated garlic hung overhead.

Mia could finally get a good look at Santiago. She'd heard so much about him, she was surprised to see how ordinary he seemed. He could have been any guy from Las Anclas, except that he wore the black Voske uniform. He and Kerry were holding hands like she and Ross were, as if something terrible would happen if they let go.

Paco also wore the Voske uniform. He looked older. Harder. Becky looked older too: thin, tired, her hair dull. Dad had lines in his forehead that Mia didn't remember seeing before. At least Meredith peered around with her usual enthusiasm. She was clearly ready for action, the sooner the better. She and Summer exchanged grins.

Everyone sat down on the floor except for Summer, who roamed around poking at everything, making comments like, "Pickled peaches! Who pickles peaches?"

"Kerry, there's something you should know," said Becky. "When I was in your mother's room, I touched something she'd handled, and I felt what she'd been thinking."

"You felt her *thinking?*" Kerry exclaimed. "You can do that?"

"It was a secret." Becky turned to the others. "Only Brisa and Sheriff Crow and Dr. Lee knew. Please don't let it get out. But the Rats need to know this about Min Soo. She was thinking about how much she loves you. Everything she's doing is to protect you."

Kerry's voice, which was usually so controlled,

choked with emotion. "Thank you for telling me."

"Did you touch anything else at Wolfe House?" Jennie asked.

"No. I'm scared to. Voske knows I can see the past of an object. He made me touch the table leg that Paco teleported with, to see who'd handled it last." Becky shivered. "I saw his thoughts."

"You saw Voske's *thoughts?*" Jennie exclaimed. "What were they?"

"Just obsessing over who could be plotting against him." Becky repeated the snatches she remembered. Even that second-hand glimpse into his mind spooked Mia.

"Interesting," said Jennie. "Becky, anything he thinks might be useful. Can you touch more things when he's not looking, and tell us everything you see?"

As Becky doubtfully nodded, Dad said, "Good idea, Jennie. You never know what might help our plans."

"What are your plans?" Jennie asked.

Paco faced her. "An uprising. We'll do it the same way Voske took the town, by surprise. Each of us will have a target. But we need more weapons."

"When?" Jennie asked. "Or hasn't it gotten that far?"

"We have a deadline," Meredith said. "Before the next Opportunity Day."

"Or Voske will make me pick the next victim," said Paco. "And we need more people we can count on, each to take out a target. Fast. At the same time."

Take out a target, Mia thought. *He means, kill a person.* She'd killed in battle herself, probably—it had been so chaotic that she wasn't sure—but there was something unsettling about how Paco spoke about it.

"I have a list—" When Jennie looked appalled, Santiago tapped his head. "In here. My cousin Manuel, my brother-in-law's sister—there's quite a few soldiers here who'd love to get out from under Voske. But the only person I trust here who doesn't have to worry about hostages is Luis. He's not close to his family. His hostage was Sophie, his fiancée, and she was killed in the invasion."

"He's a good guy," Kerry said. "I trust him."

Ross touched the scars on his throat. "He saved my life. I trust him."

Dad said after a slight hesitation, "I'll discuss it with the adults. We have to be careful. All it takes is a single weak link, and Voske will break the chain."

Jennie leaned forward, elbows on her knees. "Paco. You said the plan was to select people to each take out a target. What do you mean by target?"

Paco's expression didn't change as he looked at her. *That* was what was unsettling. Paco had always been so expressive, with his body and with his voice. Now his body made no unnecessary movements, and his voice was flat. "The targets are Voske and his captains. If they're gone, the soldiers can't fight effectively. They aren't trained to think for themselves."

Santiago added, "Once they realize that Voske is dead, and so is anyone else who could order his commands carried out, I think lots of them will run. Just like some people did when Ross blew up the dam."

Jennie rubbed her chin. "So, we're talking about the simultaneous assassinations of multiple people. Paco, we don't even have a watch to coordinate the timing!"

Paco said sharply, "If you think there's another way, I'd love to hear it."

Mia held her breath. Suddenly the room had filled with tension.

"Have you chosen the assassins?" Jennie asked. "Are they trained? Are they willing to kill in cold blood?"

"I was a Ranger trainee." Meredith folded her arms. "*I* don't have a problem with it. Yolanda and Jose Riley wouldn't either. We all fought the first time Voske attacked this town."

"I'll do it," Summer spoke up. "I'll strangle Voske with my bare hands! Just like I strangled that sand tiger."

"No," said Dad. "You're too young to make this kind of decision. And so is Yolanda. This is very different from how any of you have fought before."

"I've killed people." Meredith shrugged. "I assume. It wasn't like I could stop to check."

"In a battle, you're defending your own life or someone else's," said Dad. "This is deliberate killing in cold blood. It's not the same, and it doesn't feel the same. Many people who fight in battle find that when faced with taking a life in cold blood, they're unable to do it."

Mia wondered how Dad could possibly know that. Had he been having private discussions with Gold Point soldiers? Then she remembered that Mr. Preston and Sera Diaz—and Uncle Omar, who had died when she was a child—had come from Gold Point. And Las Anclas did have the death penalty, though it had never been used in her lifetime. The penalty for committing cold-blooded murder was to be killed in cold blood.

Becky said softly, "I try not to kill when I fight in battle, but I could if I had to. But I could never kill like that. Not even the way Dr. Lee does it, when a dying patient asks you to make it quick."

Mia imagined sneaking up on a sleeping person and…stabbing them? Driving a knife through their blanket and into their body? She wasn't sure if she could do it. Well, she could if it was Voske himself. She'd think of what he'd done to Ross and stab hard. But it wasn't as if they'd assign Voske to *her*.

Paco spoke up sharply, "I'll kill Voske. I've wanted to ever since he took over—since before then, when he killed my mother. I know I can do it."

"No." Dad held his hand out. "No. Not you, and not Kerry. I know he's not your father in any way that truly matters, but—"

"Why not?" Paco's voice had gone low. The back of Mia's neck prickled. "You really think I'd hesitate?"

"I know you're capable," Dad said in his calm, steady manner. "Both of you. But I'm trying my best to avoid it."

"I get it," Kerry said suddenly. "My father's first kill was his own brother. Then his mother. Everyone said she deserved it, but maybe that doesn't matter. Maybe once you start, it gets easier and easier, and then you just keep going. I want to be useful, but…not like that."

"Let's table the matter of who kills the king for now," said Dad. "Our second problem is gathering weapons."

Mia knew she'd never be considered for the assassinations. That was fine with her. But like Kerry, she wanted to be useful. "If someone can bring some of the things in my cottage here, I can build weapons—"

"No." Jennie spoke in her leader voice. Everyone fell silent, looking to her. "It won't work. This plan will do nothing but get us all killed."

·33·

JENNIE

LAS ANCLAS – THE CALLAHAN HOUSE

JENNIE HATED THE WAY everyone stared at her. Summer was outright glaring. But they were talking about risking their lives. And not just theirs. The lives of the other Rats, and the people of Las Anclas and their families. Jennie was willing to risk her own life to save the town—she had done so—but she was not willing to throw her life away.

"This entire plan is based on wishful thinking," she said. "It assumes the army will surrender or flee once their leaders are dead. What if they don't? They'll still have all the weapons. It assumes we can assassinate ten or more leaders simultaneously, so none of them raise an alarm. Voske managed a lightning takeover here because he had a full army of trained soldiers, his captains had synchronized watches, we were taken by surprise, and one of our main leaders and half our best fighters were gone. None of that will be true for us."

"But we do have an army," Meredith protested. "The town will rise up."

"With what weapons?" Jennie asked. "His new armory is surrounded by guards. If all our trained fighters are using all the weapons we've salvaged to do assassinations, then who attacks the armory?"

It felt so disrespectful to tell Dr. Lee he was wrong. But he was a doctor, with no training in military thinking. Paco, Meredith, Santiago, and Maria-Pilar were soldiers, not strategists. They carried out orders, they didn't make them. Only Jennie and Kerry had been trained in strategic thinking, and Kerry's training had been more in mind games than in military strategy.

Jennie turned to her. "Kerry? Do you agree?"

Slowly, Kerry nodded. "I hadn't put it together like that, but… Yes. I hate to say it, but you're right."

And everyone, including Kerry, looked expectantly at Jennie.

It was up to her. *Again.*

She wished she wasn't in this position — she wished she would stop landing in this position. Why was it always her who got stuck making decisions that she'd regret, no matter what they were?

But if she hadn't spoken up, the Rats would have gone ahead with their original plan. And they'd probably all have been killed, along with their hostages. It was a good thing she'd been there.

It *was* a good thing she was there!

"What do you suggest, Jennie?" Dr. Lee asked. "We need a workable plan that we can launch before the next Opportunity Day. We were very lucky with Jack last time. There's an excellent chance that the next Opportunity Day will lead to tragedy."

She knew everyone would hate what she was going to say next. Her plan might lead to some innocent person dying. But that wasn't because of her. That was because of the situation they were in, which she hadn't caused. Voske had.

"We can't stop the next Opportunity Day," Jennie said. When a hushed outburst rose up, she said firmly, "We need *at least* a hundred trained fighters to reinforce us. More would be better. And we need to get them armed and in position. That takes time."

"Where are they supposed to come from?" Paco demanded.

"We have to find Mr. Preston and the Rangers with him." It was all so clear in her mind. "They're not dead, or their heads would be over the gate. Mr. Preston knows he's not welcome at Catalina, so he'd go to the next-nearest town that's big enough to have some kind of trained defense like our Rangers. That's Dai La. They're probably there right now. We need to send someone to go find them. Sheriff Crow might be there, too."

"Paco?" Mia said hopefully. "Could you do it in

stages, so you don't arrive with no head?"

Despite the serious topic, Jennie had to stifle a snicker. Only Mia would phrase it like that!

"I don't think so." Paco didn't show any sign of finding it funny. "It's too far, and it takes too much out of me. Plus, I can't take supplies. By the time I was a quarter of the way there, I'd be collapsed in the middle of the desert with no water."

"I'll go," Meredith offered. "I can take supplies."

"You stand out too much, and they'll want to know where you are." Once Jennie herself had graduated, Meredith had become the leader of the schoolhouse girls. "We need someone quieter, whose absence won't be noticed."

Sean spoke up, making everyone jump. Jennie had completely forgotten he was there: the "don't notice me" at work. "I could go, but would Mr. Preston trust me?"

"Probably not," Jennie said reluctantly. "It should be a Las Anclas citizen. My cousin Naomi used to go to Dai La with her dad, back when we traded with them. She knows how to get there, if Sean can take her out of town."

"She'll have to go on foot," Sean warned. "I can't make people not notice a horse."

"That's fine," Jennie said. "It'll take her longer, but she'll get there."

"I'll vouch that she has an unpleasant and very contagious illness, which will keep her locked in her own bedroom for a month." Dr. Lee gave a meditative smile. "With oozing sores, I think."

"Can Mr. Preston get a hundred or more people?" Ross asked. "Everyone we talked to in Dai La hated him."

"It's in their best interests to stop Voske." But as soon as Jennie spoke, she wondered if she was also falling into the wishful thinking trap.

"What about Gold Point?" Santiago suggested. "If there's a real chance of killing the king, some people might be willing to take the risk. Especially if he's not there to condemn their families immediately."

"Do you really think so?" Kerry asked.

Santiago squeezed her hand. "You weren't in a position to know what got whispered in closets and behind closed doors. But trust me, some would."

"I'll go to Gold Point after I get Naomi past the gate," said Sean. "I know a lot of people there. My mom's there — she's a military commander."

"We still don't have someone to take on the king once this attack happens," said Santiago. "I'd do it, but he's too fast for me. He has reflexes like a sand viper."

Grimly, Maria-Pilar said, "I'd love to do it."

Summer snickered. "Don't you think Voske will notice a giant mushroom?"

Maria-Pilar's form blurred, and a fancy chair stood where she had been. Then she blurred back to herself.

Kerry shook her head. "You can get close to him, but there's still that moment when you blur. For Voske, that's plenty of time to strike. And — sorry, Maria-Pilar — but Santiago's quicker than you, and he's not quick enough."

"Still so sure it should be anyone but me?" Paco remarked with some bitterness.

Jennie studied him for a long moment. She could understand his anger at Voske, and why he wanted Voske dead. But it unnerved her how much he wanted to kill Voske himself. She flashed on Paco drumming at Luc's when Sera was alive, teasing the dancers by going faster and faster until they couldn't keep up, and wondered what Sera would think if she could see her son now.

"What about Jennie?" Meredith suggested.

Jennie turned the same realistic appraisal on herself that she had on their plans. "If speed is the key factor, we want Ross, not me."

"I agree," said Santiago. "I saw him attack Voske with his entire honor guard right there, and he nearly succeeded. He might be as fast as the king."

"Might be," Jennie thought. *"As fast as." Santiago is the only person who's seen Ross and Voske fighting each other, and he knows Ross isn't faster. Did I just suggest sending Ross to his death?*

Ross's gaze dropped. His long, sooty lashes hid his eyes as he said quietly, "I'll do it."

·34·
KERRY

LAS ANCLAS – THE CALLAHAN HOUSE

AS DR. LEE AND Becky got up to leave, Kerry caught hold of Sean's arm. "I'm so glad to see you!"

He hugged her tight. "Same here. Want to come to Gold Point with me? I know it sounds dangerous, but I could keep you safe."

Kerry shook her head. "Someday, maybe. Right now, I want to stay here. With Santiago. But before you go, could you help me be not-noticed?"

"Not near our father!"

"No, the opposite. Once he's out of Wolfe House for a while, could you get me in to see my mother?"

Sean's expression changed from wariness to understanding. "Sure. I overheard that he's going to inspect the company riding to reinforce Lake Perris in the morning."

Jennie spoke up. "Kerry, don't tell your mother about the Rats."

Indignant, Kerry said, "I know that. She's the one who taught me discretion. "

"I know. You learned a lot in Gold Point." Jennie's jaw muscles flexed, as if she was biting back anything else.

Kerry also could have said more, but she too kept it back. Jennie's life was on the line. Everyone's was. Not long ago, they had been enemies. Trust was one of the hardest things to build, and easiest to lose. *Don't you trust me?* her father whispered in memory.

"Sorry," said Jennie. "We're all tense. See if you can learn anything useful from her. We know she wants to help *you*."

Sean returned after dawn, and they headed for the Hill. It was eerie how people walked past them, their gaze slipping away to focus on something just to the side or behind or in front of them. As long as they didn't touch anyone, they were perfectly safe. None of these townspeople were looking for Sean.

What would happen if someone was looking for *her?* She couldn't ask. But her father and his army believed she was still in the ruined forest. No need to scare herself unnecessarily. It was dangerous enough, given that their father could always come home early. And he was always looking for Sean.

They walked through the Wolfe House garden to avoid bumping into soldiers, and came upon the well. Kerry ran her free hand along its weathered stone edge. Could Felicité really have thrown herself down it?

They went in through the servants' entrance at the back and slipped through the kitchen, dodging a spill of flour where they would have left footprints. Sean nudged Kerry toward her mother's room, then stood watch at the door.

Her mother's familiar scent enveloped he when she went in, closing the door behind her. And not only the scent, but a mix of emotions: old frustration, newer appreciation. Love.

Her mother sat at the desk, dressed in an exquisite hanbok embroidered with dogwood blossoms, writing rapidly.

"Mom," Kerry whispered.

Her mother stilled, then slowly raised her head. Her eyes were dark with painful expectation. When she saw Kerry, she dropped the pen splattering ink over the beautiful handwriting. "Kerry?"

"I can't stay long," Kerry whispered.

She got no farther, because Min Soo was on her, moving faster than Kerry had thought possible, gripping her in a tight hug. Then she laughed a little. "Oh, you *are* real. No ghost would be quite so...I take it wherever you were, there was no bathing facility?"

"We've been on the run, Mom," Kerry said. The old annoyance and new love rose up in her, but the love was stronger, putting her on the verge of tears. "I'd love a hot bath, but how would you explain the pound of mud in the tub?"

Min Soo glanced at the door. "Is someone on guard out there?"

"Sean."

"He's here? Ah, good." Mom drew Kerry to the satin-covered sofa. "At least these pillows are a dark shade of blue. Sit. Tell me everything. Then you must go. Your father will return before noon."

"I know. But I wanted to see you."

Her mother said with a sigh, "If only our meetings weren't always so brief. It seems tragic that as soon as we began seeing eye to eye, we were always forced to part."

Kerry considered what her mother was not quite saying: was she implying that she wanted Kerry to stay? No, that was a given. Was she implying that she'd like the obstacle between them—Voske—to be removed?

Kerry said carefully, "Yes, I wish that too."

With another sigh, one that sounded distinctly… social, Mom said, "Well, we must make the best use of the time we have. So much mother-to-daughter talk to be boiled down into a few moments. Let me think. What is most important for a girl your age. The subject of love, of course."

Kerry raised her hand. "Mom, do I have to hear this?"

Mom's smile was brief and fierce. "Yes. You do. Many mothers would warn their daughters against making a foolish love match too young. But I have a different perspective. I would warn you against the opposite. I would warn you against turning away from love to gain other benefits."

Kerry realized, to her relief, that Mom was not talking about Santiago. She'd never given much thought to her parents' marriage. Ugh, who likes to think about that? But it made sense that Mom hadn't married for love. So…was Mom implying that she'd be happy if Voske went away?

Was she implying that she might help Kerry?

Kerry wished it was possible to talk plainly. But she couldn't even hint that there was a resistance. She'd promised—and her mother obviously did not feel safe speaking plainly. Just being there endangered them both.

Mom said carefully, "I'm very glad you're not alone. You have your brother. You have...support." She gave Kerry an inquiring glance.

A tap at the door made Min Soo still. Kerry jumped. "I have to go."

Mom gave her the sweetest smile. "Come back when you can."

Kerry bolted out the door. Sean grabbed her hand, and just in time, too. They flattened themselves against the wall to avoid a procession of maids.

Once the maids were in Mom's room, Sean headed back to the kitchen. Kerry nudged him, indicating the pantry. Kerry had figured that since the whole house was lit, all the rooms were occupied. Therefore, the most likely place to hold a secret prisoner was the basement. If Felicité wasn't there, she'd try the attic next.

The basement door was unlocked. Well, maybe Felicité was tied up. Leaving Sean on guard, Kerry peered down the steps. It was dark except for the soft glow of bright-moths in one corner, and a girl's silhouette. But it was too small to be Felicité. Kerry's nerves chilled. Was it a child hostage slated for execution?

Kerry descended the steps. The girl bent over a dish of phosphorescent worms, which cast a green glow over her familiar face. It was Bridget. A spider as big as a kitten was delicately plucking up the worms and feeding them to its swarm of offspring.

Kerry was amused and touched at the sight of her little sister being herself. Reluctantly, she decided that it was too dangerous to greet Bridget. She started to back away, and the spiders skittered in all directions, their feet ticking on the stone floor. Bridget looked to see what had startled them, and gasped.

"Kerry?" Bridget whispered. "Is that really you?"

"Yeah. It's me." Kerry was poised to run. There was every chance that Bridget would try to turn her in.

"Kerry!" Bridget flung herself into Kerry's arms and began to babble at her in a whisper. "I missed you so much. Everyone hates me here. Hattie Salazar saw me watching her brother — because he can create fire! It's cool! And she started crying and begging me not to rot him alive! I asked Dr. Lee if I could learn surgery from him and be his apprentice, and he gave me such a sad look. I thought *he* thought Father wouldn't let me, so I asked Father, and he said he'd order Dr. Lee to teach me because surgery would be a wonderful hobby for me. He said it would be *terrifying!* And he looked so proud!"

Kerry shuddered. Voske would expect Bridget to graduate to surgical experiments on prisoners. He'd love that. She remembered him saying, *"Torture is a highly unreliable way to get information. But it's one of the best ways to keep your subjects compliant. And the more unusual the method, the more disturbing."* Then he'd assigned her to invent three original methods of torture.

Bridget looked around wildly, then pushed Kerry away. "You better go. Father could be back at any time. But I'm so glad you're alive! We—well, *I* thought you might be dead! Father announced that you were, but I don't think he really believes it. I should have known better, too." In an eerie echo of Voske's voice, she said, "'No one is dead until you see a body.'"

Kerry wondered how well Bridget had learned Father's lessons. It was dangerous, but she needed to know. "If you tell him you saw me, there will be a body. You're the crown princess now. Do you want to be the queen one day?"

"But I love you," Bridget said. Kerry was startled; such raw emotion was not encouraged in Voske's family. "Anyway, crown princes and princesses don't last long. Sean was crown prince. Then it was you and Deirdre fighting for Father's attention. He told us it was good training."

"Oh, I remember."

"And Uncle Colum was crown prince once. Now he's a skull over the gate at home. Father put him there when he was your age."

Kerry was astonished that she was having this conversation with Bridget. She wondered how far she could push it without endangering herself—or Bridget. Cautiously, she said, "Father always called Uncle Colum a traitor. But I wonder what that really meant. How did he betray Gold Point?"

Bridget cast Kerry a scornful look, "We both know it meant that he opposed Father. What else could it be? I've been thinking a lot, ever since me and Becky became friends." Bridget petted the big spider, which had returned and was creeping up her dress. "If I become queen, I could do whatever I liked. I could keep as many insects as I like. But Father pays more attention to me now, and I always feel like I'm not good enough. Because I might be the crown princess, but he talks to Liam the same—"

"Paco," Kerry corrected.

"I know that was his old name," Bridget began.

"It's his name. The name he wants. Father is…wants him to be a different identity. But we were talking about how Father speaks to you."

"Yes," Bridget said. "He talks to me sometimes like I'm not really what he wants. He says my heart's in the right place, but I think too small. What does that mean? Does it mean I'll have to fight, or maybe even kill, Owen and Fiona someday?"

"It might," Kerry said. "That's how Father grew up. He always told me it made him strong."

Bridget kept her gaze on the spider. "When I say what I know he wants, I don't really like myself."

"I felt that way, too." Kerry hesitated, then added, "Eventually."

"And you left. Like Sean. Do you think he felt the same?"

"I know he did." Kerry hesitated. Bridget was only thirteen. Where could she even go? Kerry couldn't take her anywhere. Maybe Sean could spirit her away…?

Bridget gave her a look that Kerry knew very well. Bridget was trying to read her face. In a small voice, she said, "I know you can't take me with you."

It wasn't safe to tell Bridget why, or even suggest that maybe Sean could take her away later. Kerry now trusted her sister not to reveal anything on purpose, but she knew how good her father was at getting secrets out of people once he knew they were there. But she couldn't leave Bridget with no hope at all. "You won't be thirteen forever."

"I know." Bridget sounded discouraged. In a forcedly cheerful tone, she said, "I'm not really alone. Becky and Alfonso and Dr. Lee are awfully nice to me. And I don't think anything will happen to them, because Dr. Lee has such a unique, useful Change talent, and Alfonso is so smart, and Father likes me and Becky being friends."

The shadow of their father's will fell over them both. Kerry knew she had to go soon, but she had one more task first. "Bridget, do you know what's in the attic?"

Bridget grinned. "Lots of cool spiders! A few giant dust mites."

"Do you know if any prisoners are kept here?"

"Nobody is in the attic but the spiders. Mrs. Wolfe and her mother are in the room next to William," said Bridget. "Becky brings them medicine. That's how we got to be friends."

"Anyone else up there?" Kerry asked.

"No, the officers are all gone. Mrs. Wolfe and old Mrs. Wolfe are the only prisoners. There aren't even any prisoners in the jail now. They all got flogged and released."

"Bridget, you know not to talk like this to anyone else, right?"

Her sister rolled her eyes. "Of course I do! I only told you because you already ran away!"

"Good. Be careful, but don't forget what you said, either. Keep on thinking but keep it to yourself. Someday, you'll be able to do something about it."

Before Bridget could start sniffling again, Kerry pointed down. "The baby spiders are back." Then she ghosted out to where Sean was waiting.

·35·

FELICITÉ

LAS ANCLAS

AS THE OFFICIALLY ACCREDITED envoy of the Saigon Alliance, Felicité had been entrusted with one of Saigon's precious butterfly horses, known for their speed and endurance. Her little mare's translucent wings fluttered constantly, sending a cool breeze that kept the mosquitos off Felicité's skin and kept the flies out of the mare's own eyes. Brushing flies off a horse was not only disgusting, but beneath the dignity of an envoy.

Felicité sat up straight in the saddle, resisting the old impulse to adjust her hat.

She had no hat. She no longer needed one.

She traced the subtle spirals of the mare's twin horns. In the old days, she might have worried that the mare would upstage her. But she was quite confident that the butterfly horse would only add to her impressive entrance.

Felicité and her party had ridden out ahead of her father, the Rangers, and the allies, as an army could only go as fast as its supply wagons. The experienced couriers who accompanied her could camp without leaving a trace, and her father knew all the hidden routes from his years of patrolling. They'd managed to avoid Voske's patrols until they were a mere day away from Las Anclas.

Felicité had worried that Voske would have them shot on sight, despite their white flag. But the Saigon Alliance had insisted on attempting diplomacy before resorting to war, and they and her father had assured her that not even Voske would murder an envoy.

"*Every* town would come after him if he did," her father had told her. "He may not agree to your request for a parley, and he certainly won't give up Las Anclas. But he won't harm you. Think of it as a chance to get valuable information."

And he was right. When they finally did encounter a patrol, the Gold Point soldiers had looked at the white flag, listened to her request for a parley, sent a messenger to ride ahead, and assigned two more to accompany Felicité and her companions to Las Anclas.

When they came in sight of the town, the gates creaked open. Felicité let her gaze go out of focus so she could count the sentries without quite looking at the skulls over the gates. At least there weren't any new ones.

Gold Point soldiers were everywhere. As Felicité and her escort rode slowly in, citizens stopped and stared, first in surprise — and then in shock, when they recognized her, and realized that she was alive.

And Changed.

She started to duck her head, instinctively trying to shield her face with her hair, then forced herself to straighten. She was Changed. Let everyone see that. Let them see her scales. She stretched out a hand and watched them glitter in the sun. They were *not* disgusting. They were beautiful.

The shock in everyone's faces slowly altered into individual expressions.

Mrs. Hernandez sneered, then angrily turned her back. Because Felicité had told Henry about the tunnel? Or on behalf of her daughter Laura, with her black cat claws, who had been killed in Voske's first attack?

Familiar faces slid by, some wary, others puzzled. Mrs. Horst's lip curled with outright loathing. Felicité could practically feel acid fire scorching where Mrs. Horst's gaze touched. Anger flared up in her, but she calmed herself, thinking of the skull above the gate.

Then Felicité locked eyes with Mrs. Callahan, Henry's mother. Felicité briefly thought she was Grandma Ida, before remembering that Grandma Ida was dead. Mrs. Callahan seemed to have aged twenty years within the last month.

Felicité expected more anger from her. How soon

before Henry's head joined the others? But in that heartbeat as Felicité stared down into Mrs. Callahan's face, she didn't see anger or hatred. Instead, the woman's gaze lifted with painful expectation.

You see me, and think my father is not far behind, Felicité thought. *You're right. But if you hope he's going to sweep in and make everything as it once was, think again.*

She gave Henry's mother a polite nod. This, after all, was what she had come for. She had to think ahead, as her mother had taught her. In diplomatic usage, if a visitor was met at the gates by the person they'd come to visit, that meant a reception with the greatest respect. But Voske was nowhere in sight. He was treating her less like an envoy, and more like a mere messenger.

Very well. Let the game begin.

Several soldiers flanked her party of three. "This way," one said, without even a Miss or a Ma'am.

Felicité nodded regally and spoke as if addressing a minion. "Lead on."

A quick, assessing glance from that minion shot her way, as her escort remained silent. Felicité looked around slowly, mentally assessing everything. She noted new electrical searchlights. She counted patrols along Main Street. She noted the wall placed around the south generator, which had been rebuilt. Sentries stood thick around Weavers' Row. That many armed guards wouldn't be protecting looms. That building undoubtedly had been taken over for some military purpose.

They proceeded up the path toward her home. She did not let a speck of recognition or expectation into her expression. She was an envoy in enemy territory. Nothing else mattered.

The minion said curtly, "Dismount here. We'll stable the horses."

Felicité said to her escorts, "Please go with the horses. They're not accustomed to mounts like ours here." To Voske's minion, she said, "Lead the way."

The soldier, her own age, rudely jerked his thumb toward the house, then set off. She followed at a deliberately sedate pace, so he had to stand in the rose garden until she caught up.

"Wait here." He pointed to a bench. "The king will

summon you when he's ready."

Felicité sat, taking care to arrange her robe neatly, and smiled at the children who gathered to stare at her.

"Is that really you, Felicité?" Alfonso Medina's little sister asked.

"It is," Felicité said cheerfully.

"They said you were dead!"

"They said wrong," Felicité replied sweetly.

The two scampered off, and Felicité counted under her breath. Voske might have taken over, but she knew Las Anclas, and how fast gossip spread. She'd reached thirty-seven when the first looky-loo showed up. Oh, good, it was Carlos, her very first date, his knees dusty. He'd obviously been weeding.

"Hello, Carlos," she said, smiling as if he was dressed in his best for a Welcome Dance.

"You're an envoy?" Carlos asked, then cut an anxious gaze toward Wolfe House.

Felicité suppressed the urge to look behind her. Searching for her mother's face at a window would reveal her chief concern, and Voske would use it against her.

As she chatted with Carlos, more townspeople turned up. Some pretended they were stopping on their way to other errands. Others made no pretense at all. Jack and Anna-Lucia brought from the saloon a tray table with an enormous jug of lemonade and began to pour out glasses. Felicité sipped hers, smiling. Voske had obviously intended to insult her by making her wait outside and not offering her any refreshment. Instead, he'd given her the opportunity to hold court.

The onslaught of questions began.

"How did you get out?"

"How did you become an envoy?"

"Why did Henry say you jumped down a well?"

"So, you just Changed this month, Felicité?" Carlos spoke hesitantly, as if he wasn't sure what he really wanted to say.

Felicité smiled and held up her hands, letting the sunlight sparkle off her bronze scales. "Permanent rings. Do you like them?"

"They're beautiful," exclaimed Brisa's little sister Nita. "I hope I get some just like yours. Gold!"

"Gold would be lovely on you. I hope you get them, too." Out of the corner of her eye, Felicité saw Grandpa Appel looking disgusted.

Becky came running up and flung herself into Felicité's arms. "Felicité, you're *alive!* You're *here!*"

Becky was thinner than ever, and her tears fell hot against Felicité's cheek. For the first time since she'd come back to Las Anclas—maybe for the first time since Voske had invaded—she was with a real friend. A friend whom she had hurt, long before Voske had invaded. And yet Becky had clearly grieved for her supposed death—the death that Felicité had intended and had been saved from only by her Change. The death that would have forever prevented them from speaking the truth and understanding each other.

A rush of guilt made her cling even harder to Becky. Forgetting her role as an envoy, Felicité whispered, "I'm sorry, Becky. I'm so sorry. About everything."

"I'm just so glad you're alive," Becky whispered tremulously as she pulled away, searching Felicité's face. "Wow, you're really beautiful. Especially your hair! It's like the sea! Is that part of your Change?"

"No, it's a fashion in Catalina. I wish I could take you there—"

A guard pushed through the chatting crowd. "The king will see you now." He raised his voice. "Disperse, or you'll be arrested for loitering."

Most of the crowd fled, glasses still clutched in their hands. Their fear struck a painful resonance in Felicité's heart. Anna-Lucia took the lemonade jug. Jack disassembled the tray table and walked away without looking at the soldier.

A massive desk now dominated the parlor. There were maps on the walls, and a board with military rosters. Felicité tried to memorize them, though it was possible that they were fakes set up to mislead her—or rather, to mislead her father.

The dining room had new Korean screens hiding the entryway to the kitchen. She started toward her old chair, but the guard said, "You'll sit here." He pointed to Will's chair, at what used to be Mother's left.

Felicité sat regally, wondering if Mother was still in

the house, and if Felicité could get a message to her. She hoped her mother and Grandmère had at least seen her through a window.

She considered the rights and rules of envoys. Technically, she had the right to request a meeting with her family, even if it was supervised, but it didn't have to be accepted. Her only inviolable rights were that she and her party could not be harmed, she could not be prevented from leaving, and she could retrieve any of her personal possessions that she could carry with her. Everything was a matter of tradition and courtesy with the force of law. Voske was heeding the minimum requirements, but at least he *was* heeding them. So far.

A short, graceful woman entered. She wore a silk robe embroidered with swallows and plum blossoms, but that wasn't what caught Felicité's eye. Kerry strongly resembled her father, but the shape of her mouth and eyes were the same as this woman's. They had the same black hair, too, smooth as a raven's wing.

"Welcome, dear. I am Min Soo Cho. And you are…"

"Felicité Noelle Wolfe."

"Ah," Min Soo replied, her expression impossible to read. "Would you care for something to drink?" She rang a little bell, and servants in Voske livery came out with heavy trays of gold. They served tea and more lemonade, along with a porcelain dish of candied rose petals.

Felicité had eaten them before, when Grandmère had made them. They were more of a statement than a treat. She'd seen her mother use this form of social intimidation as mayor. Felicité knew exactly which bush they came from.

"How lovely. These are my favorites." Delicately, she helped herself.

Min Soo looked at her with interest. "You're quite young to be an envoy. But I can certainly see why you were chosen. Have you always been interested in diplomacy?"

"Always." Felicité heard the ghost of a gold coin clinking and took another rose petal. "I see that you love the finer things in life. How are you finding Las Anclas?"

"There is much to admire here. And room for improvement, too. I always welcome an interesting project.

Of course, this home and garden was one of those finer things already. Your mother's hand at work, I believe."

Was this woman hinting that Mother was still alive?

"Mother loves roses." She put a little emphasis on *loves*, instead of *loved*.

Min Soo did not correct her. She didn't reply at all. Felicité was reminded of the school training yard when the students writhed in the dirt, drenched in sweat, locked in a wrestling match that neither could win or lose.

Felicité's heart jolted as Becky entered, her face unhappy, with Henry right behind her, dressed in that Gold Point uniform. He looked as thin as Becky, if not more so, his cheekbones sharply outlined, with dark circles under his eyes. Which widened, startled, when they encountered Felicité's gaze. He stood still in the middle of the floor. "Becky told me — but I couldn't believe —"

"Hello, Henry," Felicité said brightly.

"How did you get out of the well?" he asked, his voice going high.

"What well?"

"The well outside!" He pointed a shaking finger. "That you threw yourself down."

Felicité put on a puzzled look. "Who told you I did that?"

"I saw you! You fell straight down! Did you cling to the sides until I left?"

He looked so upset that she began to feel sorry for him. Then she reminded herself of the heads on the gate. Coolly, she said, "Henry, you don't need to repeat whatever story you came up with to cover my escape. It doesn't matter now. I'm an envoy, and there are rules that protect me."

Henry's eyes bulged. He opened his mouth and shut it.

Voske walked and sat at the head of the table. Felicité had prepared herself for the moment when she'd see him, reminding herself again and again that she was an envoy and he had no power over her, but terror still jolted her. She crushed it down, hoping it hadn't shown on her face.

A girl with the familiar Voske fox face entered. Was this part of Voske's family, the reason Felicité had been kicked out of her own home? She appeared to be around thirteen, wearing a bell-skirted dress embroidered with...were those spiders? Ugh! The embroidery was very fine, but what a repulsive purpose to put it to. Exactly what one would expect of a child of Voske.

Min Soo directed the seating arrangement. Voske was at the head, of course, and Min Soo at the foot, as hostess. The spider princess was by Voske's right hand, the seat that should have been given to Felicité. Becky was at Voske's left hand. Felicité was seated next to the spider girl. And Henry was next to Becky and across from Felicité. The goggle-eyed stare was still fixed on his face.

Felicité had to admire whoever had come up with this setting. It was perfectly calculated to elevate Voske, insult Felicité, and make both her and Henry deeply uncomfortable. But understanding its purpose helped her regain her sense of balance.

As a line of silent servants brought more refreshments in, Voske said, "So, Felicité, how did you escape?"

Felicité pointedly waited until the servants had closed the door behind them before she said, "I climbed over the wall."

She enjoyed the tightening of annoyance in Voske's face as she forced him to ask for the details. Crunch! She bit into a jicama stick.

"Exactly how did you manage that without being seen?" Voske asked.

Felicité chewed and swallowed in a leisurely manner before she said, "As you can see, I am Changed. If I have enough time to spend in deep concentration, I can make more scales grow, and alter them to match my surroundings. With a few hours to spare, I can make myself almost invisible."

Henry was still staring at her with the bulging eyes of a dead fish.

Voske said, "Yes, your scales. They're hard to miss. Where were they before?"

"I hid them." She made herself look Voske in the eye. "I choose not to hide now."

"I see. And how does your father feel about them?"

Felicité had expected that. She was certain that her face betrayed nothing. But the image of her father instinctively drawing back from her still flashed in her mind. "I'm not here to discuss personal matters."

Voske shifted his gaze to Henry as a muscle ticked in his jaw. He said, "Exactly what was the purpose of your absurd lie, Henry?"

"I didn't lie." A sheen of tears gleamed in his eyes. "I *didn't* lie. I *saw* her fall down that well. She must have changed her scales to match the well, and climbed up as soon as the sun went down."

Felicité hardened her heart. She could not let anyone start thinking too hard about the well. "Henry, that lie has served its purpose. You don't have to keep telling it." Putting a note of irritation into her voice, she said, "Why do you refuse to admit the truth, even when everyone knows you're lying? You've been doing it since you were a little boy." Staring straight at him, she said, "Grow up."

Min Soo said softly, "The boy was clearly hoping to protect her. I must admit, my romantic heart admires gallantry."

Voske turned to Becky. "Anything to say in your brother's defense?"

Becky's face blanched nearly to the color of her lifeless hair. In a barely audible voice, she said, "Henry loved Felicité. He wanted her to go with him when he was exiled. He'd do anything for her. I mean, almost anything. Not anything against you." She darted a terrified look at Voske.

Voske looked annoyed rather than angry. He turned to his daughter. "Bridget?"

Bridget barely glanced at Henry. She seemed entirely focused on Becky, and her gaze was surprisingly sympathetic. Could the spider girl be Becky's *friend?*

"He's clearly not capable of clever plotting. Look how he's sticking to his ridiculous story, when we all just heard the truth. I think Becky's right. He's just in love with the envoy." Bridget leaned uncomfortably close, eyeing Felicité in the same revolting way that Alfonso Medina inspected animal skeletons. "I can understand that. Her scales are fascinating. Er, and very pretty. I expect she only showed them to him."

Voske waved a hand as if brushing away noisy flies. "Enough. Felicité, take your pretty scales into the interview room. It's time for us to talk in private."

·36·
BECKY

LAS ANCLAS

BECKY HAD TO STOP herself from running flat-out to the infirmary. Dr. Lee and Luis had undoubtedly already heard about the arrival of Felicité the envoy.

"Luis," Dr. Lee called. "Do you have the heart medicine?"

Luis handed a basket to Becky as he slipped his boots on. She was surprised to see that he looked…not cheerful, exactly…but hopeful. She hadn't been alone with Dr. Lee since they'd discussed recruiting him, but the adults had obviously voted to do it.

The three of them set out for Grandma Lowell's house. Grandma Lowell answered the door herself. She dramatically clutched her chest, saying loudly, "I've had the most terrible pains! And I feel so weak! Maybe this time it's really my time to go!"

"No, no," Dr. Lee said, soothingly, a little louder than he needed to. "You've got good years left in you yet. As long as we examine you every time you have an attack, so we can adjust the dosage, I believe that you can keep on ticking."

Becky didn't see anyone on the street, but in Las Anclas, you never knew. A nosy neighbor and three soldiers could be behind every shrub. Grandma Lowell showed them into her kitchen, where she drank down her tonic. She stayed there while the others slipped into her back yard, keeping to the narrow path between the kitchen vegetables and the raspberry canes. The blackberry bushes that surrounded the yard had grown tall and wild, right up to the tall juniper that surrounded the back yard of the Callahan house. Becky had always hated that prickly, spidery hedge. It had felt like a prison wall. But now she was grateful for it.

They shoved their way through, crossed the gloomy shadows of the neglected yard, and slipped inside the house. Jennie and the others were gathered in the equally gloomy parlor.

Everyone welcomed Luis. "I'm so glad you're with us," said Ross. Luis didn't smile at him, but he did seem pleased.

Summer hopped to her feet. "Is school out already?"

Dr. Lee said, "No. This is an emergency meeting. We can't wait for Meredith, and I don't know where Santiago and Paco are. We'll have to proceed without them."

Becky burst out, "Felicité is alive!"

"I knew it!" Kerry exclaimed.

Summer made a terrible face. "Ugh. Her!"

Jennie looked like she'd spotted a lone giant cockroach in a kitchen where she'd thought she'd gotten rid of them all. "What's she up to now?"

"I'm *glad* she's alive," Mia said. "I didn't want to believe she killed herself."

Ross stirred uneasily. "Why did she turn up now?"

Becky was finally able to get a word in. "She rode straight through the gates on a winged horse from the Saigon Alliance. She's an envoy."

Summer said blankly, "What's that?"

In his best teaching tone, Dr. Lee said, "An envoy is an official representative who comes under flag of truce to present messages from one government to another."

The silence that created was finally broken by Ross saying incredulously, *"Felicité?"*

"And that's not all," Becky said. "She's Changed. She has these gorgeous bronze scales. She says she used to hide them, but she's stopped hiding now. She can use them to camouflage herself. That's how she got over the wall and away."

"Ahh," murmured Jennie. "That explains so much!"

Summer blurted, "Felicité? Changed? And she knew all the time? What a hypocrite!"

"I can understand her keeping that a secret," Ross

said. "Her own father hates Changed people."

Mia shoved her glasses back up her nose. "You're right. Poor Felicité. I bet she felt like she had to be mean to Changed people, to make sure no one guessed she was one. How awful. I'm glad she doesn't have to hide it anymore."

Kerry turned to her. "Let's not jump to conclusions. We know she's Changed now, but people can Change late. Like Becky. It would be just like Felicité to have a late Change she couldn't conceal, then claim she always had it, so everyone would excuse the way she's acted up till now."

Dr. Lee said mildly, "As you say, let's not jump to conclusions. What's important is that she's here as an envoy. She's made it quite public that she is the official representative of both Catalina and the Saigon Alliance. We can assume she's come to demand that Voske leave Las Anclas."

"I saw her ride in," said Luis. And there was that look on his face again: hope. Becky thought she finally saw what he'd been like before Min Soo had Changed him.

"I wonder if Naomi ran into Felicité on the road," said Jennie. "Maybe not. They'd both have avoided the main paths. But if Felicité came from the Saigon Alliance, I'm sure she met up with Mr. Preston."

"And they got allies!" Kerry was beaming.

Luis looked even more hopeful. "The Saigon Alliance is huge, right? Are they big enough to drive the king back to Gold Point?"

The happiness that had lit Jennie's face faded. "Depends how many of their people are willing to fight for us. But no matter what, it'll be a terrible, bloody battle, with big losses on both sides."

"But—" Luis began.

Jennie spoke over him; Becky didn't think she had even heard him. "We have to get a message to Mr. Preston. If the Saigon Alliance knows there's a resistance inside the town, that makes the odds much better for them. It could tip the balance toward them deciding to fight for us."

Luis said in a quick, eager voice, "Then this is the time to assassinate the king! And the captains. Then there won't have to be a battle at all. We tell Saigon to bring their army, and we kill the leaders here. Gold Point will see that they're leaderless and there's an army outside the gates, and they'll surrender. No more killing. No one else has to die. And we'll go home again."

Jennie gave him a long, sad look. She'd looked like that when she'd visited the infirmary to talk to Dr. Lee after Sera Diaz had been killed. "Yes, we should try that. But Voske thinks three steps ahead; we can't count on the assassinations succeeding. And he won't back down. If we want Las Anclas back, we have to accept that there will be a bloody, brutal battle, and other people will die. Not just the Gold Point leaders."

Becky's own dismay was reflected on everyone else's faces. Luis and Dr. Lee, who had been in the infirmary after the invasion, looked the grimmest of all.

Kerry nodded, her mouth tight. "Jennie's right. My father's orders will be to fight to the last. As for Felicité, he'll extract all the information from her he can get, and then he'll throw her out."

Jennie leaned forward. "We need to get a message to her right now."

Becky frowned. "I wish we'd been able to have this meeting earlier. I could have slipped her a note. I was close enough. But I can't do that now. Voske sent her to wait in a room. Under guard."

Jennie steepled her fingers. "However we get it to her, it has to be phrased so if Voske gets hold of it, he won't know who we are."

Mia's hand shot up. "A cipher! Maybe with the periodic table! Or, hmmm, maybe that's too obvious. Oh, if only Yuki was here, he could write it in Japanese."

Dr. Lee smiled. "I think we just won't mention any names."

Mia fished in her overall pockets and produced a crumpled sheet of paper, a pencil, a pair of scissors, and a slide rule. "In case you do a mathematical cipher. Indra could decipher it. He was always good at the academic decathlons."

Jennie bent over the paper. "How about this? 'Resistance inside, ready to move. Not enough people. Need weapons. Meet at Stargazing Ridge." She ducked her head, hiding an odd expression. Was she...

embarrassed? "Indra will know what that means."

A brief silence ensued, then Summer rolled her eyes. "Baaaaarf."

Kerry stifled her. "Sounds great. Let's do it."

"How do we get it to her?" Ross asked.

"Stick it in her giant hat!" Summer exclaimed.

Becky turned to her. "She's not wearing a hat. And she's really different now."

Kerry stroked Whisper, who was sleeping in her lap, "Voske's got to be expecting someone to pass her a message. He'll watch for that. I don't like Felicité, Changed or not, but she loves Wu Zetian. Probably she can only camouflage herself, and she'd have taken her rat if she could. But envoys can requisition personal belongings. I'll bet you anything she'll demand her rat back."

"And Wu Zetian wears those fancy collars," Mia said excitedly. "Someone could stuff the note under it!"

Becky's heart slammed against her ribs. But only she and Paco could go into Wolfe House, and he was far more closely watched.

"I'll do it," she said. Her voice didn't sound squeaky at all.

·37·
FELICITÉ

LAS ANCLAS – WOLFE HOUSE

FELICITÉ WISHED SHE HADN'T eaten the candied rose petals. The lemonade hadn't helped. Her mouth felt coated in sugary glue. But she knew better than to ask for water. *"Voske will stick you somewhere uncomfortable to get you rattled,"* her father had warned her.

She tried to plan her response to each possibility, but she didn't get far. It was Voske's responses she had trouble figuring out. Father had cautioned her that Voske thought three steps ahead in mind games. She had to keep her own focus on the goal: to reveal as little as possible, and to notice as much as she could.

The door opened suddenly. A slanting beam of afternoon sunlight shafted in. She'd been stuck here since morning! Hearing her mother's calm voice in her mind, she straightened her back. She was ready for battle.

"In here," a soldier said shortly. "The king will deal with you now."

Felicité rose with dignity. Mother always wore her Button Dress when a tough Council meeting lay ahead. Felicité's robe with the bronze five-clawed king dragons was her button dress. She was ready to face Voske.

He sat in a huge leather chair, very much at his ease. The soldier pointed to an uncomfortable wooden chair. Her father had predicted this, too. Felicité sat down with deliberate grace. "The Saigon Alliance and Catalina join in offering a choice to—"

"Is your father squatting out there?" Voske interrupted rudely. 'Of course he is."

Felicité gritted her teeth. It was one thing to plan out speeches, and another thing to actually face the enemy. Her heart banged against her ribs, but she kept her hands flat on her thighs. *"Hands give you away,"* Mother had said a long time ago, *"People who disguise their facial expressions often don't think about their hands."*

"A choice to withdraw from Las Anclas," Felicité continued, a little louder. "In which case they are prepared to lift the embargo on trade with the Gold Point empire."

"Or else?" Voske asked.

"Or else the Alliance is prepared to aid Las Anclas in recovering its sovereignty."

"What are we talking about? Ten shiploads, hovering off the peninsula?" He was watching her very closely, as if he could gain valuable information by seeing how many times she blinked. Father had warned her of that, too. But she'd been excluded from all discussion of military preparations. She didn't need to know that, and what she didn't know, she couldn't reveal.

"I'm not here to discuss that. If you wish to negotiate, we can arrange another meeting at a higher level."

Voske went on as if she hadn't spoken, "Ten companies? Twenty? Hard to provision at such short notice, twenty. But I imagine Catalina could arrange it."

Felicité's hands twitched, but she kept them from making fists. *"You never got involved with the military,"* her father had said as they sat on a cliff watching the whales in their slow dance out to sea, the night before she left. *"That will be your strength."*

"...or chariots?" Voske went on. He stopped, his mouth tightening. He knew she hadn't been listening. "What sort of envoy can do nothing but parrot out a message?"

"I can carry a message back," she said. That seemed to annoy him even more.

"Did your father know about your Change? Or did you live camouflaged in your own house?" he asked derisively.

Her fists had clenched after all. She relaxed them, but of course it was too late. Voske missed nothing.

"You did," he remarked with a caustic laugh. "What a comedy. And such a long one. You're what, eighteen?

Nineteen?"

Felicité thought she had made no response whatsoever, but obviously she had given something away. Voske nodded. "Nineteen. And you Changed when you were... thirteen?"

Thirteen was the most common age to Change. He was doing nothing but making a very obvious guess. But her stomach still churned when he went on, "So you've been hiding for six years. What a long time that's been to lie to your 'daddy.'" His tone made a mockery of the word.

Felicité shook her hair back. "Enough about my father. I request a meeting with my mother."

"Give me something worth listening to, and you can go sob in her lap. I'll toss in your grandmother for free." He waited to see if she'd take the bait.

He's trying to rattle me, just as Father predicted. She searched her mind for something harmless that would satisfy him. Except he wouldn't accept anything harmless. This was exactly why the military leaders of the alliance hadn't told her anything of the plans. Fury burned through her. Mother was probably in this house, maybe right overhead, but she might as well be at Corymbia City.

Felicité gritted her teeth. She wore the Button Dress. She was in control of herself, and that was all that mattered. "I demand the right to take all of my possessions that I can carry on the horses that I have with me, and I demand the right to personally select what those possessions are."

Voske's smile flattened to a line for just an instant before it curved up again. But Felicité hadn't failed to notice. Just like her fists clenching, he hadn't meant to drop that smile. Inwardly, she exulted. This battle wasn't quite so one-sided after all.

And she'd won more than just angering him. He didn't know it, but she was about to get the one thing she wanted: her rat. Pets were personal possessions. No matter what, she'd leave with her darling Wu Zetian.

Voske folded his arms. "This is the message you'll carry back: Las Anclas shares sovereignty with all my other towns, under my rule. I'll give you one hour to pack up your belongings and get out."

·38·
BECKY

LAS ANCLAS – WOLFE HOUSE

BECKY COULDN'T STOP THINKING about the note in her pocket as she walked Bridget back from the schoolhouse. Bridget chattered the entire way about the Opportunity Day play the school was rehearsing.

"I wanted to give the hero the power to make people's heads explode! I had it all planned out. First, you get a really ripe watermelon…" Bridget mournfully kicked a rock. "But the teacher said if there was watermelon juice all over the stage when the student playing Father came in to save the day, he might slip in it. She said it risked making the king look undignified." Bridget chuckled. "I guess she's right. That silver wig doesn't fit him very well. It might fly off."

She cheerfully greeted the guards as they came in through the kitchen, then turned to Becky. "Want to visit my spiders? Florabella had babies! Lots of them!"

Exactly what Becky had hoped for. She forced a smile. "I'd love to see them."

"Oh, Father's still in with the envoy." Bridget lowered her voice as they passed the office. "I thought he'd have kicked her out by now. Father never negotiates. He talks to them until he gets information out of them. She must be talking up a storm in there."

Becky didn't think Felicité was going to give him anything. But if she didn't, he'd throw her out at any moment. Becky had to hurry and find Wu Zetian.

Becky gave the rainbow spiders and their bulgy-eyed babies what she hoped was an enthusiastic inspection, then said, "I have to get back to work. You stay with your spiders."

Becky passed the sentry at the stair, her heart banging. She'd hoped they were so used to seeing her come and go that she wouldn't be stopped, and that's what happened. She hurried upstairs to Will's room. It was unguarded, the door ajar. She slipped inside, her hands sweating and her stomach twisting. Wu Zetian was snoozing on Will's bed. She wore a black leather collar painted with daisies, striking against her golden fur.

"Hold still, there's a good little rat," Becky whispered, and slipped the note under her collar, which fit snugly against the rat's back.

As she straightened, she caught the muffled sound of women's voices from Felicité's room. She pressed her ear up against the wall to make sure they were the only two inside the room.

"...quite beautiful." It was Min Soo's sweet voice! "And she can will them to camouflage. She said that's how she escaped, by assuming the color of the wall at night."

"And made her way across the desert or the sea, alone." That was Mayor Wolfe. She sounded proud.

"And acquired allies." That voice was Grandma Wolfe's. With satisfaction, she added, "My granddaughter was always clever."

"She is a very good envoy," Min Soo said. "Curious how she got the position, given her age."

"I expect her Change helped," said Grandma Wolfe. There was a pause before she added, "So she was Changed all along. Maybe even before me. But she had the scales even when she wasn't camouflaging herself?"

Min Soo replied, "She said she chose not to hide anymore."

Becky was enthralled—was Min Soo an ally of the mayor and Grandma Wolfe? Or just being kind? But the house was full of enemies, and she didn't dare to linger—especially near the concealed note. She forced herself to walk calmly back downstairs and out of the house.

As she passed the stone well that Felicité had supposedly drowned in, she realized that Henry must have made up that story so no one would search for her. For once, his lies had been well-meant. She regretted that they no longer spoke. He was still her brother, and it hurt every time she saw how miserable he looked. She wished he'd gotten that fresh start that exile was supposed to give him. But of course, it was too late for that.

Barely an hour after Becky had left the note, she glimpsed Felicité leaving town. She rode proudly with her entourage, their horses piled with her possessions. Wu Zetian perched atop a giant hat box, her black collar stark against her golden fur.

·39·
PACO

LAS ANCLAS

PACO WAS DREAMING OF Yuki again. They were at Luc's. He was drumming, harder and faster. The drumstick cracked, and the drum began to bleed…

"Wake up."

He sat bolt upright. An insistent hand withdrew from his arm. A pair of guards were standing over him. "Get dressed," one said, and they both went out.

Paco shivered in the cold air as he looked out the window. The moon had dipped low, almost hidden by the south wall. It had to be past midnight. He dressed and left with the soldiers, wondering what was going on. Shouldn't Voske have sent Santiago?

The entire ground floor of Wolfe House was lit up. Paco's stomach dropped. This had to be something big. It had been a week since Felicité had left, so Voske couldn't have discovered the note in her rat's collar.

Don't give more than you get, Paco reminded himself. For all he knew, Voske might have lit up the house just to unnerve him and get his mind racing.

Voske was waiting for him, smiling his eerie smile. "Come along, Paco. I think you'll find this a very interesting lesson in leadership."

Paco was both relieved and unsettled that Voske had finally stopped calling him Liam. It couldn't have been a slip of the tongue — this was Voske. It had to be the start of yet another mind game. A bribe, maybe? Voske would use Paco's real name, and expect some concession in return?

The honor guard fell in behind them as they left the

house — the full guard, enough soldiers to ride out with.

"Tell me," Voske said. "Do you regret not having Changed?"

Paco was startled. Where had that come from? "I don't think about things that can't happen."

"Did you dream of Changing when you were young?"

"Who doesn't?" Paco asked.

"Some people don't," Voske said. "Bigots. Cowards. Some people fear holding power. Not people like us, of course."

This was such an odd conversation. "Well, it's too late now."

Voske stopped. The Callahan house was not ten paces away. Paco looked away, then wondered if he was obviously avoiding looking at it.

"I always found my Change disappointing." Voske touched his silver hair.

White light exploded across Paco's vision. He was mashed flat to the ground, unable to breathe as what felt like a hundred bodies ground his joints into the gravel. Several hands on each arm wrenched them behind him, and a heavy metallic manacle locked around his wrists. Someone else yanked his head up by the hair.

"Gently," Voske said. Paco could hear the smile in his soft voice. "I don't want him to miss anything."

A heavy wooden something closed around Paco's neck with a click, and he was hauled to his feet. His vision whirled, checked, whirled, then settled as shock gave way to sick awareness: they'd been betrayed.

·40·
ROSS

LAS ANCLAS – THE CALLAHAN HOUSE

HIS AWARENESS SPREAD OUT to the entire desert. He could sense all the animals, from the tiniest mouse to the birds soaring above his trees. Only cold-blooded creatures were invisible to him. He needed hot blood to seed his grove…

The tinkle of shattering crystal resolved into shattering glass. He rolled out of bed and leaped to his feet, searching for the heat signatures of whatever was attacking.

He was blind. No. He couldn't see heat. He was human, in the dark.

Ross heard screams. Doors smashing. Steel against steel. They were under attack.

He always slept fully dressed, with his gauntlet on and his knives in his belt, in case of exactly this. He slipped on his boots, a knife already in his right hand, and ran to the bedroom door. Ross jumped back as it crashed open, and soldiers burst in.

Light from the hallway flooded the room. Soldiers surrounded him, forcing him further back. But they moved with caution rather than going for the kill. So, they had orders to capture him. In the shifting of eyes and the grip of hands, he could tell they knew he had no such limitation.

The suffocating weight of the hell cell flashed into his mind. He wouldn't let himself be taken alive.

Summer's shrill voice rose up, shrieking insults. Ross had to protect her, and it was easier to kill than to disable. He feinted with his left hand, then came down with his knife in a lethal arc toward the nearest soldier's throat.

Time slowed. He sensed the network of connections he'd summoned up to escape the ruined city. This soldier too was part of that web of life. Ross pulled away from the web, snapping the connections. He *had* to kill.

He could sense the soldier's blood heat. The pulse of his heartbeat, squeezing and releasing, squeezing and releasing. He no longer thought about his sister. Trees had no family. Trees did not love. Trees had only had the ringing of crystal, the songs they sang to each other, and the instinctive desire to feed and seed themselves in hot blood. He slashed out with his crystal shard. He'd kill and feed on that soldier's blood.

"Ross!" a voice shrieked.

Mia!

Ross wrenched himself out of that crystal awareness. Tiny crystalline roots snapped in his mind, an instant before they'd have grown too deep and strong to break.

He was *not* a singing tree. He was human. That crystal awareness had felt eternal, but he was still fighting the same man, his knife still on its lethal trajectory toward the soldier's throat.

Crystal chimed in a rising, hungry chorus. Thoughts of Mia and Summer and his friends faded, and he was no longer fighting to protect. He was fighting to feed.

Ross wrenched the blade aside, slicing through the man's shoulder. His enemy dropped his sword as the crystalline pull faded. Ross slid forward, swinging his knife toward the second soldier. Once more, he saw a death opening. And once more, crystal chimed, and Ross felt his humanity slipping away.

In a very human panic, Ross jerked his blade upward. The blade grated against the soldier's jawbone, and she dropped her sword to clutch at her face — wounded, not dead.

At last, he understood. This was the price he'd paid to regain his power and escape the crystal forest. He could only stay human if he remained connected to all of humanity. If he took a life, he would take it in the cold, crystalline way that a singing tree took life. He was too entangled in the mesh of crystal to kill and still remain human.

As he turned his blade to strike a non-lethal blow, he saw a new assurance press the soldiers forward: they had seen that he couldn't kill.

They rushed him in a mob, knocking him down with the sheer press of their bodies. In an instant, he was pinned under their weight. The long-healed break in his arm ached at the memory as they disarmed him and yanked off his gauntlet.

Ross kept struggling, but it was hopeless. They dragged him into the parlor. He looked around frantically. Summer was held by so many soldiers that she could do nothing but writhe uselessly. Jennie was barely visible under the soldiers who'd pinned her to the floor. He caught Mia's gaze, and her worry tightened to panic when she saw him. She, too, was held fast. A mass of soldiers hauled Kerry in, struggling, her long black braids lashing.

But Voske didn't have them all. Maria-Pilar was missing. Kerry's rat Whisper was also nowhere to be seen. And Paco had surely escaped: his Change was geared toward doing exactly that.

The soldiers dragged them all outside. And Ross saw Paco's head on a platter.

Ross froze, chilled to the heart. Then he saw Paco blink. Ross jerked his head, tossing his hair out of his eyes. Paco was alive, on his knees and surrounded by soldiers. A heavy wooden square was fitted around his neck, hiding his shoulders and creating the illusion that his head had been severed. Below it, Paco's hands were partially visible, contained in heavy metal manacles. Soldiers knelt on his legs and gripped his arms beneath that wooden thing.

Ross's gaze met Paco's in the soft starlight. A trickle of blood dripped down Paco's forehead, black in the silvery light. Ross couldn't read his expression. Defiant? Despairing? In shock?

Ross kept his gaze on Paco. He refused to look at Voske, even when he heard the tyrant's voice. "You'll join the rest of your Rats in jail. And at dawn, you'll join them on the execution platform."

"The rest of your Rats." Voske hadn't discovered them by a chance search of the house. They'd been betrayed.

Paco could teleport out from a net of sticky vines.

Were the manacles and that wooden torture device really keeping him there? Ross shaped his lips voicelessly: *"Go."*

Paco's eyes closed.

A wooden square, a pair of manacles, and a shirt and pants in Voske's colors hit the ground, forming a moat around Paco's empty boots.

·41·
ROSS

LAS ANCLAS - JAIL

ROSS WOKE TO A throbbing headache. He lay still, eyes closed, and ran a mental check over his body. He lay on a cold, hard floor. His hands were tied behind his back, and his gauntlet was gone. He ached all over, but nothing was broken. His feet were bare. They'd taken his boots and their knives.

He probably ought to let everyone go on believing he was unconscious, but he had to know what had happened to the others. Ross opened his eyes, then winced against the glare of electric lights. He was in a cell in the Las Anclas jail, with a pair of guards watching. Santiago was with him, unconscious and badly beaten.

They'd crammed Mia, Summer, Becky, and Alfonso into the two-cot cell opposite him. He was just able to see Dr. Lee, Jennie, and Meredith in the cell beside them. At least they were all alive and appeared to be without serious injuries, though Jennie and Summer looked cut and bruised. Their hands were bound behind their backs. He didn't see Kerry.

"Kerry?" Ross's voice was hoarse.

"I'm here. In the cell next to you, where we can't see each other." Kerry's tone was ironic, but in her tight voice, Ross sensed the terror she was trying to hide.

The other Rats were there, so Luis and Maria-Pilar must have been betrayed, too. All the same, he shouldn't risk saying their names. "Are there others in with you?"

"No, I'm alone," said Kerry. "Ross, can you check on Santiago?"

One of the guards gave a jeering snort. Ross spoke over him. "He's unconscious, but he's breathing fine."

It seemed deliberately cruel that Kerry had been placed where she couldn't see Santiago. Kerry had claimed to be in love with Ross, and she'd been placed so she couldn't see him, either. Had Voske hoped Ross and Santiago would attack each other out of jealousy? If so, it was almost funny how wrong he'd gotten it.

But the rest of them had been broken up along similar lines, and Voske had figured out some things. Ross could see Summer, Mia, and Jennie, but he couldn't reach them. Mia had been separated from her father. And Dr. Lee had been separated from the people with the worst injuries.

Ross pushed awkwardly to his knees. His fingers prickled agonizingly as blood returned to them. He pressed his face against the bars to see as much as he could. The back wall was at one end, and the door at the other. He couldn't see the sheriff's room, but he knew it was beyond the door. The two guards stood in the short corridor between the cells and the door, so they could see anyone coming in—or going out. They looked alert, each holding a rifle.

If he could get the ropes loose, he might be able to pick the old lock. But if he got free, those guards would shoot him on the spot. Ross shrugged inwardly. That would be better than Voske's public torture show. He began to rub the ropes against the cell wall.

"If you get out of the cell, we'll break your knee," said the sneering guard, tossing something metallic on his palm. The other stood stoically, his face a blank. "Hope the princess manages it. Bullet or rifle butt, I'm glad to oblige for a traitor."

The other guard said, "Everett, the king ordered us not to touch them."

"Lighten up, Ken! He didn't say not to talk to them," Everett retorted. He began to play with the metallic thing, flipping it between his fingers, back and forth, back and forth. Ross recognized the round, barbed throwing star. It was an assassin's weapon.

Santiago groaned and stirred. Ross glanced from him to Dr. Lee in the opposite cell. Belatedly, he wondered if he shouldn't have mentioned Luis and Maria-Pilar. His head felt like a white-hot hammer was pounding the backs of his eyes, and he was terribly thirsty.

Santiago sat up, wincing. He squinted up at Ross through one good eye, the other swollen shut. Blood trickled down his face. But he shook his shoulders and wiggled his fingers behind his back. Ross flicked a glance at the guards. Everett was busy with his throwing star, and Ken was watching him. Trying to look casual, Ross turned so his back was against Santiago's. They fumbled at each other's ropes, but their own hands got in the way. Why did people have so many *fingers?*

Everett stopped playing, and both guards looked up. Meredith abruptly burst into song. "Oh, my darlin', oh my darlin, oh my dar-r-r-rlin' Clementine…"

Ha. Trust Meredith to keep fighting, no matter how hopeless it seemed. Which reminded Ross that there was another last-ditch fighter, besides Summer, one with a far cooler head. He twisted slightly and peered at Jennie. She sat with her back to the wall, knees up. With your hands tied behind you, that was the least uncomfortable way to sit—and also afforded a clear field for defensive kicking. Nothing moved but her eyes, reflecting the overhead light.

Frustrated, Ross tried to get his fingers to work. After the fifth time his thumb slid off the knot, he relaxed and kept still so Santiago—with two good hands—could try. As Meredith bellowed on, Santiago managed to undo the knots around Ross's wrists. Then Ross went to work on Santiago's bonds.

"…lost and gone forever—" Meredith broke into a loud coughing fit.

Ross tried to drop the rope down the back of his pants, but an end flipped to the floor.

"Ken!" Everett exclaimed. "Where's the extra rope? That idiot got loose."

"The king said not to get within their reach," said Ken. "Don't do it."

Meredith started singing again. Everett shouted, "Shut up!"

"Or what?" Meredith mocked, "You'll shoot me?"

"That skunk couldn't hit the broad side of a barn," Summer jeered.

"No one's shooting anyone," Everett snarled. "That's

too fast. The king intends the fun to last all day. But maybe I can have a little fun of my own."

The jail door opened, and Luis walked in. He wasn't dragged by guards. He wasn't bruised. His face wore that flat, dead expression Ross had seen in Gold Point. If anything, it was flatter. Deader. His hands flexed once, then he said, "I thought you should know. I turned you in."

There was a moment of stunned silence. Then Dr. Lee said, "Luis, I'm so sorry."

"*You're* sorry!" Summer yelped. "*He's* the traitor! He's the double-crossing, two-timing rat of a…no, NOT a Rat. Cockroach! Slug! Did Maria-Pilar turn on us, too?"

"No," Luis said flatly.

Ross hoped she'd escaped, like Paco. It was possible, with her power. With any luck, the two of them would meet up in the desert and get away.

"Why, Luis?" Santiago's voice was hoarse with grief.

Luis looked not at him but at Jennie, his eyes like dark pits. "Because your plan was to have 'a brutal, bloody battle!' Your plan was 'lots of people on both sides will die!' The king *never* gives up, you said. So the killing will *never* stop!" His mouth was a rictus over his teeth. This wasn't smugness or triumph. It was the moon and the stars distant from triumph.

"We were your friends, Luis," Kerry said softly.

"So was Sophie. She was going to be *my wife*." He drew in a harsh breath. "You weren't going to stop; the king wasn't going to stop. Better twelve dead than hundreds."

"You didn't count our families," Santiago said.

Luis flexed his gloved hands, then walked out.

"It's my fault," Ross muttered. "I vouched for him."

Dr. Lee said gently, "Your intention was good, Ross. I'm afraid that we all misunderstood Luis."

"What's to misunderstand?" Meredith demanded. "He ratted us out because he'd rather have us and our families die instead of more Gold Point soldiers."

Dr. Lee sighed. "I think it's more that if he protects the status quo, Sophie's death won't be meaningless."

Everett sniggered. "Keep talking. This is better than a show."

Silence fell.

·42·
KERRY

LAS ANCLAS - JAIL

KERRY IGNORED EVERETT DOLAN, who'd always been a bully, and stared angrily at the door Luis had closed behind him. He'd been a friend. It was pointless to blame herself for not having guessed what he was planning, but she couldn't help it. She'd been taught by a master to observe and read people's motivations. But she hadn't even tried with Luis. She'd just assumed that she knew him.

At least one person had gotten some good out of his confession. While everyone had been watching Luis, Kerry had been grimly pleased to spot Alfonso quietly using his gecko fingers and toes to untie first himself, then the others in his cell. Even Summer kept her hands behind her back, giving nothing away. Maybe Mia, Alfonso, and Becky could create a distraction if their cell was opened, allowing Summer to attack the guards.

"Kerry." Santiago's voice was hoarse and pained. "Come to the corner near me."

Kerry pressed her face and body against the cold iron bars by the wall that separated them. A warm, sticky hand groped close, and then cupped her cheek. She leaned into his touch, reveling in its comfort. They pressed against one another, hand to cheek, as if they were drowning.

Kerry closed her eyes — then opened them when she felt Santiago tense. Everett had cocked his arm, sighting on Santiago's hand with the throwing star.

"Let 'em be," Ken Vu said. "The king won't want either of them damaged. More than they already are."

Everett dropped his hand. "Go on with the lovey dovey, you traitors. Want to lay bets on which of you goes first?"

The outer door opened with an imperious smack that could only belong to one person. Voske's silhouette stood framed in the doorway. The guards leaped to attention. Kerry's breath caught like a bone in her throat. But rather than enter, Voske stood where he was while his honor guard entered and patted down every wall, door, chair, and object in the jail. One ran his hand along all the bars.

Kerry met Jennie's steady gaze from the cell across from her. They exchanged little nods. Those guards were checking for Maria-Pilar. Fierce joy burned through Kerry. Her father was *afraid*.

Kerry thought, *Are you sorry now that you threatened Maria-Pilar's little sister?*

Santiago broke away from her. She saw Voske take that in.

"All clear, sir," spoke the honor guard leader. They'd known each other since she was five years old. He didn't meet her eyes.

Voske walked into the jail, looking closely at each prisoner. He'd taught Kerry about making observations before assembling a tactical approach, whether in fighting or in verbal combat, and she automatically observed along with him. She couldn't see Ross or Santiago, but those two wouldn't reveal anything anyway. She knew from experience that Ross wouldn't even look up.

In the cell across from Kerry, Dr. Lee sat composedly. Meredith sneered; her red hair wild. Jennie's expression was utterly unreadable, her gaze unwinking as she stared straight at Voske.

In the cell next to Jennie's, Alfonso looked away. Becky stared at the cell floor. Mia tipped her head back, trying unsuccessfully to shake her glasses up her nose.. Summer stood glaring at Voske, her face pressed against the iron bars. Kerry could *feel* her desire to attack him.

Voske let his gaze encompass them all. "If you weren't so pig-headed, every one of you could have been a general by the age of twenty-five."

Summer shrilled, "Let me go! I'll fight you in single combat!"

"That could be arranged. I need to have all of you present, though. To watch. Where are my son Liam and Maria-Pilar?"

Summer's eyes widened as she stared over his shoulder. "Behind you!"

Kerry caught the tiniest twitch at the corner of his eye. Oh yes, her instinct was right. He was afraid — and further, he knew she'd seen the reaction. And he didn't like it.

Summer's jeering laughter rose. "You fell for it! The oldest trick in the world!"

Voske snapped his fingers. "Gag her."

Ken unlocked the door, and the honor guard used their rifle butts to knock Mia, Becky, and Alfonso away from Summer. Kerry winced. Mia let out a squeak as she slammed against the wall. Ross must have moved instinctively to save her, judging by the sudden scrape from that cell — a movement that Kerry barely kept herself from making.

Keeping her hands gripped on the ropes behind her back, Summer made a valiant attempt to leap over their heads. The two honor guards smacked her down with their weapons. Summer fell with a painful splat. They were on her at once, holding her down as another gagged her with brutal efficiency.

It must have been incredibly tempting to lunge for Voske, but Summer had resisted that urge, knowing she didn't have a chance with the entire honor guard present. Instead, she'd made sure to react in character without giving away that her hands were actually untied. Kerry was proud of her. She hoped she'd get the chance to tell her so.

Voske watched them all with narrow-eyed intensity, observing their reactions more than Summer's actions. Kerry's neck hairs prickled, and she rapidly reviewed what he must have seen. She hadn't moved when Mia had cried out. Had she? She definitely hadn't made the revealing noise that Ross had. She kept her face absolutely blank and reminded herself not to react no matter what happened.

The cell door was locked with a clang.

"Now, where were we? Mia Lee. Have you any idea where my son might have gone?" When she didn't reply, he said, "Do you need some inspiration?"

Mia's gaze darted to Ross's cell. Kerry hoped that looked like a quick, random glance. But she couldn't warn anyone to hide their reactions. At least, Voske didn't know Mia. He'd have little interest in her. But he gave her the smile that always meant terrible things. "I'm sure you're very close to your father."

Kerry cursed inwardly as Mia glanced nervously toward Dr. Lee's cell. Anyone would worry about a family member, but would Voske match that glance with the one Mia had turned toward Ross?

"Or are you closer to some boy in town? Some girl? Someone here?"

Mia's startled gaze flicked again toward Ross's cell. She quickly jerked it back to Voske, but Kerry knew it was too late.

Voske's smile deepened. "You care much more about what happens to Ross than you do about yourself, don't you?" He let the question hang in the air. Was he planning to start torturing Ross right now, and make Mia watch?

Mia spoke in a nervous squeak, but her words belied her tone. "It doesn't matter who I care about. You're going to kill us all anyway. As for *Paco*, I have no idea where he is, and neither does anyone else. Torture us all you want. It won't help you find him."

As if that had taken all her energy, she sat down hard on the cot and glared at him.

Kerry was proud of Mia, too, and again wished she could say so. She'd rarely seen anyone figure out Voske so fast, and she'd seen almost no one stand up to him.

"Becky," Voske spoke with real-sounding regret. "I'm sorry to see you here. I really am. It'll hurt Bridget so much to learn that you betrayed her."

Becky stared silently down at her feet.

Voske turned to Jennie next. "Jennie Riley. I've heard so much about you. You had so much promise. So much responsibility invested in you. We will find out very soon how your family feels about your whim to snatch my daughter from her home."

Jennie looked him square in the eyes, unflinching. "I already know how they feel. They're proud of me. And I'm proud to be their child."

Her words weren't aimed at Kerry, but they hit her, nonetheless. That was the pride Kerry could never have. She was the child of a tyrant. But as Voske began to reply, Kerry reminded herself that she was someone else's child, too.

I am Kerry Cho, she told herself. *And my mother is proud of me.*

"Proud of bringing ruin to the ones you love?" Voske replied. "If you hadn't decided to kidnap Kerry, I wouldn't be here now."

"None of this is my fault. And the entire town knows it." Jennie sounded like she believed it. "*You're* the one who brought ruin."

Ross spoke up at last. "You were already coming back. That's why you had me kidnapped."

Voske turned to Ross. "And you. You're the most powerful person here. You used the singing trees as a weapon. But you're helpless to save the ones you love."

"I'm not helpless," said Ross.

In the distance, crystal chimes rang out in an eerie chorus.

Kerry jumped. Voske froze. Then he smiled, though she thought it looked forced. "Unless you can make those trees walk, everyone you care about is going to die today."

"You have no idea what I can do," Ross said. "And you have no idea what Las Anclas is doing right now."

In the brief silence that fell, Kerry heard distant shouting and running footsteps, followed by a crash and a yell. What *was* going on in Las Anclas? For the first time since their capture, hope lifted her spirit. Maybe Ross was right.

Voske turned to her, and she realized what a terrible mistake she'd made. He'd seen that hope. And he was going to use it.

He smiled at her, but it wasn't the viper's smile that came before he struck. This was a fatherly smile, the one that only his children saw, and only when he was pleased with them. "Are you thinking it's too late to come back? I can forgive a little rebellion. Testing your powers. I did the same at your age."

"By murdering Uncle Colum?" Kerry retorted. Her mind jumped to the next logical step. He liked to make people prove their loyalty. "I'd die before I'd kill Bridget."

"What about Paco?" Voske countered, quick as a striking snake.

Kerry opened her mouth to retort, but he raised his hand. She flinched back before she could stop herself. Almost gently, he said, "I would never want you to harm Bridget. She looks up to you. As she should. All your brothers and sisters do. Come home with me, Kerry. You could have breakfast with me and Bridget and your mother today."

She realized that he was serious. She'd thought he was only toying with her, but his voice held genuine hope. He actually wanted her to say yes.

"And watch Santiago be executed!" she exclaimed.

"Santiago can come, too. He's loyal to you. We can work with that."

She didn't want to believe that it was a real offer. It was too tempting to imagine the bars swinging open, putting her arm around Santiago's waist, and walking out of that jail forever, with his warm, living body pressed against hers. She wanted it so much; she could almost feel his chest rising and falling against hers.

She could watch Bridget's delight when Kerry walked right in through the door. Kerry had friends now, but there was nothing dearer than weird little Bridget and her spider obsession. And she could see Mom again. Enjoy hot baths and delicate tea. She could have the mother-daughter conversation that kept getting interrupted.

But it would be a mother-daughter conversation like their last one, with the shadow of Voske between them. Kerry was abruptly very conscious of that shadow, watching her right now. He had to have been reading every flicker of emotion she'd felt. She schooled her face into the hope she'd felt only an instant before. This could be her one chance at real freedom.

She looked up at Voske—at Father, she had to think of him as Father now—and said, "And Santiago really goes free?"

Voske held out his hand to Ken, who surrendered the keys. Voske held them up. "You can let him out yourself."

This is the carrot.

Kerry tried not to even think of what she really

planned: *The instant he unties my hands, he's getting my sword right through his heart.*

"Thank you, Father." She let her body sag with relief, then straighten as she remembered her dignity. "I accept."

"I trust you don't still have doubts," he replied. "I'll prove myself to you, as soon as you prove yourself to me."

And here comes the stick.

She'd have to use every bit of her training to deal with whatever was coming next.

"It's quite simple," Father said. "I need to know that your loyalties lie with me, not these traitors. Choose any two of them, except Ross. He's mine. Whichever two you select; we will put into that cell with you. As soon as they are dead, you walk out, perfectly free."

Summer grunted; her face purple as she struggled to yell her way past the gag.

Kerry couldn't help letting her gaze dart across the other prisoners. She expected to see fear on at least some faces, the ones who weren't good at controlling their emotions. Alfonso stared at the ground; his shoulders tight. He was clearly afraid. Becky looked miserable. But Mia gazed right back at Kerry with that same trusting look she'd given her before she'd set Kerry free. Kerry could kill her with a word, but Mia's trust never wavered.

Kerry tried to think of some way to trick Voske. If she asked for two prisoners from Summer's cell, the door would open and all four of them could attack with their hands untied…and be flung down and tied up again. Or killed. She could say she'd do it if the honor guard left? Voske would never agree. He wanted to watch.

Her mind spun like pinwheels. This was her final test, and she could neither pass nor avoid it.

Kerry looked Voske in the eyes. "My loyalty lies with my friends."

She was startled to see a flash of genuine regret. She'd expected nothing but fury. But no. He'd actually wanted her back. The offer had been real — or as real as anything ever was with him.

"Your mother will be sorry to hear it," he said, with that small smile that always made her heart bang against her ribs. He turned his back on her and took a step toward the door. At least he was leaving.

Then, quick as a striking rattler, he snatched the throwing star from Everett's fingers, turned, and flung it. Cold metal flashed in the air. Kerry instinctively ducked. Meredith shrieked in horror. Kerry whirled to stare at Mia. The throwing star had shattered one lens of her glasses and lodged deep in her eye socket.

Voske walked out. The door slammed behind him.

Blood pouring down her face, Mia crumpled slowly to the floor.

·43·
ROSS

LAS ANCLAS - JAIL

ROSS NEVER SAW MIA fall. He hit the bars so hard that he knocked himself down. Lights flashed across his vision as he staggered to his feet, screaming her name, willing her to answer. But all he heard was everyone else yelling, and Everett's laughter.

Becky and Alfonso bent over Mia, preventing Ross from being able to see if she was still breathing. He wanted to ask, but the words stuck in his throat. Then he saw one of her hands twitch. She was alive.

"There's so much blood," Becky said worriedly. "I can't stop it."

Ross ground his face into the bars, wishing with all his strength that he could shove himself through them. Why couldn't that be his power, instead of one that was useless unless he was near a crystal tree?

The moment that Voske had thrown the star at Mia played over and over in his head. The star flashing through the air. Sharp metal in her *eye*. Mia falling. Mia's hand groped toward her face.

Ross jerked his gaze away, unable to bear the thought of her touching the blade in her eye, then forced himself to look.

Alfonso caught Mia's wrist. "Don't touch it."

"Everyone, be quiet!" Dr. Lee's voice was sharp with fear and frustration. "Mia? Where was she hit? Alfonso, what do you see?"

Everett was *still* laughing. "Let's just say no one'll ask her to a dance anytime soon!"

Dr. Lee cut past that, his voice steady. "Alfonso, where was she hit?"

Everett drowned him out with a crow of admiration. "One throw. Perfectly placed. Not into the brain, which would kill her right away. Exactly deep enough so you can all watch her slowly bleed to death—"

Ross flung himself against the bars again, and again knocked himself to the floor. His throat was raw from shouting, but he had no idea what he'd said.

Everett whooped. "What a show! I'm good, but the king is so much better."

"You *are* good," Ken said. "But you only had that one throwing star, right? Why don't you go get another? No, get a couple. Get me one, too."

"Good idea! I can't wait to tell those slackers in Team B what the king did. And without even stopping to taking aim!" Everett whooped again, then went out. The door clanged shut behind him.

"He hit her eye." Alfonso's voice was surprisingly steady. "The throwing star's still in there. If I take it out, it'll make the bleeding worse, won't it? But we can't put any pressure on the area without pushing it farther in."

Mia coughed wetly.

"Turn her head," Dr. Lee said urgently. "Don't let blood run into her sinus cavities. She needs to breathe."

As Dr. Lee continued giving orders, his voice faded into the rush of a river. Ross felt as if he was trapped in a nightmare. He wished it was only a nightmare. Mia was dying, and in such a hideous way. Mia was dying without those who loved her most being able to touch her, helpless to do anything but watch. Ross was trapped, only a few feet away but unable to touch her.

The rushing river faded into the sweet chime of the trees. They rang in his ears, drowning out everything but his fury and grief and frustration and love. He wanted to smash something. He wanted to kill someone. He wanted to hold her hand. He wanted to cradle her in his arms. He'd gladly sacrifice his humanity if it would save Mia, but he couldn't even do that. She was suffering, she was dying, and he couldn't even reach her to give her the small comfort of touch.

He wanted to *reach*.

The chimes rose louder, resonating through his whole body and making his chest vibrate. His blood pulsed to the rhythm of the chimes. He could feel Mia's blood soaking into the hard-packed earth of the cell floor. The singing trees yearned to suck it up, mix it with minerals taken from the soil, and give life to new crystal. Ross instinctively fought against that idea. He didn't want to use Mia's blood, he wanted to stop her from bleeding at all…

The trees were puzzled at that. Of course you used blood. That was how you made crystal. They sent him an image of the crystal elements in his own blood, which was also dripping to the dirt floor. You could use crystal for anything. It was a building block. It was life.

He could use crystal.

Instinctively — desperately — Ross drew on the knowledge of the trees. He followed his own blood, with its tiny bits of crystal, into the soil, then stretched his awareness out further. It was like his consciousness reaching into the trees the very first time. Using that awareness, he reached through the soil, toward the blood he sensed that wasn't his own. That blood had no crystal in it, so he drew minerals from the earth and created a single tiny crystal. It touched the blood and multiplied within it.

The tiny crystals reached eagerly for the source of the blood. They'd turn everything to crystal! Ross reached with them, forcing them to slow down.

You will not become a tree. She will not become a tree. He shared the thought with the trees. *Grow slowly. This is healing, not killing. Stop the bleeding, but don't make crystal out of any part of her that's still alive.*

A piercing scream shook Ross out of the tree-awareness. He jolted back into his body, dizzy and confused. He strove to recover the world around him: he was in the cell. Someone was screaming. *Summer* was screaming.

"Get it off her," Summer shrieked. She'd clawed out the gag. "It's crystal! Those trees are trying to *eat* Mia!"

"No." Ross's tongue was heavy as a rock. He wasn't sure he'd spoken aloud, or if he'd been audible if he had.

"Ross?" Dr. Lee said.

Ross fought to move. To speak. "Don't touch her."

Alfonso said softly, "The bleeding stopped."

"There's red crystal growing around the throwing star," Becky added, her voice high and worried. "Ross? Did you do that?"

"Yes." His human thoughts were coming back slowly, along with human speech. "Take the star out now. I can stop the bleeding."

"Alfonso?" Dr. Lee called. "Pull it out. Nice and smooth."

Ross gritted his teeth. How much was this hurting Mia? How much damage was it doing? He sank back into crystal awareness, and felt the blood begin to flow. The metal had been a barrier holding it back, and now that barrier was gone. But he was in her body with the crystal. He could make a new barrier of crystal. A smaller one, only big enough to hold back the blood, a barrier that would not hurt or harm.

Someone was calling his name. Dr. Lee?

"Ross," Dr. Lee was saying. "Can you hear me? Can you sense what's happening inside her body?"

Ross reached back to the trees and found the knowledge he needed. The trees knew all about the human body. They knew the anatomy of every creature they'd ever killed and grown a tree from. The crystals grew in the blood, branching out until they devoured everything but themselves.

Ross's own body trembled as he tried to maintain that tree awareness while still keeping enough awareness to hear and respond. It was like standing on a wire stretched between two buildings. "I could. If I used crystal, I could put some in her blood. Use it to sense, but not harm. Then I'd know."

The trees liked that idea. Except for the part about not harming. That was as alien to the trees as their awareness had been for Ross. He'd have to fight them if he wanted to do that and keep her safe. "I think I can protect her."

He wasn't sure if his sense of time was still a human one. But it felt like a long time before Dr. Lee said, "Do it."

Ross fought against sinking all the way into tree awareness. They were so vast, an entire community, beyond count. They were all eager for him to break the ban he had imposed. It was unnatural to all the trees but the first one, the scarlet tree that had grown from his own blood. That tree knew Ross. And because it knew Ross, it remembered that Mia was not food. It would not hurt her. He withdrew his awareness to his crimson tree, the one he knew best. The one the crystal in his own blood belonged to.

He reached farther, carrying his own blood, with its tiny crystals, toward Mia's warm, living blood. There was no more blood flowing from the inside of her body to the outside. He'd stopped that. But there was still blood where it shouldn't be, pooling inside her head, pushing at her brain.

Ross tried to explain that, uncertain whether he was conveying what he felt or even speaking out loud. But he must have said something that made sense, because he distantly heard Dr. Lee say, "That blood has to come out. Can you use the crystal like a scalpel — like a tiny knife — and make a small cut, to let it drain?"

Ross hated the idea of using the crystal to cut into Mia. It felt far too close to harming her. Even his own singing tree balked at the idea.

Dr. Lee said, "If I had a scalpel, I'd do it myself. Go ahead."

Working as delicately as if he was bracing a half-collapsed building he planned to crawl inside, Ross created a tiny crystal blade inside Mia's head and cut into the area where the blood was pooled, from the inside out. He heard Summer give a little shriek, and Becky say, "It's fine. He's doing what Dr. Lee told him to do."

Dr. Lee said, "Now stop the bleeding entirely."

That was easier. Ross had already done that in other places. Crystal grew in a thin, protective film over the injured area. He sent out another tiny strand of crystal to search for other injuries. He found none and started to withdraw.

Then he sensed a new awareness. Curious. Bewildered. Delighted.

The awareness spiraled upward, then outward, giving him vertigo. He could sense the heat forms of the living humans from two different angles, one looking forward and one looking upward. He could sense the heat forms of everyone but himself... He could sense the heat forms of everyone but Mia.

Mia!

He was seeing from her point of view, but not as a human saw. With dawning horror, he realized that he'd lost control of the crystal he'd put in her blood. It was a part of her now. He could never get it out. She was like him, no longer completely human. Alone with this strange awareness.

What had he done? He'd tried to save her, and he'd cursed her instead. It was the worst thing he could imagine.

An image came to him, of two heat forms close together. One reached out, and then the other did the same. They touched each other and drew so close that their separate forms could no longer be distinguished.

Not alone.

·44·
MIA

LAS ANCLAS - JAIL

MIA HAD KNOWN VOSKE planned to kill them, of course. But somehow it hadn't occurred to her that Voske would kill *her* right then and there.

It was like someone punched her in the face while a knife sliced into her eye and cheekbone. Everyone had started screaming, and she discovered that Everett's round barbed blade was stuck in her *face*.

And then, nothing.

Until she felt Ross. Felt? Was 'felt' the right word? They hadn't physically touched, but she knew it was him. She'd…*sensed* him. It was like the way she knew when he walked into a room, even if his feet made no sound. She could feel what he felt No, that wasn't right. She didn't experience his emotions. But she knew what they were. He'd been so lonely. And guilty. And glad she was alive, but he'd thought he'd done something bad to her. She'd tried to tell him that he hadn't.

Mia struggled to open her eyes, to tell him everything was fine. Ross was right next to her. Except he wasn't, really. She heard his voice coming from the other cell. Yes, that part was real. She was in the jail, lying on the ground. She could feel it, hard and cold beneath her.

And she could feel *into* the ground, following her own blood where it had soaked in. There were tiny bits of crystal in her blood, and that was the part that sensed. Those tiny bits were like her eyes and ears and nose and tongue and skin, all at once.

"It's incredible," she said.

She heard gasps and squeaks, then everyone calling her name. She forced her eyes open.

Everything was flat. No depth. She blinked, trying to restore it, but it didn't come back. One of her eyelids felt strange. No. Her *eye* felt strange. Or rather, her eyelid and her eye socket could feel her eye. It was cool and had smooth facets. Like crystal!

"Wow, Mia," Summer breathed. "You've got a ruby eye. And a ruby scar."

Fascinated, Mia traced the line of tiny cool crystals that split her eyebrow and eyelid, joined with her eye of solid crystal, and ran down her cheek, almost to her jaw. There was no pain. The crystal had no sensation. It was like touching an earring.

Summer hurriedly added, "It's a cool eye. And a cool scar. The coolest scar!"

Mia began to push herself up. Becky and Alfonso supported her. The world spun, then settled into that strange flatness. It was like looking at a painting. She knew Ross's cell was farther away, and she even knew exactly by how much, but that was because she knew the dimensions of the jail already. She couldn't *see* the distance.

She'd never be able to see distances again. It wasn't necessary—she could always measure them, as everyone else did—but it was something she'd always been able to do, and now it was gone. It was a permanent loss, like when she'd dropped her favorite screwdriver into the Hassans' well.

Then she saw Ross, and she forgot all about dimensions and distances. His face was pressed into the bars, with tears and blood smeared all over it.

"I'm sorry." His voice was low and choked.

Mia wanted to comfort him, but he looked so upset that she couldn't think what she could possibly say to make him feel better. Then she remembered that sense of his nearness, before she woke up. She closed her eyes, and there it was again. As if she stood right next to him. She heard a slow intake of breath from Ross, and she smiled. She didn't need to say anything. He knew.

Of course, everyone else didn't know. In case anyone else was worried, she said, "I'm fine! Actually, it's great."

"Yeah!" Summer said. "And if anyone's ever mean about it, I'll punch them so hard they'll wished they had a ruby eye!"

"It's not the eye," Mia said. "I mean, the eye is part of it, but—"

The door rattled. Kerry hissed, "Mia! Lie down and play dead. Everyone else—she's dead."

"But…" Mia began. That guard Ken was still standing blank-faced at his post. He'd already seen everything.

"Do it!" Kerry ordered.

Mia dropped to the blood-muddied dirt. Ugh, it was cold. She buried her face in her outflung arms to hide the crystal. Now she'd have no idea what was going on. Then her lips moved into a little smile. This was the perfect opportunity to practice seeing—*sensing*—with crystal.

·45·

JENNIE

LAS ANCLAS - JAIL

EVERETT STRODE IN, GRINNING. Jennie barely stopped herself from launching into the bars like Ross had. Her hands twitched with the desire to grab him by the throat. She couldn't remember ever hating someone so much. She might even hate him more than Voske.

"Here, Ken! Brought another for you." Everett handed Ken a throwing star. "In case the king lets us play." He sauntered between the cells, smirking. "I'd love to target the noisy girl. Right in that big mouth. Which one do you want?"

Ken shrugged. "All the same to me. I'm not picking my target until the king gives us the go-ahead."

"Aw, you're no fun." Everett peered in at Mia. "Already dead? Too bad."

He strolled back, and silence fell.

Jennie shut her eyes, trying to compose herself. She'd finally met Voske, a man who would murder a helpless prisoner just to get petty revenge on the people who loved her. Soon he'd come back and order her own execution. Jennie forced her thoughts off that path. She couldn't think of herself as already dead. She was alive, and as long as she was, she could act. And Mia was alive. Jennie wouldn't let her die.

She leaned over so her mouth was at Meredith's ear and whispered, "When they open the door, let's charge them."

Meredith gave a fierce nod.

Dr. Lee was watching them. Jennie felt confident that

even with their hands tied, she and Meredith could put up a good fight. Maybe good enough to give Dr. Lee a chance to participate, if he was willing. Maybe now he would be. If they all fought as hard as they could — and she knew Ross and Kerry would fight to the death rather than be tortured to death — maybe Mia could get away. She'd try to believe that.

As if shifting her position, Jennie leaned against the wall by Dr. Lee. She whispered, "Meredith and I are going to fight. Should we push anyone to your hands?"

Dr. Lee glanced at the wall between him and Mia. Very softly, he said, "I had a chance during the invasion. I actually had my fingers on a soldier's face. But he was just one man. Killing him wouldn't have changed anything."

"I don't know if it will change anything now," Jennie whispered. "But when they come for us, I'll get Becky and Alfonso and Summer to help Mia get away. It'll be worth it if we can cover their escape. Or go down trying."

Dr. Lee's dark eyes reflected the light from the overhead lamp. "I know why many of these soldiers are here. I won't take a life, but I'll compromise. Push them at me. If they go from the age of twenty to fifty in an instant, that'll take them out of the fight."

"Shut up!" Everett clanged his rifle against the iron bars. "A gun butt in the teeth will leave you alive enough for the king to play with. Just give me an excuse."

If only that guy knew Dr. Lee was refusing to kill him on principle. If Jennie had his power, she'd age him to a hundred and fifty.

The jail door clanged open. Jennie braced herself to face Voske again. But instead of the thud of boots, she heard the rustle of silk, followed by a waft of perfume, and she pressed against the bars to peer toward the jail door. Dr. Lee joined her. A tiny woman had entered, dressed in a gorgeous hanbok like the ones Kerry and Mia treasured. Her shining black hair was held in a knot by enamel pins.

The two guards snapped to attention but didn't salute. So, this woman was important, but not military. Just as Jennie realized who she must be, Ken said respectfully, "Madam Cho."

A flicker of shock widened Min Soo Cho's eyes when she looked into Mia's cell, but her face smoothed immediately. She turned to the guards. "There is a fire at the front gate. Possibly an attack from outside. The king has ordered half the guards to reinforce the defense. You must go. Other guards are coming to take your place."

Ken started toward the door, but Everett yanked him back. "Ma'am, we can't. The king ordered us not to leave this post until he personally releases us."

Min Soo's fingers twitched slightly. Jennie wondered if the fire was a ploy to break out her daughter, or a real attack. Jennie's heart lifted with hope. Maybe Mr. Preston was out there with an army from the Saigon Alliance.

"I see. I shall let him know." Min Soo glanced at Kerry's cell and gave a disapproving cluck, then swept past Jennie's cell, so close that her skirts rustled against the iron bars. The outer door thudded shut, and she was gone.

Dr. Lee had an odd look on his face. He leaned close to Jennie, and something small and hard pressed into her side.

It was a key.

Running footsteps and shouting sounded outside the jail. The ground beneath her feet gave a rippling lurch.

"That's Jose!" Meredith exclaimed.

A voice boomed from outside, "Jennie! You ready?"

Abandoning caution, Jennie shouted, "*Pa!*"

Everett cocked his arm, a throwing star ready in his fingers. She froze.

"Not yet," Ken said urgently. "The king won't want them killed unless they actually escape."

"I can kneecap one, at least. I'd love to do that. Starting with *him*." Everett swung the throwing star toward Ross.

Ken knocked his wrist up. "The king will flog us if we mess with prisoners he wants untouched!"

While the guards argued, Dr. Lee turned his back on the cell bars and reached through. He wasn't trying for the lock to their own cell, but stretched his hands painfully toward the cell beside them. Someone in there saw the key, and two heartbeats later that cell door opened with a soft click.

Alfonso leaped out of the cell and onto the wall. As Ken and Everett swung around, he scuttled up the wall and toward the outer door. The guards lunged for him.

Becky jumped up, the ropes that had bound her hands dropping to the floor. She dashed into Jennie's cell, holding something shiny. It was the throwing star they'd taken from Mia's eye. Becky used it to slice through Jennie's bonds, then dashed to Meredith.

Jennie launched herself at Everett. The hot singe of his throwing star nicked her cheek, and then she was on him. After being so helpless for so long, it was glorious to finally get to fight. She used her body weight to slam him into the floor, then pinned him with her knees.

Everett howled hoarsely, "Back-up!"

Jennie straight-armed a palm-heel strike to his sternum. He jerked himself out of her grip and tried to level the rifle at her. She slammed her hands downward as she gave a fierce yank with her Change power, wrenching the barrel to the floor. Everett tried to drag it back up.

Jennie lunged up from her knees. With her fists doubled, she threw her entire body into striking him under the chin. His head snapped back with a shocking crack, and he slumped lifeless to the floor.

She snatched his rifle and dashed toward the door. It burst inward, sending her staggering back. Several soldiers rushed in. Meredith dodged them and struck Ken across the back of his head. He slumped to the floor. Jennie blinked. Ken had not only had a chance to shoot Meredith and not taken it, he'd sidestepped so Meredith's blow had only tapped him. Playing dead to save himself? Or secretly on their side?

Jennie had no more time to wonder. She smashed a soldier's head with the rifle butt—*he* didn't side-step the blow—and side-kicked another in the ribs. She was peripherally aware of Dr. Lee opening the other cells. Ross was out like a shot, and instantly swept the legs out from under a guard.

Santiago slumped against the bars, leaving a smear of blood. Kerry gave him an anguished glance, then yelled, "Someone cut my ropes!" Becky dashed to her side.

Jennie shot a glance at Dr. Lee and saw him helping Mia sit up. Jennie froze. Mia's right eye was gone, replaced by a glittering, faceted ruby. A gleaming ruby scar slashed across her eye socket, running from forehead to jaw. She was white as a sheet of paper, and her lips looked bruised. But she blinked her good eye and fumbled with her broken glasses in a very Mia way.

As Jennie fought to cover them, Dr. Lee spoke. Surreally, he sounded as calm as if he was in the surgery. "You lost a lot of blood, and you've had a severe shock to the body. I'll take two months. And you ought to spend another two months in bed."

When Jennie glanced back, a little color had returned to Mia's face, and her lips had gone from blue to pink.

"Get the princess!" a soldier yelled, then grunted as Ross whacked him with a rifle butt. Summer leaped to attack another looming at his side—a soldier twice her size.

Meredith dove back into the cell. She flipped up the cot and slammed it against the guy fighting Summer. It was too lightweight to do any damage, but it was a perfect distraction. As the soldier fought the enveloping blankets, Jennie kicked him in the gut. He doubled over, and she brought the rifle butt down behind his ear.

"I was going to do that," Summer protested. "But thanks."

All the soldiers inside the jail were down or dead. Dr. Lee had taken Ken's canteen. He held it to Mia's lips.

The door banged open. It was Pa, side by side with Jose. "Come on!" Jose's voice rose shrilly.

Jennie plunged outside, sweeping her gaze over the fight as she checked the rifle she'd picked up. It was loaded. Pa and a bunch of townspeople had driven the soldiers back, but they were already regrouping.

"Jennie!" Pa exclaimed, coming to her side.

"Pa, the family?"

"Safe," he said.

Relief warmed her heart like a hearth fire. "And the Lees?"

"They're safe, too," he said. "So's Rosa Callahan. They got the Medinas, but—"

A bullet zinged past Jennie's head, and she and Pa sprang apart. The soldiers were attacking again. She caught sight of a fiery glow in the distance. So there really was an attack at the front gate!

Hope surged within her. They needed to get to the

gate to join whoever was fighting there — almost certainly Mr. Preston and the Rangers. For once in her life, Jennie would be delighted to see him.

But of all people, the one who appeared was Min Soo Cho, crying out, "Don't shoot! I have a message from the king!"

The fighting was too chaotic for anyone to heed her. More townspeople ran to attack the soldiers. Jennie's heart lifted. These reinforcements were exactly what they'd needed. She turned to Ross. "Let's get to the gate —"

An enormous mob of Gold Point soldiers appeared at a dead run, shouting, "Secure the prisoners!"

Now they were completely outnumbered. In another instant, everyone would be surrounded. Jennie and the others fighting directly in front of the jail had already lost their chance to escape. Swinging her rifle to clear space in front of her, she saw Alfonso supporting Mia at Pa's side.

"Pa!" Jennie yelled. "Take Mia and run! Get help!"

She had no time to watch them go. To the others beside her, Jennie shouted, "Fall back! Fall back! Back into the jail!"

Summer screamed from the roof, where she was hurling tiles at the enemy, "I'm *not* going back in there!"

Jennie shouted, "Summer, you run! The rest of you, get back inside. It's our fortress!"

"Fortress?" Summer shrieked. "It's a prison!"

As Meredith dashed in, she yelled over her shoulder, "The weapons are inside!"

Summer gave a wild laugh, leaped off the roof, and hurtled through the door. Too late, Ross yelled, "Not you!"

Min Soo was trapped with her back to the wall, looking terrified. Kerry grabbed her arm and pulled her in. Jennie and Ross, working together to guard the retreat, were the last inside. Jennie locked the door, then turned around. Three dead soldiers lay on the floor. Ken was gone. Min Soo stood by Kerry, suspiciously calm for a woman who'd been in mortal terror moments before. Alfonso wasn't there, but the rest of the former prisoners were back inside — including Mia, now supported by Becky.

"Mia," said Jennie. "I told you to go with Pa."

Mia blinked at her, brushing a finger over her new ruby eye. "I couldn't leave Dad and you and Ross behind. I pushed Alfonso at Mr. Riley and grabbed on to Becky."

"Mia, you almost died," Jennie burst out. "You should be resting!"

Summer cut in, "Oh, sure, let's all take a nap! It's so relaxing with half the Gold Point army right outside the door!"

Ross muttered, "Summer, that isn't helping."

Becky set Mia down in a guard's chair. She slumped in it, covered in drying blood, including her hair, which stuck out in stiff strands. But she didn't seem to be in pain. Mia held up her hand, turning it slowly from side to side. "Wow. Weird. But cool."

"Can you see out of that eye?" Jennie asked.

Mia shook her head, then winced. "Ooh, that's weird. I have to remember not to do that. No. I can only see with my regular eye. Everything seems flat, like a painting. My depth perception is completely gone."

Dr. Lee put his hand on her shoulder. "Yes, that happens when you lose vision in one eye. But you can learn to compensate…"

Mia broke in, "Oh, but I won't have to. I can use anything that's hotter than the air as a marker to judge depth. You see, I can see—well, not *see*, exactly—no, it is a kind of vision—anyway, I have depth perception when I look with my crystal!"

Jennie started to say, *You just said you don't have vision in that eye*, but when she saw Ross's expression, she understood what Mia meant. "Ross gave you his power?"

"No, no, he didn't *give* it to me. He just shared it." Mia swung around, looking anxiously at Ross. "You didn't lose it yourself, did you? No, you couldn't. I saw you in there. I mean, I felt you."

Jennie stared at them both: Mia, covered in blood, but looking delighted; Ross, also with blood all over his face, looking stunned.

Jennie laid a hand on their backs. "I think the two of you will have to come up some whole new words."

·46·
ROSS

LAS ANCLAS - JAIL

ROSS WAS NUMB FROM the whipsaw emotions of this endless night. Until Mia's small, grubby hand slid into his. "Ross, isn't it exciting how much more you can do with your power? You can reach through the earth and touch people. You can use it to heal!"

"Not if it gives people my power!" he exclaimed.

"Does it bother you?" Mia sounded hurt.

He jerked his gaze to her face. Mia was still Mia, and her earnest expression was the same as ever, even with one brown eye and one scarlet. "No! Not like that. But I never—I don't want you to—"

Memories flooded through his mind, drenched with the scarlet of blood and crystal. All the agonizing deaths he'd experienced through crystal memories. Voske watching the experiments that had killed his own people, all to give them the power Ross had now inflicted on Mia. Slicing open his own arm to get at the shard. He didn't want Mia to suffer as he'd suffered, and now she would.

She was with him in the memories, not experiencing them herself but as if she were peeking over his shoulder. The shard in his arm had grown tiny rootlets that had snapped when he ripped it out—had those been the bits that had stayed in his body and given him his power? Her scientific curiosity washed over the pain of the memory like cool and soothing water.

Their shared mental world shifted, so he was in her memories as she lay on the cold cell floor and explored a wonderful new world. It was three-dimensional, like her normal vision used to be, though she could see only heat shapes. But she could use those heat shapes to calculate distances and had happily noted the distances between the heat shape that was Ross and the heat shape that was her father, the heat shape that was Kerry and the heat shape that was Santiago.

And that wasn't all. She couldn't see underground, but she could *feel* underground. No, she could *sense* underground. And not only underground! So long as she could use her blood as a sensory organ, she could sense any minerals within its reach. She hadn't lost a sense; she had gained one.

It was all because of Ross. Once she'd saved his life, and now he'd saved hers. And he'd given her such a gift, too. She could spend a lifetime exploring the marvels of minerals, which had such fascinating structures and properties when you could sense and manipulate them the way she now could. Mia gloried in quartz and mica, granite and sandstone, agate and obsidian and all the rest, and while they were together in that crystalline world, Ross gloried in them, too.

"Ross?"

He was startled back into awareness by Jennie's hand on his shoulder. Apparently, only a moment or so had passed in the real—well, the outside world.

"I'm fine," he said, though a little dazed.

"Me too," Mia piped up. "Very fine." Ross looked at her doubtfully. She sounded happy, but she didn't look fine. She was still very pale, and he doubted that she could get out of that chair without help.

Meredith leaned against a wall; her arms crossed over her blood-smeared, grimy nightgown. "Well, here we are again. I'm glad of the weapons, but...here we are."

"We have allies," Jennie pointed out. "There really was a fire at the gates. Mr. Preston must be here with the rest of the Rangers and whatever army he's raised."

Min Soo gave a delicate cough. "I regret to tell you that there is no army. The fire at the gate was set by Lili Wolfe." It took Ross a bewildered moment to remember Grandma Wolfe's first name. "It was a ruse and a distraction. Half of the guards who were supposed to be here are loyal to me. Unfortunately, the king changed the roster without informing me. I was forced to move to Plan B and give Dr. Lee a key. Plan C failed, and Plan D…"

Ross half-expected her to recite Plans D-Z, and then move on to numbers. Instead, Min Soo continued smoothly, "But Ken Vu got away, and he will let Hwa Yong know. Let us put our heads together and start from there, shall we?"

Jennie's eyebrows were raised so high, they almost touched her hairline. Then she shook her head and said, "Pa said my family and the Lees escaped — I guess Voske tried to arrest all our families — so we have allies outside."

"Yes," said Dr. Lee. "The adults made plans in case Voske did just that. Grandma Lowell is a light sleeper. She was to run and warn the Rileys if Voske entered Callahan House. The Rileys would then disperse and warn our other families. There are hiding places. I won't mention where, just yet."

Meredith looked appalled. "You think *another* one of us is a traitor?"

"No." Dr. Lee glanced at Summer.

Min Soo said delicately, "Ian can be quite… persuasive."

Ross thought of the hell cells, and shuddered.

Summer rolled her eyes. "I know what torture is. I dare him to try it with *me*, and see what he gets!"

A loud thud startled them all. The door shook in its frame.

"Battering ram," Jennie shouted.

She and Meredith snatched up the guards' rifles and ammo. They each sprang to a window and fired. Ross heard the unmistakable thud of the battering ram being dropped, then retreating footsteps.

A gunshot cracked, and the bullet zinged off a bar in a window. Meredith ducked as she reloaded. The bullet ricocheted and buried itself in the wall between the jail and Sheriff Crow's quarters.

Min Soo said quickly, "We should withdraw to the inner room."

"There's a window in there, too," said Becky. "We'll need to guard or block it."

Jennie dared a glance over her shoulder. "Are Sheriff Crow's weapons still in there?"

"Yes," Becky said. "And the ones they took from us, too."

"Load a rifle and defend that back window," said Jennie. "They'll remember it pretty quick."

Becky darted into the back room.

Kerry helped Santiago ease into a chair. "Is there any first aid stuff here?"

Becky called back, "Sheriff Crow has field kits for deputies. I'll bring one."

Santiago twisted in Kerry's arms. "Dr. Lee." His voice was barely audible. "Heal me. Don't care how many years you take off."

"I care," Kerry said softly.

"It always sounds like a little at the time, but it adds up," said Dr. Lee. He ducked as bullets whined through the front windows. Jennie and Meredith popped up and returned fire. There was a yell, cut off, from outside.

Meredith grinned fiercely. "Winged one!"

"Winged you, too." Jennie pointed to Meredith's arm, which was stippled with blood from the chipped adobe window frame.

Meredith glanced down in surprise, then shrugged. She racked another bullet into the chamber and shot again.

Dr. Lee cautiously sat beside Santiago. "Broken ribs take longer to heal because they move every time you breathe. Santiago, hold your breath and keep perfectly still."

Dr. Lee laid his hand on Santiago's side. Color returned to his face, his cuts closed over, and the bruising vanished. "You can breathe now. That was one month. You still need recovery time, but you are no longer in danger."

Santiago sucked in an easy breath. Ross had a sudden, visceral memory of how agonizing it had been to try to breathe past broken ribs, until Luis had healed him. That was a set of memories he wished he didn't have. Luis. Torture. Being trapped in the hell cell. He shivered, and Mia took his hand.

"As I suspected, broken ribs heal faster when they don't move," said Dr. Lee with satisfaction. "I'm only sorry I had to take as much time as I did."

Another bullet hit the bars and ricocheted between

Mia and Min Soo. Mia let out a squeak, recoiling. Jennie called, "Can everyone who's not returning fire get those benches from the cells and block up these windows?"

"On it," Santiago said, shaking himself as he got out of the chair. "Oh, I feel *so* much better. Just thirsty."

"These deputy kits have canteens," Meredith exclaimed. "Here."

"Mia and Santiago first," Dr. Lee said. "They lost a great deal of blood."

The canteens were small, and Ross's share didn't quench his raging thirst. Still, he only drank a few swallows, then pushed the canteen into Mia's hands. She needed it more.

Kerry, Summer, and Santiago each dragged a bench from the cells. Ross couldn't lift benches with one hand. Awkwardly, he grabbed the fourth bench with his right hand, and hooked his left elbow around the other side. The bench lifted, then tipped over with a crash. Santiago and Kerry sprang to help him. They arranged the benches to block all but two cracks for Meredith and Jennie to shoot through.

Ross needed his gauntlet. He darted into the back room, followed by Kerry and Santiago. Becky stood beside the window, using the thick adobe wall as her shield as she leaned out to shoot. By the downward angle of her rifle barrel, she was shooting their feet as they tried to storm the back area. From the yells and cursing, she was making every shot count. Becky Callahan had become a sharpshooter.

Kerry and Santiago wrestled up Sheriff Crow's bed to stand against the window, with a narrow space on either side. Becky took another shot, and a soldier let out a curse.

Ross found the shelf where their things had been set. There was Jennie's favorite sword, the one he and Mia had given to her. It lay next to Mia's stench gun and his prospecting tools. But much as he wanted to grab his tools, he left them. They'd weigh him down when he needed to move fast. There were his knives, and his boots.

As he buckled on his gauntlet, he considered his knives. He could certainly hit a moving soldier's feet with them, but he was hardly going to throw them through the windows. With a rifle, he couldn't reliably hit someone in the leg, let alone the foot. Ross doubted that Jennie and Meredith were taking any particular care not to kill. But if he picked up a rifle…

His nerves chilled with the cold bloodthirst of the singing trees. He could *feel* the crystal chimes tinkling. Their roots were still in him. Their crystal was in his blood. The bargain he'd made to get everyone safely into and out of the ruined city wasn't one he could take back. If he made the choice to kill, he'd get pulled into that cold, crystalline shared awareness, and he'd never make his way out again.

As he comprehended this, his awareness widened — and there was Mia's consciousness joined to his, gentle, curious, trusting. Understanding.

Meredith called, "Bring more ammo. I'm low. And is there any more water? Those canteens were tiny, and I'm drier than a snakeskin in summer drought."

Mia's awareness dissolved, and Ross was back in the human world. He went to the little table that had been beside the Sheriff's bed. "There's a water cup with about an inch left in it. Probably weeks old."

Becky called over her shoulder, "The sheriff used to keep the snacks Jack brought her in the drawer."

Ross opened the drawer in the little table. He found a carved box containing crumbs and half a very stale cookie. With teeth marks in it. Summer floated in and looked over his shoulder. "Yuck!" Then, reconsidering, she said, "Never mind. I've had worse." She began noisily crunching it.

Ross brought a box of bullets to Jennie and Meredith. Jennie reloaded, then gave him a serious look. "No water really puts a limit on how long we can hold out."

"It'll be even shorter if Voske rolls up a cannon," Meredith remarked, then shot again.

Min Soo spoke up. "I expect the king believes that I'm a hostage. Perhaps we can use that to negotiate for food and water. Threaten to kill me. The king will understand *that*."

"You hear what I hear, Ross?" Jennie flashed a brief, fierce grin. "Kerry's mother is a strategist. Did you know that, Kerry?"

"I do now. It took me far too long to realize that my mom has been playing the most dangerous long game of all." Kerry made a low bow to her mother, her hands sweeping to the side of her pajamas as if she wore a full-skirted hanbok. "Can I just say, you are wonderful?"

Min Soo curved her hand around her daughter's cheek. "I only regret that my best plan did not work. But we are not defeated yet."

Santiago said to Jennie and Meredith, "Do either of you want me to spell you while you get your wounds wrapped up?"

Meredith glanced over at Jennie. "Yours are worse. You go."

Jennie handed her rifle off to Santiago. Mia said, "I'll do the first aid."

"Are you sure?" Jennie glanced at Mia's gory overalls, then at her new ruby eye.

"I can. *This* eye sees just fine." She turned her head, presenting Jennie with her warm brown eye.

"Thanks, Mia," said Jennie. "Let's do it in the other room."

Ross suspected that Jennie just wanted to get Mia to a slightly safer place, and he agreed. He helped her into the sheriff's room, relieved that she only needed a steadying hand. He deposited her in a chair, and she gave his hand a grateful squeeze. He fetched the first aid kit as Jennie laid her hand on the side table. Mia uncorked a bottle of pungent witch hazel.

Jennie glanced at him. "Ross, can you take over for Meredith?"

"I will!" Summer yelled.

"You're a wild shot," Jennie said. "I want Ross."

Ross gritted his teeth. His entire body was tense. "I can't."

Jennie looked up sharply. "Are *you* hurt, Ross? Or did they break your gauntlet?"

"I'm fine. The gauntlet is fine." He tried not to snap, though he hated this conversation. He hated thinking about how useless he was, let alone talking about it—and once more, Mia was right there in his mind, a gentle presence. Reassuring, unquestioningly supportive.

Ross drew a deep, shaky breath. Everyone expected

Mia to take time getting used to her crystal eye—but he needed time to adjust to not being alone anymore in the world of crystal trees. Mia was there, too.

He was *not* alone.

He made himself speak loudly enough so everyone could hear, even the people shooting or in other rooms. The last thing he wanted was to have to explain this more than once. "I can't kill anymore. I can never kill a human being again. Remember when we were in the ruined city, and I had to pay some price to get you all safely through? I've figured out what it is. I'm connected to the trees deeper than ever—so deep that if I do things that are…tree-like…such as taking a life…I really will become one of them."

"WHAT?" Meredith yelped from the other room.

"I don't mean I'll physically turn into one." That hadn't even occurred to Ross, and he wished it hadn't occurred to her. "I hope. But inside of me. When I think about killing someone, it feels like it would tip me into becoming…not human anymore."

Mia had finished bandaging Jennie's hand. She took his free hand in both of hers. Her fingers were warm, her grip tight as she said earnestly, "I know. I felt it, too, when I was exploring the crystal world. I thought of killing Voske and that awful guard, and the trees *really* liked that." Then she brightened. "But then I thought of just wounding them, and the trees thought that was weird and unnatural and pushed me away instead of pulling me in. So that's still okay."

"Yeah, but I'm not a good enough shot with a gun to be sure of just wounding," Ross said glumly.

Becky called over her shoulder, "If I was acting as sheriff's apprentice, I'd be using my cloud viper gun. That won't kill anyone no matter where the darts hit."

Ross glanced to the shelf where the viper gun lay and sighed. It was a peacetime weapon, paralyzing people for just long enough to allow the sheriff to handcuff them, but useless in their current situation.

Eagerly, Mia said, "I'll make you a cloud viper gun, Ross. When we find another cloud viper."

"I'll catch one for you," Summer called.

"Thanks, Summer," Mia said. "You can borrow my

heavy gloves."

Jennie pulled Ross close to her, so her warm cheek pressed against his. With her other arm, she pulled in Mia. It was as if they were in a magic circle, just the three of them. "Ross. You saved Mia. That's worth any price. We'll figure out the rest."

He was relieved that Jennie was taking it so calmly. Some old part of him had imagined that she might recoil from him. But she wouldn't, any more than she'd recoil from Mia and her crystal eye. Their bond was as strong as ever.

Jennie straightened up, breaking the circle. Rifle shots echoed outside. No more bullets were coming inside, at least. But Ross found it very hard to believe that he would ever get a chance to use a cloud viper gun. He wasn't alone, but the enemy was closing in on all of them.

If only they had Paco's power, to escape any confinement. But where was Paco now?

·47·
PACO

DESERT - SOUTH OF LAS ANCLAS

PACO JOLTED FROM THE bone-aching chill of another teleport into cold air on his bare skin. He tried to scan for danger, but vertigo knocked him off-balance. He staggered and braced himself against the boulder he'd used as his mental image for Ranger Camp Five.

He'd been teleporting and running all night. It had to be near dawn. The sun's heat had been sucked out of that boulder hours ago, but it still felt warmer than his bare skin. He tried to rub out the goosebumps, but all he did was smear sticky drying blood all over him. With no shoes or clothing to protect his skin from cacti and sharp stones and sand leeches, he was scraped and cut all over. He also had a new slice on his cheek from being forced to teleport a risky distance after spotting Voske scouts ranging the desert.

Since Felicité's reappearance, Voske had become convinced Mr. Preston was hiding out in the desert and had sent scouts to search for him. Paco really hoped Voske was right. He'd spent the night checking old Ranger campsites, but all were deserted and empty. After spending an entire night naked and freezing, he'd have seized upon even the smelliest, most moth-eaten single sock with delight. The soles of his feet were bruised from hidden pebbles and scraped raw from walking over sand.

A soft rustle made more goosebumps pop up on his skin. The deliberate approach meant a predator, and Paco knew he smelled like blood. He waited, his heart pounding. The last thing he wanted to do was panic and teleport straight into a sand tiger's claws.

The hiss of shifting sand warned him. He backed away stealthily, then caught a waft of rot on the breeze. It was the fetid stench of a pit mouth. And the rustle and hiss was a huge snake trying to drive him toward it.

Paco braced himself, visualized the Ranger camp from the other side, and teleported. He fell to the ground, sick and dizzy. Every teleport made him thirstier as well as colder. He lay in the sand, exhausted and shivering.

Paco didn't know if he had another teleport in him. He'd been pushing himself to the limit all night. And for what? Mr. Preston could be days away—if he was out there at all. He might already be dead. Voske had certainly sent enough soldiers after him. And even if he was alive, what could he do? Would Saigon risk enough of its own people to take on Voske?

Now that Paco could no longer distract himself with action, an icy tide of hopelessness hit him. Ranger Camp Six was too far away. In the shape he was in now, he'd never make it. Everyone he'd abandoned at the Callahan house must already be dead. His entire life felt pointless. He hadn't saved his mother. He hadn't saved her town. He'd driven away the person he loved the most, and he'd never see Yuki again.

He stared at the cold stars glittering overhead. They were dimmer toward the east. The sun would be up soon, which would make the thirst an agony. But he had to keep moving. He could no longer teleport, so he'd have to walk. He'd go from camp to camp until he couldn't even do that. Death was coming for him, but he wouldn't go easy.

He forced himself to his hands and knees, until the dizziness subsided enough for him to stagger to his feet. He shut his eyes, his other senses reaching out. The taste of dust in his dry mouth. The smell of cold granite. The feel of...

He looked down at his feet, blinking. Was that his heartbeat thrumming through the sand? No, that was the rhythm of a cantering horse. He was about to dive behind a cluster cactus, but he registered that it was a single horse. Voske sent out his scouts in teams.

Paco wouldn't have guessed that he could recognize a horse by its hoofbeats, but he knew he'd heard that particular canter before. He tried to remember what Tom Preston's horse sounded like — no. That was wrong. Those hoofbeats made him think of bright sun and a feeling in his heart, sadness and love and pride…

It couldn't be.

He straightened up, his head whipping toward the pale strip of sky above a ridge. Tiny shapes winked in and out of the rising light, making him blink and shake his aching head. Was he seeing things? The glint of dawn on shimmering bronze. A twisting shape rising into the air. And, mounted straight and proud on the bronze mare Tigereye, was a silhouette Paco would know anywhere.

His voice cracked in his dry throat. "Yuki?"

·48·
YUKI

DESERT – SOUTH OF LAS ANCLAS

YUKI STARED INCREDULOUSLY DOWN the ridge at the naked guy alone in the desert, with his hand shading his eyes and hiding his face. Had he been robbed by bandits? The figure straightened, and his hand dropped.

It was Paco.

Naked.

Yuki couldn't believe it. After a year of adventures — both those he'd hoped to have, and those he'd never dreamed he'd have — close calls, two duels, and new friends, the only person who appeared consistently in his dreams was Paco. Sometimes naked. *Often* naked. But he'd never imagined actually stumbling on Paco naked in the desert.

The rising light illuminated Paco more clearly, and Yuki saw that he was streaked with blood. Horrified, Yuki tightened his knees on Tigereye, and they cantered down the ridge. He didn't take his gaze from Paco for an instant, half-hoping and half-fearing that he was a mirage. But even if that was merely illusion, he would never not ride to the rescue.

Paco leaned against a boulder, his hair hanging in his eyes, then forced himself upright. He took a step forward. And another. Tigereye began to slow, but Yuki couldn't wait. He leaped out of the saddle, Kogatana right on his heels, ran the few steps to Paco, and threw his arms around him.

Paco sank into Yuki's grip. His entire body trembled, and his flesh was horribly chilled. Yuki put his hands on either side of Paco's face. Their gazes met, and Yuki looked into those deep dark eyes he'd so often pictured on his travels. He'd never seen eyes as beautiful as Paco's. Or lips, so perfect…

Then they were kissing. Quick, desperate, gulping kisses, until Paco fell against Yuki, gasping, "It's you. It's really you. I thought I was hallucinating."

"I thought *I* was dreaming. But Paco, how the hell did you get *here?* Like this? No—don't talk. You're shivering. And bleeding. Were you attacked?"

As Yuki spoke, he was already rummaging in his pack for his first aid kit. He began to disinfect the cuts and scrapes, then took a closer look at the one on his cheek and then some of the older ones. They weren't sword or knife slashes, as he'd first thought. They were more like surgical incisions. Yuki took Paco's shoulders, a cold rage building in him. "Who did this to you?"

"No one." Paco hesitated, then said, "Me, I guess. Not like that. It's a hazard of my Change power."

"But you're too old." Then several pieces of information he'd heard fell into place, and Yuki shivered with horror. "Did Voske do this to you? Is he holding Opportunity Days in Las Anclas?"

Paco nodded, still trembling. Biting back an exclamation, Yuki yanked impatiently at the buttons on his shirt. He got it off, then helped Paco into it. Paco breathed, "Oh, that feels good. I was so cold."

As Tigereye nosed at a patch of stubby grass, Yuki opened his saddlebag and got out his last pair of clean pants. Paco was soon bandaged and dressed, wearing Yuki's house slippers; Paco's feet were too big to fit his spare boots. Kogotana sniffed Paco all over, then jumped into his arms. He cradled the rat, burying his face in her soft gray fur.

Yuki held Paco like Paco was holding Kogatana. He couldn't let go. Though Paco was real to all five senses, Yuki was still afraid he'd turn out to be a yokai, a ghost. Only constant contact banished the fear. Shoulder to shoulder and hip to hip, they sank down with their backs to a boulder. Kogatana curled up in Paco's lap. "She's so warm. *You're* so warm. Yuki, where did you come from?"

"Drink first. You sound awful." Yuki gave Paco his

canteen.

Paco gulped down half of it, then held it back out. "I don't want to empty it."

"Go ahead. There's a stream not far back, where we camped last night."

"We?"

"Sheriff Crow, Mr. Vilas, and—"

"You're with Sheriff Crow?" Paco looked so astonished; it would have been comical in other circumstances. "And the *bounty hunter?*"

"And some fighters they hired, to help them take back Las Anclas," Yuki said. Paco looked even more stunned at that news. "The sheriff had a hard time finding Mr. Vilas, and then they had to find the people they wanted to hire. I know she feels bad about how long it's taken—"

"No, no. I'm not mad that she didn't come sooner. It's that..." Paco seemed to struggle for words. "All this time, she's been trying to help us. Maybe if I'd known for sure that someone was, I wouldn't have felt so alone."

Yuki held him tight. "I wish I'd been here."

Paco went stiff in his arms, the horror in his eyes evident in his entire body. "Oh, Yuki, I'm so glad you weren't. Voske would have made you a hostage against me. And knowing that you were safe somewhere else was a lot of what kept me going."

Mixed emotions churned inside Yuki's belly. He still wished he'd been with Paco, he was aghast at the implications of what Paco had been through, he wished Voske was there so Yuki could kill him on the spot, and he was more glad than he'd ever been that Paco was with him now.

He fell back on holding Paco tighter. "I wish I'd heard what had happened sooner. When the news finally got to me, I was closer to Dai La, so I stopped there first. I'd just missed Mr. Preston. So had a letter Sheriff Crow sent him. They gave it to me to pass on to him. I came here looking for him and found her instead."

Paco gave a shaky laugh. "What a mess!"

"I know. It's what Grandma Wolfe used to call a comedy of errors. Remember Rabbi Litvak?" Because of the rabbi's power of empathy, which he was unable to control, he lived outside of the town. People went to visit him rather than the other way around. Yuki had half-forgotten him, but Rabbi Litvak had not forgotten Las Anclas. "I ran into him. He tipped me off that he'd sensed Sheriff Crow in the next canyon over. She told me where the old Ranger camps are, so I've been searching them in the hope that Mr. Preston was camped out in one."

"So was I," said Paco. "I thought I had the worst luck ever. But now I feel like it was the best."

"Me too. I couldn't believe it when I saw you. What happened to your clothes?"

Paco managed to smile. "You didn't seem to mind that when you first saw me."

"I thought I was dreaming." Yuki admitted, "I had a lot of dreams like that."

"Me too." Paco rubbed his face against Yuki's, as if he couldn't get close enough.

Yuki kissed him again, breathing in his scent. They'd traded clothes often enough before that it felt surreally as if they'd been transported back in time. They could have been out on a campout before Yuki left. Before Kerry came to town. Before they'd broken up—Yuki realized that he'd completely forgotten that they'd broken up. And from the way that Paco was kissing, it seemed that he had, too.

A flitting noise broke Yuki's attention. Yumiya settled on the boulder behind them, her babies on either side of her. Their wings folded and their tails curled as they faded from dark blue to boulder gray.

"Cloud vipers!" Paco's free hand scrabbled for a knife he didn't have.

"They're mine," Yuki said.

Paco turned wide eyes to him.

"I rescued Yumiya from a vampire tree. Her wing was broken, so I had to keep her while she healed. Turned out she was pregnant. I thought they'd all leave as soon as she could fly again, but they stuck around. I even taught them to scout for me."

"Yumiya," Paco repeated. Yuki couldn't imagine that he had been practicing Japanese with anyone else while Yuki was away, but his pronunciation was perfect on the first try. "What's it mean?"

"Bow and arrow. The little ones are Shuriken and

Kunai. That's throwing star and throwing knife." Hearing their names, the baby cloud vipers lifted their heads, and Kunai leaped down to perch on Yuki's shoulder.

"You must have had so many adventures." Paco's dark eyes glittered as if he was holding back tears. "I wish I'd gone with you."

"I wish you had, too." Yuki hesitated, a bit afraid to ask, then said, "How bad is it in Las Anclas?"

Paco's eyes closed. He began shivering again, though he was dressed, and the air was starting to warm. "Voske murdered people on stage. He took away my name. We created the Rats to fight back. Me and Meredith and Becky. Then I went to the ruined city, and it was me and Jennie and Ross. Voske caught us all. Ross told me to go, and I went. I don't know what happened to any of them. Maybe they're all dead."

Yuki had never seen Paco so distraught, not even after the battle where his mother had been killed. Then he'd been angry as well as grief-stricken. Now he seemed to be in shock, his story coming out in incoherent fragments.

Yuki took his food pack from the saddlebag. "How about some jerky and flatbread? You look like you haven't eaten in months."

"It feels like I haven't eaten in months." Paco wolfed down a piece of plain cold flatbread like it was a hot taco from Luc's. "Voske made me eat breakfast with him. I could barely choke down a bite."

"Breakfast with *Voske?*"

"Dinner too, sometimes."

"That *is* a nightmare," Yuki said. "Eat up. We've got more."

Yuki watched Paco wolf down the food. He'd wished he'd had something better to offer when he'd handed it to Paco, but now he realized that it wasn't the food that mattered, it was being with someone safe. Being with someone he cared about. Being with someone he loved? It had sure felt like love when they'd kissed.

Yuki hoped their love was back. But he couldn't ask now. There would be time for that later, after the battle to save Las Anclas.

He hoped there'd be a later.

·49·

FELICITÉ

BEACH – PRESTON CAMP

FELICITÉ HADN'T HAD TO search for her father, or she'd still be wandering the desert. Even the couriers had found no signs of anyone other than the Gold Point patrollers. But they followed their instructions—and Father found *her*.

Camped in a hollow along a shoreline palisade that he seemed to know as well as Wolfe House, she gave him her report. At the end, she asked, "Does anything I learned help? It's days old now."

"Everything helps," Father said. "That message in Wu Zetian's collar, especially. It changes everything to know there's an organized resistance inside Las Anclas, ready to fight from within. And that at least one of them can get inside Wolfe House."

Felicité stroked her golden rat. It was so good to be reunited. And Wu Zetian had even participated in the effort to defeat Voske!

"Your sharp eye for changes in Las Anclas helps, too," her father went on. "The soldiers around Weaver's Row, for instance. My guess is that Voske's made it into his new armory. Our old one wouldn't be big enough for his army. Yes, you did very well." He smiled at her. "Tomorrow we'll go over your part in the attack."

"My part?" She was startled to learn that she wasn't done. "Does it have to do with the well? You told me to draw attention away from it. And I did." She only wished she hadn't had to call Henry a liar when they both knew he'd told the truth.

"Smart girl. You're going to lead the amphibious

team in, so they can get to the gate from the inside. Now get some rest. I need to talk to the Rangers."

Felicité had seen the Rangers, but they hadn't even waved at her, let alone greeted her. Once upon a time, she'd have stayed awake to catch up with Sujata after the military talk was concluded. But that would never happen again.

The sun was well above the horizon when her father brought her a breakfast of hard biscuits and jerky. "Awake? Good! Let's talk about the plans—"

Indra ran up with a furry body cradled in his arms. "Kerry's rat just arrived. In bad shape, too. He must have tracked your scent, Felicité."

Felicité laid Whisper in her lap. The dust-colored rat panted, overheated. Her father passed her a canteen, and she trickled water into the rat's mouth.

Her father crouched over the exhausted rat. "No note. Kerry must not have had time to write one. Or..."

Or she's dead. It was the only reason a rat would leave of its own accord. Felicité stroked Wu Zetian, thinking of how she'd sent her darling rat away. "Then Kerry can't be *that* far."

"We don't know how far the little thing traveled," Indra pointed out. "He looks like he's been wandering the desert for weeks."

Father blew out a frustrated breath. "I wish we'd found Kerry herself instead of her rat. She could tell us where the rest of them are. What weapons they have."

Felicité imagined Jennie and Ross and Kerry striding into camp like heroes out of a ballad, the sun at their backs. She could just see Jennie leading with her sword held high. Felicité pressed her lips together to stop a giggle escaping as she remembered that Jennie's sword hand probably still bore the marks of Felicité's teeth. That incident seemed like it had happened a hundred years ago.

Despite everything that had gone down between Felicité and Jennie, Felicité and Kerry, Felicité and Ross, Felicité and Summer—at least Felicité hadn't had any horrific interactions with Mia—if they showed up, no matter how obnoxiously magnificent they looked, she would welcome them. Sincerely.

Sujata ran up, breathless and grinning. "Scout report! Outer perimeter east. Six to ten riders. And—"

"Enemies?" Felicité's dad snapped, straightening up.

"No! Paco is riding in front. He gave me the 'friends' whistle. I bet he met up with Kerry! And Ross and Jennie! I hope they brought extra ammo."

So, the heroes really were coming. Felicité set Whisper down in a shaded nest, and they hurried to meet the riders. Paco was riding with a guy who had flying snakes twisting through the air around his head.

"Are those *cloud vipers?*" Sujata gasped. "No way."

Indra peered under his hand. "Nobody can tame those things!"

Felicité recognized the voice that shouted back, "We brought friends!"

"Yuki!" Felicité exclaimed. "He wasn't supposed to come back for another year!"

Her dad was grinning in a way Felicité hadn't seen since her graduation night. "Yuki," he exclaimed, striding forward. "Welcome back."

"Look who he brought!" Paco waved at the riders emerging from the settling dust.

Sheriff Crow and the bounty hunter rode at the head of a group of six, all bristling with weapons. Felicité didn't recognize the others. One had antlers, and another was surrounded by a soft glow.

As her father let out a laugh of delight, Felicité met Sheriff Crow's cool gaze—one eye brown, the other a yellow snake eye. Felicité looked straight at the sheriff, conscious of her own eyes ringed with bronze scales. It wasn't often that she'd seen the sheriff startled, but she saw it now.

"Welcome, welcome, welcome," her father declared. He looked genuinely glad to see them all—Changed and Norms.

"Tom," the bounty hunter said. "Been a while."

"It has indeed," said Father. "Paco, what can you tell me?"

"You've got to attack now! Voske captured the entire resistance—Ross, Jennie, Dr. Lee, Becky—he'll execute them soon, if he hasn't—" Paco cut off his own words with a snap of his teeth.

Father frowned. "I planned to attack after midnight tonight. Once you correct our map and give me numbers, we can re-evaluate—"

Paco broke in, "You can't wait that long. Voske will kill them *today*. Mia. Meredith. Kerry. He's probably arrested their families, too. The Rileys. The Lees. The Medinas—" His voice cracked.

Sheriff Crow held up one hand. "We understand, Paco."

It was exactly what Felicité had been afraid of. Voske was going to execute *Becky?* She remembered Voske's eerie smile. And the casual way he'd had Becky's grandmother shot where she stood. He'd do it.

Felicité had lost Sujata. She couldn't lose Becky. She *wouldn't* lose Becky.

Her father beckoned to the newcomers. "Let's go down to the shore and look at the map. We're too visible up here anyway. Especially with the horses."

Indra and Sujata took the horses to a makeshift picket in a large cave.

"Where have you been, Sheriff?" Father asked.

"I escaped over the wall during the invasion," said Sheriff Crow. "I went looking for Furio. I ended up at a trade town up north."

The bounty hunter broke in, unasked. "She showed around the token I gave her. I've got some friends up that way. One sent a messenger bat. I brought a couple of reinforcements. Handy in a fight."

The man with the antlers gave a brief grin.

Sheriff Crow added, "I also hired some mercenaries while I worked at an inn, guarding the door. I figured you'd go to Dai La, so I sent a message there. It missed you, but that doesn't matter now."

Father spread out his rough map. Paco gave a precise report while Father wrote in corrections. Felicité was glad to see most of her guesses proved true. As her father, Sheriff Crow, and the volunteer captains from Catalina and the Saigon Alliance began discussing logistics, Felicité turned to Paco, who sat shoulder to shoulder with Yuki. He looked hard and grim, emphasizing his resemblance to Voske.

"What happened, Paco?" she asked quietly.

"I got a Change power. Teleporting. When Voske smashed our resistance, I teleported out. I looked for Mr. Preston all night, but I ran into Yuki instead." The boys' hands moved together, clasping tightly.

Felicité wished she had someone to hold hands with. Not that she wished Isais had come into danger with her! Unexpectedly, a vivid sense-memory gripped her, of a different hand holding hers. A bigger hand, one not surrounded by phosphorescence. *Henry*. She flinched.

"Ross and Kerry were in Las Anclas?" Felicité asked. "And *Becky* was in the resistance?"

With a slight smile, Paco said, "Becky put the note in Wu Zetian's collar."

Sheriff Crow glanced over. "She also covered my escape."

Felicité wasn't the only person who was different now. Paco was Changed. Kerry had unselfishly returned to the place that was most dangerous for her. And Becky was the magnificent hero! Felicité couldn't help smiling at that. Becky had fought so hard for everything that she'd become. She was much more heroic than Jennie, who had practically been born with a sword in her hand.

"Gear up, everyone," said Father. "We're on the march."

Paco breathed a huge sigh of relief.

"Good," murmured Yuki. To Paco, "See? He did change his plan."

Father went on, "But our objectives remain the same. First, we must secure the armory to get its weapons for ourselves. The town gates must be opened, so our army can get in. And, of course, we must take down Voske."

Sheriff Crow's eyebrow rose. "And the jail? The prisoners slated for execution must be held there."

"Voske likes his public executions long and lingering," replied Father. "And with no interruptions. Once we knock on the door, he'll stash them to deal with us. The jail's not a priority, unless we see an opportunity."

Sheriff Crow frowned, the skin around her brown eye crinkling. "I'll keep an eye out for that opportunity."

Yuki and Paco exchanged uncertain nods. They probably didn't like her father's reasoning but understood it. Felicité wasn't so sure. She kept thinking about Voske—

not his smile, but the moment when he stopped smiling. Father was probably right that Voske would prefer a long public execution, but he might settle for a quick one just to have them dead. And Becky was in the jail now, waiting to be dragged out and killed. Or shot out of hand, right there in the cell.

Father glanced her way. "Felicité, you'll swim out to sea, then retrace your escape route from Las Anclas. You'll lead an amphibious team to the Wolfe House well." When she nodded, her throat tight, he turned to the others. "It's an absolutely essential task — she tells me the underwater caverns are like a labyrinth — and she's the only one who can find her way."

Felicité heard in his voice that he didn't merely accept her Change, he'd actually become proud of it. But she couldn't bask in that knowledge. She had another essential task ahead of her — one she'd chosen for herself.

"Once you show them the well, swim straight back here," her father went on. "Hold the camp for our return."

Felicité nodded. It took all the practice she'd had hiding her thoughts to keep herself looking obedient. But they didn't need her to hold the camp. She intended to follow that team of assassins out of the well — in broad daylight — into her town that was now ruled by the enemy. If she wanted to save Becky, it was her only chance.

·50·
BRIDGET

LAS ANCLAS – WOLFE HOUSE

BRIDGET SAT IN THE kitchen, watching the cook crisp the breakfast bacon. When she pinched a piece for her darling spiders, the cook shot her a revolted look.

"Spiders have to eat, just like we do," Bridget pointed out. Why did everyone have so much difficulty understanding that simple biological fact?

"Well, I don't have to cook for them," the cook muttered, then said more politely, "Princess, will you take a tray to the king? Half my help has disappeared."

As Bridget neared Father's office, she heard him saying, "Flaubert, ride to the crystal forest and pull Mortensen back to reinforce us."

Bridget brought the tray in. "Good morning, Father. Here's your breakfast!"

Father's guards looked tired and stressed. Bridget put that together with the cook saying half her help was missing, and asked, "Is something interesting going on?"

"We're stamping out another rebellion," Father said. "The rebel traitors are holed up in the jail, surrounded by our soldiers. Liam was one of the rebels. He gained a Change power after all. He was secretly a teleporter. But I have scouts sweeping the desert, so he'll be back soon."

Bridget instantly pictured him onstage, getting his head chopped off. And she'd have to watch. And look glad. She wondered if she ought to look glad now because he'd be caught soon, or angry because he was a rebel. Her face muscles twitched uncertainly.

"Yes, it's a lot to take in," said Father. "And there's

more. The rebels are holding Min Soo hostage at the jail. I suspect she went there to try to reason with Kerry."

"Kerry?" Bridget blurted out, horrified that Father knew she was here, then quickly added, "She's here?"

"Yes. She joined the rebels. I gave her a chance." Father sounded sad. But of course, he could make himself sound however he liked. "She could have come back and taken her rightful place as crown princess. But she refused to prove her loyalty. Bridget, imagine that you had Kerry locked in jail, along with other traitors, and you wanted to find out if she was loyal to you. How would you do that?"

Her heart banged like a death-watch beetle. She knew the correct answer, but what if this whole conversation was actually a test of *her* loyalty? What if Father knew she'd talked to Kerry? "Well, Father, *you* can always tell if people are lying."

She could see that that answer pleased him. "I can. But I hoped that I was wrong. I asked her to choose two of her comrades to execute herself. She refused to do it. You wouldn't be so weak, would you, Bridget?"

For a sickening moment, she thought he was about to ask her to take out two of her spiders and step on them. Hoping he only wanted a reply and not a demonstration, she said, "Of course not, Father."

"I can't understand her reasoning. She could have everything. I even offered to spare the traitor Santiago." He seemed to be speaking more to himself than to her.

Bridget was so relieved that he wasn't going to ask her to kill her spiders that she blurted out, "Maybe Kerry regrets it. How about if I go talk to her?"

Father looked at her like she was stupid. "And give them *two* hostages? Absolutely not. There's no rush, Bridget. They aren't going anywhere. I want to capture Liam before I execute them, anyway. And the family members burrowed in some rat hole." He gave an irritated snort. "There are too many traitors for a long execution. I'll select the youngest from each of their families for that and put the others up against a wall after they finish watching. Anyway, Kerry made her choice. I just have to extricate Min Soo safely."

Father's words echoed in Bridget's ears. *Up against a wall. Until I find Liam. The youngest from each of their families.*

Kerry made her choice.

She knew that tone. The conversation was over. Sure enough, he said, "Go to your room and stay there. I've got work to do."

Bridget retrieved her spiders and bolted to her room. But not even their hairy bodies could comfort her. She couldn't bear the thought of Kerry letting Father execute her. Probably, Kerry and Father were furious and not listening to each other. Bridget bet Kerry would calm down and think again if she was talking to her little sister.

With so many servants gone, would anyone notice if Bridget walked out? Or *climbed* out? She'd always wanted to sneak out a window. But after that, she'd have to get into the jail. Normally, anyone in Gold Point who wasn't a member of the royal family would do anything even a baby princess ordered. But the jail was surrounded by soldiers. They might send a messenger to Father to make sure Bridget was allowed in. She needed something more than just being a princess...

Bridget slipped down the hall to her father's bedroom. It was empty, so nobody was guarding the door. She snuck inside and looked around. Father's swords rested on a wooden rack. A selection of knives and throwing stars lay on the bureau. There was a whole shelf of books, including some she recognized from lessons on military strategy.

She found what she was looking for on a tray on a side table. There were the military tokens, gold circles worked into the shape of a crown. She stashed one in her pocket and ducked out the back window. It was every bit as thrilling as she'd imagined.

The town was deserted except for soldiers, who saluted her. She smiled at them. She heard gunfire long before she saw the jail, which was indeed completely surrounded by soldiers. As she watched, several shot at the windows, whose edges looked chewed up. The walls were pockmarked with bullet holes.

Bridget almost retreated. They looked ready to fire at her if a butterfly took off from a leaf. But this was her own test. She was Princess Bridget, and she was going to prove herself to Father and save Kerry's life.

She held up the gold crown token and said, "The king

sent me to negotiate with my sister." Bridget tried to speak loudly enough to be heard inside the jail, but her voice came out high and thin.

"Go on, Princess," said the captain. She spoke to the soldiers in a low voice. "Ready. Wait for the door to open, and a clear shot. Do *not* endanger the princess."

The clack of rifles being readied sounded all around her. The first line of soldiers dropped to one knee, and a second line formed behind them, all training their weapons toward the jail door.

Bridget's gaze strayed back to the jail windows, which were barred and blocked. A voice shouted from within, "Back off twenty-five paces!"

She reached the door. No one moved. She stood there, her heart in her throat. Was she going to fail now?

The same voice yelled, "Do it!" The soldiers moved back; their weapons still trained on the door. It jerked open, and rifles poked out above Bridget's head. They fired, making her ears ring. A hand yanked her inside, and the door slammed behind her, nearly catching her skirt.

Bridget looked around. Kerry was the one who had pulled her in. The girl beside her must be a fierce fighter — she was covered in blood. Her eye and a part of her face were made of ruby. What an amazing Change!

There were other people Bridget didn't know, none as interesting to look at as the blood-splashed girl with the ruby eye. Santiago and Meredith glanced at her, then retreated to a back room. Bridget was baffled to see Dr. Lee and Becky and astonished to see Ross. As usual, he was sitting glumly in a corner. She dismissed him from her mind.

Min Soo stepped forward and frowned at her. "Your father did not send you."

Bridget admitted, "No. But I had to talk to Kerry." Eagerly, she turned to her sister. "I know you and Father are mad at each other. But you can't just throw away your life. I have an idea. I'm sure Father will agree. If you offer to let Madam Cho go free and you come back to him, I think he'll be happy. He said he was very sorry you were here."

She waited for Kerry's grim expression to turn hopeful, but it only deepened. Her mother didn't look pleased at the prospect of going free, either.

"Did he tell you about his loyalty test for me?" Kerry asked.

"Yes, but—"

"Did he tell you what he did to Mia?" Kerry indicated the girl with the ruby eye.

"That's Mia? Dr. Lee's daughter?" Bridget exclaimed. "And the blood is hers? Um, he flogged her?"

"He put out her eye with a throwing star." Kerry spoke very precisely, as if each word was broken off with a chisel. "She was in the cell, completely helpless. He meant her to die while we all watched. If Ross hadn't been able to use his Change power in a new way, she would have."

Now the crystal in Mia's face looked like an open wound. Bridget turned to Becky. "I don't understand. Why are *you* here? Where are the rebel soldiers?"

"There aren't any rebel soldiers," Kerry said. "It's just people like Becky and Dr. Lee. Father will execute them both, and their families with them. Slowly, making a show out of their suffering."

Bridget's insides hurt. Dr. Lee had taught her so much, and Becky was her friend. She'd seen executions before. Plenty of them. But those had been criminals and rebels—traitors. This was *Becky*. And *Dr. Lee*. They weren't criminals, but they were in jail, so Father had decided that they were.

Bridget imagined Becky on that stage, getting her head cut off. Or worse.

She wanted to run away—from the jail, and from everything. But if she left, she'd have to sit on stage all day to watch Kerry and Becky and Dr. Lee tortured to death.

She couldn't do it.

"I wish I'd brought my spiders," Bridget said fiercely, her throat aching. "The most venomous ones. I could send them to scuttle after the torturers—well, I could release them and shoo them in the right direction."

"It's a nice thought," Kerry said. "But you need to leave now. Someday, you can run away and go some-where better. Like Sean did."

Bridget planted her fists on her hips. "No. I'm not going back. I want to help you, even without my spiders.

I wish I could use my power from a longer distance. I'd make all their guns rust into nothing."

Kerry turned away, looking desperate and unhappy. But Mia leaned forward eagerly, her ruby eye glittering. "You can rust things? What's your range?"

"Five feet. Maybe if I went out and pretended I needed to inspect their guns...? But I could only make one fall apart before they noticed."

"Ah!" Mia exclaimed. "A gun isn't just metal. It's wood, too. Can you affect both?"

"I can decay anything that isn't alive," Bridget said with pride.

"Sand? Cement? Adobe?"

The tall girl guarding the window turned around. "Hold on, Mia. It's not going to help if she drops the roof on our heads."

"I wouldn't have her do that! But I can show her exactly what to decay to bring this building down safely." Mia turned to Ross, who was now listening with interest. "Right, Ross? It'd be like blowing up a building, only with accelerated decay in place of explosives." She frowned, fingering the tiny rubies leading down from her eye. "And going off one by one, rather than all at once. Hmm. That does make it more difficult."

Bridget bounced on her toes. "What if I partially decayed some spots, until they were almost ready to collapse, then ran back and forth finishing the decay as fast as I could? Then they'd almost come down at once."

Mia beamed at her. "That could work!"

Ross got up. "Let me get my slide rule. It should still be in my pack."

"YES!" yelled the girl a little older than Bridget, her long black hair swirling. "We're blowing up the jail!"

Meredith Lowenstein poked her head back in. "I'm all for blowing up buildings, but not with us inside."

The tall girl with the commanding presence said, "You haven't seen Mia and Ross prospect with explosives. I have. If they think they can do it safely, we should do it."

Mia grabbed Bridget's hands with glee. "Then let's get started!"

Dr. Lee gave them a bemused smile. "I thought you two would get along."

·51·
FELICITÉ

BEACH - PRESTON CAMP

FELICITÉ STOOD BAREFOOT ON the beach, facing her father, Sheriff Crow, the bounty hunter, and the Saigon Alliance captains. She wore only a short summer nightgown, and beneath it, a waterproof pack made of kelp. It contained a tightly-rolled dress and a pair of lightweight shoes, for her to wear when she returned from the mission, and a canteen, a knife, and some jerky, in case an undercurrent pulled her off course on her way back.

"Let's review the plan for the final time," Father announced. "From now on, there will be no communication."

Choosing her words carefully, Felicité said, "My role is to escort the amphibious team to the well in our garden."

"And then come straight back here." To her relief, Father sounded like it really was a review, not a warning.

Felicité used Mother's best council voice. "That's the plan."

Father turned to the captain of the amphibious team. "Galen, you and your team will emerge in front of my house. If possible, get inside, take out Voske, and rescue my son William and my wife."

When Father didn't go on, Felicité put in, "And Grandmère."

"And my mother-in-law."

Felicité remembered the terrible fight over dinner last year, when Father had objected to Grandmère lighting the candles with her power, and Grandmère had reminded Father that it was *her* house. Would it be different now?

He went on, "If it isn't possible, go to the front gate. Do whatever you need to do to get it open. If we time it right, we'll be waiting for you outside."

Galen's green skin was smooth and shiny in the sunlight. When he nodded, the tentacles growing in a crest over his head made their own gentle nod. The other two in his team also nodded briskly, fins and tentacles bouncing.

Father turned to Sheriff Crow and the bounty hunter. "Sheriff Crow, go over the wall wherever it's least guarded. Furio, take your covert team through the desert to the back gate. Furio attacks the back gate from the outside while Sheriff Crow attacks from the inside. Once it's open, converge on the new armory. Secure its weapons and back us up." He lifted his voice to address everyone at the top of the palisade. "It's time to take back Las Anclas!"

The amphibious team walked into the sea and vanished beneath the waves. Felicité couldn't help glancing at her father. He'd never seen her mermaid form. And he still didn't have to. She could transform beneath the surface, so no one would see.

She walked into the sea. The salt water was smooth and welcoming on her skin. She sank down, letting the water close over her head. The Change rippled through her internal organs. Her legs pulled together and melded, extending into a fluke.

Felicité lifted her head above the surface. She looked straight at her father and blinked, letting the nictitating membranes slide across her eyes. Then she lifted her fluke into the air and waved it at him before slapping it down with a huge splash.

Father raised his hand in salute, then turned to join the moving army.

Felicité's pleasure in her mermaid form melded with her relief at her father's acceptance. She dove down, reveling in the power of her fluke as she shrugged out of her nightie. It settled down over a twist of coral. She swam swiftly to Galen's team and gestured: *This way.*

They fell in behind her as she swam along the underwater caverns pocking the shore. They passed over half-sunken artifacts of the old days. Cement slabs of road. The beetle-like shells of cars and buses, which had become homes for fish and eels and shellfish. Sea anemones open-ed like flowers. She both sensed and saw the fissure she had first swum out of, with seawater surging against freshwater currents. She led the way through. Phosphor-escent stone marked treacherous spires of rock. Glowing sea slugs crawled up a spire in the world's slowest race.

Felicité swam through all those wonders until she reached the underwater lake. Lancing beams of gold marked the entrance to the well. Sunlight highlighted the rough stone walls of the well. She pointed to it, then swam out of the team's way. The team quickly scrambled up the well shaft and vanished over the edge.

Felicité waited. The last thing she wanted to do was emerge too soon, and have the amphibious team send her straight back down the well. She fidgeted, her tail swish-ing back and forth. Now that she wasn't preoccupied with leading the way, she had time to worry. Was the team finding her mother right now? Was Voske murdering the team right now? She hoped the utter silence was a good sign. Surely the sound of gunshots would carry to the bottom of the well.

When she was sure that at least half an hour had passed, Felicité swam upward. She glanced nervously at the circle of sky. It looked so bright and blue, she felt terribly exposed. She'd have to climb fast. It had only taken the team a minute or so.

Felicité surged up, got a good grip on a projecting stone, and tried to haul herself out of the water. Her tail flapped involuntarily, making a splash that echoed loudly. She flinched, hoping no one had heard. Once again, she tried to drag herself upward. She had to get her tail out of the water before it would turn back into legs that could climb.

It hadn't occurred to her that climbing out might be a problem. But trying to lift her entire body upward with her hands alone was incredibly difficult. It was particular-ly hard to do it silently. Every splash and grunt of effort echoed horribly, making her imagine that guards would stick their heads over the well's edge at any moment. Felicité had strained her shoulders and both wrists, and scraped herself all over, before she finally managed to lift her tail out of the water for long enough to make it turn back into legs. She jammed the tender skin of her soles hard into the rock wall, terrified that if she fell, she'd have to do it all over again.

And then she actually had to climb up the sides. She hadn't climbed anything since she was ten or eleven years old. The amphibious team had made it look easy, but they were trained soldiers. For Felicité, it was difficult, exhausting, and terrifying. She had to stop halfway to catch her breath and was seriously tempted to give up the entire idea and let herself fall back into the welcoming water.

For Becky, she reminded herself. Climbing up a wall was nothing compared to what Becky must going through. With stifled groan, Felicité forced herself to go on. There was nothing quite so wretched and miserable as climbing the wet, rough sides of a well while naked. The stone scraped every inch of skin.

With a combination of triumph and terror, she finally heaved herself over the edge and flopped down onto the grass.

But she couldn't take even a moment to rest, naked and exposed to view. With utter loathing, she crept to the garden shed. She ducked inside and dressed faster than she ever had in her life, ignoring her many scrapes. A little seawater had gotten into the supposedly waterproof pack, and her dress and shoes were unpleasantly damp.

She slipped out and darted behind an enormous rose bush. From there she could see the north side of Wolfe House. There were three guards in sight. The closest one stifled a yawn, then straightened up with an effort Felicité could almost feel. Had they been up all night, too?

More black-clad figures moved across the windows inside. There was no way the amphibious team could have gotten inside. They must have given up on rescuing her family and were sneaking their way to the front gate. So Voske was still alive, and Felicité was alone in a town full of enemies.

She longed to dive back into the well. No one would blame her. It was what she was supposed to do.

Felicité traced the scale mask around her eyes. There were so many bad choices she couldn't undo; she couldn't make another one. If she didn't at least try to rescue Becky, she'd regret it for the rest of her life.

She belly-crawled from bush to bush. As a child, she had explored all the gardens on the Hill. She remembered where to go, and how to stay hidden. When she reached the orchard behind Jack's saloon, she caught sight of the jail. It was surrounded by what looked the entire Gold Point army.

Felicité's heart sank. What had she expected to do—swim into it? Fight an army with a small knife that she'd never even trained with?

"Felicité," a voice whispered.

She whipped around. There was no one in sight.

"Look up." There was Henry, sitting in a big apple tree. He was nearly invisible in his black fatigues, but his blond hair stood out against the bark.

"A patrol's coming," he whispered urgently. "Climb up."

She scrambled up into the tree, wincing at the rough bark on her raw hands. She reached Henry's branch just before a troop of soldiers jogged down the pathway.

Once the soldiers were gone, Felicité forced herself to say, "Thanks."

"Any time," Henry said, with a ghost of his old sweetness. He was even skinnier than when she'd seen him last, his cheekbones sharp and his wrists bony.

He offered her a handkerchief. "You're bleeding."

"Thanks," she said again. It felt surreal to be thanking him for anything. She took the handkerchief and mopped at the worst of her scrapes.

"How did you get back into town?" he asked.

She considered lying—it wasn't as if he deserved the truth—then remembered his confused and betrayed look when she'd denied jumping into the well. He was a traitor, but she still felt bad about her lie. And he obviously had no intention of turning her in. "I climbed back up the well," she said, her gaze meeting his.

His head dropped against the bole of the tree. "You almost convinced me that I'd gone crazy. Or that I was lying about it and somehow, I'd forgotten."

Guilt stabbed at Felicité. Defensively, she said, "I had to lie. I was sitting at Voske's table!"

"You could have told me. I mean, before. You really were Changed all along, right? Like me?"

Felicité was ready to snap at him, but the *like me* doused her annoyance. "I was. Ever since I was thirteen. I thought of telling you, but I was sure you hated the Changed."

Glumly, Henry said, "Right back at you."

"I wish I had the power to turn back time." Felicité sighed. And then everything she'd been turning over in her mind burst out of her. "If I'd told you I was Changed, would you have told me you were? Would you have listened if I'd told you not to set any fires? If I'd told you the truth, would that have made everything different?"

"Felicité, I *had* to set those fires. I mean, I felt like I had to. I wanted so badly to be a Ranger…to impress your father…to impress everyone. But I really did mean to save the town by putting them out."

She believed him. The fires hadn't been her fault in any way. There was nothing she could have done to stop Henry. She ought to have been relieved, but she just felt sad.

Henri bumped his head gently against the tree trunk. "I've had nothing but time to think about it. And think, and think, and think. Nobody talks to me. It's the one thing both sides agree on: I'm a scummy traitor." His smile was crooked. "If we could go back in time, there's a lot of stuff I'd do differently."

Felicité had plenty of experience with regrets spining endlessly in her head. Now she knew how to halt that cycle. "Well, we can't. What are you going to do now?"

Henry shrugged. "There's nothing I can do. It's too late—"

A tremendous explosion made Felicité jump. She had to clutch at the branches to stop herself from falling out of the tree.

The roof of the jail collapsed with awful slowness, crumbling from within. An even louder crash shook the earth as its walls fell outward. An enormous cloud of dust rose up, completely enveloping the surrounding soldiers. A chorus of startled shouts arose, then a few gunshots. A woman yelled, "Cease fire! Cease fire! Madam Cho and Princess Bridget are in there!"

Had Voske blown up the jail to dispose of all his prisoners at once?

·52·
BECKY

LAS ANCLAS

DUST BILLOWED UP INTO her face as objects thundered and crashed. She could see nothing but gray dust. It was as if a giant had dropped a bag of flour. Then someone grabbed her forearm, someone else clutched the back of her shirt, and yet another person slid their hands down her arm until they found her hand.

Becky reached out with her free hand, touched something that was probably someone's side, and fumbled until she found fingers. She clutched tightly, and then nearly lost her balance when that person tugged her up and began running. Becky ran, her ears still ringing from the crash. They stumbled over splintered beams, moving in such a tight mass that anyone who fell was instantly hauled back to their feet.

They jolted to a stop. Becky could see better now, making out the plaster walls and kick wheels of the pottery. A tall figure—that had to be Jennie—yanked the door open and dragged them all in.

The door slammed behind them. Everyone was coughing and gasping. Becky sneezed violently. Her ears were ringing, and even her eyelashes were covered in dust. Jennie went from person to person, checking for injuries and counting everyone.

"…and Kerry," Jennie concluded. "That's everyone."

"Good!" said Dr. Lee. "Now—"

The pottery door slammed open. Jennie leveled her rifle at the door, Santiago dropped into a fighting crouch, and Kerry's hands closed over the shape of a hilt and a shield handle. Somewhat to her own surprise, Becky found that she too had instantly aimed her rifle at the door.

The figure standing in the doorway kicked it shut behind her. She raised her empty hands, her head lifting. Glossy blue-black braids fell back from a face Becky knew as well as her own.

Becky gasped with surprise and sheer delight. "Sheriff Crow!"

"Deputy," said the sheriff with a nod and a smile. "Good reflexes."

For the first time since the invasion, Becky stopped feeling small and inadequate. She was the sheriff's apprentice. And the sheriff was back.

Dr. Lee smiled. "Elizabeth, you're the most welcome sight I've ever seen. Where did you come from?"

"I jumped the wall just as the jail fell," the sheriff explained. "I spotted you all from the town hall roof, before the dust rose high enough to hide you."

Becky pictured Sheriff Crow running from the town hall to the pottery. She'd have moved faster than a hawk stooping.

Sheriff Crow surveyed everyone, with only cool curiosity rather than surprise as she noted Santiago, Min Soo, and Bridget, whom she'd never met. Then Mia stopped fiddling with her broken glasses and dropped her hands, revealing her ruby eye and scar. It was the first time Becky had seen the sheriff look shocked.

"Voske tried to kill me," Mia explained. "Ross saved my life. I'd have lost the eye anyway."

Summer, crouching precariously on a tall shelf otherwise occupied by casserole dishes, called down, "Isn't it cool?"

Sheriff Crow's half-smile encompassed both Summer and Mia. "Very cool. Good work, Ross."

Ross ducked his head, and dust fell from his hair.

The sheriff addressed them all. "Tom Preston has an army — a very small one, unfortunately — approaching the front gate. A team headed by Mr. Vilas is on its way to break through the back gate. I was sent to help him, then head to the armory."

Jennie spoke as confidently as the sheriff herself. "I

was planning to rally my family. Dr. Lee? Where are they?"

"At the schoolhouse," Dr. Lee said.

"What if I take them to the back gate, to help the boun—er, to help Mr. Vilas's team?" Jennie suggested. "Sheriff Crow, Dr. Lee can tell you where to find the rest of the people in hiding, and you can take them straight to the armory."

"Let's do it," Sheriff Crow said. "Where should I look?"

"Ms. Lowenstein's hidden basement and Luc's second attic," said Dr. Lee.

"And the Medinas' barn," said Becky. "Brisa will be there…I hope. She and I planned that." She turned to Sheriff Crow. Now that she was back, Becky didn't want to be anywhere but by her side.

Sheriff Crow glanced at Min Soo and Bridget. "And you are…?"

"Min Soo Cho and Bridget Voske," Min Soo said with perfect calm. "We do not have time to recount our story; perhaps Becky can explain later. But as far as the king is concerned, I am an escaped hostage, and Bridget is the brave princess who tried to rescue me. We shall return to the king's house, where Bridget will be safe."

Sheriff Crow's eyebrow rose even higher. "You can walk straight into the king's house? Can you…?" She discreetly laid her hand on her belt knife.

"I cannot," said Min Soo coolly. "Even if I had been trained to fight, I could never hope to prevail against him on my own. But I might be able to provide some crucial misdirection."

Kerry turned to the sheriff. "Mom and Bridget were wonderful—Bridget blew up the jail—but they can't kill Voske. You might as well ask a kitten to fight a pit mouth."

Becky recalled the kitten-like creature that had turned out to *be* a pit mouth, and suppressed what would have been a wildly inappropriate giggle.

"Go on, then," said the sheriff to Min Soo and Bridget. "And thank you." She turned to the rest of them. "Let's divide up the strongest fighters. Becky's with me."

The strongest fighters, Becky thought. Sheriff Crow had named her first.

Summer tossed her long black hair. "I'll go take out Voske."

Jennie, Sheriff Crow, and Ross all spoke at once. "No, you won't."

Summer crossed her arms, saying defiantly, "Then I'll go with the sheriff. She can deputize me."

Becky had never seen Sheriff Crow look afraid, and she didn't now—exactly—but she did look somewhat horrified.

"Summer, you're with me," said Jennie. "We'll find something good for you to do. Sheriff, I'd also like Kerry with me, if you don't mind."

Santiago immediately said, "Then I want to go with Jennie, too."

"And you are…?" the sheriff inquired.

"Santiago Flores. I was in the king's honor guard, before I joined the resistance."

Sheriff Crow gave him an approving nod. "Take them, Jennie. In that case, I'll take Ross and Meredith."

Meredith joined Becky beside the sheriff, but Ross hesitated. He pushed his hair back and straightened. "You should know something, sheriff. I can't kill anymore. Not won't. *Can't.*"

Mia jumped in. "It's because of the singing trees. Ross made a deal with them. It's why we're here—and why he can do more with crystal now and it hurts him less, he got so much deeper in—but if he kills anyone now, he'll turn into a tree. And so will I. I mean I'll turn into a tree if I kill someone. Not that I'll turn into a tree if Ross does. Er, a crystal tree. Not a regular one."

Sheriff Crow was visibly taken aback. "You'll literally…"

"No, no! Not literally," Mia said hastily. "I hope. But we wouldn't be *us* anymore."

"I can still fight to disable," Ross said. "But I'm not a good enough shot to do that with a gun, and I only have four throwing knives."

"Hmm." The sheriff rubbed her chin. "I need long-distance fighters for the armory. Becky and Meredith are two of the best shots in Las Anclas, so that works out."

"I'll get you the third," said Dr. Lee. "Ms. Lowenstein is still lying helpless in the infirmary. She was the only patient there last night. The soldiers who arrested me jeered at her, saying she'd be left there alone, with no one to fetch her food or water."

Meredith shot Dr. Lee a horrified look. "You didn't tell me!"

"There was no point." He sounded calm, but Becky could only imagine how much stress he'd been under, knowing that all along. "I'll go heal her so she can meet up with you. Please send any wounded to the infirmary. I'll hide if I see soldiers."

"Sounds good," said the sheriff. "Ross, Mia, go with Jennie."

"Actually," Dr. Lee said, "I'd rather Mia didn't fight at all. She has a serious injury, and she should rest. Mia, come with me."

"I'll rest at my cottage," Mia piped up. "I have the parts for a non-lethal weapon Ross can use. I promise I'll put it together sitting down."

"I'll protect you," Ross said immediately.

Sheriff Crow nodded. "Let's go before the dust settles and we lose our cover."

Becky fell into place beside her as they exited in twos and threes out the pottery's back door. The dust cloud had not dispersed — if anything, it was thicker. She could hear enemy soldiers shouting in frustration. Becky exulted, wondering if some Las Anclas citizen was resisting by using a Change power.

Watch out, Voske, she thought. *Rats could be anywhere.*

·53·
BRIDGET

LAS ANCLAS - MAIN STREET

MIN SOO PAUSED BY the empty saloon, touching her dusty skirts and once-perfectly dressed hair. "We can use this dishevelment. Let us discover the disposition of affairs," she said to Bridget with a smile. "Shall we, my dear?"

Bridget straightened her back. Min Soo had not lost any of her poise. She could be at a garden party, not an awful battle.

They headed out of the slowly dissipating dust cloud and found the captain shouting at her soldiers to stop shooting. She snapped off a salute. "Madam Cho! I thought you were a hostage —"

"Bridget and I escaped under cover of the explosion. I saw our captors making hand signals to each other. I believe they were planning to run that way." Min Soo pointed back toward headquarters. In a worried voice, she said, "I think they intended to harm the king. I do hope he's well protected there."

The captain's head turned sharply. "A and B Teams! To headquarters, on the double. That's where the prisoners went. Protect the king!"

Two sets of soldiers emerged from the dust and ran off.

"Madam Cho, permit me to escort you safely," said the captain.

"Thank you, captain, that would be a relief. Such a dreadful experience." Min Soo patted Bridget's shoulder. "Princess Bridget was a great comfort. She was so brave."

The captain frowned slightly. "What caused that

explosion?"

"Evidently someone had planted explosives inside the jail," Min Soo said. "I believe the rebels had originally intended to blow up the jail before they were caught in it themselves. They were gloating about the explosives they had planted all around town when I was dragged in. After that, they communicated only in whispers and hand signals. I'm afraid I know no more."

"Explosives all over town?" The captain's eyes rounded. "I have to report this."

"Do," Min Soo urged. "The king will want to know as soon as possible."

The captain turned to a pair of soldiers. "You two. Escort Madam Cho and the princess to HQ. I need to report directly to the king." She turned to the rest of the company. "You come with me."

They ran off, weapons clattering. During her time in the jail, Bridget had discovered that there was a lot more to Min Soo than she'd ever realized. But it was still impressive to see her dispatch all those soldiers on a useless mission.

Another soldier started to run past, coming from another direction. Min Soo called, "Lieutenant Samuels!"

The soldier stopped short and saluted. His eyes were red-rimmed, as though he hadn't slept in days. "Madam Cho. I'm glad to see you free."

"Thank you. I'll only keep you for a moment. Can you give me a report on the general situation?"

"I'm on my way to report to the king now," Lt. Samuels said. "An enemy army has just been sighted, according to the outer perimeter riders."

"I won't keep you, then," Min Soo said. "Bridget, my dear, will you run to the infirmary? I would like a draught of willow bark elixir. I have the most dreadful headache and must lie down for a bit."

Bridget nodded, realizing that Min Soo must want her to report to Dr. Lee.

One of their guards said, "I'll go with the princess."

Alarmed, Bridget was about to object when Min Soo said, "That would be lovely." To Bridget, she said, "You can have some candied rose petals when you get back, as a token of my regard."

Bridget nodded, nervous and confused. She didn't like rose petals and had no idea how to get rid of the soldier so she could talk to Dr. Lee. What had Min Soo meant about the rose petals being a token of her regard? It was such an odd way to phrase it…Token!

When they reached the infirmary, Bridget held up her military token. "You can rejoin your company now. I'll get another escort after I get the medicine."

The soldier saluted and ran off down Main Street, toward the front gate.

Bridget heard Dr. Lee's voice coming from the surgery. "Luis? What are you doing with that?"

She told herself that Luis was a very common name. It wasn't necessarily *that* Luis, Father's torturer, who could burn you to the bone with a touch. But she recognized the dull, toneless voice that replied, "You know what I'm doing."

It *was* that Luis. Father must have sent him to capture and torture Dr. Lee. Bridget looked around frantically for a weapon, though she didn't know if she'd dare to use one against *him*.

But Dr. Lee didn't sound frightened. He sounded calm. Gentle, even. "Yes, I had worried that you were thinking of taking your life."

"Why shouldn't I?" Luis retorted. "I wanted to stop the violence. Instead, I caused the loss of more lives than the night we came to this town. *I* did it. I can't live with that. I *shouldn't* live with that."

"You didn't cause it, Luis. That responsibility lies with the king, and with those who voluntarily choose to obey him. Did you ever do that?"

There was a gulping sound, then another. Luis was sobbing. Bridget's body chilled worse than when she'd fallen into a pond during a sleet storm. The last time she'd heard the sound was when her brother Sean had chosen his friend on Opportunity Day, and she'd died on the stage. Bridget pressed herself against the wall.

After a while, Dr. Lee said, "I believe I know something about how you feel."

"You can't," Luis said unsteadily. "I've lost everything. Everybody I loved died or is going to die. Sophie's dead. We were going to get married, but some Ranger killed her. If the king finds out I'm talking to you, he'll kill my entire family. We're not close, but I don't want them *dead*. Santiago is my friend, and he'll be tortured to death because of *me*."

"I was supposed to be tortured to death, and yet here I am," Dr. Lee pointed out. "Your family is not dead yet. Neither is Santiago. Things can change."

"The king will never let any of you go." Luis drew in a breath loud enough for Bridget to hear. "And Sophie is *gone*. She's never coming back."

"Yes. It's terrible to lose someone you love that much. I lost my wife and my newborn son in a single night. I thought that I should have been able to save them, because I'm a doctor and I have a healing power. Like you. And yet it wasn't enough."

Bridget dared a peek inside the surgery. Dr. Lee was holding up a bottle of essence of poppy, used to kill pain and induce sedation. He had warned her how dangerous it was and showed her the safe doses for people of different weights. She'd been fascinated by how you could figure out the difference between helping someone or killing them just by calculating a ratio. It had never occurred to her that anyone would take it to try to kill *themselves*.

"I picked up this bottle, too," said Dr. Lee. Once again, Bridget's nerves chilled. "I sat there looking at it for a long time. You're not the only one who has felt this temptation."

"Why didn't you?" Luis asked.

Dr. Lee looked up at the ceiling, then down again. "I knew how much it would hurt my family. Whether you're close or not, is there anyone in your family who'd feel the same pain that you feel now when they hear that you weren't killed, but chose to take your own life?"

Luis gave another muffled sob. Bridget pressed against the door frame, unable to move. Almost unable to breathe. Dr. Lee waited in silence while Luis covered his face with his hands.

Finally, he mumbled, "They might be sad. But Santiago won't be. And Ross. Becky. You saw them when I came into the jail. They think I'm a traitor—I *am* a traitor—and they hate my guts. If I ever see any of them again, they'll probably come at me with a knife. And I won't blame them."

Dr. Lee shook his head. "I know Ross very well, and I've gotten to know Santiago. I've known Becky since she was a baby. They all understand how people can make what turns out to be the wrong choice, for what they thought was the best of reasons. They're angry and upset, but I think they'd be willing to sit down and talk to you. No knives involved."

"I can't face them," Luis said quickly.

"How about this?" Dr. Lee asked. "I have a friend outside of town who I could send you to. His name is Rabbi Litvak. He's one of the best listeners I know, and he doesn't know your history. Just say I sent you, and he'll take you in."

Luis gave a great, shuddering sigh.

Dr. Lee began taking things from shelves and slipping them into a cloth bag. He slung it over Luis's shoulder, and said, "You can walk out the gate. You're in uniform, with special status. Follow the pipe toward the water tower on the hill. He can feel emotions—he'll know you're coming."

He led Luis to the back door, patted him on the shoulder, and closed the door behind him. Then he replaced the essence of poppy in the medicine cabinet, and called, "Bridget? You can come in now."

Startled, Bridget said, "You saw me."

"Yes. Luis would have, too, if he hadn't been so distracted." Dr. Lee put a hand on her back and led her in. "I'm sorry you had to listen to that. But I couldn't risk a distraction."

Bridget nodded uncertainly.

"What I did with him was a form of healing. Perhaps one day I'll teach it to you, when you're a little older." He smiled. "It's a little advanced for you right now."

Though Bridget still felt shaken up, that reassured her. He'd told her about advanced and difficult surgeries, and said he'd teach them to her later. This was just another lesson she wasn't quite ready for.

"Did you come for a specific purpose?" he asked.

"Oh!" she exclaimed. "I completely forgot! I'm sorry. I couldn't move."

"Are there other times when you've felt that way?"

Bridget thought back. "When Father gets in a scary mood. I always want to be invisible, even though I know he's not mad at me."

Dr. Lee nodded. She thought he looked sad.

"Min Soo sent me." Bridget passed on the soldier's report. Then she told him what Min Soo did, and Dr. Lee smiled.

"A perfect use of non-violent strategy," he said. "Good work, Princess Bridget."

Bridget abruptly realized that all the work she was doing, if she succeeded, would mean her father might no longer be the king. Would she still be a princess if Father lost power? Did she actually care about being one? She gave Dr. Lee an awkward smile. "Thanks. Can I stay with you? They're sending the wounded here. I could help. If you think I've learned enough to be useful."

Dr. Lee looked at her thoughtfully, then nodded. "You have. In fact, I'd be very grateful for your help. You have good hands."

·54·

HENRY

LAS ANCLAS - MAIN STREET

HENRY LEANED PAST A branch, blinking stinging eyes. The dust cloud was slowly dissipating; he could see soldiers digging in the rubble. The entire jail had collapsed. All those heavy adobe walls had crumbled into a giant heap. Nobody inside could have survived that.

His sister was under that pile.

Felicité had jumped down and rushed into the dust cloud. He'd frozen, afraid of finding Becky's body, and then he'd wished he'd gone with her. Now it was almost like he'd dreamed that conversation in the tree. He hoped she hadn't been captured.

He realized he'd been gripping the tree branch when his hand cramped, and he let go without taking his eyes from that rubble. He strained to see through the dust, hoping painfully to make out Becky's skinny form stumbling out. Anyone stumbling out. But he knew no one would.

On the other hand, nobody had shouted about finding any bodies. Henry dropped out of the tree and ran toward the jail. When he reached the rubble, with a dust pall still hanging above it, he saw a team systematically turning over chunks of adobe.

"Get out of here."

Henry turned to find a patrol leader behind him, his uniform gray. Dust clung to the man's eyebrows.

"I can help dig."

"You're in the way."

"My sister might be in there," Henry protested.

The man's mouth twisted. "Your sister the sneaking, lying rebel? Let's hope she's still alive so you can watch her execution. Or maybe we'll just find a hand. Or her head. That might be fun—"

The company commander jerked her thumb at Henry. "Out of our way," she snapped.

Henry retreated down Main Street. A patrol jogged past him; their rifles carried in ready position. They didn't slow until they reached the swarm of soldiers gathering around the jail. Henry looked around the now empty Main Street. The dust cloud had settled over the vegetables in the patches, making them a uniform light gray.

Something huge slammed into his back, knocking him flat. Heavy knees pinned him down, and a thick arm pressed into his throat. Henry stared up into Tommy Horst's rage-distorted face as Tommy pulled back his big fist. Henry braced for that fist to smash into his face.

"Don't you dare yell for help," Tommy ground out.

"Help from who?" Henry said bitterly.

"From your friend Voske," Tommy snarled. "The guy you sold out the town to!"

"He's not my friend," Henry said. "And I didn't—"

"Jennie's dead under all that rubble because of you. Mia is dead. Because of *you!*"

"So's my sister." Henry regretted it the instant he said it.

"That's *your* fault! And my dad's skull is staring out at the desert because of you! You were *there* when they cut off his head, sitting with *him*. Dressed in *that*." Tommy looked with loathing at the uniform that Henry wished he could rip off and burn.

"Go ahead. Smash my face in." Henry still saw the execution in his dreams, mixed up with memories of school and pranks with Tommy, when the worst thing in life once his dad was gone was hiding his Change.

Tommy grabbed a handful of the hated black shirt. "I want to know why you sold us out."

It was the question that circled around Henry's mind every time he closed his eyes to try to sleep. The more he asked himself, the less he felt like he knew the answer. "I don't know. I really don't."

"How can you not know? You did it!" Tommy's fist tightened as he pulled it back.

"Go on. Hit me. You can beat me bloody, but I still won't know."

"But why did you tell him about some tunnel that *I* didn't even know about? And my dad was defense chief!" Tommy's voice cracked on the word *dad.*

The weirdest thing was, Henry didn't remember ever making a decision to tell Voske about it. "I don't know that either. I knew he was the enemy. But he didn't *feel* like one."

Tommy snarled, "Yeah, I saw you looking at him like he was your new dad—" He gazed back at Henry with sudden understanding. "Oh."

Henry closed his eyes, his mind filling with memories of dinners and overnights at the Horsts' place. Mr. Horst had a big store of jokes about Changed people, and no matter how often he told the same ones, Tommy always laughed. And Henry had laughed even louder, wishing he had a dad who told jokes instead of hitting....

Tommy grunted and rose to his feet. Henry got up more slowly, shrugging as dirt dribbled down the back of his neck.

Tommy froze. Henry glanced back and saw Voske. He was surrounded by his elite guards, walking up to the soldiers milling around the ruins of the jail. Everyone stopped what they were doing to salute. Though Voske usually ignored him, except during those horrible meals, Henry backed away, all the way on to the shady porch of the infirmary. Tommy followed.

"No bodies?" Voske pointed at a soldier. "Your squad keep digging, just in case. The rest of you, fan out and search the area."

He began walking down Main Street. Henry pressed back on the infirmary porch, Tommy with him. When Voske reached the execution stage, he stopped so abruptly that a few of his guards were forced to take a quick step backward. Henry peered in the direction Voske was staring.

Voske's bloody corpse lolled on the throne onstage.

Henry's gaze jerked from Voske's body to the living man who stood staring at it, then back to the corpse.

Henry immediately realized that it wasn't a real corpse. It was a sort of scarecrow, a set of black and red clothing stuffed to approximate the shape of a person. Its burlap head was painted with a grotesquely exaggerated grin and wore a wig of spookily realistic silver hair. Fake blood—at least Henry assumed it was fake—was splashed all over it. Its intestines dangled to the stage floor—Henry saw now that they were socks sewn together—and a table leg protruded from its heart.

"What *is* that?" one of the honor guard exclaimed, then choked herself off.

A deadly silence gripped everybody.

"An effigy," said Voske. His calm tone gripped Henry with terror.

Several of the guards took a step back.

Voske stepped onto the stage. His heels rang over the boards. For a long moment, he bent over the figure sprawled on his throne. Then he straightened and addressed his guards. "It's broad daylight. Exactly how did it get here without anyone noticing?"

There was a long silence. A guard said, "Sir, we've all been with you."

Voske shot a glare at his honor guard. "*You've* all been with me." He waved a hand at the soldiers who had been searching the area. "What were all of *you* doing?"

Every soldier froze, staring at Voske.

Voske pulled his pistol, raised it, and fired. Henry recoiled as the company commander dropped dead, a red hole in her forehead.

Tommy grabbed Henry's arm.

"I assume she was the leader of the traitors." Voske's tone was terrifyingly calm. "Who else is working with the rebels? Whoever has information will be spared."

The soldiers looked at each other. Nobody spoke.

Henry's heart stuttered as the king turned his head and looked straight at him. He lifted his voice. "Henry. How long has Tommy been with you?"

Henry felt Tommy flinch. "Since right after I tried to help search for—search the rubble." He pointed at the dead company commander. "She didn't want me around. Tommy jumped me right as I was leaving."

Voske turned to the soldiers. "Can anyone

corroborate that?"

Voices of assent rose up. Speaking in a low voice, as if to himself, Voske said, "Then the effigy must have already been there. Yes. That makes sense. It was placed under the cover of the dust cloud. It couldn't have been in the jail, so it must have come from one of the homes behind the shops, where everyone is locked down." Raising his voice, he demanded, "Search them!"

Henry and Tommy froze as soldiers rushed into the Trans' house. They soon came back out, shaking their heads. Their leader said nervously, "Empty, sir."

Voske's hand settled on his pistol. The soldier flinched. In a soft, ominous voice, Voske said, "A family lives there. So, they were allowed to escape. Next house!"

The soldiers ran up the alley behind the Trans' store—they looked like they were fleeing—and emerged dragging Mrs. Hernandez.

"Let me go," she protested. "I was in my own house, minding my own business!"

"What do you know about this?" Voske pointed toward the effigy.

Mrs. Hernandez looked at it and gave a startled bark of laughter.

Voske moved so quickly that Henry never saw him draw. There was just the crack of a pistol shot, and Mrs. Hernandez dropped in the middle of her laugh.

Henry stared at the crumpled body. Laura's mom! She'd always brought snacks to the schoolhouse along with Laura's lunch, when Laura was training to be a teacher. Mrs. Hernandez had never liked Henry, as she was fiercely protective of her daughter, and Henry used to mock Laura's black cat claws. Laura had died defending Las Anclas the first time Voske attacked, and now Voske had killed her mother, too. Henry heard Tommy's voice echoing in his mind: *This is your fault.*

"I'm going to kill him," Tommy muttered, and took a step toward the street.

Henry caught him by the arm. "Don't." If he had to see Tommy lying there in the dust with a bullet hole in his head, he'd lose his mind.

Voske replaced the pistol in his belt. As if nothing had happened, he raised his voice. "The traitors have been executed. Dispose of the effigy and—"

Voske spun around. "Who said that?"

Henry hadn't heard anything. Apparently, no one else had, either. He shrank back toward the wall, hoping Voske had forgotten he was there.

After a tense silence, Voske said, "Get rid of this. Now, I want—"

He stopped, his head jerking toward his shoulder. This time, when he spun about, it was with the pistol in his hand. To Henry's astonishment, he fired at the effigy. Several holes appeared in the stuffed shirt, and bits of hay flew everywhere. Voske then adjusted his aim slightly and fired at his throne. Splinters flew. He didn't stop shooting until the gun clicked, empty.

Voske glared at his soldiers, who were all staring at him. He shouted, "The traitor Maria-Pilar is here! Find her!"

The soldiers all scattered and began feeling everything. Several of them flung themselves down on hands and knees and began touching every brick on the street. Others stooped from vegetable to vegetable in the nearest plot, fingering beans and pumpkins. As they did so, Voske quickly left the stage.

"Who's Maria-Pilar?" Tommy whispered.

Henry shrugged. "Guess Voske's invisible son isn't the only one with that power."

A soldier stepped onto the infirmary porch, shoving Tommy aside. "Go home. You're under lockdown." Ignoring Henry, he began feeling the benches and the shoe rack.

Tommy cast Henry a last glance and vanished around the side of the infirmary. Realizing that no one was paying any attention to him, Henry took the opportunity to get out of there. Since he already knew no one was in the Trans' house, he ducked into their backyard. What now? He'd better grab this chance to sit and think. Voske was killing random citizens as well as his own people. Henry wished he could just get away…

He *could.* If Becky was dead, she was no longer a hostage. He could grab food and water from the Trans' house, jump the wall, and get as far away as he could before dawn. It could be days before anyone even noticed he was missing, and he doubted that chasing after him would be high on Voske's list of priorities. He could get to another town and start over. No one would ever know who he was or what he'd done.

But what if Becky wasn't dead? Voske sure didn't think she was.

Even if she was alive, it wasn't like Henry could do anything to help her. If Henry just left, and Voske killed Becky, it wouldn't be his fault.

Henry could hear his own voice, his own inflections, in his mind, as if he was explaining it to someone: "*It wasn't my fault.*"

Then the voice shifted to his mother's: "*It's your father's fault. It's Becky's fault. It's Becky's mutant girlfriend's fault.*"

And then back to Henry's own voice. "*Voske said I'd be doing the town a favor. I was just kidding. It was just a little fire.*"

He couldn't run, if there was any chance that staying would make a difference for Becky. But he couldn't stay. Everyone hated him. Sooner or later, someone would kill him. And he deserved it, because it really was all his fault. Nobody else's. His.

Henry sank down onto the Trans' back porch, his head in his hands.

·55·

JENNIE

LAS ANCLAS - SCHOOLHOUSE

JENNIE RE-ADJUSTED THE LOAD of weapons she'd brought out of the jail. She slipped into the schoolhouse, followed by Kerry, Santiago, and Summer. There was the desk she and Mia had shared long ago. There was the bigger desk that Jennie had taught from. And there was the chalkboard. Two columns were written in a neat, unfamiliar hand, headed with THINGS THE KING PROVIDES and WHAT WE OWE TO THE KING.

Jennie's stomach crawled when she recognized her little brother Tonio's handwriting under the second list: *loyultee*.

Below that, Dee's writing: *gratiturd*. Jennie couldn't help grinning at that. Dee knew perfectly well how to spell "gratitude."

"Gratiturd," Summer exclaimed, cackling. "He does deserve gratiturds. All the other turds, too."

Jennie looked up at the ceiling. A hidden crawl space had been added at Mr. Preston's insistence, after Voske's first attack. She moistened her lips, spitting out dust, and gave the Ranger whistle. Once, twice.

A panel slid open overhead, and Pa's head appeared.

"Pa!" Jennie cried, delighted. "I'm so glad you made it here! Is everyone else here? We've got work to do!"

Pa smiled and a rope ladder descended. Down came a whole lot of Rileys, led by Pa, Ma, Aunt Flora, Uncle Joe, and Cousin Susie. They were followed by the Terrible Trio, then Mr. and Mrs. Tran, Alfonso, and Grandma Lowell. Three-year-old April spread her wings and fluttered down, just out of reach of her parents' grasping hands. Mia's aunt Olivia and her cousins Renata and Lorenzo were the last ones down.

Jennie quickly said, "Everyone who was in the jail with me is fine. They're…" Remembering Dr. Lee and Min Soo's warning, she concluded, "Doing other things."

Dee began jumping up and down. "Jennie! Jennie! You know what we did, Jennie? Me and Nhi and Z made an *effigy!* Of Voske! It's *disgusting!*"

Eagerly, Z added, "We left it right on the stage. He must have seen it by now!"

Nhi piped up, "I painted his horrible smile! And we threw blood all over him! Well, it was paint, but it looked like blood!"

"Yeah, he's *disemboweled*," Dee added proudly.

Z beamed. "We used socks. I sewed them myself."

"Great work." Summer clapped Dee on the back. "I *wish* I could've helped. I would've made it ten times grosser!"

Dee said indignantly, "You didn't see it! You don't know how gross it was."

Jennie put up a hand. "Wait. When did you do this?"

Dee spoke gleefully. "That teacher was making us practice a play for the next Opportunity Day, with Voske as the hero. Yesterday we swiped his costume and his silver wig, and we made an effigy of him!"

Nhi added, "We were having a sleepover at my house when they came around saying we had to stay inside. Then there was a big explosion, and all the soldiers ran off."

Z bounced on her toes. "Main Street was completely empty! So we took the effigy out of the attic and dumped it right on his throne on stage!"

Mr. and Mrs. Tran looked astonished and horrified. Mr. Tran said, "You did what?" Mrs. Tran scowled at all three girls. "I take my eyes off you for a *moment…*"

Z hastily said, "And then we ran back, and Mr. and Mrs. Tran said to come to our hiding place here."

Jennie was at a loss for words, imagining Voske confronted by an effigy of himself made by thirteen-year-olds. Forcing her mind back to the immediate goal, she said, "Never mind the effigy. All of us who can fight need to get to the back gate—"

The door slammed open, and Tommy Horst burst in, crimson-faced. He gasped, "Oh, good! You *are* here. Dr. Lee said you'd be, but..."

"I'm glad to see you. We need you—" Jennie began.

Tommy blurted out, "Voske's gone crazy. He's shooting his own people! He murdered Mrs. Hernandez!"

Everyone looked at him, then at each other. "What?" someone said. "Why?"

Mrs. Hernandez? Jennie's gaze shot to the teacher desk where Laura Hernandez had sat so briefly, when Jennie had first joined the Rangers. Then she looked at Laura's own desk where she'd scratched designs with her black cat claws. That was all that was left of that entire family.

Tommy stood looking bewildered as people bombarded him with questions.

Pa said, "Quiet, everybody."

And Jennie said, "Tommy, tell us what happened from the beginning."

Tommy rubbed his face with his hands. "After the jail blew up, Voske saw this scarecrow that had been dumped on the stage. It had a silver wig. He called it an effigy."

Jennie's nerves turned to ice. She hadn't taken the Terrible Trio's story seriously. But anything having to do with Voske would have serious consequences.

"He accused his own commander and shot her in the head," Tommy went on. "Then his solders dragged out Mrs. Hernandez and he shot her, too. For no reason. She was just *there*."

Everybody turned their eyes toward the Terrible Trio.

"We didn't want that," Dee said in a tiny voice. "We just wanted to...do something."

Tommy looked from the others to Dee. "*You* made the effigy?"

Z wiped the back of her hand across her eyes as Nhi said, "We all did."

All three girls turned their faces to Jennie. She had known these girls since they were born, and she could read their thoughts in their faces. Horror. Guilt. Regret. Fear. Dee's gaze pleaded with Jennie, as if to say, *Fix it,*

Jennie. You're my big sister.

A clamor of voices rose, most talking, no one listening.

"How could you be so irresponsible?" Olivia Lee demanded.

"Don't *ever* do anything like that again!" Mr. Tran was saying.

Mrs. Tran added fiercely, "We raised you better than that."

Jennie turned to Pa. He met her gaze and nodded, and she knew he was giving her the chance to handle this herself. Not as Dee's older sister, but as the teacher of all the children. And as the leader of the mission that all these people were about to undertake.

Jennie held up her hand. "Everybody, quiet. What's done is done. We can't change it by scolding the girls right now. They understand why it was wrong." She glanced at them, all three blinking back tears, and knew that they would bear this scar for the rest of their lives. "And I know they won't ever do anything like that again. But they were trying to strike a blow against Voske. Just like all of us."

"One more thing, Jennie," Tommy said. "Voske really is going crazy. After he shot those people, he suddenly acted like he was hearing voices. He had all the soldiers start feeling around for someone named Maria-Pilar. I ran off and Dr. Lee stopped me. He was hiding, too, after they dragged out Laura's mom!"

At the mention of Maria-Pilar, Jennie had the briefest impulse to smile. It was good to know that she was alive and stalking Voske — and that Voske was falling apart in front of his own soldiers.

"Mr. Preston has brought an army to the front gate," Jennie said. "And he's sent a team to the back gate. It's up to us to open the back gate and let them in."

Immediately, Summer said, "I'll scout."

"I can, too," Alfonso said. "I'll climb anywhere you like."

Pa spoke up. "We'll go together. How's that? You two can go high, and I'll scout from ground level."

Summer scowled, but before she could protest, Jennie said, "Great idea, Pa. You've got the best eyes in Las Anclas."

Summer subsided, as Jennie had hoped she would — Summer had ridden on patrol with Pa enough times to know that this was true.

"I brought weapons." Jennie laid her stash on the teacher's desk.

Tommy picked up a rifle. Aunt Flora went for a pair of single-sticks, and Pa took a rifle. Grandma Lowell and Ma stepped back. Everyone else looked at the weapons doubtfully. April's mother put her arm around her husband and said, "We practiced in Mr. Preston's drills, but neither of us have ever fought."

"Same for me," said Olivia Lee. "And honestly, I wasn't much good. Now, if you want your plumbing fixed, I'm your woman."

Trying not to let her dismay show, Jennie said, "But you all know how to load and shoot a rifle, right?"

She got several nods of varying levels of confidence. Olivia scrunched up her face and said, "Um…"

Jennie forced herself not to sigh. "Aunt Olivia, stay with Ma, Grandma Lowell, and April. The rest of you adults, take a rifle. Mr. and Mrs. Tran, can you stay and guard the schoolhouse?"

"We will," Mrs. Tran said. Her husband nodded.

Jennie turned to the Terrible Trio. Dee gave her a pleading look. "We have to help, Jennie. To make up for…I mean, nothing can ever make up for — what happened. But…"

"Please let us help." Nhi raised her hand as if she were in school. "My brother's been taking me target shooting. I'm good! I can hit a rock at twenty-five paces."

"Me, too," Z said, ranging herself alongside Nhi. "Well, not *twenty-five* paces. But I can hit a rock!"

"Me three!" Dee exclaimed. "Pa makes me strip and clean the rifles after every drill. And you know I've been practicing my dust devils. I can get them pretty big now. I could blow dust in those soldiers' faces and blind them."

The three girls stood so hopefully, shoulder to shoulder. The consequences had been dreadful, but they had made a plan, carried it out in enemy territory, and returned alive — so fast that not even the people in the same house had noticed. And if they wanted to help, Jennie thought it would be good for them to do so. She didn't want their memory of their effort in defense to end up being the inadvertent means of getting an innocent woman killed.

But they were still children. Killing a human being — even someone like Voske — was different from making an effigy. She'd do her best to give them something useful to do that wouldn't put them in the position of having to kill.

She gave them a solemn nod. "You three will back me up. Choose your weapons."

As everyone sorted through the weapons, Jennie moved to Pa's side. Quietly, she said, "I don't intend to use the kids except to scout or guard the perimeter."

"I know," Pa said. "They're proud of themselves. And you didn't take that away from them."

"But I wanted to," Jennie said fiercely. "Did you hear them talk about disemboweling? Voske's made life so cheap. I hate hearing children talking about killing so casually, let alone actually doing it." She took a deep breath. "*I* killed someone today. I was so furious, I enjoyed it. He laughed when Mia was dying." She still felt that anger, co-existing with more complicated feelings. "Afterward, I realized that even he must have someone waiting for him to come home. And he won't. Ever. But he was trying to kill me. And the others."

Pa cupped her face, his thumb brushing the blood-smear from one cheekbone. The quiet affection in his touch threw her back to her earliest memories, and her eyes stung.

Fighting had been a part of her life since she was younger than the Terrible Trio, and she and Indra had led classroom defense exercises. Later, they'd volunteered for Ranger training. She could see for herself how Mr. Preston felt about Changed people, and yet he kept giving her command of Ranger exercises. He didn't stop even when she lost, again and again. She sometimes wondered if he wanted her to quit, but then he'd speak of his own defeats in similar exercises, and crouch down, using pebbles in the dust to illustrate how he'd place his team to achieve the objective.

And it was she he'd sent to execute the vital mission to blow up Voske's ammo when he'd attacked Las Anclas the first time. It was then — when Sera Diaz did not come back—that she truly understood the difference between a mission and an exercise. In a mission, people might die. People *she'd* given orders to. The same realization had struck her again when she led the team to Gold Point to rescue Ross.

She looked up at Pa. "Why didn't you ever want to command? Is it the killing?"

He shook his head. "It made sense for me to be a scout, since my distance vision was the best in town. I had some training in command, until Tom Preston turned up. He was better than any of us, and I preferred scouting. Are your qualms about your ability to lead?"

"No. I know I have the skills. But that doesn't guarantee bringing everyone back safely."

Pa met her gaze. "It doesn't. Can you accept that?"

She *still* wasn't sure. And now she had the lives of three children in her hands. "I'll place those girls as far from danger as I can—"

"Of course you will," Pa interrupted gently. "Your tactical knowledge is excellent. You'll place them in the least danger. And yourself in the most."

"I'm the best fighter. I *should* put myself front and center, to defend this town."

"Exactly. And everyone who volunteers to follow you is also willing to put themselves in danger to defend this town. And not just to fight. They'll lead if they have to. Even Grandma Lowell would, if no one else stepped up."

Jennie smiled briefly at the image of feisty, white-haired Grandma Lowell leading a sneak attack. Then her smile faded. Grandma Lowell *would* do it. Even if she had no real chance of carrying out the mission.

"Noah Horst badly wanted to command," Pa went on. "And he did. But his plan got everyone he led killed."

"I wish I'd been there," Jennie said. "I'd have told him…"

Pa nodded. "You'd have given him a better plan. Noah might not have listened to you, of course. Even if he had, you know that the best plans seldom survive first contact with the enemy. We *can't* guarantee we'll all make it. But you're the best at command, and accepting responsibility is a part of that. That's what divides tyrants like Voske, who force obedience if they can't win loyalty, from commanders whom people choose to trust. It's better to be trusted, even if the cost to you is higher."

Jennie remembered the guard Kevin Vu doing nothing while Ross and Dr. Lee tried to heal Mia, when he ought to have sent a messenger to Voske. She thought of Santiago, and of Kerry. Even Luis, who had betrayed them not out of loyalty to the king, but because he'd been so damaged by Voske that he lashed out in desperation.

"I've tried so hard not to make choices I'd regret," Jennie said. "But that's not possible, is it?"

"Regret is a part of life. It's a part of command. The pain spurs you to try not to repeat mistakes. That's the cost of leadership."

"It's in the Ranger's oath. 'I will have the courage to hold myself and others accountable for our actions.'" She hugged her father hard, burying her face in his long dreadlocks. "I will, Pa."

Pa clapped her on the shoulder, then left with Summer and Alfonso. Jennie faced the others. "Those staying behind, get back in the attic. Everyone else, follow me."

Dee bounced, clutching her rifle. The others gave her tight nods, hands gripping weapons, shoulders tense. They were ready.

Someone had to pay the cost of leadership. She'd been trained to do it, and she was proud of her skills. Time to put it to the test.

"Let's go," Jennie said.

Her team slipped out, bending low over ready weapons, looking around alertly. The Terrible Trio ran last in a perfect single file.

As Ma pulled up the rope ladder, Jennie took a last look at the blackboard. She grabbed an eraser, and scrubbed out everything but WHAT WE OWE THE KING.

Below that, she printed: A SWORD IN THE HEART.

·56·

YUKI

LAS ANCLAS – OUTSIDE THE FRONT GATE

UNDER THE HOT DESERT sun, Yuki and Paco searched for more rocks for the two trebuchets the Saigon Alliance had loaned to Mr. Preston. The trebuchets had been brought in pieces but were now assembled and catapulting stones at the front gate.

Yuki had once defended Las Anclas from an army trying to break down that same gate. It felt bizarre to be part of an army trying to break *in*.

"How about this?" With a grunt of effort, Paco pulled up a stone half-buried in sand. Several centipedes scuttled away, and a toad splotched green and purple let out a tiny puff of flame.

Yuki pointed to the underside. "Too uneven. There's a jagged edge beneath."

Paco let the boulder fall with a thump, taking care not to drop it on the fire toad. When the trebuchet launched a lopsided rock, it spun crazily off to one side, missing the wall entirely.

"We've used all the good ones around here," Yuki said, wiping his hair back. "I wish Mr. Preston had been able to pry a battering ram out of the Saigon people."

"Can't pry what doesn't exist," Paco said.

"He couldn't just cut down an oak?" Yuki asked.

"They're not big or tall enough. A battering ram is a single piece of straight wood, the larger the better. It has to be banded with iron, so it doesn't splinter on impact. They're offensive weapons. Saigon doesn't conquer towns, so it doesn't need them."

Yuki gave him a covert glance. That little speech could have come straight out of Mr. Preston's mouth—and probably had. Paco hadn't been that much of a soldier when Yuki had last seen him. He'd altered from the carefree drummer Yuki had first fallen in love with. But this much?

I never should have left him, he thought bleakly.

They began searching a gully. Yuki wanted to say something, anything, that wasn't about war, but he found it impossible to think about anything else. Maybe it had been like that for Paco, too.

"Here's one," Paco exclaimed. The boulder had been smoothed by water, and was round enough that the two of them, could roll it up the lip of the gully.

They worked together to push the boulder out of sand. With their shoulders and arms touching, Yuki could feel the heat of Paco's skin and breathe in the scent of his sweat. He longed to be this close to Paco forever, doing something, anything other than fighting a war.

The boulder flipped over, and something beneath it let out a piercing shriek. Yumiya plummeted from the sky, scooped up the creature, and flew away with it before Yuki even got a good look at it. All he could tell was that it was bright yellow and had either multiple tails or tentacles. Kunai and Shuriken hissed happily over head as their mother hovered so they could eat it.

Paco squinted upward. Yuki expected him to say something—about the weird creature, about the cloud vipers, about how every rock concealed some colony of insects or reptiles—but he only said, "Yeah, this should do some damage."

They rolled it to the rear of the attack force. Indra ran up and lent a hand. Mr. Preston remarked, "Good. We needed more ammunition."

In the glaring light of noon, the orange flash from the sharpshooters along the sentry walk looked weak. Bullets kicked up the sand well short of the team maneuvering the boulder into the sling. Other than a few gouges, it seemed that the trebuchets had done little damage.

Mr. Preston wiped his glasses and squinted at the gates. "A little to the right. A little more. Go!"

The enemy soldiers along the sentry walk ducked as

the trebuchet team released the mighty spring. The trebuchet snapped forward, hurling the boulder high into the air. It arced up, spinning, then down at an angle. The boulder thumped against the top of the wall, then fell to the ground. Once again, it had missed the gate. From behind the wall, the soldiers laughed and yelled insults.

But as soon as the trebuchet team had touched the lever, Mr. Preston had beckoned the sharpshooters to come closer. Now he said calmly, "Fire."

Just as the enemies' heads popped up again, the line of sharpshooters fired, then ran back. The soldiers ducked — one not fast enough. There was a yelp, and a space appeared in the line of snipers. The others returned fire. Dirt kicked up the sand in front of their force.

The trebuchets would take days to break down the front gate, if they could at all. There had been no sign of the amphibious team that was supposed to attack the gate from the inside, and Yuki wondered bleakly if Voske had caught and killed them.

Paco gazed at the wall, a muscle in his jaw jumping. "Mr. Preston, I'm close enough to teleport inside."

Yuki's heart tried to slam its way out of his chest. He'd seen what Paco looked like after teleporting out of Las Anclas. And to teleport in, when everyone would recognize him, and he would be shot on sight?

"No, Paco," said Mr. Preston. "Let's wait on our friends elsewhere. In the meantime, why don't we entertain our unwanted visitors, the same way they entertained us last year?" He turned. "Leapfrog formation!"

Yuki was glad not to be on boulder duty anymore. He and Paco ran for their rifles and took their place in the first line. On the signal, the front line each targeted one figure on the wall and shot. Then they sidestepped, and the second row stepped past and shot. By the time they had reloaded, the other line shot, keeping up a steady fire. It used a lot of ammunition, but for a short time they cleared the wall.

Yuki remembered being on the wall with Meredith, and how many defenders had been shot or wounded early in Voske's attack. Unlike Mr. Preston's army, Gold Point had enough weapons and ammunition to keep it up indefinitely.

"Fire!"

Paco moved fast and fluidly as he'd once drummed, firing, reloading, taking a step, and firing again, a lethal rhythm. Yuki matched his movements to Paco's. Whatever had happened, whatever would happen, at least they were together again.

"Fire!"

·57·

MIA

LAS ANCLAS - MIA'S COTTAGE

ROSS SUPPORTED MIA AS they staggered through the pocket gardens. She wished Dad had used more of his power on her. At least another month. Not that she wanted to lose another month off her life. But it had been so interesting to experience his power, which she'd often watched him use but never felt herself. It had been like a thousand breaths taken at once.

"Lean on me," Ross said.

His warm, strong arm was all the support Mia needed as they hurried into her yard. She tripped over a piece of rusted iron and nearly fell into a broken turbine. Ross kept her upright at the price of his cuts and bruises—she felt him clench his jaw.

"Are you okay?" He sounded worried.

"*I'm* fine. I'm just not used to seeing in two dimensions."

Everything in the yard was exactly where she'd left it, even the mattress under the sheet of metal. She wished she hadn't left it out. It had mildewed in the winter rains.

The crack of rifle fire echoed as they scrambled inside. Her cottage looked undisturbed, but a slower sweep revealed tools out of order, and all her cutting blades pilfered. She lunged for the concealed panel in the floor and came up triumphantly with the book Ross had first brought to Las Anclas. "Voske probably knew you sold it to the town. But I bet he thought Mr. Preston kept it, rather than handing it right back to me."

"Yes." Ross was as tense as he'd been when he first

came to Las Anclas. She'd have to move slowly around him, or he'd panic and bolt…

No. He wasn't *afraid*. He was worried. About her. "I'm okay. I can work."

"First drink this," Ross said, pumping a glass of water.

She drank it down—and then another one. When her insides sloshed, she said, "I'm really okay. Ross. You remember that skunk gun I took with us was a prototype."

"I remember," he said absently, fishing around in one of her tool kits. "Ah! Right where you put it. Eat this, Mia."

Mia had forgotten that she'd stashed extra jerky there before they took off. It was still perfectly good. Dad's jerky was always delicious. It was hard to do anything too weird to jerky.

She sank down onto the bed between the two engines, her mouth full of jerky. She got a pair of pliers, straightened the lens frame for her new eye, and knocked out the remaining bits of glass. "I didn't tell you what the skunk gun was a prototype of. I'd wanted it to be, well, it's based on a drawing in your book of an oil spray cannon. I was going to mount it on the walls by the front gate and power it with electricity."

Ross looked deeply alarmed. "I remember that drawing."

"I won't light the oil on fire, like in the book. It'll just be slippery, so enemies can't keep their balance or hold their weapons. With salt added, so it burns their eyes. And it stinks, which is distracting. But it can't kill anyone."

She polished the remaining lens and put her glasses back on. "This oil cannon will shoot a fine spray with much more force than the skunk gun. Spread spectrum. It'll clog guns so they won't fire. Directed, so it won't clog *our* guns."

"But how heavy is this cannon? Will I be able to handle it on my own?" He held up his hand in its gauntlet.

"No, but you won't have to," she assured him. "I'll be there, too."

"You can't even stand up by yourself."

"Dad said I just needed some rest." Mia hoped Ross wouldn't remember that the amount Dad had suggested was one month. Two. "I'll be fine by the time it's ready."

Ross looked deeply dubious, and Mia stuffed more jerky into her mouth. "See? I'm already feeling better."

He eyed her, then glanced at the door. "How long will it take to put that together?"

"If I stuck to the original design, maybe a week. But that was mostly the electrical engine! Obviously, we can't use that *now*. But! I have a hand pump around here somewhere. Under the bed?"

The worry crease in his forehead cleared. "I know where it is." He lifted up a sheet of corrugated tin that leaned behind the bed and took out the hand pump.

Mia smiled up at him. "You remember everything in here."

He had such an odd look at that, part wistful, part...

"What?" she asked.

"I was remembering us, here, when you gave me the multiple-arrow crossbow."

"The night of the dance," Mia said—and abruptly recalled that pink ruffled dress that had turned transparent in the rain.

The door banged open. Mia flung her hands over her breasts. Ross slammed the intruder up against the wall with a forearm against her throat and a hand over her mouth.

Then Mia remembered that the dress had long since been handed off to a cousin. And Ross stared, dropped his arms, and said incredulously, "Felicité?" Then, "Are you being followed?"

"No." Felicité primly brushed paint chips out of her hair.

Mia echoed Ross. "Felicité? That's really you?"

No amount of bronze scales could disguise that utterly Felicité expression. Then it shifted to shock. "Mia? What happened to *you*? Is that *blood*?"

For the first time in her life, Mia wished she had an actual mirror. She pulled up the sheet metal and examined the blurry image, noting then dismissing the blood-stiffened spikes of her hair and her gore-splattered overalls. The interesting part was the glittering ruby in her eye socket, with the fine line of tiny crystals above and below, all the way from her forehead to her jawline. Like a slash. It *was* from a slash.

Felicité grabbed Mia's arm. "What happened to the others in the jail? You're the only ones I saw. Are they…?"

"They're fine," Mia said quickly. "I brought down the jail on purpose. Everyone else went…where they were supposed to go."

Ross found his voice again. "Where did *you* come from?"

"I came to rescue Becky," Felicité said. "But all I saw was you two."

Despite the very Felicité way that Felicité said "you two," Mia suddenly almost liked her. She had returned to a city under siege, without any weapons that Mia could see, because Becky was her friend, or had used to be her friend. "Becky's fine. She's with Sheriff Crow."

Felicité looked immensely relieved. And also unsurprised to learn that Sheriff Crow was there. "Good. However, did you get explosives into the jail?"

"I didn't. Princess Bridget rotted the jail supports with her Change power. Ross and I showed her where to rot."

Ross nudged her. "Mia, the oil cannon."

She got back to work. It went twice as fast because Ross fetched what she needed, sometimes before she asked for it. But as her hands assembled the cannon, her mind skipped back through everything that had happened. She had to stop herself from saying stuff like, "So, you're Changed. How long have you been lying to us about that? Were you Changed when you called Ross a mutant?"

Felicité's head turned sharply, and Mia clapped her hand over her mouth, almost banging herself in the nose with a wrench. Had that last question actually come out?

Ross bent over the engine until his nose was practically pressed against the metal.

Stiffly, Felicité said, "Yes, I was. I can't tell you how much I regret it. Ross, I apologize —"

Ross muttered, "It's fine, it's fine."

"It isn't fine, actually. I don't know if I can ever make amends. I mean to try."

At that, Ross glanced up. Mia suspected that it was the first time those two had ever looked each other in the eyes. "Okay."

Felicité broke the silence first. In her old, sprightly

scribe voice, she asked, "What are you building? Can I help?"

"It's an oil cannon. I'm hooking the oil barrels to the hand pump because we can't use electricity when it's mobile." As she looked at the cannon, which was hooked up to heavy barrels of oil, she turned to Ross. "And I just realized…"

Ross nodded. "I saw it, too. I'll have to cover us while you shoot it. That leaves…"

They turned to Felicité. Mia said, "…you to handle the pump. If you're willing."

Felicité looked from Ross to Mia to the wheeled barrels and gave an audible sniff. Mia had forgotten how smelly the oil was. She was already trying to think of someone else who could handle the pump when Felicité said, "Just tell me what to do."

After a short, intensely busy interval, Mia told herself that time was not actually repeating itself. True, she was in a battle and running as fast as she could while lugging an incredibly heavy weapon, with Ross protecting her. But she was in overalls, not a party dress. Also, she wasn't lugging it all by herself. She had help. She had…Felicité.

She had something else, too. She'd figured out how to walk without tripping. Everything looked distractingly flat, and it made her lose her balance when she looked down. So, she determinedly didn't look down, reminding herself that she could walk just fine without staring at the ground. That worked much better. As for gauging distances, which she'd need to do to know what was within range, she knew Las Anclas well enough to do it from memory rather than calculating them on the spot. They might not be exact, but they'd be close.

Ross guarded them as they sneaked from Primrose Lane toward Saguaro. There were no enemies in sight, or allies either.

"This reeks," Felicité muttered as she pushed the oil

cannon. "Why does it smell like old fish?"

"Because the fuel is the used oil we collect from people's houses, after they fry fish in it," Mia explained.

"Ugh!" Felicité exclaimed.

"It's an efficient use of resources," Mia pointed out.

"That's true," Felicité admitted.

The old Felicité would never have conceded the point. But the old Felicité wouldn't have gone around with her bronze scales shining for everybody to see. Mia wondered how she had managed to hide her Change for so long, when it must have happened when she'd hit puberty. Mia remembered it because Felicité had developed a figure, and Mia hadn't. Felicité had been so proud of her new curves, she'd started dressing extra fancy, with those enormous hats…

"Oh!" Mia exclaimed, getting that zing that happened when she realized a new way to make an engine work. "You wore those giant hats to hide your face in case you Changed, right?"

Felicité glanced at her over the cannon. It was strange to see her eyes shining within that bronze mask of scales, and it was even stranger to see their expression. Mia couldn't figure out what it was, but it wasn't proud or sneering or haughty. "Yes. And so everyone would believe I was obsessed with keeping my hair nice, and they wouldn't think anything of it when I ran away from rain. That's what triggered my Change before: water."

"Oh. How clever." Then Mia thought about it. "And sad. You know, if you'd told me, I wouldn't have cared."

"But I would have," Felicité said.

"Eyes sharp," Ross said softly. "We're coming into the open."

"Head for our garden," Mia whispered. "We can hide behind the greenhouse."

They pushed the oil cannon across the alley between the adobe buildings and the pocket gardens behind the Main Street stores. Ross ran ahead, then returned. "No-one's in the space between the saddler and the cobbler. We have to be ready when we come out on Main Street."

"Ready," Mia said, with the hose tucked firmly under her arm. She turned to Felicité. "Can you take the whole weight?"

"As long as the wheels don't get stuck," said Felicité.

Nothing impeded the wheels as Mia counted off the steps under her breath. The clash and roar of fighting got louder. Then there was a loud thud.

"What was that?" Mia said.

"A Change power?" Ross hazarded.

"I know," Felicité said, totally unexpectedly. "My father got two trebuchets from the Saigon Alliance."

Mia gasped. "Trebuchets! I'd love to see those—"

She was interrupted by another loud thud. They emerged onto Main Street and raced toward the wall. Mia counted under her breath. She was up to thirty-nine when a lot of black-clad figures turned smartly and headed their way, the leader shouting, "Halt! Raise your hands!"

When the soldiers passed the lightning-struck oak tree, Mia knew they had to be within range. She jerked up the hose and braced her feet. "Now!"

Felicité began pumping. With a glutinous burble, the oil surged up into the hose, stiffening it. Out came a fine spray, glistening in the sun. Mia coughed at the stench, eyes watering—then the oil hit the soldiers.

"Fire!" the leader yelled, then started gagging.

Mia ducked her head and kept spraying. She heard triggers clicking, followed by curses and yells. Some soldiers dropped their weapons to wipe at their faces. Others banged the rifle butts on the ground, then leveled them again. But no weapons fired. The oil cannon worked, and so did her distance memory!

Ross had darted off the moment Mia's oil drenched the soldiers. He kicked weapons away, dodging between enemies. His knives flickered as he cut gunpowder horns and ammo belts, then stomped them, spilling the dry gunpowder on the oil-slick ground.

Mia and Felicité passed by, trundling on. Ross caught up with them and called, "Mia, to the right!"

Felicité pumped furiously as Mia aimed to the right and caught a pair of soldiers running at them. One skidded in the oil and fell hard. The other stumbled to a halt, scrubbing at her eyes. Mia pushed past them, and Ross continued to call out obstacles. Mia aimed, shot, and ran, periodically checking the gauge on the oil barrel. She hoped they wouldn't run out of oil before they got to the gate.

"That's really just cooking oil?" Felicité asked.

"I added some salt to it," Mia said proudly. "For extra sting. Skunk oil for stench. And—"

"How are we on ammo?" Ross asked. "Wall ahead."

Mia risked a glance. Up on the wall, where she had spent so much time working on the gate, enemy sentries were firing down at the other side of the wall, presumably at Mr. Preston and his army. She wondered who else was with him. The rest of the Rangers? Paco?

"We're almost in range," Ross said. "To the left!"

Soldiers rounded the stable. Mia sprayed them from top to toe, then turned to the wall. "Felicité, pump as hard as you can."

"I'll help." Ross sprang to Felicité's side.

Mia's hose stiffened, almost yanking free of her hands. She gritted her teeth, braced it against her body, and sprayed the soldiers atop the wall, right up to the edge of the gate. A series of satisfying yells and shouts and clicks resulted.

"Right!" Felicité shrieked. Ross yelled, "Left!"

Mia whirled to the left, aiming blindly—and caught a soldier square in the face as she raised a sword. Ross knocked the sword aside and kicked the side of her knee. She fell hard.

Mia turned to the right, but whoever Felicité had seen had retreated. She kept pumping, and Mia kept shooting—she looked at the gauge—still a third of a barrel—

CRACK!

The hose flew out of Mia's arms. The entire oil cannon had split in half as if sliced by a giant scalpel. Oil poured out onto the ground. She staggered back, looking around wildly. A soldier faced them, his bare palm out.

"Duck," Ross snapped.

Mia crouched down, arm over her head, as one of his knives arced through the air. Someone yelped, while someone else shouted, "I got it!"

Ross grabbed her hand and hauled her away. She ran so fast her breath burned in her lungs. They fetched up on the other side of the stable, gasping. She looked around wildly—no soldiers—and saw that only Ross had come with her.

"Where's Felicité?"

·58·
FELICITÉ

LAS ANCLAS – MAIN STREET

FELICITÉ STAGGERED BACK FROM the oil cannon an instant before it exploded.

Oil sprayed everywhere. Mia and Ross bolted. Felicité ran the other way, desperately looking for a hiding place. She spotted an elegant coach backed off Main Street. After a quick glance to make sure no one was looking her way, she jumped in.

Shock nearly flung her right out again when she saw someone else inside. A woman in a maid's uniform – *"Mother?"*

"Felicité!" Mother held out her arms.

Felicité threw herself into Mother's embrace. Laughing and crying, she said, "Sorry about the smell."

Mother gave a shaky laugh. "What is it?"

"Mia's fish oil cannon. It exploded. I was helping — oh, never mind. I'm so glad Father's team rescued you!"

"Ah," Mother said. "So, he did send a team. I hope they survived. No, I never saw them. Min Soo rescued me just before dawn. Some of the guards are loyal to her, and they turned a blind eye when I slipped out in these maid's clothes. We put pillows under the blankets. Hopefully, Voske has been too distracted to notice that we're gone."

It was so much to take in. Mother was alive and free. Min Soo was an ally. "We? Did she rescue Grandmère and Will, too?"

"Yes. Your grandmother is roaming about setting fires. Min Soo sent Will to safety in the custody of a trusted servant."

Felicité sat back with a sigh. Now that she knew her family was alive, she could take in that for the first time, Mother was seeing her new form. Felicité raised her face, determined not to flinch or hide.

Mother touched the mask of bronze scales around her eyes. The gesture was as maternal and tender as her hug. "Felicité, I have something to tell you. As of this morning, I too am Changed. I asked Min Soo to use her power on me, in the hope that I could help defend this town."

Felicité couldn't believe it. Her mother had deliberately Changed herself? Absurdly, she said, "But you look the same."

"Keep watching me," Mother said.

Mother's lips didn't move, but her voice sounded directly in Felicité's ear. *"Your scales are beautiful. Everything about you is beautiful. You're my brave and lovely daughter, and I couldn't be more proud of you."*

Felicité almost jumped out of her skin at the first word, then settled down to listen once she realized what was happening. It was as if Mother was speaking from right behind her. "So that's your Change," she said. "You can throw your voice."

"There's a little more to it than that," Mother said. "As you will see, I hope. But yes. That is my power."

There was so much Felicité felt, so much she wanted to say and so much that she probably shouldn't say. She couldn't believe how courageous Mother was, to voluntarily subject herself to Min Soo's terrifying power. She loved her so much for doing it, and for loving Felicité no matter what. She wondered if Mother thought Father would never love her again, and if she believed she'd destroyed her marriage just to get a useless Change.

"You're so brave." And though it felt strange to say it to her own mother, Felicité said, "I'm proud of you, too."

"Thank you, my dear." Mother tapped a carved rose on the carriage wall. "Put your eye here."

Intensely curious, Felicité did so. The rose had a spy hole, completely hidden by the carved petals. She could see the area between the stable wall and the bit of Main Street directly before the gates. No one was in sight.

"Now we wait," said Mother.

"For what? You found the perfect hiding place. Safe,

comfortable, beautiful. I don't suppose there's any food?"

"I haven't looked."

There were little cabinets beneath the plush seats. Felicité began opening the drawers. Most were empty, but one held a fan. The painted silk depicted people in hanboks sitting beside a pool, feeding colorful fish. Even the handle had a lovely little carving of a fish leaping out of water. She stroked it. The fan emitted a quiet "snick," and barbs snapped out of the fan's ribs. Felicité jumped.

"Be careful," her mother cautioned. "I think this coach is weaponized."

"I expect it's Min Soo's. Stylish and full of surprises. Like her."

"It is." Mother touched Felicité's hair. "Your Change really is beautiful, my darling."

Felicité's shoulders tightened. "Do I hear a 'but'?"

"You do," Mother said calmly. "It has nothing to do with you, but with my own regrets. How long did you live with this, believing you had to keep it hidden?"

Remorse chilled Felicité. She'd never dared to risk telling Mother about her Change. "Since I was thirteen. The scales only became permanent after I fled Las Anclas. Before, they came out when my skin got wet."

"Ah. That's why you broke the tub and the mirror."

That awful night seemed a hundred years ago, but the guilt and regret remained. Felicité wasn't going to create even more regrets by continuing to keep secrets out of shame. "That's why I showed Henry the tunnel. I was sweating and my scales were coming out. All I could think of was making sure no one knew about my awful secret. And the worst of it is, Henry was hiding his own Change, for the same reason."

"Yes. These prejudices and fears have troubled the town for years." Mother glanced through the spyhole again. "And I allowed them to fester, in the council and in my own home."

"I don't think Father is so prejudiced now," said Felicité. "I was terrified that he'd take one look and reject me. But he didn't. It wasn't easy for him to see me. My scales. My eyes. My fluke, when I was in the water. But he loves me, and he's proud of me. The Changed me. The real me."

Mother's smile was soft. "I'm glad to hear that. How is he?"

"It really hurt him to lose those Rangers. But he's determined to get the town back. He brought an army."

"As I expected," Mother said. "You're grown up enough for this conversation. I've always cautioned you to be aware of the difference between physical attraction and a relationship of mind and heart. Your father and I had all three. But the danger of such a precious relationship is that you fear losing it. I was afraid that taking a stand on the matter of the Changed might end in me telling your father that he had to choose between me and his prejudices."

Mother must not have known which Father would choose. Felicité had been certain she did know — and she'd thought it wouldn't be her.

Mother spoke more to herself than to Felicité. "Tom has always had his exceptions. He respected Dr. Lee. Jennie Riley was his protégé. You are his daughter. But he needs to go beyond exceptions. When we meet again — and I believe that we will — I will ask him to choose."

Mother glanced through the spy hole, then said, "Ah. I thought he'd head this way." She beckoned to Felicité to look through another spy hole in a rose near her.

The area before the main gate had filled with black-clad soldiers. Voske stood in their midst, silver hair glinting. As Father had said, Voske always surrounded himself by guards so no one could get a clear shot at him. But as the guards moved about, Felicité could see flashes of him.

"Team D, fall back," Voske shouted. "Replace the ruined rifles and wash that oil out of your eyes. Team A, get to the wall. Team Leader Santos, can your power extend far enough to split their trebuchets?"

Felicité almost fell off the bench when a ghostly whisper sounded behind her ear. *"Can you trust his answer? You know that Changed people can always underplay their powers. Or lie about them, like Paco."*

Felicité knew it was Mother, but she shivered. The voice didn't sound like Mother, or like any living woman. It was clear and distinct, but had an unearthly, whispery quality. And the moment she'd begun speaking, Voske had given a visible start. "Is *he* hearing it, too?"

"Yes."

So *that* was what Mother had meant when she'd said there was more to her power!

Voske shouted, "Answer me, Santos!"

"Um…" Santos looked nervous. "As I said, sir, no. I can't reach that far."

Voske gave him such a murderous glare that Felicité ducked back, then looked again.

The eerie whisper sounded in her ear. It was *exactly* like a ghost stood right behind her. *"Ross fooled you. Kerry, too. A tyrant can force superficial obedience, but never trust."*

Voske whipped around, shockingly fast. He stared at the soldiers behind him, then spun back round. "Santos, up on the wall! I want to see you destroy that trebuchet."

A soldier said, "Sir. The trebuchet can't do any real damage. It's too small."

Voske turned his glare on that soldier. "Are you questioning my judgment?"

The soldiers stiffened. In unison, they exclaimed, "No sir!"

"Then do what I say. Santos, get up there. Ming, cover up that oil spill!"

As the two soldiers ran off, the ghostly whisper again sounded in Felicité's ear. *"No one trusts you. Ever since you murdered your own brother, they realized you could turn on them, too. So, they turn on you first. Tom Preston. Sera Diaz. Omar Anders. The three you trusted most lost their trust in you. Now this generation is doing the same —"*

"Shut up!" Voske shouted.

The guards around him froze. Furtive gazes flickered his way, then away. He stared out into the distance, his mouth pressed in a thin white line.

"Deirdre died trying to prove herself to you. Sean ran away from you. He was the first to abandon the Voske name, but not the last. Paco Diaz hates you. There is no Liam Voske. Kerry Ji Sun Cho is trying to kill you. She'll never again be Kerry Voske. You're losing all your children, one by one. Who will be —"

"Come! This way!" Voske shouted. He ran off with the soldiers grouped tightly around him.

Felicité gazed at her mother in admiration. "You're going to drive him mad."

Mother patted her shoulder. "That's the plan."

·59·
BECKY

LAS ANCLAS – DAIRY BARN

BECKY TOUCHED HER DART gun as she ran with the sheriff. She'd kept the rifle, but she was still a sheriff's apprentice. Someday this would all be over, and the dart gun would be the only weapon she'd ever use again.

If only Brisa was safe…

"Go," said Sheriff Crow. "I'll keep guard."

Becky eased inside, whispering, "Brisa?"

"Becky?" Brisa whispered back from the loft.

Becky threw herself at the ladder, swarming up faster than she ever had in training. Brisa emerged from a pile of hay. They tumbled into a heap together, hay flying as they clutched each other, kissing desperately. Becky was laughing and crying. Brisa's kisses were sweet but tasted like tears.

"You're alive, you're really alive," Brisa whispered between kisses, then coughed and pulled a piece of hay out of her mouth. "I came here as soon as I heard you'd been arrested, as we promised, so I have no idea what's been going on. I brought a bunch of rocks, in case they searched. I was going to throw them until I ran out of ammo."

"Oh, Brisa." Becky's heart squeezed at the thought of her sweet Brisa lying there alone, preparing to make her last stand.

"How'd you get out of jail?" Brisa asked.

"Mia and Princess Bridget made it collapse." Becky remembered guiltily how she'd mistrusted Brisa's instincts and kept so much from her. "Min Soo helped.

You were right about her, Brisa."

"I'm glad. She was so kind to me! I couldn't make myself hate her." Brisa kissed Becky again, then wrinkled her nose. "Not like Voske. I have no trouble hating *him*. Were you really in a resistance? Why didn't you tell me? I'd have helped!"

"I couldn't. It would've put you in danger."

"Voske was going to kill me anyway, if *you* got caught," Brisa pointed out. "I assumed he tried."

A flush scorched Becky's cheeks. "Um. I was also worried that you're not, well, the best at keeping secrets."

Brisa looked hurt. "Maybe for little things, but not for important ones! I kept *your* secrets, didn't I?"

"You did. I'm sorry, Brisa." Becky's throat clogged with tears. "I was too scared to tell you. To burden you. But I should have."

"I wish you had. I'd rather have been in the jail with you than here alone. But it's okay, Beck. I'm not mad. You're here now, and that's what's important." Brisa held Becky close, letting her breathe in the hay-sweet scent of her skin, then straightened. "Can I help now? I want to help!"

"You can." Relief washed through Becky. She and Brisa were good again. Whatever else happened, she'd have Brisa by her side. "Sheriff Crow is back—"

"She is? That's so exciting! Does she need us?"

"Yes. We're going to attack the armory."

"Ooh! I'll get my rocks." Brisa staggered to the ladder under the weight of a backpack crammed with fist-sized rocks, puffing with effort and refusing Becky's offer to take some. Becky was very relieved when Brisa and her rocks made it down.

Sheriff Crow glanced at the backpack, and the side of her face that could smile did. "Brisa! Excellent idea." To Brisa, she said, "Dr. Lee healed Rivka Lowenstein. She and some others are waiting in the orchard. We'll meet up, then attack the armory."

She led the way toward the orchard. The trees, planted at intervals for better harvesting, had big gaps between them. Becky felt horribly exposed, as if enemy eyes crawled over her back. She kept her gaze on the Sheriff. As long as she was calm, Becky would be—

A voice shouted, "Halt!"

Sheriff Crow whipped up her sword as black-clad figures emerged from the trees. Becky planted her feet, brought her dart gun up, supporting it with the other hand, and shot, targeting mid-body. One. Two. Three soldiers keeled over, unconscious, but the rest charged. Sheriff Crow whirled to the attack, so fast that she blurred.

Brisa was struggling to get her heavy backpack off. Becky slapped more darts into her gun, her fingers trembling, and stepped in front of Brisa. She shot again — missed — and the soldier dropped with an arrow in his back. Ms. Lowenstein ran up, shooting as she went, with Meredith right behind her. Other citizens of Las Anclas were running behind them to join the battle.

"Got it," Brisa muttered as her backpack dropped to the ground, leaving a dent in the earth. She snatched up a rock and hurled it into the midst of the enemies. It exploded in a puff of flame, sending fragments in all directions. Soldiers reeled away, blood splashing from tattered uniforms. Some fell, and others dropped their weapons. The rest backed out of range. Becky warmed with pride. Her girlfriend was formidable!

Jack Lowell panted up. "Give me the pack, Brisa. I'll hand you rocks."

He looked past her to Sheriff Crow, his sudden smile like a dawn sky. Becky couldn't remember ever seeing an adult smile like that. Sheriff Crow stepped up to him, one hand running up his arm to cup his face.

"Aw, they're so sweet," Brisa murmured.

"Attack!" shouted the enemy captain. The soldiers charged.

Brisa hurled another rock. Becky stood beside her, keeping a steady rate of fire. She had no attention to spare for any battle but her own, but she knew her friends were fighting hard. Abruptly, a soldier gave a sharp whistle. In disciplined order, the soldiers turned and retreated. It happened so fast that Becky could barely believe it was real.

Brisa broke the silence with a yell. "We won! Yay!"

Ms. Lowenstein shook her head. "They're getting reinforcements."

Mr. Preciado, Brisa's father, ran up and hugged her.

"The family's safe. Your mother has Nita."

"Come on," the sheriff said, her hand reaching for Jack's. "Let's take the armory."

They ran to the jumble of sheds and storage areas behind Voske's armory, which used to be Weavers' Row. It was infuriating and upsetting to see the building where Aunt Rosa had once worked with her friends, now desecrated. But a fierce joy rose in Becky at the thought of taking it back.

Sheriff Crow gathered everyone into a tight circle. "There're at least twenty soldiers on guard, all with rifles and swords. And we have…" She looked around. Two rifles. A dart gun. Three bows. An axe. Three knives."

"I have rocks." Brisa patted her sack.

Sheriff Crow smiled. "And rocks."

Yolanda and Jose dashed up. Becky was startled to see that Bridget was with them. Yolanda clapped Bridget on the shoulder, announcing proudly, "She's with us!"

Bridget was beaming. "I was going to help Dr. Lee at the infirmary, but soldiers came and searched it. Dr. Lee and I had to run and hide. I ran into Yolanda, and she thought I'd be more useful here!"

"And we found *them*," Yolanda said. Three strangers joined the circle. One had tentacles, one had streamlined fins, and one had green skin *and* tentacles.

"Galen," Sheriff Crow greeted the one with the green skin. "Report?"

He gave a frustrated shake of his head, sending little dripping tentacles flying. "We couldn't get into Wolfe House. Too many guards. And we couldn't even get near the front gate. Too many soldiers."

But Sheriff Crow looked pleased, the normal side of her face smiling and the yellow snake eye in the skull side narrowing. "Now we have a force that can take them on." To Galen's amphibious team, she said, "Bridget can decay matter. She made the jail collapse." And to Bridget, "We need just one wall of the armory to come down. If you bring down the entire building, the weapons will be buried."

Bridget said, a little nervously, "Even one wall takes a while. But Mia taught me what parts to decay."

"I can speed things along by making a quake under

the walls, once you rot the joints," Jose offered. Bridget gave him a delighted clap on the back.

"Excellent," said the sheriff. "Some of us will cover you, and the rest will decoy the guards."

"I can shock them." One of the amphibious people held up a hand ridged with delicate fins.

"If I shift my upper body toward my octopus, I can squirt ink in their eyes," said Galen.

The tall woman with wet, orange tentacles instead of hair said in mild apology, "My Change is just breathing underwater. I'll use my crossbow."

"I'll take the decoy group," Ms. Lowenstein said. "Brisa, come with me. Nothing like a shower of exploding rocks for a diversion."

Jack Lowell gave a smile with no humor in it. "I'm worthless as a fighter, but I can pass rocks to Brisa."

Sheriff Crow took him by the shoulders. "You're not worthless, Jack. As a fighter. Or as a man."

Jack and the sheriff gazed into each other's eyes.

"Er, it really would be helpful if you could pass me rocks, though," Brisa said.

Jack laughed, this time with genuine warmth, and went to her. Becky was torn between wanting to fight by her side and wanting to back up Sheriff Crow. Before she could ask where she was more needed, Jose said, "Ready when you are."

"Just let me get started on rotting that wall," said Bridget. Becky smiled at the princess, proud of her. Bridget smiled back, a little tremulously.

The stationary guards and the roaming patrol froze at the first explosion. The next came an instant later. A woman shouted orders as the guards raised their rifles. Someone yelled, "My eyes! What *is* that?"

The commander shouted, "Take cover!"

Two soldiers fell, pierced by arrows. The others retreated behind wagons and barrels and returned fire from there. The enemy was focused on the far side of the building, where dust and gun smoke rose—leaving the closer side unguarded.

"Now," whispered Sheriff Crow.

They dashed to the unguarded side. Bridget stood motionless for an instant, and Becky had the panicked thought that she'd lost her nerve. Then she darted close to the wall and pointed to one spot after another on the wooden support. Where Bridget pointed, the wood began to blacken, as if ink bled into it. Wood splinters began to crumble. Wood creaked. Then a louder creak.

Bridget hissed, "Jose!"

Jose whispered, "Brace yourselves."

Becky had already taken up her proper stance for shooting, feet apart, weight distributed evenly, center of gravity low. She loosened her knees—and the ground rippled under her feet. She swayed, almost falling. Someone behind her yelped as they toppled. The wall collapsed with an ear-splitting crash. The rest of the building was completely intact. Through a haze of dust, Becky could see into it as if it was a dollhouse.

"Other side!" yelled the enemy commander. "Go, go!"

Sheriff Crow and Becky guarded the townspeople jumping over the chunks of wall and rushing into the armory. They emerged staggering under piles of weapons up to their chins.

"Don't forget ammo!" Sheriff Crow shouted as she shot twice in rapid succession.

Becky spotted soldiers moving from wagon to barrel, the small round holes of their rifles like wicked eyes pointing right at her. She suppressed the instinct to shoot at those eyes, holding her fire until a soldier charged. Then Becky gripped her dart gun in both hands and shot.

The woman tumbled to the ground, her rifle clattering.

The ground rippled again as Jose sent another quake toward a fresh set of soldiers. Yolanda raised her hands. Dust and grit rose up at the feet of the charging soldiers, blowing straight into their eyes.

"Hold them off," Sheriff Crow ordered Becky, Yolanda, and Jose.

She darted into the armory and emerged almost instantly, carrying more weapons than all three townspeople had brought out. She sped off into the trees, emerged empty-handed, and repeated her run into the armory. If Becky, Yolanda, and Jose could hold off the soldiers for a few more minutes, the sheriff might empty the entire armory.

Becky shot, shot, and shot, each dart to a target like Sheriff Crow had taught her. Like she had during the initial attack. She remembered Voske praising her for that and froze for an instant. Then she gritted her teeth and focused as she slapped more darts into her gun. He'd said that stuff on purpose, to get into her head. She wouldn't let him stay.

Sheriff Crow appeared at her shoulder. "We've got enough. Reinforcements are on the way. Get the fallen enemies' weapons, then retreat."

Becky approached the closest slumped figure, a teenage girl with an arrow in her neck. Her stomach lurched. Mr. Preciado took the rifle from the dead girl's hands. He already had a load of rifles under one burly arm.

"I'll get them, Becky," he said. "I can carry the lot."

He meant the rifles, but for a dreamlike instant Becky thought he meant memories. Could one man really carry the memories of all those human beings who would never get up again, like that girl Becky's age with an arrow — who knew whose — through her throat?

She was jarred out of that idea by the sight of a familiar silhouette in the drifting smoke — Felicité! Becky pelted toward her and opened her arms. Felicité walked straight into them. They hugged like they were ten years old again, making blanket forts in Felicité's room at Wolfe House.

"How did you get here?" Becky gasped. "I thought you were gone. Safe."

"I came back," Felicité said. "For you. It was silly, I suppose. I don't know one end of a rifle from another, but all I could think of was you in that jail. I had to come."

Becky gulped back tears. "It wasn't silly at all. It was brave."

Felicité had come back — for *her*. Sheriff Crow had chosen Becky to accompany her into battle. Brisa had forgiven her. The Rats had trusted her. Unexpectedly, on this terrible battleground, Becky felt surrounded by love and caring.

Mayor Wolfe had come with Felicité. Surreally, she wore a maid's outfit made for someone much bigger. They all headed for the denser woods where Sheriff Crow had stashed the weapons. Meredith, Mr. Preciado, and two of Becky's neighbors dumped their loads onto the stash. Some were sticky with blood. Jack passed out weapons and ammunition. Several townspeople clutched armloads to their chests and vanished into the trees.

Sheriff Crow turned to Mayor Wolfe and Ms. Lowenstein. "Tom Preston's plan was to attack both gates simultaneously. Furio Vilas is leading the team to break through the back gate from the outside. Jennie Riley is gathering volunteers to reinforce that effort from the inside. Since Galen's team couldn't open the front gate, we'll take over that task. I'll divide you into—"

Sheriff Crow's yellow snake eye and brown human eye darted to the side. She took off like an arrow, pounced on someone in the woods, and dragged out a black-clad figure out in a hammer lock.

Becky gasped. "Henry?"

He tried to look up, but the sheriff held him too tightly for that. His lips were bloody as if he'd bitten them, his eyes bloodshot and circled with dull, dark skin. "I want to help."

"The way you helped Voske take this town?" Alfonso's sister Tania asked coldly.

"Nice try, traitor," Mrs. Vardam said in a hard voice.

"I bet he's here to assassinate the mayor," said Amy Chen, the butcher.

"Becky," Henry said. "Please. I want to help."

He didn't sound like the Henry who'd bragged and bullied and set fires and lied. This was another Henry, the one she'd known when they were small.

"Help how?" Becky asked. But she was drowned out by the rising accusations.

Sheriff Crow looked at Becky, her expression remote. "What did you say, Becky? Everyone else, be quiet."

Becky fingered her dart gun as she tried to get her thoughts in order. She was Henry's sister and the sheriff's apprentice; she could be both those things, so long as the good of the town was her first concern.

"He's been fighting us all morning," Ricardo Horst said. "Now he's here to spy."

"Did you *see* him fighting, Ricardo?" Becky asked. He

scowled and shook his head. She looked straight at the circle of angry faces. "Have any of you *seen* him fighting for Voske?"

"I saw him earlier," Dan Valdez said. "He was hiding from Voske's soldiers."

"Coward," snarled Carlos Garcia.

Felicité raised her voice. "I saw him, too, and I dare anyone to call *me* a coward. Henry saved me from getting caught by a patrol."

"He's unarmed," put in Sheriff Crow. "When I grabbed him, he had his hands clasped. He needs them open to throw fire."

"Why are we wasting time with this?" Mr. McVey said loudly. "Shoot him!"

The mayor stepped forward, standing straight and tall. "We do not form lynch mobs in this town. Henry Callahan has a right to speak in his own defense."

The sheriff loosened her hold on him, allowing him to stand up straight. But she kept a grip on his hands. Henry said hoarsely, "I really do want to help, if you'll let me. You could use my Change power —"

"He's just trying to get out of being executed," said Ricardo Horst. "This entire war is because of *him*."

Mayor Wolfe spoke up. "This war was going to happen anyway. Every one of you knows that." She gazed from face to face. "How well do you think *you* would have done, alone in a room with Voske himself?"

"It wasn't like that," Henry muttered. "He didn't torture me. He didn't threaten me. I just…told him. I'd do anything to take it back, but I can't. But if you can use me, I'll do whatever you want."

"Set fire to the gates, since you like arson so much," jeered Ricardo Horst.

"Okay," Henry said. "I will."

To Becky's surprise, Sheriff Crow released him. Henry straightened his back and began walking toward Main Street, alone.

·60·
HENRY

LAS ANCLAS – FRONT GATE

HENRY HEARD FOOTSTEPS BEHIND him. He tightened his shoulders, bracing for the knife in the back he'd been expecting for so long. He didn't even feel afraid, only mildly disappointed that he wouldn't even get to die fighting.

Becky panted up beside him. "You can't walk out there alone. They'll kill you before you get anywhere near the gates."

"Great. I'll die a hero. That'll annoy Ricardo." Henry summoned up his best 'just kidding' grin.

"I want you to *live* a hero." Becky unslung a rifle. *Becky with a rifle*. He still hadn't gotten used to it. "Go ahead. We'll cover you."

He didn't want her to die trying to protect him. What a waste that would be. "The royal 'we!' When did you get to be a princess?"

"Henry." Becky pointed. "Look behind you."

He turned and saw Brisa Preciado, tossing a rock on her palm. Of course. Brisa would do anything for Becky. Her father walked beside her, rifle at the ready. That made sense too: he was there to protect Brisa. And Sheriff Crow—she'd come to protect Becky. And Meredith and Ms. Lowenstein were following to…protect the sheriff?

More people followed them. Tania Medina. Henry couldn't think of a reason for her to come along, unless she meant to be the stabber. Jack Lowell. He couldn't even fight. Mrs. Vardam. She hated Henry. Ricardo Horst. He hated Henry even more.

Becky yelped, "Duck!"

He ducked as two arrows from the wall sentries whizzed by. Becky smacked one away with the rifle barrel.

He was now in range. Leaving the others to defend him or not, he shut his eyes. His hands tingled. Deep inside him, the fire churned, a warmth that spread through his nerves. He tensed every muscle in his body, pulling that fire into his hands. He raised them, shaping the fireballs. They hovered above his palms, hot enough to blister the skin, before he dug his heels into the ground and hurled the fireballs at the gate.

WHUMP! They hit the gates, splashing fire outward and leaving glowing star-shaped craters. Flames rose—

And began to die down. Wouldn't you know it. Henry laughed sourly; the terrifying arsonist was defeated at the last by fire-resistant varnish.

But before his flames could go out, a pair of new fires flared up. One burned a small hole all the way through the gate, leaving a ring of flame. The other set a small fire that stuck there, burning like a candle. The fires he'd started merged with these new ones, and there was Grandma Wolfe. He gritted his teeth and fed the fires with a new blast—

BOOM!

A rock hit the center of the fire and exploded, sending burning shards flying. The gate sentries dove for cover.

BOOM! BOOM!

Brisa was flinging rocks as fast as she could. Jack stood beside her with a heavy sack, passing her a new rock the instant one left her hand. Each explosion shook the gate.

An enormous boulder arced into view, hurled from outside, and struck the gate with a tremendous crash.

The gate broke into flaming pieces and tumbled to the dust.

A man's voice rose above the shouts and cheers. From beyond the ruins of the gate, Mr. Preston yelled, "CHARGE!"

·61·
PACO

LAS ANCLAS – FRONT GATE

PACO RAN THROUGH THE dust and smoke of the shattered gate, Yuki close beside him. He glimpsed Becky Callahan yanking Henry to one side. Brisa, her dad, and Jack Lowell dived to the other side.

Beyond them, a mass of enemy soldiers formed up. The front line dropped to one knee and fired, halting the advance of the allies amid the smoking rubble. Around Paco, people staggered. He kept shooting, fast and steady. Like a machine, making every shot count. He only spared glances to make sure Yuki was unharmed and noted Yuki's look of concern. But there was no time for talk, even if they could have heard anything over the roar of gunfire and the shouts and screams.

He shot an enemy taking a bead on Tania Medina, and watched him fall, lifeless. Paco felt no triumph. No remorse. Nothing. Another enemy saw the one Paco had just killed and dropped to his knees beside the corpse, his face anguished.

Voske feels nothing when he kills, Paco thought. *Voske sees the fallen as nothing.*

Paco deliberately looked back at the man he had killed, then at the one who mourned him, this time seeing them not as stuffed Gold Point uniforms, but as people. Like Santiago. Like Maria-Pilar. Even like Luis, once a nice guy like Santiago, and now a wreck. Nausea surged in Paco. And the bitterness of regret, But he welcomed it.

Yuki shouted a word in Japanese. It took Paco an instant to remember that it meant, "Attack!"

The cloud vipers appeared out of nowhere, camouflaged in the smoke. They looked like shapes of rain as they dove, bit, and rose up again. Three Gold Point soldiers collapsed. But all around Paco, allies staggered and fell, fired on not only from the enemy lines on Main Street, but from the sentries above. Ms. Lowenstein dashed up the sentry stairway with Meredith at her heels.

"Protect them!" Yuki called. "I'll cover you."

Paco fired and reloaded, fired and reloaded, his hands faster than his mind, until Ms. Lowenstein shouted, "Clear! Get up here, both of you!"

He and Yuki bolted up, avoiding the noisome oil splashed on the stairs and the sentry walk. The four of them took out the remaining sentries. The instant the last one fell, Meredith shoved her bow on her back and flung her arms around Yuki, squeezing him so hard his breath huffed out. "You came back! I missed you!"

"I missed you, too." Yuki ruffled her wild copper hair.

"Good timing, Yuki." His mother's cat eyes only flicked to him as she kept a lookout, but she pulled him into a one-armed hug. Then she let him go to shoot at Voske's firing line.

Brisa and Jack panted up the stairs, Jack lugging a sack of rocks. Brisa hurled a rock that exploded in the midst of the firing line, briefly scattering their disciplined rows. Voske's soldiers had Mr. Preston's force bottlenecked between the gateposts. Sheriff Crow straight-armed through them, breaking up their lines and leaving them scattered on the ground, but there were too many of them. They reformed instantly, firing in fast and disciplined lines, under the hard eyes of...

Paco searched for the telltale glint of silver. And there he was, surrounded as always by his elites, just out of rifle range as he commanded the firing line. Would *nobody* go after him?

Ms. Lowenstein caught Paco's arm. "Concentrate your fire on the front lines. Voske's out of reach."

Hatred burned through Paco. If he charged Voske now, he'd be shot down for sure. But at least he'd have tried. He stood poised, then turned to Yuki, who gazed back steadily. Side by side, he'd said — and Paco knew he meant it. If Paco went for Voske, Yuki would go with him. That was real loyalty. Freely given.

Did Voske have that, in spite of his empire and his army? Not that Paco could see.

Paco reloaded. He was needed here. "Can you tell your cloud vipers to go bite the guy with the silver hair?"

Yuki shook his head. "They only know 'attack'. They're not as bright as rats."

"Stop yapping and start shooting," Ms. Lowenstein said. "Here come more."

Paco saw with dismay that she was right. Enemy reinforcements were coming down Main Street from the town hall.

Las Anclas was losing the battle.

·62·

JENNIE

LAS ANCLAS – BACK GATE

JENNIE COULDN'T ASK FOR better team leaders than Pa, Aunt Flora, and Kerry. Unfortunately, they, Santiago, and Tommy were also the only experienced fighters she had. Well, and Summer.

Sera had taught Jennie that when dealing with inexperienced fighters, it was best to calmly tell them exactly what would happen. Mr. Preston had added, *"It conveys a semblance of order in a situation where chaos is imminent."*

"This is the plan," said Jennie. "Thanks to Summer, Alfonso, and Pa, we know where Voske's three covert teams are lying in wait to attack anyone trying to open the back gate." Summer beamed proudly. Alfonso just looked scared and miserable. Trying not to think of imminent chaos, Jennie went on, "Pa's team will take the enemy team by the harvest barn."

Pa nodded. At his elbow, Summer stood with her knives bare. Only Pa could keep her from dashing out to be the gunslinger who single-handedly defeated Gold Point—and getting herself killed. She'd only fought animals and bandits, not skilled soldiers. Mia's cousin Lorenzo rounded out that group. He held his rifle awkwardly, looking sick.

"Aunt Flora will take on Voske's team by the north forge."

Aunt Flora tapped her singlesticks together. Behind her, Mia's cousin Renata licked her lips. Alfonso rubbed his gecko pads over his face. This was Jennie's most vulnerable group. She wished she could switch out Alfonso or Renata for Santiago or Tommy. But Kerry's group would force open the back gate, which was heavily guarded, so it had to be the strongest.

Strongest, Jennie thought with an inward wince. It had Kerry, Santiago, Tommy, and the toddler April's parents. Jennie could only hope that would be enough.

Jennie also worried about her own group—specifically, the Terrible Trio. It would be no trouble giving them something useful to do, since they were so undermanned, but harder to ensure that they didn't get involved in the fighting. The rest of Jennie's group had also never fought before, but at least Uncle Joe could briefly blind people with a brilliant flash of light. Jennie suppressed a gulp of laughter at the thought of her cousin Susie's power, which was to summon frogs.

"My group will take the team hiding behind the old oak." Jennie saw agreement in tight little nods, readiness in set shoulders, and fear in the tension of hands gripping weapons. She turned to Kerry, flashing a quick grin. "It's up to your team to get the gates open. Ever wanted to lead a charge?"

"I was all set to lead one into Las Anclas, once." Kerry gave a brief smile, then looked solemn. "I'd be honored to lead one in its defense."

They separated off. Even Summer and the Terrible Trio were quiet. Dee's soft breathing was audible on Jennie's right.

At the hedgerow, Jennie addressed the Terrible Trio. "It's up to you three to guard our backs. If anyone sneaks up on us from behind, we're dead. If you spot anyone, screech like a red jay. When you hear me whistle, come to me. Until then, you cannot move from this position. Guard it *with your lives.* Each of you, face outward, standing in a triangle back to back." Jennie turned to Z, who wanted to be a Ranger. "When you get into Ranger training, you'll learn that this defense is called The Deadly Triangle."

Dee's and Nhi's eyes widened, and Z jutted her jaw. Jennie had to hope they'd stay there—and that no soldiers would come across them.

She motioned for the rest of her team to follow her

single file. As always, the anticipation was far worse than the actual battle. When she spotted the soldiers in black uniforms, she felt no fear, only a sense of *at last* and *now*. Jennie charged, sword in hand.

Her first stroke took off one enemy's head. The backswing was met by a huge soldier with an axe. Jennie whirled her blade around in a fast bind before he could swing the awkward axe again and took the man under the jaw.

The third soldier had driven Uncle Joe back. Uncle Joe raised his palm, and Jennie dropped her gaze. A blinding flash glowed redly against her eyelids. She opened her eyes to see the soldier staring blindly. She raised her free hand and yanked the rifle out of her hands and into Jennie's. Uncle Joe and Susie tackled the woman, and Jennie brought her sword down, breaking her shoulder. The soldier collapsed—dead or alive, Jennie didn't know. But she would fight no more this day.

Susie turned away, her throat working as she tried not to throw up. A scream rose in the distance, abruptly cut off. Jennie flinched, hoping it was one of Voske's people rather than hers. She charged past the spreading tree under which she'd had so many school picnics and ran for the gate. Shouts rose. Shots rang, weapons clashed. Then, as suddenly as the noise had risen, it died.

She burst through the underbrush, and nearly stumbled over a body. Soldiers were strewn around the gate, some dead, others alive and tied up. Jennie was relieved to see that April's parents were alive and collecting weapons from the fallen soldiers. Santiago and Tommy, muscles bunching in their backs, strained to open a massive gate that required four people. Beside them, Kerry pushed with what seemed to be an invisible lever. From the sounds, people were helping from the other side.

The gate creaked open, and in spilled Mr. Vilas and a group of Changed people she didn't know. Jennie had never in her life expected to be relieved at the sight of that bounty hunter.

Mr. Vilas gave her a short nod. "Jennifer Riley."

She abruptly remembered how she'd once threatened to murder him. "Er, thank you for coming."

Dead Gold Point soldiers lay in the road outside the

gate. The bounty hunter jerked his thumb at them. "Reinforcements. They met us first."

Pa appeared from behind the ruined forge, blood splashed down his shirt, one hand clasped over the other arm, which bled sluggishly. Summer was unhurt and supporting Mia's cousin Lorenzo, who had a bullet wound in his leg.

Aunt Flora ran up, tears streaking her face. Alfonso limped by her side, gripping a bloody knife in his gecko fingers.

Lorenzo looked up; his face twisted in pain. "Where's Renata?"

"She didn't make it," Aunt Flora said. "Lorenzo, I'm so sorry. She was so brave."

The others closed around Lorenzo, offering comfort. Jennie wanted to join them, but the bounty hunter and his tough-looking band waited expectantly. She had to keep moving forward. She whistled between her teeth. The Terrible Trio pounded up, looking around wildly. Nhi paled at the sight of all the blood.

Jennie spoke before they could get any ideas of their own. "I have a very important job for you three. And you, Summer. I need you to accompany the wounded to the schoolhouse. Defend them and guard the door. That includes you, Pa." Pa gave a wry nod. Jennie turned to Kerry. "Over to you, Kerry."

Sharp angles of bone stood out on Kerry's tense and haggard face. Once Jennie would have thought it made her look like Voske. Now she thought that Voske was a caricature of Kerry, with her strength twisted into tyranny and her irony into cruelty.

Kerry took Santiago's hand. "We're ready."

·63·
KERRY

LAS ANCLAS – BACK GATE

KERRY HELD TIGHT TO Santiago's hand. He squeezed back, lending her strength. "We're ready."

"Good." Jennie raised her voice. "Everyone who's not wounded or accompanying them, go to the front gate with Kerry and the—Mr. Vilas. Aunt Flora and I will make sure there's no more assassins lurking around here, then catch up at the front gate."

Kerry met the gaze of the bounty hunter, who had once worked for her father. But then, so had she. A group of well-armed Changed people were at his back, looking like an army all in themselves.

"Is Sheriff Crow down there?" The bounty hunter pointed down Main Street, where they could hear and even see some of the fighting around the front gate. "The plan was for her to raid the armory."

"She'd take the weapons to the front gate once she got them," said Jennie.

"Then that's where we're headed." The bounty hunter and his team began jogging down Main Street. Kerry and Santiago fell in with them, followed by Tommy, April's parents, and Joe and Susie Riley.

So much for leading the charge! Now Kerry was just one of many. Well, she'd left Gold Point because she didn't want to be the princess at the head of an army. Being one of many was fine.

They passed the dead soldiers that Jennie's team had taken out. Voske had taught her to never look at the faces of the dead until the battle was over. It was defiance as much as anything that made her stop to look. Except for Santiago, the procession continued without her. He flinched from the head of Larry Gonzalez, lying on its ear. "Come on, Kerry."

"Wait." She knew Larry's team and was unsurprised to find Shao Meghe dead nearby. Terra Aguila was still alive, but unconscious. It was such a *waste*. If Kerry had led that team instead of Jennie, she could have said, "Larry, tell your team to stand down. No one has to know." She bet he'd have done it.

She grabbed Santiago's arm. "I need a horse."

"What?" Santiago began. Then his face cleared, and she knew he understood. "We've got the secondary captains' mounts behind the forge. You should take the white stallion."

They ran hand in hand. Kerry mounted the white stallion, and Santiago took a handsome roan. She held the reins with one hand and shielded them with the other as they rode toward the town hall — now the main barracks.

"I hope this works," Santiago muttered.

They caught up with the soldiers who had been summoned to reinforce the battle at the front gate. Up ahead, Kerry heard the rhythm of leapfrogging firing lines. As one soldier fell, they were instantly replaced by the soldier behind them. She had to keep these soldiers from reinforcing them.

Trying to project the royal confidence she had once felt, Kerry bellowed, "Attention!"

The soldiers turned and stared at her with the utter astonishment she'd hoped for. Before they could start thinking, she shouted, "I won't harm you! Lay down your weapons! You'll have amnesty!"

"Santiago? I thought you were dead," his cousin Manuel exclaimed.

"Nope, alive and kicking." Santiago yelled, "I'm here to save your lives! Do what Kerry says. Lay down your weapons. We'll protect you."

Manuel dropped his rifle with a clatter. A man leaped at Manuel, swinging his rifle to knock him down. "Coward! You're betraying the king!"

"The king is betraying you!" Kerry shouted. "How many of you are only fighting to save a hostage? A child?"

Rifle fire flashed. The bullet hit Kerry's shield, nearly knocking her out of the saddle. Santiago grabbed her arm and steadied her.

"Who shot at the princess?" Manuel demanded.

Before a melee could break out, Kerry yelled, "Stand down! Who's lost someone they loved to the king's wars? Who's lost someone to the king's bad mood? Show of hands!"

The soldiers looked around warily, then one hand rose. Then another. More began going up.

Another shot rang out and bounced off her shield. She yelled, "Disarm the one who fired at me! But don't harm them. The killing has to stop! NOW!"

Santiago roared, "Lay down your weapons!"

Swords and rifles clattered to the ground.

Kerry lifted her voice. "Let's convince our brothers and sisters in arms to join us."

A woman shouted, "How?"

"Disperse," Kerry called. "Look for small groups, where there's no active fighting. Tell them there will be amnesty for anyone who lays down their arms. Stay away from the main fighting, or someone will shoot you by accident. If you see anyone from Las Anclas, raise your hands. If you see wounded, get them to the infirmary." She pointed at the woman. "You, take a team to the rear gate. There's a wounded soldier there, and more tied up. If the bound ones agree to surrender, untie them."

The crowd began to disperse. Two soldiers stooped to pick up their weapons in long-trained habit. Santiago shouted, "Divak! Put it down. You too, Xiao Hu. The only way anyone can know which side you're on is whether or not you're armed."

Some ran to catch up with their teams, empty-handed. Others emerged from the barracks in twos, carrying stretchers.

Kerry spoke for Santiago's ears only. "Even better than leading a charge."

·64·
Ross

LAS ANCLAS - MAIN STREET

ROSS WISHED MIA HAD agreed to stay in her cottage when they'd gone back to look for more weapons. Or at least brought fewer weapons. Or let him carry all of them.

Though her balance had improved, the running and fighting had exhausted her. But she was determined to help. Weapons and tools rattled around her as she and Ross stumbled together, arms around each other. Despite the many bruises he'd taken when he was captured, he did his best to take her weight. Their progress was slow. Other than a few running figures, they saw no one. Then a tremendous crash startled them. Dust and smoke rose above Old Pottery Circle.

"I think that was the gate," Mia gasped.

They cut through Old Pottery Circle. Between two bungalows, they slowed, spotting black uniforms ahead. And in the middle of them, a glint of silver hair. Voske was giving orders. "Send another team to reinforce them. I want that sheriff boxed in and taken down."

Ross snatched out a knife, but Voske was well out of throwing range. Voske turned, and his eyes met Ross's across the short distance. Then his gaze shifted to Mia, and his jaw dropped.

"I'm not dead!" Mia yelled. Then, after a brief pause, "So there!"

Voske drew the pistol in his belt and took aim at Mia. "Not for long."

Ross yanked Mia back and came face to face with several soldiers. He instantly sank the knife into the shoulder of the nearest one and spun to attack the other. In the back of his mind, he wondered why he hadn't heard a pistol shot.

"SHUT UP!" Voske yelled.

All three soldiers jerked around, staring at Voske. Someone grabbed Ross and yanked him behind the bungalow, dragging Mia with him. His hand whipped up to strike, then dropped when Ross recognized Sean.

Sean murmured, "Don't speak." He had one hand on Ross's elbow, and the other on Mia's shoulder. Stepping softly, he led them into the orchard.

Once they were out of earshot, Ross said, "Thank you. So, you're back from Gold Point—Did you—"

Sean interrupted him. "Never mind that. Where's Kerry?"

"The last we heard, she was going to the back gate," said Mia.

"No idea where she is now," Ross added.

Sean gave an exasperated sigh. "Okay. I'll go look for her."

Mia grabbed his sleeve. "Wait! Can you get us somewhere first?"

"I suppose," Sean said reluctantly. "Where do you want to go?"

Mia rubbed her chin. "Wherever the most soldiers are. Gold Point soldiers, I mean."

Ross turned to her in dismay. "Mia…"

"I think I have an idea! I mean, I *definitely* have an idea, and I *think* it'll work. But we need you, Sean."'

"I didn't come here to fight," said Sean. "I'm just trying to rescue my family."

"Oh, this will help rescue Kerry," Mia assured him.

"Mia," Ross said warningly. "What is this idea?"

"Well," Mia began. "It has to do with crystal…"

·65·
MIA

LAS ANCLAS – MAIN STREET

THERE WAS NOTHING LIKE having whirling, impractical pieces form into a plan. It was harder to get it into words.

"I have a new power. Actually, it's Ross's old power, only used in a new way. I've been thinking about how we could use it to get rid of Voske, like maybe create a crystal wall to block off his soldiers or make a giant crystal cube and embed Voske in it, or create a crystal seed pod I could hold—" She broke off, seeing Ross's look of horror. Hastily, she said, "It was just a thought. But—"

Sean turned to Ross, his expression bewildered. His lips shaped the word, *Help*.

If only she wasn't so tired! It made it hard to figure out how to put words together in a way other people could understand. It would probably be easier just to show him.

Mia took one of Ross's knives, plopped down on the ground, nicked her finger, and laid her palm on the dirt. She closed her eyes and felt Ross's warm touch on her hand, and then inside her mind. She shared the shape of her plan and felt the warmth of his agreement like a lovely hot bath. Together, they sent a tiny bit of crystal out from the drop of blood, and had it collect the minerals it needed to make more of itself. They shaped it and pushed it upward through the earth.

Mia opened her eyes—her eye—well, the lids raised up from both of them—and was thrilled to see Sean looking very impressed with the little crystal cube that had grown out of the earth.

"Could you really embed Voske in a giant crystal cube?" Sean asked.

"Well, if he stood still long enough..." Mia began.

Ross said quickly, "That's not what we're doing. Can you get us near the gate, where we can see the front lines of the Gold Point army?"

"Kerry might be there," Mia added. "Wouldn't surprise me at all."

Sean led them around the broken remains of Weavers' Row. It was fascinating how people's gazes slid off them, as if they were part of the scenery. She tried to stop watching that so she could think over her plan and make sure it was perfect. But she instead remembered the look on Voske's face when he'd seen her, and how, in her only chance ever to defy him, she had completely failed to think of anything heroic or witty to say. Had she really said, "So there!" to the tyrant king? Jennie would have said something heroic. Mia's only consolation was that Ross hadn't said anything at all.

They rounded the corner of the ruined building. Mr. Preston was only...she briefly dropped into the crystal world to get the distance...forty-six feet away, directing a lot of people Mia had never seen before. They were trying to push forward, but rifle flashes thundered and four of Mr. Preston's people went down.

The Gold Point army stood in a disciplined block, first one row shooting, then another, a steady, lethal fire. Mr. Preston's army fired back with everything they had as they tried to win a foot at a time, but the cost was so high.

"There," she whispered, pointing to the killing ground between the two armies. "Right there."

"Got it," Ross breathed.

"Can your crystal stand up to rifle fire?" Sean asked.

That was an interesting question. But before Mia could get sidetracked into considering it, Ross said, "We're not building a wall."

He pulled Mia down beside him, nicked his finger with his knife, and handed her the blade. Mia stuck her own finger with it, remembering too late that she probably should have pricked the same finger twice, and laid her hands down beside to his.

Together, they sent their awareness, along with the

crystal in their blood, into the earth. Chains of tiny crystal particles spread through the earth, gathering minerals and pushing them together. It took a lot of minerals to do what they were planning. But Ross could see the scarlet tree that had grown from his own blood as if it was standing right in front of him. He had the design. All Mia needed to do was help him build it.

They made it grow out of the ground. Mia saw the heat shapes of people hurriedly backing up. But they weren't running yet. She wanted them to run. Ross reached delicately up through the crystal branches and made the leaves chime.

Then the heat shapes ran.

·66·

JENNIE

LAS ANCLAS – MAIN STREET

JENNIE EASED ALONG THE stable wall, followed by the townspeople she'd rounded up. The royal horses were kicking their stalls inside. They didn't like the constant gunfire. "Neither do I," she muttered, and peered out toward Main Street.

Shock chilled her. It was worse than she'd thought.

Gold Point's mighty army stood in disciplined rows, the front lines executing a perfect firing line. The gate lay in smoking ruins. There was Mr. Preston—she'd never been so glad to see him—with Indra, Sujata, and the rest of the surviving Rangers, plus the army from Catalina and the Saigon Alliance, firing as fast as they could. Mr. Preston was trying to get the Saigon people organized in a firing line. But they were clearly not trained to fight that way, in addition to being outnumbered and outgunned. Voske was nowhere in sight, but his army was functioning perfectly.

From behind her, Mr. Nguyen muttered, "They're gonna wipe us all out."

Jennie privately agreed. Well, she intended to go down fighting. What was the most effective way she could use her group? Twelve people—four rifles—two axes, two swords… She should hit that lethal firing line on the flank and split their focus.

As she turned to give the orders, the relentless roar of gunfire from the firing line stuttered, then stopped. Jennie whipped around. And stared.

The firing line had broken up. The first row was

pushing back in total disorganization, as the rows behind stirred, also trying to back up. Someone shouted, "Reform the line! Stay where you are!"

Then she saw what was scaring them. A slender trunk of red crystal slowly but relentlessly speared up from the ground. As she watched in astonishment, it grew several slim branches. A fierce joy filled her. She couldn't see Ross, but he had to be hiding somewhere. Undoubtedly with Mia.

A few people screamed in terror, including one from her group. Jennie spun and hissed, "It's Ross! He won't let it harm us!"

She looked back at the crystal tree. In the instant it had taken her to get control of her group, the tree had grown noticeably, and added leaves and seed pods to the branches. The leaves clashed together, sending out the chime that meant that anyone within range was going to die in shrieking agony.

It was like a bomb dropped in the middle of the Gold Point army. They fled in all directions.

Mr. Preston's army was also terrified, trying to back up through the wall. Jennie leaped onto the stable wall. Her trained voice projected over the screams and chimes as she shouted, "Defenders of Las Anclas! The tree won't harm you! Ross Juarez is controlling it!"

She was gratified to see Mr. Preston instantly begin marshalling his troops. Jennie raised her voice again, hoping it would project far beyond the area she could see. "The crystal tree will only kill Gold Point soldiers!"

Then she got an even better idea. She shouted so loudly that it felt like her throat was tearing, "ALL those crystal trees, SPRINGING UP THROUGHOUT TOWN, will only kill Gold Point soldiers! Ross has them ALL under his complete control!!!"

Jennie broke off, coughing. The Gold Point army had scattered, despite captains bellowing orders and threats. Mr. Preston led his people forward, though with caution. As she jumped down, she saw him send one company off toward the south forge, and another in her direction.

"Come on," she said to her group. They ran into Main Street, giving the tree a wide berth.

The moment Mr. Preston saw her, his face relaxed.

"Jennie! I'm so glad to see you." And, in a low voice, "Are those things really springing up throughout the town?"

She said quietly, "Not that I'm aware. But maybe I gave Ross an idea."

Mr. Preston actually paled beneath his tan. But all he said was, "Situation report?"

"We cleared the north side of town." Jennie looked around. She saw the bounty hunter and his people, but where were Kerry and Santiago? She had to hope they were elsewhere, not killed on the way here. More people ran up. Ms. Lowenstein, Meredith, Paco, and… "Yuki!"

"Jennie!" Ms. Lowenstein exclaimed. "Now we've got a chance."

Mr. Preston jerked his chin down in a decisive nod. "Right. We need to press our advantage, slim as it is."

Jennie agreed. "Keep them from reforming the line."

Mr. Preston pointed. "I'll take Vilas and the Rangers." The Rangers stepped out of line. "*All* the Rangers." He looked at Paco, who turned to Yuki. Mr. Preston glanced at the sky, then said, "Yuki? Come along." And to them all, "We're going after the captains."

"And Voske?" Paco asked.

"He keeps moving. But if we sight him, of course he's our main objective." Mr. Preston turned back to Jennie. "Jennie, take charge of the army."

"Take charge of the army?" Jennie repeated blankly.

Mr. Preston spoke as if it was a perfectly normal task. "Yes. Keep advancing in a wedge formation, splitting the ground so they can't reform their lines."

The military terminology calmed her. Yes. She knew exactly how to do that.

Mr. Preston grabbed her wrist and held their hands up. He shouted, "I'm turning command over to Jennie Riley! Jennie Riley is in command!"

His group headed for the pocket garden, where a Gold Point captain was waving a group of soldiers back toward Main Street with his sword.

Jennie looked at all those expectant faces, some she'd known all her life, and many she'd never seen before. All those people ready to retake Las Anclas. And she knew what to do.

She began giving orders.

·67·
KERRY

LAS ANCLAS – MAIN STREET

KERRY AND SANTIAGO REINED up at the town hall-turned-barracks, trailed by an ever-growing crowd of surrendered soldiers. Santiago suggested, "How about we leave them here, and I go with you?"

Much as Kerry longed to have him stay with her, she had to shake her head. "You need to make sure anybody else who turns up gets the message—and see that the wounded get picked up. Ours as well as theirs."

"Which 'ours'?" Santiago commented in one of his rare sardonic moments.

"Everybody," Kerry corrected.

"Right. But if I see someone from Las Anclas who can take over, I'm handing them off. No one needs protection more than you."

Kerry shivered. She had no doubt that her father would kill her in a heartbeat. Like he'd killed his own brother, when Voske had been younger than she was now. At least she had weapons no one could take from her.

Halfway to the front gate, her horse began to plunge and buck. She fought for control, but experienced a rider as she was, the horse was too panicked to heed anything but the instinct to flee. Then her own nerves chilled as she heard the sweet chime of crystal leaves clashing.

She leaped free just before her horse bolted. Soldiers dashed past her in the same blind panic that had seized the horse. She didn't see any singing tree, but Ross had to be responsible. Gritting her teeth to overcome her gut-level fear, she ran toward the chimes.

Kerry almost collided with a fleeing soldier. "Armando?"

"Run, Princess!" he gasped. "Crystal trees! They're everywhere!"

She grabbed his arm before he could run off. "Lay down your arms and go to the barracks. You'll be safe there."

He flung down his rifle and bolted for the barracks. She yelled after him, "Spread the word!" Remembering her vocal training, Kerry breathed from the diaphragm and shouted, "Everyone under my protection is safe from Ross Juarez's crystal trees! Lay down your arms and go to the barracks or die screaming!"

She repeated the message every few feet as she continued forward. Soon she could make out the glinting scarlet of the singing tree, right in the middle of Main Street, wreathed in smoke. Mr. Preston and some Rangers passed within range of its shards. But the tree did nothing to harm them.

That was Ross, all right.

Several soldiers she'd known all her life dropped their arms and followed her rather than going to the barracks. More soldiers followed them. Kerry was soon trailed by her own small, unarmed army, their hands in the air.

Then she caught sight of several members of the elite guard. That meant her father was nearby. She spotted him by the jumble of bungalows called Old Pottery Circle—and he caught sight of her.

His lips moved into a thin smile of triumph. She knew what he was thinking: she wanted to be a princess again. She was bringing him reinforcements.

Kerry pointed at him and screamed, "IT'S VOSKE!"

She had just enough time to see his white-lipped fury before he and his guards disappeared behind a bungalow. Mr. Preston and the Rangers charged after them. Kerry was about to follow when a hand seized her arm. She started, instinctively creating a shield.

"Kerry. It's me," Sean said quickly. With his hand on her arm, she saw that Ross and Mia were also with him. They leaned on each other, looking utterly exhausted.

"No one can see any of us, right?" Kerry asked.

Sean nodded. "I was going to leave Ross and Mia somewhere safe."

Ross swayed, and terror flashed through her. She grabbed him by the shoulders and shook him hard. "Stay awake! You have to keep control of that tree!"

"It's okay, Kerry." Mia flicked a wan smile at her. "It's not real. I mean, it's not an illusion. It's solid. But the seed pods are hollow. It's a statue, basically."

Ross had sent the Gold Point army running for their lives by erecting a statue? Kerry fought a wild urge to laugh.

"Listen, Kerry," said Sean. "We need to get to Wolfe House. I left Fiona and Owen there with Bridget and Min Soo while I came to find you. We need to go pick them up and get out before Father thinks of going back there."

Kerry could only gape at him.

"Who are Fiona and Owen?" Mia asked.

"Our little sister and brother," Kerry said. "What are they doing here?"

"Come on." Sean took her arm and tugged.

"Wait, can you hide us all like this?" Kerry stepped up beside Mia and helped Ross support her. When Sean nodded, they set out in an awkward four-person line. "Sean? What did you do?"

"I showed Owen and Fiona a command token and told them I was Father's aide, and he'd sent for them. Luckily, they're too young to pay much attention to adult faces and resemblances. We walked straight out the gates. They never even noticed that no one saw them."

Frustrated, Kerry said, "Yes, but why bring them *here?*"

"I hoped you and Min Soo could get them to see the truth about Father," Sean said. "Bridget, too. I didn't know all this was going to happen *now*. I thought I had until the next Opportunity Day—"

"But what was your plan?"

Sean stopped, staring at her as if she'd said that she didn't understand why people needed to breathe. "To get them away. *All* of you away. You know whatever happens here, he's going to retaliate, and I can at least protect our siblings. But that's if we go far beyond his reach."

Kerry bit back a sharp response. Sean meant well. But

she'd already told him she wouldn't leave Las Anclas. And now he'd brought an enormous amount of trouble down on their heads—as if they didn't have enough already!

"Sean, your mother got put in charge at Gold Point, and Owen and Fiona are *her children*. Half the Gold Point home guard is probably on your heels!"

"They're not," said Sean. "I left Mom a note. I said I'd keep them safe until the revolt is over and there's no danger of retaliation. Will you talk to them, or not?"

"I will." Kerry sighed. "But I'm still staying—"

Mia stumbled, yanking the line off-balance. Ross swung his free hand around her waist, then froze, staring past her shoulder. Kerry snapped her head around and caught the glint of silver hair. Surrounded by his honor guard, Voske was weaving through the trees, going up the Hill.

"He's headed for Wolfe House," said Ross.

Kerry remembered her father's fury when he'd seen Mr. Preston. She sucked in a breath. "He's going to kill Mr. Preston's wife."

Sean said bleakly, "He'll find the kids, and I promised Min Soo I'd get them away as soon as I found you and Bridget. We have to get there first."

If she'd been alone, Kerry could have easily outpaced the honor guards, who were more concerned with security than speed. But dragging along two people close to collapse slowed them down. At least Sean had learned some shortcuts during his secret visits. He led them unerringly, though Mia stumbled, gasping. "Leave me. I'll hide."

"No." Ross didn't look much better, but he held her slight form against him. "We'll stay together."

They arrived at Wolfe House at the same time as Voske and his elite guards. Kerry's heart sank. They were too late. But rather than stream inside with Voske safely in their midst, the guards formed a ragged bunch in front of the house. The house guards remained in the background; weapons ready.

Voske's voice rang out in fury and—was that fear? "You're traitors! All of you! Call yourselves my honor guard. All the time you're whispering to me—lying to me—getting ready to stab me in the back!"

The gleam of his silver hair was joined by the glint of metal as he drew his sword. His honor guard inched back. One elite guard said, "Sir, I swear—"

"Traitors!" Voske yelled. "Who put that effigy on my stage? Who gave the prisoners explosives? *Who's been whispering in my ear?*"

Kerry glanced at Sean, Ross, and Mia, but they looked as bewildered as she was. Other than the prison collapse, she had no idea what her father was raving about.

"Which of you is plotting with Ross Juarez?" Voske went on. "Which of you is plotting with Kerry? With Liam? You're *all* conspiring!"

"Sir, I'm loyal!" exclaimed one of the elite guard. That broke the dam. They all began wildly protesting their loyalty. Voske raised his hand, and they instantly fell silent.

"I'll sort that out later," he said. "Drop your weapons!"

They gaped at him. One said, "But sir…"

"Drop. Your. Weapons." Voske's icy tone was more frightening than his shouting. Kerry couldn't suppress a shudder.

The honor guard's weapons clattered to the ground.

Voske turned to the gaping house guards. "Arrest them. I'll interrogate them myself when I'm through here."

He strode inside the house. The door slammed behind him. Kerry realized that finally, *finally,* Voske had been separated from his elite guard. If they were ever going to have a chance at him, it was now.

They. Kerry's stomach felt heavy as a rock. There was no *they.* Sean had been trained as a soldier, but he'd renounced violence. Mia was no fighter, and she was fainting on her feet. Ross was as well, and anyway he could no longer kill.

Kerry was their only chance.

·68·
ROSS

ROSS'S BODY THRUMMED WITH tension as Sean led them into Wolfe House through the kitchen door. This was the best possible chance to kill Voske, and Ross couldn't do it. Sean wouldn't. Mia couldn't even stand up by herself.

Kerry was the only person capable of killing Voske, and he was her own father. Even an instant of hesitation would allow Voske to strike a death blow. *He* wouldn't hesitate. Maybe Ross could injure or pin down Voske to give Kerry a better chance. He fingered the knives at his belt with his free hand. He was fast. But, injured and exhausted, he wasn't sure he'd be faster than Voske. Their only chance was to take him completely by surprise.

At least they didn't need to worry about their footfalls. Voske was yelling loudly enough to cover all manner of noises. "I did *not* give orders for you two to be brought here!"

A young boy spoke up. Ross recognized Owen's voice from his imprisonment in Gold Point. "But the aide had a command token, Father."

"The aide was a traitor! Owen, you're old enough to suspect treachery *everywhere*. How many times have I—"

Min Soo said sweetly, "Bridget, please take the children to the kitchen for a—"

Voske snapped, "Bridget, don't move."

Ross, Mia, Sean, and Kerry crossed the hall. Ross's heart slammed into his chest as they crept past a pair of guards at the staircase. If anyone's hand slipped free, they'd be seen. If a guard reached out for any reason, they'd be touched and the illusion would fail.

He held his breath as they flattened themselves against the wall across from the open door. Two more guards stood on either side of the door, looking straight in Ross's direction without seeing him. That blank gaze made his skin crawl.

He looked into a bedroom full of fancy furniture that had to belong to Min Soo. Bridget was in the corner with Fiona and Owen pressed close to her, big-eyed with terror.

Ross let a slow trickle of breath escape his lips as he saw that Voske, as usual, had placed himself in the best defensive position, half-concealed by an ornate chest of drawers, with no direct path to him. They couldn't sneak up on him, and there was too much furniture in the way to throw a knife. Voske had sheathed his sword, which would be awkward to use in close quarters, but he had knives in his sleeves and boot tops. And the instant there was any commotion, the guards right outside the door would rush in to defend him.

"That traitor aide must be in league with the traitors among the guards," Voske muttered. "And Kerry. And Ross. And Preston. Why did they bring Owen and Fiona here instead of killing them outright?"

"An excellent question," said Min Soo. "Shall we sit down and consider it?"

Voske ignored her. "It was a strike against me, of course. Maybe they meant to gather you together as hostages and make me choose which one of you was to die. Or choose which one was to stay alive."

Ross gritted his teeth. The sound of them scraping together seemed horribly loud. Mia squeezed his hand; he could feel her trembling beside him.

"Whatever they meant to do, it failed." Voske took a deep breath, then smiled. "Actually, I'm glad you're here. Now, all three of you can share in a special lesson. Would you like to see how to break an enemy's spirit?"

Voske's tone promised a special treat. Fiona took Owen's hand and clung tight. Ross realized that the children knew what was coming. Owen said, "Yes, Father." Nervously, Fiona added, "Yes, please!"

Voske snapped his fingers and called, "Bring me the prisoners."

Ross and the others flattened themselves even closer against the wall as the door guards saluted and headed for the stairs. The instant they were out of the way, Ross and Kerry yanked the others toward the room. A jerk—a stumble—and they passed inside and pressed themselves against the wall. Kerry's free hand closed around air: she had materialized a sword.

Min Soo beckoned to Voske, murmuring, "Ian, dear, I need to tell you something not for children's ears."

Impatient, Voske stepped toward her.

A little carved table by Min Soo wavered and vanished. Maria-Pilar lunged for Voske, knife in hand.

Voske leaped backward, drawing his sword unnervingly fast. He struck at Maria-Pilar. She dodged, but not quite fast enough. Steel slashed her forehead, and she fell. Voske tried to stomp on her knife hand, but Maria-Pilar rolled under the bed. His boot crashed to the floor.

Kerry let go of Mia and vaulted over the bed, her arm raised high to strike with her invisible sword. Anyone but Voske would have lost time to the sheer astonishment of someone materializing out of nowhere, but he didn't hesitate. Voske easily dodged her invisible blade, and side-kicked her viciously in the ribs. She staggered back, bent double. Ross dropped Mia's other hand and threw a dagger at Voske's shoulder. The king sidestepped, and the knife only shattered a mirror.

Kerry lunged upright, pale and grim. She swung her sword with her entire body. Once again Voske dodged, and the blade struck the chest of drawers. Splinters of wood and glass flew everywhere, some stinging Ross's face. Kerry staggered, clutching her ribs as she struggled for breath.

Voske had managed to get behind the chest of drawers again, with his back against the wall. He could easily hold his position from there. All he needed to do was shout for the guards, and they'd be there in an instant.

But he didn't call for help. Instead, he bared his teeth in a cruel smile. "Ross Juarez. Right at the center of the conspiracy. Which of you was behind the effigy? Don't try to lie to me—"

Voske gave a start as if he'd been stung by a bee. He

yelled, *"I'll shut you up!"*

The veins in his forehead stood out as he whipped free a throwing knife. Everything seemed to be happening so slowly. It was as if Ross was in a dream, trying to run through water up to his chest. He pulled his second knife as Kerry raised her sword. Neither of them was fast enough—which one would Voske kill—

Me.

Ross flung himself to the floor, dragging Mia with him. The knife thudded into the wall where he'd been a heartbeat before. A glass vase on a shelf fell off and smashed, sending shards clinking across the floor.

Mia's gaze locked with his, and their minds met. Ross's hand was already bleeding; Mia slapped her palm down on a fragment of glass. Then she was with him in that crystal world. He sensed her fear, her desperation, her fierce appreciation of the idea he sent her, and her cool scientific appraisal of how to help him do it. There were minerals under the floorboards. They only needed a little bit.

Now. And they focused.

Voske's scream of shock and agony jolted Ross back into the world.

Kerry was still raising her sword as Voske recoiled. The crystal blade that Ross and Mia had created had stabbed all the way through the floorboards to pierce through his foot. Voske's sword clattered to the floor as he bent over in agony.

An overturned chair blurred and transformed into Maria-Pilar. Her face was a mask of blood, her hand steady as she doubled her fists on her knife. Just as Voske reached for his sword, his foot still pinned to the floor, she slammed her blade into his heart.

Voske collapsed slowly. His eyes were open. They shifted from Kerry to Sean, then to Min Soo, who stared back, expressionless. He looked from his two younger children to Bridget, and then back to Kerry, and he opened his mouth. To rage? To make one final threat? But he choked on his own blood. His last words were lost forever as his head fell back, his eyes staring sightlessly upward.

The utter silence that followed was broken by Owen, who stood pale and trembling by his little sister Fiona.

Min Soo had pressed Fiona to her side, hiding her face. Owen turned away from them, toward Kerry. "Is he…okay?"

Kerry leaned against the bed, struggling for breath with one hand pressed against her ribs. She said nothing.

Owen turned to Maria-Pilar, who stood shivering violently, the bloody knife still gripped in one hand. "Why did you do that?"

Maria-Pilar's voice was harsh as she wiped the blood off her face, then gazed down at Voske. "Because *he* was the traitor."

·69·
Ross

LAS ANCLAS – WOLFE HOUSE

MARIA-PILAR'S WORDS MET ringing silence.

"He's dead," Ross said, numb. It had seemed like the threat of Voske would never end. But there he was, dead on the floor.

Min Soo said, in a thin semblance of her usual calm, "Bridget, take the children to the kitchen." Bridget led them out. "Thank you," Min Soo said to Ross and Mia, her gaze wide and shocked. "I could not have done that, no matter how much I wanted to."

"The guards," Mia said, sitting up painfully.

Ross could hear their footsteps upstairs. "I don't know why they're still up there. They had to hear what was going on."

"Nobody interrupts the king's…exercises, no matter how noisy it gets," Min Soo said, low. "Their orders were to bring down the prisoners. They don't know that I helped them get away hours ago. They are searching in a panic up there, no doubt. They know better than to come downstairs empty-handed."

"They'll kill us if we don't get out," Kerry whispered painfully. She waved a hand toward the door — and the elites outside the house, waiting for an interrogation that would never come. "But if the guards find him dead, they'll blame Mom."

"Not if the killer already escaped." Ross pointed at the window behind Voske's body.

"Right." Maria-Pilar picked up a chair and smashed the window, then set the chair back neatly in its place.

"The shard," Mia hissed. "If they see it…"

Ross knelt beside her. Once again, he sensed her presence, warm and comforting. Together, they dissolved the shard into sand, then dust. When he left the world of crystal, he saw nothing but a pool of blood around the king's foot. The puncture in his boot looked like a stab wound.

Sean put his arm around Kerry and helped her to Ross and Mia. He took Mia's hand, and Mia took Ross's. "Ready."

"I'll be a table," said Maria-Pilar. She crouched down and blurred.

Min Soo let out the most shrill, horrifying shriek of horror that Ross had ever heard. He jumped so violently that Sean's fingers dug into his shoulder to keep him in place. Min Soo kept on screaming.

Footsteps pounded down the stairs, and the four house guards burst into the room. They took one look at the body and gasped in shock. One turned at the broken window. "Assassins? Did they get out that way?"

Min Soo burst into hysterical sobs, gasping, "In and out… A huge Changed man, with great Changed legs… He moved like lightning… The king only had time to send the children away… He fought so bravely…" She flung herself on her knees beside Voske's body, weeping hysterically.

Ross was amazed and impressed. He could see real tears.

The guard who had first spoken said, "I'll guard her highness."

The other three guards rushed to the window. One of them turned, furious. "Your highness. Did you see which way he went?"

Another barked, "We need more of a description!"

Gulping back tears, Min Soo said, "He headed for the walls. I think he could jump straight over it. He had legs like a grasshopper." She dashed the tears from her eyes. "I know what the king would want from his trusted honor guard. Get a message to Captain Perault to capture the assassin before he vanishes into the desert."

"Yes, Madam Cho!"

Three of the guards ran out. Min Soo stood up,

smoothed trembling fingers down her silken robe, and turned to the final guard. "Xue, please spread the word that the king is dead, and the army is to stand down and retreat to the barracks."

Xue took a moment to stare down at Voske. Ross saw the utter satisfaction on the man's face before he saluted Min Soo and ran off.

Kerry leaned against a wall, rubbing her ribs. "Mom, how long has Xue Murphy been *your* man?"

"Since Ian had his youngest brother executed," said Min Soo. "I promised it would never happen in his family again, and I kept that promise."

Kerry stared down at the body. "Santiago and I were getting people to lay down their arms…" She winced as she forced herself upright. "I'll spread the word too. I want to save as many lives as I can."

The table once again became Maria-Pilar. "I'll help."

She too looked down at the body. Maria-Pilar still held the bloody dagger, her other hand pressed to the deep cut on her forehead. She cast the blade down on the corpse with an exclamation of disgust.

"You killed him," Mia said. "You're a hero!"

Maria-Pilar shook her head. "It was all of us. If Kerry hadn't distracted him, he'd have killed me. And I was only able to do it because Ross stabbed him in the foot."

"Me and Ross both stabbed him, actually," said Mia, with some pride. "But Maria-Pilar, you struck the death blow! When everyone in Las Anclas finds out, they'll carry you through the streets."

"I don't want them to find out." Maria-Pilar looked sick. "Those kids in the kitchen were scared of Voske, sure, but they loved him, too. I killed their dad in front of them. Those guards who just took off admired Voske, and there's more like them. I'd rather not spend the rest of my life looking over my shoulder. And I don't want to be famous for being an assassin. Please don't tell anyone who killed the king."

Ross, who knew all about being famous for the wrong reasons, said, "No one will hear it from us."

Mia nodded hard. "I won't tell a soul."

"You will always be a hero to me, my dear," said Min Soo. "The children won't tell if I ask them not to. They are terribly upset now, but they've been seeing executions since they were small. I will explain to them that their father lived and died by his own rules. And that it is time for new rules."

"Thank you. I'll go spread the word." Maria-Pilar walked out.

Ross retrieved his knife and kicked Maria-Pilar's under a fold of Voske's coat, so no one who had initially seen him lying dead would notice that anything new had appeared.

Min Soo said, "Sean, please come with me. You can help me take the children to a quiet room in the infirmary. I think it's best if no one sees them now."

"Good idea," said Ross. Dr. Lee was so good at talking to people who had been wounded, physically or mentally. "They can stay in my room. It's the one with the glass ceiling. I need to get Mia to the infirmary anyway."

"I'm fine," Mia said unconvincingly.

Min Soo addressed Ross. "Please tell Dr. Lee I'd like to speak to him. Discreetly."

"I will." He turned to Kerry. "He could do something about those ribs."

Kerry winced again. "No. I want to remember Voske's last gift to me. So, I'll *never* tempted to be like him."

Ross couldn't wait to get out of that house. Even with Voske dead, it was filled with his presence. He wanted to be out in the open air, and he wanted to look for Summer. He doubted that she'd obeyed her orders, whatever they'd ended up being. She was probably flitting around the town, looking for chances to be a hero.

Min Soo and Sean went to the kitchen. Ross turned to Kerry. "Need a hand?"

"Looks like you've got yours full. Anyway, I'm not going to the infirmary. I need to find Santiago." Kerry set off briskly, a forearm pressed to her ribs.

Ross and Mia left at a slower pace, Ross supporting her. Mia wearily pushed her glasses up. "I can't believe he's really gone. I keep thinking he'll pop up as a ghost."

Oh, Mia, Ross thought. *I really wish you hadn't put that image into my head.*

Sorry. I'll try not to think of any images. Instantly, she imagined a Voske-shaped shadow, with elongated arms outstretched. Ross shuddered.

"Sorry!" Mia said aloud. "And sorry I was inside your head. I didn't mean to be. Oh! That's interesting. I didn't realize we could be in each other's minds when we're not doing crystal things. Maybe it's because we're touching. Do you mind?"

Ross had spent so much time creating inner doors and barriers and walls that he immediately knew what to do. He created a mental door—not a heavy reinforced one, like he'd used on the crystal trees—but an ordinary door, the door of his own room, which could be opened and shut by nothing more than turning a knob.

"You mind," said Mia, crestfallen.

"I mind when it happens whether we want it to or not. I can teach you to make your own door. You don't want me accidentally reading your mind, either."

Her entire face turned almost as red as her crystal eye. "No! No! Definitely not!"

They both stopped to look when they reached the Callahan house. It hadn't even been a full day since they'd been dragged out of there, but it felt like a lifetime. Grandma Lowell was limping toward her house next door, a poker dangling from one veined hand.

"Grandma Lowell," Mia called. "Voske is dead!"

The old woman halted. "You're alive! I thought Voske killed you! Mia, your eye—Wait, did you say he's dead? *Really* dead?"

"Really dead," Ross confirmed. "I saw his body."

"Did you get him?" Grandma Lowell asked with the relish of a kid of twelve.

Ross froze, but Mia spoke up. "Madam Cho said an assassin jumped in through a window."

"Wonderful! I'll spread the word." She tossed the poker into the bushes and bustled off at a brisk pace.

"It's not a lie," Mia said. "She did say that. Do you mind not going straight to the infirmary? I'd love to tell more people."

Ross wavered. He was anxious about Mia, but he was equally anxious to find Summer. "Let's try the gate."

They proceeded cautiously. As they passed the remains of Weavers' Row, they spotted Jennie shouting orders at a huge group of weaponless Gold Point soldiers. "Go inside your barracks! None of you will be harmed!"

Ross was immensely relieved to see her alive and uninjured. She stood on a tree stump, gesturing with the sword he and Mia had given her. Even covered with dust and with her clothes ripped, she commanded the eye.

Especially with her clothes ripped, he thought, and was instantly glad that Mia was no longer reading his mind.

"Jennie looks so heroic." Mia's tone was half-admiring, half-wistful. "She always does. If I stood on that same stump and waved around the same sword — well, or a sword I could actually lift — people either wouldn't notice me at all, or they'd ask me if I could fix their squeaky clothes mangle."

Ross kissed her cheek. "You helped with Voske. And you did something even more heroic than that. You told him off to his face."

Mia brightened. "That's right. I did. It wasn't very heroic language, though."

"He was probably even more insulted because it wasn't."

She grinned. Then Jennie spotted them. Her tired, anxious face split into a smile of relief, and Ross warmed when his eyes met hers. They'd only been separated for hours, but it felt like an eternity. And now they were back together again, alive and free.

The bells rang out the pattern for Stand Down.

"I bet that's Kerry," remarked Mia.

Ross shouted, "Jennie! Voske is dead!" His words seemed to echo through the crowd: "Voske is dead! The king is dead?"

Yolanda and Jose dashed up, yelling, "Stand down! Stand down! Voske is dead!"

Jennie eyed Ross and Mia sharply. Then she took up the shout, lifting the bullhorn to her lips. "Voske is dead! Pass the word!"

She handed off the bullhorn and elbowed her way through the milling defenders. Jennie put her arms around Ross and Mia and hugged them both.

Ross spotted a graceful figure bounding from rooftop to rooftop, hair streaming behind her — Summer! He let out a breath of relief as she saw him, leaped down, then swerved as she caught sight of the scarlet tree. "You have control of that, right?"

Seeing some Gold Point soldiers within earshot, Ross said, "Yes. It won't harm anyone unless I want it to."

"Ah-HA!" Summer leaped and landed at the base of the tree. Nobody else was anywhere near it. She spread her arms wide. "This is my brother's tree! He killed Voske with it! At one blow!"

Ross began, "I didn't—"

But Summer's imagination was already off and running. "He made it sprout! From the ground! It grabbed Voske by the feet and ATE HIM!"

Jennie covered her eyes with one hand, but it occurred to Ross that Summer wasn't *that* far off from the truth. He glanced at Mia and didn't need mind-reading to know she was thinking the same thing. When he looked up, he saw Jennie watching them both with an expression of *I'll get that story later.*

"Take Mia to the infirmary, Ross," Jennie said. "She looks dead on her feet, and you don't look much better. I'll wrangle the storyteller."

They continued toward the infirmary. Las Anclas citizens and Gold Point soldiers worked together to carry away the wounded and the dead. Younger children were picking up debris, and older students collected discarded weapons. Ross and Mia found Bridget in the infirmary lobby, sorting the wounded. With calm assurance, she directed the seriously injured into the surgery, and the minor injuries to sit on the porch.

"I'm not an emergency," Mia said. "I just want to sit down and get some water."

Ross took her to the kitchen. He was handing Mia her water when Luis walked in. He froze on the threshold when he saw Mia.

She touched her eye. "Ross did it to save my life."

Luis's gaze shifted to Ross. He stood very still, as if he thought Ross might go for a knife. But he made no effort to protect himself. He wasn't even armed. Ross remembered how he'd asked Luis to kill him, back at the hell cell in Gold Point. Luis had same look of dull resignation that Ross had felt.

"I know this…" Ross gestured at the lobby. "The

wounded. The dead. The destruction. I know this was what you were trying to prevent."

Luis muttered, "And I did such a good job of it."

"Everyone but Voske was trying to prevent it. You were right, he was never going to let it go. You know he's dead, right?"

Luis nodded. "People are shouting about it all over town. Rabbi Litvak could feel their emotions all the way out in the desert. Everyone was so relieved. Almost everyone."

"You came to help, didn't you?" Ross asked.

"If Dr. Lee will accept it from me."

Mia set down her empty cup. "Accept it? He'll be thrilled. Go on. Every minute is important when people are bleeding."

Luis went into the other room as if he was walking to his execution.

Dr. Lee's delighted exclamation was loud enough to be clear all the way to the kitchen. "Luis! I'm so glad you came. Quick, I need your help over here!"

·70·
FELICITÉ

LAS ANCLAS – MAIN STREET

FELICITÉ GRINNED FIERCELY AS she hid with her mother behind the law guild's veil of purple bougainvillea. There was something so exhilarating about turning the tables on Voske, searching for him until they spotted him, and then watching him twitch and yell when Mother used her power on him.

They'd last caught sight of him through the window of a downstairs bedroom at Wolfe House — only a glint of his silver hair, but that was enough for Mother's power to work. Then they'd heard breaking glass and shouting, and Mother had insisted that they run and hide.

"Should we go back to Wolfe —" Felicité began now. She was interrupted by the bell ringing out the pattern for Stand Down. Doubtfully, she said, "Voske would never order his army to stand down. Do you think it's a ruse?"

"Let's go find out," Mother said.

The gunfire, which had been constant, became sporadic, then stopped altogether. They left their shelter and hurried toward Main Street. There were no sounds of battle, and the tone of the shouting sounded excited and happy. Soon she could distinguish the words: "Voske is dead! The king is dead!"

One voice rose above the rest, amplified by a bullhorn. It was Jennie Riley, shouting loud enough to be heard in Catalina. "Lay down your weapons! Voske is dead!"

Felicité wanted to believe it was true. "Maybe one of his own guards killed him."

"Let's hope someone did," Mother replied.

"If Jennie Riley says it, I believe it," said a familiar voice.

Father walked up behind them, accompanied by Indra, Sujata, and other Rangers. To Felicité's astonishment, he ran the last few steps, grabbed Mother around the waist, and swung her around so her feet left the ground. And Mother *laughed!* Then they kissed, not a proper-for-public peck but a real kiss, clutching at each other until Mother's always-tidy hair tumbled out of the last of its pins and swung wildly about her shoulders.

They broke apart, both breathing fast. Father said, "I was gathering the Rangers to go rescue you, but it seems you rescued yourself. Where's Will?"

"Will was spirited to safety by Min Soo. She also aided my escape." Mother brushed her hands over the ill-fitting maid's dress.

Father gave a sigh of relief and turned to Felicité. "I'd thought you were safe at our camp until I saw you just now. Well—you really are taking the initiative, darling. That's a good quality in an envoy." He and pulled Felicité in for a three-way hug.

Mother stepped back and cleared her throat, then hesitated. Her usual self-possession had given way to tension. "I have something to tell you. I requested Min Soo to use her power on me. And I Changed."

Father's lips tightened, but he looked more worried than disgusted. "I can see you're all right. What kind of Change?"

Mother said nothing that Felicité could hear. But Father jumped, looked behind him, then looked back at her. "That's…unsettling."

"It was even more unsettling for Voske," Felicité put in. She still wasn't sure how her father was taking the news. "You should have heard him bellowing at people who weren't there. He sounded like a madman."

"I used some of the very personal details you disclosed to me many years ago, Tom. Things I'm sure he believed had been forgotten." Mother looked positively wicked, with her hair hanging every which way and that rumpled maid dress bunching in all the wrong places.

"I wonder if that's part of what led to his death," her

father mused. "He had so many unexpected setbacks, and it must have been days since he'd slept. Your whispers might have pushed him over the cliff."

"Perhaps they did."

Quietly, Father said, "That was a heroic deed. You might have been killed. I'm so glad you weren't, Valeria. I'm so glad to see you again. I missed you so much."

"I missed you too, Tom." Her parents embraced again, holding each other tight.

It was such an intimate moment that Felicité turned away—and was startled to see Henry approaching. He still wore black fatigues, now gray with smoke. Her heart twisted painfully at how exhausted he looked. How resigned. The old grin seemed gone for good. Sheriff Crow and Becky flanked him. They also looked exhausted, and Sheriff Crow was bruised and bloody. Felicité was relieved to see that Becky was only disheveled.

"Mr. Preston," Henry said awkwardly. "Mayor. I'm here to surrender myself. To justice."

Felicité bit her lip. The penalty for assisting an enemy to damage to the town was execution. Her heart banged against her ribs. She waited for his excuses, but none came.

Sheriff Crow stepped up. "He presented himself to me of his own accord. I didn't arrest him and bring him here."

Father folded his arms. "Henry, what do you have to say on your own behalf?"

"Nothing," Henry said. "There's no excuse."

Sheriff Crow spoke up. "I just want to say that Henry fought hard under fire. If he hadn't used his Change power to raise smoke to foul the aim of the firing line, we'd have lost a lot more people. He also used fireballs to help bring down the gate."

The sheriff nodded at Felicité's parents, then walked away. Becky lingered, coming to stand by Felicité.

Sternly, Father said, "Henry, do you know the penalty for what you've done?"

Henry nodded, swallowed, and shut his eyes. "Can I ask you to…make it quick?"

Mother laid her hand on Father's arm, and the two of them walked away a few steps. When Felicité started to follow, Mother held out a hand to halt her. Felicité was left standing there with Henry, the boy she'd once dreamed of spending her life with. But almost every aspect of that dream had been built on lies. The attraction between them had been real. But that was the flimsiest of foundations on which to base the rest of your life.

Henry stared after Felicité's parents. His hands shook. She wanted to run to her parents to point out that some of the responsibility for what he'd done was *hers*. But they had to be talking about exactly that. When they returned, both looked so grim that Henry blanched. Becky thumbed tears from her eyes.

Father folded his arms. "Henry, I'd be a hypocrite not to acknowledge that I'm also culpable in what you did. The chain of responsibility is rather long." He didn't look at Felicité, but she knew she was included in that chain. "It's interesting that the sheriff presented you to me, when I'm not the defense chief and have no council vote, and to Valeria, who has only one vote. Sheriff Crow has a vote, too, which she seems to have cast, in a way…"

Felicité realized where this was going. Becky clearly did too; she once again breathed easily. But Henry just looked scared and confused.

"Arson doesn't impress me," Father said bluntly. "Heroism in defense of Las Anclas does. So. Speaking citizen to citizen, I suggest you take off. As quickly and discreetly as possible."

He turned his back on Henry and slid his hand under Mother's arm. "What we don't see, we don't have to report. Shall I escort you to address those Gold Point soldiers crowding into our town hall, Madam Mayor?" They walked away, Mother fingering the snarls out of her hair with her free hand.

So, Henry was to live. And this was the last time Felicité might ever see him. "Henry. Remember our talk at the jail, before you left?"

Henry was standing uncertainly, staring after her parents, but when she spoke, he turned quickly. "I asked you to go with me."

"We both know that isn't going to happen." She spoke firmly, but without anger.

"Yeah." He breathed out the word in a shaky sigh.

"What I said then is still true. If you get out now, you get to start over. With a new name, if you want. Nobody will know who you are, or anything about your past." Felicité glanced at Becky. "And it doesn't mean you'll never see anyone from Las Anclas again. There'll be a lot more travel between towns now. Wherever you settle down, you can always send a message."

Becky said steadily, "I'd come see you, if you wanted. And if you write to me, I'll write back."

Henry drew another shaky breath. "All right." He looked with loathing at his Gold Point uniform. "I want to get rid of this. And I should fill a canteen. Grab some food."

Becky's chin lifted. "I'll walk with you." And Felicité heard *I'll protect you* in Becky's gritty determination.

"Thanks." Henry sounded sincerely grateful, not joking; he knew Becky could and would protect him. In a softer voice, he said, "Good-bye, Felicité."

"Bye, Henry. I do wish you good luck," Felicité said.

He turned away; his shoulders tight. His sister walked away beside him.

Felicité was surprised to find her eyes stinging. She was glad that Becky would see him safely out. It was so chaotic and there were so many strangers in town, he might escape notice. But if anyone did spot him, nobody would attack him with the sheriff's apprentice at his side.

Felicité followed her parents to the town hall. Several Gold Point soldiers stood side by side with Rangers, keeping order at the doors. Inside, Las Anclas citizens lined the walls. Gold Point soldiers sat on the floor in neat, tightly packed rows. Her parents climbed onto a makeshift stage of tables shoved together. Min Soo was already there, in a hanbok embroidered with golden phoenixes and lotus blossoms. She was surrounded by an honor guard of Gold Point soldiers. Kerry stood with her, a shocking contrast in filthy, blood-stained clothes, her face drawn in pain.

Min Soo pitched her soft voice to be heard. "As Kerry promised, no citizens of Gold Point will be harmed as long as you do not take up arms against Las Anclas."

Some Las Anclas citizens murmured angrily. Others reproved them with, "They surrendered!"

Felicité admired Min Soo's poise as she addressed the crowd. "Citizens of Las Anclas, you may not be aware that King Voske held families hostage to insure obedience in his soldiers as well as citizens. That practice ends today. I am now the queen of Gold Point, and I hold no hostages. Gold Point will become an open town. Anyone may leave if they choose, with no retribution."

Voices rose in surprise and relief and disbelief.

Min Soo went on, "I will return to Gold Point in a few days. Everyone who wishes to come with me may do so. Anyone who wishes to stay in Las Anclas or move here with your family has permission from me. However, you will also need permission from the rulers of Las Anclas."

Mother stepped forward. She had managed to wind up her hair again, and though nothing would make that maid uniform fit any better, she stood tall and dignified as if she wore the Button Dress. "Citizens of Gold Point, I am Valeria Wolfe, the mayor of Las Anclas. I would like to respectfully offer one correction to Madam Cho: I am not a ruler. Nor is my husband. I am an elected official. We will be holding a new election soon, to replace the members we lost. As for staying here, we have a procedure for that."

There was more murmuring. She raised her voice. "Anyone who wishes to stay as a peaceful citizen of Las Anclas may request to be accepted on probation. During that period, you must become a productive citizen and obey the laws of the town. Then you will be granted citizenship, which enables you to vote in our elections."

"I'm a citizen," Kerry put in. "I liked it here enough to give up my crown for it."

"We have never prevented anyone from leaving," Mother added. "And that will not change. Are there any questions?"

A voice from the back shouted, "This town is tiny. Where would we even stay?"

Mother had clearly thought about this already. "We need to repair the destruction anyway, so expanding the walls at the same time is reasonable. It would be the third expansion in our history. And we will need workers to help with the construction."

"What about Changed people?" someone shouted.

Father came forward. "I imagine that this is addressed to me."

He beckoned to Felicité. Doing her best to mirror Mother's dignity, Felicité stepped up on the table and stood between her parents.

"This is our daughter, Felicité," he said. "Some of you saw her come to town as an envoy. I expect the town council will confirm her in that position. If so, she'll regularly visit Gold Point, along with Catalina and the Saigon Alliance. As you can see, she is Changed. It took me longer than it should have to accept Changed people, but I'm doing that work. I think a lot of us will be reviewing old prejudices as we move forward."

Mother spoke up. "I am also Changed. So are two members of our council whose positions are not up for election, our sheriff and our doctor."

A man stood up from the front row. "I've heard enough. I want to stay."

"Me, too," said a woman.

More and more people stood up, saying things like, "Can I put my name down now? What about my family? Do you need their names, too?"

Felicité said, "I'll go fetch my scribe tools."

·71·
PACO

LAS ANCLAS

PACO LAY IN BED, his eyes closed, nestled against Yuki. The soft sound of Yuki's breathing and the touch of his skin filled Paco with peace. The early morning sunlight cast a pleasant warmth on his face. Three days ago, he'd dreaded each sunrise, as it had brought the burden of another day with Voske.

That burden had lifted. He was just so damn *happy*.

His eyes stung. His throat ached. His breathing must have changed, because Yuki flung an arm over his chest, murmuring, "It's okay. It's over."

"Not entirely," Paco said. "Mom is still gone. The people I killed are still dead. And nobody in Las Anclas will ever look at me the same way again."

Yuki rose on his elbow, his long hair falling over his shoulder as he studied Paco intently. "You think they're stupid enough to hold Voske's deeds against you?"

"That last Opportunity Day, when Voske forced me to hand Jack over to Min Soo, everyone glared at me. They blamed *me*."

"I'm sure Jack has already told everyone that he volunteered."

"Oh, sure," Paco replied. "But that's the least of it. I had to ride around town with Voske. Wearing his colors. Wearing his *face*. He treated me like his heir, pretending that one day he'd hand over the town to me. Every time I had to ride on patrol with his soldiers, I was sick with dread that I'd have to watch them kill someone I knew."

Yuki's dark eyes studied Paco. "What did people

actually look like, when they looked at you?"

Paco could see them so clearly. "Angry. So angry. Disgusted. Distrustful. And afraid. Terrified. They were terrified of *me*."

Yuki put his hands on either side of Paco's face. "Paco, they were afraid *for* you. They were angry and disgusted at what Voske was doing *to* you. Everyone remembers how your mom died. And how you changed after…" He stopped himself. "Sorry."

"But you're right." Paco thought back to those bleak, angry days. "You're absolutely right. That was the worst of it. How much I was becoming like him."

"Never," Yuki began, his grip tightening.

Paco shook his head, determined to get the words out. Just this once. "I was. My whole life was shaped by wanting revenge. Voske tried to make me into his son, and yeah, I resisted, but for how long? Even in my dreams I was angry, wanting Voske dead at my feet. If I'd been the one to do it, who knows what I would have become?"

Yuki's hands jerked convulsively as he started to protest. Paco spoke over him. "It's like you said yourself. I was changing before Voske even got here. All I thought about was getting stronger. Faster. Better at weapons, not just to defend the town but to kill Voske. I thought so *much* about killing him. Did he think about killing his brother when he was our age? All I know is, I'd have given up everything to take him out—I *did* give up everything. Even you."

Yuki, who was always so poised, looked unsettled. Paco remembered that the last time they'd had a conversation about how he'd changed after his mother's death, he'd broken up with Yuki.

Paco stroked Yuki's hair. "But that's all done. Voske is gone. The anger is gone. I'm glad that I wasn't the one who killed him. Everyone's trying to figure out who finally got him, but I don't give a damn who did it." As he said it, he knew that it was true. He was just glad the town was safe again. "As for being a Ranger, it's a good calling, but it's not really mine. It never was. When you're ready to take off prospecting again, I want to go with you."

"You do?" Yuki murmured, his gaze searching. "Really?"

"Really. And not just to get away from here. I want to be with you. I want to play music again, and explore new places, and find beautiful, useless things." In Japanese, he said, "Flowers over dumplings."

Yuki smiled. "You remembered."

"Of course I remember. I remember every word you've ever said. Thinking of you was the only thing that kept me sane. Yuki…I want you back."

Yuki held out his arms, his voice husky. "I'm here."

A hug turned into a kiss, and a kiss turned into their own celebration. Afterward, as they lay together, limbs entwined, Paco realized that he was absently drumming a rhythm on Yuki's arm.

He looked up and saw Yuki's grin. "Let's get some breakfast."

Paco got up and opened his closet and was faced by clothes in Voske colors. His stomach clenched. Yuki came to stand beside him. Paco knew what he wanted to do, but a lifetime of training made him hesitate. "It's perfectly good cloth…"

Yuki yanked a shirt off a hanger and ripped it from collar to hem. "It'll make even better cleaning rags."

Paco took hold of a sleeve, Yuki took the other, and they tore the shirt to bits between them. They destroyed every piece of Voske clothing, until the closet was bare except for a pair of outgrown pants and the folklórico shirt Ross had given him for Christmas, which he'd never worn.

He put it on, along with the too-tight pants, and caught Yuki's look of amused admiration. "Those pants look like they're about to rip right off your legs. I like it."

Paco laughed, kicking the pile of rags up at him, and they went out. The three cloud vipers, which had been perched along the edge of the roof, flew down to Yuki's shoulders. Paco petted them, marveling at Yuki's ability to tame wild creatures. "Stay out in the desert long enough, and you'll end up adopting a baby sand tiger."

"Just so long as it isn't a baby pit mouth," Yuki said wryly.

They walked to Luc's. The sound of construction filled the air, along with drifting odors of good food. Luc had set up tables outside his café. As they approached,

Luc stared, and Sebastien Nguyen nearly dropped his tray.

Yuki said loudly, "The cloud vipers are tame! They're my pets!"

"Still not getting close to them," said Luc. "Hungry, boys? Jack and I are feeding everyone. Ready for some breakfast tacos?"

Paco gritted his teeth. Everyone was staring at him. No. Everyone was staring at *them*. Nobody had ever seen tame cloud vipers before. And Yuki had been gone for six months. From the chorus of "Yuki! You're back!" and "Yuki! Welcome home!" a lot of people hadn't even realized he'd returned. Most of the attention wasn't on Paco. And when people did catch his eye, it was only to wave and smile, or to give him and Yuki the "what adorable lovebirds" look that had annoyed Yuki so much when they'd first started dating. Even the occasional Gold Point person looked at him with no particular animosity.

"You were right," Paco said quietly. Yuki squeezed his hand.

They sat down amongst a crowd of townspeople, Saigon Alliance allies, and Gold Point soldiers who meant to stay in Las Anclas. Some of the former soldiers wore donated pieces of civilian clothing to supplement their uniforms, whether it was a shirt or a pair of pants or a bandanna, and the rest had a piece of cloth tied around their wrists, in any color but black. He guessed that what had started as practicality had become symbolism: they were part of Las Anclas now.

"Paco! Yuki!" Ricardo Horst called, hefting a jug. "Want some tamarindo?"

Meredith sat down and raised her glass in a single, fluid motion, then blinked at the cloud vipers. "Can I pet them?"

"Hold out your hand first," Yuki cautioned. "Let them get your scent."

She offered her hand to the cloud vipers, who flicked out their forked tongues. Kunai jumped and settled on her wrist. Meredith grinned and petted her. "Where's Kogatana?"

"I left her in camp, to stay safe," said Yuki. "Someone will fetch her."

Ricardo poured out the tamarindo. "Once you eat, we could use some strong arms to sweep out the north forge. It's full of debris from the exploded jail."

"Lucky," Meredith remarked. "Mom's already roped me into helping pick up all the rocks around the gate."

"Think of it as weight-lifting," Yuki advised.

"Only less fun," Paco couldn't help adding.

He was on his fourth taco when Santiago and Kerry came up, looking dusty and tired. And sad. "Are you guys all right?"

"We were on burial duty," Santiago said.

"Someone has to bury the Gold Point dead, and keep a tally of who they are," said Kerry. "We thought it'd be right to be able to tell their families we did it ourselves."

Paco was startled. "You're going back?"

"Only for a week," Kerry said. "My mom asked me to ride in as Princess Kerry for the last time. She thinks it'll help make the changeover peaceful."

"When Voske took over from his mother, there was a lot of fighting," Santiago said. "And then a lot of executions."

He went to the taco platter, and served Kerry before he took some for himself. As soon as he was back within touching range, she put her hand on his wrist, as if she couldn't stand to let go of him for longer than she absolutely had to. Paco felt the same way about Yuki, whose left hand was on his thigh under the table as his right held a taco.

For almost the entire time he'd been separated from Yuki, she'd been separated from Santiago. Neither of them had known whether they'd ever be reunited with the person they loved. When Paco and Kerry had both been in Las Anclas before Voske's invasion, he'd wanted nothing to do with her. But if anyone could understand the burden of the time he'd spent under Voske's thumb, it would be her.

As she joked with Meredith and asked Yuki questions about his travels, Paco realized that he wanted to get to know her better. He again tested the idea of *sister*. Not to be spoken yet. If ever. But the awareness was there.

"In other news," Kerry said, holding up Santiago's hand, "Don't spread it around, but I wanted you to know…" She looked from Meredith to Yuki to Paco, her gaze resting last on him. "We're getting married!"

The radiance on her face and Santiago's made Paco spontaneously join in the chorus of "Congratulations!"

"Why's it a secret?" Meredith asked.

Kerry grinned. "I don't want my mom finding out until the last minute. If I tell her now, she'll plan an enormous wedding that'll delay it for ten years."

"I don't want to be superstitious," Santiago said more soberly, "But we both want it done as soon as possible. So, we'll never be parted again."

"I get that," Paco murmured, and Yuki smiled, his hand tightening on Paco's leg.

After breakfast, he and Yuki walked down Main Street toward the north forge. They both halted at the sight of the blood-red crystal tree—or rather, the statue of a crystal tree. All the same, it made his skin crawl. Everyone else was also giving it a wide berth. Except for a group of four—the Terrible Trio and Summer—who were heading straight for it. They carried four small fenceposts, a length of rope, a painted wooden square, and a toolbox.

"Dee?" Paco asked. "What are you doing?"

"We've made a monument," Dee proclaimed.

"To the tree that won the war!" Nhi exclaimed.

"Ross will be so thrilled when he gets out of the infirmary and sees *this!*" Summer held up the wooden plaque. It read: ROSS'S TRYUMPH! THE TREE THAT GREW FROM THE TIERRANT VOSKE'S HEART!

Paco was certain that when Ross got out of the infirmary, that plaque would disappear.

After a hard day of work, Paco and Yuki headed to Jack's. Tables had been set up outside. Lamps and bright-moth terrariums cast light on tired but happy faces. Sheriff Crow sat down with a sigh, looking as if she'd been on her feet all day. Everyone in town had been on their feet all day. Jack and Anna-Lucia brought out beef stew, cornbread, cactus salad, and lemonade. Jack glanced at Sheriff Crow before he and Anna-Lucia went back into the kitchen.

The Gold Point soldiers at the next table gazed gloomily at the food rather than digging in immediately as everyone from Las Anclas had. One said, "Well, if we survived the battle..." and grimly picked up a spoon.

As the soldiers began to eat, Paco watched their expressions change to surprise and appreciation, then dawning realization. He braced himself for anger — retaliation — but one sighed, another gave Jack a wry glance, and the third let out a bark of laughter, muttering something about prune whip.

The bounty hunter seemed to materialize from out of the shadows. He stepped up to Sheriff Crow. "Elizabeth."

"Furio," she said. "Have a seat."

He remained standing. "I just wanted to say goodbye. Most of our team will stay for a while. One or two might stay permanently. But I'm leaving tonight."

"Are you sure?" she asked. "You're welcome to stay."

He shook his head. "If you ever want me, you know where to find me."

The sheriff gave him a wistful smile. "Goodbye, Furio."

The bounty hunter faded into the night. Paco suspected that most of the people present hadn't even realized he was there.

Jack returned, carrying a glass of lemonade and a footstool. He set the glass on the table and knelt at her feet with the footstool. "Foot rub?"

The sheriff sighed with contentment as he began removing her boots.

Anna-Lucia and her assistants emerged from the kitchen with dishes of plum crumble. One of the soldiers looked up. "What, no prune whip?"

"It's permanently off the menu," Jack said. "I promise."

Just as Paco was loading his plate, Felicité walked up. It was startling to see her with her bronze scales, blue-green hair, and bare head and throat. She carried Kogatana, and Wu Zetian and Whisper trotted at her heels. Her tone was natural rather than sticky-sweet as she said, "Look who just arrived!"

Kogatana leaped from her arms to Yuki's. The gray rat climbed all over Yuki, nuzzling and squeaking at him. Paco scratched behind her ears, and she curled her tail around his wrist. Felicité headed for Kerry's table,

Whisper running ahead.

"When do you think you want to leave?" Yuki asked. "I'd like to stay awhile, if you don't mind. I've missed Meredith and my mom. And I want to help rebuild."

"I do, too," Paco replied. "And I want to stay for Kerry and Santiago's wedding."

"So would I," said Yuki.

Paco was surprised. Yuki had only met Santiago that morning and had left Las Anclas soon after Kerry had become a citizen. But they'd shared some important moments, Yuki helping Jennie and Mia engineer Kerry's escape from Las Anclas when she'd been slated for execution. He'd even sent Kogatana along to help Kerry cross the desert alone. On her return to Las Anclas, Kerry had given Yuki the beautiful bronze mare Tigereye, so he could fulfill his dream of becoming a prospector. It did feel right for him to stay for the wedding.

The lone sound of a banjo tuning drifted through the air. Mr. Salazar began strumming a fast ballad. Cisco Preciado played his flute in accompaniment. Heads nodded, feet tapped, and Paco leaned over the table, beating out a counterpoint. He started softly, aware that he was totally out of practice. But as Nasreen Hassan took up a clap to his beat, he played louder, using his fists and palms to get different sounds. Soon he was playing against the back of his chair, on top of a jug, and all over the table.

A slim figure soared from the shadows. Summer Juarez began to whirl and leap, dancing with her eyes closed, light and graceful as a leaf on the wind. Jack moved out as well, drawing Sheriff Crow by the hand. They began dancing together, moving gracefully to the beat. Kerry and Santiago were the first to join them. Kerry moved with a stiffness unlike her usual athletic strength, and Santiago held her tenderly as they swayed together. In ones and twos, others joined them.

The lamplight reflected in Yuki's eyes as he smiled. "Sure you want to go wandering? Seems to me we'd be taking off right when the town is turning into what we'd always wanted it to be."

"I want to go exploring. With you," Paco said, smiling back. "But I want to play with the band again, while I get my rhythm back and we wait for Kerry's wedding. And there's something else I want to do. Will you come?"

"Yes," Yuki said instantly, without asking what or where.

They went to his room to get the drums from the cabinet where they'd sat for over a year. Together, they walked to his mother's grave. He'd barely visited it since she'd died. There were fresh flowers on it, roses and lupines and softly glowing night poppies. Paco had no idea who had put them there. But he liked knowing that others would visit his mother while he was gone.

As he set up his drums, he remembered her listening to him playing at Luc's, and thought that she wouldn't mind his being rusty. He didn't need to tell her how he had changed or where he was going or that he understood now that all she'd ever wanted was for him to be happy. He was certain that she knew, and that wherever he went, she would be with him, sharing his joy.

Paco picked up the drumsticks and began to play.

·72·

KERRY

GOLD POINT

KERRY RODE BESIDE MIN SOO's carriage, followed by a company led by Santiago and Sean. Whisper perched on his saddle platform, sniffing the air. In the royal carriage, Min Soo sat with Owen and Fiona, who were taking turns reading aloud. Kerry suspected that the book Min Soo had chosen had nothing to do with war.

Dr. Lee had spent some time with Owen and Fiona before their departure from Las Anclas. After his visits, they'd begun to sound more like kids and less like obedient and frightened puppets. Min Soo had been impressed enough to give in to Bridget's badgering to leave her behind with him. Dr. Lee had promised, "We'll take good care of her. And she's needed here, with so many wounded."

Bridget had looked so proud. Kerry wondered if anyone had ever told her before that she was needed.

They rounded a brush-covered slope, and she saw Gold Point. It felt like only months ago that she'd ridden that road with Santiago, before her older sister Deirdre had Changed. Santiago had only been a foot soldier and she'd only been the second princess. Riding with him had been her escape from the tension of the palace, even if it did come with the occasional pit mouth or creeping cactus.

Santiago reined up beside her. She wondered if he was also remembering those rides. He asked, "Ever think we'd ride back together?"

"Never," she breathed, rubbing absently at her

healing ribs.

They were close enough now to see the high walls of Gold Point. When she squinted, she could spot the white dots of skulls gleaming in the sunlight. When they'd left Las Anclas, the heads Voske had put on its gates had been gone. They must have been taken down almost as soon as the battle had ended.

"What are you thinking about?" Santiago broke into her thoughts.

She indicated the distant walls. "Heads."

Santiago grimaced. "You heard your mom. Those are coming down. And there will never be any more."

Their shadows will stay, Kerry thought. No matter what her mother did, Gold Point wouldn't become a happy, peaceful place overnight.

The sentries at the gates peered at them, and she straightened her spine. For the very last time, she had to be Princess Kerry. She urged Nugget into a trot. She'd loaned silver Sally to Sean, and copper Penny to Santiago. Voske's silver Coronet had stayed in the Las Anclas stables, being spoiled by Ma Riley.

"Riding the king's horse into Gold Point would make a statement," Min Soo had said. "One which we do not want to make. You'll be returning to Las Anclas, not reigning in Gold Point."

Kerry glanced back. The Gold Point soldiers returning home had also straightened up, their easy talk replaced by a familiar guarded blankness. But though Sean, who led them, looked a little strained from the effort of keeping himself visible, he seemed hopeful. He urged his horse to trot up on her other side and smiled at her.

"Ready?" he asked.

"Ready."

Gold Point's outer patrol had already seen them, of course. Word would have raced ahead that Madam Cho's carriage had been sighted, along with a sizable honor guard and Princess Kerry. And that the king wasn't there. But they'd have known that could mean anything, including that he was still in Las Anclas.

He was. Sean and Kerry had scattered his ashes in the sea the night before they left. Fiona and Owen had gone with them, and they'd cried. Bridget had refused to go, saying she'd rather stay with Dr. Lee, Becky, and her spiders.

Immediately after the battle, Min Soo had sent a trusted messenger to Gold Point with a note for Commander Thandi, Sean and Fiona's birth mother and Owen's adopted mother. The commander had been in charge of Gold Point in Voske's absence, ever since he'd executed the bloody-handed Custer Bern.

Kerry had wondered what was in that note, and exactly how unexpected its contents had been. She'd never forget Min Soo's complete lack of surprise when the little table had turned into Maria-Pilar. Kerry had always known her father's wives spent a lot of time plotting, but she'd always assumed they were plotting against each other, to advance their own positions and those of their children. Probably that was what everyone had always been led to think.

When they reached the gates, she heard whispers carried on the wind.

"Is that Prince Sean?"

"It really is Princess Kerry!"

"So those stories were true after—" That whisper was followed by shushing.

Kerry made sure she sounded properly royal when she spoke. "Make way for Madam Cho, the Queen of Gold Point!"

The carriage swept through the gate to a chorus of gasps and exclamations. They halted in a large courtyard where Commander Thandi waited with two companies of soldiers. Min Soo's one company was thoroughly out-numbered. Kerry tensed. If her mother had misunder-stood the situation or been betrayed, they'd have no hope of fighting their way out.

Commander Thandi came forward, and Min Soo stepped daintily down from the carriage. The commander gracefully knelt before Min Soo. Even in the midst of her relief, Kerry noted the lack of surprise on the comm-ander's face.

Oh, yes, Kerry thought. *Those two were plotting, all right. Together.*

"Thank you," Min Soo said. Kerry admired how her seemingly soft voice made itself heard clear to the walls.

"I am desolated to report that King Voske died heroically in battle. As Queen of Gold Point, my first act is to promote Commander Thandi to General of the Army."

The Gold Point soldiers saluted. That was habit, but Kerry reflected that it was also an unconscious acceptance of the new reign. Min Soo—and Commander Thandi—had done it. Though Kerry didn't intend to relax completely until she was back in Las Anclas, it seemed like for once, the change of ruler would be bloodless.

Min Soo spoke again. "My second proclamation is to invite all of Gold Point to a banquet in the parade court at sunset. You are dismissed to spread the word and get ready."

General Thandi bawled, "Dis-missed!"

The soldiers departed with a susurrus of whispers fading behind them. Owen and Fiona jumped out of the carriage and dashed to the general.

"Mommy!" Fiona shouted, flinging herself in Thandi's arms. Owen was right behind her. Thandi hugged and kissed her children.

Sean approached more slowly. Thandi looked up, her eyes moist. Huskily, she said, "Sean."

Sean embraced his mother. She murmured into his shoulder, "I never thought I'd see this day. Thank you for your note. I was right to trust you to keep them safe."

Leaving Sean to his reunion, Kerry turned to Santiago. "Let's go get a bath. My tub fits two."

They had a very long and satisfying bath. Afterward, Santiago went to help spread the word about the new queen, and Kerry assured Bridget's mother that no one had forced her to write her three-page letter—complete with surgical diagrams—begging to stay and become a Las Anclas citizen and the doctor's apprentice.

"You should see her practicing surgery on plums," Kerry said. "And taking care of real patients. I've never seen her so happy."

"That *is* Bridget's style." Her mother eyed a finely detailed sketch of a foot amputation.

"Dr. Lee says you're welcome to visit her, any time and for as long as you like." Kerry suppressed the urge to ask if she liked experimental kimchi.

She returned to her bedroom. It had been kept clean

but was otherwise untouched since the night she'd left. She remembered her frantic packing for a trip she'd been certain she'd never return from, and how afterward she'd regretted all the things she hadn't had room to take. Now she could retrieve everything. She packed every book she owned and topped them with her second-best hanbok. She'd also regretted leaving her best dancing outfit. But when she opened the closet, she flinched away from all the red and black. Those were Voske colors. She'd never wear them again.

Kerry had thought she'd want to take more, but she already had all the furniture and everyday clothes she needed. The tapestries wouldn't fit in with her plain room, and she rarely wore a hanbok. But Jennie would love looking through her books. Kerry might even give her one or two. Then it occurred to her that she didn't need to part with her own books to get Jennie a gift. Deirdre had also collected books.

The first thing she noticed in Deirdre's room were the iron bars in the windows. They had been installed to keep Ross from escaping. She remembered him sitting on the floor after refusing to eat for three days, thin and despairing yet quietly determined. Kerry shuddered. The room felt like a big, fancy hell cell.

Her gaze shifted to those iron bars. How could she have seen those, and not thought there was anything wrong with them? How could she have spent all that time in Las Anclas as a hostage, and still intended to return to Gold Point and take up her old life? Of course, Las Anclas hadn't seemed so great then. A majority of the townspeople had voted to allow the council to murder her!

Most of those townspeople were still there. And while the Gold Point citizens who wanted to move to Las Anclas hadn't liked living under Voske, were they so different from the citizens of Las Anclas? Some of them undoubtedly also were the sort of people who would vote to kill a teenage girl in cold blood.

There was no voting in Gold Point. But the point of elections was that everyone got to participate and have a say, not that they always made the right decision.

Eyeing the iron bars, Kerry thought, *I could participate.*

Not just by voting, as she'd failed to do in her first election. But by doing her best to make sure that Las Anclas never became another Gold Point.

She swept Deirdre's books into her bag. Las Anclas would have those books, and Deirdre's ghost could keep that room.

At sunset, everyone gathered in the great parade court, where Opportunity Day and executions had once been held. Where once all the citizenry had had to gather in rows, hundreds of tables of every size and description had been brought out in a massive community effort. Every eatery in the city had contributed food, at crown expense.

The platform where so many people had died was tastefully decorated with what Kerry suspected were all of Min Soo's prize roses. Min Soo sat on a throne on the platform, exquisitely dressed in an embroidered hanbok. With Whisper in her lap, Kerry sat with her brothers and sisters and their mothers at the royal banquet table behind the platform.

Min Soo stood up and nodded to the steward, whose Change power was to amplify sound. He stepped behind her. Min Soo's voice still sounded soft, but everyone could hear it, as if she spoke to them from across the table.

"Good people of Gold Point," she said. "It is time to issue my first general proclamations."

Everyone looked nervous, and there was a clatter as some dropped their utensils.

"First: there will be no more Opportunity Days. We will leave nature to take its course." A hubbub of whispers arose, some relieved and some suspicious. "Second: Gold Point is now an open town. Anyone can leave if they wish. No one will stop you or punish you. There will be no more family members used as hostages." With a smile, Min Soo added, "You are also free to come back."

A burst of voices rang out. Some people looked around fearfully, but others spoke normally rather than whispering.

Kerry nudged Santiago. "I really admire Mom's tactics. And her vision. How long has she been planning this, I wonder?"

Santiago shrugged. "Who knows. But if it wasn't for you, it would still be just planning."

Kerry kissed him. "You're sweet, but it was Ross as much as me. Maybe more. I never would have thought of blowing up the dam."

"He never would have gotten to the dam without you," Santiago said.

Min Soo turned to them. "Princess Kerry will now address you."

She joined her mother on the platform. The steward shifted to stand behind Kerry. She spoke normally but knew the entire town would hear. "My last act as Crown Princess Kerry is to renounce my title. I'm moving to Las Anclas, to live there as an ordinary..." She suppressed a smile, thinking that she could never see herself that way, and smoothly continued, "...citizen. I will depart in one week, with a wagon train of guards and supplies. If anyone wishes to join me, they are welcome to do so."

She paused to let the uproar die down. "For anyone who comes with me and wants to become a citizen of Las Anclas, there will be a short period of probation. After that, you can become a citizen and vote in their upcoming election."

The word "election" ricocheted around the gathering, in tones of disbelief, surprise, skepticism, and curiosity. She'd had all those feelings at her first election. She'd been so convinced it was fake that she hadn't even bothered to vote. And that election had had consequences.

Sean stepped up beside her. "Hello." Kerry had known he was there, but the entire audience jumped. "I'm Prince Sean, for those who don't recognize me."

"Sean!" A shrill voice exclaimed. "You're baaaaack!"

Sean grinned. "I am, but not for long. I've been living in Catalina, operating my own fishing boat. I love living on the sea. I, too, renounce my title. And I've been deputized by our sister Bridget to inform you that she is also renouncing hers. Bridget will remain in Las Anclas to train to become a surgeon. Our brother Owen is now the

Crown Prince."

As exclamations of wonder broke out, many hastily shushed by people who still believed they'd be punished for their opinions, Owen and General Thandi joined Min Soo. Kerry looked out over Gold Point's population for the last time. The wariness and cautious whispering didn't bother her. They'd learn.

She and Sean stepped down from the platform.

"Okay, duty done," said Kerry to Santiago. "Let's go to your house."

Santiago eyed a platter of custard tarts. "And miss the banquet?"

"I'm sure we can scrounge something out of the pantry."

Santiago piled several tarts in a napkin. With Whisper at her heels, they walked hand in hand through the garden. She had been right. The rose bushes had been stripped of their flowers. But they'd bud soon.

His hand tightened on hers as they approached the garrison. It was a walk she had taken so many times that she could probably make it with her eyes closed. She'd stopped noticing the grounds long ago. But now, everything caught her eye. The whipping post. The hell cells. The torture annex. The army's own execution ground, when Voske didn't want to make a public exhibition.

Kerry shuddered, first in horror and then at her own callousness. She'd seen it all before, but she hadn't cared. "I don't understand how you could have loved me when I just walked past all this."

"We all walked past it," Santiago pointed out. "Maybe we didn't like it, but it was just how life was. We thought—I thought—nothing else was possible."

She turned her back on the hell cells. "I don't ever want to see this place again."

"It won't exist much longer. I heard your mother saying she'll tear it down and build a school."

Kerry faltered at the place where she, Santiago, and Shanti Bankar had once stood talking. Kerry and Santiago had always thought Bankar had been a brat, but it had still been a shock when she'd been killed trying to rescue Kerry from Las Anclas. "I wonder what Bankar would be doing now if she'd survived."

Santiago shrugged. "I expect she'd have tried to stir up trouble. And if no one joined her, she'd have run off and become a bandit."

"Or found a town more to her liking." It occurred to Kerry that some people would leave Gold Point not to go to a town with more freedom, but to a town with less.

At Santiago's house, they rustled up some leftovers and made burritos. As they finished eating, the entire Flores clan returned. Little Maria-Elena held her parents' hands, her face grave. Kerry wondered if the child had understood that her life had been in danger—or that she was safe now.

The front door slammed, and Maria-Elena flinched. Oh, yes. She'd known. She'd probably dreaded soldiers coming through that door ever since she'd been old enough to eavesdrop on her parents.

Everyone hugged Santiago, exclaiming and firing questions at him. His mother kept commenting on how skinny he was and how he needed feeding up.

"Where's Maria-Pilar?" his aunt Maria-Luisa asked, then clapped her hand to her mouth. "She isn't—"

"She's fine!" Santiago said hurriedly. "She stayed in Las Anclas. She wants to become a citizen."

His voice was admirably bland. Maybe too bland? Kerry noticed looks passing between some of the adults, but none of them said anything.

"I want to move to Las Anclas," Santiago's younger brother Diego announced.

"So do I," said Maria-Luisa.

"I do too!" squeaked Maria-Elena.

Santiago's dad slapped his hands on his knees. "What are we standing around for? I've always wished to see the ocean. Let's pack!"

·73·
JENNIE

LAS ANCLAS

IT WAS GOOD TO be back on the Ranger field. The obstacle course had been expanded during Voske's tyranny, but unlike the whipping post, which had been removed, the additions had been left as they were. The eight original Rangers stood with the new candidates from both Las Anclas and Gold Point.

Santiago's brother Diego hooted at Jose and Yolanda, "Get used to the sight of my back. You'll be chasing it the entire way with your tiny little legs."

"I'm gonna laugh so hard when you eat my dust." Yolanda raised her hand and whirled dust into Diego's face. "Starting now."

Sujata nudged Maria-Pilar. "Why don't you turn into a wall for us to climb?"

Maria-Pilar retorted, "Maybe I'll be a rock for you to trip over."

She looked so ordinary—short and solid, with blunt features—much like Santiago. Ross and Mia had told Jennie what had really happened to Voske. Jennie had been astonished that their original backup plan had actually worked, when nothing else had gone according to plan. Later, when she'd seen Maria-Pilar and her little sister Maria-Elena walking hand-in-hand, Jennie had thought there was a rightness to it.

Jose turned, serious as usual. "Mr. Preston, can we use Change powers?"

Mr. Preston gestured with the bullhorn. "Not during warmups. We'll work on integrating Change powers later."

Jennie caught Indra's eye, trying to convey her complicated emotions. She was amazed at how much things had changed, glad they had, and exasperated at how much it had taken to make Mr. Preston give up his prejudices. Indra winked, and she thought he understood.

Mr. Preston turned to her. "Jennie? Over to you!"

Here she was again, in the place where she had worked hardest to achieve. She reveled in how good it felt. Jennie shot a challenging grin at the Rangers and candidates and took off like a bolt from a crossbow. Her feet pounded as she headed for the first obstacle, vaulting over it with inches to spare. Her peripheral vision caught the others striving to catch up. Several ran full out, purple in the face as they pulled ahead. She let them pass, knowing that they'd be blown by the time they reached the mud pit.

Indra kept pace with her. They fell into the old rhythm, leaping, running, ducking, crawling. When everyone had finished, she jogged to the starting line.

"Good warmup," Mr. Preston called. "Now let's see some real work. Jennie, divide them up for the carry."

From old habit, Jennie turned to Indra, who gave a nod. She paired the rest up, putting Maria-Pilar with Sujata and Diego with Tommy Horst, matching Rangers with newcomers and Las Anclas people with candidates from Gold Point.

Jennie remembered the last time she'd done it with Sera, and using Sera's words, she called out, "One of each pair, lie down! Okay, your comrade is down. But you never abandon a fellow Ranger. Pick them up and get them to safety."

Indra flopped to the ground. She knelt and pulled him over her shoulders, then straightened her knees. Either she'd gotten stronger, or Indra had lost weight, because though he felt heavy, he wasn't the impossible weight she remembered him being.

All around her, candidates and Rangers were groaning, complaining, and teasing. Once again, Jennie shouted Sera's words, "Lift with your knees, not with your back! If you really can't lift someone, drag them! We never abandon our own!"

She began to run. The others followed, some staggering. More moans, grunts, and breathless jokes rose as they approached the obstacles.

As she approached the mud pit, Indra commented, "I just washed my hair. Don't drop me."

Jennie retorted, "Quiet, dead boy."

She carried him across most of the pit, then couldn't resist launching them both into the mud. She slid to the end of the pit, then hauled him out, covered from eyebrows to boots with mud.

Indra grabbed his braid and used it to flick more mud into her face. "Just wait."

"I dare you." She ran the last section and set him on his feet.

Jennie jogged toward those struggling at the back. "Come on, you can do it," she shouted, and there was Sera again in memory. "There's always one more drop of lemon juice! SQUEEZE!"

They squeezed.

Now that they were warmed up, it was time for sparring. Jennie reveled in the old exhilaration as she sparred with Indra, then Santiago. It was so much fun to spar with someone she hadn't been practicing with her entire life. She'd only experienced that once before, with Ross. It was too bad he had no interest in being a Ranger, but she could always spar with him in private.

Time raced by until the bell began to peal. They broke up, as Mr. Preston called out, "Excellent first day. That's the bell for assembling at the town hall in one hour. I'll see you all there."

Everyone dispersed, chatting in groups. Jennie found Indra next to her, and sensed in his lagging step that he had something to say. She laughed at the sight of him. He was always so sleek, from his long, glossy braid to his boots, but now he was thoroughly enslimed. Even so, she was aware of some of old feelings stirring. Feelings that had never completely gone away.

She sensed the same in him as he said, "It's good to be back where we were." He indicated the Rangers' field.

"It is."

"How far back?" he asked quietly, and then, as if aware that he was making things awkward, he forced a laugh and added, "My mom wants to know when the real *El Heraldo* is coming back."

Jennie considered what to say. What was true. Her feelings for Indra were there, but so were her feelings for Ross. She and Mia and Ross had found a balance that felt right, and she had no desire to mess that up. "Right now, things are great as they are. But hey, we've got our whole lives ahead of us."

"That's true." His gaze was steady, and she felt the "*I can wait*" that remained unspoken. She was also aware of a leap of flame within her, and wondered with a suppressed laugh why human life was so *messy?*

"As for *El Heraldo*, someone set fire to its paper supply during the battle. I guess it was a comment on the Voske *Heraldo*." She gave a wry nod at Indra's lip curl of disgust. "So, we'll need to trade with Saigon Alliance for paper. But also, I'd like to wait for some news that doesn't involve Voske's war."

Indra ducked his head in a nod. "I'll pass that on."

Jennie ran down Jackalope Row to her home to bathe and change, then ran back to Mia's cottage. She found not only Ross and Mia, but Kerry, Becky, Brisa, Sujata, and Meredith wedged inside. When Jennie came in, everyone was forced to squish closer together. Mia grabbed a jar of tools before it could topple.

Ross looked like he was about to jump out through a window. Jennie squeezed herself next to him as Kerry teased, "Really, Ross. If you run for council, you're sure to get elected."

"That's what he's afraid of," Meredith cracked.

Jennie remembered her earlier regret that Ross had no interest in the Rangers. He was one of the best fighters in town, maybe *the* best, aside from Sheriff Crow, but he had no interest in making it his job. He'd fight when he had to, but he didn't seek it out, and shied away from recognition of his deeds, let alone from fame. If he did run for office, a lot of people would vote for him, but he seemed content to leave governing to others.

But it would be a mistake to think he didn't have influence. That ruby tree glittering in the sunlight just inside the new gates was evidence of that. And so were the prospecting finds he brought back from the ruined city. There were many ways of contributing to a town other than the military or the government.

As often happened, Mia's thoughts seemed to be paralleling hers. "Ross has a job," she said firmly, cutting through the jokes and cajolery. "He's a prospector. He's not running for council. And neither am I. I'd rather run into a pit mouth. If you're so interested, why don't *you* run?"

Kerry grinned wickedly. "I *am* running."

Mia gasped. "For defense chief?"

Kerry grinned. "I'd love to run against Mr. Preston. But no. I'm running for the empty council seat."

"I'll campaign for you," Becky said instantly.

"So will I," Brisa added.

"You don't even know who's running against her," Jennie pointed out. "No one's announced yet."

Brisa shrugged. "It'll be some grandma or grandpa. Or uncle or aunt, I guess. Whoever it is, I'd rather have Kerry."

Jennie met Kerry's gaze across the small space, as everyone but Ross began talking on top of each other. They had come to understand each other in all the time they'd spent together—not in a Jennie-and-Mia way, but in a Jennie-and-Kerry way. She could tell that Kerry had been looking forward to her reaction.

"Let's go out in Mia's yard," Jennie suggested. "There's more space there."

"Thank you," Ross muttered, as everyone filed outside.

Jennie caught up with Kerry. "Why are you running?"

Kerry perched on a sheet of metal. "I want to keep Las Anclas a place where people—all sorts of people— would want to live. And I think people from Gold Point should have a voice on the council."

Jennie nodded. "Those are good reasons."

"Why aren't *you* running?" Kerry asked.

Jennie was startled. "I'm with the Rangers now. They never run for council—they're gone too much. You have to be present to vote."

Kerry steepled her fingers. "When you and Mia and Yuki decided to set me free, knowing the consequences, wouldn't it have been better if you could have argued your case on the council?"

Jennie thought back, not to setting Kerry free, but to the final battle against Voske. She'd once again accepted the responsibility that had been so disastrous for her before, with even more people's lives in her hands, and with even higher stakes. She'd done her best, and when she looked back at it now, she still felt that she'd done her best. She'd never before truly believed that. "I wasn't ready for that before."

Kerry pounced. "But you are now?"

"Yeah. I think I am. But seriously, Rangers can't be on the council."

As Kerry kept watching her, Jennie supposed that she might not be a Ranger forever. In just a few years, she'd already been so many things. And as she'd said to Indra, she had her whole life ahead of her. "You want me on the council with you, huh?"

Kerry nodded, absolutely serious. "Of course. I want to work with the best."

The bell rang out the pattern for Assemble, and they headed out. Voske's execution platform had been dismantled, the wood used to build the bigger stable and corrals for the horses the new citizens had brought. The old platform had been restored with new wood, at the other end of the town hall.

Everyone was gathered. The council sat on benches on the platform. Mayor Wolfe, immaculate in the Button Dress, spoke from the stage. "Welcome! We are gathered to introduce the current members of the council, and the candidates running for defense chief and for the council seat that had been served so ably by Marina Lopez."

There was a moment of silence for Judge Marina Lopez, who had been killed in the battle. Then Mayor Wolfe introduced the council: herself, Dr. Lee, Sheriff Crow, Grandma Wolfe, and Mr. Appel the guild chief. "Will the candidates for defense chief please come forward?"

Jennie was relieved when Mr. Preston wasn't the only person who stepped onto the stage. She had hoped that someone would run against him, to show the newcomers that they really did have a choice, and was surprised to see that the other two candidates were from Gold Point.

Mr. Preston stepped forward. "I'm Tom Preston. I once lived in Gold Point, but I moved here twenty years ago, partly because this town had elections. The previous election voted me out. Since defense chief is now an open slot, I'm running again. I promise to defend this town for all its people—wherever they came from, and whether they're Changed or Norms."

A middle-aged woman took his place. "I'm Inez Orlando. My position in Gold Point was similar to defense chief—I was home guard captain of the East Garrison. That was a defensive position that I held for fifteen years. I was brought here as night watch captain in charge of the walls. I stayed in Las Anclas because I like your way of life, and I hope to bring my skills to benefit my new town."

Kerry murmured, "Captain Orlando would be a good choice. Too bad no one in Las Anclas will get a chance to know her before the election."

"Give her five years," Jennie whispered back. "She'll have another chance."

"Right. I'll have to get used to that."

A young man from Gold Point swaggered up. "I'm Burton Ruiz, and I'm obviously the best choice here. Do I even need to explain why? Just look at me!" He paused, sending Mr. Preston a challenging grin. There were a few chuckles, and more exasperated sighs. He paused as if he was waiting for something. When nothing happened but a few impatient murmurs, he said, "See you on election day!"

"What was that about?" Jennie whispered. "Does he think this is all a joke?"

"No." Kerry looked grim. "He's hoping to demon-strate—or learn for himself—that he can challenge and even mock the rulers without getting murdered."

Chilled, Jennie realized what he might have been expecting in that pause.

Mayor Wolfe said graciously, "Thank you. And now, will the candidates for the open council seat please come forward?"

Mr. Hassan and Grandma Thakrar stepped up. Amu-sed, Jennie saw that Kerry deliberately walked behind them, so the crowd only saw her when she emerged from between them. There was a series of gasps and startled exclamations.

Mr. Hassan said, "I'm Amir Hassan, and I've lived in Las Anclas my entire life. I'm a beekeeper, but I took up arms to defend my town. I hope to never do that again. If elected to the council, I'll bring my life experience and intention to keep the peace."

Grandma Thakrar said, "My name is Radha Thakrar, and I have thirty years of experience on Mr. Hassan. I'm a brewer and a grandmother and a great-grandmother. I too plan to bring my life experience to the council."

There was a shout from the back. "Will there be free beer if you win?"

"Not for you, Peter! You still have to wait till you're eighteen," Grandma Thakrar shot back. "And I'm locking down my barrels extra tight today."

Kerry lifted her voice effortlessly. "I'm Kerry Ji Sun Cho. As you know, I was once a princess of Gold Point. I have renounced that title and am now a citizen of Las Anclas. I understand how difficult it was — and how diffi-cult it still is — to move from Gold Point to Las Anclas. I also understand what it means to be a citizen of Las Anclas and love it enough to risk my life to defend it. If elected to the council, I will be a voice for *all* of Las Anclas." A rustle of whispers ran through the crowd as Kerry stepped back.

Felicité stepped up beside her mother in a beautiful blue-green dress that matched her hair. It was still start-ling for Jennie to see her new Changed face, and even more startling that Felicité didn't try to hide it. No hat. No veil. No scarf. She didn't even have her hair brushed so it partly hid her face, as Sheriff Crow once had.

She spoke with all her old precision and pride, "I am Felicité Wolfe. I will be joining the council as Envoy, a new position. It's not up for election, as I will not have a vote on the council. I will travel too often to attend many meetings, so it's a purely advisory position. I look forward to being the voice of Las Anclas in other towns."

"Thank you, Felicité." Mayor Wolfe turned to the gathering. "The election will be held here in one week. You'll have all day to cast your votes. In the past, the counting was done in private by retired council members. But this year, we will count the votes on this stage, before anyone who wishes to witness. Thank you."

The crowd dispersed, all talking at once. Jennie had promised to join Mia, Ross, and Dr. Lee for dinner at Jack's. But Felicité stepped down from the platform, taking care not to brush the expensive fabric of her skirts against the wood, and said, "Jennie? Will you come with me?"

Surprised, Jennie said, "Sure."

As they started walking, Felicité asked, "Why aren't you running for a council seat?" And, lowering her voice, she added, "I think you'd beat all three of them."

"Thank you," Jennie responded, wondering why everyone was so interested in her running. "But you know that Rangers can't be on council."

Felicité gave a delicate shudder. "I'll never understand what you see in it. You or Sujata, or any of the others." There was nothing accusatory in her voice, just honesty.

Jennie said, testing the waters, "Well, I'll never understand how anyone could want to sit down all day, or wear a dress so fine you have to be careful with it all the time. Though it's very pretty."

Felicité preened a little. "I've always been this way. Even before I Changed."

Jennie mentally begged Dr. Lee's, Mia's and Ross's pardon. Felicité wanted to talk, and Jennie was intrigued enough to follow her lead. "I can try to explain why I'm happy where I am right now, if you're willing to answer a question for me."

Felicité nodded. "Let's go to my house. It's hot out here."

They walked up the hill. Wolfe House had always represented everything Jennie disliked about the Hill. The last time she'd entered it, she'd been soaked in beer. But she was curious to see what the Wolfe-Prestons had done with it. She put her shoes on the rack by the door and followed Felicité inside. There was no sign of Voske ever having been there. The ancient rugs seemed even brighter, if anything, as if they'd been newly cleaned. They sat down in the parlor, which was, Jennie noted with amusement, still Mia-proof, with the breakables placed safely on high shelves.

She tried to put her thoughts into order, more for herself than for Felicité. "I'm not running for council because right now, I want to be with the Rangers. I've gone through so much with them—good and bad and complicated—I earned a place with them, I got banned from them, I had the worst moment of my life with them—and I feel like I'm not done with them yet. They're like a family. They're part of me, and I'm part of them. Does that make sense to you?"

Felicité nodded, though she looked a little dubious. *Probably thinking of all that running and sweating,* Jennie thought with an inward grin.

"I think I know what you're going to ask," said Felicité. Before Jennie could reply, she went on, "I Changed when I was thirteen, but I hid it. I thought that as long as I thought of myself as a Norm, I was a Norm. But I was always afraid of water. Even my own sweat."

Jennie instantly remembered every time she'd despised Felicité for what she'd believed was laziness and vanity. Jennie had even been her teacher. How could she not have noticed that Felicité was afraid?

"I will always regret what I said to Ross that time," Felicité went on. "But when the word mutant came out of my mouth, it was really about me. And how much I hated myself for that Change that I couldn't really control." She gave a little shrug. "That's it."

"That was very honest," Jennie said. "Thank you. But it wasn't what I was going to ask about. I assumed you'd Changed at puberty—unless you got pregnant and none of us knew."

"Certainly not," Felicité said indignantly. "I would never be so careless."

Jennie stifled a grin. Felicité was still Felicité. "I wanted to ask how you escaped from Las Anclas. I've heard a lot of different stories, and I have no idea what's true."

Felicité looked away, out the window. Jennie thought she wasn't going to answer. But she said, slowly, "The only people who know the truth are my parents. And Becky."

"I'm glad you and Becky are close again," Jennie said. "She was devastated before you came back. She really believed you'd committed suicide."

Felicité met Jennie's gaze straight on. "I did. I mean, I tried."

Jennie flinched inside.

"I trust you not to spread that around. I'm not proud of it. Voske threw me out of the house, but that that wasn't why. I'd told Henry about the tunnel to protect my secret, so I thought the invasion was my fault. I hated myself. My body. Everything about me. I sat on the edge of the well and I just...gave up."

Jennie abruptly remembered Ross after he'd come back from Gold Point, so thin and with his throat bandaged, saying, *"I gave up."* He'd been ashamed, too.

"It didn't even occur to me what it would do to my family," Felicité went on. "Or to Becky."

Jennie imagined the water closing over her and shivered. For the first time, she thought she saw the real Felicité beneath the fancy dresses and the practiced voice and the pride. Jennie wasn't sure she liked her, but she understood some of what drove her.

"Did your Change save you?" Jennie asked.

Felicité nodded. "I'd never let myself be immersed in water for long enough to complete it before."

"You know, my family believes — I believe — that the Change is a blessing from God."

Felicité looked thoughtful. "Maybe that's true." She shook her head, sending her blue-green hair flying. In a lighter tone, she said, "I'd never have believed I'd ever say those words. But I do love being a mermaid. Everyone in Catalina says it's so special to swim with me."

·74·
FELICITÉ

LAS ANCLAS - WOLFE HOUSE

IT WAS THE FIRST time since Felicité turned thirteen that she had looked at Jennie without resentment. Jennie the hero. Jennie the strong. Jennie, who had always used her Changed power—one everyone thought was useful and cool.

Jennie Riley, with her Riley beliefs. Changed powers as a gift from God. It was Jennie's Riley side, Felicité acknowledged, that accepted Felicité's confession. Resentment stung her at the thought that it was easy for Jennie to be accepting. *She'd* never had to closely guard what she thought a hideous secret, day and night.

Well. Those days were gone forever. Felicité could be as open and accepting as the Rileys now. She had even been heroic, in her own way. Climbing up from that well and venturing into Las Anclas while Voske was on the rampage was the sort of thing that people expected of Jennie, but Felicité had been the one to do it. She felt that a balance had been achieved between them.

Jennie pushed her braids back, and Felicité saw the pink half-crescents on the dark skin of her hand. Jennie, following her gaze, smiled. "Sharp teeth you've got."

Felicité smiled back, showing them. "Yes. Well, it's been a long time since the Vardams' fruit shed."

"What's that about fruit sheds?" Her father walked in. "Hello, Jennie. Nice work at the Ranger field today. We're off to a good start."

Jennie nodded, her expression smoothing into the face she'd worn when she became a Ranger. In those days, she'd stood beside Indra, one half of the power couple of the future. But her expression had never hinted at what she was thinking.

Father sat down and leaned forward, elbows on his knees. "We can hold the candidate test soon, judging by the eagerness displayed today. I didn't see anyone we'll have to weed out. What did you think, Jennie? Particularly of the newcomers?"

Jennie said slowly, "They look good. I'd been concerned, but I guess the ones who believed in Voske's ways all left. Either they're in Gold Point or they're riding into other towns, looking for another Voske."

"I agree. So, I realize it's early days yet. Anything can happen in an election, as we found out a few months ago. But assuming I'm voted back in, I'd like to look ahead to the future. With both of you, actually." He turned to Felicité, with his old smile. She'd almost stopped bracing for him to flinch at her scales.

"It's good to be back in the saddle, so to speak," he said. "But Jennie, I meant what I said earlier today. I want you to take over the lion's share of the training."

"I'd like that very much, Mr. Preston," Jennie replied.

"I thought you might. You and Indra are both captain material. But you…in five or ten years, if all goes well…I'd like to see you run for defense chief, so I can retire with a clean conscience."

Jennie's expression blanked in shock. As if she had not thought that far ahead. As if Felicité had seen Jennie's future years before Jennie herself had even considered it. "You want to put the safety of Las Anclas in my hands?"

Father gave a slow but firm nod. "Whose hands would be better? You come from one of the most respected families in town. You're respected in your own right. You're a natural leader—"

Jennie laughed. "Got it. Got it. Thanks for the confidence. I think…I think I've got to think about it. You know what I mean?"

"I do indeed. But in the meantime, let's have you studying strategy. With Voske gone, I believe we have the luxury of time. But one never knows." Father turned to Felicité. "That's why I wanted to have this conversation with you here, Envoy. The strategy Jennie will learn involves alliances with other towns. And you're the person who will represent these strategies before other town councils."

Felicité realized what he was getting at. She couldn't stifle a laugh. "So, Jennie and I will be taking classes together. Again."

Jennie said with a brief grin, "I think it'll go better this time. Thank you, Mr. Preston. See you in class, Felicité." Jennie gave her a casual wave as she walked out.

Father turned to Felicité. "That's the future down the road. Right now, we've got this election."

"Do you think Kerry could win? That was a good speech."

"I wish Amir and Radha hadn't both signed up to run. They're likely to split the Las Anclas vote, which raises Kerry's chances of winning."

"Do you think she's a danger?" Felicité asked.

"No, no." Father waved a hand. "Not since she made a point of telling me, and not Horst, about Voske planning an attack from the sea. But she's ambitious."

Felicité smiled. "I know. I actually look forward to her being on the council, if she wins. It'll be fun."

Father sat up looking surprised. "Fun?"

"Fun in the way you liked sparring with Sera. And Uncle Omar. They were as good as you. You always said sparring with them kept you sharp. Having Kerry on the council will keep me sharp. I mean, all of us," Felicité quickly corrected herself.

Father smiled. "You sound exactly like your mother, twenty years ago. One of these days, you'll be every bit as good a mayor as she."

"That's the plan," Felicité said in her sweetest voice.

The gong rang for dinner, and they went to the dining room. Mother said, "Will's reading is done, and he's upstairs washing his hands. I don't know what that awful teacher was teaching him, but I'm thankful to say nothing stuck."

"Oh, I'm sure she had strict orders to flatter him and make him grateful," said Father. "Ian Voske was determined to turn one of my kids against me the way Kerry turned on him. It was easier to blame me for that, rather than believe he was the cause."

Mother affected a shudder. "Please, let us not discuss that man over dinner."

Grandmère breezed in, her silk fluttering. "Why not gloat a little that he's gone?"

Will ran downstairs and thumped into his seat. "We killed him right here in this house! Everyone wants to know exactly where! Peter and Hans said they'd give me a bottle of bee—jamaica!—if I can show them the real, true Voske bloodstains."

"A bottle of *what?*" Mother inquired.

Grandmère said with a smile, "Oh, those have been thoroughly scrubbed away."

The day Voske had died, Felicité'd spent hours recording the names of the Gold Point people who wanted to stay. By the time she got home, Voske's corpse had been carried off, and Mother, Grandmère, and Min Soo were marshalling servants to scrub and rearrange everything. Felicité didn't even know what room he'd been killed in, and she didn't want to know. She'd think of him every time she was in it if she did.

"At least tell me who killed him, Daddy?" Will pleaded. "Everybody at school wants to know."

Based on how friendly Gold Point had become once Min Soo was in charge, Felicité's guess was that she'd killed Voske herself. Probably she'd stabbed him with one of her golden hairpins. But of course, no one would ever breathe a word of it.

"Come on!" Will begged. "Who killed him?"

"Let us have another topic of conversation at the table, please," said Mother.

"Can you tell me after dinner?" Will begged.

"Will, I don't know, and that's the truth," said Father. "All I can tell you is that he's dead and gone. And within a few years, he'll be forgotten."

"Not as long as the crystal tree still stands in the middle of Main Street," proclaimed Grandmère. With a flair of a gesture, she lit the candles in the chandelier.

Father just laughed. "True. Is that roast duck? My favorite. Let's eat."

·75·

FROM *EL HERALDO DE LAS ANCLAS*

ELECTION RESULTS

Defense chief: Tom Preston

Council member: Kerry Ji Sun Cho

In a landmark election, which was both un-precedented and familiar, Tom Preston was once again elected as defense chief. Newcomer Kerry Cho was elected as council member by a mere yet crucial two votes.

Radha Thakrar and Amir Hassan split the vote, allowing Kerry Cho to reach the finish with her nose under the wire. Tom Preston easily won his election, with Inez Orlando coming in second. The complete totals are… *(see page 2)*.

NEW NUPTIAL NEWS

Wedding bells will ring twice in Las Anclas in one month, on Midsummer Night!

New council member Kerry Cho and Ranger Santiago Flores will marry in a double wedding with Las Anclas's longtime couple, Sheriff Elizabeth Crow and popular saloon owner Jack Lowell.

The festivities are not to be missed! The Old

Town Band will provide the music. All Las Anclas is invited.

Rare Chance to name new Street

Only Daisy O'Connor and Jens Lee, the oldest citizens of Las Anclas, remember the last vote to name a street. As Ms. O'Connor recollects, "The choice came down to Saguaro Lane and Montgomery Vista, named for the town architect at that time, but which no one liked except Mr. Montgomery, his dad. Saguaro Lane was my first vote." Jens Lee stated that he did not remember which name he voted for.

Interested citizens are encouraged to submit names to the Council. Suggestions will close and voting will take place when the last stone is laid.

Mysterious artifacts Found

During the excavation of the desert for the expansion of the southwestern wall, three hitherto unknown artifacts were uncovered. They were handed over to mechanic Mia Lee and prospectors Ross Juarez and Yuki Nakamura for inspection. All three pronounced themselves mystified. Mia Lee stated, "I think I can figure them out eventually. Once I take them apart. I just need to make sure they won't explode."

Ross Juarez hastened to reassure the onlookers that any taking apart would be done under safe conditions and outside of the town walls. He also added that the new homes being built in that area will be guaranteed free of all suspicious artifacts before construction.

(See page 2 for a sketch of the artifacts, by Mia Lee.)

NEW BOOKS IN LIBRARY

Twenty-six books have been added to the library of Las Anclas—its single largest expansion in the town's history! All the books are fully intact artifacts in excellent condition. They were an extremely generous gift to the town from new councilmember Kerry Cho.

Come by the library to view or *carefully* read them. Normal rules for handling artifact books apply.

HIDDEN HEROES

Everyone knows of the spectacular heroics of the battle to win back the freedom of Las Anclas. But in the midst of the fighting, many people were busy with quieter yet no less crucial great deeds. This article will highlight just a few of them. If we missed your friend or family member, please contact Jennie Riley for a future article.

RISKY RESCUE OF MEDINA FAMILY!

At the height of the battle, Sam Riley, Jack Lowell, and beer brewer Radha Thakrar joined forces to rescue the Medina family, who had been imprisoned in the north harvest barn. Using whiskey supplied from a secret still run by Brewer Thakrar, the intrepid rescuers were able to torch off a wave of whiskey! Faced by the fearsome furnace of flaming fluid, Voske's guards were forced to fight the deadly diversion, allowing the three heroes to rescue the prisoners.

Brewer Thakrar wishes readers to note that the legal drinking age is still eighteen. As Brewer Thakrar states, "This means YOU, P— — and H—-!"

NEW DOCTOR'S APPRENTICE PROVES PROFICIENCY

Bridget Austin (formerly Bridget Voske) underwent trial by fire on her very first day as Dr. Dante Lee's apprentice. After escaping from the tyrant, she went to the infirmary, where Dr. Lee had been unofficially teaching her.

As stated by Dr. Lee, "Bridget ran triage entirely unsupervised, sorting patients to determine who needed immediate treatment and who could wait. She also assisted in multiple surgeries, where she displayed both her calm under fire and her unwavering surgeon's hands. When I retire — which I don't intend to do any time soon — I will have complete confidence leaving the health of Las Anclas in the very capable hands of Bridget (chief surgeon) and Alfonso Medina (chief doctor)."

THE TIRELESS TREK OF NAOMI RILEY

While Las Anclas was still in Voske's hands, Naomi Riley heroically volunteered to trek to the Saigon Alliance in the hopes of raising allies to help free our town.

But when she reached Dai La, she was informed that the allies had already been raised and had begun marching on Las Anclas the day before her arrival. Naomi had not spotted them on her way, as she had taken a secret trail to avoid the tyrant's roaming soldiers. But Naomi refused to spend even a single night resting! She turned around and went straight back to Las Anclas, arriving just as the battle began!

Despite her exhaustion, Naomi fought hard in that battle.

As she said later, "I was so tired, when I woke up afterward, someone else had to tell me that I was actually awake and not dreaming. I still dream that I am on that road."

PSYCHOLOGICAL POWER PROVES POTENT

What do the three girls informally known as the Terrible Trio and the mayor of Las Anclas have in common? All four deployed unusual tactics to demoralize and distract the dictator!

Z Kabbani, Dee Riley, and Nhi Tran secretly constructed a fine specimen of the tyrant's likeness, playing upon his fear of mockery, and bravely deployed it on the very stage on which he murdered citizens of Las Anclas.

As observed by new Las Anclas citizen Gloria Ruiz, "I was one of Voske's guards, and he went white as a ghost when he saw that effigy with a table leg stuck through its chest. I'm still not sure exactly what was up with his table leg obsession, but it definitely scared him. I'm convinced that seeing that effigy was a big factor in how he died."

As Z Kabbani stated for our reporter, "We think he died of sheer fright."

Meanwhile, our own mayor, Valeria Wolfe, was doing her part to disturb and divert the devilish desperado. Earlier in the day of doom, Mayor Wolfe became the last person

Changed by the often-deadly power of Min Soo Cho (now our ally, the queen of Gold Point).

Mayor Wolfe used her new power to taunt and terrify the tyrant by whispering into his ear from a distance, unseen. The modest mayor declined to comment, stating that all citizens did their part.

Ernesto Flores, the father of Ranger Santiago Flores, stated: "I think she accused him of all the crimes none of us were ever able to charge him with. Beginning with murdering his own brother. And holding my little niece hostage. I like to think that he died with the names of all his hostages ringing in his ears."

THE TREE OF TERROR!

BY SUMMER JUAREZ

(edited by Jennie Riley)

You probably think you know the true story of the blood-red crystal tree in the middle of Main Street. You probably heard it's a fake, just a rock shaped like a singing tree. You probably heard my brother made it to scare off the invaders, and he hasn't paid any attention to it since. And you probably have no idea there were any sand tigers in the battle.

That's all wrong!

And you probably have no idea what else was going on when he made it. Well, I do. And you will be the first to find out at the Harvest Festival, when the first production of the Las Anclas Players presents a new play, "The Tree of Terror!" Written by and starring me, Summer Juarez.

·76·
BECKY

LAS ANCLAS

AUNT ROSA SHOOED BECKY out of the kitchen. "It's your party. Go sit down and enjoy it. I'll bring out the food."

Becky protested, "It's not a party. There's just four of us."

Aunt Rosa guided her firmly to the door. "It's your fancy garden brunch."

"You can do it, Beck," Brisa said, hugging Becky as she hustled her out to the back garden. "I'll throw myself between them if they start hurling dishes."

Becky smiled, but her heart was pounding. A year ago, she'd never have dared to invite anyone over, let alone those two. Let alone those two *at the same time.*

A year ago, she'd lived in a house where no one ever invited anyone.

Kerry and Felicité sat side by side in Aunt Rosa's garden. It was small and hot, but the roses were beautiful, and the sun brought out the scents of the herbs. Much better than the closed-in gloom of the huge backyard she'd grown up with. Becky wondered how her mother was doing with that yard. She'd been forced to move back into the old Callahan house, after she'd said one too many mean things to Grandma Ida's relatives and they'd kicked her out.

Felicité was gazing around with interest, or possibly avoiding looking at Kerry. "Lovely roses. My mother would adore these."

Kerry smiled, looking hard at Felicité. "So would mine."

Aunt Rosa came out with the teapot and cups on a tray. "Here you go, girls. Becky has a real treat—Fudong from the first tea delivery from Dai La. Bought with her sheriff's apprentice pay."

"I adore Fudong," Kerry said.

Felicité shot her a look, and Becky caught a blink from Aunt Rosa. It took Becky a moment to realize that Gold Point and the Saigon Alliance had been enemies and did not trade together. Exactly how had Kerry, or rather Voske, obtained tea from Dai La?

"Shall I pour?" Becky asked hastily.

By the time everyone had tea—and it was as good as Becky hoped—Aunt Rosa returned with pan dulce and poached eggs on toast with chopped herbs. Kerry and Felicité each took a bite, complimented the food, then flicked their gazes at each other. Becky hoped she hadn't made a horrible mistake by inviting them both. Was her brunch going to turn out to be a war of glares across the table, like those nightmare meals with her mother and Grandma Ida, and before that, Grandma Ida and Grandma Alice? Or the gut-wrenching silences between her parents when she was small?

"Felicité, will you pass the teapot?" Kerry said. "The tea is lovely."

"Gladly," Felicité said, in her mayor voice.

Becky relaxed. Whatever they thought about the other, they weren't bringing it to the table. It was awkward, but they were both making an effort.

A treble voice yelled, "Delivery! *El Heraldo!*"

A rolled-up paper flew into the yard, accompanied by a burst of Tonio Riley's bioluminescence. Kerry caught *El Heraldo* in an invisible net, and they all pored over it. When they got to the story about Mayor Wolfe, Brisa exclaimed, "Felicité, your mom fought Voske herself with her new Change power! That's *so cool!*"

"It is," said Kerry. Becky glanced at her, alert for sarcasm, but there was none. "I didn't realize what was happening at the time, but yeah. Your mom made a difference."

The quiet way Kerry spoke made the back of Becky's neck prickle. Becky wondered if Kerry had been there when Voske was killed, but she'd never ask. If Kerry wanted to tell her someday, she would.

Felicité replied in the same serious manner, "I'm glad. It took a lot of persuading to get Mother to make that public. But I was with her, and I know how dangerous it was for her to keep following Voske. I wanted people to know how brave she was."

Becky relaxed. Felicité and Kerry might never be friends, but it looked like Becky's hope of getting them to at least not openly hate each other was on its way to working.

There was a loud bang at the door. Becky recognized that impatient, demanding knock. The roil in her stomach returned. "That has to be my mom." The mention of her mother cast an instant pall over the party. But she didn't blame any of the girls. "No one else bangs like that. I'd better go see what she wants."

"You don't have to," Kerry said. "She'll go away eventually."

"And lie in wait for you," said Felicité.

Becky stood up. "Felicité's right. I'd rather see her now than have it hanging over my head."

"I'll come with you," Brisa said instantly.

"It's okay." Becky hated it when her mother was rude right to Brisa's face.

"We'll all come with you. How's that?" Kerry offered.

Felicité, too, was already on her feet. She fluffed out her sea-green hair and said, again in her mayor's daughter—no, in her envoy voice, "Yes. We're all coming."

Becky had always felt like a dog slinking to a cruel master when she was summoned by her mother. But this time she felt like she was going into battle with an army at her back. Brisa's hand stole into hers, and Becky resisted the urge to let go. If her mother wanted her, she could see Becky as she was, with her girlfriend and her friends.

Aunt Rosa met them in the kitchen. "Becky, if you don't want to see her, I won't let her in."

"No," Becky sighed. "I'll deal."

She opened the door, and her mother stalked in. "Rebecca Callahan, it's about time for you to give up your selfish and childish hiding." She made a sour face at Brisa. "I see you're freeloading here, as usual."

Aunt Rosa said, "Brisa is always welcome in my

home."

"And so is *Voske's daughter?*" Mom made a spitting sound.

"What is it you want, Mom?" Becky said, suddenly tired.

"It's time for you to come home." Mom made a visible effort to soften her tone. "I forgive you. I've even forgiven you for choosing to be a mutant."

It had been such a long time since Becky had experienced forgiveness used as a weapon. It hurt as if she'd been stabbed. But she did not have to let it hurt.

"No." It didn't come out small. It came out like a sheriff giving an order.

Her mother stared at her. "What do you mean, no!"

"No," Becky repeated. "I live *here* now. *This* is my home."

Mom glared. "You'd abandon the only family you have left? I can't cope with that house on my own, and you threw your brother out of town. I hope you can live with yourself after you force me to leave the only home I've ever known since I entered as a bride."

"I *can* live with myself. No matter what you choose to do." With distant surprise, Becky registered that her voice hadn't trembled a bit.

"You'll be sorry!" Mom slammed the door so hard that a picture fell off the wall.

Unexpectedly, Aunt Rosa laughed. Not a giggle or a titter, but a full guffaw. "Same old Martha. When we were little girls at school, she used to throw her slate on the ground when she didn't get her way, then flounce out and slam the doors."

Brisa snickered. "I can see her doing it right now!"

Felicité added, "With her petticoats flying."

Aunt Rosa wiped her eyes. "I ought not to laugh. It's sad, really."

Becky had been on the verge of tears, but Aunt Rosa's laugh had startled her out of it. She imagined her mother as a little girl, expecting to find the image funny, but it made her sadder. Becky hung up the fallen picture, which was a sketch of her great-grandmother.

"I like her face," Brisa commented.

"She was my grandmother," said Aunt Rosa. "I don't

remember her well, but I liked her. The rest of my family? They weren't so kind."

Becky thought of her dad—Aunt Rosa's brother—and his awful temper. It had been a relief when she'd realized he was never coming back.

Aunt Rosa went on, "I used to sit at the dinner table and promise myself that I'd be different."

"Of course you're different," Brisa said.

"I am now." Aunt Rosa looked straight at Becky. "It wasn't easy."

"Mom doesn't want to be different. I wish she *would* leave," Becky admitted. "But she won't, of course."

"She might." Kerry traced her fingers along her ribcage, wincing as if it hurt. "Maybe, she's finally realized that she's driven all her children away."

It felt appropriate that it was Kerry who triumphantly brought Becky the news a week later that Mom was not only selling her house, but she was leaving town. The house had been purchased by the Flores family, who had been living in leftover military tents while they looked for a place big enough to hold them all.

Becky hadn't believed it would really happen. Even now, seeing a covered wagon outside her old home and the entire Flores family squared off with her mother, she half-expected Mom to change her mind.

"This is the price we agreed on." Mrs. Flores gestured at the covered wagon with oxen hitched to it and a half-grown calf tied to the back. "One wagon. Two oxen. One female calf. Three sacks of wheat. Three sacks of beans. Four barrels of salt pork."

"Very fair!" a man shouted. As always happened in Las Anclas whenever it looked like something interesting might be happening, a crowd had gathered.

Kerry remarked, "It's more than enough to get you to some bigoted Norm town."

Mom crossed her arms over her chest, flushing.

"Where I go or don't go is none of your business, Kerry *Voske*. And it's *four* sacks of wheat."

"*Three* sacks." Mrs. Flores folded her arms. "Take it or leave it."

Mr. Flores laid a hand on his wife's arm, murmuring, "Let's just get this done." Louder, he said, "Four sacks, though we did agree on three. Do we have a deal?"

An onlooker yelled, "Don't do it, Mr. Flores! It's not too late to back out!"

"Yeah, that house is haunted," another shouted.

Maria-Elena piped up, "I hope there's a ghost. I'll make friends with it."

Mom's gaze jerked back and forth, her mouth pursed grimly. If she was expecting support from the crowd, she was clearly disappointed. She shot an extra glare at Becky, who made herself gaze back, her heart hurting, until Mom turned her back on her.

"She loved me once," Becky whispered. Her eyes stung. "I felt it in her memory. I don't know what I did to make her stop."

Brisa rubbed her shoulders, warm and reassuring, and murmured, "You were just a baby. Whatever made her switch out love for anger wasn't your fault."

"My house is better than you deserve." Mom glared at Kerry. "We should have shot you when we had the chance. It's *your* fault your father ruined this town."

Paco stepped out of the crowd. "The town's not ruined. And a lot of that is thanks to my sister. Now take your extra wheat and hit the road."

"YAY!" Santiago yelled so loudly that Becky jumped. The Flores family and most of the onlookers joined in the cheer.

"Do we have a deal?" Mr. Flores repeated.

"Deal," Mom snapped, her voice trembling with rage. "The house is yours."

Maria-Pilar heaved a sack into the wagon. "There you go. Your *extra* wheat."

As Mom climbed up, Summer yelled, "You forgot the pickled peaches!"

The wagon slowly bumped toward Main Street, and the gate beyond. It struck Becky that her mother was dragging all her anger with her, along with her wagon.

Becky consciously breathed out, trying to let all those old feelings go.

"Nobody made her go, Becky," Kerry pointed out. "She's kicking herself out."

"Who knows, maybe someday she'll decide to be nicer and come back." Brisa gave Kerry a meaningful glance. "People do change."

Becky doubted that her mom would. But she hoped that the Flores family—and Kerry, who was moving in with them—would be happy in that house. As far as Becky was concerned, it was haunted by bitter memories. No one had been happy in that house for generations.

Mr. Flores clapped his hands. "Get out the axes and clippers, everyone! The first thing to go is that prison of a hedge!"

Santiago ran inside and pulled the curtains open. For the first time in Becky's memory, sunlight flooded inside. The windows were flung wide, letting in fresh air, as laughter and happy chatter floated out. It was hard to imagine any ghost standing up to that.

·77·
MIA

LAS ANCLAS

MIA STOOD ON THE sentry walk, looking down at the new gate. *Her* new gate. The newly planted scarlet eater roses beside it strained up from the ground, their hungry mouths snapping. She caught the eye of the old mechanic, Josiah Rodriguez. He looked so proud of her.

She almost jumped out of her skin when Felicité stuck a bunch of scarlet roses in her face. Felicité cleared her throat, and Mia hastily clutched at the bouquet, which of course was non-carnivorous. The townspeople gathered below applauded, some chuckling. But not in a mean way. They undoubtedly understood that anyone could have made that mistake under the circumstances.

Felicité gave a tiny sigh, then announced, "We are gathered here for the first opening of the new gate. Designed by town mechanic Mia Lee. Mia? A few words?"

Mia realized, with some horror, that she was expected to give a speech. "Um. This is the new gate. Which I designed. It's easy to open from the inside. But it's very sturdy, so it's hard to blow up or break down from the outside. Even if an attacking army could get close with a trebuchet and perfectly round rocks—"

Felicité interrupted her. "Mia! Please do the honor of demonstrating the new mechanism?"

Mia shoved the bouquet back at Felicité and eagerly reached for the mechanism. "Look! One hand!" She took the lever in her left hand to demonstrate that anyone could use it, braced her feet, and shoved it up. The gate opened easily.

A roar from the crowd made her jump. All those people were cheering for the gate. For *her* gate. Mia beamed. Then she remembered what she'd brought. "Oh! I made something special for the opening!"

She pulled a bouquet of crystal eater roses from her satchel. She'd spent hours getting the crystals to grow in just the right sinuous shapes, and making sure the stems and leaves were green, and the roses were red, and the fangs were white. "I grew it myself! Solid crystal! Very sturdy! And decorative."

There was no cheer. Most of the crowd looked surprised, but some seemed downright unnerved. All of them were staring more at her than at her crystal bouquet.

A shout rose up. It was Jennie, yelling in her Ranger command voice. "Hurrah for Mia! Engineer! *Sculptor!*"

A ragged cheer followed. Mia stuck the bouquet in the crystal holder she'd made for it and ran down the stairs. Only then did she recall that she'd left Felicité up there, still clutching the real roses. Oh, well. Mia didn't care for cut flowers. If you put them in water, the vase was sure to get knocked over on top of her blueprints, and if you didn't put them in water, they died, and petals got everywhere.

Her friends surrounded her, congratulating and hugging her. Ross stepped smiling to her side. He'd helped her enough with the gate that he ought to have gone up with her, but of course, he'd refused.

To Mia's surprise, her friends and family weren't the only ones who approached her. Random townspeople politely waited their turn to congratulate her as if she was...well, she *was* an adult. As if she was a *respected* adult. Others hung back, staring at her ruby scar and crystal eye. It occurred to her that it had been a long time since she'd been overlooked little Mia, whom no one had taken seriously. Now people would take her seriously whether she wanted them to or not.

She'd wanted that so much. But now that she had it, she figured she could stand about ten more minutes of serious attention before she'd want to hide in her cottage.

Ross nudged her. "Do you want to tell them about the...?"

Mia brightened. She had an excellent use for that ten

more minutes. She announced, "I have something new! Something even more amazing than the gate! Something *unprecedented!* I mean, it's actually very precedented! Come to my cottage if you want to view its virgin voyage!"

"Three Vs," Jennie remarked. "You've been reading *El Heraldo.*"

"Of course," Mia said, grinning. "I adore alliteration."

She ran to her yard, feeling like she was walking on air. She'd dreamed of this moment for so long, and she and Ross had worked so hard lugging pieces out of the ruined city, then building it. With a flourish, she and Ross moved aside some sheet metal, revealing the greatest construction of her entire life.

A presumably awestruck silence fell.

Mia hadn't told Jennie or Kerry what she'd been building. She'd wanted to surprise them. Now she ushered them into the two seats in the back.

"I know what this is," Jennie breathed. "Mia, you're incredible."

Kerry stroked the seat, marveling. "I know too, from pictures in books. But I never thought I'd ride in one!"

Ross took the passenger seat and Mia took the driver's seat. The solar panels on the roof had been soaking up summer sunshine, and she'd already tested the vehicle in the middle of the night. All the same, her heart pounded as she pulled the lever. The hum of electricity was soft, but it seemed loud to her. She turned the wheel, and the vehicle slowly rolled onto the street.

"Look!" Mia shouted. "It's a CAR! An ancient vehicle brought back to life! Moving all by itself! No horses or oxen needed!"

There were gasps and murmurs, followed by an odd quiet. Summer's voice rose up. "Does it go any faster? It's slower than a cow."

"It doesn't need to go fast," Mia said. "It's for carrying heavy objects. Look! There's four people in it!"

There was a sudden jolt, and the car tipped forward. And stopped. She jumped out to investigate. The front wheels were stuck in a deep rut.

Ross examined the wheels. "We might need a team of

oxen to get it out."

A loud snicker was heard from the crowd.

Mia whirled around and glared. Whoever had snickered didn't do it again. She touched her ruby scar with satisfaction. People might laugh once at her car needing to be pulled by oxen, but they wouldn't laugh twice.

"It's amazing, Mia," said Kerry. "It really does look like the pictures of ancient cars. Except the wheels are metal, not that black stuff. And there's no walls. But I wouldn't want to be trapped inside a metal box anyway."

Jennie spoke loudly, for the crowd. "It's the most impressive feat of engineering that Las Anclas has ever seen. Can I interview you about it for *El Heraldo*? And can you do a sketch of it?"

"Of course!" Mia said.

By the time a team of oxen arrived from the Medinas to extract the car, the crowd had wandered off. Mia returned to her cottage, followed by Summer, Ross, Kerry, and Jennie.

"I loved the crystal eater roses," Summer said. "I just wish you'd included a crystal slug for Felicité."

Mia perked up. "I could make you some crystal eater roses, Summer."

"Yeah!" Summer turned to Ross. "Why don't you ever make any crystal things?"

"I do." He lifted a pane of transparent crystal from a table. "See, it's an unbreakable window."

"Why don't you ever make anything cool, I mean?" Summer demanded. "What about another fake crystal tree for Mia's yard? What about a grove of them?"

Jennie tried to fold her arms to take up less space, and accidentally elbowed Ross. "I think Mia's yard is crowded enough as it is."

It's my cottage that's crowded, Mia thought.

Ross had moved in with her so Luis could have his room in the infirmary. Mia had been thrilled for exactly one night. Then she'd discovered that there was a mysteriously big difference between Ross practically living in her cottage, and Ross actually living in it. It was fine when they were working, but he was also there when she was used to being alone. She didn't *mind* having him around. But she liked it better when she could ask him if he'd like to come over, instead of him always already being there. And she knew he missed the glass ceiling in his old bedroom.

As if Summer had read Mia's mind, she complained, "It *is* crowded. It's crowded everywhere. I hate sharing a room with Bridget and her disgusting bugs. Spring doesn't mind them, but I do. I found a huge…Bridget had some fancy name for it. Anyway, it was in my bed, clacking its pincers. And when I threatened to throw it out the window, Bridget threatened to rot my clothes!"

"I know, Summer," said Ross. "We all could use a little more space. I had an idea about that."

"Build another room on Mia's cottage?" Jennie asked.

"No. Build a house. I can afford it, with everything I've been bringing out of the ruined city, plus the scrip I saved from selling my book. There's room beyond the Ranger field, overlooking the ocean. It's not a long walk from your cottage, Mia. Or from your house, Jennie." He turned to his sister. "It would have a room for you, Summer. If you'd like to live with me."

Summer immediately demanded, "No bugs?"

"No bugs," Ross promised.

Mia liked the idea of having Ross near her, close enough to come over whenever they wanted. And she could see that Jennie liked it, too.

"We could move the glass ceiling out of Luis's room," Mia said. "I'm sure he doesn't care about it. Paco could help, since he installed it, before he and Yuki take off."

Jennie shot a glance at Ross. In a voice pitched low, she said, "You could get a bigger bed."

"Baaaaarrrrrff," groaned Summer.

·78·
ROSS

LAS ANCLAS

UNTIL A YEAR OR so ago, Ross had never believed he'd have a home, much less a house. But now he lived in his own house. His own home.

He'd lived in it for a month, and he'd helped build it. But he still sometimes woke up wondering where he was, certain that he was about to get kicked out of the comfortable bed with its clean sheets. Then he'd glance up through the skylight, see the stars or the dawn sky, and the happiness he still wasn't used to would come rushing back.

That joy didn't come from ownership. It was too easy to lose possessions for him to get attached to them. And he found the idea of humans owning land absurd. The land belonged to itself. When he'd mentioned that to Summer, she'd nodded and said, "I feel the same way. Mom said our father believed that, too. She said everyone in his tribe did." Ross had replied, "Everyone in our tribe does," heartened at her sudden smile.

The happiness Ross found in his home came from people, not things. So many people had unexpectedly insisted on contributing to the construction of this house.

Paco had installed the skylight, and Ross's new bed was directly under it. The Preciado family had cleared his plot of land, as they knew the soil of Las Anclas. Yolanda and her Riley cousins had laid out his kitchen garden for him. The Vardams had contributed precious saplings; someday he'd pick apples, plums, oranges, and lemons. Mr. Flores, Santiago's dad, had supervised the adobe construction. And Mia had designed and installed gadgets all over the house, so Ross didn't have to wear his gauntlet inside unless he wanted to.

All these people and many more had cheerfully volunteered their labor. After a hard day's work, Jack would appear with crispy fried chicken, hot biscuits, and apple crumble, claiming it merely leftovers. At their lunch breaks, Dr. Lee brought noodles, kimchi, and seasoned greens, claiming that his reward would be an honest vote for their favorite kimchi. Ross hadn't even been allowed to pay for the materials, though he had plenty of scrip.

"Your scrip stays right where it is," Olivia Lee had said, laughing, as she packed up her plumbing tools.

"It's no good to us," Tommy had said with a meaningful look, before he and Ricardo left.

When the adobe had set properly, Mr. Flores had said soberly, "Say what you want, but we all know who took down the tyrant."

"He dueled the wicked king with a crystal tree branch against his sword!" Hattie Salazar piped up before her mother Constanzia shushed her.

Ross wondered what Mr. Flores would think if he knew the tyrant had been taken down by his own niece. But the witnesses respected Maria-Pilar's wishes. They only had to see little Maria-Elena, once so grave-faced and scared of sudden noises, running and shouting in the schoolyard, to know her big sister had all the reward she wanted.

And now the house was finished. Ross took pleasure in pumping hot water over himself from the solar-heated shower designed by Mia and installed by Olivia Lee, hanging up the towel woven by Constanzia Salazar on the rack forged by Tommy Horst, and putting on the shirt Jennie had given him.

Ross called up the stairs, "Summer? You ready? It's time to go!"

The bedrooms were upstairs. There was another way the siblings were alike: both loved open air and the sky. Ross had his skylight, and Summer had a balcony where she liked to dance or lie down to watch the stars.

Summer floated down the stairs, hair swinging about her leather jacket. She wore it over a sky-blue dress Kerry had given her—Spring's favorite color, Summer had said. But because she was Summer, she wore black work pants and boots beneath it. Ross smiled, sure that if he asked her why, she'd say something like, "Because you never know when you'll have to fight sand tigers, of course!"

She gave him a suspicious look. "Are we going alone?"

"I told Mia I'd stop by to walk with her."

"Then *I'm* going alone. Mia is cool, but when you're with her—or Jennie—you're all disgusting." With that, Summer flitted through the door and away.

Ross left his house—his house!—and walked down the path lined with flourishing saplings. Maybe next year he'd have fruit. A red jay swooped low, taunting a pair of squirrels, then gave a reverberating shriek. A patch of earth crumbled, became dust, and blew away, exposing a pair of tiny carrots. The jay snatched one up and flew away. The other carrot vanished, then reappeared in the paws of one of the squirrels. The squirrels promptly began fighting over it.

Ross resolved to drape netting over his carrots before the feathered and furry thieves ate them all. Then he spotted pawprints leading to a half-built house hidden within a raspberry bush. He'd have to ask Mia for help in chasing off the raccoons. He'd already evicted them from the city they'd begun to build in the branches of his old oak tree, but they'd only moved to new territory.

At Mia's cottage, he found her dressed in overalls, pacing in a circle and picking up and putting down the crimson silk dress Kerry had given her. Ross cleared his throat, making her jump, and asked, "Aren't you wearing that?"

"Yes." Mia picked up the dress. "No." She dropped it back on the bed. "Every time I wear a dress, something awful happens. A battle. A fire. If I put it on, we'll probably get attacked by flying sand tigers."

"Summer would love to fight them for you. Mia, nothing bad is going to happen." It was only after Ross spoke that he realized that he believed his own words.

She eyed the dress doubtfully. "Maybe the curse is just on ruffled dresses."

"There you go. No ruffles. And Summer called you

cool before she took off. She'll love seeing you in it."

"Because it matches my eye." Mia met his gaze with one brown eye and one scarlet gem. Her glasses still had two panes; for balance, she'd said. "Kerry checked with me first, to see if I'd love it or be horrified. That's why I showed it to you early."

All he'd registered then was how beautiful it would look on Mia and how happy she'd been with it. It was the color of his scarlet tree, of Mia's scarlet eye, of blood. But her crystal eye and scar were the marks of how he'd saved her life. Mia had confided that for the first time ever, she actually did look cool. And thinking of the singing trees mostly reminded him of how different his power felt now that Mia shared it. It was as if some of her delight in it had gotten into him, just as some of his crystal had gotten into her.

"Okay," Mia said decisively, snatching it up. "I'm wearing it."

Automatically, Ross turned his back.

A small finger tapped his shoulder. "You don't need to do that."

A short time later, they walked hand in hand down Main Street, toward the stage outside the town hall. It had been decorated with bunting and flowers. Half the town was already gathered, along with guests from Gold Point, Dai La, and Catalina. Everyone was dressed in their best clothes, whether that meant fine silk or home-dyed cotton-wool.

The Old Town Band was playing on one side of the stage. Paco sat behind his drums, wearing the folklórico shirt Ross had given him for Christmas, his face relaxed and happy as his hands moved in a blur. Yuki sat nearby, absorbed in Paco's music, with a pair of cloud vipers on his shoulders and Kogatana in his lap.

A gleam of iridescence caught Ross's eye. A giant jellyfish descended toward the Ranger field, a gondola swinging below it. *El Heraldo* had announced that some wedding guests from Catalina would arrive by boat and some by flying jellyfish, but it was still startling to see.

All the nearby kids took off to get a closer look. They dodged like sparrows around the Riley family, who were walking together to join the wedding party. The winged toddler April flew several feet above the ground, with her parents running beside her.

Jennie spotted Ross and peeled away. She wore a brilliant yellow dress like a dandelion, and the stone beads he'd given her swung and clicked in her braids.

She and Mia hugged. Jennie remarked, "You look great in that dress. Did Kerry tell you she had Min Soo bring the fabric from Gold Point?"

Kerry walked up, arm in arm with Santiago. They were in their wedding clothes, she in a crimson hanbok embroidered in golden phoenixes, he in an embroidered blue shirt and pants.

"Did I hear my name?" Kerry asked.

"We were talking about my dress," said Mia. "I love it!"

With a rather sly smile, Kerry said, "I designed Becky's outfit, too."

Jennie caught Kerry's eye as if the two of them were sharing a joke. "I see."

Ross followed their gaze to where Felicité stood surrounded by friends from both Las Anclas and Catalina. The guy with the phosphorescent aura, wearing an intricately embroidered outfit color-coordinated with Felicité's, was clearly her date. The other boy from Catalina seemed to have struck up a romance with Dan Valdez. The Catalina girl with the opalescent wings was chatting with Nasreen, while the other Catalina girl was in an earnest conversation with Becky and Brisa.

Kerry added, "It suits Becky very well, don't you think?"

"It does," said Jennie. "I expect Felicité appreciates where she got it."

Ross didn't see anything special about Becky's fancy shirt and pants, but he supposed they did look nice on her.

"Who invited all those people from Catalina?" Mia asked. "You don't know them, do you? Are they friends of Sheriff Crow or Jack?"

Kerry said dryly, "They're friends of Felicité. Santiago and I got asked if we had any objection to extra guests, and of course Santiago said the more the merrier."

"Kerry invited me."

Ross almost jumped out of his skin before he

recognized Sean.

"Sorry, Ross," Sean said. "I wasn't trying to sneak up on you."

"I know," Ross said, his hammering heartbeat slowing down. "Just an old habit."

He still hadn't gotten used to seeing so many people in Las Anclas. It wasn't only the visitors from other towns; there were so many new citizens, he hadn't learned all their names yet. Once, strangers had been so unusual in Las Anclas that Ross had been stared at wherever he went. Now the town was full of new people, but none of them were strangers. All of them belonged.

The mayor approached, arm in arm with Mr. Preston. He looked tall and intimidating in his long coat and polished black boots, and she looked just as intimidating, if not tall, in a heavily embroidered dress.

"There you are," said Mayor Wolfe to Kerry and Santiago. "The guests are almost all here. The ceremony will begin soon."

"Come on, Santiago," said Kerry. "Let's go say hi to Mom. There she is, with your mom."

The people who'd disembarked from the jellyfish arrived, surrounded by squealing kids. Ross was unsurprised that about half of them were visibly changed. After all, they were from Catalina. He hoped no one would stare rudely—or worse. At least the kids didn't care. One shrill voice persisted, "Can I *please* pet the jellyfish?"

Mayor Wolfe and Mr. Preston approached the new arrivals. For all that Mr. Preston clearly wasn't bothered by Felicité's Change, Ross was still surprised and relieved to see them go to the skeletal woman and the man with glistening gray skin, greet them pleasantly and by name, and show them to prime reserved seats.

Once everyone was seated, the band stopped playing. The crowd grew quiet and expectant.

"It's starting," Mia said. "It's so strange to have a wedding with someone our age instead of the grownups."

Jennie chuckled. "We're the grownups now, Mia."

Mia touched her eye and straightened up. "I'm still trying to get used to that."

The drums gave a reverberating roll, and the band began to play a wedding march. Ross gave a startled laugh as trained rats ran onto the stage with tiny baskets strapped to their backs, scattering flower petals as they went. The rats assembled in a formation and shook themselves vigorously. Petals flew. The rats ran offstage to the accompaniment of ripples of laughter.

The grooms came out first, each with his escort. Mr. and Mrs. Flores beamed proudly as they walked with Santiago. Jack was escorted by Grandma Lowell and Anna-Lucia. When the escorts exited the stage, the brides appeared. Kerry was escorted by Min Soo, who seemed to float beside her daughter. Whisper trotted at Kerry's heels, and Bridget walked on her other side in a black dress.

"That's not the predator dress," Mia whispered.

Jennie muttered, "It looks like…"

Mia closed her eyes, and Ross could feel her observing with her other vision. She'd been practicing sensing patterns of heat transferred from bodies to their clothing. When she opened them, she was snickering. "It has a beautiful, very accurate depiction of a caesarian surgery on the front. The back has an appendix removal."

"Very educational," Jennie said dryly.

Ross turned to Sheriff Crow, who was escorted by her mothers and several more rats. The sheriff wore a slinky white dress that made her pregnancy very obvious.

Jennie murmured, "That's brave of her. I've never seen a woman in Las Anclas show off her pregnancy like that."

"She is brave," said Ross. The first person from Las Anclas he'd ever seen was Sheriff Crow. She could have run away and left him, like he'd told her to, but instead she'd rescued him and brought him into town. The new life he'd gotten — the new life the entire town had gotten — had come from that one moment of courage and compassion.

The priest from Gold Point began the ceremony. Ross recognized bits of the liturgy as each couple gave their vows. Words that had been repeated down the years, from times completely lost. He found it comforting now that he knew why he knew them.

At the end, the two couples kissed very enthusiastically. Ross heard, coming from somewhere behind him, a very soft but totally recognizable, "Barrrrff!"

The drums rolled once more. Kerry called out, "Let's dance!"

Everyone hurried to move the chairs and benches to the sides. The two couples were the first to take the floor. As Sheriff Crow and Jack swept past him, Ross heard someone mutter, "Showing off a pregnancy is a bad omen."

He didn't see who had spoken, but he recognized Dr. Lee's sharp reply. "She's already Changed, so she can't Change again. There's no reason to believe anything will go wrong."

"Also, none of your business," put in Grandma Wolfe.

"I don't believe in that superstition," said Maria-Pilar. "Nobody in my family has ever kept a pregnancy secret. When I carry a child, I plan to tell everybody who matters to me."

When, Ross thought. *Not if.* After all that Maria-Pilar had endured to protect her little sister, she had to feel truly safe if she was thinking ahead about having kids.

All around him, people moved to the dance floor. Maria-Pilar. Felicité and her friends. Dr. Lee and Anna-Lucia. It reminded Ross of the welcome dance Felicité thrown when he'd first arrived in Las Anclas. So much had changed since then. So much had stayed the same.

Ross put out his hands to Mia and Jennie. "Dance?"

They spun him around the floor. The drumming pulsed through his body, matching the rhythm of his heartbeat. He danced until he could barely feel his feet hitting the floor, until he felt like he was flying. His shirt and hair were damp with sweat when the music stopped. Jennie's dark skin glistened, and Mia's cheeks were bright red. The dancers staggered to a halt, laughing and gasping, then headed for the food tables.

It was a spread such as he'd never seen before. A cask of beer towered over bottles of wine and whiskey and tequila, all fiercely guarded by Grandma Thakrar. The other half of the drinks table held plain lemonade and mint lemonade and watermelon lemonade and (Mia wrinkled her nose) lavender lemonade, barley tea and herbal tisanes, corn silk tea and jamaica and tamarindo and a white drink that looked like skimmed milk, though he couldn't think why anyone would serve that at a wedding.

"It's horchata," said Kerry, appearing at his elbow. "It's made from rice. Try it."

Ross tasted the horchata. It was flavored with cinnamon, sweet and refreshing. He filled his glass, then turned to the food tables. Jack had clearly cooked for his own wedding, providing carne asada and potato salad and of course apple crumble, but he wasn't the only one represented. The fourteen dishes of kimchi could only have come from Dr. Lee.

Mia nudged Ross, grinning. "Are you going to rank Dad's kimchi in order of deliciousness?"

"Half of them are from my personal chef, whom I brought for the occasion." Min Soo gave Ross a sweet smile. "I'm certain he'd appreciate your thoughts."

Ross, certain that he would not, muttered, "I'm not going to rank them."

Min Soo gave a delicate sigh. "That was a joke, Ross. But—and I am quite serious about this—I would like to speak with you later. And you, too, Mia."

Unnerved, Ross said, "About what?"

"About the ruined city by Gold Point," said Min Soo. "I wish to invite you both to prospect it, in exchange for giving me the first chance to make an offer on whatever you bring out. No obligation to sell, but I will offer a *very* fair price."

"Ohh." Mia drew in an excited breath and shot a hopeful glance at Ross. "Oh, I'd love to see it. But I'm not a prospector. Ross is. I mean, I could get in by myself. But I wouldn't. It's both of us or nothing."

If Mia hadn't looked so thrilled, Ross would have refused. He wanted nothing to do with Gold Point or its ruined city…or rather, he wanted nothing to do with Voske. But Voske was gone. Min Soo had helped them. And that ruined city *was* a prospector's dream. Cautiously, he said, "We can talk about it. Later. Not tonight."

"Certainly not tonight," Min Soo agreed. Sweetly, she said, "Do try the kimchi."

As she swept away, Mia said, "We could help Yuki get in, too!"

"I don't think Paco would want to go near Gold Point," Ross pointed out. "And Yuki's not going anywhere without him."

"Oh. Right." Mia turned to the kimchi, inspected every dish closely, and took only the cucumber and radish to go with her grilled beef and noodles in black bean sauce. Ross couldn't resist taking a spoonful of each, along with spicy pork, pumpkin with salted egg, carne asada, corn bread, roast chicken, and stir-fried rice with preserved lobster. He would have taken some steamed fish, too, but his plate was overflowing. He'd save the fish for seconds.

He and Mia sat down with Jennie, who immediately beckoned the Rangers to join them. Paco came with them, sitting between Yuki and Indra, Meredith arriving shortly after with a giant pie, which she plonked down in front of Ross.

"Remember how I promised you a pie at Christmas?" Meredith asked. "Here it is! It's peach with crumb topping."

Ross eyed it. "It's for me?"

"Well," Meredith said, grinning. "I assume you'll share."

Summer dangled by her ankles from an overhanging tree branch and ate a slice of pie upside down. Crumb topping rained down like hail. Ross decided not to say anything.

Twilight slowly closed in, the sky deepening to blue overhead as golden lamps were lit. Faces glowed in the light, merry with laughter. The scents of night-blooming jasmine mixed with buttery pastry crust filled the air. Voices rose and fell, with an undertone of enjoyment. Laughter—Ross glanced across to where Kerry and Paco sat under one of the trees, talking. Kerry laughed again. Friendship. Maria-Pilar was dancing with Sujata Vardam. A year ago, they'd have been forced to be enemies. Luis and Santiago sat together, apart from the crowd. Santiago spoke. Luis didn't, but he was listening.

It was a beautiful night, as peaceful as the stars overhead.

"No, it's not our second honeymoon," Mr. Preston said to Grandma Thakrar. "It'll be our first. Twenty years ago, it didn't seem a good idea to travel. But the Ambassadors of Catalina offered us a guest suite in their palace, and Cathy and Jim offered us a ride, so we…" His voice was drowned by a swell of congratulatory voices from the adults.

Jennie was right, Ross thought. He and Jennie and Mia were adults now. So were Felicité and Becky and Paco and Yuki. All those he'd first met in the schoolyard, now beginning their adult lives as they found their places in the town.

Ross glanced at Mia, who was drawing on the table with her finger, outlining some invention as Jennie watched intently. Their heads were almost touching, bead-tipped black braids against fine black hair.

Summer sat with Jose, watching as Yolanda tried out a dance step. Then Summer glided over beside Yolanda, light and graceful as they executed the step together. It was the first time Ross had ever seen her dance with another person. But maybe she'd never danced alone; one of her hands clasped Yolanda's, and the other curled around empty air. Summer was dancing with her friend, and with her sister Spring.

His awareness spread across the entire gathering, hearing snatches of voices, and catching glimpses of faces in the golden light. Ross remembered how he'd needed to see everyone in Las Anclas connected to him to save his humanity. Once again, he welcomed that connection. He closed his eyes and beheld the sparks of life all around him, brilliant as the stars.

The lamps were burning low when Summer walked up to him, yawning, and plopped down by his side. "It's been fun, but I'm tired now."

Ross took his sister's hand. "Let's go home," he said.

ABOUT THE AUTHORS

RACHEL MANIJA BROWN is the author of the memoir *All the Fishes Come Home to Roost: An American Misfit in India*. She writes paranormal romance for adults under the pen names of Lia Silver and Zoe Chant. She has worked as a stage manager, a television writer, and a trauma therapist, and currently works as a life coach. Rachel lives in a little house in the big woods with two cats and six chickens.

SHERWOOD SMITH has published more than forty novels for teenagers and adults, including *Crown Duel* and the Mythopoeic Award Finalist *The Spy Princess*. A retired teacher, she lives in Southern California, and her website is www.sherwoodsmith.net.

If you would like to be notified of future works in this world, sign up here: http://eepurl.com/Tzv25

About Book View Café

Book View Café Publishing Cooperative is an author-owned cooperative of over fifty professional writers, publishing in a variety of genres such as fantasy, romance, mystery, and science fiction.

BVC authors include *New York Times* and *USA Today* best-sellers; Nebula, Hugo, and Philip K. Dick Award winners; World Fantasy Award, Campbell Award, and RITA Award nominees; and winners and nominees of many other publishing awards.

Since its debut in 2008, BVC has gained a reputation for producing high-quality e-books, and is now bringing that same quality to its print editions